The Collected Supernatural and Weird Fiction of Rudyard Kipling

The Collected Supernatural and Weird Fiction of Rudyard Kipling

Thirty-Eight Short Stories of the Strange and Unusual

Rudyard Kipling

LEONAUR

The Collected
Supernatural and Weird
Fiction of
Rudyard Kipling
Thirty-Eight Short Stories of the Strange and Unusual
by Rudyard Kipling

FIRST EDITION

Leonaur is an imprint
of Oakpast Ltd

ISBN: 978-1-78282-074-1 (hardcover)
ISBN:978-1-78282-075-8 (softcover)

http://www.leonaur.com

Publisher's Notes

The views expressed in this book are not necessarily
those of the publisher.

Contents

The Dream of Duncan Barrenness

Like Mr. Bunyan of old, I, Duncan Parrenness, writer to the Most Honourable the East India Company, in this God-forgotten city of Calcutta, have dreamed a dream, and never since that Kitty my mare fell lame have I been so troubled. Therefore, lest I should forget my dream, I have made shift to set it down here. Though Heaven knows how unhandy the pen is to me who was always readier with sword than ink-horn when I left London two long years since.

When the governor-general's great dance (that he gives yearly at the latter end of November) was finished, I had gone to mine own room which looks over that sullen, un-English stream, the Hoogly, scarce so sober as I might have been. Now, roaring drunk in the West is but fuddled in the East, and I was drunk Nor'-Nor' Easterly as Mr. Shakespeare might have said. Yet, in spite of my liquor, the cool night winds (though I have heard that they breed chills and fluxes innumerable) sobered me somewhat; and I remembered that I had been but a little wrung and wasted by all the sicknesses of the past four months, whereas those young bloods that came eastward with me in the same ship had been all, a month back, planted to Eternity in the foul soil north of Writers' Buildings.

So then, I thanked God mistily (though, to my shame, I never kneeled down to do so) for license to live, at least till March should be upon us again. Indeed, we that were alive (and our number was less by far than those who had gone to their last account in the hot weather late past) had made very merry that evening, by the ramparts of the fort, over this kindness of Providence; though our jests were neither witty nor such as I should have liked my mother to hear.

When I had lain down (or rather thrown me on my bed) and the fumes of my drink had a little cleared away, I found that I could get no sleep for thinking of a thousand things that were better left alone. First, and it was a long time since I had thought of her, the sweet face of Kitty Somerset, drifted, as it might have been drawn in a picture, across the foot of my bed, so plainly, that I almost thought she had been present in the body. Then I remembered how she drove me to this accursed country to get rich, that I might the more quickly marry her, our parents on both sides giving their consent; and then how she thought better (or worse may be) of her troth, and wed Tom Sanderson but a short three months after I had sailed.

From Kitty I fell a-musing on Mrs. Vansuythen, a tall pale woman with violet eyes that had come to Calcutta from the Dutch Factory at Chinsura, and had set all our young men, and not a few of the factors, by the ears. Some of our ladies, it is true, said that she had never a husband or marriage-lines at all; but women, and specially those who have led only indifferent good lives themselves, are cruel hard one on another. Besides, Mrs. Vansuythen was far prettier than them all. She had been most gracious to me at the governor-general's rout, and indeed I was looked upon by all as her *preux chevalier*—which is French for a much worse word. Now, whether I cared so much as the scratch of a pin for this same Mrs. Vansuythen (albeit I had vowed eternal love three days after we met) I knew not then nor did till later on; but mine own pride, and a skill in the small sword that no man in Calcutta could equal, kept me in her affections. So that I believed I worshiped her.

When I had dismissed her violet eyes from my thoughts, my reason reproached me for ever having followed her at all; and I saw how the one year that I had lived in this land had so burnt and seared my mind with the flames of a thousand bad passions and desires, that I had aged ten months for each one in the Devil's school. Whereat I thought of my mother for a while, and was very penitent: making in my sinful tipsy mood a thousand vows of reformation—all since broken, I fear me, again and again. Tomorrow, says I to myself, I will live cleanly forever. And I smiled dizzily (the liquor being still strong in me) to think of the dangers I had escaped; and built all manner of fine castles in Spain, whereof a shadowy Kitty Somerset that had the violet eyes and the sweet slow speech of Mrs. Vansuythen, was always queen.

Lastly, a very fine and magnificent courage (that doubtless had its birth in Mr. Hastings' Madeira) grew upon me, till it seemed that I could become Governor-General, Nawab, Prince, ay, even the Great Mogul himself, by the mere wishing of it. Wherefore, taking my first steps, random and unstable enough, towards my new kingdom, I kicked my servants sleeping without till they howled and ran from me, and called Heaven and Earth to witness that I, Duncan Parrenness, was a writer in the service of the company and afraid of no man. Then, seeing that neither the moon nor the Great Bear were minded to accept my challenge, I lay down again and must have fallen asleep.

I was waked presently by my last words repeated two or three times, and I saw that there had come into the room a drunken man, as I thought, from Mr. Hastings' rout. He sate down at the foot of my bed in all the world as it belonged to him, and I took note, as well as I could, that his face was somewhat like mine own grown older, save when it changed to the face of the governor-general or my father, dead these six months. But this seemed to me only natural, and the due result of too much wine; and I was so angered at his entry all unannounced, that I told him, not over civilly, to go. To all my words he made no answer whatever, only saying slowly, as though it were some sweet morsel: 'Writer in the company's service and afraid of no man.'

Then he stops short, and turning round sharp upon me, says that one of my kidney need fear neither man nor Devil; that I was a brave young man, and like enough, should I live so long, to be governor-general. But for all these things (and I suppose that he meant thereby the changes and chances of our shifty

life in these parts) I must pay my price. By this time I had sobered somewhat, and being well waked out of my first sleep,
was disposed to look upon the matter as a tipsy man's jest. So,
says I merrily: 'And what price shall I pay for this palace of
mine, which is but twelve feet square, and my five poor *pagodas*
a month? The Devil take you and your jesting: I have paid my
price twice over in sickness.'

At that moment my man turns full toward me: so that by the
moonlight I could see every line and wrinkle of his face. Then
my drunken mirth died out of me, as I have seen the waters of
our great rivers die away in one night; and I, Duncan Parrenness,
who was afraid of no man, was taken with a more deadly terror
than I hold it has ever been the lot of mortal man to know. For
I saw that his face was my very own, but marked and lined and
scarred with the furrows of disease and much evil living—as I
once, when I was (Lord help me) very drunk indeed, have seen
mine own face, all white and drawn and grown old, in a mirror.
I take it that any man would have been even more greatly feared
than I. For I am in no way wanting in courage.

After I had lain still for a little, sweating in my agony and
waiting until I should awake from this terrible dream (for dream
I knew it to be) he says again, that I must pay my price: and a
little after, as though it were to be given in *pagodas* and *sicca rupees*: 'What price will you pay?'

Says I, very softly: 'For God's sake let me be, whoever you are,
and I will mend my ways from tonight.'

Says he, laughing a little at my words, but otherwise making
no motion of having heard them: 'Nay, I would only rid so brave
a young ruffler as yourself of much that will be a great hindrance
to you on your way through life in the Indies; for believe me,'
and here he looks full on me once more, 'there is no return.'

At all this rigmarole, which I could not then understand, I
was a good deal put aback and waited for what should come
next. Says he very calmly: 'Give me your trust in man.' At that
I saw how heavy would be my price, for I never doubted but
that he could take from me all that he asked, and my head was,

through terror and wakefulness, altogether cleared of the wine I had drunk. So I takes him up very short, crying that I was not so wholly bad as he would make believe, and that I trusted my fellows to the full as much as they were worthy of it.

'It was none of my fault,' says I, 'if one half of them were liars and the other half deserved to be burnt in the hand, and I would once more ask him to have done with his questions.' Then I stopped, a little afraid, it is true, to have let my tongue so run away with me, but he took no notice of this, and only laid his hand lightly on my left breast and I felt very cold there for a while. Then he says, laughing more: 'Give me your faith in women.'

At that I started in my bed as though I had been stung, for I thought of my sweet mother in England, and for a while fancied that my faith in God's best creatures could neither be shaken nor stolen from me. But later, myself's hard eyes being upon me, I fell to thinking, for the second time that night, of Kitty (she that jilted me and married Tom Sanderson) and of Mistress Vansuythen, whom only my Devilish pride made me follow, and how she was even worse than Kitty, and I worst of them all—seeing that with my life's work to be done, I must needs go dancing down the Devil's swept and garnished causeway, because, forsooth, there was a light woman's smile at the end of it. And I thought that all women in the world were either like Kitty or Mistress Vansuythen (as indeed they have ever since been to me) and this put me to such an extremity of rage and sorrow, that I was beyond word glad when myself's hand fell again on my left breast, and I was no more troubled by these follies.

After this he was silent for a little, and I made sure that he must go or I awake ere long: but presently he speaks again (and very softly) that I was a fool to care for such follies as those he had taken from me, and that ere he went he would only ask me for a few other trifles such as no man, or for matter of that boy either, would keep about him in this country. And so it happened that he took from out of my very heart as it were, looking all the time into my face with my own eyes, as much as remained to me of my boy's soul and conscience.

This was to me a far more terrible loss than the two that I had suffered before. For though, Lord help me, I had travelled far enough from all paths of decent or godly living, yet there was in me, though I myself write it, a certain goodness of heart which, when I was sober (or sick) made me very sorry of all that I had done before the fit came on me. And this I lost wholly: having in place thereof another deadly coldness at the heart. I am not, as I have before said, ready with my pen, so I fear that what I have just written may not be readily understood.

Yet there be certain times in a young man's life, when, through great sorrow or sin, all the boy in him is burnt and seared away so that he passes at one step to the more sorrowful state of manhood: as our staring Indian day changes into night with never so much as the gray of twilight to temper the two extremes. This shall perhaps make my state more clear, if it be remembered that my torment was ten times as great as comes in the natural course of nature to any man. At that time I dared not think of the change that had come over me, and all in one night: though I have often thought of it since.

'I have paid the price,' says I, my teeth chattering, for I was deadly cold, 'and what is my return?' At this time it was nearly dawn, and myself had begun to grow pale and thin against the white light in the east, as my mother used to tell me is the custom of ghosts and Devils and the like.

He made as if he would go, but my words stopped him and he laughed as I remember that I laughed when I ran Angus Macalister through the sword-arm last August, because he said that Mrs. Vansuythen was no better than she should be. 'What return?' says he, catching up my last words 'Why, strength to live as long as God or the Devil pleases, and so long as you live my young master, my gift.' With that he puts something into my hand, though it was still too dark to see what it was, and when next I looked up he was gone.

When the light came I made shift to behold his gift, and saw that it was a little piece of dry bread.

The Lost Legion

When the Indian Mutiny broke out, and a little time before the siege of Delhi, a regiment of Native Irregular Horse was stationed at Peshawur on the frontier of India. That regiment caught what John Lawrence called at the time 'the prevalent mania' and would have thrown in its lot with the mutineers, had it been allowed to do so The chance never came, for, as the regiment swept off down south, it was headed off by a remnant of an English corps into the hills of Afghanistan, and there the newly conquered tribesmen turned against it as wolves turn against buck. It was hunted for the sake of its arms and accoutrements from hill to hill, from ravine to ravine, up and down the dried beds of rivers and round the shoulders of bluffs, till it disappeared as water sinks in the sand— this officerless rebel regiment. The only trace left of its existence today is a nominal roll drawn up in neat round hand and countersigned by an officer who called himself, ' Adjutant, late—— Irregular Cavalry.' The paper is yellow with years and dirt, but on the back of it you can still read a pencil-note by John Lawrence; to this effect:

See that the two native officers who remained loyal are not deprived of their estates.—J. L.

Of six hundred and fifty sabres only two stood strain, and John Lawrence in the midst of all the agony of the first months of the mutiny found time to think about their merits.

That was more than thirty years ago, and the tribesmen across the Afghan border who helped to annihilate the regiment are now old men. Sometimes a graybeard speaks of his share in the massacre. 'They came,' he will say, 'across the border, very proud, calling upon us to rise and kill the English, and go down to the sack of Delhi. But we who had just been conquered by the same English knew that they were over bold, and that the government could account easily for those down-country dogs. This Hindustani regiment, therefore, we treated with fair words, and kept standing in one place till the redcoats came after them very hot and angry. Then this regiment ran forward a little more into our hills to avoid the wrath of the English, and we lay upon their flanks watching from the sides of the hills till we were well assured that their path was lost behind them. Then we came down, for we desired their clothes, and their bridles, and their rifles, and their boots—more especially their boots. That was a great killing—done slowly.'

Here the old man will rub his nose, and shake his long snaky locks, and lick his bearded lips, and grin till the yellow tooth-stumps show. 'Yes, we killed them because we needed their gear, and we knew that their lives had been forfeited to God on account of their sin—the sin of treachery to the salt which they had eaten. They rode up and down the valleys, stumbling and rocking in their saddles, and howling for mercy. We drove them slowly like cattle till they were all assembled in one place, the flat wide valley of Sheor Kôt. Many had died from want of water, but there still were many left, and they could not make any stand. We went among them pulling them down with our hands two at a time, and our boys killed them who were new to the sword. My share of the plunder was such and such—so many guns, and so many saddles. The guns were good in those days. Now we steal the government rifles, and despise smooth barrels. Yes, beyond doubt we wiped that regiment from off the face of the earth, and even the memory of the deed is now dying. But men say—'

At this point the tale would stop abruptly, and it was impossible to find out what men said across the border. The Afghans were always a secretive race, and vastly preferred doing something wicked to saying anything at all. They would be quiet and well-behaved for months, till one night, without word or warning, they would rush a police-post, cut the throats of a constable or two, dash through a village, carry away three or four women, and withdraw, in the red glare of burning thatch, driving the cattle and goats before them to their own desolate hills. The Indian Government would become almost tearful on these occasions. First it would say, 'Please be good and we'll forgive you.' The tribe concerned in the latest depredation would collectively put its thumb to its nose and answer rudely.

Then the government would say:—'Hadn't you better pay up a little money for those few corpses you left behind you the other night?' Here the tribe would temporise, and lie and bully, and some of the younger men, merely to show contempt of authority, would raid another police-post and fire into some frontier mud-fort, and, if lucky, kill a real English officer. Then the government would say:—'Observe; if you really persist in this line of conduct, you will be hurt.' If the tribe knew exactly what was going on in India, it would apologise or be rude, according as it learned whether the government was busy with other things or able to devote its full attention to their performances. Some of the tribes knew to one corpse how far to go. Others became excited, lost their heads, and told the government to come on.

With sorrow and tears, and one eye on the British taxpayer at home, who insisted on regarding these exercises as brutal wars of annexation, the government would prepare an expensive little field-brigade and some guns, and send all up into the hills to chase the wicked tribe out of the valleys, where the corn grew, into the hill-tops where there was nothing to eat. The tribe would turn out in full strength and enjoy the campaign, for they knew that their women would never be touched, that their wounded would be nursed, not mutilated, and that as soon as each man's bag of corn was spent they could surrender and palaver with the English general as though they had been a real enemy.

Afterwards, years afterwards, they would pay the blood-money, driblet by driblet, to the government and tell their children how they had slain the redcoats by thousands. The only drawback to this kind of picnic-war was the weakness of the redcoats for solemnly blowing up with powder their fortified towers and keeps. This the tribes always considered mean.

Chief among the leaders of the smaller tribes—the little clans who knew to a penny the expense of moving white troops against them—was a priest-bandit-chief whom we will call the Gulla Kutta Mullah. His enthusiasm for border murder as an art was almost dignified. He would cut down a mail-runner from pure wantonness, or bombard a mud fort with rifle-fire when he knew that our men needed to sleep. In his leisure moments he would go on circuit among his neighbours, and try to incite other tribes to devilry. Also, he kept a kind of hotel for fellow-outlaws in his own village, which lay in a valley called Bersund.

Any respectable murderer on that section of the frontier was sure to lie up at Bersund, for it was reckoned an exceedingly safe place. The sole entry to it ran through a narrow gorge which could be converted into a death-trap in five minutes. It was surrounded by high hills, reckoned inaccessible to all save born mountaineers, and here the Gulla Kutta Mullah lived in great state, the head of a colony of mud and stone huts, and in each mud hut hung some portion of a red uniform and the plunder of dead men. The government particularly wished for his capture, and once invited him formally to come out and be hanged on account of the many murders in which he had taken a direct part. He replied:—

'I am only twenty miles, as the crow flies, from your border. Come and fetch me.'

'Some day we will come,' said the government, 'and hanged you will be.'

The Gulla Kutta Mullah let the matter from his mind. He knew that the patience of the government was as long as a summer day; but he did not realise that its arm was as long as a winter night. Months afterwards, when there was peace on the border, and all India was quiet, the Indian Government turned in its sleep and remembered the Gulla Kutta Mullah at Bersund, with his thirteen outlaws. The movement against him of one single regiment—which the telegrams would have translated as war—would have been highly impolitic. This was a time for silence and speed, and, above all, absence of bloodshed.

You must know that all along the north-west frontier of India there is spread a force of some thirty thousand foot and horse, whose duty it is to quietly and unostentatiously shepherd the tribes in front of them. They move up and down, and down and up, from one desolate little post to another; they are ready to take the field at ten minutes' notice; they are always half in and half out of a difficulty somewhere along the monotonous line; their lives are as hard as their own muscles, and the papers never say anything about them. It was from this force that the government picked its men.

One night, at a station where the mounted night patrol fire as they challenge, and the wheat rolls in great blue-green waves under our cold northern moon, the officers were playing billiards in the mud-walled club-house, when orders came to them that they were to go on parade at once for a night-drill. They grumbled, and went to turn out their men—a hundred English troops, let us say, two hundred Goorkhas, and about a hundred cavalry of the finest native cavalry in the world.

When they were on the parade-ground, it was explained to them in whispers that they must set off at once across the hills to Bersund. The English troops were to post themselves round the hills at the side of the valley; the Goorkhas would command the gorge and the death-trap, and the cavalry would fetch a long march round and get to the back of the circle of hills, whence, if there were any difficulty, they could charge down on the *mullah's* men. But orders were very strict that there should be no fighting and no noise. They were to return in the morning with every round of ammunition intact, and the *mullah* and the thirteen outlaws bound in their midst. If they were successful, no one would know or care anything about their work; but failure meant probably a small border war, in which the Gulla Kutta

Mullah would pose as a popular leader against a big bullying power, instead of a common border murderer.

Then there was silence, broken only by the clicking of the compass-needles and snapping of watch-cases, as the heads of columns compared bearings and made appointments for the rendezvous. Five minutes later the parade-ground was empty; the green coats of the Goorkhas and the overcoats of the English troops had faded into the darkness, and the cavalry were cantering away in the face of a blinding drizzle.

What the Goorkhas and the English did will be seen later on. The heavy work lay with the horses, for they had to go far and pick their way clear of habitations. Many of the troopers were natives of that part of the world, ready and anxious to fight against their kin, and some of the officers had made private and unofficial excursions into those hills before. They crossed the border, found a dried riverbed, cantered up that, walked through a stony gorge, risked crossing a low hill under cover of the darkness, skirted another hill, leaving their hoof-marks deep in some ploughed ground, felt their way along another water-course, ran over the neck of a spur praying that no one would hear their horses grunting, and so worked on in the rain and the darkness, till they had left Bersund and its crater of hills a little behind them, and to the left, and it was time to swing round.

The ascent commanding the back of Bersund was steep, and they halted to draw breath in a broad level valley below the height. That is to say, the men reined up, but the horses, blown as they were, refused to halt. There was unchristian language, the worse for being delivered in a whisper, and you heard the saddles squeaking in the darkness as the horses plunged.

The subaltern at the rear of one troop turned in his saddle and said very softly:—

'Carter, what the blessed heavens are you doing at the rear? Bring your men up, man.'

There was no answer, till a trooper replied:—

'Carter Sahib is forward—not there. There is nothing behind us.'

'There is,' said the subaltern. 'The squadron's walking on its own tail.'

Then the major in command moved down to the rear swearing softly and asking for the blood of Lieutenant Halley—the subaltern who had just spoken.

'Look after your rearguard,' said the major. 'Some of your infernal thieves have got lost. They're at the head of the squadron, and you're a several kinds of idiot.'

'Shall I tell off my men, sir?' said the subaltern sulkily, for he was feeling wet and cold.

'Tell 'em off!' said the major. '*Whip* 'em off, by Gad! You're squandering them all over the place. There's a troop behind you *now!*'

'So I was thinking,' said the subaltern calmly. 'I have all my men here, sir. Better speak to Carter.'

'Carter Sahib sends *salaam* and wants to know why the regiment is stopping,' said a trooper to Lieutenant Halley.

'Where under heaven *is* Carter?' said the major.

'Forward with his troop,' was the answer.

'Are we walking in a ring, then, or are we the centre of a blessed brigade?' said the major.

By this time there was silence all along the column. The horses were still; but, through the drive of the fine rain, men could hear the feet of many horses moving over stony ground.

'We're being stalked,' said Lieutenant Halley.

'They've no horses here. Besides they'd have fired before this,' said the major. 'It's— it's villagers' ponies.'

'Then our horses would have neighed and spoilt the attack long ago. They must have been near us for half an hour,' said the subaltern.

'Queer that we can't smell the horses,' said the major, damping his finger and rubbing it on his nose as he sniffed up wind.

'Well, it's a bad start,' said the subaltern, shaking the wet from his overcoat. 'What shall we do, sir?'

'Get on,' said the major. 'We shall catch it tonight.'

The column moved forward very gingerly for a few paces.

Then there was an oath, a shower of blue sparks as shod hooves crashed on small stones, and a man rolled over with a jangle of accoutrements that would have waked the dead.

'Now we've gone and done it,' said Lieutenant Halley. 'All the hillside awake and all the hillside to climb in the face of musketry-fire! This comes of trying to do night-hawk work.'

The trembling trooper picked himself up and tried to explain that his horse had fallen over one of the little cairns that are built of loose stones on the spot where a man has been murdered. There was no need to give reasons. The major's big Australian charger blundered next, and the column came to a halt in what seemed to be a very graveyard of little cairns, all about two feet high. The manoeuvres of the squadron are not reported. Men said that it felt like mounted quadrilles without training and without the music; but at last the horses, breaking rank and choosing their own way, walked clear of the cairns, till every man of the squadron reformed and drew rein a few yards up the slope of the hill.

Then, according to Lieutenant Halley, there was another scene very like the one which has been described. The major and Carter insisted that all the men had not joined rank, and that there were more of them in the rear, clicking and blundering among the dead men's cairns. Lieutenant Halley told off his own troopers again and resigned himself to wait. Later on he said to me:

'I didn't much know, and I didn't much care what was going on. The row of that trooper falling ought to have scared half the country, and I would take my oath that we were being stalked by a full regiment in the rear, and *they* were making row enough to rouse all Afghanistan. I sat tight, but nothing happened.'

The mysterious part of the night's work was the silence on the hillside. Everybody knew that the Gulla Kutta Mullah had his outpost-huts on the reverse side of the hill, and everybody expected, by the time that the major had sworn himself into quiet, that the watchmen there would open fire. When nothing happened, they said that the gusts of the rain had deadened the sound of the horses, and thanked Providence. At last the major satisfied himself (*a*) that he had left no one behind among the cairns, and (*b*) that he was not being taken in the rear by a large and powerful body of cavalry. The men's tempers were thoroughly spoiled, the horses were lathered and unquiet, and one and all prayed for the daylight.

They set themselves to climb up the hill, each man leading his mount carefully. Before they had covered the lower slopes or the breast-plates had begun to tighten, a thunderstorm came up behind, rolling across the low hills and drowning any noise less than that of cannon. The first flash of the lightning showed the bare ribs of the ascent, the hill-crest standing steely-blue against the black sky, the little falling lines of the rain, and, a few yards to their left flank, an Afghan watchtower, two-storied, built of stone, and entered by a ladder from the upper story. The ladder was up, and a man with a rifle was leaning from the window. The darkness and the thunder rolled down in an instant, and, when the lull followed, a voice from the watchtower cried, 'Who goes there?'

The cavalry were very quiet, but each man gripped his carbine and stood beside his horse. Again the voice called, 'Who goes there?' and in a louder key, 'O, brothers, give the alarm!' Now, every man in the cavalry would have died in his long boots sooner than have asked for quarter, but it is a fact that the answer to the second call was a long wail of '*Marf karo! Marf karo?*' which means, 'Have mercy! Have mercy!' It came from the climbing regiment.

The cavalry stood dumbfoundered, till the big troopers had time to whisper one to another: ' Mir Khan, was that thy voice? Abdullah, didst thou call?' Lieutenant Halley stood beside his charger and waited. So long as no firing was going on he was content. Another flash of lightning showed the horses with heaving flanks and nodding heads; the men, white eye-balled, glaring beside them, and the stone watchtower to the left. This time there was no head at the window, and the rude iron-clamped shutter that could turn a rifle bullet was closed.

' Go on, men,' said the major. 'Get up to the top at any rate!' The squadron toiled forward, the horses wagging their tails and the men pulling at the bridles, the stones rolling down the hillside and the sparks flying. Lieutenant Halley declares that he never heard a squadron make so much noise in his life. They scrambled up, he said, as though each horse had eight legs and a spare horse to follow him. Even then there was no sound from the watchtower, and the men stopped exhausted on the ridge that overlooked the pit of darkness in which the village of Bersund lay. Girths were loosed, curb-chains shifted, and saddles adjusted, and the men dropped down among the stones. Whatever might happen now, they held the upper ground of any attack.

The thunder ceased, and with it the rain, and the soft thick darkness of a winter night before the dawn covered them all. Except for the sound of falling water among the ravines below, everything was still. They heard the shutter of the watchtower below them thrown back with a clang, and the voice of the watcher calling, 'Oh, Hafiz Ullah!'

The echoes took up the call, '*La-la-la!*' and an answer came from the watchtower hidden round the curve of the hill, 'What is it, Shahbaz Khan?'

Shahbaz Khan replied in the high-pitched voice of the mountaineer: 'Hast thou seen?'

The answer came back: 'Yes. God deliver us from all evil spirits!'

There was a pause, and then: 'Hafiz Ullah, I am alone! Come to me.'

'Shahbaz Khan, I am alone also; but I dare not leave my post!'

'That is a lie; thou art afraid.'

A longer pause followed, and then: 'I am afraid. Be silent! They are below us still. Pray to God and sleep.'

The troopers listened and wondered, for they could not understand what save earth and stone could lie below the watchtowers.

Shahbaz Khan began to call again: 'They are below us. I can

see them! For the pity of God come over to me, Hafiz Ullali! My father slew ten of them. Come over!'

Hafiz Ullah answered in a very loud voice, 'Mine was guiltless. Hear, ye Men of the Night, neither my father nor my blood had any part in that sin. Bear thou thine own punishment, Shahbaz Khan.'

'Oh, someone ought to stop those two chaps crowing away like cocks there," said the lieutenant shivering under his rock.

He had hardly turned round to expose a new side of him to the rain before a bearded, long-locked, evil-smelling Afghan rushed up the hill, and tumbled into his arms. Halley sat upon him, and thrust as much of a sword-hilt as could be spared down the man's gullet. 'If you cry out, I kill you,' he said cheerfully.

The man was beyond any expression of terror. He lay and quaked, gasping. When Halley took the sword-hilt from between his teeth, he was still inarticulate, but clung to Halley's arm, feeling it from elbow to wrist.

'The *rissala!* The dead *rissala!*' he gasped. 'It is down there!'

'No; the *rissala*, the very much alive *rissala*. It is up here,' said Halley, unshipping his watering-bridle, and fastening the man's hands. Why were you in the towers so foolish as to let us pass?'

'The valley is full of the dead,' said the Afghan. 'It is better to fall into the hands of the English than the hands of the dead. They march to and fro below there. I saw them in the lightning.'

He recovered his composure after a little, and whispering, because Halley's pistol was at his stomach, said: 'What is this? There is no war between us now, and the *mullah* will kill me for not seeing you pass!'

'Rest easy,' said Halley; 'we are coming to kill the *mullah*, if God please. His teeth have grown too long. No harm will come to thee unless the daylight shows thee as a face which is desired by the gallows for crime done. But what of the dead regiment?'

'I only kill within my own border,' said the man, immensely relieved. 'The Dead Regiment is below. The men must have passed through it on their journey—four hundred dead on horses, stumbling among their own graves, among the little heaps—dead men all, whom we slew.'

'Whew!' said Halley. 'That accounts for my cursing Carter and the major cursing me. Four hundred sabres, eh? No wonder we thought there were a few extra men in the troop. Kurruk Shah,' he whispered to a grizzled native officer that lay within a few feet of him, ' Hast thou heard anything of a dead *Rissala* in these hills?'

'Assuredly,' said Kurruk Shah with a grim chuckle. 'Otherwise, why did I, who have served the queen for seven and twenty years, and killed many hill-dogs, shout aloud for quarter when the lightning revealed us to the watchtowers? When I was a young man I saw the killing in the valley of Sheor-Kôt there at our feet, and I know the tale that grew up therefrom. But how can the ghosts of unbelievers prevail against us who are of the Faith? Strap that dog's hands a little tighter *sahib*. An Afghan is like an eel.'

'But a dead *rissala*,' said Halley, jerking his captive's wrist. 'That is foolish talk, Kurruk Shah. The dead are dead. Hold still. *Sag!*' The Afghan wriggled.

'The dead are dead, and for that reason they walk at night. What need to talk? We be men; we have our eyes and ears. Thou canst both see and hear them down the hillside,' said Kurruk Shah composedly.

Halley stared and listened long and intently. The valley was full of stifled noises, as every valley must be at night; but whether he saw or heard more than was natural Halley alone knows, and he does not choose to speak on the subject.

At last, and just before the dawn, a green rocket shot up from the far side of the valley of Bersund, at the head of the gorge, to show that the Goorkhas were in position. A red light from the infantry at left and right answered it, and the cavalry burnt a white flare. Afghans in winter are late sleepers, and it was not till full day that the Gulla Kutta Mullah's men began to straggle from their huts, rubbing their eyes. They saw men in green, and red, and brown uniforms, leaning on their arms, neatly arranged all round the crater of the village of Bersund, in a cordon that not even a wolf could have broken. They rubbed their eyes the more when a pink-faced young man, who was not even in the army, but represented the Political Department, tripped down the hillside with two orderlies, rapped at the door of the Gulla Kutta Mullah's house, and told him quietly to step out and be tied up for safe transport. That same young man passed on through the huts, tapping here one *cateran*, and there another lightly with his cane; and as each was pointed out, so he was tied up, staring hopelessly at the crowned heights around where the English soldiers looked down with incurious eyes. Only the *Mullah* tried to carry it off with curses and high words, till a soldier who was tying his hands said:—

'None o' your lip! Why didn't you come out when you was ordered, instead o' keeping us awake all night? You're no better than my own barrack-sweeper, you white-'eaded old polyanthus! Kim up!'

Half an hour later the troops had gone away with the *Mullah* and his thirteen friends. The dazed villagers were looking ruefully at a pile of broken muskets and snapped swords, and wondering how in the world they had come so to miscalculate the forbearance of the Indian Government.

It was a very neat little affair, neatly carried out, and the men concerned were unofficially thanked for their services. Yet it seems to me that much credit is also due to another regiment whose name did not appear in brigade orders, and whose very existence is in danger of being forgotten.

Wireless

It's a funny thing, this Marconi business, isn't it?" said Mr. Shaynor, coughing heavily. "Nothing seems to make any difference, by what they tell me—storms, hills, or anything; but if that's true we shall know before morning."

"Of course it's true," I answered, stepping behind the counter. "Where's old Mr. Cashell?"

"He's had to go to bed on account of his influenza. He said you'd very likely drop in."

"Where's his nephew?"

"Inside, getting the things ready. He told me that the last time they experimented they put the pole on the roof of one of the big hotels here, and the batteries electrified all the water-supply, and"—he giggled—"the ladies got shocks when they took their baths."

"I never heard of that."

"The hotel wouldn't exactly advertise it, would it? Just now, by what Mr. Cashell tells me, they're trying to signal from here to Poole, and they're using stronger batteries than ever. But, you see, he being the guvnor's nephew and all that (and it will be in the papers too), it doesn't matter how they electrify things in this house. Are you going to watch?"

"Very much. I've never seen this game. Aren't you going to bed?"

"We don't close till ten on Saturdays. There's a good deal of influenza in town, too, and there'll be a dozen prescriptions coming in before morning. I generally sleep in the chair here.

26

It's warmer than jumping out of bed every time. Bitter cold, isn't it?"

"Freezing hard. I'm sorry your cough's worse."

"Thank you. I don't mind cold so much. It's this wind that fair cuts me to pieces." He coughed again hard and hackingly, as an old lady came in for ammoniated quinine. "We've just run out of it in bottles, madam." said Mr.Shaynor, returning to the professional tone, "but if you will wait two minutes, I'll make it up for you, madam."

I had used the shop for some time, and my acquaintance with the proprietor had ripened into friendship. It was Mr. Cashell who revealed to me the purpose and power of Apothecaries' Hall what time a fellow-chemist had made an error in a pre-scription of mine, had lied to cover his sloth, and when error and lie were brought home to him had written vain letters.

"A disgrace to our profession," said the thin, mild-eyed man, hotly, after studying the evidence. "You couldn't do a better serv-ice to the profession than report him to Apothecaries' Hall."

I did so, not knowing what *djinns* I should evoke; and the result was such an apology as one might make who had spent a night on the rack. I conceived great respect for Apothecaries' Hall, and esteem for Mr. Cashell, a zealous craftsman who mag-nified his calling. Until Mr. Shaynor came down from the North his assistants had by no means agreed with Mr. Cashell.

"They forget," said he, "that, first and foremost, the com-pounder is a medicine-man. On him depends the physician's reputation. He holds it literally in the hollow of his hand. Sir."

Mr. Shaynor's manners had not, perhaps, the polish of the grocery and Italian warehouse next door, but he knew and loved his dispensary work in every detail. For relaxation he seemed to go no farther afield than the romance of drugs—their discovery, preparation packing, and export—but it led him to the ends of the earth, and on this subject, and the Pharmaceutical Formu-lary, and Nicholas Culpepper, most confident of physicians, we met.

Little by little I grew to know something of his beginnings

and his hopes—of his mother, who had been a schoolteacher in one of the northern counties, and of his red-headed father, a small job-master at Kirby Moors, who died when he was a child; of the examinations he had passed and of their exceeding and increasing difficulty; of his dreams of a shop in London; of his hate for the price-cutting Co-operative stores; and, most interesting, of his mental attitude towards customers.

"There's a way you get into," he told me, "of serving them carefully, and I hope, politely, without stopping your own thinking. I've been reading Christie's *New Commercial Plants* all this autumn, and that needs keeping your mind on it, I can tell you. So long as it isn't a prescription, of course, I can carry as much as half a page of Christie in my head, and at the same time I could sell out all that window twice over, and not a penny wrong at the end. As to prescriptions, I think I could make up the general run of 'em in my sleep, almost."

For reasons of my own, I was deeply interested in Marconi experiments at their outset in England; and it was of a piece with Mr. Cashell's unvarying thoughtfulness that, when his nephew the electrician appropriated the house for a long-range installation, he should, as I have said, invite me to see the result.

The old lady went away with her medicine, and Mr. Shaynor and I stamped on the tiled floor behind the counter to keep ourselves warm. The shop, by the light of the many electrics, looked like a Paris-diamond mine, for Mr. Cashell believed in all the ritual of his craft. Three superb glass jars—red, green, and blue—of the sort that led Rosamund to parting with her shoes—blazed in the broad plate-glass windows, and there was a confused smell of orris, Kodak films, vulcanite, tooth-powder, sachets, and almond-cream in the air. Mr. Shaynor fed the dispensary stove, and we sucked cayenne-pepper jujubes and menthol lozenges. The brutal east wind had cleared the streets, and the few passers-by were muffled to their puckered eyes. In the Italian warehouse next door some gay feathered birds and game, hung upon hooks, sagged to the wind across the left edge of our window-frame.

"They ought to take these poultry in—all knocked about like that," said Mr. Shaynor. "Doesn't it make you feel fair perishing? See that old hare! The wind's nearly blowing the fur off him."

I saw the belly-fur of the dead beast blown apart in ridges and streaks as the wind caught it, showing bluish skin underneath. "Bitter cold," said Mr. Shaynor, shuddering. "Fancy going out on a night like this! Oh, here's young Mr. Cashell."

The door of the inner office behind the dispensary opened, and an energetic, spade-bearded man stepped forth, rubbing his hands.

"I want a bit of tin-foil, Shaynor," he said. "Good-evening. My uncle told me you might be coming." This to me, as I began the first of a hundred questions.

"I've everything in order," he replied. "We're only waiting until Poole calls us up. Excuse me a minute. You can come in whenever you like—but I'd better be with the instruments. Give me that tin-foil. Thanks."

While we were talking, a girl—evidently no customer—had come into the shop, and the face and bearing of Mr. Shaynor changed. She leaned confidently across the counter.

"But I can't," I heard him whisper uneasily—the flush on his cheek was dull red, and his eyes shone like a drugged moth's. "I can't. I tell you I'm alone in the place."

"No, you aren't. Who's *that?* Let him look after it for half an hour. A brisk walk will do you good. Ah, come now, John."

"But he isn't—"

"I don't care. I want you to; we'll only go round by St. Agnes. If you don't—"

He crossed to where I stood in the shadow of the dispensary counter, and began some sort of broken apology about a lady-friend.

"Yes," she interrupted. "You take the shop for half an hour—to oblige *me*, won't you?"

She had a singularly rich and promising voice that well matched her outline.

"All right," I said. "I'll do it—but you'd better wrap yourself up, Mr. Shaynor."

"Oh, a brisk walk ought to help me. We're only going round by the church." I heard him cough grievously as they went out together.

I refilled the stove, and, after reckless expenditure of Mr. Cashell's coal, drove some warmth into the shop. I explored many of the glass-knobbed drawers that lined the walls, tasted some disconcerting drugs, and, by the aid of a few cardamoms, ground ginger, chloric-ether, and dilute alcohol, manufactured a new and wildish drink, of which I bore a glassful to young Mr. Cashell, busy in the back office. He laughed shortly when I told him that Mr. Shaynor had stepped out—but a frail coil of wire held all his attention, and he had no word for me bewildered among the batteries and rods. The noise of the sea on the beach began to make itself heard as the traffic in the street ceased. Then briefly, but very lucidly, he gave me the names and uses of the mechanism that crowded the tables and the floor.

"When do you expect to get the message from Poole?" I demanded, sipping my liquor out of a graduated glass.

"About midnight, if everything is in order. We've got our installation-pole fixed to the roof of the house. I shouldn't advise you to turn on a tap or anything tonight. We've connected up with the plumbing, and all the water will be electrified." He repeated to me the history of the agitated ladies at the hotel at the time of the first installation.

"But what *is* it?" I asked. "Electricity is out of my beat altogether."

"Ah, if you knew *that* you'd know something nobody knows. It's just It—what we call electricity, but the magic—the manifestations—the Hertzian waves—are all revealed by *this*. The coherer, we call it."

He picked up a glass tube not much thicker than a thermometer, in which, almost touching, were two tiny silver plugs, and between them an infinitesimal pinch of metallic dust. "That's all," he said, proudly, as though himself responsible for the wonder.

"That is the thing that will reveal to us the powers—whatever the powers may be—at work—through space—a long distance away."

Just then Mr. Shaynor returned alone and stood coughing his heart out on the mat.

"Serves you right for being such a fool," said young Mr. Cashell, as annoyed as myself at the interruption. "Never mind—we've all the night before us to see wonders."

Shaynor clutched the counter, his handkerchief to his lips. When he brought it away I saw two bright red stains.

"I—I've got a bit of a rasped throat from smoking cigarettes," he panted. "I think I'll try a cubeb."

"Better take some of this. I've been compounding while you've been away." I handed him the brew.

"'Twon't make me drunk, will it? I'm almost a teetotaller. My word! That's grateful and comforting."

He sat down the empty glass to cough afresh.

"Brr! But it was cold out there I I shouldn't care to be lying in my grave a night like this. Don't you ever have a sore throat from smoking?" He pocketed the handkerchief after a furtive peep.

"Oh, yes, sometimes," I replied, wondering, while I spoke, into what agonies of terror I should fall if ever I saw those bright-red danger-signals under my nose. Young Mr. Cashell among the batteries coughed slightly to show that he was quite ready to continue his scientific explanations, but I was thinking still of the girl with the rich voice and the significantly cut mouth, at whose command I had taken charge of the shop. It flashed across me that she distantly resembled the seductive shape on a gold-framed toilet-water advertisement whose charms were unholily heightened by the glare from the red bottle in the window. Turning to make sure, I saw Mr. Shaynor's eyes bent in the same direction, and by instinct recognised that the flamboyant thing was to him a shrine. "What do you take for your—cough?" I asked.

"Well, I'm the wrong side of the counter to believe much in

patent medicines. But there are asthma cigarettes and there are pastilles. To tell you the truth, if you don't object to the smell, which is very like incense, I believe, though I'm not a Roman Catholic, Blaudett's Cathedral Pastilles relieve me as much as anything."

"Let's try." I had never raided a chemist's shop before, so I was thorough. We unearthed the pastilles—brown, gummy cones of benzoin—and set them alight under the toilet-water advertisement, where they fumed in thin blue spirals.

"Of course," said Mr. Shaynor, to my question, "what one uses in the shop for one's self comes out of one's pocket. Why, stock-taking in our business is nearly the same as with jewellers—and I can't say more than that. But one gets them—he pointed to the pastille-box—"at trade prices." Evidently the censing of the gay, seven-tinted wench with the teeth was an established ritual which cost something.

"And when do we shut up shop?"

We stay like this all night The gov—old Mr. Cashell—doesn't believe in locks and shutters as compared with electric light. Besides it brings trade. I'll just sit here in the chair by the stove and write a letter, if you don't mind. Electricity isn't my pre-scription."

The energetic young Mr. Cashell snorted within, and Shaynor settled himself up in his chair over which he had thrown a staring red, black, and yellow Austrian jute blanket, rather like a table-cover. I cast about, amid patent medicine pamphlets, for something to read, but finding little, returned to the manufacture of the new drink. The Italian warehouse took down its game and went to bed. Across the street blank shutters flung back the gaslight in cold smears; the dried pavement seemed to rough up in goose-flesh under the scouring of the savage wind, and we could hear, long ere he passed, the policeman flapping his arms to keep himself warm. Within, the flavours of cardamoms and chloric-ether disputed those of the pastilles and a score of drugs and perfume and soap scents.

Our electric lights, set low down in the windows before the

tunbellied Rosamund jars, flung inward three monstrous daubs of red, blue, and green, that broke into kaleidoscopic lights on the facetted knobs of the drug-drawers, the cut-glass scent flagons, and the bulbs of the sparklet bottles. They flushed the white-tiled floor in gorgeous patches; splashed along the nickel-silver counter-rails, and turned the polished mahogany counter-panels to the likeness of intricate grained marbles—slabs of porphyry and malachite. Mr. Shaynor unlocked a drawer, and ere he began to write, took out a meagre bundle of letters. From my place by the stove, I could see the scalloped edges of the paper with a flaring monogram in the corner and could even smell the reek of chypre. At each page he turned toward the toilet-water lady of the advertisement and devoured her with over-luminous eyes. He had drawn the Austrian blanket over his shoulders, and among those warring lights he looked more than ever the incarnation of a drugged moth—a tiger-moth as I thought.

He put his letter into an envelope, stamped it with stiff mechanical movements, and dropped it in the drawer. Then I became aware of the silence of a great city asleep—the silence that underlaid the even voice of the breakers along the sea-front—a thick, tingling quiet of warm life stilled down for its appointed time, and unconsciously I moved about the glittering shop as one moves in a sick-room. Young Mr. Cashell was adjusting some wire that crackled from time to time with the tense, knuckle-stretching sound of the electric spark. Upstairs, where a door shut and opened swiftly, I could hear his uncle coughing abed.

"Here," I said, when the drink was properly warmed, "take some of this, Mr. Shaynor."

He jerked in his chair with a start and a wrench, and held out his hand for the glass. The mixture, of a rich port-wine colour, frothed at the top.

"It looks," he said, suddenly, "it looks—those bubbles-like a string of pearls winking at you— rather like the pearls round that young lady's neck." He turned again to the advertisement where the female in the dove-coloured corset had seen fit to put on all her pearls before she cleaned her teeth.

"Not bad, is it?" I said.

"Eh?"

He rolled his eyes heavily full on me, and, as I stared, I beheld all meaning and consciousness die out of the swiftly dilating pupils. His figure lost its stark rigidity, softened into the chair, and, chin on chest, hands dropped before him, he rested open-eyed, absolutely still.

"I'm afraid I've rather cooked Shaynor's goose," I said, bearing the fresh drink to young Mr. Cashell. "Perhaps it was the chlorio-ether."

"Oh, he's all right." The spade-bearded man glanced at him pityingly. "Consumptives go off in those sort of doses very often. It's exhaustion . . . . I don't wonder. I dare say the liquor will do him good. It's grand stuff," he finished his share appreciatively. "Well, as I was saying—before he interrupted—about this little coherer. The pinch of dust, you see, is nickel-filings. The Hertzian waves, you see, come out of space from the station that despatches 'em, and all these little particles are attracted together—cohere, we call it—for just so long as the current passes through them. Now, it's important to remember that the current is an induced current. There are a good many kinds of induction—"

"Yes, but what is induction?"

"That's rather hard to explain untechnically. But the long and the short of it is that when a current of electricity passes through a wire there's a lot of magnetism present round that wire; and if you put another wire parallel to, and within what we call its magnetic field—why then, the second wire will also become charged with electricity."

"On its own account?"

"On its own account."

"Then let's see if I've got it correctly. Miles off, at Poole, or wherever it is—"

"It will be anywhere in ten years.

"You've got a charged wire—"

"Charged with hertzian waves which vibrate, say, two hun-

34

dred and thirty million times a second." Mr. Cashell snaked his forefinger rapidly through the air.

"All right—a charged wire at Poole, giving out these waves into space. Then this wire of yours sticking out into space—on the roof of the house—in some mysterious way gets charged with those waves from Poole—"

"Or anywhere—it only happens to be Poole tonight."

"And those waves set the coherer at work, just like an ordinary telegraph-office ticker?"

"No! That's where so many people make the mistake. The hertzian waves wouldn't be strong enough to work a great heavy Morse instrument like ours. They can only just make that dust cohere, and while it coheres (a little while for a dot and a longer while for a dash) the current from this battery—the home battery"—he laid his hand on the thing—"can get through to the Morse printing-machine to record the dot or dash. Let me make it clearer. Do you know anything about steam?"

"Very little. But go on."

"Well, the coherer is like a steam-valve. Any child can open a valve and start a steamer's engines, because a turn of the hand lets in the main steam, doesn't it? Now, this home battery here ready to print is the main steam. The coherer is the valve, always ready to be turned on. The hertzian wave is the child's hand that turns it."

"I see. That's marvellous."

"Marvellous, isn't it? And, remember, we're only at the beginning. There's nothing we sha'n't be able to do in ten years. I want to live—my God, how I want to live, and see it develop!" He looked through the door at Shaynor breathing lightly in his chair. "Poor beast! And he wants to keep company with Fanny Brand."

"Fanny *who?*" I said, for the name struck an obscurely familiar chord in my brain—something connected with a stained handkerchief, and the word "arterial."

"Fanny Brand—the girl you kept shop for." He laughed. "That's all I know about her, and for the life of me I can't see what Shaynor sees in her, or she in him."

"*Can't* you see what he sees in her?" I insisted.

"Oh, yes, if *that's* what you mean. She's a great, big, fat lump of a girl, and so on. I suppose that's why he's so crazy after her. She isn't his sort. Well, it doesn't matter. My uncle says he's bound to die before the year's out. Your drink's given him a good sleep, at any rate." Young Mr. Cashell could not catch Mr. Shaynor's face, which was half turned to the advertisement.

I stoked the stove anew, for the room was growing cold, and lighted another pastille. Mr. Shaynor in his chair, never moving, looked through and over me with eyes as wide and lustreless as those of a dead hare.

"Poole's late," said young Mr. Cashell, when I stepped back. "I'll just send them a call."

He pressed a key in the semi-darkness, and with a rending crackle there leaped between two brass knobs a spark, streams of sparks, and sparks again.

"Grand, isn't it? That's the power—our unknown power—kicking and fighting to be let loose," said young Mr. Cashell. "There she goes—kick—kick—kick into space. I never get over the strangeness of it when I work a sending-machine—waves going into space, you know. T. R. is our call. Poole ought to answer with L. L. L."

We waited two, three, five minutes. In that silence, of which the boom of the tide was an orderly part, I caught the clear "*kiss—kiss—kiss*" of the halliards on the roof, as they were blown against the installation-pole.

"Poole is not ready. I'll stay here and call you when he is."

I returned to the shop, and set down my glass on a marble slab with a careless clink. As I did so, Shaynor rose to his feet, his eyes fixed once more on the advertisement, where the young woman bathed in the light from the red jar simpered pinkly over her pearls. His lips moved without cessation. I stepped nearer to listen. "And threw—and threw—and threw," he repeated, his face all sharp with some inexplicable agony.

I moved forward astonished. But it was then he found

words—delivered roundly and clearly. These:—

And threw warm gules on Madeleine's young breast.

The trouble passed off his countenance, and he returned lightly to his place, rubbing his hands.

It had never occurred to me, though we had many times discussed reading and prize-competitions as a diversion, that Mr. Shaynor ever read Keats, or could quote him at all appositely. There was, after all, a certain stained-glass effect of light on the high bosom of the highly-polished picture which mighty by stretch of fancy, suggest, as a vile chromo recalls some incomparable canvas, the line he had spoken. Night, my drink, and solitude, were evidently turning Mr. Shaynor into a poet. He sat down again and wrote swiftly on his villainous note-paper, his lips quivering.

I shut the door into the inner office and moved up behind him. He made no sign that he saw or heard. I looked over his shoulder, and read, amid half-formed words, sentences, and wild scratches:—

—Very cold it was. Very cold
The hare—the hare—the hare—
The birds

He raised his head sharply, and frowned toward the blank shutters of the poulterer's shop where they jutted out against our window. Then one clear line came:—

The hare, in spite of fur, was very cold.

The head, moving machine-like, turned right to the advertisement where the Blaudett's Cathedral pastille reeked abominably. He grunted, and went on:—

Incense in a censer—
Before her darling picture framed in gold—
Maiden's picture—angel's portrait—

"Hsh!" said Mr. Cashell guardedly from the inner office, as though in the presence of spirits. "There's something coming through from somewhere; but it isn't Poole." I heard the crackle of sparks as he depressed the keys of the transmitter. In my own brain, too, something crackled, or it might have been the hair on my head. Then I heard my own voice, in a harsh whisper: "Mr. Cashell, there is something coming through here, too. Leave me alone till I tell you."

"But I thought you'd come to see this wonderful thing—Sir," indignantly at the end.

"Leave me alone till I tell you. Be quiet."

I watched—I waited. Under the blue-veined hand—the dry hand of the consumptive—came away clear, without erasure:

And my weak spirit fails
To think how the dead must freeze—

He shivered as he wrote—

Beneath the churchyard mould.

Then he stopped, laid the pen down, and leaned back.

For an instant, that was half an eternity, the shop spun before me in a rainbow-tinted whirl, in and through which my own soul most dispassionately considered my own soul as that fought with an over-mastering fear. Then I smelt the strong smell of cigarettes from Mr. Shaynor's clothing, and heard, as though it had been the rending of trumpets, the rattle of his breathing. I was still in my place of observation, much as one would watch a rifle-shot at the butts, half-bent, hands on my knees, and head within a few inches of the black, red, and yellow blanket of his shoulder I was whispering encouragement, evidently to my other self, sounding sentences, such as men pronounce in dreams.

"If he has read Keats, it proves nothing. If he hasn't—like causes *must* beget like effects. There is no escape from this law. *You* ought to be grateful that you know 'St. Agnes Eve' without the book; because, given the circumstances, such as Fanny Brand, who is the key of the enigma, and approximately represents the latitude and longitude of Fanny Brawne; allowing also for the bright red colour of the arterial blood upon the handkerchief, which was just what you were puzzling over in the shop just now; and counting the effect of the professional environment, here almost perfectly duplicated—the result is logical and inevitable. As inevitable as induction."

Still, the other half of my soul refused to be comforted. It was cowering in some minute and inadequate corner—at an immense distance.

Hereafter, I found myself one person again, my hands still gripping my knees, and my eyes glued on the page before Mr. Shaynor. As dreamers accept and explain the upheaval of landscapes and the resurrection of the dead, with excerpts from the evening hymn or the multiplication-table, so I had accepted the facts, whatever they might be, that I should witness, and had devised a theory, sane and plausible to my mind, that explained them all. Nay, I was even in advance of my facts, walking hurriedly before them, assured that they would fit my theory. And all that I now recall of that epoch-making theory are the lofty words: "If he has read Keats it's the chloric-ether. If he hasn't, it's the identical *bacillus*, or hertzian wave of tuberculosis, *plus* Fanny Brand and the professional status which, in conjunction with the mainstream of subconscious thought common to all mankind, has thrown up temporarily an induced Keats."

Mr. Shaynor returned to his work, erasing and rewriting as before with swiftness. Two or three blank pages he tossed aside. Then he wrote, muttering:

The little smoke of a candle that goes out.

"No," he muttered. "Little smoke—little smoke—little smoke. What else?" He thrust his chin forward toward the advertisement, whereunder the last of the Blaudett's Cathedral pastilles fumed in its holder. "Ah!" Then with relief:—

The little smoke that dies in moonlight cold.

Evidently he was snared by the rhymes of his first verse, for he wrote and rewrote "gold—cold—mould" many times. Again he sought inspiration from the advertisement, and set down, without erasure, the line I had overheard:

And threw warm gules on Madeleine's young breast.

As I remembered the original it is "fair"—a trite word—instead of "young," and I found myself nodding approval, though I admitted that the attempt to reproduce "*its little smoke in pallid moonlight died*" was a failure.

Followed without a break ten or fifteen lines of bald prose—the naked soul's confession of its physical yearning for its beloved—unclean as we count uncleanliness; unwholesome, but human exceedingly; the raw material, so it seemed to me in that hour and in that place, whence Keats wove the twenty-sixth, seventh, and eighth *stanzas* of his poem. Shame I had none in overseeing this revelation; and my fear had gone with the smoke of the pastille.

"That's it," I murmured. "That's how it's blocked out. Go on! Ink it in, man. Ink it in!"

Mr. Shaynor returned to broken verse wherein "loveliness" was made to rhyme with a desire to look upon "her empty dress." He picked up a fold of the gay, soft blanket, spread it over one hand, caressed it with infinite tenderness, thought, muttered, traced some snatches which I could not decipher, shut his eyes drowsily, shook his head, and dropped the stuff. Here I found myself at fault, for I could not then see (as I do now) in what manner a red, black, and yellow Austrian blanket coloured his dreams.

In a few minutes he laid aside his pen, and, chin on hand, considered the shop with thoughtful and intelligent eyes. He threw down the blanket, rose, passed along a line of drug-drawers, and read the names on the labels aloud. Returning, he took from his desk Christie's *New Commercial Plants* and the old Culpepper that I had given him, opened and laid them side by side with a clerky air, all trace of passion gone from his face, read first in one and then in the other, and paused with pen behind his ear.

"What wonder of Heaven's coming now?" I thought

"Manna—manna—manna," he said at last, under wrinkled brows. "That's what I wanted. Good! Now then! Now then! Good! Good! Oh, by God, that's good!" His voice rose and he spoke rightly and fully without a falter:—

> *Candied apple, quince and plum and gourd,*
> *And jellies smoother than the creamy curd,*
> *And lucent syrups tinct with cinnamon,*
> *Manna and dates in Argosy transferred*
> *From Fez; and spiced dainties, every one*
> *From silken Samarcand to cedared Lebanon.*

He repeated it once more, using "blander" for " smoother" in the second line; then wrote it down without erasure, but this time (my set eyes missed no stroke of any word) he substituted "soother" for his atrocious second thought, so that it came away under his hand as it is written in the book—as it is written in the book.

A wind went shouting down the street, and on the heels of the wind followed a spurt and rattle of rain.

After a smiling pause—and good right had he to smile—he began anew, always tossing the last sheet over his shoulder:—

> *The sharp rain falling on the window-pane,*
> *Rattling sleet—the wind-blown sleet.*

Then prose:

> It is very cold of mornings when the wind brings rain and sleet with it. I heard the sleet on the window-pane out-side, and thought of you, my darling. I am always thinking of you. I wish we could both run away like two lovers into the storm and get that little cottage by the sea which we are always thinking about, my own dear darling. We could sit and watch the sea beneath our windows. It would be a fairyland all of our own—a fairy sea—a fairy sea. . . .

He stopped, raised his head, and listened. The steady drone of the Channel along the sea-front that had borne us company so long leaped up a note to the sudden fuller surge that signals the change from ebb to flood. It beat in like the change of step throughout an army—this renewed pulse of the sea—and filled our ears till they, accepting it, marked it no longer.

41

A fairyland for you and me
Across the foam—beyond . . .
A magic foam, a perilous sea.

He grunted again with effort and bit his underlip. My throat dried, but I dared not gulp to moisten it lest I should break the spell that was drawing him nearer and nearer to the high-water mark but two of the sons of Adam have reached. Remember that in all the millions permitted there are no more than five— five little lines—of which one can say: "These are the pure Magic. These are the clear Vision. The rest is only poetry." And Mr. Shaynor was playing hot and cold with two of them!

I vowed no unconscious thought of mine should influence the blindfold soul, and pinned myself desperately to the other three, repeating and re-repeating:

A savage spot as holy and enchanted
As e'er beneath a waning moon was haunted
By woman wailing for her demon lover.

But though I believed my brain thus occupied, my every sense hung upon the writing under the dry, bony hand, all brown-fingered with chemicals and cigarette-smoke.

Our windows fronting on the dangerous foam,

(—he wrote, after long, irresolute snatches), and then—

Our open casements facing desolate seas
Forlorn—forlorn

Here again his face grew peaked and anxious with that sense of loss I had first seen when the Power snatched him. But this time the agony was tenfold keener, As I watched it mounted like mercury in the tube. It lighted his face from within till I thought the visibly scourged soul must leap forth naked between his jaws, unable to endure. A drop of sweat trickled from my forehead down my nose and splashed on the back of my hand.

"Our windows facing on the desolate seas
And pearly foam of magic fairyland—"

"Not yet—not yet," he muttered, "wait a minute. *Please* wait a minute. I shall get it then—

Our magic windows fronting on the sea,
The dangerous foam of desolate seas . . .
For aye.

"*Ouh*, my God!"

From head to heel he shook—shook from the marrow of his bones outwards—then leaped to his feet with raised arms, and slid the chair screeching across the tiled floor where it struck the drawers behind and fell with a jar. Mechanically, I stooped to recover it.

As I rose, Mr. Shaynor was stretching and yawning at leisure.

"I've had a bit of a doze," he said. "How did I come to knock the chair over? You look rather—"

"The chair startled me," I answered. "It was so sudden in this quiet."

Young Mr. Cashell behind his shut door was offendedly silent.

"I suppose I must have been dreaming," said Mr. Shaynor.

"I suppose you must," I said. "Talking of dreams—I—I noticed you writing—before—"

He flushed consciously.

"I meant to ask you if you've ever read anything written by a man called Keats."

"Oh! I haven't much time to read poetry, and I can't say that I remember the name exactly. Is he a popular writer?"

"Middling. I thought you might know him because he's the only poet who was ever a druggist. And he's rather what's called the lover's poet."

"Indeed. I must dip into him. What did he write about?"

"A lot of things. Here's a sample that may interest you."

Then and there, carefully, I repeated the verse he had twice spoken and once written not ten minutes ago.

"Ah. Anybody could see he was a druggist from that line about the tinctures and syrups. It's a fine tribute to our profession."

"I don't know," said young Mr. Cashell, with icy politeness, opening the door one half-inch, "if you still happen to be interested in our trifling experiments. But, should such be the case—"

I drew him aside, whispering, "Shaynor seemed going off into some sort of fit when I spoke to you just now. I thought, even at the risk of being rude, it wouldn't do to take you off your instruments just as the call was coming through. Don't you see?"

"Granted—granted as soon as asked," he said unbending. "I *did* think it a shade odd at the time. So that was why he knocked the chair down?"

"I hope I haven't missed anything," I said.

"I'm afraid I can't say that, but you're just in time for the end of a rather curious performance. You can come in, too, Mr. Shaynor. Listen, while I read it off."

The Morse instrument was ticking furiously. Mr. Cashell interpreted: "'*K.K.V. Can make nothing of your signals.*'" A pause. "'*M.V. M.M.V. Signals unintelligible. Purpose anchor Sandown Bay. Examine instruments tomorrow.*' Do you know what that means? It's a couple of men-o'-war working Marconi signals off the Isle of Wight. They are trying to talk to each other. Neither can read the other's messages; but all their messages are being taken in by our receiver here. They've been going on for ever so long. I wish you could have heard it."

"How wonderful!" I said. " Do you mean we're overhearing Portsmouth ships trying to talk to each other—that we're eavesdropping across half South England?"

"Just that. Their transmitters are all right, but their receivers are out of order, so they only get a dot here and a dash there. Nothing clear."

"Why is that?"

"God knows—and Science will know tomorrow. Perhaps the induction is faulty; perhaps the receivers aren't tuned to receive just the number of vibrations per second that the transmitter sends. Only a word here and there. Just enough to tantalise."

Again the Morse sprang to life.

"That's one of 'em complaining now. Listen:'*Disheartening—most disheartening.*' It's quite pathetic. Have you ever seen a spiritualistic *séance?* It reminds me of that sometimes—odds and ends of messages coming out of nowhere—a word here and there—no good at all."

" But mediums are all impostors," said Mr. Shaynor, in the doorway, lighting an asthma-cigarette. "They only do it for the money they can make. I've seen 'em."

"Here's Poole, at last—clear as a bell. L.L.L. *Now* we sha'n't be long." Mr. Cashell rattled the keys merrily. "Anything you'd like to tell 'em?"

"No, I don't think so," I said. "I'll go home and get to bed. I'm feeling a little tired."

Uncovenanted Mercies

If the Order Above be but the reflection of the Order Below, as that ancient affirms who has had experience of the orders, it follows that in the administration of the universe all departments must work together.

This explains why Azrael, Angel of Death, and Gabriel, Adam's First Servant and Courier of the Thrones, were talking with the Prince of Darkness in the office of the Archangel of the English, who—Heaven knows—is more English than his people.

Two guardian spirits had been reported to the Archangel for allowing their respective charges to meet against Orders. The affair involved Gabriel, as official head of all guardian spirits, and also Satan, since guardian spirits are exhuman souls, reconditioned for re-issue by the Lower Hierarchy. There was a doubt, too, whether the orders which the couple had disobeyed were absolute or conditional. And, further, Ruya'il, the female spirit, had refused to tell the Archangel of the English what the woman in her charge had said or thought when she met the man, for whom Kalka'il, the male guardian spirit, was responsible. Kalka'il had been equally obstinate; both spirits sheltering themselves behind the old ruling:—'Who knoweth the spirit of man that goeth upward, and the spirit of the beast that goeth downward to the earth?' The Archangel of the English, ever anxious to be just, had therefore invited Azrael, who separates the Spirit from the Flesh, to assist at the inquiry.

The four Powers were going over the case in detail.

'I am afraid,' said Gabriel at last, 'no Guardian Spirit is obliged to—er—give away, as your people say, his or her charge. But'—he turned towards the Angel of Death—'what's your view of the ruling?'

"'Ecclesiastes, Three, Twenty-one,'" Satan prompted.

'Thank you so much. I should say that it depends on the interpretation of "Who,"' Azrael answered. 'And it is certainly laid down that Whoever Who may be'—his halo paled as he bowed his head—'it is not any member of either hierarchy.'

'So I have always understood,' said Satan.

'To my mind'—the Archangel of the English spoke fretfully—'this lack of—er—loyalty in the rank and file of the G.S. comes from our pernicious system of employing reconditioned souls on such delicate duties.'

The shaft was to Satan's address, who smiled in acknowledgment.

'They have some human weaknesses, of course,' he returned. 'By the way, where on earth were that man and the woman allowed to meet?'

'Under the clock at——Terminus, I understand.'

'How interesting! 'By appointment?'

'Not at all. Ruya'il says that her woman stopped to look for her ticket in her bag. Kalka'il says that his man bumped into her. Pure accident, but a breach of Orders—trivial, in my judgment, for—'

'Was it a breach of Orders for Life?' Azrael asked.

He referred to that sentence, written on the frontal sutures of the skull of every three-year-old child, which is supposed, by the less progressive departments, to foreshadow his or her destiny.

'As a matter of detail,' said the Archangel, 'there were Orders for Life—identical in both cases. Here's the copy. But nowadays we rely on training and environment to counteract this sort of auto-suggestion.'

'Let's make sure,' Satan picked up the typed slip, and read aloud:—"'If So-and-so shall meet So-and-So, their state at the last shall be such as even Evil itself shall pity." H'm! That's not absolutely prohibitive. It's conditional—isn't it? 'There's great virtue in your "if," and'—he muttered to himself—'it will all come back to me.'

'Nonsense!' the Archangel replied. 'I intend that man and that woman for far better things. Orders for Life nowadays are no more than Oriental flourishes—aren't they?'

But the level-browed Gabriel, in whose department these trifles lie, was not to be drawn.

'I hope you're right,' Satan said after a pause. 'So you intend that couple for better things?'

'Yes!' the Archangel of the English cleared his throat ominously. 'Rightly or wrongly, I'm an optimist. I do believe in the general upward trend of life. It connotes, of course, a certain restlessness among my people—the English, you know.'

'The English I know,' said Satan.

'But in my humble judgment, they are developing on new planes. They must be met and guided by new methods. Surely in your dealings with the—er—more temperamental among them, you must have noticed this new sense of a larger outlook.'

'In a measure—ye-es,' Satan replied. 'But I remember much the same sort of thing after printing was invented. Your people used to come down to me then, reeking—positively Caxtonised—with words. Some of 'em were convinced they had invented new sins. We-ell! Boiled and peeled (we had to do a little of that, of course) their novelties were only variations on the Imperfect Octave—Pride, Envy, Anger, Sloth, Gluttony, Covetousness, Lust. Technique, I grant you. Originality, nil. You may find it so with this new Zeitgeist of theirs.'

'Ah, but you're such a pessimist,' the Archangel retorted, smiling. 'I do wish you could meet these two I have in my eye. Charmin' people. Cultured, capable, devout, of the happiest influences on their respective entourages; practical, earnest, and—er—so forth—they will each, in their spheres, supply just that touch which my people need at the present moment for their development. Therefore, I am giving them each full advantages for self-expression and realisation. These will include impeccable surroundings, wealth, culture, health, felicity (unhappy people can't make other people happy, can they?), and—everything else commensurate with the greatness of the destiny for which I—er—destine them.'

The Archangel of the English rubbed his soft hands and beamed on his colleagues.

'I hope you're justified,' said Satan. 'But are you quite sure that your method of—may I call it cosseting people, gets the best out of them?'

"Rather what I was thinking,' said Azrael. 'I've seen wonderful work done—with my sword practically at people's throats—even when I've had to haggle a bit. They're a hard lot sometimes.'

'Let's take Job's case.' Satan continued. 'He didn't reach the top of his form, as your people say, till I had handled him a little—did he?'

'Possibly not—by the standards of his age. But nowadays we don't give very high marks to the man of Uz. Qua Literature, rhetorical, Qua Theology, anthropomorphic and unobserved. No-o, you can't get away from the fact that new standards demand new methods, new outlooks, and above all, enlarged acceptances—yes, enlarged acceptances. That reminds me'—the Archangel of the English addressed himself to Azrael 'I've sent in-perhaps it hasn't come up to you yet—a demi–official asking if you can't see your way towards mitigating some of your departmental methods, so far as those affect your—er—final despatch-work. My people's standards of comfort have risen, you know; and they're complaining of the—the crudity of certain vital phenomena which lie within your provenance.'

For one instant Azrael lifted his eyes full on the hopeful countenance of the Archangel of the English, but no muscle twitched round his mouth as he replied:—'Death is a little crude. For that matter, so's Birth; but the two seem, somehow, to hang together. What would you say to an Inter–Departmental Committee—'

'Or commission—that gives ampler powers—to explore all possible avenues with a view to practical co-ordination? The very thing,' the Archangel ran on. 'As a matter of fact, I've had the terms of reference for such a conference drafted in the office. I'll run through 'em with you—if you can spare a few minutes.'

"Nothing I should like better,' Satan cried whole-heartedly. 'Unluckily, I'm not always master of my time.' He rose. The others followed his example and, due leave taken, launched into the void that lay flush with the office windows.

******

'Now, that,' Satan observed after an interval which had sunk three universes behind them, 'is a perfect example of the dyer's hand being subdued to what it works in. "We don't give high marks to the man of Uz." Don't we? I'm glad I've always dealt faithfully with all schoolmasters.'

'And he objects to my methods!' Azrael muttered. 'If he weren't immortal—unfortunately—I—I could show him something.'

The notion set them laughing so much that the ruler of an unconditioned galaxy hailed them from his throne; and to Satan's half-barked 'No!—No!'—sign that they were Powers in flight and not halting—returned a courteous 'On You be the Blessing.'

'He has left out "and the Peace,"' said Azrael critically.

'There is no need. They've never conceived of Your existence in these parts,' Gabriel explained, as one free of all the creations.

'Really?' Azreal seemed a little dashed. 'Our young English friend ought to apply for a transfer here. I fancy I should have to follow him before long.'

'Oh no,' Gabriel chuckled. 'He'd eliminate you by training and environment. You're only an Oriental flourish—like Orders for Life to a soul. D'you suppose there's no one in his office who knows what *Kismet* means?'

'I should say not—from the quality of the stuff he sends down to us,' Satan complained. 'Did you notice his dig at me about "our pernicious system" of guardian spirits? I do my best to recondition his damned souls for reissue, but—'

'You do it very thoroughly indeed,' said Gabriel. 'I've said as much in my last report on our personnel.'

'Thank you. It's heavier work than you'd imagine. If you're free for a little, I'd like to show you how heavy—'

'You're sure it wouldn't—?' Gabriel began politely.

'Not in the least. Come along, then! . . . Take Space! Drop Time! Forgive my going first . . . Now!'

The Three nose-dived at that point where Infinity returns upon itself, till they folded their wings beneath the foundations of Time and Space, whose double weight bore down on them through the absolute Zeroes of Night and Silence.

Gabriel breathed uneasily; for, the greater the glory, the more present the imperfections.

'It's the pressures,' Satan reassured him. 'We came down too quickly. Swallow a little and they'll go off. Meantime, we'll have some light on our subjects.'

The glare of the halo he wore in His Own Place fought against the Horror of Great Darkness.

'Have we gone beyond The Mercy?' Azrael whispered, appalled at the little light it won.

'They're delivered into *my* hands now,' Satan answered.

'Usen't there to be a notice hereabouts, requesting visitors to leave all their hopes behind them?' Gabriel peered into the gulf as he spoke.

'We've taken it down. We work on hope deferred now,' Satan answered. 'It acts more certainly.'

'But I'm not conscious of anything going on,' Azrael remarked.

'The processes are largely mental. But now and again . . . For example!' There was a minute sound, hardly louder than the parting of fever-gummed lips in delirium, but the silence multiplied it like thunders in a nightmare. 'That is one reconditioning now,' Satan explained.

'A hard lot. They frighten me sometimes,' said Azrael.

'And me always,' Gabriel added. 'I suppose that is because We are their servants.'

'Of whom I am the hardest-worked,' Satan insisted.

'Oh, but you've every sort of labour-saving device, these days, haven't you?' Gabriel said vaguely.

'None that eliminate responsibility. Take the case of that man and that woman we were talking about just now. What conclusion did you draw from the evidence of their guardian spirits?'

'There was only one conclusion possible—if they should meet,' Gabriel replied. 'You yourself read the copy of their Orders for Life.'

'And what did our young friend do? 'Rode off on glittering generalities about uplift and idealism and his precious scheme for debauching them both with all the luxuries, because "unhappy people can't make others happy." You heard him say it? He's hopeless.' Satan spoke indignantly.

'Oh, I wouldn't go as far as that. He's English.' Gabriel smiled.

'And then,' Satan held on, 'did you see him look at me when I read out "Evil itself shall pity?" That means, if and when the worst comes to the worst I shall have to put it straight again. I shall be expected to do the whole of his dirty work—unofficially—and shoulder the unpopularity—officially. I shall have to give that couple Hell—and our young friend will take the credit of my success.'

'The attitude is not unknown elsewhere,' said Azrael. 'Very little would persuade our worthy Michael, for instance, that his sword is as effective as mine.'

'I'll prove my contention now,' Satan turned to Gabriel, 'if you'll permit—we don't need both of 'em—the woman's guardian, Ruya'il, to report here for a moment. It's night in England now. I can jam "all ill dreams" while she's off duty. We shall have to manage the interview like one of their own cinemas, but you'll overlook that, I hope.'

Gabriel gave the permission without which no guardian spirit may quit station, even for a breath, and on the instant, monstrously enlarged upon space, her eyes shut against the glare that revealed her, stood Ruya'il in her last human shape as a woman upon earth.

Azrael moved forward.

'One instant,' said he. 'I think I have had the pleasure of meeting you, Mrs.—' (he gave her her name, address, and the date of her death). 'You called for me at the time. You seemed glad to meet me. Why?'

'Because I wanted to meet Gregory,' came the answer, in the flat tones of the held.

'There's our trouble in a nutshell,' said Satan, and took over the inquiry, saying:—'You were under Our Hand for recondition and re-issue, Mrs.—. For what cause?'

'Because of Gregory.'

'Who was re-issued as Kalka'il. And he because of you?'

'Yes.'

'On what terms were you issued as guardian spirits, please?'

'There were no terms. Gregory and I were free to meet in the course of our duties, if we could. So we did. It wasn't his fault.'

'Those, by the way, were the last words Eve ever spoke to me,' Azrael whispered to Gabriel.

'Indeed!' Satan resumed. 'So you met and, incidentally, your charges met, too. I think that will be all—oh, one minute more. You know—?' he named a railway terminus.

'Yes.' The eyelids quivered.

'In London and—Ours here?'

'Oh, please, don't! Yes!' A tear forced its way out, and glittered horribly on the cheek.

'I beg your pardon! Thank you so much. I needn't detain you any longer.'

'Now you see my position,' said Satan to the others. 'Our young friend should have had all this information on his blotter before his inquiry began. When he called me in, he should have communicated it to me. Then I should have known where I stood. But he didn't. He makes my job ten times more difficult than it need be by burking the essentials of it—stabs me in the back with his crazy schemes of betterment—and expects me to carry on!'

'I'm afraid my department must be responsible for the original error of detailing those two particular guardian spirits to those two particular people,' said Gabriel. 'At any rate, I accept the responsibility, and apologise.'

Satan laughed frankly. 'No need. We've been opposite numbers since Adam. Mistakes will happen. I merely wished to show you something of our young friend's loyal and helpful nature.'

'Meantime, what steps are you taking with that man and that woman?' Azrael asked.

'Tentative, only. Listen!'

He lifted his hand for silence. A broken whisper that seemed one with all space fought itself into their hearing:

'My God! My God! Why hast Thou forsaken me?'

'Was that an echo?' said Gabriel presently. 'Or was it in duplicate?'

'In duplicate. But we don't attach too much value to that class of expression. Very often it's only hysteria—or vanity. One can't be sure till much later.'

'What were those curious metallic clicks after the message?' Azrael asked.

'In the woman's case,' Satan explained, 'it was one of her rings against her tiara as she was putting it on to go to court. In the second, it was the star of some order that the man was being invested with by his sovereign. That proves how happy they are!'

A certain amount of human time passed.

'Surely there's music, too,' Gabriel went on. 'And words?'

Both were most faint, but quite clear:

'I have a song to sing, oh!

Sing me your song, oh!'

A break, a patter of verse, and then—on an almost unendurable movement that seemed to brush the heart-strings:

'Misery me! Lackaday-dee!

He died for the love of a lady!'

Last, the fall of a body.

'Oh, that's on a stage somewhere,' said Satan. 'They must be enjoying themselves now at a theatre. Everything's coming their way. "Unhappy people can't make people happy, y'know." Well! Now you've heard them, I suggest that, if it doesn't bore you too much, you meet me here on—Azrael must know the dates—they are due for filing and we'll watch the result.'

After a glance into the future, Azrael gave a date in time as earth reckons it, and they parted.

As Death returned to his own sphere, by way of that galaxy which had been denied knowledge of his existence, its ruler heard a voice under the stars framing words, to him meaningless, such as these

'His speech is a burning fire.
With his lips he travaileth.
At his heart is a blind desire.
In his eye foreknowledge of Death.'

★★★★★★

The Archangel of the English, to whom, as to his people, the years had brought higher education, was more optimistic than ever. This time, he confided to the Three Archangels that, since Mass–action was the note of the age, he had discovered and was training an entire battalion of hand-picked souls, whose collective efforts towards the world's well-being he would aid with improved sanitary appliances and gratuitous sterilised public transport.

'What grasp and vision you have!' said Satan. 'By the way, do you remember a man and a woman you were rather interested in, some time ago? "Male and female created He them"—didn't He? Ruya'il, I think, was the woman's guardian spirit.'

'Perfectly,' said the Archangel of the English. 'They had a certain—not quite so large, perhaps, as they thought, but a certain—share in paving the way towards these present developments, which I have the honour to direct a little, perhaps, from my inconspicuous post in the background.'

'Good! I remember you spoke rather highly of them.'

'None the less'—the Archangel joined his hands across a stomach that insisted a little—'none the less I should *hardly* mark those two definitely as among the saviours of society. We say in the department that social service can be divided into two categories—saviours and paviours. Ha! Ha!'

'How very neat!' and Satan laughed, too.

'You see it? As a matter of fact, it arose out of one of my own marginal notes on an Hierarchical docket. No-o! I think I should be constrained to mark that couple as first-class among second-class paviours of society.'

'And what has happened to them?' Satan pursued.

The Archangel of the English glanced towards Azrael, who replied: 'Both filed.'

"Sorry for that—'sorry for that,' the Archangel chirped briskly. 'But of course I was only concerned to get the best work out of them which their limitations permitted. And I think, without unduly vaunting my methods, I have succeeded. By the way, I have just drafted a little bit of propaganda on the Interdependence of True Happiness and Vital Effort. It won't take ten minutes to—'

But once again it appeared that his hearers had business elsewhere. And indeed they met, soon after, on the edge of the abyss.

'If I had nerves,' said Satan, 'my young friend would arride them, as he'd say. What was he telling you when we left?'

'Oh,' said Azrael, 'our Interdepartmental Commission hadn't come up to his expectations. We couldn't agree on a form of words for a *modus moriendi*.'

'And then,' Gabriel added, 'he said Azrael hadn't the judicial mind.'

'How can! have?' said Azrael simply. 'I'm strictly executive. My instructions are to dismiss to the Mercy. *Apropos*—what has happened to that couple you were talking over with him, just now?'

'I'll show you in a minute.' Satan looked about him. The light from his halo was answered by a throb of increased productivity through all the Hells. He shaped some wordless questions across space, and nodded. 'It's all right,' he said. 'She's been in one of our shops, on test for breaking strain. He's due for final test too.

We'—Satan parodied the manner of the Archangel of the English—'took the liberty of thinking that there was a little more work to be got out of him in the paviour line, after our young friend above had dropped him. So we made him do it—rather as Job did—on an annuity bought by his friends, in what they call a Rowton lodging house, with an incurable disease on him. In our humble judgment, his last five years' realisation-output was worth all his constructive efforts.'

'Does—did he know it?' Gabriel asked.

'Hardly. He was down and out, as the English say. I'll show them both to you in a little. They met first at——Terminus; didn't they? . . . Good! . . . Follow me till you see me check!—So I . . . And here we are!'

'But this is the terminus! Line for line and'—Gabriel pointed to the newspaper posters—'letter for letter!'

'Of course it is. We don't babble about progress. We keep up with it.'

'Then why'—Gabriel coughed as a locomotive belched smoke to the roof—'why don't you electrify your system? I never smelt such fuel.'

'I have,' said Azrael, expert in operations. 'It's ether—'he sniffed again—'it's nitrous oxide—it's—it's every sort of anaesthetic.'

'It is. Smells wake memory,' said Satan.

'But what's the idea?' Gabriel demanded.

'Quite simple. A large number of persons in Time have weaknesses for making engagements—on oath, I regret to say—to meet other persons for all Eternity. Most of these appointments are forgotten or overlaid by later activities which have first claim on our attention. But the residue—say two *per cent*—comes here. Naturally, it represents a high level of character, passion, and tenacity which, *ipso facto,* reacts generously to our treatments. At first we used to put 'em into pillories and chaff 'em. When coaches came in, we accommodated them in replicas of roadside inns. With the advance of transportation, we duplicated all the leading London stations. (You ought to see some of 'em on a Saturday night!) But that's a detail. The essence of our idea is that every soul here is waiting for a train, which may or may not bring the person with whom they have contracted to spend Eternity. And, as the English say, they don't half have to wait either.'

Satan smiled on Hell's own——terminus as that would appear to men and women at the end of a hot, stale, sticky, petrol-scented summer afternoon under summer-time—twenty past six o'clock standing for twenty past seven.

A train came in. Porters cried the number of its platform; many of the crowd grouped by the barriers, but some stood fast under the clock, men straightening their ties and women tweaking their hats. An elderly female with a string-bag observed to a stranger: 'I always think it's best to stay where you promised you would. 'Less chance o' missing 'im that way.' 'Oh, quite,' the other answered. 'That's what I always do'; and then both moved towards the barrier as though drawn by cords.

The passengers filed out—they and the waiting crowd devouring each other with their eyes. Some, misled by a likeness or a half-heard voice, hurried forward crying a name or even stretching out their arms. To cover their error, they would pretend they had made no sign and bury themselves among their uninterested neighbours. As the last passenger came away, a little moan rose from the assembly.

A fat Jew suddenly turned and butted his way back to the ticket-collector, who was leaving for another platform.

'Every living soul's out, sir,' the man began, 'but—thank ye, sir—you can make sure if you like.'

The Jew was already searching beneath each seat and opening each shut door, till, at last, he pulled up in tears at the emptied luggage-van. He was followed on the same errand by a looseknit person in golfing-kit, seeking, he said, a bag of clubs, who swore bitterly when a featureless woman behind him asked: 'Was you looking for a sweetheart, ducky?'

Another train was called. The crowd moved over—some hopeful in step and bearing; others upheld only by desperate will. Several ostentatiously absorbed themselves in newspapers and magazines round the bookstalls; but their attention would not hold and when people brushed against them they jumped.

'They are all under moderately high tension,' Satan said. 'Come into the hotel—it's less public there—in case any of them come unstuck.'

The Archangels moved slowly till they were blocked by a seedy-looking person button-holing the stationmaster between two barrows of unlabelled luggage. He talked thickly. The official disengaged himself with practised skill. 'That's all right, Sir. I understand,' he said. 'Now, if I was you I'd slip over to the hotel and sit down and wait a bit. You can be quite sure, Sir, that the instant your friend arrives I'll slip over and advise you.'

The man, muttering and staring, drifted on.

'That's him,' said Satan. '"And behold he was in *my* hand"— with a vengeance. Did you hear him giving his titles to impress the stationmaster?'

'What will happen to him?' said Gabriel.

'One can't be certain. My departmental heads are independent in their own spheres. They arrange all sorts of effects. There's one, yonder, for instance, that 'ud never be allowed in the other station up above.'

A woman with a concertina and a tin cup took her stand on the kerb of the road by Number One platform, where a crowd was awaiting a train. After a pitiful flourish she began to sing:—

The Sun stands still in Heaven—
Dusk and the stars delay.
There is no order given
To cut the throat of the day.
My Glory is gone with my Power.
Only my torments remain.
Hear me! Oh, hear me!
All things wait on the hour
That sets me my doom again.'

But the song seemed unpopular, and few coins fell into the

cup.

'They used to pay anything you please to hear her—once,' Satan said, and gave her name. 'She's saving up her pennies now to escape.'

'Do they ever?' Gabriel asked.

'Oh, yes—often. They get clear away till—the very last. Then they're brought back again. It's an old Inquisition effect, but they never fail to react to it. You'll see them in the reading–rooms making their plans and looking up continental Bradshaws. By the way, we've taken some liberties with the decorations of the Hotel itself. I hope you'll approve.'

He ushered them into an enormously enlarged terminus hotel with passages and suites of public rooms, giving on to a further confusion of corridors and saloons. Through this maze men and women wandered and whispered, opening doors into hushed halls whence polite attendants reconducted them to continue their cycle of hopeless search elsewhere. Others, at little writing-tables in the suites of overheated rooms, made notes for honeymoons, as Satan had said, from the Bradshaws and steamer-folders, or wrote long letters which they posted furtively. Often, one of them would hurry out into the yard, with some idea of stopping a taxi which seemed to be carrying away a known face. And there were women who fished frayed correspondence out of their vanity-bags and read it with moist eyes close up to the windows.

'Everything is provided for—"according to their own imaginations,"' said Satan with some pride. 'Now I wonder what sort of test our man will—'

The seedy-looking person was writing busily when a page handed him a telegram. He turned, his face transfigured with joy, read, stared deeply at the messenger, and collapsed in a fit. Satan picked up the paper which ran:—'Reconsidered. Forgive. Forget.'

'Tck!' said Satan. 'That isn't quite cricket. But we'll see how he takes it.'

Well-trained attendants bore the snorting, inert body out,

into a little side-room, and laid it on a couch. When Satan and the others entered they found a competent-looking doctor in charge.

"'He that sinneth—let him fall into the hands of the physician,'" said Satan. 'I wonder what choice he'll make?'

'Has he any?' said Gabriel.

'Always. This is his last test. I can't say I exactly approve of the means, but if one interferes with one's subordinates it weakens initiative.'

'Do you mean to say, then, that that telegram was forged?' cried Gabriel hotly.

"'There are lying spirits also, was the smooth answer." Wait and see.'

The man had been brought to with brandy and *sal volatile*. As he recovered consciousness he groaned.

'I remember now,' said he.

'You needn't;' the doctor spoke slowly. 'We can take away your memory—'

'If—if,' said Satan, as one prompting a discourteous child.

'If you please,' the doctor went on, looking Satan full in the face, and adding under his breath:—'Am I in charge here or are You? "Who knoweth—"'

'If I please?' the man stammered.

'Yes. If you authorise me,' the doctor went on.

'Then what becomes of me?'

'You'll be free from that pain at any rate. Do you authorise me?'

'I do not. I'll see you damned first.'

The doctor's face lit, but his answer was not cheering.

'Then you'd better go.'

'Go? Where in Hell to?'

'That's not my business. This room's needed for other patients.'

'Well, if that's the case, I suppose I'd better.' He rebuttoned his loosed flannel shirt all awry, rolled off the couch, and fumbled towards the door, where he turned and said thickly:—'Look here—I've got something to say—I think . . . 'I—I charge you at the Judgment—make it plain. Make it plain, y'know . . . I charge you—'

But whatever the charge may have been, it ended in indistinct mutterings as he went out, and the doctor followed him with the bottle of spirits that had clogged his tongue.

'There!' said Satan. 'You've seen a full test for Ultimate Breaking Strain.'

'But now?' Gabriel demanded.

'Why do you ask?'

'Because it was written: "Even Evil itself shall pity."'

'I told you long ago it would all be laid on me at last,' said Satan bitterly.

Here Azrael interposed, icy and resplendent. 'My orders,' said he, 'are to dismiss to the Mercy. Where is it?'

Satan put out his hand, but did not speak.

The Three waited in that casualty room, with its porcelain washstand beneath the glass shelf of bottles, its oxygen cylinders tucked under the leatherette couch, and its heart-lowering smell of spent anaesthetics—waited till the agony of waiting that shuffled and mumbled outside crept in and laid hold; dimming, first, the lustre of their pinions; bowing, next, their shoulders as the motes in the never-shifted sunbeam filtered through it and settled on them, masking, finally, the radiance of Robe, Sword, and very Halo, till only their eyes had light.

The groan broke first from Azrael's lips. 'How long?' he muttered. 'How long?' But Satan sat dumb and hooded under cover of his wings.

There was a flurry of hysterics at the opening door. An uniformed nurse half supported, half led a woman to the couch.

'But I can't! I mustn't!' the woman protested, striving to push away the hands. 'I—I've got an appointment. I've got to meet the 7.12. I have really. It's rather—you don't know how important it is. Won't you let me go? Please, let me go! If you'll let me go, I'll give you all my diamonds.'

'Just a little lay-down and a nice cup o' tea. I'll fetch it in a minute,' the nurse cooed.

'Tea? How do I know it won't be poisoned. It will be poisoned—I know it will. Let me go I I'll tell the police if you don't let me go! I'll tell—I'll tell! Oh God!—who can I tell? . . . Dick! Dick! They're trying to drug me! Come and help me! Oh, help me! It's me, Dickie!'

Presently the unbridled screams exhausted themselves and turned into choking, confidential, sobbing whispers: 'Nursie! I'm so sorry I made an exhibition of myself just now. I won't do it again—on my honour I won't—if you'll just let me—just let me slip out to meet the 7.12. I'll be back the minute it's in, and then I'll be good. Please, take your arm away!'

But it was round her already. The nurse's head bent down as she blew softly on the woman's forehead till the grey hair parted and the Three could see the Order for Life, where it had been first written. The body began to relax for sleep.

'Don't—don't be so silly,' she murmured. 'Well, only for a minute, then. You mustn't make me late for the 7.12, because— because . . . Oh! Don't forget . . . "I charge you at the Judgment make it plain—I charge you—"'She ceased. The nurse looked as Kalka'il had done, straight into Satan's eyes, and:—'Go!' she commanded.

Satan bowed his head.

There was a knock, a scrabbling at the door, and the seedy-looking man shambled in.

'Sorry!' he began, 'but I think I left my hat here.'

The woman on the couch waked and, turning, chin in hand, chuckled deliciously:—'What does it matter now, dear?'

. . . . .

The Three found themselves whirled into the Void—two of them a little ruffled, the third somewhat apologetic.

'How did it happen?' Gabriel smoothed his plumes.

'Well—as a matter of fact, we were rather ordered away,' said Satan.

'Ordered away? I?' Azrael cried.

'Not to mention your senior in the Service,'

Satan answered. 'I don't know whether you noticed that that nurse happened to be Ruya'il—'

'Then I shall take official action.' But Azrael's face belied his speech.

'I think you'll find she is protected by that ruling you have so lucidly explained to our young friend. It all turns upon the interpretation of "Who," you know.'

'Even so,' said Gabriel, 'that does not excuse the neck-and-crop abruptness—the cinema—like trick—of our—our expulsion.'

'I'm afraid, as the little girl said about her spitting at her nurse, that that was my invention. But, my Brothers'—the Prince of Darkness smiled—'did you really think that we were needed there much longer?'

The Phantom Rickshaw

May no ill dreams disturb my rest,
Nor Powers of Darkness me molest.
                    —Evening Hymn

One of the few advantages that India has over England is a certain great knowability. After five years' service a man is directly or indirectly acquainted with the two or three hundred civilians in his province, all the messes of ten or twelve regiments and batteries, and some fifteen hundred other people of the non-official *castes*. In ten years his knowledge should be doubled, and at the end of twenty he knows, or knows something about, almost every Englishman in the empire, and may travel anywhere and everywhere without paying hotel-bills.

Globe-trotters who expect entertainment as a right, have, even within my memory, blunted this open-heartedness, but, none the less, today if you belong to the inner circle and are neither a bear nor a black sheep all houses are open to you and our small world is very kind and helpful.

Rickett of Kamartha stayed with Polder of Kumaon, some fifteen years ago. He meant to stay two nights only, but was knocked down by rheumatic fever, and for six weeks disorganized Polder's establishment, stopped Polder's work, and nearly died in Polder's bedroom. Polder behaves as though he had been placed under eternal obligation by Rickett, and yearly sends the little Ricketts a box of presents and toys. It is the same everywhere. The men who do not take the trouble to conceal from you their opinion that you are an incompetent ass, and the women who blacken your character and misunderstand your wife's amusements, will work themselves to the bone in your behalf if you fall sick or into serious trouble.

Heatherlegh, the doctor, kept, in addition to his regular practice, a hospital on his private account—an arrangement of loose-boxes for Incurables, his friends called it—but it was really a sort of fitting-up shed for craft that had been damaged by stress of weather. The weather in India is often sultry, and since the tale of bricks is a fixed quantity, and the only liberty allowed is permission to work overtime and get no thanks, men occasionally break down and become as mixed as the metaphors in this sentence.

Heatherlegh is the nicest doctor that ever was, and his invariable prescription to all his patients is "lie low, go slow, and keep cool." He says that more men are killed by overwork than the importance of this world justifies. He maintains that overwork slew Pansay who died under his hands about three years ago. He has, of course, the right to speak authoritatively, and he laughs at my theory that there was a crack in Pansay's head and a little bit of the Dark World came through and pressed him to death. "Pansay went off the handle," says Heatherlegh, "after the stimulus of long leave at home. He may or he may not have behaved like a blackguard to Mrs. Keith-Wessington. My notion is that the work of the Katabundi Settlement ran him off his legs, and that he took to brooding and making much of an ordinary P. & O. flirtation. He certainly was engaged to Miss Mannering, and she certainly broke off the engagement. Then he took a feverish chill and all that nonsense about ghosts developed itself. Overwork started his illness, kept it alight, and killed him, poor devil. Write him off to the system—one man to do the work of two-and-a-half men."

I do not believe this. I used to sit up with Pansay sometimes when Heatherlegh was called out to visit patients and I happened to be within claim. The man would make me most unhappy by describing in a low, even voice the procession of men, women, children, and devils that was always passing at the bottom of his bed. He had a sick man's command of language. When he recovered I suggested that he should write out the whole affair from beginning to end, knowing that ink might assist him to ease his mind. When little boys have learned a new bad word they are never happy till they have chalked it up on a door. And this also is literature.

He was in a high fever while he was writing, and the blood-and-thunder magazine style he adopted did not calm him. Two months afterwards he was reported fit for duty, but, in spite of the fact that he was urgently needed to help an undermanned commission stagger through a deficit, he preferred to die; vowing at the last that he was hag-ridden. I secured his manuscript before he died, and this is his version of the affair, dated 1885:—

My doctor tells me that I need rest and change of air. It is not improbable that I shall get both ere long—rest that neither the red-coated orderly nor the mid-day gun can break, and change of air far beyond that which any homeward-bound steamer can give me. In the meantime I am resolved to stay where I am; and, in flat defiance of my doctor's orders, to take all the world into my confidence. You shall learn for yourselves the precise nature of my malady; and shall, too, judge for yourselves whether any man born of woman on this weary earth was ever so tormented as I.

Speaking now as a condemned criminal might speak ere the drop-bolts are drawn, my story, wild and hideously improbable as it may appear, demands at least attention. That it will ever receive credence I utterly disbelieve. Two months ago I should have scouted as mad or drunk the man who had dared tell me the like. Two months ago I was the happiest man in India. Today, from Peshawar to the sea, there is no one more wretched. My doctor and I are the only two who know this. His explanation is that my brain, digestion and eyesight are all slightly affected; giving rise to my frequent and persistent "delusions." Delusions, indeed! I call him a fool; but he attends me still with the same unwearied smile, the same bland professional manner, the same neatly-trimmed red whiskers, till I begin to suspect that I am an ungrateful, evil-tempered invalid. But you shall judge for yourselves.

Three years ago it was my fortune—my great misfortune—

to sail from Gravesend to Bombay, on return from long leave, with one Agnes Keith-Wessington, wife of an officer on the Bombay side. It does not in the least concern you to know what manner of woman she was. Be content with the knowledge that, ere the voyage had ended, both she and I were desperately and unreasoningly in love with one another. Heaven knows that I can make the admission now without one particle of vanity. In matters of this sort there is always one who gives and another who accepts. From the first day of our ill-omened attachment, I was conscious that Agnes's passion was a stronger, a more dominant, and—if I may use the expression—a purer sentiment than mine. Whether she recognized the fact then, I do not know. Afterwards it was bitterly plain to both of us.

Arrived at Bombay in the spring of the year, we went our respective ways, to meet no more for the next three or four months, when my leave and her love took us both to Simla. There we spent the season together; and there my fire of straw burnt itself out to a pitiful end with the closing year. I attempt no excuse. I make no apology. Mrs. Wessington had given up much for my sake, and was prepared to give up all. From my own lips, in August, 1882, she learnt that I was sick of her presence, tired of her company, and weary of the sound of her voice. Ninety-nine women out of a hundred would have wearied of me as I wearied of them; seventy-five of that number would have promptly avenged themselves by active and obtrusive flirtation with other men. Mrs. Wessington was the hundredth. On her neither my openly-expressed aversion, nor the cutting brutalities with which I garnished our interviews had the least effect.

"Jack, darling!" was her one eternal cuckoo-cry, "I'm sure it's all a mistake—a hideous mistake; and we'll be good friends again someday. *Please* forgive me. Jack, dear."

I was the offender, and I knew it. That knowledge transformed my pity into passive endurance, and, eventually, into blind hate—the same instinct, I suppose, which prompts a man to savagely stamp on the spider he has but half killed. And with this hate in my bosom the season of 1882 came to an end.

Next year we met again at Simla—she with her monotonous

face and timid attempts at reconciliation, and I with loathing of her in every fibre of my frame. Several times I could not avoid meeting her alone; and on each occasion her words were identically the same. Still the unreasoning wail that it was all a "mistake;" and still the hope of eventually making friends." I might have seen, had I cared to look, that that hope only was keeping her alive. She grew more wan and thin month by month. You will agree with me, at least, that such conduct would have driven any one to despair. It was uncalled for, childish, unwomanly. I maintain that she was much to blame. And again, sometimes, in the black, fever-stricken night watches, I have begun to think that I might have been a little kinder to her. But that really is a "delusion." I could not have continued pretending to love her when I didn't; could I? It would have been unfair to us both.

Last year we met again—on the same terms as before. The same weary appeals, and the same curt answers from my lips. At least I would make her see how wholly wrong and hopeless were her attempts at resuming the old relationship. As the season wore on, we fell apart—that is to say, she found it difficult to meet me, for I had other and more absorbing interests to attend to. When I think it over quietly in my sick-room, the season of 1884 seems a confused nightmare wherein light and shade were fantastically intermingled—my courtship of little Kitty Mannering; my hopes, doubts and fears; our long rides together; my trembling avowal of attachment; her reply; and now and again a vision of a white face flitting by in the 'rickshaw with the black and white liveries I once watched for so earnestly; the wave of Mrs. Wessington's gloved hand; and, when she met me alone, which was but seldom, the irksome monotony of her appeal. I loved Kitty Mannering, honestly, heartily loved her, and with my love for her grew my hatred for Agnes. In August Kitty and I were, engaged. The next day I met those accursed "magpie" *jhampanies* at the back of Jakko, and, moved by some passing sentiment of pity, stopped to tell Mrs. Wessington everything. She knew it already.

"So I hear you're engaged, Jack dear." Then, without a moment's pause: "I'm sure it's all a mistake—a hideous mistake. We shall be as good friends some day, Jack, as we ever were."

My answer might have made even a man wince. It cut the dying woman before the like the blow of a whip. "Please forgive me, Jack; I didn't mean to make you angry; but it's true, it's true!"

And Mrs. Wessington broke down completely. I turned away and left her to finish her journey in peace, feeling, but only for a moment or two, that I had been an unutterably mean hound. I looked back, and saw that she had turned her 'rickshaw with the idea, I suppose, of overtaking me.

The scene and its surroundings were photographed on my memory. The rain-swept sky (we were at the end of the wet weather), the sodden, dingy pines, the muddy road, and the black powder-riven cliffs formed a gloomy background against which the black and white liveries of the *jhampanies*, the yellow-panelled 'rickshaw and Mrs. Wessington's down-bowed golden head stood out clearly. She was holding her handkerchief in her left hand and was leaning back exhausted against the 'rickshaw cushions. I turned my horse up a bypath near the Sanjowlie Reservoir and literally ran away. Once I fancied I heard a faint call of "Jack!" This may have been imagination. I never stopped to verify it. Ten minutes later I came across Kitty on horseback; and, in the delight of a long ride with her, forgot all about the interview.

A week later Mrs. Wessington died, and the inexpressible burden of her existence was removed from my life. I went Plainsward perfectly happy. Before three months were over I had forgotten all about her, except that at times the discovery of some of her old letters reminded me unpleasantly of our bygone relationship. By January I had disinterred what was left of our correspondence from among my scattered belongings and had burnt it. At the beginning of April of this year, 1885, I was at Simla—semi-deserted Simla—once more, and was deep in lover's talks and walks with Kitty. It was decided that we should be married at the end of June. You will understand, therefore, that, loving Kitty as I did, I am not saying too much when I pronounce myself to have been, at the time, the happiest man in India.

Fourteen delightful days passed almost before I noticed their flight. Then, aroused to the sense of what was proper among mortals circumstanced as we were, I pointed out to Kitty that an engagement ring was the outward and visible sign of her dignity as an engaged girl; and that she must forthwith come to Hamilton's to be measured for one. Up to that moment, I give you my word, we had completely forgotten so trivial a matter. To Hamilton's we accordingly went on the 15th of April, 1885. Remember that—whatever my doctor may say to the contrary—I was then in perfect health, enjoying a well-balanced mind and an absolutely tranquil spirit. Kitty and I entered Hamilton's shop together, and there, regardless of the order of affairs, I measured Kitty's finger for the ring in the presence of the amused assistant. The ring was a sapphire with two diamonds. We then rode out down the slope that leads to the Combermere Bridge and Peliti's shop.

While my Waler was cautiously feeling his way over the loose shale, and Kitty was laughing and chattering at my side—while all Simla, that is to say as much of it as had then come from the plains, was grouped round the reading-room and Peliti's veranda—I was aware that someone, apparently at a vast distance, was calling me by my Christian name. It struck me that I had heard the voice before, but when and where I could not at once determine. In the short space it took to cover the road between the path from Hamilton's shop and the first plank of the Combermere Bridge I had thought over half-a-dozen people who might have committed such a solecism, and had eventually decided that it must have been some singing in my ears.

Immediately opposite Peliti's shop my eye was arrested by the sight of four *jhampanies* in black and white livery, pulling a yellow-panelled, cheap, bazaar 'rickshaw. In a moment my mind flew back to the previous season and Mrs. Wessington with a sense of irritation and disgust. Was it not enough that the woman was dead and done with, without her black and white servitors reappearing to spoil the day's happiness? Whoever employed them now I thought I would call upon, and ask as a personal favor to change her *jhampanies'* livery. I would hire the men myself, and, if necessary, buy their coats from off their backs. It is impossible to say here what a flood of undesirable memories their presence evoked.

"Kitty," I cried, "there are poor Mrs. Wessington's *jhampanies* turned up again! I wonder who has them now?"

Kitty had known Mrs. Wessington slightly last season, and had always been interested in the sickly woman.

"What? Where?" she asked. "I can't see them anywhere."

Even as she spoke, her horse, swerving from a laden mule, threw himself directly in front of the advancing 'rickshaw. I had scarcely time to utter a word of warning when, to my unutterable horror, horse and rider passed *through* men and carriage as if they had been thin air.

"What's the matter?" cried Kitty; "what made you call out so foolishly, Jack? If I *am* engaged I don't want all creation to know about it. There was lots of space between the mule and the veranda; and, if you think I can't ride—There!"

Whereupon wilful Kitty set off, her dainty little head in the air, at a hand-gallop in the direction of the bandstand; fully expecting, as she herself afterwards told me, that I should follow her. What was the matter? Nothing, indeed. Either that I was mad or drunk, or that Simla, was haunted with devils. I reined in my impatient cob, and turned round. The 'rickshaw had turned too, and now stood immediately facing me, near the left railing of the Combermere Bridge.

"Jack! Jack, darling." (There was no mistake about the words this time: they rang through my brain as if they had been shouted in my ear.) "It's some hideous mistake, I'm sure. *Please* forgive me Jack, and let's be friends again."

The 'rickshaw-hood had fallen back, and inside, as I hope and daily pray for the death I dread by night, sat Mrs. Keith-Wessington, handkerchief in hand, and golden head bowed on her breast.

How long I stared motionless I do not know. Finally, I was aroused by my groom taking the Waler's bridle and asking whether I was ill. I tumbled off my horse and dashed, half fainting, into Peliti's for a glass of cherry-brandy. There two or three couples were gathered round the coffee-tables discussing the gossip of the day. Their trivialities were more comforting to me just then than the consolations of religion could have been. I plunged into the midst of the conversation at once; chatted, laughed and jested with a face (when I caught a glimpse of it in a mirror) as white and drawn as that of a corpse. Three or four men noticed my condition; and, evidently setting it down to the results of over many pegs, charitably endeavoured to draw me apart from the rest of the loungers. But I refused to be led away. I wanted the company of my kind—as a child rushes into the midst of the dinner-party after a fright in the dark. I must have talked for about ten minutes or so, though it seemed an eternity to me, when I heard Kitty's clear voice outside inquiring for me. In another minute she had entered the shop, prepared to roundly upbraid me for failing so signally in my duties. Something in my face stopped her.

"Why, Jack," she cried, "what *have* you been doing? What *has* happened? Are you ill?" Thus driven into a direct lie, I said that the sun had been a little too much for me. It was close upon five o'clock of a cloudy April afternoon, and the sun had been hidden all day. I saw my mistake as soon as the words were out of my mouth: attempted to recover it; blundered hopelessly and followed Kitty, in a regal rage, out of doors, amid the smiles of my acquaintances. I made some excuse (I have forgotten what) on the score of my feeling faint; and cantered away to my hotel, leaving Kitty to finish the ride by herself.

In my room I sat down and tried calmly to reason out the matter. Here was I, Theobald Jack Pansay, a well-educated Bengal civilian in the year of grace 1885, presumably sane, certainly healthy, driven in terror from my sweetheart's side by the apparition of a woman who had been dead and buried eight months ago. These were facts that I could not blink. Nothing was further from my thought than any memory of Mrs. Wessington when Kitty and I left Hamilton's shop. Nothing was more utterly commonplace than the stretch of wall opposite Peliti's. It was broad daylight. The road was full of people; and yet here, look you, in defiance of every law of probability, in direct outrage of Nature's

73

ordinance, there had appeared to me a face from the grave.

Kitty's Arab had gone *through* the 'rickshaw: so that my first hope that some woman marvellously like Mrs. Wessington had hired the carriage and the *coolies* with their old livery was lost. Again and again I went round this tread mill of thought; and again and again gave up baffled and in despair. The voice was as inexplicable as the apparition. I had originally some wild notion of confiding it all to Kitty; of begging her to marry me at once; and in her arms defying the ghostly occupant of the 'rickshaw. "After all," I argued, "the presence of the 'rickshaw is in itself enough to prove the existence of a spectral illusion. One may see ghosts of men and women, but surely never of *coolies* and carriages. The whole thing is absurd. Fancy the ghost of a hill-man!"

Next morning I sent a penitent note to Kitty, imploring her to overlook my strange conduct of the previous afternoon. My Divinity was still very wroth, and a personal apology was necessary. I explained, with a fluency born of night-long pondering over a falsehood, that I had been attacked with a sudden palpitation of the heart—the result of indigestion. This eminently practical solution had its effect; and Kitty and I rode out that afternoon with the shadow of my first lie dividing us.

Nothing would please her save a canter round Jakko. With my nerves still unstrung from the previous night I feebly protested against the notion, suggesting Observatory Hill, Jutogh, the Boileaugunge road—anything rather than the Jakko round. Kitty was angry and a little hurt, so I yielded from fear of provoking further misunderstanding, and we set out together towards Chota Simla. We walked a greater part of the way, and, according to our custom, cantered from a mile or so below the convent to the stretch of level road by the Sanjowlie Reservoir. The wretched horses appeared to fly, and my heart beat quicker and quicker as we neared the crest of the ascent. My mind had been full of Mrs. Wessington all the afternoon; and every inch of the Jakko road bore witness to our old-time walks and talks. The boulders were full of it; the pines sang it aloud overhead; the rain-fed torrents giggled and chuckled unseen over the shameful story; and the wind in my ears chanted the iniquity aloud.

As a fitting climax, in the middle of the level men call the La-dies' Mile, the Horror was awaiting me. No other 'rickshaw was in sight—only the four black and white *jhampanies*, the yellow-panelled carriage, and the golden head of the woman within—all apparently just as I had left them eight months and one fortnight ago! For an instant I fancied that Kitty must see what I saw—we were so marvellously sympathetic in all things. Her next words undeceived me—"Not a soul in sight! Come along, Jack, and I'll race you to the reservoir buildings!" Her wiry little Arab was off like a bird, my Waler following close behind, and in this order we dashed under the cliffs. Half a minute brought us within fifty yards of the 'rickshaw. I pulled my Waler and fell back a little. The 'rickshaw was directly in the middle of the road: and once more the Arab passed through it, my horse following. "Jack, Jack, dear! *Please* forgive me," rang with a wail in my ears, and, after an interval: "It's all a mistake, a hideous mistake!"

I spurred my horse like a man possessed. When I turned my head at the reservoir works the black and white liveries were still waiting—patiently waiting—under the gray hillside, and the wind brought me a mocking echo of the words I had just heard. Kitty bantered me a good deal on my silence throughout the remainder of the ride. I had been talking up till then wildly and at random. To save my life I could not speak afterwards naturally, and from Sanjowlie to the church wisely held my tongue.

I was to dine with the Mannerings that night and had barely time to canter home to dress. On the road to Elysium Hill I overheard two men talking together in the dusk—"It's a curious thing," said one, "how completely all trace of it disappeared. You know my wife was insanely fond of the woman (never could see anything in her myself) and wanted me to pick up her old 'rick-shaw and *coolies* if they were to be got for love or money. Morbid sort of fancy I call it, but I've got to do what the *memsahib* tells me. Would you believe that the man she hired it from tells me that all four of the men, they were brothers, died of cholera, on the way to Hardwár, poor devils; and the 'rickshaw has been broken up by the man himself. Told me he never used a dead *memsahib's* 'rickshaw. Spoilt his luck. Queer notion, wasn't it? Fancy poor little Mrs. Wessington spoiling anyone's luck except her own!" I laughed aloud at this point; and my laugh jarred on me as I uttered it. So there *were* ghosts of 'rickshaws after all, and ghostly employments in the other world! How much did Mrs. Wessington give her men? What were their hours? Where did they go?

And for visible answer to my last question I saw the infernal thing blocking my path in the twilight. The dead travel fast and by short-cuts unknown to ordinary *coolies*. I laughed aloud a second time and checked my laughter suddenly, for I was afraid I was going mad. Mad to a certain extent I must have been, for I recollect that I reined in my horse at the head of the 'rickshaw, and politely wished Mrs. Wessington "good evening." Her answer was one I knew only too well. I listened to the end; and replied that I had heard it all before, but should be delighted if she had anything further to say. Some malignant devil stronger than I must have entered into me that evening, for I have a dim recollection of talking the commonplaces of the day for five minutes to the thing in front of me.

"Mad as a hatter, poor devil—or drunk. Max, try and get him to come home,"

Surely *that* was not Mrs. Wessington's voice! The two men had overheard me speaking to the empty air, and had returned to look after me. They were very kind and considerate, and from their words evidently gathered that I was extremely drunk. I thanked them confusedly and cantered away to my hotel, there changed, and arrived at the Mannerings' ten minutes late. I pleaded the darkness of the night as an excuse; was rebuked by Kitty for my unlover-like tardiness; and sat down.

The conversation had already become general; and, under cover of it, I was addressing some tender small talk to my sweetheart when I was aware that at the further end of the table a short red-whiskered man was describing with much broidery his encounter with a mad unknown that evening. A few sentences convinced me that he was repeating the incident of half an hour ago. In the middle of the story he looked round for applause, as professional story-tellers do, caught my eye, and straightway collapsed. There was a moment's awkward silence, and the red-whiskered man muttered something to the effect that he had "forgotten the rest;" thereby sacrificing a reputation as a good story-teller which he had built up for six seasons past. I blessed him from the bottom of my heart and—went on with my fish.

In the fullness of time that dinner came to an end; and with genuine regret I tore myself away from Kitty—as certain as I was of my own existence that It would be waiting for me outside the door. The red-whiskered man, who had been introduced to me as Dr. Heatherlegh of Simla, volunteered to bear me company as far as our roads lay together. I accepted his offer with gratitude.

My instinct had not deceived me. It lay in readiness in the Mall, and, in what seemed devilish mockery of our ways, with a lighted head-lamp. The red-whiskered man went to the point at once, in a manner that showed he had been thinking over it all dinner time.

"I say, Pansay, what the deuce was the matter with you this evening on the Elysium road?" The suddenness of the question wrenched an answer from me before I was aware.

"That!" said I, pointing to It.

"*That* may be either *D. T.* or eyes for aught I know. Now you don't liquor. I saw as much at dinner, so it can't be *D. T.* There's nothing whatever where you're pointing, though you're sweating and trembling with fright like a scared pony. Therefore, I conclude that it's eyes. And I ought to understand all about them. Come along home with me. I'm on the Blessington lower road."

To my intense delight the 'rickshaw instead of waiting for us kept about twenty yards ahead—and this, too, whether we walked, trotted, or cantered. In the course of that long night ride I had told my companion almost as much as I have told you here.

"Well, you've spoilt one of the best tales I've ever laid tongue to," said he, "but I'll forgive you for the sake of what you've gone through. Now come home and do what I tell you; and when I've cured you, young man, let this be a lesson to you to steer clear of women and indigestible food till the day of your death."

The 'rickshaw kept steadily in front; and my red-whiskered friend seemed to derive great pleasure from my account of its exact whereabouts.

"Eyes, Pansay—all eyes, brain and stomach; and the greatest of these three is stomach. You've too much conceited brain, too little stomach, and thoroughly unhealthy eyes. Get your stomach straight and the rest follows. And all that's French for a liver pill. I'll take sole medical charge of you from this hour; for you're too interesting a phenomenon to be passed over."

By this time we were deep in the shadow of the Blessington lower road and the 'rickshaw came to a dead stop under a pine-dad, overhanging shale diff. Instinctively I halted too, giving my reason. Heatherlegh rapped out an oath.

"Now, if you think I'm going to spend a cold night on the hillside for the sake of a stomach-*cum*-brain-*cum*-eye illusion . . . Lord ha' mercy! What's that?"

There was a muffled report, a blinding smother of dust just in front of us, a crack, the noise of rent boughs, and about ten yards of the cliff-side—pines, undergrowth, and all—slid down into the road below, completely blocking it up. The uprooted trees swayed and tottered for a moment like drunken giants in the gloom, and then fell prone among their fellows with a thunderous crash. Our two horses stood motionless and sweating with fear. As soon as the rattle of falling earth and stone had subsided, my companion muttered: "Man, if we'd gone forward we should have been ten feet deep in our graves by now! *There are more things in , heaven and earth* . . . Come home, Pansay, and thank God. I want a drink badly."

We retraced our way over the Church Ridge, and I arrived at Dr. Heatherlegh's house shortly after midnight.

His attempts towards my cure commenced almost immediately, and for a week I never left his sight. Many a time in the course of that week did I bless the good fortune which had thrown me in contact with Simla's best and kindest doctor. Day by day my spirits grew lighter and more equable. Day by day, too, I became more and more inclined to fall in with Heatherlegh's "spectral illusion" theory, implicating eyes, brain, and stomach. I wrote to Kitty, telling her that a slight sprain caused by a fall from my horse kept me indoors for a few days; and that I should be recovered before she had time to regret my absence.

Heatherlegh's treatment was simple to a degree. It consisted of liver-pills, cold-water baths and strong exercise, taken in the dusk or at early dawn—for, as he sagely observed: "A man with a sprained ankle doesn't walk a dozen miles a day, and your young woman might be wondering if she saw you."

At the end of the week, after much examination of pupil and pulse and strict injunctions as to diet and pedestrianism, Heatherlegh dismissed me as brusquely as he had taken charge of me. Here is his parting benediction:

Man, I certify to you: mental cure, and that's as much as to say I've cured most of your bodily ailments. Now, get your traps out of this as soon as you can; and be off to make love to Miss Kitty.

I was endeavouring to express my thanks for his kindness. He cut me short:

"Don't think I did this because I like you. I gather that you've behaved like a blackguard all through. But, all the same you're a phenomenon, and as queer a phenomenon as you are a blackguard. Now, go out and see if you can find the eyes-brain-and-stomach business again. I'll give you a *lakh* for each time you see it."

Half an hour later I was in the Mannerings' drawing-room with Kitty—drunk with the intoxication of present happiness and the foreknowledge that I should never more be troubled with It's hideous presence. Strong in the sense of my new-found security, I proposed a ride at once; and, by preference, a canter round Jakko.

Never have I felt so well, so overladen with vitality and mere animal spirits as I did on the afternoon of the 30th of April. Kitty was delighted at the change in my appearance, and complimented me on it in her delightfully frank and outspoken manner. We left the Mannerings' house together, laughing and talking, and cantered along the Chota Simla road as of old.

I was in haste to reach the Sanjowlie Reservoir and there make my assurance doubly sure. The horses did their best, but seemed all too slow to my impatient mind. Kitty was astonished at my boisterousness. "Why, Jack!" she cried at last, "you are behaving like a child! What are you doing?"

We were just below the convent, and from sheer wantonness I was making my Waler plunge and curvet across the road as I tickled it with the loop of my riding-whip.

"Doing," I answered, "nothing, dear. That's just it. If you'd been doing nothing for a week except lie up, you'd be as riotous as I.

Singing and murmuring in your feastful mirth.
Joying to feel yourself alive;
Lord over nature, Lord of the visible Earth,
Lord of the senses five.

My quotation was hardly out of my lips before we had rounded the corner above the convent; and a few yards further on could see across to Sanjowlie. In the centre of the level road stood the black and white liveries, the yellow-panelled 'rickshaw and Mrs. Keith-Wessington. I pulled up, looked, rubbed my eyes, and, I believe, must have said something. The next thing I knew was that I was lying face downward on the road, with Kitty kneeling above me in tears.

"Has it gone, child?" I gasped. Kitty only wept more bitterly.

"Has what gone? Jack dear: what does it all mean? There must be a mistake somewhere, Jack. A hideous mistake." Her last words brought me to my feet—mad—raving for the time being.

"Yes, there is a mistake somewhere." I repeated, "a hideous mistake. Come and look at It!"

I have an indistinct idea that I dragged Kitty by the wrist along the road up to where It stood, and implored her for pity's sake to speak to it; to tell It that we were betrothed! that neither Death nor Hell could break the tie between us; and Kitty only knows how much more to the same effect. Now and again I appealed passionately to the Terror in the 'rickshaw to bear witness to all I had said, and to release me from a torture that was killing me. As I talked I suppose I must have told Kitty of my old relations with Mrs. Wessington, for I saw her listen intently with white face and blazing eyes.

"Thank you, Mr. Pansay," she said, "that's *quite* enough. Bring my horse."

The grooms, impassive as Orientals always are, had come up with the recaptured horses; and as Kitty sprang into her saddle I caught hold of the bridle entreating her to hear me out and forgive. My answer was the cut of her riding-whip across my face from mouth to eye, and a word or two of farewell that even now I cannot write down. So I judged, and judged rightly, that Kitty knew all; and I staggered back to the side of the 'rickshaw. My face was cut and bleeding, and the blow of the riding-whip had raised a livid blue weal on it. I had no self-respect. Just then, Heatherlegh, who must have been following Kitty and me at a distance, cantered up.

"Doctor," I said, pointing to my face, "here's Miss Mannering's signature to my order of dismissal and ... I'll thank you for that *lakh* as soon as convenient."

Heatherlegh's face, even in my abject misery, moved me to laugh.

"I'll stake my professional reputation"—he began.

"Don't be a fool," I whispered. "I've lost my life's happiness and you'd better take me home."

As I spoke the 'rickshaw was gone. Then I lost all knowledge of what was passing. The crest of Jakko seemed to heave and roll like the crest of a cloud and fall in upon me.

Seven days later (on the 7th of May, that is to say) I was aware that I was lying in Heatherlegh's room as weak as a little child. Heatherlegh was watching me intently from behind the papers on his writing table. His first words were not very encouraging; but I was too far spent to be much moved by them.

"Here's Miss Kitty has sent back your letters. You corresponded a good deal, you young people. Here's a packet that looks like a ring, and a cheerful sort of a note from Mannering

Papa, which I've taken the liberty of reading and burning. The old gentleman's not pleased with you."

"And Kitty?" I asked dully.

"Rather more drawn than her father from what she says. By the same token you must have been letting out any number of queer reminiscences just before I met you. Says that a man who would have behaved to a woman as you did to Mrs. Wessington ought to kill himself out of sheer pity for his kind. She's a hot-headed little *virago*, your mash. Will have it too that you were suffering from *D. T.* when that row on the Jakko road turned up. Says she'll die before she ever speaks to you again."

I groaned and turned over on the other side.

"Now you've got your choice, my friend. This engagement has to be broken off; and the Mannerings don't want to be too hard on you. Was it broken through *D. T.* or epileptic fits? Sorry I can't offer you a better exchange unless you'd prefer hereditary insanity. Say the word and I'll tell 'em it's fits. All Simla knows about that scene on the Ladies' Mile. Come! I'll give you five minutes to think over it."

During those five minutes I believe that I explored thoroughly the lowest circles of the Inferno which it is permitted man to tread on earth. And at the same time I myself was watching myself faltering through the dark labyrinths of doubt, misery, and utter despair. I wondered, as Heatherlegh in his chair might have wondered, which dreadful alternative I should adopt. Presently I heard myself answering in a voice that I hardly recognized:

"They're confoundedly particular about morality in these parts. Give 'em fits, Heatherlegh, and my love. Now let me sleep a bit longer."

Then my two selves joined, and it was only I (half crazed, devil-driven I) that tossed in my bed, tracing step by step the history of the past month.

"But I am in Simla," I kept repeating to myself. "I, Jack Pansay, am in Simla, and there are no ghosts here. It's unreasonable of that woman to pretend there are. Why couldn't Agnes have left me alone? I never did her any harm. It might just as well have been me as Agnes. Only I'd never have come back on purpose to kill *her*. Why can't I be left alone—left alone and happy?"

It was high noon when I first awoke: and the sun was low in the sky before I slept—slept as the tortured criminal sleeps on his rack, too worn to feel further pain.

Next day I could not leave my bed. Heatherlegh told me in the morning that he had received an answer from Mr. Mannering, and that, thanks to his (Heatherlegh's) friendly offices, the story of my affliction had travelled through the length and breadth of Simla, where I was on all sides much pitied.

"And that's rather more than you deserve," he concluded pleasantly, "though the Lord knows you've been going through a pretty severe mill. Never mind; we'll cure you yet, you perverse phenomenon."

I declined firmly to be cured. "You've been much too good to me already, old man," said I; "but I don't think I need trouble you further."

In my heart I knew that nothing Heatherlegh could do would lighten the burden that had been laid upon me.

With that knowledge came also a sense of hopeless, impotent rebellion against the unreasonableness of it all. There were scores of men no better than I whose punishments had at least been reserved for another world and I felt that it was bitterly, cruelly unfair that I alone should have been singled out for so hideous a fate. This mood would in time give place to another where it seemed that the 'rickshaw and I were the only realities in a world of shadows; that Kitty was a ghost; that Mannering, Heatherlegh, and all the other men and women I knew were all ghosts and the great, gray hills themselves but vain shadows devised to torture me: From mood to mood I tossed backwards and forwards for seven weary days, my body growing daily stronger and stronger, until the bedroom looking-glass told me that I had returned to everyday life, and was as other men once more. Curiously enough, my face showed no signs of the struggle I had gone through. It was pale indeed, but as expressionless and commonplace as ever. I had expected some permanent alteration—visible evidence of the disease that was eating me away. I found nothing.

On the 15th of May I left Heatherlegh's house at eleven o'clock in the morning; and the instinct of the bachelor drove me to the club. There I found that every man knew my story as told by Heatherlegh, and was, in clumsy fashion, abnormally kind and attentive. Nevertheless I recognized that for the rest of my natural life I should be among, but not of, my fellows; and I envied very bitterly indeed the laughing *coolies* on the Mall below. I lunched at the club, and at four o'clock wandered aimlessly down the Mall in the vague hope of meeting Kitty.

Close to the bandstand the black and white liveries joined me; and I heard Mrs. Wessington's old appeal at my side. I had been expecting this ever since I came out; and was only surprised at her delay. The phantom 'rickshaw and I went side by side along the Chota Simla road in silence. Close to the bazaar, Kitty and a man on horseback overtook and passed us. For any sign she gave I might have been a dog in the road. She did not even pay me the compliment of quickening her pace; though the rainy afternoon had served for an excuse.

So Kitty and her companion, and I and my ghostly Light-o'-Love, crept round Jakko in couples. The road was streaming with water; the pines dripped like roof-pipes on the rocks below, and the air was full of fine, driving rain. Two or three times I found myself saying to myself almost aloud: "I'm Jack Pansay on leave at Simla—*at Simla!* Everyday, ordinary Simla. I mustn't forget that—I mustn't forget that." Then I would try to recollect some of the gossip I had heard at the club; the prices of So-and-So's horses—anything, in fact, that related to the work-a-day Anglo-Indian world I knew so well. I even repeated the multiplication-table rapidly to myself, to make quite sure that I was not taking leave of my senses. It gave me much comfort; and must have prevented my hearing Mrs. Wessington for a time.

Once more I wearily climbed the convent slope and entered the level road. Here Kitty and the man started off at a canter, and I was left alone with Mrs. Wessington. "Agnes," said I, "will you put back your hood and tell me what it all means?" The hood dropped noiselessly and I was face to face with my dead and buried mistress. She was wearing the dress in which I had last seen her alive: carried the same tiny handkerchief in her right hand; and the same card-case in her left. (A woman eight months dead with a card-case!) I had to pin myself down to the multiplication-table, and to set both hands on the stone parapet of the road to assure myself that that at least was real.

"Agnes," I repeated, "for pity's sake tell me what it all means." Mrs. Wessington leant forward, with that odd, quick turn of the head I used to know so well, and spoke.

If my story had not already so madly overleaped the bounds of all human belief I should apologize to you now. As I know that no one—no, not even Kitty, for whom it is written as some sort of justification of my conduct—will believe me, I will go on. Mrs. Wessington spoke and I walked with her from the Sanjowlie road to the turning below the commander-in-chief's house as I might walk by the side of any living woman's 'rickshaw, deep in conversation. The second and most tormenting of my moods of sickness had suddenly laid hold upon me, and like the prince in Tennyson's poem, "*I seemed to move amid a world of ghosts.*" There had been a garden-party at the commander-in-chief's, and we two joined the crowd of homeward-bound folk.

As I saw them then it seemed that *they* were the shadows— impalpable fantastic shadows that divided for Mrs. Wessington's 'rickshaw to pass through. What we said during the course of that weird interview I cannot—indeed, I dare not—tell. Heatherlegh's comment would have been a short laugh and a remark that I had been "mashing a brain-eye-and-stomach chimera." It was a ghastly and yet in some indefinable way a marvellously dear experience. Could it be possible, I wondered, that I was in this life to woo a second time the woman I had killed by my own neglect and cruelty?

I met Kitty on the homeward road—a, shadow among shadows.

If I were to describe all the incidents of the next fortnight in their order, my story would never come to an end; and your patience would be exhausted. Morning after morning and evening after evening the ghostly 'rickshaw and I used to wander through Simla together. Wherever I went, there the four black and white liveries followed me and bore me company to and from my hotel. At the theatre I found them amid the crowd of yelling *jhampanies*; outside the club veranda, after a long evening of whist; at the birthday ball, waiting patiently for my reappearance; and in broad daylight when I went calling. Save that it cast no shadow, the 'rickshaw was in every respect as real to look upon as one of wood and iron. More than once, indeed, I have had to check myself from warning some hard-riding friend against cantering over it. More than once I have walked down the Mall deep in conversation with Mrs. Wessington to the unspeakable amazement of the passers-by.

Before I had been out and about a week I learnt that the "fit" theory had been discarded in favor of insanity. However, I made no change in my mode of life. I called, rode, and dined out as freely as ever. I had a passion for the society of my kind which I had never felt before; I hungered to be among the realities of life; and at the same time I felt vaguely unhappy when I had been separated too long from my ghostly companion. It would be almost impossible to describe my varying moods from the 15th of May up to today.

The presence of the 'rickshaw filled me by turns with horror, blind fear, a dim sort of pleasure, and utter despair. I dared not leave Simla; and I knew that my stay there was killing me. I knew, moreover, that it was my destiny to die slowly and a little every day. My only anxiety was to get the penance over as quietly as might be. Alternately I hungered for a sight of Kitty and watched her outrageous flirtations with my successor—to speak more accurately, my successors—with amused interest. She was as much out of my life as I was out of hers. By day I wandered with Mrs. Wessington almost content. By night I implored Heaven to let me return to the world as I used to know it. Above all these varying moods lay the sensation of dull, numbing wonder that the seen and the unseen should mingle so strangely on this earth to hound one poor soul to its grave.

August 27th,—Heatherlegh has been indefatigable in his attendance on me; and only yesterday told me that I ought to send in an application for sick-leave. An application to escape the company of a phantom! A request that the government would graciously permit me to get rid of five ghosts and an airy 'rickshaw by going to England! Heatherlegh's proposition moved me to almost hysterical laughter. I told him that I should await the end quietly at Simla; and I am sure that the end is not far off. Believe me that I dread its advent more than any word can say; and I torture myself nightly with a thousand speculations as to the manner of my death.

Shall I die in my bed decently and as an English gentlemen should die; or, in one last walk on the Mall, will my soul be wrenched from me to take its place forever and ever by the side of that ghastly phantasm? Shall I return to my old lost allegiance in the next world, or shall I meet Agnes loathing her and bound to her side through all eternity? Shall we two hover over the scene of our lives till the end of time? As the day of my death draws nearer, the intense horror that all living flesh feels towards escaped spirits from beyond the grave grows more and more powerful. It is an awful thing to go down quick among the dead with scarcely one half of your life completed. It is a thousand times more awful to wait as I do in your midst, for I know not what unimaginable terror. Pity me, at least on the score of my "delusion," for I know you will never believe what I have written here. Yet as surely as ever a man was done to death by the Powers of Darkness I am that man.

In justice, too, pity her. For as surely as ever woman was killed by man, I killed Mrs. Wessington. And the last portion of my punishment is even now upon me.

The House Surgeon

On an evening after Easter Day, I sat at a table in a homeward bound steamer's smoking-room, where half a dozen of us told ghost stories. As our party broke up a man, playing patience in the next alcove, said to me: "I didn't quite catch the end of that last story about the Curse on the family's first-born."

"It turned out to be drains," I explained. "As soon as new ones were put into the house the Curse was lifted, I believe. I never knew the people myself."

"Ah! I've had my drains up twice; I'm on gravel too."

"You don't mean to say you've a ghost in your house? Why didn't you join our party?"

"Any more orders, gentlemen, before the bar closes?" the steward interrupted.

"Sit down again, and have one with me," said the patience player. "No, it isn't a ghost. Our trouble is more depression than anything else."

"How interesting! Then it's nothing anyone can see?"

"It's—it's nothing worse than a little depression; And the odd part is that there hasn't been a death in the house since it was built—in 1863. The lawyer said so. That decided me—my good lady, rather—and he made me pay an extra thousand for it."

"How curious. Unusual, too!" I said.

"Yes; ain't it? It was built for three sisters—Moultrie was the name—three old maids. They all lived together; the eldest owned it. I bought it from her lawyer a few years ago, and if I've spent a pound on the place first and last, I must have spent five thousand. Electric light, new servants' wing, garden—all that sort of thing. A man and his family ought to be happy after so much expense, ain't it?" He looked at me through the bottom of his glass.

"Does it affect your family much?"

"My good lady—she's a Greek, by the way—and myself are middle-aged. We can bear up against depression; but it's hard on my little girl. I say little; but she's twenty. We send her visiting to escape it. She almost lived at hotels and hydros last year, but that isn't pleasant for her. She used to be a canary—a perfect canary—always singing. You ought to hear her. She doesn't sing now. That sort of thing's unwholesome for the young, ain't it?"

"Can't you get rid of the place?" I suggested.

"Not except at a sacrifice, and we are fond of it. Just suits us three. We'd love it if we were allowed."

"What do you mean by not being allowed?"

"I mean because of the depression. It spoils everything."

"What's it like exactly?"

"I couldn't very well explain. It must be seen to be appreciated, as the auctioneers say. Now, I was much impressed by the story you were telling just now."

"It wasn't true," I said.

"My tale is true. If you would do me the pleasure to come down and spend a night at my little place, you'd learn more than you would if I talked till morning. Very likely 'twouldn't touch your good self at all. You might be—immune, ain't it? On the other hand, if this influenza—influence *does* happen to affect you, why, I think it will be an experience."

While he talked he gave me his card, and I read his name was L. Maxwell M'Leod, Esq., of Holmescroft. A City address was tucked away in a corner.

"My business," he added, "used to be furs. If you are interested in furs—I've given thirty years of my life to 'em."

"You're very kind," I murmured.

"Far from it, I assure you. I can meet you next Saturday afternoon anywhere in London you choose to name, and I'll be only too happy to motor you down. It ought to be a delightful run at this time of year—the rhododendrons will be out. I mean it. You don't know how truly I mean it. Very probably—it won't affect you at all. And—I think I may say I have the finest collection of narwhal tusks in the world. All the best skins and horns have to go through London, and L. Maxwell M'Leod, he knows where they come from, and where they go to. That's his business."

For the rest of the voyage up-channel Mr. M'Leod talked to me of the assembling, preparation, and sale of the rarer furs; and told me things about the manufacture of fur-lined coats which quite shocked me. Somehow or other, when we landed on Wednesday, I found myself pledged to spend that weekend with him at Holmescroft.

On Saturday he met me with a well-groomed motor, and ran me out, in an hour and a half, to an exclusive residential district of dustless roads and elegantly designed country villas, each standing in from three to five acres of perfectly appointed land. He told me land was selling at eight hundred pounds the acre, and the new golf links, whose Queen Anne pavilion we passed, had cost nearly twenty-four thousand pounds to create.

Holmescroft was a large, two-storied, low, creeper-covered residence. A verandah at the south side gave on to a garden and two tennis courts, separated by a tasteful iron fence from a most park-like meadow of five or six acres, where two Jersey cows grazed. Tea was ready in the shade of a promising copper beech, and I could see groups on the lawn of young men and maidens appropriately clothed, playing lawn tennis in the sunshine.

"A pretty scene, ain't it?" said Mr. M'Leod. "My good lady's sitting under the tree, and that's my little girl in pink on the far court. But I'll take you to your room, and you can see 'em all later."

He led me through a wide parquet-floored hall furnished in pale lemon, with huge *Cloisonné* vases, an ebonized and gold grand piano, and banks of pot flowers in Benares brass bowls, up a pale oak staircase to a spacious landing, where there was a green velvet settee trimmed with silver. The blinds were down, and the light lay in parallel lines on the floors.

He showed me my room, saying cheerfully: "You may be a little tired. One often is without knowing it after a run through traffic. Don't come down till you feel quite restored. We shall all be in the garden."

My room was rather warm, and smelt of perfumed soap. I threw up the window at once, but it opened so close to the floor and worked so clumsily that I came within an ace of pitching out, where I should certainly have ruined a rather lop-sided laburnum below. As I set about washing off the journey's dust, I began to feel a little tired. But, I reflected, I had not come down here in this weather and among these new surroundings to be depressed; so I began to whistle.

And it was just then that I was aware of a little grey shadow, as it might have been a snowflake seen against the light, floating at an immense distance in the background of my brain. It annoyed me, and I shook my head to get rid of it. Then my brain telegraphed that it was the forerunner of a swift-striding gloom which there was yet time to escape if I would force my thoughts away from it, as a man leaping for life forces his body forward and away from the fall of a wall. But the gloom overtook me before I could take in the meaning of the message. I moved toward the bed, every nerve already aching with the foreknowledge of the pain that was to be dealt it, and sat down, while my amazed and angry soul dropped, gulf by gulf, into that horror of great darkness which is spoken of in the Bible, and which, as auctioneers say, must be experienced to be appreciated.

Despair upon despair, misery upon misery, fear after fear, each causing their distinct and separate woe, packed in upon me for an unrecorded length of time, until at last they blurred together, and I heard a click in my brain like the click in the ear when one descends in a diving bell, and I knew that the pressures were equalised within and without, and that, for the moment, the worst was at an end. But I knew also that at any moment the darkness might come down anew; and while I dwelt on this speculation precisely as a man torments a raging tooth with his tongue, it ebbed away into the little grey shadow on the brain of its first coming, and once more I heard my brain, which knew what would recur, telegraph to every quarter for help, release or diversion.

The door opened, and M'Leod reappeared. I thanked him politely, saying I was charmed with my room, anxious to meet Mrs. M'Leod, much refreshed with my wash, and so on and so forth. Beyond a little stickiness at the corners of my mouth, it seemed to me that I was managing my words admirably, the while that I myself cowered at the bottom of unclimbable pits. M'Leod laid his hand on my shoulder, and said: "You've got it now already, ain't it?"

"Yes," I answered. "It's making me sick!"

"It will pass off when you come outside. I give you my word it will then pass off. Come!"

I shambled out behind him, and wiped my forehead in the hall.

"You musn't mind," he said. "I expect the run tired you. My good lady is sitting there under the copper beech."

She was a fat woman in an apricot-coloured gown, with a heavily powdered face, against which her black long-lashed eyes showed like currants in dough. I was introduced to many fine ladies and gentlemen of those parts. Magnificently appointed landaus and covered motors swept in and out of the drive, and the air was gay with the merry outcries of the tennis players.

As twilight drew on they all went away, and I was left alone with Mr. and Mrs. M'Leod, while tall men-servants and maid-servants took away the tennis and tea things. Miss M'Leod had walked a little down the drive with a light-haired young man, who apparently knew everything about every South American railway stock. He had told me at tea that these were the days of financial specialisation.

"I think it went off beautifully, my dear," said Mr. M'Leod to his wife; and to me : "You feel all right now, ain't it? Of course you do."

Mrs. M'Leod surged across the gravel. Her husband skipped

nimbly before her into the south verandah, turned a switch, and all Holmes croft was flooded with light.

"You can do that from your room also," he said as they went in. "There is something in money, ain't it?"

Miss M'Leod came up behind me in the dusk. "We have not yet been introduced," she said, "but I suppose you are staying the night?"

"Your father was kind enough to ask me," I replied.

She nodded. "Yes, *I* know; and you know too, don't you? I saw your face when you came to shake hands with mamma. You felt the depression very soon. It is simply frightful in that bedroom sometimes. What do you think it is—bewitchment? In Greece, where I was a little girl, it might have been; but not in England, do you think? Or *do* you?"

"I don't know what to think," I replied. "I never felt anything like it. Does it happen often?"

"Yes, sometimes. It comes and goes."

"Pleasant!" I said, as we walked up and down the gravel at the lawn edge. "What has been your experience of it?"

"That is difficult to say, but—sometimes that—that depression is like as it were"—she gesticulated in most un-English fashion—"a light. Yes, like a light turned into a room—only a light of blackness, do you understand?—into a happy room. For sometimes we are so happy, all we three—so very happy. Then this blackness, it is turned on us just like—ah, I know what I mean now—like the head-lamp of a motor, and we are eclipsed. And there is another thing—"

The dressing-gong roared, and we entered the over-lighted hall. My dressing was a brisk athletic performance, varied with outbursts of song—careful attention paid to articulation and expression. But nothing happened. As I hurried downstairs, I thanked Heaven that nothing had happened.

Dinner was served breakfast fashion; the dishes were placed on the sideboard over heaters, and we helped ourselves.

"We always do this when we are alone, so we talk better," said Mr. M'Leod.

"And we are always alone," said the daughter.

"Cheer up, Thea. It will all come right," he insisted.

"No, papa." She shook her dark head. "Nothing is right while *it* comes."

"It is nothing that we ourselves have ever done in our lives—that I will swear to you," said Mrs. M'Leod suddenly. "And we have changed our servants several times. So we know it is not them."

"Never mind. Let us enjoy ourselves while we can," said Mr. M'Leod, opening the champagne.

But we did not enjoy ourselves. The talk failed. There were long silences.

"I beg your pardon," I said, for I thought someone at my elbow was about to speak.

"Ah! That is the other thing!" said Miss M'Leod. Her mother groaned.

We were silent again, and, in a few seconds it must have been, a live grief beyond words—not ghostly dread or horror, but aching, helpless grief—overwhelmed us, each, I felt, according to his or her nature, and held steady like the beam of a burning-glass. Behind that pain I was conscious there was a desire on somebody's part to explain something on which some tremendously important issue hung.

Meantime I rolled bread pills and remembered my sins; M'Leod considered his own reflection in a spoon; his wife seemed to be praying, and the girl fidgeted desperately with hands and feet, till the darkness passed on—as though the malignant rays of a burning-glass had been shifted from us."

"There," said Miss M'Leod, half rising. "Now you see what makes a happy home. Oh, sell it—sell it, father mine, and let us go away!"

"But I've spent thousands on it. You shall go to Harrogate next week, Thea dear."

"I'm only just back from hotels. I am *so* tired of packing."

"Cheer up, Thea. It is over. You know it does not often come here twice in the same night. I think we shall dare now to be comfortable."

He lifted a dish-cover, and helped his wife and daughter. His face was lined and fallen like an old man's after debauch, but his hand did not shake, and his voice was clear. As he worked to restore us by speech and action, he reminded me of a grey-muzzled collie herding demoralised sheep.

After dinner we sat round the dining-room fire—the drawing-room might have been under the Shadow for aught we knew—talking with the intimacy of gipsies by the, wayside, or of wounded comparing notes after a skirmish. By eleven o'clock the three between them had given me every name and detail they could recall that in any way bore on the house, and what they knew of its history.

We went to bed in a fortifying blaze of electric light. My one fear was that the blasting gust of depression would return—the surest way, of course, to bring it. I lay awake till dawn, breathing quickly and sweating lightly, beneath what De Quincey inadequately describes as "*the oppression of inexpiable guilt.*" Now as soon as the lovely day was broken, I fell into the most terrible of all dreams—that joyous one in which all past evil has not only been wiped out of our lives, but has never been committed; and in the very bliss of our assured innocence, before our loves shriek and change countenance, we wake to the day we have earned.

It was a coolish morning, but we preferred to breakfast in the south verandah. The forenoon we spent in the garden, pretending to play games that come out of boxes, such as croquet and clock golf. But most of the time we drew together and talked. The young man who knew all about South American railways took Miss M'Leod for a walk in the afternoon, and at five M'Leod thoughtfully whirled us all up to dine in town.

"Now, don't say you will tell the Psychological Society, and that you will come again," said Miss M'Leod, as we parted. "Because I know you will not."

"You should not say that," said her mother. "You should say, 'Goodbye, Mr. Perseus. Come again.'"

"Not him!" the girl cried. "He has seen the Medusa's head!"

Looking at myself in the restaurant's mirrors, it seemed to me that I had not much benefited by my weekend. Next morning I wrote out all my Holmescroft notes at fullest length, in the hope that by so doing I could put it all behind me. But the experience worked on my mind, as they say certain imperfectly understood rays work on the body.

I am less calculated to make a Sherlock Holmes than any man I know, for I lack both method and patience, yet the idea of following up the trouble to its source fascinated me. I had no theory to go on, except a vague idea that I had come between two poles of a discharge, and had taken a shock meant for someone else. This was followed by a feeling of intense irritation. I waited cautiously on myself, expecting to be overtaken by horror of the supernatural, but myself persisted in being humanly indignant, exactly as though it had been the victim of a practical joke. It was in great pains and upheavals—that I felt in every fibre—but its dominant idea, to put it coarsely, was to get back a bit of its own. By this I knew that I might go forward if I could find the way.

After a few days it occurred to me to go to the office of Mr. J. M. M. Baxter—the solicitor who had sold Holmescroft to M'Leod. I explained I had some notion of buying the place. Would he act for me in the matter?

Mr. Baxter, a large, greyish, throaty-voiced man, showed no enthusiasm. "I sold it to Mr. M'Leod," he said. "It 'ud scarcely do for me to start on the running-down tack now. But I can recommend—"

"I know he's asking an awful price," I interrupted, "and atop of it he wants an extra thousand for what he calk your clean bill of health."

Mr. Baxter sat up in his chair. I had all his attention.

"Your guarantee with the house. Don't you remember it?"

"Yes, yes. That no death had taken place in the house since it was built. I remember perfectly."

He did not gulp as untrained men do when they lie, but his

jaws moved stickily, and his eyes, turning towards the deed boxes on the wall, dulled. I counted seconds, one, two, three—one, two, three—up to ten. A man, I knew, can live through ages of mental depression in that time.

"I remember perfectly." His mouth opened a little as though it had tasted old bitterness.

"Of course *that* sort of thing doesn't appeal to me." I went on. "I don't expect to buy a house free from death."

"Certainly not. No one does. But it was Mr. M'Leod's fancy—his wife's rather, I believe; and since we could meet it—it was my duty to my clients—at whatever cost to my own feelings—to make him pay."

"That's really why I came to you. I understood from him you knew the place well."

"Oh, yes. Always did. It originally belonged to some connections of mine."

"The Misses Moultrie, I suppose. How interesting! They must have loved the place before the country round about was built up."

"They were very fond of it indeed."

"I don't wonder. So restful and sunny. I don't see how they could have brought themselves to part with it."

Now it is one of the most constant peculiarities of the English that in polite conversation—and I had striven to be polite—no one ever does or sells anything for mere money's sake.

"Miss Agnes—the youngest—fell ill" (he spaced his words a little), "and, as they were very much attached to each other, that broke up the home."

"Naturally. I fancied it must have been something of that kind. One doesn't associate the Staffordshire Moultries" (my Demon of Irresponsibility at that instant created 'em), "with—with being hard up."

"I don't know whether we're related to them," he answered importantly. "We may be, for our branch of the family comes from the Midlands."

I give this talk at length, because I am so proud of my first attempt at detective work. When I left him, twenty minutes later, with instructions to move against the owner of Holmescroft, with a view to purchase, I was more bewildered than any Doctor Watson at the opening of a story.

Why should a middle-aged solicitor turn plovers' egg colour and drop his jaw when reminded of so innocent and festal a matter as that no death had ever occurred in a house that he had sold? If I knew my English vocabulary at all, the tone in which he said the youngest sister "fell ill" meant that she had gone out of her mind. That might explain his change of countenance, and it was just possible that her demented influence still hung about Holmescroft; but the rest was beyond me.

I was relieved when I reached M'Leod's City office, and could tell him what I had done—not what I thought.

M'Leod was quite willing to enter into the game of the pretended purchase, but did not see how it would help if I knew Baxter.

"He's the only living soul I can get at who was connected with Holmescroft," I said.

"Ah! Living soul is good," said M'Leod. "At any rate our little girl will be pleased that you are still interested in us. Won't you come down some day this week?"

"How is it there now?" I asked.

He screwed up his face. "Simply frightful!" he said. "Thea is at Droitwich."

"I' should like it immensely, but I must cultivate Baxter for the present. You'll be sure and keep him busy your end, won't you?"

He looked at me with quiet contempt. "Do not be afraid. I shall be a good Jew. I shall be my own solicitor."

Before a fortnight was over, Baxter admitted ruefully that M'Leod was better than most firms in the business. We buyers were coy, argumentative, shocked at the price of Holmescroft, inquisitive, and cold by turns, but Mr. M'Leod the seller easily met and surpassed us; and Mr. Baxter entered every letter, telegram, and consultation at the proper rates in a cinematograph-film of a bill. At the end of a month he said it looked as though M'Leod, thanks to him, were really going to listen to reason. I was many pounds out of pocket, but I had learned something of Mr. Baxter on the human side. I deserved it. Never in my life have I worked to conciliate, amuse, and flatter a human being as I worked over my solicitor.

It appeared that he golfed. Therefore, I was an enthusiastic beginner, anxious to learn. Twice I invaded his office with a bag (M'Leod lent it) full of the spelicans needed in this detestable game, and a vocabulary to match. The third time the ice broke, and Mr. Baxter took me to his links, quite ten miles off, where in a maze of tramway lines, railroads, and nursery-maids, we skelped our divotted way round nine holes like barges plunging through head seas. He played vilely and had never expected to meet any one worse; but as he realised my form, I think he began to like me, for he took me in hand by the two hours together.

After a fortnight he could give me no more than a stroke a hole, and when, with this allowance, I once managed to beat him by one, he was honestly glad, and assured me that I should be a golfer if I stuck to it. I was sticking to it for my own ends, but now and again my conscience pricked me; for the man was a nice man. Between games he supplied me with odd pieces of evidence, such as that he had known the Moultries all his life, being their cousin, and that Miss Mary, the eldest, was an unforgiving woman who would never let bygones be. I naturally wondered what she might have against him; and somehow connected him unfavourably with mad Agnes.

"People ought to forgive and forget," he volunteered one day between rounds. "Specially where, in the nature of things, they can't be sure of their deductions. Don't you think so?"

"It all depends on the nature of the evidence on which one forms one's judgment," I answered.

"Nonsense!" he cried. "I'm lawyer enough to know that there's nothing in the world so misleading as circumstantial evidence. Never was."

"Why? Have you ever seen men hanged on it?"

"Hanged? People have been supposed to be eternally lost on it," his face turned grey again. "I don't know how it is with you, but my consolation is that God must know. He *must*! Things that seem on the face of 'em like murder, or say suicide, may appear different to God. Heh?"

"That's what the murderer and the suicide can always hope—I suppose."

"I have expressed myself clumsily as usual. The facts as God knows 'em—may *be* different—even after the most clinching evidence. I've always said that—both as a lawyer and a man, but some people won't—I don't want to judge 'em—we'll say they can't—believe it; whereas *I* say there's always a working chance—a certainty—that the worst hasn't happened." He stopped and cleared his throat. "Now, let's come on! This time next week. I shall be taking my holiday."

"What links?" I asked carelessly, while twins in a perambulator got out of our line of fire.

"A potty little nine-hole affair at a hydro in the Midlands. My cousins stay there. Always will. Not but what the fourth and the seventh holes take some doing. You could manage it, though," he said encouragingly. "You're doing much better. It's only your approach shots that are weak."

"You're right. I can't approach for nuts! I shall go to pieces while you're away—with no one to coach me," I said mournfully.

"I haven't taught you anything," he said, delighted with the compliment.

"I owe all I've learned to you, anyhow. When will you come back?"

"Look here," he began. "I don't know your engagements, but I've no one to play with at Burry Mills. Never have. Why couldn't you take a few days off and join me there? I warn you it will be rather dull. It's a throat and gout place—baths, massage, electricity, and so forth. But the fourth and the seventh holes really take some doing."

"I'm for the game," I answered valiantly; Heaven well knowing that I hated every stroke and word of it.

"That's the proper spirit. As their lawyer I must ask you not to say anything to my cousins about Holmescroft. It upsets 'em. Always did. But speaking as man to man, it would be very pleasant for me if you could see your way to "

I saw it as soon as decency permitted, and thanked him sincerely. According to my now well-developed theory he had certainly misappropriated his aged cousins' monies under power of attorney, and had probably driven poor Agnes Moultrie out of her wits, but I wished that he was not so gentle, and good-tempered, and innocent-eyed.

Before I joined him at Burry Mills Hydro, I spent a night at Holmescroft. Miss M'Leod had returned from her Hydro, and first we made very merry on the open lawn in the sunshine over the manners and customs of the English resorting to such places. She knew dozens of hydros, and warned me how to behave in them, while Mr. and Mrs. M'Leod stood aside and adored her.

"Ah! That's the way she always comes back to us," he said. "Pity it wears off so soon, ain't it? You ought to hear her sing 'With mirth thou pretty bird.'"

We had the house to face through the evening, and there we neither laughed nor sang. The gloom fell on us as we entered, and did not shift till ten o'clock, when we crawled out, as it were, from beneath it.

"It has been bad this summer," said Mrs. M'Leod in a whisper after we realised that we were freed. "Sometimes I think the house will get up and cry out—it is so bad."

"How?"

"Have you forgotten what comes after the depression?"

So then we waited about the small fire, and the dead air in the room presently filled and pressed down upon us with the sensation (but words are useless here) as though some dumb and bound power were striving against gag and bond to deliver its soul of an articulate word. It passed in a few minutes, and I fell to thinking about Mr. Baxter's conscience and Agnes Moultrie, gone mad in the well-lit bedroom that waited me. These reflections secured me a night during which I rediscovered how, from purely mental causes, a man can be physically sick; but the sickness was bliss compared to my dreams when the birds waked. On my departure, M'Leod gave me a beautiful narwhal's horn, much as a nurse gives a child sweets for being brave at a dentist's.

"There's no duplicate of it in the world," he said, "else it would have come to old Max M'Leod," and he tucked it into the motor. Miss M'Leod on the far side of the car whispered, "Have you found out anything, Mr. Perseus?"

I shook my head.

"Then I shall be chained to my rock all my life," she went on. "Only don't tell papa."

I supposed she was thinking of the young gentleman who specialised in South American rails, for I noticed a ring on the third finger of her left hand.

I went straight from that house to Burry Mills Hydro, keen for the first time in my life on playing golf, which is guaranteed to occupy the mind. Baxter had taken me a room communicating with his own, and after lunch introduced me to a tall, horse-headed elderly lady of decided manners, whom a white-haired maid pushed along in a bath-chair through the park-like grounds of the Hydro. She was Miss Mary Moultrie, and she coughed and cleared her throat just like Baxter. She suffered— she told me it was a Moultrie caste-mark—from some obscure form of chronic bronchitis, complicated with spasm of the glottis; And, in a dead, flat voice, with a sunken eye that looked and saw not, told me what washes, gargles, pastilles, and inhalations she had proved most beneficial.

From her I was passed on to her younger sister, Miss Elizabeth, a small and withered thing with twitching lips, victim, she told me, to very much the same sort of throat, but secretly devoted to another set of medicines. When she went away with Baxter and the bath-chair, I fell across a major of the Indian army with gout in his glassy eyes, and a stomach which he had taken all round the Continent. He laid everything before me; and him I escaped only to be confided in by a matron with a tendency to follicular tonsilitis and eczema. Baxter waited hand and foot on his cousins till five o'clock, trying, as I saw, to atone for his treatment of the dead sister. Miss Mary ordered him about like a dog.

"I warned you it would be dull," he said when we met in the smoking-room.

"It's tremendously interesting," I said. "But how about a look round the links?"

"Unluckily damp always affects my eldest cousin. I've got to buy her a new bronchitis-kettle. Arthurs broke her old one yesterday."

We slipped out to the chemist's shop in the town, and he bought a large glittering tin thing whose workings he explained.

"I'm used to this sort of work. I come up here pretty often," he said. "I've the family throat too."

"You're a good man," I said. "A very good man."

He turned towards me in the evening light among the beeches, and his face was changed to what it might have been a generation before.

"You see," he said huskily, "there was the youngest—Agnes. Before she fell ill, you know. But she didn't like leaving her sisters. Never would." He hurried on with his odd-shaped load and left me among the ruins of my black theories. The man with that face had done Agnes Moultrie no wrong.

★★★★★★

We never played our game. I was waked between two and three in the morning from my hygienic bed by Baxter in an ulster over orange and white pyjamas, which I should never have suspected from his character.

"My cousin has had some sort of a seizure," he said. "Will you come? I don't want to wake the doctor. Don't want to make a scandal. Quick!"

So I came quickly, and led by the white-haired Arthurs in a jacket and petticoat, entered a double-bedded room reeking with steam and Friar's Balsam. The electrics were all on. Miss Mary—I knew her by her height—was at the open window, wrestling with Miss Elizabeth, who gripped her round the knees. Miss Mary's hand was at her own throat, which was streaked with blood.

"She's done it. She's done it too!" Miss Elizabeth panted. "Hold her! Help me!"

"Oh, I say! Women don't cut their throats," Baxter whispered.

"My God! Has she cut her throat?" the maid cried out, and with no warning rolled over in a faint. Baxter pushed her under the wash-basins, and leaped to hold the gaunt woman who crowed and whistled as she struggled toward the window. He took her by the shoulder, and she struck out wildly.

"All right! She's only cut her hand," he said. "Wet towel—quick!"

While I got that he pushed her backward. Her strength seemed almost as great as his. I swabbed at her throat when I could, and found no mark; then helped him to control her a little. Miss Elizabeth leaped back to bed, wailing like a child.

"Tie up her hand somehow," said Baxter. "Don't let it drip about the place. She"—he stepped on broken glass in his slippers, "she must have smashed a pane."

Miss Mary lurched towards the open window again, dropped on her knees, her head on the sill, and lay quiet, surrendering the cut hand to me.

"What did she do?" Baxter turned towards Miss Elizabeth in the far bed.

"She was going to throw herself out of the window," was the answer. "I stopped her, and sent Arthurs for you. Oh, we can never hold up our heads again!"

Miss Mary writhed and fought for breath. Baxter found a shawl which he threw over her shoulders.

"Nonsense!" said he. "That isn't like Mary;" but his face worked when he said it.

"You wouldn't believe about Aggie, John. Perhaps you will

now!" said Miss Elizabeth. "I saw her do it, and she's cut her throat too!"

"She hasn't," I said. "It's only her hand."

Miss Mary suddenly broke from us with an indescribable grunt, flew, rather than ran, to her sister's bed, and there shook her as one furious schoolgirl would shake another.

"No such thing," she croaked. "How dare you think so, you wicked little fool?"

"Get into bed, Mary," said Baxter. "You'll catch a chill."

She obeyed, but sat up with the grey shawl round her lean shoulders, glaring at her sister. "I'm better now," she panted. "Arthurs let me sit out too long. Where's Arthurs? The kettle."

"Never mind Arthurs," said Baxter. "*You* get the kettle." I hastened to bring it from the side table. "Now, Mary, as God sees you, tell me what you've done."

His lips were dry, and he could hot moisten them with his tongue.

Miss Mary applied herself to the mouth of the kettle, and between indraws of steam said: "The spasm came on just now, while I was asleep. I was nearly choking to death. So I went to the window. I've done it often before, without waking any one. Bessie's such an old maid about draughts. I tell you I was choking to death. I couldn't manage the catch, and I nearly fell out. That window opens too low. I cut my hand trying to save myself. Who has tied it up in this filthy handkerchief? I wish you had had my throat, Bessie. I never was nearer dying!" She scowled on us all impartially, while her sister sobbed.

From the bottom of the bed we heard a quivering voice: "Is she dead? Have they took her away? Oh, I never could bear the sight o' blood!"

"Arthurs," said Miss Mary, "you are an hireling. Go away! "

It is my belief that Arthurs crawled out on all fours, but I was busy picking up broken glass from the carpet.

Then Baxter, seated by the side of the bed, began to cross-examine in a voice I scarcely recognised. No one could for an instant have doubted the genuine rage of Miss Mary against

105

her sister, her cousin, or her maid; and that a doctor should have been called in—for she did me the honour of calling me doctor—was the last drop. She was choking with her throat; had rushed to the window for air; had near pitched out, and in catching at the window bars had cut her hand. Over and over she made this clear to the intent Baxter. Then she turned on her sister and tongue-lashed her savagely.

"You mustn't blame me," Miss Bessie faltered at last. "You know what we think of night and day."

"I'm coming to that," said Baxter. "Listen to me. What *you* did, Mary, misled four people into thinking you—you meant to do away with yourself."

"Isn't one suicide in the family enough? Oh God, help and pity us! You *couldn't* have believed that!" she cried.

"The evidence was complete. Now, don't you think," Baxter's finger wagged under her nose—"*can't* you think that poor Aggie did the same thing at Holmescroft when she fell out of the window?"

"She had the same throat," said Miss Elizabeth. "Exactly the same symptoms. Don't you remember, Mary?"

"Which was her bedroom?" I asked of Baxter in an undertone.

"Over the south verandah, looking on to the tennis lawn."

"I nearly fell out of that very window when I was at Holmescroft—opening it to get some air. The sill doesn't come much above your knees," I said.

"You hear that, Mary? Mary, do you hear what this gentleman says? Won't you believe that what nearly happened to you must have happened to poor Aggie that night? For God's sake—for her sake—Mary, *won't* you believe?"

There was a long silence while the steam kettle puffed.

"If I could have proof—if I could have proof," said she, and broke into most horrible tears.

Baxter motioned to me, and I crept away to my room, and lay awake till morning, thinking more specially of the dumb Thing at Holmescroft which wished to explain itself. I hated

Miss Mary as perfectly as though I had known her for twenty years, but I felt that, alive or dead, I should not like her to condemn me.

Yet at mid-day, when I saw Miss Mary in her bath-chair, Arthurs behind and Baxter and Miss Elizabeth on either side, in the park-like grounds of the Hydro, I found it difficult to arrange my words.

"Now that you know all about it," said Baxter aside, after the first strangeness of our meeting was over, "it's only fair to tell you that my poor cousin did not die in Holmescroft at all. She was dead when they found her under the window in the morning. Just dead."

"Under that laburnum outside the window?" I asked, for I suddenly remembered the crooked evil thing.

"Exactly. She broke the tree in falling. But no death has ever taken place *in* the house, so far as we were concerned. You can make yourself quite easy on that point. Mr. M'Leod's extra thousand for what you called the 'clean bill of health' was something toward my cousins' estate . when we sold. It was my duty as their lawyer to get it for them—at any cost to my own feelings."

I know better than to argue when the English talk about their duty. So I agreed with my solicitor.

"Their sister's death must have been a great blow to your cousins," I went on. The bath-chair was behind me.

"Unspeakable," Baxter whispered. "They brooded on it day and night. No wonder. If their theory of poor Aggie making away with herself was correct, she was eternally lost!"

"Do you believe that she made away with herself?"

"No, thank God! Never have! And after what happened to Mary last night, I see perfectly what happened to poor Aggie. She had the family throat too. By the way, Mary thinks you are a doctor. Otherwise she wouldn't like your having been in her room."

"Very good. Is she convinced now about her sister's death?"

"She'd give anything to be able to believe it, but she's a hard woman, and brooding along certain lines makes one groovy. I have sometimes been afraid of her reason—on the religious side, don't you know. Elizabeth doesn't matter. Brain of a hen. Always had."

Here Arthurs summoned me to the bath-chair, and the ravaged face, beneath its knitted Shetland wool hood, of Miss Mary Moultrie.

"I need not remind you, I hope, of the seal of secrecy—absolute secrecy—in your profession," she began. "Thanks to my cousin's and my sister's stupidity, you have found out—" she blew her nose.

"Please don't excite her, sir," said Arthurs at the back.

"But, my dear Miss Moultrie, I only know what I've seen, of course, but it seems to me that what you thought was a tragedy in your sister's case, turns out, on your own evidence, so to speak, to have been an accident—a dreadfully sad one—but absolutely an accident."

"Do you believe that too?" she cried. "Or are you only saying it to comfort me?"

"I believe it from the bottom of my heart. Come down to Holmescroft for an hour—for half an hour—and satisfy yourself."

"Of what? You don't understand. I see the house every day—every night. I am always there in spirit—waking or sleeping. I couldn't face it in reality."

"But you must," I said. "If you go there in the spirit the greater need for you to go there in the flesh. Go to your sister's room once more, and see the window—I nearly fell out of it myself. It's—it's awfully low and dangerous. That would convince you," I pleaded.

"Yet Aggie had slept in that room for years," she interrupted.

"You've slept in your room here for a long time, haven't you? But you nearly fell out of the window when you were choking."

"That is true. That is one thing true," she nodded. "And I might have been killed as—perhaps—Aggie was killed."

"In that case your own sister and cousin and maid would have said you had committed suicide, Miss Moultrie. Come down to Holmescroft, and go over the place just once."

"You are lying," she said quite quietly. "You don't want me to come down to see a window. It is something else. I warn you we are Evangelicals. We don't believe in prayers for the dead. 'As the tree falls—'"

"Yes. I daresay. But you persist in thinking that your sister committed suicide—"

"No! No! I have always prayed that I might have misjudged her."

Arthurs at the bath-chair spoke up: "Oh, Miss Mary! you *would* 'ave it from the first that poor Miss Aggie 'ad made away with herself; an', of course, Miss Bessie took the notion from you. Only Master—Mister John stood out, and—and I'd 'ave taken my Bible oath you was making away with yourself last night."

Miss Mary leaned towards me, one finger on my sleeve.

"If going to Holmescroft kills me," she said, "you will have the murder of a fellow-creature on your conscience for all eternity."

"I'll risk it," I answered. Remembering what torment the mere reflection of her torments had cast on Holmescroft, and remembering, above all, the dumb Thing that filled the house with its desire to speak, I felt that there might be worse things.

Baxter was amazed at the proposed visit, but at a nod from that terrible woman went off to make arrangements. Then I sent a telegram to M'Leod bidding him and his vacate Holmescroft for that afternoon. Miss Mary should be alone with her dead, as I had been alone.

I expected untold trouble in transporting her, but to do her justice, the promise given for the journey, she underwent it without murmur, spasm, or unnecessary word. Miss Bessie, pressed in a corner by the window, wept behind her veil, and from time to time tried to take hold of her sister's hand. Baxter wrapped himself in his newly found happiness as selfishly as a bridegroom, for he sat still and smiled.

"So long as I know that Aggie didn't make away with herself," he explained, "I tell you frankly I don't care what happened. She's as hard as a rock—Mary. Always was. *She* won't die."

We led her out on to the platform like a blind woman, and so got her into the fly. The half-hour crawl to Holmescroft was the most racking experience of the day. M'Leod had obeyed my instructions. There was no one visible in the house or the gardens; and the front door stood open.

Miss Mary rose from beside her sister, stepped forth first, and entered the hall.

"Come, Bessie," she cried.

"I daren't. Oh, I daren't."

"Come!" Her voice had altered. I felt Baxter start. "There's nothing to be afraid of."

"Good heavens!" said Baxter. "She's running up the stairs. We'd better follow."

"Let's wait below. She's going to the room."

We heard the door of the bedroom I knew open and shut, and we waited in the lemon-coloured hall, heavy with the scent of flowers.

"I've never been into it since it was sold," Baxter sighed. "What a lovely, restful place it is! Poor Aggie used to arrange the flowers."

"Restful?" I began, but stopped of a sudden, for I felt all over my bruised soul that Baxter was speaking truth. It was a light, spacious, airy house, full of the sense of well-being and peace—above all things, of peace. I ventured into the dining-room where the thoughtful M'Leod's had left a small fire. There was no terror there, present or lurking; and in the drawing-room, which for good reasons we had never cared to enter, the sun and the peace and the scent of the flowers worked together as is fit in an inhabited house. When I returned to the hall, Baxter was sweetly asleep on a couch, looking most unlike a middle-aged solicitor who had spent a broken night with an exacting cousin.

There was ample time for me to review it all—to felicitate

myself upon my magnificent acumen (barring some errors about Baxter as a thief and possibly a murderer), before the door above opened, and Baxter, evidently a light sleeper, sprang awake.

"I've had a heavenly little nap," he said, rubbing his eyes with the backs of his hands like a child. "Good Lord! That's not *their* step!"

But it was. I had never before been privileged to see the Shadow turned backward on the dial—the years ripped bodily off poor human shoulders—old sunken eyes filled and alight—harsh lips moistened and human.

"John," Miss Mary called, "I know now. Aggie didn't do it!" and "She didn't do it!" echoed Miss Bessie, and giggled.

"I did not think it wrong to say a prayer," Miss Mary continued. "Not for her soul, but for our peace. Then I was convinced."

"Then we got conviction," the younger sister piped.

"We've misjudged poor Aggie, John. But I feel she knows now. Wherever she is, she knows that we know she is guiltless."

"Yes, she knows. I felt it too," said Miss Elizabeth.

"I never doubted," said John Baxter, whose face was beautiful at that hour. "Not from the first. Never have!"

"You never offered me proof, John. Now, thank God, it will not be the same any more. I can think henceforward of Aggie without sorrow." She tripped, absolutely tripped, across the hall. "What ideas these Jews have of arranging furniture!" She spied me behind a big *Cloisonné* vase.

"I've seen the window," she said remotely. "You took a great risk in advising me to undertake such a journey. However, as it turns out . . . I forgive you, and I pray you may never know what mental anguish means! Bessie! Look at this peculiar piano! Do you suppose, doctor, these people would offer one tea? I miss mine."

"I will go and see," I said, and explored M'Leod's new-built servants' wing. It was in the servants' hall that I unearthed the M'Leod family, bursting with anxiety.

"Tea for three, quick," I said. "If you ask me any questions

111

now, I shall have a fit!" So Mrs. M'Leod got it, and I was butler, amid murmured apologies from Baxter, still smiling and self-absorbed, and the cold disapproval of Miss Mary, who thought the pattern of the china vulgar. However, she ate well, and even asked me whether I would not like a cup of tea for myself.

They went away in the twilight—the twilight that I had once feared. They were going to an hotel in London to rest after the fatigues of the day, and as their fly turned down the drive, I capered on the door step, with the all-darkened house behind me.

Then I heard the uncertain feet of the M'Leods and bade them not to turn on the lights, but to feel—to feel what I had done; for the Shadow was gone, with the dumb desire in the air. They drew short, but afterwards deeper, breaths, like bathers entering chill water, separated one from the other, moved about the hall, tiptoed upstairs, raced down, and then Miss M'Leod, and I believe her mother, though she denies this, embraced me. I know M'Leod did.

It was a disgraceful evening. To say we rioted through the house is to put it mildly. We played a sort of Blind Man's Buff along the darkest passages, in the unlighted drawing-room, and little dining-room, calling cheerily to each other after each exploration that here, and here, and here, the trouble had removed itself. We came up to *the* bedroom—mine for the night again—and sat, the women on the bed, and we men on chairs, drinking in blessed draughts of peace and comfort and cleanliness of soul, while I told them my tale in full, and received fresh praise, thanks, and blessings.

When the servants, returned from their day's outing, gave us a supper of cold fried fish, M'Leod had sense enough to open no wine. We had been practically drunk since nightfall, and grew incoherent on water and milk.

"I like that Baxter," said M'Leod. "He's a sharp man. The death wasn't in the house, but he ran it pretty close, ain't it?"

"And the joke of it is that he supposes I want to buy the place from you," I said. "Are you selling?"

"Not for twice what I paid for it—now," said M'Leod. "I'll keep you in furs all your life, but not our Holmescroft."

"No—never our Holmescroft," said Miss M'Leod. "We'll ask *him* here on Tuesday, mamma." They squeezed each other's hands.

"Now tell me," said Mrs. M'Leod—"that tall one I saw out of the scullery window—did *she* tell you she was always here in the spirit? I hate her. She made all this trouble. It was not her house after she had sold it. What do you think?"

"I suppose," I answered, "she brooded over what she believed was her sister's suicide night and day—she confessed she did—and her thoughts being concentrated on this place, they felt like a—like a burning glass."

"Burning glass is good," said M'Leod.

"I said it was like a light of blackness turned on us," cried the girl, twiddling her ring. "That must have been when the tall one thought worst about her sister and the house."

"Ah, the poor Aggie!" said Mrs. M'Leod. "The poor Aggie, trying to tell everyone it was not so! No wonder we felt Something wished to say Something. Thea, Max, do you remember that night—"

"We need not remember any more," M'Leod interrupted. "It is not our trouble. They have told each other now."

"Do you think, then," said Miss M'Leod, "that those two, the living ones, were actually told something—upstairs—in your—in the room?"

"I can't say. At any rate they were made happy, and they ate a big tea afterwards. As your father says, it is not our trouble any longer—thank God!"

"Amen!" said M'Leod. "Now, Thea, let us have some music after all these months. '*With mirth, thou pretty bird*,' ain't it? You ought to hear that."

And in the half-lighted hall, Thea sang an old English song that I had never heard before.

With mirth, thou pretty bird, rejoice

113

Thy Maker's praise enhanced;
Lift up thy shrill and pleasant voice,
Thy God is high advanced!
Thy food before He did provide,
And gives it in a fitting side,
Wherewith be thou sufficed!
Why shouldst thou now unpleasant be,
Thy wrath against God venting,
That He a little bird made thee,
Thy silly head tormenting,
Because He made thee not a man?
Oh, Peace! He hath well thought thereon,
Therewith be thou sufficed!

The Finest Story in the World

Or ever the knightly years were gone
With the old world to the grave,
I was a king in Babylon
And you were a Christian slave.'
W. E. Henley.

His name was Charlie Mears; he was the only son of his mother who was a widow, and he lived in the north of London, coming into the City every day to work in a bank. He was twenty years old and suffered from aspirations. I met him in a public billiard-saloon where the marker called him by his first name, and he called the marker 'Bullseyes.' Charlie explained, a little nervously, that he had only come to the place to look on, and since looking on at games of skill is not a cheap amusement for the young, I suggested that Charlie should go back to his mother.

That was our first step towards better acquaintance. He would call on me sometimes in the evenings instead of running about London with his fellow-clerks; and before long, speaking of himself as a young man must, he told me of his aspirations, which were all literary. He desired to make himself an undying name chiefly through verse, though he was not above sending stories of love and death to the penny-in-the-slot journals. It was my fate to sit still while Charlie read me poems of many hundred lines, and bulky fragments of plays that would surely shake the world. My reward was his unreserved confidence, and the self-revelations and troubles of a young man are almost as holy as those of a maiden.

Charlie had never fallen in love, but was anxious to do so at the first opportunity; he believed in all things good and all things honourable, but at the same time, was curiously careful to let me see that he knew his way about the world as befitted a bank-clerk on twenty-five shillings a week. He rhymed 'dove' with 'love' and 'moon' with 'June,' and devoutly believed that they had never so been rhymed before. The long lame gaps in his plays he filled up with hasty words of apology and description and swept on, seeing all that he intended to do so clearly that he esteemed it already done, and turned to me for applause.

I fancy that his mother did not encourage his aspirations, and I know that his writing-table at home was the edge of his washstand. This he told me almost at the outset of our acquaintance; when he was ravaging my bookshelves, and a little before I was implored to speak the truth as to his chances of 'writing something really great, you know.' Maybe I encouraged him too much, for, one night, he called on me, his eyes flaming with excitement, and said breathlessly:—

'Do you mind—can you let me stay here and write all this evening? I won't interrupt you, I won't really. There's no place for me to write in at my mother's.'

'What's the trouble?' I said, knowing well what that trouble was.

'I've a notion in my head that would make the most splendid story that was ever written. Do let me write it out here. It's *such* a notion!'

There was no resisting the appeal. I set him a table; he hardly thanked me, but plunged into the work at once. For half an hour the pen scratched without stopping. Then Charlie sighed and tugged his hair. The scratching grew slower; there were more erasures; and at last ceased. The finest story in the world would not come forth.

'It looks such awful rot now,' he said mournfully. 'And yet it seemed so good when I was thinking about it. What's wrong?'

I could not dishearten him by saying the truth. So I answered: 'Perhaps you don't feel in the mood for writing.'

'Yes, I do—except when I look at this stuff. Ugh!'

'Read me what you've done,' I said.

He read, and it was wondrous bad, and he paused at all the specially turgid sentences, expecting a little approval; for he was proud of those sentences, as I knew he would be.

'It needs compression,' I suggested cautiously.

'I hate cutting my things down. I don't think you could alter a word here without spoiling the sense. It reads better aloud than when I was writing it.'

'Charlie, you're suffering from an alarming disease afflicting a numerous class. Put the thing by, and tackle it again in a week.'

'I want to do it at once. What do you think of it?'

'How can I judge from a half-written tale? Tell me the story as it lies in your head.'

Charlie told, and in the telling there was everything that his ignorance had so carefully prevented from escaping into the written word. I looked at him, wondering whether it were possible that he did not know the originality, the power of the notion that had come in his way? It was distinctly a Notion among notions. Men had been puffed up with pride by ideas not a tithe as excellent and practicable. But Charlie babbled on serenely, interrupting the current of pure fancy with samples of horrible sentences that he purposed to use. I heard him out to the end. It would be folly to allow his thought to remain in his own inept hands, when I could do so much with it. Not all that could be done indeed; but, oh so much!

'What do you think?' he said at last. 'I fancy I shall call it *The Story of a Ship*.'

'I think the idea is pretty good; but you won't be able to handle it for ever so long. Now I—'

'Would it be of any use to you? Would you care to take it? I should be proud,' said Charlie promptly.

There are few things sweeter in this world than the guileless, hot-headed, intemperate, open admiration of a junior. Even a woman in her blindest devotion does not fall into the gait of the man she adores, tilt her bonnet to the angle at which he wears his hat, or interlard her speech with his pet oaths. And Charlie did all these things. Still it was necessary to salve my conscience before I possessed myself of Charlie's thought.

'Let's make a bargain. I'll give you a fiver for the notion,' I said.

Charlie became a bank clerk at once.

'Oh, that's impossible. Between two pals, you know, if I may call you so, and speaking as a man of the world, I couldn't. Take the notion if it's any use to you. I've heaps more.'

He had—none knew this better than I—but they were the notions of other men.

'Look at it as a matter of business—between men of the world,' I returned. 'Five pounds will buy you any number of po-etry books. Business is business, and you may be sure I shouldn't give that price unless—'

'Oh., if you put it *that* way,' said Charlie, visibly moved by the thought of the books. The bargain was clinched with an agree-ment that he should at unstated intervals come to me with all the notions that he possessed, should have a table of his own to write at, and unquestioned right to inflict upon me all his po-ems and fragments of poems. Then I said, 'Now tell me how you came by this idea.'

'It came by itself.' Charlie's eyes opened a little.

'Yes, but you told me a great deal about the hero that you must have read before somewhere.'

'I haven't any time for reading, except when you let me sit here, and on Sundays I'm on my bicycle or down the river all day. There's nothing wrong about the hero, is there?'

'Tell me again and I shall understand clearly. You say that your hero went pirating. How did he live?'

'He was on the lower deck of this ship-thing that I was tell-ing you about.'

'What sort of ship?'

'It was the kind rowed with oars, and the sea spurts through the oar-holes and the men row sitting up to their knees in water.

Then there's a bench running down between the two lines of oars and an overseer with a whip walks up and down the bench to make the men work.'

'How do you know that?'

'It's in the tale. There's a rope running overhead, looped to the upper deck, for the overseer to catch hold of when the ship rolls. When the overseer misses the rope once and falls among the rowers, remember the hero laughs at him and gets licked for it. He's chained to his oar of course—the hero.'

'How is he chained?'

'With an iron band round his waist fixed to the bench he sits on, and a sort of handcuff on his left wrist chaining him to the oar. He's on the lower deck where the worst men are sent, and the only light comes from the hatchways and through the oar-holes. Can't you imagine the sunlight just squeezing through between the handle and the hole and wobbling about as the ship rolls?'

'I can, but I can't imagine your imagining it.'

'How could it be any other way? Now you listen to me. The long oars on the upper deck are managed by four men to each bench, the lower ones by three, and the lowest of all by two. Remember it's quite dark on the lowest deck and all the men there go mad. When a man dies at his oar on that deck he isn't thrown overboard, but cut up in his chains and stuffed through the oar-hole in little pieces.'

'Why?' I demanded amazed, not so much at the information as the tone of command in which it was flung out.

'To save trouble and to frighten the others. It needs two over-seers to drag a man's body up to the top deck; and if the men at the lower-deck oars were left alone, of course they'd stop row-ing and try to pull up the benches by all standing up together in their chains.'

'You've a most provident imagination. Where have you been reading about galleys and galley-slaves?'

'Nowhere that I remember. I row a little when I get the chance. But, perhaps, if you say so, I may have read something.'

119

He went away shortly afterwards to deal with booksellers, and I wondered how a bank-clerk aged twenty could put into my hands with a profligate abundance of detail, all given with absolute assurance, the story of extravagant and bloodthirsty adventure, riot, piracy, and death in unnamed seas. He had led his hero a desperate dance through revolt against the overseers, to command of a ship of his own, and the ultimate establishment of a kingdom on an island 'somewhere in the sea, you know;' and, delighted with my paltry five pounds, had gone out to buy the notions of other men, that these might teach him how to write. I had the consolation of knowing that this notion was mine by right of purchase; and I thought that I could make something of it.

When next he came to me he was drunk—royally drunk—on many poets for the first time revealed to him. His pupils were dilated, his words tumbled over each other, and he wrapped himself in quotations—as a beggar would enfold himself in the purple of Emperors. Most of all was he drunk with Longfellow.

'Isn't it splendid? Isn't it superb?' he cried, after hasty greetings. 'Listen to this—'

"Wouldst thou,"—so the helmsman answered,
" Know the secret of the sea?
Only those who brave its dangers
Comprehend its mystery."

'By gum!'

"Only those who brave its dangers
Comprehend its mystery,"'

He repeated twenty times, walking up and down the room and forgetting me. 'But *I* can understand it too,' he said to himself. 'I don't know how to thank you for that fiver. And this; listen—

"I remember the black wharves and the slips
And the sea-tides tossing free;
And the Spanish sailors with bearded lips.

And the beauty and mystery of the ships,
And the magic of the sea."

'I haven't braved any dangers, but I feel as if I knew all about it.'

'You certainly seem to have a grip of the sea. Have you ever seen it?'

'When I was a little chap I went to Brighton once; we used to live in Coventry, though, before we came to London. I never saw it,

"When descends on the Atlantic
The gigantic
Storm-wind of the Equinox."

He shook me by the shoulder to make me understand the passion that was shaking himself.

'When that storm comes,' he continued, 'I think that all the oars in the ship that I was talking about get broken, and the rowers have their chests smashed in by the oar-heads bucking. By the way, have you done anything with that notion of mine, yet?'

'No. I was waiting to hear more of it from you. Tell me how in the world you're so certain about the fittings of the ship. You know nothing of ships.'

'I don't know. It's as real as anything to me until I try to write it down. I was thinking about it only last night in bed, after you had lent me *Treasure Island*; and I made up a whole lot of new things to go into the story.'

'What sort of things?'

'About the food the men ate; rotten figs and black beans and wine in a skin-bag, passed from bench to bench.'

'Was the ship built so long ago as *that?*'

'As what? I don't know whether it was long ago or not. It's only a notion, but sometimes it seems just as real as if it was true. Do I bother you with talking about it?'

'Not in the least. Did you make up anything else?'

'Yes, but it's nonsense.' Charlie flushed a little.

121

'Never mind; let's hear about it.'

'Well, I was thinking over the story, and after awhile I got out of bed and wrote down on a piece of paper the sort of stuff the men might be supposed to scratch on their oars with the edges of their handcuffs. It seemed to make the thing more life-like. It is so real to me, y'know.'

'Have you the paper on you?'

'Ye—es, but what's the use of showing it? It's only a lot of scratches. All the same, we might have 'em reproduced in the book on the front page.'

'I'll attend to those details. Show me what your men wrote.'

He pulled out of his pocket a sheet of notepaper, with a single line of scratches upon it, and I put this carefully away.

'What is it supposed to mean in English?' I said.

'Oh, I don't know. I mean it to mean "I'm beastly tired." It's great nonsense,' he repeated, 'but all those men in the ship seem as real as real people to me. Do do something to the notion soon; I should like to see it written and printed.'

'But all you've told me would make a long book.'

'Make it then. You've only to sit down and write it out.'

'Give me a little time. Have you anymore notions?'

'Not just now. I'm reading all the books I've bought. They're splendid.'

When he had left I looked at the sheet of notepaper with the inscription upon it. Then I took my head tenderly between both hands, to make certain that it was not coming off or turning round. Then . . . but there seemed to be no interval between leaving my rooms and finding myself arguing with a policeman outside a door marked *Private* in a corridor of the British Museum. All I demanded, as politely as possible, was 'the Greek antiquity man.' The policeman knew nothing except the rules of the museum, and it became necessary to forage through all the houses and offices inside the gates. An elderly gentleman called away from his lunch put an end to my search by holding the notepaper between finger and thumb and sniffing at it scornfully.

'What does this mean? H'mm,' said he. 'So far as I can ascertain it is an attempt to write extremely corrupt Greek on the part'—here he glared at me with intention—'of an extremely illiterate—ah—person.' He read slowly from the paper, '*Pollock, Erckmann, Tauchnitz, Henniker*'—four names familiar to me.

'Can you tell me what the corruption is supposed to mean— the gist of the thing?' I asked.

'I have been—many times—overcome with weariness in this particular employment. That is the meaning.' He returned me the paper, and I fled without a word of thanks, explanation, or apology.

I might have been excused for forgetting much. To me of all men had been given the chance to write the most marvellous tale in the world, nothing less than the story of a Greek galley-slave, as told by himself. Small wonder that his dreaming had seemed real to Charlie. The Fates that are so careful to shut the doors of each successive life behind us had, in this case, been neglectful, and Charlie was looking, though that he did not know, where never man had been permitted to look with full knowledge since Time began.

Above all, he was absolutely ignorant of the knowledge sold to me for five pounds; and he would retain that ignorance; for bank-clerks do not understand metempsychosis, and a sound commercial education does not include Greek. He would supply me—here I capered among the dumb gods of Egypt and laughed in their battered faces—with material to make my tale sure—so sure that the world would hail it as an impudent and vamped fiction. And I—I alone would know that it was absolutely and literally true. I—I alone held this jewel to my hand for the cutting and polishing. Therefore I danced again among the gods of the Egyptian court, till a policeman saw me and took steps in my direction.

It remained now only to encourage Charlie to talk, and here there was no difficulty. But I had forgotten those accursed books of poetry. He came to me time after time, as useless as a surcharged phonograph—drunk on Byron, Shelley, or Keats.

Knowing now what the boy had been in his past lives, and desperately anxious not to lose one word of his babble, I could not hide from him my respect and interest. He misconstrued both into respect for the present soul of Charlie Mears, to whom life was as new as it was to Adam, and interest in his readings: he stretched my patience to breaking point by reciting poetry—not his own now, but that of others. I wished every English poet blotted out of the memory of mankind. I blasphemed the mightiest names of song because they had drawn Charlie from the path of direct narrative, and would, later, spur him to imitate them; but I choked down my impatience until the first flood of enthusiasm should have spent itself and the boy returned to his dreams.

'What's the use of my telling you what I think, when these chaps wrote things for the angels to read?' he growled, one evening.

'Why don't you write something like theirs?'

'I don't think you're treating me quite fairly,' I said, speaking under strong restraint.

'I've given you the story,' he said shortly, replunging into *Lara*

'But I want the details.'

'The things I make up about that damned ship that you call a galley? They're quite easy. You can just make 'em up for yourself. Turn up the gas a little, I want to go on reading.'

I could have broken the gas-globe over his head for his amazing stupidity. I could indeed make up things for myself did I only know what Charlie did not know that he knew. But since the doors were shut behind me I could only wait his youthful pleasure and strive to keep him in good temper. One minute's want of guard might spoil a priceless revelation: now and again he would toss his books aside—he kept them in my rooms, for his mother would have been shocked at the waste of good money had she seen them—and launched into his sea dreams.

Again I cursed all the poets of England. The plastic mind of the bank-clerk had been overlaid, coloured, and distorted by that which he had read, and the result as delivered was a confused tangle of other voices most like the mutter and hum through a City telephone in the busiest part of the day. He talked of the galley—his own galley had he but known it—with illustrations borrowed from the *Bride of Abydos*. He pointed the experiences of his hero with quotations from *The Corsair*, and threw in deep and desperate moral reflections from *Cain* and *Manfred*, expecting me to use them all. Only when the talk turned on Longfellow were the jarring cross-currents dumb, and I knew that Charlie was speaking the truth as he remembered it.

'What do you think of this?' I said one evening, as soon as I understood the medium in which his memory worked best, and, before he could expostulate, read him nearly the whole of *The Saga of King Olaf*.

He listened open-mouthed, flushed, his hands drumming on the back of the sofa where he lay, till I came to the Song of Einar Tamberskelver and the verse:—

Einar then, the arrow taking
From the loosened string,
Answered, "That was Norway breaking
'Neath thy hand, King."

He gasped with pure delight of sound.
'That's better than Byron, a little?' I ventured.
'Better! Why it's *true*! How could he have known?'
I went back and repeated:—

"What was that?" said Olaf, standing
On the quarter-deck,
"Something heard I like the stranding
Of a shattered wreck."

'How could he have known how the ships crash and the oars rip out and go *z-zzp* all along the line? Why only the other night . . . But go back please and read *The Skerry of Shrieks* again.'

'No, I'm tired. Let's talk. What happened the other night?'

'I had an awful dream about that galley of ours. I dreamed I was drowned in a fight. You see we ran alongside another ship in harbour. The water was dead still except where our oars whipped it up. You know where I always sit in the galley?' He spoke haltingly at first, under the fine English fear of being laughed at.

'No. That's news to me,' I answered meekly, my heart beginning to beat.

'On the fourth oar from the bow on the right side on the upper deck. There were four of us at that oar, all chained. I remember watching the water and trying to get my handcuffs off before the row began. Then we closed up on the other ship, and all their fighting men jumped over our bulwarks, and my bench broke and I was pinned down with the three other fellows on top of me, and the big oar jammed across our backs.'

'Well?' Charlie's eyes were alive and alight. He was looking at the wall behind my chair.

'I don't know how we fought. The men were trampling all over my back, and I lay low. Then our rowers on the left side— tied to their oars, you know—began to yell and back water. I could hear the water sizzle, and we spun round like a cock-chafer and I knew, lying where I was, that there was a galley coming up bow-on, to ram us on the left side. I could just lift up my head and see her sail over the bulwarks. We wanted to meet her bow to bow, but it was too late. We could only turn a little bit because the galley on our right had hooked herself on to us and stopped our moving. Then, by gum! there was a crash! Our left oars began to break as the other galley, the moving one y'know, stuck her nose into them. Then the lower-deck oars shot up through the deck planking, butt first, and one of them jumped clear up into the air and came down again close at my head.'

'How was that managed?'

'The moving galley's bow was plunking them back through their own oar-holes, and I could hear no end of a shindy in the decks below. Then her nose caught us nearly in the middle, and we tilted , sideways, and the fellows in the right-hand galley unhitched their hooks and ropes, and threw things on to our upper deck—arrows, and hot pitch or something that stung, and we went up and up on the left side, and the right side dipped, and I twisted my head round and saw the water stand still as it topped the right bulwarks; and then it curled over and crashed down on the whole lot of us on the right side, and I felt it hit my back, and I woke.'

'One minute, Charlie. When the sea topped the bulwarks, what did it look like?' I had my reasons for asking. A man of my acquaintance had once gone down with a leaking ship in a still sea, and had seen the water-level pause for an instant ere it fell on the deck.

'It looked just like a banjo-string drawn tight, and it seemed to stay there for years,' said Charlie.

Exactly! The other man had said: 'It looked like a silver wire laid down along the bulwarks, and I thought it was never going to break.' He had paid everything except the bare life for this little valueless piece of knowledge, and I had travelled ten thousand weary miles to meet him and take his knowledge at second hand. But Charlie, the bank-clerk on twenty-five shillings a week, who had never been out of sight of a made road, knew it all. It was no consolation to me that once in his lives he had been forced to die for his gains. I also must have died scores of times, but behind me, because I could have used my knowledge, the doors were shut!

'And then?' I said, trying to put away the devil of envy.

'The funny thing was, though, in all the row I didn't feel a bit astonished or frightened. It seemed as if I'd been in a good many fights, because I told my next man so when the row began. But that cad of an overseer on my deck wouldn't unloose our chains and give us a chance. He always said that we'd all be set free after a battle, but we never were; we never were.' Charlie shook his head mournfully.

'What a scoundrel!'

'I should say he was. He never gave us enough to eat, and sometimes we were so thirsty that we used to drink salt-water. I can taste that salt-water still.'

'Now tell me something about the harbour where the fight

was fought.'

'I didn't dream about that. I know it was a harbour though; because we were tied up to a ring on a white wall and all the face of the stone under water was covered with wood to prevent our ram getting chipped when the tide made us rock.'

'That's curious. Our hero commanded the galley, didn't he?'

'Didn't he just! He stood by the bows and shouted like a good 'un. He was the man who killed the overseer.'

'But you were all drowned together, Charlie, weren't you?'

'I can't make that fit quite,' he said, with a puzzled look. 'The galley must have gone down with all hands, and yet I fancy that the hero went on living afterwards. Perhaps he climbed into the attacking ship. I wouldn't see that, of course. I was dead, you know.'

He shivered slightly and protested that he could remember no more.

I did not press him further, but to satisfy myself that he lay in ignorance of the workings of his own mind, deliberately introduced him to Mortimer Collinses *Transmigration*, and gave him a sketch of the plot before he opened the pages.

'What rot it all is!' he said frankly, at the end of an hour. 'I don't understand his nonsense about the Red Planet Mars and the King, and the rest of it. Chuck me the Longfellow again.'

I handed him the book and wrote out as much as I could remember of his description of the sea-fight, appealing to him from time to time for confirmation of fact or detail. He would answer without raising his eyes from the book, as assuredly as though all his knowledge lay before him on the printed page. I spoke under the normal key of my voice that the current might not be broken, and I know that he was not aware of what he was saying, for his thoughts were out on the sea with Longfellow.

'Charlie,' I asked, 'when the rowers on the galleys mutinied how did they kill their overseers?'

'Tore up the benches and brained 'em. That happened when a heavy sea was running. An overseer on the lower deck slipped from the centre plank and fell among the rowers. They choked him to death against the side of the ship with their chained hands quite quietly, and it was too dark for the other overseer to see what had happened. When he asked he was pulled down too and choked, and the lower deck fought their way up deck by deck, with the pieces of the broken benches banging behind 'em. How they howled!'

'And what happened after that?'

'I don't know. The hero went away—red hair and red beard and all. That was after he had captured our galley, I think.'

The sound of my voice irritated him, and he motioned slightly with his left hand as a man does when interruption jars.

'You never told me he was red-headed before, or that he captured your galley,' I said, after a discreet interval.

Charlie did not raise his eyes.

'He was as red as a red bear,' said he abstractedly. 'He came from the north; they said so in the galley when he looked for rowers—not for slaves, but free men. Afterwards—years and years afterwards—news came from another ship, or else he came back—'

His lips moved in silence. He was rapturously retasting some poem before him.

'Where had he been, then?' I was almost whispering that the sentence might come gently to whichever section of Charlie's brain that was working on my behalf.

'To the Beaches—the Long and Wonderful Beaches!' was the reply after a minute of silence.

'To Furdurstrandi?' I asked, tingling from head to foot.

'Yes, to Furdurstrandi,' he pronounced the word in a new fashion. 'And I too saw—' The voice failed.

'Do you know what you have said?' I shouted incautiously.

He lifted his eyes, fully roused now. 'No!' he snapped. 'I wish you'd let a chap go on reading. Hark to this:—

But Othere, the old sea-captain,
He neither paused nor stirred
Till the king listened, and then
Once more took up his pen

And wrote down every word.

And to the King of the Saxons
In witness of the truth,
Raising his noble head,
He stretched his brown hand and said,
'Behold this walrus tooth.'

'By Jove, what chaps those must have been, to go sailing all over the shop never knowing where they'd fetch the land! Hah!

'Charlie,' I pleaded, 'if you'll only be sensible for a minute or two I'll make our hero in our tale every inch as good as Othere.'

'Umph! Longfellow wrote that poem. I don't care about writing things any more. I want to read.' He was thoroughly out of tune now, and raging over my own ill-luck, I left him. Conceive yourself at the door of the world's treasure-house guarded by a child—an idle irresponsible child playing knuckle-bones—on whose favour depends the gift of the key, and you will imagine one-half my torment. Till that evening Charlie had spoken nothing that might not lie within the experiences of a Greek galley-slave. But now, or there was no virtue in books, he had talked of some desperate adventure of the Vikings, of Thorfin Karlsefne's sailing to Wineland, which is America, in the ninth or tenth century.

The battle in the harbour he had seen; and his own death he had described. But this was a much more startling plunge into the past. Was it possible that he had skipped half a dozen lives and was then dimly remembering some episode of a thousand years later? It was a maddening jumble, and the worst of it was that Charlie Mears in his normal condition was the last person in the world to clear it up. I could only wait and watch, but I went to bed that night full of the wildest imaginings. There was nothing that was not possible if Charlie's detestable memory only held good.

I might rewrite the saga of Thorfin Karlsefne as it had never been written before, might tell the story of the first discovery of America, myself the discoverer. But I was entirely at Charlie's mercy, and so long as there was a three-and-sixpenny Bohn volume within his reach Charlie would not tell. I dared not curse him openly; I hardly dared jog his memory, for I was dealing with the experiences of a thousand years ago, told through the mouth of a boy of today; and a boy of today is affected by every change of tone and gust of opinion, so that he must lie even when he most desires to speak the truth.

I saw no more of Charlie for nearly a week. When next I met him it was in Gracechurch Street with a bill-book chained to his waist. Business took him over London Bridge, and I accompanied him. He was very full of the importance of that book and magnified it. As we passed over the Thames we paused to look at a steamer unloading great slabs of white and brown marble. A barge drifted under the steamer's stern and a lonely ship's cow in that barge bellowed. Charlie's face changed from the face of the bank-clerk to that of an unknown and—though he would not have believed this—a much shrewder man. He flung out his arm across the parapet of the bridge and laughing very loudly, said:—

'When they heard *our* bulls bellow the Skroelings ran away!'

I waited only for an instant, but the barge and the cow had disappeared under the bows of the steamer before I answered.

'Charlie, what do you suppose are Skroelings?'

'Never heard of 'em before. They sound like a new kind of sea-gull. What a chap you are for asking questions!' he replied. 'I have to go to the cashier of the Omnibus Company yonder. Will you wait for me and we can lunch somewhere together? I've a notion for a poem.'

'No, thanks. I'm off. You're sure you know nothing about Skroelings?'

'Not unless he's been entered for the Liverpool Handicap.' He nodded and disappeared in the crowd.

Now it is written in the saga of Eric the Red or that of Thorfin Karlsefne, that nine hundred years ago when Karlsefne's galleys came to Leif's booths, which Leif had erected in the unknown land called Markland, which may or may not have been Rhode Island, the Skroelings—and the Lord He knows who these may or may not have been—came to trade with the Vikings, and ran away because they were frightened at the bellowing of the cattle which Thorfin had brought with him in the ships. But what in the world could a Greek slave know of that affair? I wandered up and down among the streets trying to unravel the mystery, and the more I considered it, the more baffling it grew. One thing only seemed certain, and that certainty took away my breath for the moment. If I came to full knowledge of anything at all, it would not be one life of the soul in Charlie Mears's body, but half a dozen—half a dozen several and separate existences spent on blue water in the morning of the world!

Then I walked round the situation.

Obviously if I used my knowledge I should stand alone and unapproachable until all men were as wise as myself. That would be something, but manlike I was ungrateful. It seemed bitterly unfair that Charlie's memory should fail me when I needed it most. Great Powers above—I looked up at them through the fog smoke—did the Lords of Life and Death know what this meant to me? Nothing less than eternal fame of the best kind, that comes from One, and is shared by one alone. I would be content—remembering Olive, I stood astounded at my own moderation,—with the mere right to tell one story, to work out one little contribution to the light literature of the day.

If Charlie were permitted full recollection for one hour— for sixty short minutes—of existences that had extended over a thousand years—I would forego all profit and honour from all that I should make of his speech. I would take no share in the commotion that would follow throughout the particular corner of the earth that calls itself 'the world.' The thing should be put forth anonymously. Nay, I would make other men believe that they had written it. They would hire bull-hided self-advertising Englishmen to bellow it abroad. Preachers would found a fresh conduct of life upon it, swearing that it was new and that they had lifted the fear of death from all mankind.

Every Orientalist in Europe would patronise it discursively with Sanskrit and Pali texts. Terrible women would invent unclean variants of the men's belief for the elevation of their sisters. Churches and religions would war over it. Between the hailing and restarting of an omnibus I foresaw the scuffles that would arise among half a dozen denominations all professing ' the doctrine of the True Metempsychosis as applied to the world and the New Era;' and saw, too, the respectable English newspapers shying, like frightened kine over the beautiful simplicity of the tale.

The mind leaped forward a hundred—two hundred—a thousand years. I saw with sorrow that men would mutilate and garble the story; that rival creeds would turn it upbide down till, at last, the western world which clings to the dread of death more closely than the hope of life, would set it aside as an interesting superstition and stampede after some faith so long forgotten that it seemed altogether new. Upon this I changed the terms of the bargain that I would make with the Lords of Life and Death. Only let me know, let me write, the story with sure knowledge that I wrote the truth, and I would burn the manuscript as a solemn sacrifice. Five minutes after the last line was written I would destroy it all. But I must be allowed to write it with absolute certainty.

There was no answer. The flaming colours of an Aquarium poster caught my eye, and I wondered whether it would be wise or prudent to lure Charlie into the hands of the professional mesmerist there, and whether, if he were under his power, he would speak of his past lives. If he did, and if people believed him . . . but Charlie would be frightened and fluttered, or made conceited by the interviews. In either case he would begin to lie, through fear or vanity. He was safest in my own hands.

'They are very funny fools, your English,' said a voice at my elbow, and turning round I recognised a casual acquaintance, a young Bengali law student, called Grish Chunder, whose father had sent him to England to become civilised. The old man was a

133

retired native official, and on an income of five pounds a month contrived to allow his son two hundred pounds a year, and the run of his teeth in a city where he could pretend to be the cadet of a royal house, and tell stories of the brutal Indian bureaucrats who ground the faces of the poor.

Grish Chunder was a young, fat, full-bodied Bengali, dressed with scrupulous care in frock-coat, tall hat, light trousers, and tan gloves. But I had known him in the days when the brutal Indian Government paid for his university education, and he contributed cheap sedition to *Sachi Durpan*, and intrigued with the wives of his fourteen-year-old schoolmates.

'That is very funny and very foolish,' he said nodding at the poster. 'I am going down to the Northbrook Club. Will you come too?'

I walked with him for some time. 'You are not well,' he said. 'What is there on your mind? You do not talk.'

'Grish Chunder, you've been too well educated to believe in a God, haven't you?'

'Oah, yes, *here!* But when I go home I must conciliate popular superstition, and make ceremonies of purification, and my women will anoint idols.'

'And hang up *tulsi* and feast the *purohit*, and take you back into caste again and make a good *khuttri* of you again, you advanced social free-thinker. And you'll eat *desi* food, and like it all, from the smell in the courtyard to the mustard oil over you.'

'I shall very much like it,' said Grish Chunder unguardedly. 'Once a Hindu—always a Hindu. But I like to know what the English think they know.'

'I'll tell you something that one Englishman knows. It's an old tale to you.'

I began to tell the story of Charlie in English, but Grish Chunder put a question in the vernacular, and the history went forward naturally in the tongue best suited for its telling. After all, it could never have been told in English. Grish Chunder heard me, nodding from time to time, and then came up to my rooms, where I finished the tale.

'*Beshak*,' he said philosophically. '*Lekin darwaza band hai.* (Without doubt, but the door is shut.) I have heard of this remembering of previous existences among my people. It is of course an old tale with us, but, to happen to an Englishman—a cow-fed *Mlechh*—an outcast. By Jove, that is most peculiar!'

'Outcast yourself, Grish Chunder! You eat cow-beef every day. Let's think the thing over. The boy remembers his incarnations.'

'Does he know that?' said Grish Chunder quietly, swinging his legs as he sat on my table. He was speaking in his English now.

'He does not know anything. Would I speak to you if he did? Go on!'

'There is no going on at all. If you tell that to your friends they will say you are mad and put it in the papers. Suppose, now, you prosecute for libel.'

'Let's leave that out of the question entirely. Is there any chance of his being made to speak?'

'There is a chance. Oah, yess! But *if* he spoke it would mean that all this world would end now—*instanto*—fall down on your head. These things are not allowed, you know. As I said, the door is shut.'

'Not a ghost of a chance?'

'How can there be? You are a *Christi-án*, and it is forbidden to eat, in your books, of the Tree of Life, or else you would never die. How shall you all fear death if you all know what your friend does not know that he knows? I am afraid to be kicked, but I am not afraid to die, because I know what I know. You are not afraid to be kicked, but you are afraid to die. If you were not, by God! you English would be all over the shop in an hour, upsetting the balances of power, and making commotions. It would not be good. But no fear. He will remember a little and a little less, and he will call it dreams. Then he will forget altogether. When I passed my First Arts Examination in Calcutta that was all in the cram-book on Wordsworth. *Trailing clouds of glory*, you know.'

'This seems to be an exception to the rule.'

'There are no exceptions to rules. Some are not so hard-looking as others, but they are all the same when you touch. If this friend of yours said so-and- so and so-and-so, indicating that he remembered all his lost lives, or one piece of a lost life, he would not be in the bank another hour. He would be what you called sack because he was mad, and they would send him to an asylum for lunatics. You can see that, my friend.'

'Of course I can, but I wasn't thinking of him. His name need never appear in the story.'

'Ah! I see. That story will never be written. You can try.'

'I am going to.'

'For your own credit and for the sake of money, *of* course?'

'No. For the sake of writing the story. On my honour that will he all.'

'Even then there is no chance. You cannot play with the Gods. It is a very pretty story now. As they say. Let it go on that—I mean at that. Be quick; he will not last long.'

'How do you mean?'

'What I say. He has never, so far, thought about a woman.'

'Hasn't he, though!' I remembered some of Charlie's confidences.

'I mean no woman has thought about him. When that comes; *bus—hogya*—all up! I know. There are millions of women here. Housemaids, for instance. They kiss you behind doors.'

I winced at the thought of my story being ruined by a housemaid. And yet nothing was more probable.

Grish Chunder grinned.

'Yes—also pretty girls—cousins of his house, and perhaps *not* of his house. One kiss that he gives back again and remembers will cure all this nonsense, or else—'

'Or else what? Remember he does not know that he knows.'

'I know that. Or else, if nothing happens he will become immersed in the trade and the financial speculations like the rest. It must be so. You can see that it must be so. But the woman will come first, *I* think.'

There was a rap at the door, and Charlie charged in impetu-
ously. He had been released from office; and by the look in his
eyes I could see that he had come over for a long talk; most
probably with poems in his pockets. Charlie's poems were very
wearying, but sometimes they led him to talk about the galley.

Grish Chunder looked at him keenly for a minute.

'I beg your pardon,' Charlie said uneasily; 'I didn't know you
had anyone with you.'

'I am going,' said Grish Chunder.

He drew me into the lobby as he departed.

'That is your man,' he said quickly. 'I tell you he will never
speak all you wish. That is rot—bosh! But he would be most
good to make to see things. Suppose now we pretend that it was
only play'—I had never seen Grish Chunder so excited—'and
pour the ink-pool into his hand. Eh, what do you think? I tell
you that he could see *anything* that a man could see. Let me get
the ink and the camphor. He is a seer and he will tell us very
many things.'

'He may be all you say, but I'm not going to trust him to your
gods and devils.'

'They will not hurt him. He will only feel a lit-stupid and
dull when he wakes up. You have seen boys look into the ink-
pool before.'

'That is the reason why I am not going to see it any more.
You'd better go, Grish Chunder.'

He went, insisting far down the staircase that it was throwing
away my only chance of looking into the future.

This left me unmoved, for I was concerned for the past, and
no peering of hypnotised boys into mirrors and ink-pools would
· help me to that. But I recognised Grish Chunder's point of view
and sympathised with it.

'What a big black brute that was!' said Charlie, when I returned to him. 'Well, look here, I've just done a poem; did it
instead of playing dominoes after lunch. May I read it?'

'Let me read it to myself.'

'Then you miss the proper expression. Besides, you always make my things sound as if the rhymes were all wrong.'

'Read it aloud, then. You're like the rest of 'em.'

Charlie mouthed me his poem, and it was not much worse than the average of his verses. He had been reading his books faithfully, but he was not pleased when I told him that I preferred my Longfellow undiluted with Charlie.

Then we began to go through the MS. line by line; Charlie parrying every objection and correction with:

'Yes, that may be better, but you don't catch what I'm driving at.'

Charlie was, in one way at least, very like one kind of poet.

There was a pencil scrawl at the back of the paper and 'What's that?' I said.

'Oh, that's not poetry at all. It's some rot I wrote last night before I went to bed, and it was too much bother to hunt for rhymes; so I made it a sort of blank verse instead.'

Here is Charlie's 'blank verse':—

We pulled for you when the wind was against us and the sails were low.
Will you never let us go?
We ate bread and onions when you took towns or ran aboard quickly when you were beaten back by the foe,
The captains walked up and down the deck in fair weather singing songs, but we were below.
We fainted with our chins on the oars and you did not see that we were idle for we still swung to and fro.
Will you never let us go?
The salt made the oar-handles like shark-skin; our knees were cut to the bone with salt cracks; our hair was stuck to our foreheads; and our lips were cut to our gums and you whipped us because we could not row.
Will you never let us go?
But in a little time we shall run out of the portholes as the water
runs along the oar-blade, and though you tell the others to

row after us you will never catch us till you catch the oar-
thresh and tie up the winds in the belly of the sail. Aho!
Will you never let us go?

'H'm. What's oar-thresh, Charlie?'

'The water washed up by the oars. That's the sort of song they might sing in the galley y' know. Aren't you ever going to finish that story and give me some of the profits?'

'It depends on yourself. If you had only told me more about your hero in the first instance it might have been finished by now. You're so hazy in your notions.'

'I only want to give you the general notion of it—the knocking about from place to place and the fighting and all that. Can't you fill in the rest yourself? Make the hero save a girl on a pirate-galley and marry her or do something.'

'You're a really helpful collaborator. I suppose the hero went through some few adventures before he married.'

'Well, then, make him a very artful card—a low sort of man—a sort of political man who went about making treaties and breaking them—a black-haired chap who hid behind the mast when the fighting began.'

'But you said the other day that he was red-haired.'

'I couldn't have. Make him black-haired of course. You've no imagination.'

Seeing that I had just discovered the entire principles upon which our half-memory falsely called imagination is based, I felt entitled to laugh, but forbore, for the sake of the tale. 'You're right. *You're* the man with imagination. A black-haired chap in a decked ship,' I said.

' No, an open ship—like a big boat.'

This was maddening.

'Your ship has been built and designed, closed and decked in; you said so yourself,' I protested.

'No, no, not that ship. That was open or half-decked because By Jove you're right! You made me think of the hero as a red-haired chap. Of course if he were red, the ship would be an open one with painted sails.'

Surely, I thought, he would remember now that he had served in two galleys at least—in a three-decked Greek one under the black-haired 'political man,' and again in a Viking's open sea-serpent under the man 'red as a red bear' who went to Markland. My devil prompted me to speak.

'Why, "of course," Charlie?' said I.

'I don't know. Are you making fun of me?'

The current was broken for the time being. I took up a notebook and pretended to make many entries in it.

'It's a pleasure to work with an imaginative chap like yourself,' I said, after a pause. 'The way that you've brought out the character of the hero is simply wonderful.'

'Do you think so?' he answered with a pleased flush. 'I often tell myself that there's more in me than my mo—than people think.'

'There's an enormous amount in you.'

'Then, won't you let me send an essay on The Ways of Bank-Clerks to *Tit-Bits*, and get the guinea prize?'

'That wasn't exactly what I meant, old fellow: perhaps it would be better to wait a little and go ahead with the galley-story.'

'Ah, but I sha'n't get the credit of that. *Tit-Bits* would publish my name and address if I win. What are you grinning at? They *would*.'

'I know it. Suppose you go for a walk. I want to look through my notes about our story.'

Now this reprehensible youth who left me, a little hurt and put back, might for aught he or I knew have been one of the crew of the *Argo*—had been certainly slave or comrade to Thorfin Karlsefne. Therefore he was deeply interested in guinea competitions. Remembering what Grish Chunder had said I laughed aloud. The Lords of Life and Death would never allow Charlie Mears to speak with full knowledge of his pasts; and I must even piece out what he had told me with my own poor inventions while Charlie wrote of the ways of bank-clerks.

I got together and placed on one file all my notes; and the

net result was not cheering. I read them a second time. There was nothing that might not have been compiled at second-hand from other people's books—except, perhaps, the story of the fight in the harbour. The adventures of a Viking had been written many times before; the history of a Greek galley-slave was no new thing, and though I wrote both, who could challenge or confirm the accuracy of my details? I might as well tell a tale of two thousand years hence. The Lords of Life and Death were as cunning as Grish Chunder had hinted. They would allow nothing to escape that might trouble or make easy the minds of men. Though I was convinced of this, yet I could not leave the tale alone.

Exaltation followed reaction, not once, but twenty times in the next few weeks. My moods varied with the March sunlight and flying clouds. By night or in the beauty of a spring morning I perceived that I could write that tale and shift continents thereby. In the wet windy afternoons, I saw that the tale might indeed be written, but would be nothing more than a faked, false-varnished, sham-rusted piece of Wardour Street work at the end. Then I blessed Charlie in many ways—though it was no fault of his. He seemed to be busy with prize competitions, and I saw less and less of him as the weeks went by and the earth cracked and grew ripe to spring, and the buds swelled in their sheaths. He did not care to read or talk of what he had read, and there was a new ring of self-assertion in his voice. I hardly cared to remind him of the galley when we met; but Charlie alluded to it on every occasion, always as a story from which money was to be made.

'I think I deserve twenty-five *per cent*, don't I, at least,' he said, with beautiful frankness. 'I supplied all the ideas, didn't I?'

This greediness for silver was a new side in his nature. I assumed that it had been developed in the City, where Charlie was picking up the curious nasal drawl of the underbred City man. 'When the thing's done we'll talk about it. I can't make anything of it at present. Red-haired or black-haired hero are equally difficult.'

He was sitting by the fire staring at the red coals. 'I can't understand what you find so difficult. It's all as clear as mud to me,' he replied. A jet of gas puffed out between the bars, took light, and whistled softly. 'Suppose we take the red-haired hero's adventures first, from the time that he came south to my galley and captured it and sailed to the Beaches.'

I knew better now than to interrupt Charlie. I was out of reach of pen and paper, and dared not move to get them lest I should break the current. The gas-jet puffed and whinnied, Charlie's voice dropped almost to a whisper, and he told a tale of the sailing of an open galley to Furdurstrandi, of sunsets on the open sea, seen under the curve of the one sail evening after evening when the galley's beak was notched into the centre of the sinking disc, and 'we sailed by that for we had no other guide,' quoth Charlie. He spoke of a landing on an island and explorations in its woods, where the crew killed three men whom they found asleep under the pines.

Their ghosts, Charlie said, followed the galley, swimming and choking in the water, and the crew cast lots and threw one of their number overboard as a sacrifice to the strange gods whom they had offended. Then they ate sea-weed when their provisions failed, and their legs swelled, and their leader, the red-haired man, killed two rowers who mutinied, and after a year spent among the woods they set sail for their own country, and a wind that never failed carried them back so safely that they all slept at night. This, and much more Charlie told.

Sometimes the voice fell so low that I could not catch the words, though every nerve was on the strain. He spoke of their leader, the red-haired man, as a pagan speaks of his God; for it was he who cheered them and slew them impartially as he thought best for their needs; and it was he who steered them for three days among floating ice, each floe crowded with strange beasts that 'tried to sail with us,' said Charlie, ' and we beat them back with the handles of the oars.'

The gas-jet went out, a burnt coal gave way, and the fire settled with a tiny crash to the bottom of the grate. Charlie ceased speaking, and I said no word.

'By Jove!' he said at last, shaking his head. 'I've been staring at the fire till I'm dizzy. What was I going to say?'

'Something about the galley-book.'

'I remember now. It's a quarter of the profits, isn't it?'

'It's anything you like when I've done the tale.'

'I wanted to be sure of that. I must go now. I've—I've an appointment.' And he left me.

Had not my eyes been held I might have known that that broken muttering over the fire was the swan-song of Charlie Mears. But I thought it the prelude to fuller revelation. At last and at last I should cheat the Lords of Life and Death!

When next Charlie came to me I received him with rapture. He was nervous and embarrassed, but his eyes were very full of light, and his lips a little parted.

'I've done a poem,' he said; and then, quickly: 'it's the best I've ever done. Read it.' He thrust it into my hand and retreated to the window.

I groaned inwardly. It would be the work of half an hour to criticise—that is to say praise—the poem sufficiently to please Charlie. Then I had good reason to groan, for Charlie, discarding his favourite centipede metres, had launched into shorter and choppier verse, and verse with a motive at the back of it. This is what I read:—

> The day is most fair, the cheery wind
> Halloos behind the hill
> Where he bends the wood as seemeth good,
> And the sapling to his will!
> Riot O wind; there is that in my blood
> That would not have thee still!

> She gave me herself, Earth, Sky;
> Gray sea, she is mine alone!
> Let the sullen boulders hear my cry,
> And rejoice tho' they be but stone!

> Mine! I have won her, good brown earth,

Make merry! 'Tis hard on Spring;
Make merry; my love is doubly worth
All worship your fields can bring!
Let the hind that tills you feel my mirth
At the early harrowing.'

'Yes, it's the early harrowing, past a doubt,' I said, with a dread at my heart. Charlie smiled, but did not answer.

Red cloud of the sunset, tell it abroad;
I am victor. Greet me, O Sun,
Dominant master and absolute lord
  Over the soul of one!

'Well?' said Charlie, looking over my shoulder. I thought it far from well, and very evil indeed, when he silently laid a photograph on the paper—the photograph of a girl with a curly head, and a foolish slack mouth.

'Isn't it—isn't it wonderful?' he whispered, pink to the tips of his ears, wrapped in the rosy mystery of first love. 'I didn't know; I didn't think—it came like a thunderclap.'

'Yes. It comes like a thunderclap. Are you very happy, Charlie?'

'My God—she—she loves me!' He sat down repeating the last words to himself. I looked at the hairless face, the narrow shoulders already bowed by desk-work, and wondered when, where, and how he had loved in his past lives.

'What will your mother say?' I asked cheerfully.

'I don't care a damn what she says.'

At twenty the things for which one does not care a damn should, properly, be many, but one must not include mothers in the list. I told him this gently; and he described Her, even as Adam must have described to the newly-named beasts the glory and tenderness and beauty of Eve. Incidentally I learned that She was a tobacconist's assistant with a weakness for pretty dress, and had told him four or five times already that She had never been kissed by a man before.

Charlie spoke on and on, and on; while I, separated from him by thousands of years, was considering the beginnings of things. Now I understood why the Lords of Life and Death shut the doors so carefully behind us. It is that we may not remember our first and most beautiful wooings. Were it not so, our world would be without inhabitants in a hundred years.

'Now, about that galley-story,' I said still more cheerfully, in a pause in the rush of the speech.

Charlie looked up as though he had been hit. 'The galley— what galley? Good heavens, don't joke, man! This is serious! You don't know how serious it is!'

Grish Chunder was right. Charlie had tasted the love of woman that kills remembrance, and the finest story in the world would never be written.

A Madonna of the Trenches

'Whatever a man of the sons of men
Shall say to his heart of the lords above.
They have shown man, verily, once and again.
Marvellous mercies and infinite love.
★★★★★★
'O sweet one love, O my life's delight.
Dear, though the days have divided us.
Lost beyond hope, taken far out of sight.
Not twice in the world shall the Gods do thus.'
Swinburne, Les Noyades.

Seeing how many unstable ex-soldiers came to the Lodge of Instruction (attached to Faith and Works E.C. 5837) in the years after the war, the wonder is there was not more trouble from Brethren whom sudden meetings with old comrades jerked back into their still raw past. But our round, torpedo-bearded local Doctor–Brother Keede, Senior Warden—always stood ready to deal with hysteria before it got out of hand; and when I examined Brethren unknown or imperfectly vouched for on the Masonic side, I passed on to him anything that seemed doubtful. He had had his experience as medical officer of a South London battalion, during the last two years of the war; and, naturally, often found friends and acquaintances among the visitors.

Brother C. Strangwick, a young, tallish, new-made brother, hailed from some South London Lodge. His papers and his answers were above suspicion, but his red-rimmed eyes had a puzzled glare that might mean nerves. So I introduced him particularly to Keede, who discovered in him a headquarters orderly of his old battalion, congratulated him on his return to fitness—he had been discharged for some infirmity or other—and plunged at once into Somme memories.

'I hope I did right, Keede,' I said when we were robing before Lodge.

'Oh, quite. He reminded me that I had him under my hands at Sampoux in 'Eighteen, when he went to bits. He was a runner.'

'Was it shock?' I asked.

'Of sorts—but not what he wanted me to think it was. No, he wasn't shamming. He had jumps to the limit—but he played up to mislead me about the reason of 'em . . . Well, if we could stop patients from lying, medicine would be too easy, I suppose.'

I noticed that, after lodge-working, Keede gave him a seat a couple of rows in front of us, that he might enjoy a lecture on the Orientation of King Solomon's Temple, which an earnest brother thought would be a nice interlude between labour and the high tea that we called our 'banquet.' Even helped by tobacco it was a dreary performance. About half-way through, Strangwick, who had been fidgeting and twitching for some minutes, rose, drove back his chair grinding across the tessellated floor, and yelped 'Oh, My Aunt! I can't stand this any longer.' Under cover of a general laugh of assent he brushed past us and stumbled towards the door.

'I thought so!' Keede whispered to me. 'Come along!' We overtook him in the passage, crowing hysterically and wringing his hands. Keede led him into the Tyler's room, a small office where we stored odds and ends of regalia and furniture, and locked the door.

'I'm—I'm all right,' the boy began, piteously.

"Course you are.' Keede opened a small cupboard which I had seen called upon before, mixed *sal volatile* and water in a graduated glass, and, as Strangwick drank, pushed him gently on to an old sofa. 'There,' he went on. 'It's nothing to write home about. I've seen you ten times worse. I expect our talk has brought things back.'

He hooked up a chair behind him with one foot, held the patient's hands in his own, and sat down. The chair creaked.

'Don't!' Strangwick squealed. 'I can't stand it! There's nothing on earth creaks like they do! And—and when it thaws we—we've got to slap 'em back with a spa-ade! Remember those Frenchmen's little boots under the duckboards? . . . What'll I do? What'll I do about it?'

Someone knocked at the door, to know if all were well.

'Oh, quite, thanks!' said Keede over his shoulder. 'But I shall need this room awhile. Draw the curtains, please.'

We heard the rings of the hangings that drape the passage from lodge to banquet room click along their poles, and what sound there had been, of feet and voices, was shut off.

Strangwick, retching impotently, complained of the frozen dead who creak in the frost.

'He's playing up still,' Keede whispered. 'That's not his real trouble—any more than 'twas last time.'

'But surely,' I replied, 'men get those things on the brain pretty badly. 'Remember in October—'

'This chap hasn't, though. I wonder what's really helling him. What are you thinking of?' said Keede peremptorily.

'French End an' Butcher's Row,' Strangwick muttered.

'Yes, there were a few there. But suppose we face Bogey instead of giving him best every time.' Keede turned towards me with a hint in his eye that I was to play up to his leads.

'What was the trouble with French End?' I opened at a venture.

'It was a bit by Sampoux, that we had taken over from the French. They're tough, but you wouldn't call 'em tidy as a nation. They had faced both sides of it with dead to keep the mud back. All those trenches were like gruel in a thaw. Our people had to do the same sort of thing—elsewhere; but Butcher's Row in French End was the—er—show-piece. Luckily, we pinched a salient from Jerry just then, an' straightened things out—so we didn't need to use the Row after November. You remember,

Strangwick?'

'My God, yes! When the buckboard-slats were missin' you'd tread on 'em, an' they'd creak.'

'They're bound to. Like leather,' said Keede. 'It gets on one's nerves a bit, but—'

'Nerves? It's real! It's real!' Strangwick gulped.

'But at your time of life, it'll all fall behind you in a year or so. I'll give you another sip of paregoric, an' we'll face it quietly. Shall we?'

Keede opened his cupboard again and administered a carefully dropped dark dose of something that was not *sal volatile*. 'This'll settle you in a few minutes,' he explained. 'Lie still, an' don't talk unless you feel like it.'

He faced me, fingering his beard.

'Ye-es. Butcher's Row wasn't pretty,' he volunteered. 'Seeing Strangwick here, has brought it all back to me again. 'Funny thing! We had a platoon sergeant of number two—what the deuce was his name?—an elderly bird who must have lied like a patriot to get out to the front at his age; but he was a first-class non–com., and the last person, you'd think, to make mistakes. Well, he was due for a fortnight's home leave in January, 'Eighteen. You were at B.H.Q. then, Strangwick, weren't you?'

'Yes. I was orderly. It was January twenty-first'; Strangwick spoke with a thickish tongue, and his eyes burned. Whatever drug it was, had taken hold.

'About then,' Keede said. 'Well, this sergeant, instead of coming down from the trenches the regular way an' joinin' Battalion Details after dark, an' takin' that funny little train for Arras, thinks he'll warm himself first. So he gets into a dugout, in Butcher's Row, that used to be an old French dressing-station, and fugs up between a couple of braziers of pure charcoal! As luck 'ud have it, that was the only dugout with an inside door opening inwards—some French anti-gas fitting, I expect—and, by what we could make out, the door must have swung to while he was warming. Anyhow, he didn't turn up at the train. There was a search at once. We couldn't afford to waste platoon sergeants. We found him in the morning. He'd got his gas all right. A machine-gunner reported him, didn't he, Strangwick?'

'No, Sir. Corporal Grant—o' the Trench Mortars.'

'So it was. Yes, Grant—the man with that little wen on his neck. 'Nothing wrong with your memory, at any rate. What was the sergeant's name?'

'Godsoe—John Godsoe,' Strangwick answered.

'Yes, that was it. I had to see him next mornin'—frozen stiff between the two braziers—and not a scrap of private papers on him. That was the only thing that made me think it mightn't have been—quite an accident.'

Strangwick's relaxing face set, and he threw back at once to the orderly room manner.

'I give my evidence—at the time—to you, sir. He passed—overtook me, I should say—comin' down from supports, after I'd warned him for leaf. I thought he was goin' through Parrot Trench as usual; but 'e must 'ave turned off into French End where the old bombed barricade was.'

'Yes. I remember now. You were the last man to see him alive. That was on the twenty-first of January, you say? Now, when was it that Dearlove and Billings brought you to me—clean out of your head?' . . . Keede dropped his hand, in the style of magazine detectives, on Strangwick's shoulder. The boy looked at him with cloudy wonder, and muttered: 'I was took to you on the evenin' of the twenty-fourth of January. But you don't think I did him in, do you?'

I could not help smiling at Keede's discomfiture; but he recovered himself. 'Then what the dickens was on your mind that evening—before I gave you the hypodermic?'

'The—the things in Butcher's Row. They kept on comin' over me. You've seen me like this before, sir.'

'But I knew that it was a lie. You'd no more got stiffs on the brain then than you have now. You've got something, but you're hiding it.'

'"Ow do you know, doctor?" Strangwick whimpered.

'D'you remember what you said to me, when Dearlove and

Billings were holding you down that evening?'

'About the things in Butcher's Row?'

'Oh, no! You spun me a lot of stuff about corpses creaking; but you let yourself go in the middle of it—when you pushed that telegram at me. What did you mean, f'rinstance, by asking what advantage it was for you to fight beasts of officers if the dead didn't rise?'

'Did I say "Beasts of Officers"?'

'You did. It's out of the burial service.'

'I suppose, then, I must have heard it. As a matter of fact, I 'ave.' Strangwick shuddered extravagantly.

'Probably. And there's another thing—that hymn you were shouting till I put you under. It was something about Mercy and Love. Remember it?'

'I'll try,' said the boy obediently, and began to paraphrase, as nearly as possible thus: "*Whatever a man may say in his heart unto the Lord, yea, verily I say unto you—Gawd hath shown man, again and again, marvellous mercy an'—an' somethin' or other love.*" He screwed up his eyes and shook.

'Now where did you get that from?' Keede insisted.

'From Godsoe—on the twenty-first Jan . . . 'Ow could I tell what 'e meant to do?' he burst out in a high, unnatural key—'Any more than I knew she was dead.'

'Who was dead?' said Keede.

'Me Auntie Armine.'

'The one the telegram came to you about, at Sampoux, that you wanted me to explain—the one that you were talking of in the passage out here just now when you began: "O Auntie," and changed it to "O Gawd," when I collared you?'

'That's her! I haven't a chance with you, Doctor. I didn't know there was anything wrong with those braziers. How could I? We're always usin' 'em. Honest to God, I thought at first go-off he might wish to warm himself before the leaf-train. I—I didn't know Uncle John meant to start 'ouse-keepin'.' He laughed horribly, and then the dry tears came.

Keede waited for them to pass in sobs and hiccoughs before

he continued: 'Why? Was Godsoe your Uncle?'

'No,' said Strangwick, his head between his hands. 'Only we'd known him ever since we were born. Dad 'ad known him before that. He lived almost next street to us. Him an' Dad an' Ma an'—an' the rest had always been friends. So we called him Uncle—like children do.'

'What sort of man was he?'

'One o' the best, sir. pensioned sergeant with a little money left him—quite independent—and very superior. They had a sittin'-room full o' Indian curios that him and his wife used to let sister an' me see when we'd been good.'

'Wasn't he rather old to join up?'

'That made no odds to him. He joined up as Sergeant Instructor at the first go-off, an' when the battalion was ready he got 'imself sent along. He wangled me into 'is platoon when I went out—early in 'Seventeen. Because Ma wanted it, I suppose.'

'I'd no notion you knew him that well,' was Keede's comment.

'Oh, it made no odds to him. He 'ad no pets in the platoon, but 'e'd write 'ome to Ma about me an' all the doin's. You see'— Strangwick stirred uneasily on the sofa—'we'd known him all our lives—lived in the next street an' all . . . An' him well over fifty. Oh dear me! Oh dear me! What a bloody mix-up things are, when one's as young as me!' he wailed of a sudden.

But Keede held him to the point. 'He wrote to your mother about you?'

'Yes. Ma's eyes had gone bad followin' on air-raids. 'Blood-vessels broke behind 'em from sittin' in cellars an' bein' sick. She had to 'ave 'er letters read to her by auntie. Now I think of it, that was the only thing that you might have called anything at all—'

'Was that the aunt that died, and that you got the wire about?' Keede drove on.

'Yes–Auntie Armine–Ma's younger sister, an' she nearer fifty than forty. What a mix-up! An' if I'd been asked any time about it, I'd 'ave sworn there wasn't a single sol'tary item concernin' her that everybody didn't know an' hadn't known all along. No more conceal to her doin's than—than so much shop-front. She'd looked after sister an' me, when needful—whoopin' cough an' measles just the same as Ma. We was in an' out of her house like rabbits. You see, Uncle Armine is a cabinet-maker, an' second-'and furniture, an' we liked playin' with the things. She 'ad no children, and when the war came, she said she was glad of it. But she never talked much of her feelin's. She kept herself to herself, you understand.' He stared most earnestly at us to help out our understandings.

'What was she like?' Keede inquired.

'A biggish woman, an' had been 'andsome, I believe, but, bein' used to her, we two didn't notice much—except, per'aps, for one thing. Ma called her 'er proper name, which was Bella; but Sis an' me always called 'er Auntie Armine. See?'

'What for?'

'We thought it sounded more like her—like somethin' movin' slow, in armour.'

'Oh! And she read your letters to your mother, did she?'

'Every time the post came in she'd slip across the road from opposite an' read 'em. An'—an' I'll go bail for it that that was all there was to it for as far back as I remember. Was I to swing tomorrow, I'd go bail for that! 'Tisn't fair of 'em to 'ave unloaded it all on me, because—because—if the dead do rise, why, what in 'ell becomes of me an' all I've believed all me life? I want to know that! I—I—'

But Keede would not be put off. 'Did the sergeant give you away at all in his letters?' he demanded, very quietly.

'There was nothin' to give away—we was too busy—but his letters about me were a great comfort to Ma. I'm no good at writin'. I saved it all up for my leafs. I got me fourteen days every six months an' one over . . . I was luckier than most, that way.'

'And when you came home, used you to bring 'em news about the sergeant?' said Keede.

'I expect I must have; but I didn't think much of it at the

time. I was took up with me own affairs—naturally. Uncle John always wrote to me once each leaf, tellin' me what was doin' an' what I was li'ble to expect on return, an' Ma 'ud'ave that read to her. Then o' course I had to slip over to his wife an' pass her the news. An' then there was the young lady that I'd thought of marryin' if I came through. We'd got as far as pricin' things in the windows together.'

'And you didn't marry her—after all?'

Another tremor shook the boy. 'No!' he cried. ''Fore it ended, I knew what reel things reelly mean! I—I never dreamed such things could be! . . . An' she nearer fifty than forty an' me own Aunt! . . . But there wasn't a sign nor a hint from first to last, so 'ow could I tell? Don't you see it? All she said to me after me Christmas leaf in' '18, when I come to say goodbye—all Auntie Armine said to me was: "You'll be seein' Mister Godsoe soon?" "Too soon for my likings," I says. "Well then, tell 'im from me," she says, "that I expect to be through with my little trouble by the twenty-first of next month, an' I'm dyin' to see him as soon as possible after that date."'

'What sort of trouble was it?' Keede turned professional at once.

'She'd 'ad a bit of a gatherin' in 'er breast, I believe. But she never talked of 'er body much to anyone.'

'I see,' said Keede. 'And she said to you?'

Strangwick repeated: '"Tell Uncle John I hope to be finished of my drawback by the twenty-first, an' I'm dying to see 'im as soon as 'e can after that date." An' then she says, laughin': "But you've a head like a sieve. I'll write it down, an' you can give it him when you see 'im." So she wrote it on a bit o' paper an' I kissed 'er goodbye—I was always her favourite, you see—an' I went back to Sampoux. The thing hardly stayed in my mind at all, d'you see. But the next time I was up in the front line—I was a runner, d'ye see—our platoon was in North Bay Trench an' I was up with a message to the Trench Mortar there that Corporal Grant was in charge of. Followin' on receipt of it, he borrowed a couple of men off the platoon, to slue 'er round or somethin'.

I give Uncle John Auntie Armine's paper, an' I give Grant a fag, an' we warmed up a bit over a brazier. Then Grant says to me: "I don't like it;" an' he jerks 'is thumb at Uncle John in the bay studyin' auntie's message. Well, you know, sir, you had to speak to Grant about 'is way of prophesyin' things—after Rankine shot himself with the Very light.'

'I did,' said Keede, and he explained to me 'Grant had the Second Sight—confound him! It upset the men. I was glad when he got pipped. What happened after that, Strangwick?'

'Grant whispers to me: "Look, you damned Englishman. 'E's for it." Uncle John was leanin' up against the bay, an' hummin' that hymn I was tryin' to tell you just now. He looked different all of a sudden—as if 'e'd got shaved. I don't know anything of these things, but I cautioned Grant as to his style of speakin', if an officer 'ad 'eard him, an' I went on. Passin' Uncle John in the bay, 'e nods an' smiles, which he didn't often, an' he says, pocketin' the paper "This suits me. I'm for leaf on the twenty-first, too."'

'He said that to you, did he?' said Keede.

'Precisely the same as passin' the time o' day. O' course I returned the agreeable about hopin' he'd get it, an' in due course I returned to 'eadquarters. The thing 'ardly stayed in my mind a minute. That was the eleventh January—three days after I'd come back from leaf. You remember, sir, there wasn't anythin' doin' either side round Sampoux the first part o' the month. Jerry was gettin' ready for his March push, an' as long as he kept quiet, we didn't want to poke 'im up.'

'I remember that,' said Keede. 'But what about the sergeant?'

'I must have met him, on an' off, I expect, goin' up an' down, through the ensuin' days, but it didn't stay in me mind. Why needed it? And on the twenty-first Jan., his name was on the leaf-paper when I went up to warn the leaf-men. I noticed that, o' course. Now that very afternoon Jerry 'ad been tryin' a new trench-mortar, an' before our 'eavies could out it, he'd got a stinker into a bay an' mopped up 'alf a dozen. They were bringin' 'em down when I went up to the supports, an' that blocked Little Parrot, same as it always did. You remember, sir?'

'Rather! And there was that big machine-gun behind the Half–House waiting for you if you got out,' said Keede.

'I remembered that too. But it was just on dark an' the fog was comin' off the canal, so I hopped out of Little Parrot an' cut across the open to where those four dead Warwicks are heaped up. But the fog turned me round, an' the next thing I knew I was knee-over in that old 'alf-trench that runs west o' Little Parrot into French End. I dropped into it—almost atop o' the machine-gun platform by the side o' the old sugar boiler an' the two Zoo-ave skel'tons. That gave me my bearin's, an' so I went through French End, all up those missin' buckboards, into Butcher's Row where the *poy-looz* was laid in six deep each side, an' stuffed under the buckboards. It had froze tight, an' the drippin's had stopped, an' the creakin's had begun.'

'Did that really worry you at the time?' Keede asked.

'No,' said the boy with professional scorn. 'If a runner starts noticin' such things he'd better chuck. In the middle of the row, just before the old dressin'-station you referred to, sir, it come over me that somethin' ahead on the Buckboards was just like Auntie Armine, waitin' beside the door; an' I thought to meself 'ow truly comic it would be if she could be dumped where I was then. In 'alf a second I saw it was only the dark an' some rags o' gas-screen, 'angin' on a bit of board, 'ad played me the trick. So I went on up to the supports an' warned the leaf-men there, includin' Uncle John. Then I went up Rake Alley to warn 'em in the front line. I didn't hurry because I didn't want to get there till Jerry 'ad quieted down a bit. Well, then a company relief dropped in an' the officer got the wind up over some lights on the flank, an' tied 'em into knots, an' I 'ad to hunt up me leaf-men all over the blinkin' shop. What with one thing an' another, it must 'ave been 'alf-past eight before I got back to the supports. There I run across Uncle John, scrapm' mud off himself, havin' shaved—quite the dandy. He asked about the Arras train, an' I said, if Jerry was quiet, it might be ten o'clock. "Good!" says 'e. "I'll come with you." So we started back down the old trench that used to run across Halnaker, back of the support dugouts. You know, sir.'

Keede nodded.

'Then Uncle John says something to me about seein' ma an' the rest of 'em in a few days, an' had I any messages for 'em? Gawd knows what made me do it, but I told 'im to tell Auntie Armine I never expected to see anything like her up in our part of the world. And while I told him I laughed. That's the last time I 'ave laughed." Oh—you've seen 'er, 'ave you? says he, quite natural-like. Then I told 'im about the sand-bags an' rags in the dark, playin' the trick. "Very likely," says he, brushin' the mud off his *putties*. By this time, we'd got to the corner where the old barricade into French End was—before they bombed it down, sir. He turns right an' climbs across it. "No, thanks," says I. "I've been there once this evenin'." But he wasn't attendin' to me. He felt behind the rubbish an' bones just inside the barricade, an' when he straightened up, he had a full brazier in each hand.

"'Come on, Clem," he says, an' he very rarely give me me own name. "You aren't afraid, are you?" he says. "It's just as short, an' if Jerry starts up again he won't waste stuff here. He knows it's abandoned." "Who's afraid now?" I says. "Me for one," says he. "I don't want my leaf spoiled at the last minute." Then 'e wheels round an' speaks that bit you said come out o' the burial service.'

For some reason Keede repeated it in full, slowly: '*If after the manner of men I have fought with beasts at Ephesus, what advantageth it me, if the dead rise not?*'

'That's it,' said Strangwick. 'So we went down French end to-gether—everything froze up an' quiet, except for their creakin's. I remember thinkin'—' his eyes began to flicker.

'Don't think. Tell what happened,' Keede ordered.

'Oh! Beg y' pardon! He went on with his braziers, hummin' his hymn, down Butcher's Row. Just before we got to the old dressin' station he stops and sets 'em down an' says "Where did you say she was, Clem? Me eyes ain't as good as they used to be."

157

'"In 'er bed at 'ome," I says. "Come on down. It's perishin' cold, an' I'm not due for leaf."

'"Well, I am," 'e says. "I am ..." An' then—'give you me word I didn't recognise the voice—he stretches out 'is neck a bit, in a way 'e 'ad, an' he says: "Why, Bella!" 'e says. "Oh, Bella!" 'e says. "Thank Gawd!" 'e says. Just like that! An' then I saw—I tell you I saw—Auntie Armine herself standin' by the old dressin'station door where first I'd thought I'd seen her. He was lookin' at 'er an' she was lookin' at him. I saw it, an' me soul turned over inside me because—because it knocked out everything I'd believed in. I 'ad nothin' to lay 'old of, d'ye see? An' 'e was lookin' at 'er as though he could 'ave et 'er, an' she was lookin' at 'im the same way, out of 'er eyes. Then he says: "Why, Bella," 'e says, "this must be only the second time we've been alone together in all these years."

'An' I saw 'er half hold out her arms to 'im in that perishin' cold. An' she nearer fifty than forty an' me own aunt! You can shop me for a lunatic tomorrow, but I saw it—I saw 'er answerin' to his spoken word ... Then 'e made a snatch to unsling 'is rifle. Then 'e cuts 'is hand away saying: "No! Don't tempt me, Bella. We've all Eternity ahead of us. An hour or two won't make any odds." Then he picks up the braziers an' goes on to the dugout door. He'd finished with me. He pours petrol on 'em, an' lights it with a match, an' carries 'em inside, flarin'. All that time Auntie Armine stood with 'er arms out—an' a look in 'er face! I didn't know such things was or could be! Then he comes out an' says: "Come in, my dear;" an' she stoops an' goes into the dugout with that look on her face—that look on her face! An' then 'e shuts the door from inside an' starts wedgin' it up. So 'elp me Gawd, I saw an' 'eard all these things with my own eyes an' ears!'

He repeated his oath several times. After a long pause Keede asked him if he recalled what happened next.

'It was a bit of a mix-up, for me, from then on. I must have carried on—they told me I did, but—but I was—I felt a—a long way inside of meself, like—if you've ever had that feelin'.

I wasn't rightly on the spot at all. They woke me up some-time next morning, because 'e 'adn't showed up at the train; an' someone had seen him with me. I wasn't 'alf cross-examined by all an' sundry till dinner-time.

'Then, I think, I volunteered for Dearlove, who 'ad a sore toe, for a front-line message. I had to keep movin', you see, because I hadn't anything to hold on to. Whilst up there, Grant informed me how he'd found Uncle John with the door wedged an' sand-bags stuffed in the cracks. I hadn't waited for that. The knockin' when 'e wedged up was enough for me.

'Like Dad's coffin.'

'No one told me the door had been wedged.' Keede spoke severely.

'No need to black a dead man's name, sir.'

'What made Grant go to Butcher's Row?'

'Because he'd noticed Uncle John had been pinchin' charcoal for a week past an' layin' it up behind the old barricade there. So when the 'unt began, he went that way straight as a string, an' when he saw the door shut, he knew. He told me he picked the sand-bags out of the cracks an' shoved 'is hand through and shifted the wedges before anyone come along. It looked all right. You said yourself, sir, the door must 'ave blown to.'

'Grant knew what Godsoe meant, then?' Keede snapped.

'Grant knew Godsoe was for it; an' nothin' earthly could 'elp or 'inder. He told me so.'

'And then what did you do?'

'I expect I must 'ave kept on carryin' on, till Headquarters give me that wire from ma—about Auntie Armine dyin'.'

'When had your aunt died?'

'On the mornin' of the twenty-first. The mornin' of the 21st! That tore it, d'ye see? As long as I could think, I had kep' tellin' myself it was like those things you lectured about at Arras when we was billeted in the cellars—the Angels of Mons, and so on. But that wire tore it.'

'Oh! Hallucinations! I remember. And that wire tore it?' said Keede.

'Yes! You see'—he half lifted himself off the sofa—'there wasn't a single gor-dam thing left abidin' for me to take hold of, here or hereafter. If the dead do rise—and I saw 'em—why—why, anything can 'appen. Don't you understand?'

He was on his feet now, gesticulating stiffly.

'For I saw 'er,' he repeated. 'I saw 'im an' 'er—she dead since mornin' time, an' he killin' 'imself before my livin' eyes so's to carry on with 'er for all Eternity—an' she 'oldin' out 'er arms for it! I want to know where I'm at! Look 'ere, you two—why stand we in jeopardy every hour?'

'God knows,' said Keede to himself.

'Hadn't we better ring for some one?' I suggested. 'He'll go off the handle in a second.'

'No, he won't. It's the last kick-up before it takes hold. I know how the stuff works. Hul-lo!'

Strangwick, his hands behind his back and his eyes set, gave tongue in the strained, cracked voice of a boy reciting. 'Not twice in the world shall the Gods do thus,' he cried again and again.

'And I'm damned if it's goin' to be even once for me!' he went on with sudden insane fury. 'I don't care whether we 'ave been pricin' things in the windows . . . Let 'er sue if she likes! She don't know what reel things mean. I do—I've 'ad occasion to notice 'em . . . No, I tell you! I'll 'ave 'em when I want 'em, an' be done with 'em; but not till I see that look on a face . . . that look . . . I'm not takin' any. The reel thing's life an' death. It begins at death, d'ye see. She can't understand . . . Oh, go on an' push off to Hell, you an' your lawyers. I'm fed up with it—fed up!'

He stopped as abruptly as he had started, and the drawn face broke back to its natural irresolute lines. Keede, holding both his hands, led him back to the sofa, where he dropped like a wet towel, took out some flamboyant robe from a press, and drew it neatly over him.

'Ye-es. That's the real thing at last,' said Keede. 'Now he's got it off his mind he'll sleep. By the way, who introduced him?'

'Shall I go and find out?' I suggested.

'Yes; and you might ask him to come here. There's no need for us to stand to all night.'

So I went to the banquet, which was in full swing, and was seized by an elderly, precise brother from a South London Lodge, who followed me, concerned and apologetic. Keede soon put him at his ease.

'The boy's had trouble,' our visitor explained. 'I'm most mortified he should have performed his bad turn here. I thought he'd put it be'ind him.'

'I expect talking about old days with me brought it all back,' said Keede. 'It does sometimes.'

'Maybe! Maybe! But over and above that, Clem's had postwar trouble, too.'

'Can't he get a job? He oughtn't to let that weigh on him, at his time of life,' said Keede cheerily.

"Tisn't that—he's provided for—but'—he coughed confidentially behind his dry hand—'as a matter of fact, Worshipful Sir, he's—he's implicated for the present in a little breach of promise action.'

'Ah! That's a different thing,' said Keede.

'Yes. That's his reel trouble. No reason given, you understand. The young lady in every way suitable, an' she'd make him a good little wife too, if I'm any judge. But he says she ain't his ideel or something. 'No getting at what's in young people's minds these days, is there?'

'I'm afraid there isn't,' said Keede. 'But he's all right now. He'll sleep. You sit by him, and when he wakes, take him home quietly . . . Oh, we're used to men getting a little upset here. You've nothing to thank us for, Brother—Brother—'

'Armine,' said the old gentleman. 'He's my nephew by marriage.'

'That's all that's wanted!' said Keede.

Brother Armine looked a little puzzled. Keede hastened to explain. 'As I was saying, all he wants now is to be kept quiet till he wakes.'

The Strange Ride of Morrowbie Jukes

Alive or dead there is no other way.—Native Proverb.

There is, as the conjurers say, no deception about this tale. Jukes by accident stumbled upon a village that is well known to exist, though he is the only Englishman who has been there. A somewhat similar institution used to flourish on the outskirts of Calcutta, and there is a story that if you go into the heart of Bikanir, which is in the heart of the Great Indian Desert, you shall come across not a village, but a town where the Dead who did not die but may not live have established their headquarters. And, since it is perfectly true that in the same desert is a wonderful city where all the rich money-lenders retreat after they have made their fortunes (fortunes so vast that the owners cannot trust even the strong hand of the government to protect them, but take refuge in the waterless sands), and drive sumptuous C-spring barouches, and buy beautiful girls and decorate their palaces with gold and ivory and Minton tiles and mother-o'-pearl, I do not see why Jukes's tale should not be true.

He is a civil engineer, with a head for plans and distances and things of that kind, and he certainly would not take the trouble to invent imaginary traps. He could earn more by doing his legitimate work. He never varies the tale in the telling, and grows very hot and indignant when he thinks of the disrespectful treatment he received. He wrote this quite straightforwardly at first, but he has since touched it up in places and introduced

162

moral reflections, thus:—

In the beginning it all arose from a slight attack of fever. My work necessitated my being in camp for some months between Pakpattan and Mubarakpur—a desolate sandy stretch of country as everyone who has had the misfortune to go there may know. My *coolies* were neither more nor less exasperating than other gangs, and my work demanded sufficient attention to keep me from moping, had I been inclined to so unmanly a weakness.

On the 23rd December, 1884, I felt a little feverish. There was a full moon at the time, and, in consequence, every dog near my tent was baying it. The brutes assembled in twos and threes and drove me frantic. A few days previously I had shot one loud-mouthed singer and suspended his carcass *in terrorem* about fifty yards from my tent-door. But his friends fell upon, fought for, and ultimately devoured the body: and, as it seemed to me, sang their hymns of thanksgiving afterwards with renewed energy.

The light-headedness which accompanies fever acts differently on different men. My irritation gave way, after a short time, to a fixed determination to slaughter one huge black and white beast who had been foremost in song and first in flight throughout the evening. Thanks to a shaking hand and a giddy head I had already missed him twice with both barrels of my shotgun, when it struck me that my best plan would be to ride him down in the open and finish him off with a hog-spear. This, of course, was merely the semi-delirious notion of a fever patient; but I remember that it struck me at the time as being eminently practical and feasible.

I therefore ordered my groom to saddle Pornic and bring him round quietly to the rear of my tent. When the pony was ready, I stood at his head prepared to mount and dash out as soon as the dog should again lift up his voice. Pornic, by the way, had not been out of his pickets for a couple of days; the night air was crisp and chilly; and I was armed with a specially long and sharp pair of persuaders with which I had been rousing a sluggish cob that afternoon. You will easily believe, then, that when he was let go he went quickly. In one moment, for the brute bolted as straight as a die, the tent was left far behind, and we were flying over the smooth sandy soil at racing speed. In another we had passed the wretched dog, and I had almost forgotten why it was that I had taken horse and hog-spear.

The delirium of fever and the excitement of rapid motion through the air must have taken away the remnant of my senses. I have a faint recollection of standing upright in my stirrups, and of brandishing my hog-spear at the great white moon that looked down so calmly on my mad gallop; and of shouting challenges to the camel-thorn bushes as they whizzed passed. Once or twice, I believe, I swayed forward on Pornic's neck, and literally hung on by my spurs—as the marks next morning showed.

The wretched beast went forward like a thing possessed, over what seemed to be a limitless expanse of moonlit sand. Next, I remember, the ground rose suddenly in front of us, and as we topped the ascent I saw the waters of the Sutlej shining like a silver bar below. The Pornic blundered heavily on his nose, and we rolled together down some unseen slope.

I must have lost consciousness, for when I recovered I was lying on my stomach in a heap of soft white sand, and the dawn was beginning to break dimly over the edge of the slope down which I had fallen. As the light grew stronger I saw that I was at the bottom of a horseshoe-shaped crater of sand, opening on one side directly on to the shoals of the Sutlej. My fever had altogether left me, and with the exception of a slight dizziness in the head, I felt no bad effects from the fall over night.

Pornic, who was standing a few yards away, was naturally a good deal exhausted, but had not hurt himself in the least. His saddle, a favourite polo one, was much knocked about, and had been twisted under his belly. It took me some time to put him to rights, and in the meantime I had ample opportunities of observing the spot into which I had so foolishly dropped.

At the risk of being considered tedious, I must describe it at length; inasmuch as an accurate mental picture of its peculiarities will be of material assistance in enabling the reader to understand what follows.

Imagine then, as I have said before, a horseshoe-shaped cra-ter of sand with steeply graded sand walls about thirty-five feet high. (The slope, I fancy, must have been about 65°). This crater enclosed a level piece of ground about fifty yards long by thirty at its broadest part, with a rude well in the centre. Round the bottom of a crater, about three feet from the level of the ground proper, ran a series of eighty-three semi-circular, ovoid, square, and multilateral holes, all about three feet at the mouth. Each hole on inspection showed that it was carefully shored internally with driftwood and bamboos, and over the mouth a wooden drip-board projected, like the peak of a jockey's cap, for two feet. No sign of life was visible in these tunnels, but a most sickening stench pervaded the entire amphitheatre—a stench fouler than any which my wanderings in Indian villages have introduced me to.

Having remounted Pornic, who was as anxious as I to get back to camp, I rode round the base of the horseshoe to find some place whence an exit would be practicable. The inhabit-ants, whoever they might be, had not thought fit to put in an appearance, so I was left to my own devices. My first attempt to "rush" Pornic up the steep sand-banks showed me that 1 had fallen into a trap exactly on the same model as that which the ant-lion sets for its prey. At each step the shifting sand poured down from above in tons, and rattled on the drip-boards of the holes like small shot. A couple of ineffectual charges sent us both rolling down to the bottom, half choked with the torrents of sand; and I was constrained to turn my attention to the river-bank.

Here everything seemed easy enough. The sand hills ran down to the river edge, it is true, but there were plenty of shoals and shallows across which I could gallop Pornic, and find my way back to *terra firma* by turning sharply to the right or the left. As I led Pornic over the sands I was startled by the faint pop of a rifle across the river; and at the same moment a bullet dropped with a sharp "*whit*" close to Pornic's head.

There was no mistaking the nature of the missile—a regulation Martini-Henry "picket." About five hundred yards away a country-boat was anchored in midstream; and a jet of smoke drifting away from its bows in the still morning air showed me whence the delicate attention had come. Was ever a respectable gentleman in such an *impassé?* The treacherous sand slope allowed no escape from a spot which I had visited most involuntarily, and a promenade on the river frontage was the signal for a bombardment from some insane native in a boat. I'm afraid that I lost my temper very much indeed.

Another bullet reminded me that I had better save my breath to cool my porridge; and I retreated hastily up the sands and back to the horseshoe, where I saw that the noise of the rifle had drawn sixty-five human beings from the badger-holes which I had up till that point supposed to be untenanted. I found myself in the midst of a crowd of spectators—about forty men, twenty women, and one child who could not have been more than five years old. They were all scantily clothed in that salmon-coloured cloth which one associates with Hindu mendicants, and, at first sight, gave me the impression of a band of loathsome *fakirs.* The filth and repulsiveness of the assembly were beyond all description, and I shuddered to think what their life in the badger-holes must be.

Even in these days, when local self-government has destroyed the greater part of a native's respect for a Sahib, I have been accustomed to a certain amount of civility from my inferiors, and on approaching the crowd naturally expected that there would be some recognition of my presence. As a matter of fact there was; but it was by no means what I had looked for.

The ragged crew actually laughed at me such laughter I hope I may never hear again. They cackled, yelled, whistled, and howled as I walked into their midst; some of them literally throwing themselves down on the ground in convulsions of unholy mirth. In a moment I had let go Pornic's head, and, irritated beyond expression at the morning's adventure, commenced cuffing those nearest to me with all the force I could. The wretches dropped under my blows like nine-pins, and the laughter gave place to wails for mercy; while those yet untouched clasped me round the knees, imploring me in all sorts of uncouth tongues to spare them.

In the tumult, and just when I was feeling very much ashamed of myself for having thus easily given way to my temper, a thin, high voice murmured in English from behind my shoulder:—"*Sahib! Sahib!* Do you not know me? *Sahib*, it is Gunga Dass, the telegraph-master."

I spun round quickly and faced the speaker.

Gunga Dass (I have, of course, no hesitation in mentioning the man's real name) I had known four years before as a Deccanee Brahmin lent by the Punjab Government to one of the Khalsia States. He was in charge of a branch telegraph-office there, and when I had last met him was a jovial, full-stomached, portly government servant with a marvellous capacity for making bad puns in English—a peculiarity which made me remember him long after I had forgotten his services to me in his official capacity. It is seldom that a Hindu makes English puns.

Now, however, the man was changed beyond all recognition. Caste-mark, stomach, slate-coloured continuations, and unctuous speech were all gone. I looked at a withered skeleton, turbanless and almost naked, with long matted hair and deep-set codfish-eyes. But for a crescent-shaped scar on the left cheek—the result of an accident for which I was responsible—I should never have known him. But it was indubitably Gunga Dass, and—for this I was thankful—an English-speaking native who might at least tell me the meaning of all that I had gone through that day.

The crowd retreated to some distance as I turned towards the miserable figure, and ordered him to show me some method of escaping from the crater. He held a freshly plucked crow in his hand, and in reply to my question climbed slowly on a platform of sand which ran in front of the holes, and commenced lighting a fire there in silence. Dried bents, sand-poppies, and driftwood burn quickly; and I derived much consolation from the fact that he lit them with an ordinary sulphur-match. When they were in a bright glow, and the crow was neatly spitted in front thereof, Gunga Dass began without a word of preamble:—

"There are only two kinds of men, Sar. The alive and the dead. When you are dead you are dead, but when you are alive you live." (Here the crow demanded his attention for an instant as it twirled before the fire in danger of being burnt to a cinder.) "If you die at home and do not die when you come to the *ghât* to be burnt you come here."

The nature of the reeking village was made plain now, and all that I had known or read of the grotesque and the horrible paled before the fact just communicated by the ex-Brahmin. Sixteen years ago, when I first landed in Bombay, I had been told by a wandering Armenian of the existence, somewhere in India, of a place to which such Hindus as had the misfortune to recover from trance or catalepsy were conveyed and kept, and I recollect laughing heartily at what I was then pleased to consider a traveller's tale. Sitting at the bottom of the sand-trap, the memory of Watson's Hotel, with its swinging *punkahs*, white-robed attendants, and the sallowed faced Armenian, rose up in my mind as vividly as a photograph, and I burst into a loud fit of laughter. The contrast was too absurd!

Gunga Dass, as he bent over the unclean bird, watched me curiously. Hindus seldom laugh, and his surroundings were not such as to move Gunga Dass to any undue excess of hilarity. He removed the crow solemnly from the wooden spit and as solemnly devoured it. Then he continued his story, which I give in his own words:—

"In epidemics of the cholera you are carried to be burnt almost before you are dead. When you come to the riverside the cold air, perhaps, makes you alive, and then, if you are only little alive, mud is put on your nose and mouth and you die conclusively. If you are rather more alive, more mud is put; but if you are too lively they let you go and take you away. I was too lively, and made protestation with anger against the indignities that they endeavoured to press upon me. In those days I was Brahmin and proud man. Now I am dead man and eat"—here he eyed the well-gnawed breastbone with the first sign of emotion that I had seen in him since we met—"crows, and other things. They took me from my sheets when they saw that I was too lively and gave me medicines for one week, and I survived successfully. Then they sent me by rail from my place to Okara Station with a man to take care of me; and at Okara Station we met two other men, and they conducted we three on camels, in the night, from Okara Station to this place, and they propelled me from the top to the bottom, and the other two succeeded, and I have been here ever since, two and a half years. Once I was Brahmin and proud man, and now I eat crows."

"There is no way of getting out?"

"None of what kind at all. When I first came I made experiments frequently and all the others also, but we have always succumbed to the sand which is precipitated upon our heads."

"But surely," I broke in at this point, "the river-front is open, and it is worth while dodging the bullets; while at night—"

I had already matured a rough plan of escape which a natural instinct of selfishness forbade me sharing with Gunga Dass. He, however, divined my unspoken thought almost as soon as it was formed; and, to my intense astonishment, gave vent to a long low chuckle of derision—the laughter, be it understood, of a superior or at least of an equal. "You will not"—he had dropped the Sir completely after his opening sentence "make any escape that way. But you can try. I have tried. Once only."

The sensation of nameless terror and abject fear which I had in vain attempted to strive against overmastered me completely. My long fast—it was now close upon ten o'clock, and I had eaten nothing since *tiffin* on the previous day—combined with the violent and unnatural agitation of the ride had exhausted me, and I verily believe that, for a few minutes, I acted as one mad. I hurled myself against the pitiless sand-slope. I ran round the base of the crater, blaspheming and praying by turns. I crawled out among the sedges of the river-front, only to be driven back each time in an agony of nervous dread by the rifle-bullets which cut up the sand round me—for I dared not face the death of a mad dog among that hideous crowd—and finally fell, spent and raving, at the curb of the well. No one had taken the slightest notice of an exhibition which makes me blush hotly even when I think of it now.

Two or three men trod on my panting body as they drew water, but they were evidently used to this sort of thing, and had no time to waste upon me. The situation was humiliating. Gunga Dass, indeed, when he had banked the embers of his fire with sand, was at some pains to throw half a cupful o fetid water over my head, an attention for which I could have fallen on my knees and thanked him, but he was laughing all the while in the same mirthless, wheezy key that greeted me on my first attempt to force the shoals. And so, in a semi-comatose condition, I lay till noon. Then, being only a man after all, I felt hungry, and intimated as much to Gunga Dass, whom I had begun to regard as my natural protector. Following the impulse of the outer world when dealing with natives, I put my hand into my pocket and drew out four *annas*. The absurdity of the gift struck me at once, and I was about to replace the money.

Gunga Dass, however, was of a different opinion. "Give me the money," said he; "all you have, or I will get help, and we will kill you!" All this as if it were the most natural thing in the world!

A Briton's first impulse, I believe, is to guard the contents of his pockets; but a moment's reflection convinced me of the futility of differing with the one man who had it in his power to make me comfortable; and with whose help it was possible that I might eventually escape from the crater. I gave him all the money in my possession, *Rs.* 9-8-5 nine *rupees* eight *annas* and five *pie*—for I always keep small change as *bakshish* when I am in camp. Gunga Dass clutched the coins, and hid them at once in his ragged loin-cloth, his expression changing to something diabolical as he looked round to assure himself that no one had observed us.

"*Now* I will give you something to eat," said he.

What pleasure the possession of my money could have afforded him I am unable to say; but inasmuch as it did give him evident delight I was not sorry that I had parted with it so readily, for I had no doubt that he would have had me killed if I had refused. One does not protest against the vagaries of a den of wild beasts; and my companions were lower than any beasts. While I devoured what Gunga Dass had provided, a coarse *chapatti* and a cupful of the foul well-water, the people showed not the faintest sign of curiosity that curiosity—which is so rampant, as a rule, in an Indian village.

I could even fancy that they despised me. At all events they treated me with the most chilling indifference, and Gunga Dass was nearly as bad. I plied him with questions about the terrible village, and received extremely unsatisfactory answers. So far as I could gather, it had been in existence from time immemorial—whence I concluded that it was at least a century old—and during that time no one had ever been known to escape from it. (I had to control myself here with both hands, lest the blind terror should lay hold of me a second time and drive me raving round the crater.) Gunga Dass took a malicious pleasure in emphasizing this point and in watching me wince. Nothing that I could do would induce him to tell me who the mysterious "They" were.

"It is so ordered," he would reply, "and I do not yet know anyone who has disobeyed the orders."

"Only wait till my servants find that I am missing," I retorted, "and I promise you that this place shall be cleared off the face of the earth, and I'll give you a lesson in civility, too, my friend."

"Your servants would be torn in pieces before they came near this place; and, besides, you are dead, my dear friend. It is not your fault, of course, but none the less you are dead *and* buried."

At irregular intervals supplies of food, I was told, were dropped down from the land side into the amphitheatre, and the inhabitants fought for them like wild beasts. When a man felt his death coming on he retreated to his lair and died there. The body was sometimes dragged out of the hole and thrown on to the sand, or allowed to rot where it lay.

The phrase "thrown on to the sand" caught my attention, and I asked Gunga Dass whether this sort of thing was not likely to breed a pestilence.

"That," said he, with another of his wheezy chuckles, "you may see for yourself subsequently. You will have much time to make observations."

Whereat, to his great delight, I winced once more and hastily continued the conversation:—"And how do you live here from day to day? What do you do? "The question elicited exactly the same answer as before—coupled with the information that "this place is like your European heaven; there is neither marrying nor giving in marriage."

Gunga Dass had been educated at a Mission School, and, as he himself admitted, had he only changed his religion "like a wise man," might have avoided the living grave which was now his portion. But as long as I was with him I fancy he was happy.

Here was a *sahib*, a representative of the dominant race, helpless as a child and completely at the mercy of his native neighbours. In a deliberate lazy way he set himself to torture me as a schoolboy would devote a rapturous half-hour to watching the agonies of an impaled beetle, or as a ferret in a blind burrow might glue himself comfortably to the neck of a rabbit. The burden of his conversation was that there was no escape "of no kind whatever," and that I should stay here till I died and was "thrown on to the sand." If it were possible to forejudge the conversation of the Damned on the advent of a new soul in their abode, I should say that they would speak as Gunga Dass did to me throughout that long afternoon. I was powerless to protest or answer; all my energies being devoted to a struggle against the inexplicable terror that threatened to overwhelm me again and again. I can compare the feeling to nothing except the struggles of a man against the overpowering nausea of the Channel passage—only my agony was of the spirit and infinitely more terrible.

As the day wore on, the inhabitants began to appear in full strength to catch the rays of the afternoon sun, which were now sloping in at the mouth of the crater. They assembled in little knots, and talked among themselves without even throwing a glance in my direction. About four o'clock, as far as I could judge, Gunga Dass rose and dived into his lair for a moment, emerging with a live crow in his hands. The wretched bird was in a most draggled and deplorable condition, but seemed to be in no way afraid of its master. Advancing cautiously to the river-front, Gunga Dass stepped from tussock to tussock until he had reached a smooth patch of sand directly in the line of the boat's fire. The occupants of the boat took no notice.

Here he stopped, and with a couple of dexterous turns of the wrist, pegged the bird on its back with outstretched wings. As was only natural, the crow began to shriek at once and beat the air with its claws. In a few seconds the clamour had attracted the attention of a bevy of wild crows on a shoal a few hundred yards away, where they were discussing something that looked like a corpse. Half a dozen crows flew over at once to see what was going on, and also, as it proved, to attack the pinioned bird. Gunga Dass, who had lain down on a tussock, motioned to me to be quiet, though I fancy this was a needless precaution.

In a moment, and before I could see how it happened, a wild crow, who had grappled with the shrieking and helpless bird, was entangled in the latter's claws, swiftly disengaged by Gunga Dass, and pegged down beside its companion in adversity. Curiosity, it seemed, overpowered the rest of the flock, and almost before Gunga Dass and I had time to withdraw to the tussock, two more captives were struggling in the upturned claws of the decoys. So the chase—if I can give it so dignified a name—continued until Gunga Dass had captured seven crows. Five of them he throttled at once, reserving two for further operations another day. I was a good deal impressed by this, to me, novel method of securing food, and complimented Gunga Dass on his skill.

"It is nothing to do," said he. "Tomorrow you must do it for

173

me. You are stronger than I am."

This calm assumption of superiority upset me not a little, and I answered peremptorily:—"Indeed, you old ruffian! What do you think I have given you money for?"

"Very well," was the unmoved reply. "Perhaps not tomorrow, nor the day after, nor subsequently; but in the end, and for many years, you will catch crows and eat crows, and you will thank your European Gods that you have crows to catch and eat."

I could have cheerfully strangled him for this; but judged it best under the circumstances to smother my resentment. An hour later I was eating one of the crows; and, as Gunga Dass had said, thanking my God that I had a crow to eat. Never as long as I live shall I forget that evening meal. The whole population were squatting on the hard sand platform opposite their dens, huddled over tiny fires of refuse and dried rushes. Death, having once laid his hand upon these men and forborne to strike, seemed to stand aloof from them now; for most of our company were old men, bent and worn and twisted with years, and women aged to all appearance as the Fates themselves.

They sat together in knots and talked—God only knows what they found to discuss—in low equable tones, curiously in contrast to the strident babble with which natives are accustomed to make day hideous. Now and then an access of that sudden fury which had possessed me in the morning would lay hold on a man or woman; and with yells and imprecations the sufferer would attack the steep slope until, baffled and bleeding, he fell back on the plat- form incapable of moving a limb. The others would never even raise their eyes when this happened, as men too well aware of the futility of their fellows' attempts and wearied with their useless repetition. I saw four such outbursts in the course of that evening.

Gunga Dass took an eminently business-like view of my situation, and while we were dining—I can afford to laugh at the recollection now, but it was painful enough at the time—propounded the terms on which he would consent to "do" for me. My nine *rupees* eight *annas*, he argued, at the rate of three *annas*

174

a day, would provide me with food for fifty-one days, or about seven weeks; that is to say, he would be willing to cater for me for that length of time. At the end of it I was to look after myself. For a further consideration—*videlicet* my boots—he would be willing to allow me to occupy the den next to his own, and would supply me with as much dried grass for bedding as he could spare.

"Very well, Gunga Dass," I replied; "to the first terms I cheerfully agree, but, as there is nothing on earth to prevent my killing you as you sit here and taking everything that you have" (I thought of the two invaluable crows at the time), "I flatly refuse to give you my boots and shall take whichever den I please."

The stroke was a bold one, and I was glad when I saw that it had succeeded. Gunga Dass changed his tone immediately, and disavowed all intention of asking for my boots. At the time it did not strike me as at all strange that I, a civil engineer, a man of thirteen years' standing in the service, and I trust, an average Englishman, should thus calmly threaten murder and violence against the man who had, for a consideration, it is true, taken me under his wing. I had left the world, it seemed, for centuries.

I was as certain then as I am now of my own existence, that in the accursed settlement there was no law save that of the strongest; that the living dead men had thrown behind them every canon of the world which had cast them out; and that I had to depend for my own life on my strength and vigilance alone. The crew of the ill-fated Mignonette are the only men who would understand my frame of mind. "At present," I argued to myself, "I am strong and a match for six of these wretches. It is imperatively necessary that I should, for my own sake, keep both health and strength until the hour of my release comes—if it ever does."

Fortified with these resolutions, I ate and drank as much as I could, and made Gunga Dass understand that I intended to be his master, and that the least sign of insubordination on his part would be visited with the only punishment I had it in my power to inflict—sudden and violent death. Shortly after this I went to bed. That is to say, Gunga Dass gave me a double armful of dried bents which I thrust down the mouth of the lair to the right of his, and followed myself, feet foremost; the hole running about nine feet into the sand with a slight downward inclination, and being neatly shored with timbers. From my den, which faced the river-front, I was able to watch the waters of the Sutlej flowing past under the light of a young moon and composed myself to sleep as best I might.

The horrors of that night I shall never forget. My den was nearly as narrow as a coffin, and the sides had been worn smooth and greasy by the contact of innumerable naked bodies, added to which it smelled abominably. Sleep was altogether out of question to one in my excited frame of mind. As the night wore on, it seemed that the entire amphitheatre was filled with legions of unclean devils that, trooping up from the shoals below, mocked the unfortunates in their lairs.

Personally I am not of an imaginative temperament,—very few engineers are,—but on that occasion I was as completely prostrated with nervous terror as any woman. After half an hour or so, however, I was able once more to calmly review my chances of escape. Any exit by the steep sand walls was, of course, impracticable. I had been thoroughly convinced of this some time before. It was possible, just possible, that I might, in the uncertain moonlight, safely run the gauntlet of the rifle shots. The place was so full of terror for me that I was prepared to undergo any risk in leaving it. Imagine my delight, then, when after creeping stealthily to the river-front I found that the infernal boat was not there. My freedom lay before me in the next few steps!

By walking out to the first shallow pool that lay at the foot of the projecting left horn of the horseshoe, I could wade across, turn the flank of the crater, and make my way inland. Without a moment's hesitation I marched briskly past the tussocks where Gunga Dass had snared the crows, and out in the direction of the smooth white sand beyond. My first step from the tufts of dried grass showed me how utterly futile was any hope of escape; for, as I put my foot down, I felt an indescribable drawing, sucking motion of the sand below. Another moment and my leg was swallowed up nearly to the knee. In the moonlight the whole surface of the sand seemed to be shaken with devilish delight at my disappointment. I struggled clear, sweating with terror and exertion, back to the tussocks behind me and fell on my face.

My only means of escape from the semi-circle was protected with a quicksand!

How long I lay I have not the faintest idea; but I was roused at last by the malevolent chuckle of Gunga Dass at my ear. "I would advise you, Protector of the Poor" (the ruffian was speaking English) "to return to your house. It is unhealthy to lie down here. Moreover, when the boat returns, you will most certainly be rifled at." He stood over me in the dim light of the dawn, chuckling and laughing to himself. Suppressing my first impulse to catch the man by the neck and throw him on to the quicksand, I rose sullenly and followed him to the platform below the burrows.

Suddenly, and futilely as I thought while I spoke, I asked:— "Gunga Dass, what is the good of the boat if I can't get out *anyhow?*" I recollect that even in my deepest trouble I had been speculating vaguely on the waste of ammunition in guarding an already well protected foreshore.

Gunga Dass laughed again and made answer:—"They have the boat only in day time. It is for the reason that *there is a way*. I hope we shall have the pleasure of your company for much longer time. It is a pleasant spot when you have been here some years and eaten roast crow long enough."

I staggered, numbed and helpless, towards the fetid burrow allotted to me, and fell asleep. An hour or so later I was awakened by a piercing scream—the shrill, high-pitched scream of a horse in pain. Those who have once heard that will never forget the sound. I found some little difficulty in scrambling out of the burrow. When I was in the open, I saw Pornic, my poor old Pornic, lying dead on the sandy soil. How they had killed him I cannot guess. Gunga Dass explained that horse was better than crow, and "greatest good of greatest number." is political maxim.

We are now Republic, Mister Jukes, and you are entitled to a fair share of the beast. If you like, we will pass a vote of thanks. Shall I propose?"

Yes, we were a Republic indeed! A Republic of wild beasts penned at the bottom of a pit, to eat and fight and sleep till we died. I attempted no protest of any kind, but sat down and stared at the hideous sight in front of me. In less time almost than it takes me to write this, Pornic's body was divided, in some unclean way or other; the men and women had dragged the fragments on to the platform and were preparing their morning meal. Gunga Dass cooked mine. The almost irresistible impulse to fly at the sand walls until I was wearied laid hold of me afresh, and I had to struggle against it with all my might. Gunga Dass was offensively jocular till I told him that if he addressed another remark of any kind whatever to me I should strangle him where he sat. This silenced him till silence became insupportable, and I bade him say something.

"You will live here till you die like the other *Feringhi*," he said coolly, watching me over the fragment of gristle that he was gnawing.

"What other *sahib*, you swine? Speak at once, and don't stop to tell me a lie."

"He is over there," answered Gunga Dass, pointing to a burrow-mouth about four doors to the left of my own. "You can see for yourself. He died in the burrow as you will die, and I will die, and as all these men and women and the one child will also die."

"For pity's sake tell me all you know about him. Who was he? When did he come, and when did he die? "

This appeal was a weak step on my part. Gunga Dass only leered and replied:—"I will not—unless you give me something first."

Then I recollected where I was, and struck the man between the eyes, partially stunning him. He stepped down from the platform at once, and, cringing and fawning and weeping and attempting to embrace my feet, led me round to the burrow which he had indicated.

"I know nothing whatever about the gentleman. Your God be my witness that I do not. He was as anxious to escape as you were, and he was shot from the boat, though we all did all things to prevent him from attempting. He was shot here." Gunga Dass laid his hand on his lean stomach and bowed to the earth.

"Well, and what then? Go on!"

"And then—and then, Your Honour, we carried him in to his house and gave him water, and put wet cloths on the wound, and he laid down in his house and gave up the ghost."

"In how long? In how long? "

"About half an hour, after he received his wound. I call Vishn to witness," yelled the wretched man, "that I did everything for him. Everything which was possible, that I did! "

He threw himself down on the ground and clasped my ankles. But I had my doubts about Gunga Bass's benevolence, and kicked him off as he lay protesting.

"I believe you robbed him of everything he had. But I can find out in a minute or two. How long was the *sahib* here?"

"Nearly a year and a half. I think he must have gone mad. But hear me swear, Protector of the Poor! Won't Your Honour hear me swear that I never touched an article that belonged to him? What is Your Worship going to do?"

I had taken Gunga Dass by the waist and had hauled him on to the platform opposite the deserted burrow. As I did so I thought of my wretched fellow-prisoner's unspeakable misery among all these horrors for eighteen months, and the final agony of dying like a rat in a hole, with a bullet-wound in the stomach. Gunga Dass fancied I was going to kill him and howled pitifully. The rest of the population, in the plethora that follows a full flesh meal, watched us without stirring.

"Go inside, Gunga Dass," said I, "and fetch it out."

I was feeling sick and faint with horror now. Gunga Dass nearly rolled off the platform and howled aloud.

"But I am Brahmin, *sahib*—a high-caste Brahmin. By your soul, by your father's soul, do not make me do this thing! "

"Brahmin or no Brahmin, by my soul and my father's soul, in you go!" I said, and, seizing him by the shoulders, I crammed his head into the mouth of the burrow, kicked the rest of him in, and, sitting down, covered my face with my hands.

At the end of a few minutes I heard a rustle and a creak; then Gunga Dass in a sobbing, choking whisper speaking to himself; then a soft thud—and I uncovered my eyes.

The dry sand had turned the corpse entrusted to its keeping into a yellow-brown mummy. I told Gunga Dass to stand off while I examined it. The body—clad in an olive-green hunting-suit much stained and worn, with leather pads on the shoulders—was that of a man between thirty and forty, above middle height, with light, sandy hair long moustache, and a rough unkempt beard. The left canine of the upper jaw was missing, and a portion of the lobe of the right ear was gone. On the second finger of the left hand was a ring—a shield-shaped bloodstone set in gold, with a monogram that might have been either "B. K." or "B. L." On the third finger of the right hand was a silver ring in the shape of a coiled cobra, much worn and tarnished. Gunga Dass deposited a handful of trifles he had picked out of the burrow at my feet, and, covering the face of the body with my handkerchief, I turned to examine these. I give the full list in the hope that it may lead to the identification of the unfortunate man:—

1. Bowl of a briarwood pipe, serrated at the edge; much worn and blackened; bound with string at the screw.

2. Two patent-lever keys; wards of both broken.

3. Tortoise-shell handled penknife, silver or nickel, name-plate, marked with monogram "B.K."

4. Envelope, post-mark undecipherable, bearing a Victorian stamp, addressed to "Miss Mon—" (rest illegible)— "ham"—"nt."

5. Imitation crocodile-skin note-book with pencil. First forty-five pages blank; four and a half illegible; fifteen others filled with private memoranda relating chiefly to three

persons—a Mrs. L. Singleton, abbreviated several times to "Lot Single," "Mrs. S. May," and "Garmison," referred to in places as "Jerry" or "Jack."

6. Handle of small-sized hunting-knife. Blade snapped short. Buck's horn, diamond cut, with swivel and ring on the butt; fragment of cotton cord attached.

It must not be supposed that I inventoried all these things on the spot as fully as I have here written them down. The note-book first attracted my attention, and I put it in my pocket with a view to studying it later on. The rest of the articles I conveyed to my burrow for safety's sake, and there, being a methodical man, I inventoried them. I then returned to the corpse and ordered Gunga Dass to help me to carry it out to the river-front. While we were engaged in this, the exploded shell of an old brown cartridge dropped out of one of the pockets and rolled at my feet.

Gunga Dass had not seen it; and I fell to thinking that a man does not carry exploded cartridge-cases, especially "browns," which will not bear loading twice, about with him when shooting. In other words, that cartridge-case had been fired inside the crater, Consequently there must be a gun somewhere. I was on the verge of asking Gunga Dass, but checked myself, knowing that he would lie. We laid the body down on the edge of the quicksand by the tussocks. It was my intention to push it out and let it be swallowed up—the only possible mode of burial that I could think of. I ordered Gunga Dass to go away.

Then I gingerly put the corpse out on the quicksand. In doing so, it was lying face downward, I tore the frail and rotten khaki shooting-coat open, disclosing a hideous cavity in the back. I have already told you that the dry sand had, as it were, mummified the body. A moment's glance showed that the gaping hole had been caused by a gun-shot wound; the gun must have been fired with the muzzle almost touching the back. The shooting-coat, being intact, had been drawn over the body after death, which must have been instantaneous. The secret of the poor wretch's death was plain to me in a flash. Some one of the crater, presumably Gunga Dass, must have shot him with his own gun—the gun that fitted the brown cartridges. He had never attempted to escape in the face of the rifle-fire from the boat.

I pushed the corpse out hastily, and saw it sink from sight literally in a few seconds. I shuddered as I watched. In a dazed, half-conscious way I turned to peruse the note-book. A stained and discoloured slip of paper had been inserted between the binding and the back, and dropped out as I opened the pages. This is what it contained:—

Four out from crow-dump: three left; nine out; two right; three back; two left; fourteen out; two left; seven out; one left; nine back; two right; six back; four right; seven back.

The paper had been burnt and charred at the edges. What it meant I could not understand. I sat down on the dried bents turning it over and over between my fingers, until I was aware of Gunga Dass standing immediately behind me with glowing eyes and outstretched hands.

"Have you got it?" he panted. "Will you not let me look at it also? I swear that I will return it."

"Got what? Return what?" I asked.

"That which you have in your hands. It will help us both." He stretched out his long, bird-like talons, trembling with eagerness.

"I could never find it," he continued. "He had secreted it about his person. Therefore I shot him, but nevertheless I was unable to obtain it."

Gunga Dass had quite forgotten his little fiction about the rifle-bullet. I received the information perfectly calmly. Morality is blunted by consorting with the dead who are alive.

"What on earth are you raving about? What is it you want me to give you?"

"The piece of paper in the note-book. It will help us both. Oh, you fool! You fool! Can you not see what it will do for us?

We shall escape! "

His voice rose almost to a scream, and he danced with excitement before me. I own I was moved at the chance of getting away.

"Don't skip! Explain yourself. Do you mean to say that this slip of paper will help us? What does it mean?"

"Read it aloud! Read it aloud! I beg and I pray to you to read it aloud."

I did so. Gunga Dass listened delightedly, and drew an irregular line in the sand with his fingers.

"See now! It was the length of his gun-barrels without the stock. I have those barrels. Four gun-barrels out from the place where I caught crows. Straight out; do you follow me? Then three left—Ah! how well I remember when that man worked it out night after night. Then nine out, and so on. Out is always straight before you across the quicksand. He told me so before I killed him."

"But if you knew all this why didn't you get out before?"

"I did *not* know it. He told me that he was working it out a year and a half ago, and how he was working it out night after night when the boat had gone away, and he could get out near the quicksand safely. Then he said that we would get away together. But I was afraid that he would leave me behind one night when he had worked it all out, and so I shot him. Besides, it is not advisable that the men who once get in here should escape. Only I, and *I* am a Brahmin."

The prospect of escape had brought Gunga Dass's caste back to him. He stood up, walked about and gesticulated violently. Eventually I managed to make him talk soberly, and he told me how this Englishman had spent six months night after night in exploring, inch by inch, the passage across the quicksand; how he had declared it to be simplicity itself up to within about twenty yards of the river bank after turning the flank of the left horn of the horseshoe. This much he had evidently not completed when Gunga Dass shot him with his own gun.

In my frenzy of delight at the possibilities of escape I recollect shaking hands effusively with Gunga Dass, after we had decided that we were to make an attempt to get away that very night. It was weary work waiting throughout the afternoon.

About ten o'clock, as far as I could judge, when the moon had just risen above the lip of the crater, Gunga Dass made a move for his burrow to bring out the gun-barrels whereby to measure our path. All the other wretched inhabitants had retired to their lairs long ago. The guardian boat drifted downstream some hours before, and we were utterly alone by the crow-clump. Gunga Dass, while carrying the gun-barrels, let slip the piece of paper which was to be our guide. I stooped down hastily to recover it, and, as I did so, I was aware that the diabolical Brahmin was aiming a violent blow at the back of my head with the gun-barrels. It was too late to turn round. I must have received the blow somewhere on the nape of my neck. A hundred thousand fiery stars danced before my eyes, and I fell forward senseless at the edge of the quicksand.

When I recovered consciousness, the moon was going down, and I was sensible of intolerable pain in the back of my head. Gunga Dass had disappeared and my mouth was full of blood. I lay down again and prayed that I might die without more ado. Then the unreasoning fury which I have before mentioned laid hold upon me, and I staggered inland towards the walls of the crater. It seemed that someone was calling to me in a whisper—"*Sahib! Sahib! Sahib!*" exactly as my bearer used to call me in the mornings. I fancied that I was delirious until a handful of sand fell at my feet. Then I looked up and saw a head peering down into the amphitheatre—the head of Dunnoo, my dog-boy, who attended to my collies.

As soon as he had attracted my attention, he held up his hand and showed a rope. I motioned, staggering to and fro the while, that he should throw it down. It was a couple of leather *punkah*-ropes knotted together, with a loop at one end. I slipped the loop over my head and under my arms; heard Dunnoo urge something forward; was conscious that I was being dragged, face downward, up the steep sand slope, and the next instant found myself choked and half fainting on the sand hills overlooking the crater. Dunnoo, with his face ashy gray in the moonlight, implored me not to stay but to get back to my tent at once.

It seems that he had tracked Pornic's footprints fourteen miles across the sands to the crater; had returned and told my servants, who flatly refused to meddle with anyone, white or black, once fallen into the hideous Village of the Dead; whereupon Dunnoo had taken one of my ponies and a couple of *punkah* ropes, returned to the crater, and hauled me out as I have described.

To cut a long story short, Dunnoo is now my personal servant on a gold *mohur* a month—a sum which I still think far too little for the services he has rendered. Nothing on earth will induce me to go near that devilish spot again, or to reveal its whereabouts more clearly than I have done. Of Gunga Dass I have never found a trace, nor do I wish to do. My sole motive in giving this to be published is the hope that someone may possibly identify, from the details and the inventory which I have given above, the corpse of the man in the olive-green hunting-suit.

The Gardener

One grave to me was given.
One watch till Judgement Day;
And God looked down from Heaven
And rolled the stone away.
One day in all the years.
One hour in that one day.
His Angel saw my tears.
And rolled the stone away!

Everyone in the village knew that Helen Turrell did her duty by all her world, and by none more honourably than by her only brother's unfortunate child. The village knew, too, that George Turrell had tried his family severely since early youth, and were not surprised to be told that, after many fresh starts given and thrown away, he, an Inspector of Indian Police, had entangled himself with the daughter of a retired non-commissioned officer, and had died of a fall from a horse a few weeks before his child was born. Mercifully, George's father and mother were both dead, and though Helen, thirty-five and independent, might well have washed her hands of the whole disgraceful affair, she most nobly took charge, though she was, at the time, under threat of lung trouble which had driven her to the South of France.

She arranged for the passage of the child and a nurse from Bombay, met them at Marseilles, nursed the baby through an attack of infantile dysentery due to the carelessness of the nurse, whom she had had to dismiss, and at last, thin and worn but triumphant, brought the boy late in the autumn, wholly restored, to her Hampshire home.

All these details were public property, for Helen was as open as the day, and held that scandals are only increased by hushing them up. She admitted that George had always been rather a black sheep, but things might have been much worse if the mother had insisted on her right to keep the boy. Luckily, it seemed that people of that class would do almost anything for money, and, as George had always turned to her in his scrapes, she felt herself justified—her friends agreed with her—in cutting the whole non-commissioned officer connection, and giving the child every advantage. A christening, by the Rector, under the name of Michael, was the first step. So far as she knew herself, she was not, she said, a child-lover, but, for all his faults, she had been very fond of George, and she pointed out that little Michael had his father's mouth to a line; which made something to build upon.

As a matter of fact, it was the Turrell forehead, broad, low, and well-shaped, with the widely spaced eyes beneath it, that Michael had most faithfully reproduced. His mouth was somewhat better cut than the family type. But Helen, who would concede nothing good to his mother's side, vowed he was a Turrell all over, and, there being no one to contradict, the likeness was established.

In a few years Michael took his place, as accepted as Helen had always been—fearless, philosophical, and fairly good-looking. At six, he wished to know why he could not call her 'Mummy', as other boys called their mothers. She explained that she was only his auntie, and that aunties were not quite the same as mummies, but that, if it gave him pleasure, he might call her 'Mummy' at bedtime, for a pet-name between themselves.

Michael kept his secret most loyally, but Helen, as usual, explained the fact to her friends; which when Michael heard, he raged.

'Why did you tell? Why did you tell?' came at the end of the storm.

'Because it's always best to tell the truth,' Helen answered, her arm round him as he shook in his cot.

'All right, but when the troof's ugly I don't think it's nice.'

'Don't you, dear!'

'No, I don't, and'—she felt the small body stiffen—'now you've told, I won't call you "Mummy" any more—not even at bedtimes.

'But isn't that rather unkind?' said Helen softly.

'I don't care! You've hurted me in my insides and I'll hurt you back. I'll hurt you as long as I live!'

'Don't, oh, don't talk like that, dear! You don't know what—'

'I will! And when I'm dead I'll hurt you worse!'

'Thank goodness, I shall be dead long before you, darling.'

'Huh! Emma says, "'Never know your luck.'" (Michael had been talking to Helen's elderly flat-faced maid.) 'Lots of little boys die quite soon. So'll I. Then you'll see!'

Helen caught her breath and moved towards the door, but the wail of 'Mummy! Mummy!' drew her back again, and the two wept together.

At ten years old, after two terms at a prep. school, something or somebody gave him the idea that his civil status was not quite regular. He attacked Helen on the subject, breaking down her stammered defences with the family directness.

'Don't believe a word of it,' he said, cheerily, at the end. 'People wouldn't have talked like they did if my people had been married. But don't you bother, Auntie. I've found out all about my sort in English Hist'ry and the Shakespeare bits. There was William the Conqueror to begin with, and—oh, heaps more, and they all got on first-rate. 'Twon't make any difference to you, my being that—will it?'

'As if anything could—' she began.

'All right. We won't talk about it anymore if it makes you cry.' He never mentioned the thing again of his own will, but when, two years later, he skilfully managed to have measles in the holidays, as his temperature went up to the appointed one hundred and four he muttered of nothing else, till Helen's voice, piercing at last his delirium, reached him with assurance that nothing on earth or beyond could make any difference between them.

The terms at his public school and the wonderful Christmas, Easter, and Summer holidays followed each other, variegated and glorious as jewels on a string; and as jewels Helen treasured them. In due time Michael developed his own interests, which ran their courses and gave way to others; but his interest in Helen was constant and increasing throughout. She repaid it with all that she had of affection or could command of counsel and money; and since Michael was no fool, the War took him just before what was like to have been a most promising career.

He was to have gone up to Oxford, with a scholarship, in October. At the end of August he was on the edge of joining the first holocaust of public-school boys who threw themselves into the Line; but the captain of his OTC, where he had been sergeant for nearly a year, headed him off and steered him directly to a commission in a battalion so new that half of it still wore the old army red, and the other half was breeding meningitis through living overcrowdedly in damp tents. Helen had been shocked at the idea of direct enlistment. 'But it's in the family,' Michael laughed.

'You don't mean to tell me that you believed that old story all this time?' said Helen. (Emma, her maid, had been dead now several years.) 'I gave you my word of honour—and I give it again—that—that it's all right. It is indeed.'

'Oh, that doesn't worry me. It never did,' he replied valiantly. 'What I meant was, I should have got into the show earlier if I'd enlisted—like my grandfather.

'Don't talk like that! Are you afraid of its ending so soon, then!'

'No such luck. You know what K says.'

'Yes. But my banker told me last Monday it couldn't possibly last beyond Christmas—for financial reasons.'

'Hope he's right, but our colonel—and he's a Regular—says it's going to be a long job.'

Michael's battalion was fortunate in that, by some chance which meant several 'leaves', it was used for coast-defence among shallow trenches on the Norfolk coast; thence sent north to watch the mouth of a Scotch estuary, and, lastly, held for weeks on a baseless rumour of distant service. But, the very day that Michael was to have met Helen for four whole hours at a railway-junction up the line, it was hurled out, to help make good the wastage of Loos, and he had only just time to send her a wire of farewell.

In France luck again helped the battalion. It was put down near the Salient, where it led a meritorious and unexacting life, while the Somme was being manufactured; and enjoyed the peace of the Armentieres and Laventie sectors when that battle began. Finding that it had sound views on protecting its own flanks and could dig, a prudent commander stole it out of its own division, under pretence of helping to lay telegraphs, and used it round Ypres at large.

A month later, just after Michael had written Helen that there was nothing special doing and therefore no need to worry, a shell-splinter dropping out of a wet dawn killed him at once. The next shell uprooted and laid down over the body what had been the foundation of a barn wall, so neatly that none but an expert would have guessed that anything unpleasant had happened.

By this time the village was old in experience of war, and, English fashion, had evolved a ritual to meet it. When the post-mistress handed her seven-year-old daughter the official telegram to take to Miss Turrell, she observed to the rector's gardener: 'It's Miss Helen's turn now.' He replied, thinking of his own son: 'Well, he's lasted longer than some.' The child herself came to the front-door weeping aloud, because Master Michael had often given her sweets. Helen, presently, found herself pulling down the house-blinds one after one with great care, and saying earnestly to each: 'Missing always means dead.' Then she took her place in the dreary procession that was impelled to go through an inevitable series of unprofitable emotions. The rector, of course, preached hope and prophesied word, very soon, from a prison camp. Several friends, too, told her perfectly truthful tales, but always about other women, to whom, after months and months of silence, their missing had been miraculously restored. Other people urged her to communicate with infallible secretaries of organizations who could communicate with benevolent neutrals, who could extract accurate information from the most secretive of Hun prison commandants. Helen did and wrote and signed everything that was suggested or put before her.

Once, on one of Michael's leaves, he had taken her over munition factory, where she saw the progress of a shell from blankiron to the all but finished article. It struck her at the time that the wretched thing was never left alone for a single second; and 'I'm being manufactured into a bereaved next of kin,' she told herself, as she prepared her documents.

In due course, when all the organizations had deeply or sincerely regretted their inability to trace, etc., something gave way within her and all sensation—save of thankfulness for the release—came to an end in blessed passivity. Michael had died and her world had stood still and she had been one with the full shock of that arrest. Now she was standing still and the world was going forward, but it did not concern her—in no way or relation did it touch her. She knew this by the ease with which she could slip Michael's name into talk and incline her head to the proper angle, at the proper murmur of sympathy.

In the blessed realization of that relief, the Armistice with all its bells broke over her and passed unheeded. At the end of another year she had overcome her physical loathing of the living and returned young, so that she could take them by the hand and almost sincerely wish them well. She had no interest in any aftermath, national or personal, of the war, but, moving at an immense distance, she sat on various relief committees and held strong views—she heard herself delivering them—about the site of the proposed village War Memorial.

Then there came to her, as next of kin, an official intimation, backed by a page of a letter to her in indelible pencil, a silver identity-disc, and a watch, to the effect that the body of Lieutenant Michael Turrell had been found, identified, and reinterred in Hagenzeele Third Military Cemetery—the letter of the row and the grave's number in that row duly given.

So Helen found herself moved on to another process of the manufacture—to a world full of exultant or broken relatives, now strong in the certainty that there was an altar upon earth where they might lay their love. These soon told her, and by means of time-tables made clear, how easy it was and how little it interfered with life's affairs to go and see one's grave.

'So different,' as the rector's wife said, 'if he'd been killed in Mesopotamia, or even Gallipoli.'

The agony of being waked up to some sort of second life drove Helen across the Channel, where, in a new world of abbreviated titles, she learnt that Hagenzeele Third could be comfortably reached by an afternoon train which fitted in with the morning boat, and that there was a comfortable little hotel not three kilometres from Hagenzeele itself, where one could spend quite a comfortable night and see one's grave next morning. All this she had from a central authority who lived in a board and tar-paper shed on the skirts of a razed city full of whirling lime-dust and blown papers.

'By the way,' said he, 'you know your grave, of course!'

'Yes, thank you,' said Helen, and showed its row and number typed on Michael's own little typewriter. The officer would have checked it, out of one of his many books; but a large Lancashire woman thrust between them and bade him tell her where she might find her son, who had been corporal in the A.S.C. His proper name, she sobbed, was Anderson, but, coming of respectable folk, he had of course enlisted under the name of Smith; and had been killed at Dickiebush, in early 'fifteen. She had not his number nor did she know which of his two Christian names he might have used with his *alias*; but her Cook's tourist ticket expired at the end of Easter week, and if by then she could not find her child she should go mad. Whereupon she fell forward on Helen's breast; but the officer's wife came out quickly from a little bedroom behind the office, and the three of them lifted the woman on to the cot.

'They are often like this,' said the officer's wife, loosening the tight bonnet-strings. 'Yesterday she said he'd been killed at Hooge. Are you sure you know your grave? It makes such a difference.'

'Yes, thank you,' said Helen, and hurried out before the woman on the bed should begin to lament again.

Tea in a crowded mauve and blue striped wooden structure, with a false front, carried her still further into the nightmare. She paid her bill beside a stolid, plain-featured Englishwoman, who, hearing her inquire about the train to Hagenzeele, volunteered to come with her.

'I'm going to Hagenzeele myself,' she explained . 'Not to Hagenzeele Third; mine is Sugar Factory, but they call it La Rosiere now. It's just south of Hagenzeele Three. Have you got your room at the hotel there!'

'Oh yes, thank you. I've wired.'

'That's better. Sometimes the place is quite full, and at others there's hardly a soul. But they've put bathrooms into the old Lion d'Or—that's the hotel on the west side of Sugar Factory—and it draws off a lot of people, luckily.'

'It's all new to me. This is the first time I've been over.'

'Indeed! This is my ninth time since the Armistice. Not on my own account. I haven't lost any one, thank God—but, like everyone else, I've a lot of friends at home who have. Coming over as often as I do, I find it helps them to have someone just look at the—the place and tell them about it afterwards. And one can take photos for them, too. I get quite a list of commissions to execute.' She laughed nervously and tapped her slung Kodak. 'There are two or three to see at Sugar Factory this time, and plenty of others in the cemeteries all about. My system is to save them up, and arrange them, you know. And when I've got enough commissions for one area to make it worthwhile, I pop over and execute them. It does comfort people.'

'I suppose so,' Helen answered, shivering as they entered the little train.

'Of course it does. (Isn't it lucky we've got window-seats!) It must do or they wouldn't ask one to do it, would they! I've a list of quite twelve or fifteen commissions here'—she tapped the Kodak again—'I must sort them out tonight. Oh, I forgot to ask you. What's yours!'

'My nephew,' said Helen. 'But I was very fond of him.'

'Ah, yes! I sometimes wonder whether they know after death! What do you think?'

'Oh, I don't—I haven't dared to think much about that sort of thing,' said Helen, almost lifting her hands to keep her off.

'Perhaps that's better,' the woman answered. 'The sense of loss must be enough, I expect. Well, I won't worry you anymore.'

Helen was grateful, but when they reached the hotel Mrs Scarsworth (they had exchanged names) insisted on dining at the same table with her, and after the meal, in the little, hideous salon full of low-voiced relatives, took Helen through her 'commissions' with biographies of the dead, where she happened to know them, and sketches of their next of kin. Helen endured till nearly half-past nine, ere she fled to her room.

Almost at once there was a knock at her door and Mrs Scarsworth entered; her hands, holding the dreadful list, clasped before her.

'Yes—yes—I know,' she began. 'You're sick of me, but I want to tell you something. You—you aren't married, are you? Then perhaps you won't . . . But it doesn't matter. I've got to tell someone. I can't go on any longer like this.'

'But please—' Mrs Scarsworth had backed against the shut door, and her mouth worked dryly.

In a minute,' she said. 'You—you know about these graves of mine I was telling you about downstairs, just now! They really are commissions. At least several of them are.' Her eye wandered round the room. 'What extraordinary wall-papers they have in Belgium, don't you think? . . . Yes. I swear they are commissions. But there's one, d'you see, and—and he was more to me than anything else in the world. Do you understand?'

Helen nodded.

'More than anyone else. And, of course, he oughtn't to have been. He ought to have been nothing to me. But he was. He is. That's why I do the commissions, you see. That's all.'

'But why do you tell me!' Helen asked desperately.

'Because I'm so tired of lying. Tired of lying—always lying—year in and year out. When I don't tell lies I've got to act 'em and I've got to think 'em, always. You don't know what that means. He was everything to me that he oughtn't to have been—the one real thing—the only thing that ever happened to me in all my life; and I've had to pretend he wasn't. I've had to watch every word I said, and think out what lie I'd tell next, for years and years!'

'How many years?' Helen asked.

'Six years and four months before, and two and three-quarters after. I've gone to him eight times, since. Tomorrow'll make the ninth, and—and I can't—I can't go to him again with nobody in the world knowing. I want to be honest with someone before I go. Do you understand! It doesn't matter about me. I was never truthful, even as a girl. But it isn't worthy of him. So I—I had to tell you. I can't keep it up any longer. Oh, I can't.'

She lifted her joined hands almost to the level of her mouth and brought them down sharply, still joined, to full arms' length below her waist. Helen reached forward, caught them, bowed her head over them, and murmured: 'Oh, my dear! My—' Mrs Scarsworth stepped back, her face all mottled.

'My God!' said she. 'Is that how you take it!'

Helen could not speak, and the woman went out; but it a long while before Helen was able to sleep.

Next morning Mrs Scarsworth left early on her round of commissions, and Helen walked alone to Hagenzeele Third. The place was still in the making, and stood some five or feet above the metalled road, which it flanked for hundred yards. Culverts across a deep ditch served for entrances through the unfinished boundary wall. She climbed a few wooden-faced earthen steps and then met the entire crowded level of the thing in one held breath. She did not know Hagenzeele Third counted twenty-one thousand dead already. All she saw was a merciless sea of black crosses, bearing little strips of stamped tin at all angles across their faces. She could distinguish no order or arrangement in their mass; nothing but a waist-high wilderness as of weeds stricken dead, rushing at her. She went forward, moved to the left and the right hopelessly, wondering by what guidance she should ever come to her own.

A great distance away there was a line of whiteness. It proved to be a block of some two or three hundred graves whose head-stones had already been set, whose flowers planted out, and whose new-sown grass showed green. Here she could see clear-cut letters at the ends of the rows, referring to her slip, realized that it was not here she must look.

A man knelt behind a line of headstones—evidently a gardener, for he was firming a young plant in the soft earth. She went towards him, her paper in her hand. He rose at her approach and without prelude or salutation asked: 'Who are you looking for?'

'Lieutenant Michael Turrell—my nephew,' said Helen slowly and word for word, as she had many thousands of times in her life.

The man lifted his eyes and looked at her with infinite compassion before he turned from the fresh-sown grass toward the naked black crosses.

'Come with me,' he said, 'and I will show you where your son lies.'

When Helen left the cemetery she turned for a last look. In the distance she saw the man bending over his young plants; and she went away, supposing him to be the gardener.

A Matter of Fact

And if ye doubt the tale I tell,
Steer through the South Pacific swell;
Go where the branching coral hives
Unending strife of endless lives,
Where, leagued about the 'wildered boat,
The rainbow jellies fill and float;
And, lilting where the laver lingers,
The starfish trips on all her fingers;
Where, 'neath his myriad spines ashock,
The sea-egg ripples down the rock;
An orange wonder dimly guessed.
From darkness where the cuttles rest,
Moored o'er the darker deeps that hide
The blind white Sea-snake and his bride;
Who, drowsing, nose the long-lost ships
Let down through darkness to their lips.
                                        —The Palms.

Once a priest always a priest; once a Mason always a Mason; but once a journalist always and forever a journalist.

There were three of us, all newspaper men, the only passengers on a little tramp-steamer that ran where her owners told her to go. She had once been in the Bilbao iron ore business, had been lent to the Spanish Government for service at Manilla; and was ending her days in the Cape Town *coolie*-trade, with occasional trips to Madagascar and even as far as England. We found her going to Southampton in ballast, and shipped in her because the fares were nominal. There was Keller, of an American paper, on his way back to the States from palace executions in Madagascar; there was a burly half Dutchman, called Zuyland, who owned and edited a paper up country near Johannesberg; and there was myself, who had solemnly put away all journalism, vowing to forget that I had ever known the difference between an imprint and a stereo advertisement.

Three minutes after Keller spoke to me, as the *Rathmines* cleared Cape Town, I had forgotten the aloofness I desired to feign, and was in heated discussion on the immorality of expanding telegrams beyond a certain fixed point. Then Zuyland came out of his state-room, and we were all at home instantly, because we were men of the same profession needing no introduction. We annexed the boat formally, broke open the passengers' bathroom door—on the Manilla lines the *dons* do not wash—cleaned out the orange-peel and cigar-ends at the bottom of the bath, hired a lascar to shave us throughout the voyage, and then asked each other's names.

Three ordinary men would have quarrelled through sheer boredom before they reached Southampton. We, by virtue of our craft, were anything but ordinary men. A large percentage of the tales of the world, the thirty-nine that cannot he told to ladies and the one that can, are common property coming of a common stock. We told them all, as a matter of form, with all their local and specific variants which are surprising. Then came, in the intervals of steady card-play, more personal histories of adventure and things seen and reported; panics among white folk, when the blind terror ran from man to man on the Brooklyn Bridge, and the people crushed each other to death they knew not why; fires, and faces that opened and shut their mouths horribly at red-hot window-frames; wrecks in frost and snow, reported from the sleet-sheathed rescue tug at the risk of frostbite; long rides after diamond thieves; skirmishes on the veldt and in municipal committees with the Boers; glimpses of lazy, tangled Cape politics and the mule-rule in the Transvaal; card-tales, horse-tales, woman-tales by the score and the half hundred; till the first mate, who had seen more than us all put together, but lacked words to clothe his tales with, sat open-mouthed far into the dawn.

When the tales were done we picked up cards till a curious hand or a chance remark made one or other of us say, 'That reminds me of a man who—or a business which—'and the anecdotes would continue while the *Rathmines* kicked her way northward through the warm water.

In the morning of one specially warm night we three were sitting immediately in front of the wheel-house where an old Swedish boatswain whom we called 'Frithiof the Dane' was at the wheel pretending that he could not hear our stories. Once or twice Frithiof spun the spokes curiously, and Keller lifted his head from a long chair to ask, 'What is it? Can't you get any pull on her?'

"There is a feel in the water,' said Frithiof, 'that I cannot understand. I think that we run downhills or somethings. She steers bad this morning.'

Nobody seems to know the laws that govern the pulse of the big waters. Sometimes even a lands-man can tell that the solid ocean is a-tilt, and that the ship is working herself up a long unseen slope; and sometimes the captain says, when neither full steam nor fair wind justify the length of a day's run, that the ship is sagging downhill; but how these ups and downs come about has not yet been settled authoritatively.

'No, it is a following sea,' said Frithiof; 'and with a following sea you shall not get good steerage way.'

The sea was as smooth as a duck-pond, except for a regular oily swell. As I looked over the side to see where it might be following us from, the sun rose in a perfectly clear sky and struck the water with its light so sharply that it seemed as though the sea should clang like a burnished gong. The wake of the screw and the little white streak cut by the log-line hanging over the stern were the only marks on the water as far as eye could reach.

Keller rolled out of his chair and went aft to get a pine-apple from the ripening stock that were hung inside the after awning.

'Frithiof, the log-line has got tired of swimming. It's coming home,' he drawled.

'What?' said Frithiof, his voice jumping several octaves.

'Coming home,' Keller repeated, leaning over the stern, I ran to his side and saw the log-line, which till then had been drawn tense over the stern railing, slacken, loop, and come up off the port quarter. Frithiof called up the speaking-tube to the bridge, and the bridge answered, 'Yes, nine knots.'

Then Frithiof spoke again, and the answer was, 'What do you want of the skipper?' and Frithiof bellowed, 'Call him up.'

By this time Zuyland, Keller, and myself had caught something of Frithiof s excitement, for any emotion on shipboard is most contagious. The captain ran out of his cabin, spoke to Frithiof, looked at the log-line, jumped on the bridge, and in a minute we felt the steamer swing round as Frithiof turned her.

'Going back to Cape Town?' said Keller.

Frithiof did not answer, but tore away at the wheel. Then he beckoned us three to help, and we held the wheel down till the *Rathmines* answered it, and we found ourselves looking into the white of our own wake, with the still oily sea tearing past our bows, though we were not going more than half steam ahead.

The captain stretched out his arm from the bridge and shouted. A minute later I would have given a great deal to have shouted too, for one-half of the sea seemed to shoulder itself above the other half, and came on in the shape of a hill. There was neither crest, comb, nor curl-over to it; nothing but black water with little waves chasing each other about the flanks. I saw it stream past and on a level with the *Rathmine's* bow-plates before the steamer made up her mind to rise, and I argued that this would be the last of all earthly voyages for me. Then we rose forever and ever and ever, till I heard Keller saying in my ear, 'The bowels of the deep, good Lord!' and the *Rathmines* stood poised, her screw racing and drumming on the slope of a hollow that stretched downwards for a good half-mile.

We went down that hollow, nose under for the most part, and

the air smelt wet and muddy, like that of an emptied aquarium. There was a second hill to climb; I saw that much: but the water came aboard and carried me aft till it jammed me against the smoking-room door, and before I could catch breath or clear my eyes again we were rolling to and fro in torn water, with, the scuppers pouring like eaves in a thunderstorm.

'There were three waves,' said Keller; 'and the stoke-hold's flooded.'

The firemen were on deck waiting, apparently,, to be drowned. The engineer came and dragged them below, and the crew, gasping, began to work the clumsy Board of Trade pump. That showed nothing serious, and when I understood that the *Rathmines* was really on the water, and not beneath it, I asked what had happened.

'The captain says it was a blow-up under the sea—a volcano,' said Keller.

'It hasn't warmed anything,' I said. I was feeling bitterly cold, and cold was almost unknown in those waters. I went below to change my clothes, and when I came up everything was wiped out by clinging white fog.

'Are there going to be any more surprises?' said Keller to the captain.

'I don't know. Be thankful you're alive, gentlemen. That's a tidal wave thrown up by a volcano. Probably the bottom of the sea has been lifted a few feet somewhere or other. I can't quite understand this cold spell. Our sea-thermometer says the surface water is 44°, and it should be 68° at least.'

'It's abominable,' said Keller, shivering. 'But hadn't you better attend to the fog-horn? It seems to me that I heard something.'

'Heard! Good heavens!' said the captain from the bridge, 'I should think you did.' He pulled the string of our fog-horn, which was a weak one. It sputtered and choked, because the stoke-hold was full of water and the fires were half-drowned, and at last gave out a moan. It was answered from the fog by one of the most appalling steam-sirens I have ever heard. Keller turned as white as I did, for the fog, the cold fog, was upon us, and any man may be forgiven for fearing the death he cannot see.

'Give her steam there!' said the captain to the engine-room. 'Steam for the whistle, if we have to go dead slow.'

We bellowed again, and the damp dripped off the awnings to the deck as we listened for the reply. It seemed to be astern this time, but much nearer than before.

'The *Pembroke Castle*, by gum! ' said Keller, and then, viciously, 'Well, thank God, we shall sink her too.'

'It's a side-wheel steamer,' I whispered. 'Can't you hear the paddles?'

This time we whistled and roared till the steam gave out, and the answer nearly deafened us. There was a sound of frantic threshing in the water, apparently about fifty yards away, and something shot past in the whiteness that looked as though it were gray and red.

'The *Pembroke Castle* bottom up,' said Keller, who, being a journalist, always sought for explanations. 'That's the colours of a Castle liner. We're in for a big thing.'

'The sea is bewitched,' said Frithiof from the wheel-house. 'There are two steamers.'

Another siren sounded on our bow, and the little steamer rolled in the wash of something that had passed unseen.

'We're evidently in the middle of a fleet,' said Keller quietly. 'If one doesn't run us down, the other will. Phew! What in creation is that?'

I sniffed for there was a poisonous rank smell in the cold air— a smell that I had smelt before.

'If I was on land I should say that it was an alligator. It smells like musk,' I answered.

'Not ten thousand alligators could make that smell.' said Zuyland; 'I have smelt them.'

'Bewitched! Bewitched!' said Frithiof. 'The sea she is turned upside down, and we are walking along the bottom.'

Again the *Rathmines* rolled in the wash of some unseen ship, and a silver-gray wave broke over the bow, leaving on the deck a sheet of sediment—the gray broth that has its place in the fathomless deeps of the sea. A sprinkling of the wave fell on my face, and it was so cold that it stung as boiling water stings. The dead and most untouched deep water of the sea had been heaved to the top by the submarine volcano— the chill, still water that kills all life and smells of desolation and emptiness. We did not need either the blinding fog or that indescribable smell of musk to make us unhappy—we were shivering with cold and wretchedness where we stood.

'The hot air on the cold water makes this fog,' said the captain. 'It ought to clear in a little time.'

'Whistle, oh! whistle, and let's get out of it,' said Keller.

The captain whistled again, and far and far astern the invisible twin steam-sirens answered us. Their blasting shriek grew louder, till at last it seemed to tear out of the fog just above our quarter, and I cowered while the *Rathmines* plunged bows under on a double swell that crossed.

'No more,' said Frithiof, 'it is not good any more. Let us get away, in the name of God.'

'Now if a torpedo-boat with a *City of Paris* siren went mad and broke her moorings and hired a friend to help her, it's just conceivable that we might be carried as we are now. Otherwise this thing is—'

The last words died on Keller's lips, his eyes began to start from his head, and his jaw fell. Some six or seven feet above the port bulwarks, framed in fog, and as utterly unsupported as the full moon, hung a face. It was not human, and it certainly was not animal, for it did not belong to this earth as known to man. The mouth was open, revealing a ridiculously tiny tongue—as absurd as the tongue of an elephant; there were tense wrinkles of white skin at the angles of the drawn lips; white feelers like those of a barbel sprang from the lower jaw, and there was no sign of teeth within the mouth. But the horror of the face lay in the eyes, for those were sightless—white, in sockets as white as scraped bone, and blind. Yet for all this the face, wrinkled as the mask of a lion is drawn in Assyrian sculpture, was alive with rage and terror. One long white feeler touched our bulwarks. Then the face disappeared with the swiftness of a blind worm popping into its burrow, and the next thing that I remember is my own voice in my own ears, saying gravely to the mainmast, 'But the air-bladder ought to have been forced out of its mouth, you know.'

Keller came up to me, ashy white. He put his hand into his pocket, took a cigar, bit it, dropped it, thrast his shaking thumb into his mouth and mumbled, 'The giant gooseberry and the raining frogs! Gimme a light—gimme a light! I say, gimme a light.' A little bead of blood dropped from his thumbnail.

I respected the motive, though the manifestation was absurd. 'Stop, you'll bite your thumb off,' I said, and Keller laughed brokenly as he picked up his cigar. Only Zuyland, leaning over the port bulwarks, seemed self-possessed. He declared later that he was very sick.

'We've seen it,' he said, turning round. 'That is it.'

'What?' said Keller, chewing the unlighted cigar.

As he spoke the fog was blown into shreds, and we saw the sea, gray with mud, rolling on every side of us and empty of all life. Then in one spot it bubbled and became like the pot of ointment that the Bible speaks of. From that wide-ringed trouble a *thing* came up—a gray and red thing with a neck—a *thing* that bellowed and writhed in pain. Frithiof drew in his breath and held it till the red letters of the ship's name, woven across his jersey, straggled and opened out as though they had been type badly set. Then he said with a little cluck in his throat, 'Ah, me! It is blind. *Hur illa!* That thing is blind,' and a murmur of pity went through us all, for we could see that the thing on the water was blind and in pain.

Something had gashed and cut the great sides cruelly and the blood was spurting out. The gray ooze of the undermost sea lay in the monstrous wrinkles of the back and poured away in sluices. The blind white head flung back and battered the wounds, and the body in its torment rose clear of the red and gray waves till we saw a pair of quivering shoulders streaked with weed and rough with shells, but as white in the clear spaces as the hairless, nameless, blind, toothless head. Afterwards came a dot on the horizon and the sound of a shrill scream, and it was as though a shuttle shot all across the sea in one breath, and a second head and neck tore through the levels, driving a whispering wall of water to right and left. The two *things* met—the one untouched and the other in its death throe—male and female, we said, the female coming to the male.

She circled round him bellowing, and laid her neck across the curve of his great turtle-back, and he disappeared under water for an instant, but flung up again, grunting in agony while the blood ran. Once the entire head and neck shot clear of the water and stiffened, and I heard Keller saying, as though he was watching a street accident, 'Give him air. For God's sake give him air!' Then the death struggle began, with crampings and twistings and jerkings of the white bulk to and fro, till our little steamer rolled again, and each gray wave coated her plates with the gray slime. The sun was clear, there was no wind, and we watched, the whole crew, stokers and all, in wonder and pity, but chiefly pity.

The *thing* was so helpless, and, save for his mate, so alone. No human eye should have beheld him; it was monstrous and indecent to exhibit him there in trade waters between atlas degrees of latitude. He had been spewed up, mangled and dying from his rest on the sea-floor, where he might have lived till the Judgment Day, and we saw the tides of his life go from him as an angry tide goes out across rocks in the teeth of a landward gale. The mate lay rocking on the water a little distance off, bellowing continually, and the smell of musk came down upon the ship making ns cough.

At last the battle for life ended, in a batter of coloured seas. We saw the writhing neck fall like a flail, the carcase turn sideways, showing the glint of a white belly and the inset of a gigantic hind-leg or flapper. Then all sank, and sea boiled over it, while the mate swam round and round, darting her blind head in every direction. Though we might have feared that she would attack the steamer, no power on earth could have drawn any one of us from our places that hour. We watched, holding our breaths. The mate paused in her search; we could hear the wash beating along her sides; reared her neck as high as she could reach, blind and lonely in all that loneliness of the sea, and sent one desperate bellow booming across the swells, as an oyster shell skips across a pond. Then she made off to the westward, the sun shining on the white head and the wake behind it, till nothing was left to see but a little pin point of silver on the horizon. We stood on our course again, and the *Rathmines*, coated with the sea-sediment, from bow to stern, looked like a ship made gray with terror.

★★★★★★

'We must pool our notes,' was the first coherent remark from Keller. 'We're three trained journalists—we hold absolutely the biggest scoop on record. Start fair.'

I objected to this. Nothing is gained by collaboration in journalism when all deal with the same facts, so we went to work each according to his own lights. Keller triple-headed his account, talked about our 'gallant captain,' and wound up with an allusion to American enterprise in that it was a citizen of Dayton, Ohio, that had seen the sea-serpent. This sort of thing would have discredited the Creation, much more a mere sea tale, but as a specimen of the picture-writing of a half-civilised people it was very interesting. Zuyland took a heavy column and a half, giving approximate lengths and breadths and the whole list of the crew whom he had sworn on oath to testify to his facts. There was nothing fantastic or flamboyant in Zuyland. I wrote three-quarters of a leaded *bourgeois* column, roughly speaking, and refrained from putting any journalese into it for reasons that had begun to appear to me.

Keller was insolent with joy. He was going to cable from Southampton to the New York *World*, mail his account to America on the same day, paralyse London with his three columns of loosely knitted headlines, and generally efface the earth. 'You'll see how I work a big scoop when I get it,' he said.

'Is this your first visit to England?' I asked.

'Yes,' said he. 'You don't seem to appreciate the beauty of our scoop. It's pyramidal—the death of the sea-serpent! Good heavens alive man, it's the biggest thing ever vouchsafed to a paper!'

'Curious to think that it will never appear in any paper, isn't it? I said.

Zuyland was near me, and he nodded quickly.

'What do you mean?' said Keller. 'If you're enough of a Britisher to throw this thing away, I sha'n't. I thought you were a newspaper man.'

'I am. That's why I know. Don't be an ass, Keller. Remember, I'm seven hundred years your senior, and what your grandchildren may learn five hundred years hence, I learned from my grandfathers about five hundred years ago. You won't do it, because you can't.'

This conversation was held in open sea, where everything seems possible, some hundred miles from Southampton. We passed the Needles Light at dawn, and the lifting day showed the stucco villas on the green and the awful orderliness of England—line upon line, wall upon wall, solid stone dock and monolithic pier. We waited an hour in the Customs shed, and there was ample time for the effect to soak in.

'Now, Keller, you face the music. The *Havel* goes out today. Mail by her, and I'll take you to the telegraph office,' I said.

I heard Keller gasp as the influence of the land closed about him, cowing him as they say Newmarket Heath cows a young horse unused to open country.

'I want to retouch my stuff. Suppose we wait till we get to London?' he said.

Zuyland, by the way, had torn up his account and thrown it overboard that morning early. His reasons were my reasons.

In the train Keller began to revise his copy, and every time that he looked at the trim little fields, the red villas, and the embankments of the line, the blue pencil plunged remorselessly through the slips. He appeared to have dredged the dictionary for adjectives. I could think of none that he had not used. Yet he was a perfectly sound poker player and never showed more cards than were sufficient to take the pool.

'Aren't you going to leave him a single bellow?' I asked sympathetically. 'Remember, everything goes in the States, from a trouser-button to a double eagle."

'That's just the curse of it,' said Keller below his breath. 'We've played 'em for suckers so often that when it comes to the golden truth—I'd like to try this on a London paper. You have first call there, though.'

'Not in the least. I'm not touching the thing in the papers. I shall be happy to leave 'em all to you; but surely you'll cable it home?'

'No. Not if I can make the scoop here and see the Britishers sit up.'

'You won't do it with, three column of slushy headline, believe me. They don't sit up as quickly as some people.'

'I'm beginning to think that too. Does nothing make any difference in this country?' he said, looking out of the window. 'How old is that farmhouse?'

'New. It can't be more than two hundred years at the most.'

'Um. Fields, too?'

'That hedge there must have been clipped for about eighty years.'

'Labour cheap—eh?'

'Pretty much. Well, I suppose you'd like to try the *Times*, wouldn't you?'

'No,' said Keller, looking at Winchester Cathedral. 'Might as well try to electrify a hay-rick. And to think that the *World* would take three columns and ask for more—with illustrations too! It's sickening.'

'But the *Times* might,' I began.

Keller flung his paper across the carriage, and it opened in its austere majesty of solid type—opened with the crackle of an encyclopaedia.

'Might! You *might* work your way through the bow-plates of a cruiser. Look at that first page!'

'It strikes you that way, does it?' I said. 'Then I'd recommend you to try a light and frivolous journal.'

'With a thing like this of mine—of ours? It's sacred history!'

I showed him a paper which I conceived would be after his own heart, in that it was modelled on American lines.

'That's homey,' he said, 'but it's not the real thing. Now, I should like one of these fat old *Times'* columns. Probably there'd be a bishop in the office, though.'

When we reached London Keller disappeared in the direction of the Strand. What his experiences may have been I cannot tell, but it seems that he invaded the office of an evening paper at 11.45 a. m. (I told him English editors were most idle at that hour), and mentioned my name as that of a witness to the truth of his story.

'I was nearly fired out,' he said furiously at lunch. 'As soon as I mentioned you, the old man said that I was to tell you that they didn't want any more of your practical jokes, and that you knew the hours to call if you had anything to sell, and that they'd see you condemned before they helped to puff one of your infernal yarns in advance. Say, what record do you hold for truth in this city, anyway?'

'A beauty. You ran up against it, that's all. Why don't you leave the English papers alone and cable to New York? Everything goes over there.'

'Can't you see that's just why?' he repeated.

'I saw it a long time ago. You don't intend to cable, then?'

'Yes, I do,' he answered, in the over-emphatic voice of one who does not know his own mind.

That afternoon I walked him abroad and about, over the streets that run between the pavements like channels of grooved and tongued lava, over the bridges that are made of enduring stone, through subways floored and sided with yard-thick concrete, between houses that are never rebuilt, and by river steps hewn to the eye from the living rock. A black fog chased us into Westminster Abbey, and, standing there in the darkness, I could hear the wings of the dead centuries circling round the head of Litchfield A. Keller, journalist, of Dayton, Ohio, U. S. A., whose mission it was to make the Britishers sit up.

He stumbled gasping into the thick gloom, and the roar of the traffic came to his bewildered ears.

'Let's go to the telegraph office and cable,' I said. 'Can't you hear the New York *World* crying for news of the great sea-serpent, blind, white, and smelling of musk, stricken to death by a submarine volcano, assisted by his loving wife to die in mid-ocean, as visualised by an independent American citizen, a breezy, newsy, brainy newspaper man of Dayton, Ohio? 'Rah for the Buckeye State. Step lively! Both gates! Szz! Boom—ah!' Keller was a Princeton man, and he seemed to need encouragement.

'You've got me on your own ground.' said he, tugging at his overcoat pocket. He pulled out his copy, with the cable forms—for he had written out his telegram—and put them all into my hand, groaning, 'I pass. If I hadn't come to your cursed country—if I'd sent it off at Southampton—if I ever get you west of the Alleghanies, if—'

'Never mind, Keller. It isn't your fault. It's the fault of your country. If you had been seven hundred years older you'd have done what I'm going to do.'

'What are you going to do?'

'Tell it as a lie.'

'Fiction?' This with the full-blooded disgust of a journalist for the illegitimate branch of the profession.

'You can call it that if you like. I shall call it a lie.'

And a lie it has become, for Truth is a naked lady, and if by accident she is drawn up from the bottom of the sea, it behoves a gentleman either to give her a print petticoat or to turn his face to the wall, and vow that he did not see.

Bubbling Well Road

Look out on a large scale map the place where the Chenab River falls into the Indus fifteen miles or so above the hamlet of Chachuran. Five miles west of Chachuran lies Bubbling Well Road, and the house of the *gosain* or priest of Arti-goth. It was the priest who showed me the road, but it is no thanks to him that I am able to tell this story.

Five miles west of Chachuran is a patch of the plumed jungle-grass, that turns over in silver when the wind blows, from ten to twenty feet high and from three to four miles square. In the heart of the patch hides the *gosain* of Bubbling Well Road. The villagers stone him when he peers into the daylight, although he is a priest, and he runs back again as a strayed wolf turns into tall crops. He is a one-eyed man and carries, burnt between his brows, the impress of two copper coins. Some say that he was tortured by a native prince in the old days; for he is so old that he must have been capable of mischief in the days of Run jit Singh. His most pressing need at present is a halter, and the care of the British Government.

These things happened when the jungle-grass was tall; and the villagers of Chachuran told me that a sounder of pig had gone into the Arti-goth patch. To enter jungle-grass is always an unwise proceeding, but I went, partly because I knew nothing of pig-hunting, and partly because the villagers said that the big boar of the sounder owned foot long tushes. Therefore I wished to shoot him, in order to produce the tushes in after years, and say that I had ridden him down in fair chase. I took a gun and went into the hot, close patch, believing that it would be an easy thing to unearth one pig in ten square miles of jungle. Mr. Wardle, the terrier, went with me because he believed that I was incapable of existing for an hour without his advice and countenance. He managed to slip in and out between the grass clumps, but I had to force my way, and in twenty minutes was as completely lost as though I had been in the heart of Central Africa. I did not notice this at first till I had grown wearied of stumbling and pushing through the grass, and Mr. Wardle was beginning to sit down very often and hang out his tongue very far. There was nothing but grass everywhere, and it was impossible to see two yards in any direction. The grass-stems held the heat exactly as boiler-tubes do.

In half an hour, when I was devoutly wishing that I had left the big boar alone, I came to a narrow path which seemed to be a compromise between a native footpath and a pig-run. It was barely six inches wide, but I could sidle along it in comfort. The grass was extremely thick here, and where the path was ill defined it was necessary to crush into the tussocks either with both hands before the face, or to back into it, leaving both hands free to manage the rifle. None the less it was a path, and valuable because it might lead to a place.

At the end of nearly fifty yards of fair way, just when I was preparing to back into an unusually stiff tussock, I missed Mr. Wardle, who for his girth is an unusually frivolous dog and never keeps to heel. I called him three times and said aloud, 'Where has the little beast gone to?' Then I stepped backwards several paces, for almost under my feet a deep voice repeated, 'Where has the little beast gone?' To appreciate an unseen voice thoroughly you should hear it when you are lost in stifling jungle grass. I called Mr. Wardle again and the underground echo assisted me. At that I ceased calling and listened very attentively, because I thought I heard a man laughing in a peculiarly offensive manner. The heat made me sweat, but the laughter made me shake.

There is no earthly need for laughter in high grass. It is indecent, as well as impolite. The chuckling stopped, and I took courage and continued to call till I thought that I had located the echo somewhere behind and below the tussock into which I was preparing to back just before I lost Mr. Wardle. I drove my rifle up to the triggers, between the grass-stems in a downward and forward direction. Then I waggled it to and fro, but it did not seem to touch ground on the far side of the tussock as it should have done. Every time that I grunted with the exertion of driving a heavy rifle through thick grass, the grunt was faithfully repeated from below, and when I stopped to wipe my face the sound of low laughter was distinct beyond doubting.

I went into the tussock, face first, an inch at a time, my mouth open and my eyes fine, full, and prominent. When I had overcome the resistance of the grass I found that I was looking straight across a black gap in the ground—that I was actually lying on my chest leaning over the mouth of a well so deep I could scarcely see the water in it.

There were things in the water,—black things,—and the water was as black as pitch with blue scum atop. The laughing sound came from the noise of a little spring, spouting halfway down one side of the well. Sometimes as the black things circled round, the trickle from the spring fell upon their tightly-stretched skins, and then the laughter changed into a sputter of mirth. One thing turned over on its back, as I watched, and drifted round and round the circle of the mossy brickwork with a hand and half an arm held clear of the water in a stiff and horrible flourish, as though it were a very wearied guide paid to exhibit the beauties of the place.

I did not spend more than half-an-hour in creeping round that well and finding the path on the other side. The remainder of the journey I accomplished by feeling every foot of ground in front of me, and crawling like a snail through every tussock. I carried Mr. Wardle in my arms and he licked my nose. He was not frightened in the least, nor was I, but we wished to reach open ground in order to enjoy the view. My knees were loose, and the apple in my throat refused to slide up and down. The path on the far side of the well was a very good one, though boxed in on all sides by grass, and it led me in time to a priest's hut in the centre of a little clearing. When that priest saw my very white face coming through the grass he howled with terror and embraced my boots; but when I reached the bedstead set outside his door I sat down quickly and Mr. Wardle mounted guard over me. I was not in a condition to take care of myself.

When I awoke I told the priest to lead me into the open, out of the Arti-goth patch, and to walk slowly in front of me. Mr. Wardle hates natives, and the priest was more afraid of Mr. Wardle than of me, though we were both angry. He walked very slowly down a narrow little path from his hut. That path crossed three paths, such as the one I had come by in the first instance, and every one of the three headed towards the Bubbling Well. Once when we stopped to draw breath, I heard the well laughing to itself alone in the thick grass, and only my need for his services prevented my firing both barrels into the priest's back.

When we came to the open the priest crashed back into cover, and I went to the village of Arti-goth for a drink. It was pleasant to be able to see the horizon all round, as well as the ground underfoot.

The villagers told me that the patch of grass was full of devils and ghosts, all in the service of the priest, and that men and women and children had entered it and had never returned. They said the priest used their livers for purposes of witchcraft. When I asked why they had not told me of this at the outset, they said that they were afraid they would lose their reward for bringing news of the pig.

Before I left I did my best to set the patch alight, but the grass was too green. Some fine summer day, however, if the wind is favourable, a file of old newspapers and a box of matches will make clear the mystery of Bubbling Well Road.

Swept and Garnished

When the first waves of feverish cold stole over Frau Ebermann she very wisely telephoned for the doctor and went to
bed. He diagnosed the attack as mild influenza, prescribed the
appropriate remedies, and left her to the care of her one servant in her comfortable Berlin flat. Frau Ebermann, beneath the
thick coverlet, curled up with what patience she could until
the aspirin should begin to act, and Anna should come back
from the chemist with the formamint, the ammoniated quinine,
the eucalyptus, and the little tin steam-inhaler. Meantime, every
bone in her body ached; her head throbbed; her hot, dry hands
would not stay the same size for a minute together; and her
body, tucked into the smallest possible compass, shrank from the
chill of the well-warmed sheets.

Of a sudden she noticed that an imitation-lace cover which
should have lain mathematically square with the imitation-mar-
ble top of the radiator behind the green plush sofa had slipped
away so that one corner hung over the bronze-painted steam
pipes. She recalled that she must have rested her poor head
against the radiator-top while she was taking off her boots. She
tried to get up and set the thing straight, but the radiator at once
receded toward the horizon, which, unlike true horizons, slant-
ed diagonally, exactly parallel with the dropped lace edge of the
cover. Frau Ebermann groaned through sticky lips and lay still.

'Certainly, I have a temperature,' she said. 'Certainly, I have a
grave temperature. I should have been warned by that chill after
dinner.'

She resolved to shut her hot-lidded eyes, but opened them in a little while to torture herself with the knowledge of that ungeometrical thing against the far wall. Then she saw a child—an untidy, thin-faced little girl of about ten, who must have strayed in from the adjoining flat. This proved—Frau Ebermann groaned again at the way the world falls to bits when one is sick—proved that Anna had forgotten to shut the outer door of the flat when she went to the chemist. Frau Ebermann had had children of her own, but they were all grown up now, and she had never been a child-lover in any sense. Yet the intruder might be made to serve her scheme of things.

'Make—put,' she muttered thickly, 'that white thing straight on the top of that yellow thing.'

The child paid no attention, but moved about the room, investigating everything that came in her way—the yellow cut-glass handles of the chest of drawers, the stamped bronze hook to hold back the heavy puce curtains, and the mauve enamel, New Art finger-plates on the door. Frau Ebermann watched indignantly.

'Aie! That is bad and rude. Go away!' she cried, though it hurt her to raise her voice. 'Go away by the road you came!' The child passed behind the bed-foot, where she could not see her. 'Shut the door as you go. I will speak to Anna, but—first, put that white thing straight.'

She closed her eyes in misery of body and soul. The outer door clicked, and Anna entered, very penitent that she had stayed so long at the chemist's. But it had been difficult to find the proper type of inhaler, and—

'Where did the child go?' moaned Frau Ebermann—'the child that was here?'

'There was no child,' said startled Anna. 'How should any child come in when I shut the door behind me after I go out? All the keys of the flats are different.'

'No, no! You forgot this time. But my back is aching, and up my legs also. Besides, who knows what it may have fingered and upset? Look and see.'

'Nothing is fingered, nothing is upset,' Anna replied, as she took the inhaler from its paper box.

'Yes, there is. Now I remember all about it. Put—put that white thing, with the open edge—the lace, I mean—quite straight on that—' she pointed. Anna, accustomed to her ways, understood and went to it.

'Now, is it quite straight?' Frau Ebermann demanded.

'Perfectly,' said Anna. 'In fact, in the very centre of the radiator.' Anna measured the equal margins with her knuckle, as she had been told to do when she first took service.

'And my tortoise-shell hair brushes?' Frau Ebermann could not command her dressing-table from where she lay.

'Perfectly straight, side by side in the big tray, and the comb laid across them. Your watch also in the coralline watch-holder. Everything'—she moved round the room to make sure—'everything is as you have it when you are well.' Frau Ebermann sighed with relief. It seemed to her that the room and her head had suddenly grown cooler.

'Good!' said she. 'Now warm my night-gown in the kitchen, so it will be ready when I have perspired. And the towels also. Make the inhaler steam, and put in the eucalyptus; that is good for the larynx. Then sit you in the kitchen, and come when I ring. But, first, my hot-water bottle.'

It was brought and scientifically tucked in.

'What news?' said Frau Ebermann drowsily. She had not been out that day.

'Another victory,' said Anna. 'Many more prisoners and guns.'

Frau Ebermann purred, one might almost say grunted, contentedly.

'That is good too,' she said; and Anna, after lighting the inhaler-lamp, went out.

Frau Ebermann reflected that in an hour or so the aspirin would begin to work, and all would be well. To-morrow—no, the day after—she would take up life with something to talk over with her friends at coffee. It was rare—everyone knew it—that she should be overcome by any ailment. Yet in all her distresses she had not allowed the minutest deviation from daily routine and ritual. She would tell her friends—she ran over their names one by one—exactly what measures she had taken against the lace cover on the radiator-top and in regard to her two tortoise-shell hair brushes and the comb at right angles. How she had set everything in order—everything in order. She roved further afield as she wriggled her toes luxuriously on the hot-water bottle. If it pleased our dear God to take her to Himself, and she was not so young as she had been—there was that plate of the four lower ones in the blue tooth-glass, for instance—He should find all her belongings fit to meet His eye. 'Swept and garnished' were the words that shaped themselves in her intent brain. 'Swept and garnished for—'

No, it was certainly not for the dear Lord that she had swept; she would have her room swept out tomorrow or the day after, and garnished. Her hands began to swell again into huge pillows of nothingness. Then they shrank, and so did her head, to minute dots. It occurred to her that she was waiting for some event, some tremendously important event, to come to pass. She lay with shut eyes for a long time till her head and hands should return to their proper size.

She opened her eyes with a jerk.

'How stupid of me,' she said aloud, 'to set the room in order for a parcel of dirty little children!'

They were there—five of them, two little boys and three girls—headed by the anxious-eyed ten-year-old whom she had seen before. They must have entered by the outer door, which Anna had neglected to shut behind her when she returned with the inhaler. She counted them backward and forward as one counts scales—one, two, three, four, five.

They took no notice of her, but hung about, first on one foot then on the other, like strayed chickens, the smaller ones holding by the larger. They had the air of utterly wearied passengers in a railway waiting-room, and their clothes were disgracefully dirty.

'Go away!' cried Frau Ebermann at last, after she had struggled, it seemed to her, for years to shape the words.

'You called?' said Anna at the living-room door.

'No,' said her mistress. 'Did you shut the flat door when you came in?'

'Assuredly,' said Anna. 'Besides, it is made to catch shut of itself.'

'Then go away,' said she, very little above a whisper. If Anna pretended not to see the children, she would speak to Anna later on.

'And now,' she said, turning toward them as soon as the door closed. The smallest of the crowd smiled at her, and shook his head before he buried it in his sister's skirts.

'Why—don't—you—go—away?' she whispered earnestly.

Again they took no notice, but, guided by the elder girl, set themselves to climb, boots and all, on to the green plush sofa in front of the radiator. The little boys had to be pushed, as they could not compass the stretch unaided. They settled themselves in a row, with small gasps of relief, and pawed the plush approvingly.

'I ask you—I ask you why do you not go away—why do you not go away?' Frau Ebermann found herself repeating the question twenty times. It seemed to her that everything in the world hung on the answer. 'You know you should not come into houses and rooms unless you are invited. Not houses and bedrooms, you know.'

'No,' a solemn little six-year-old repeated, 'not houses nor bedrooms, nor dining-rooms, nor churches, nor all those places. Shouldn't come in. It's rude.'

'Yes, he said so,' the younger girl put in proudly. 'He said it. He told them only pigs would do that.' The line nodded and dimpled one to another with little explosive giggles, such as children use when they tell deeds of great daring against their elders.

'If you know it is wrong, that makes it much worse,' said Frau Ebermann.

'Oh yes; much worse,' they assented cheerfully, till the smallest boy changed his smile to a baby wail of weariness.

'When will they come for us?' he asked, and the girl at the head of the row hauled him bodily into her square little capable lap.

'He's tired,' she explained. 'He is only four. He only had his first breeches this spring.' They came almost under his armpits, and were held up by broad linen braces, which, his sorrow diverted for the moment, he patted proudly.

'Yes, beautiful, dear,' said both girls.

'Go away!' said Frau Ebermann. 'Go home to your father and mother!'

Their faces grew grave at once.

'H'sh! We *can't*,' whispered the eldest. 'There isn't anything left.'

'All gone,' a boy echoed, and he puffed through pursed lips. 'Like *that*, uncle told me. Both cows too.'

'And my own three ducks,' the boy on the girl's lap said sleepily.

'So, you see, we came here.' The elder girl leaned forward a little, caressing the child she rocked.

'I—I don't understand,' said Frau Ebermann 'Are you lost, then? You must tell our police.'

'Oh no; we are only waiting.'

'But what are you waiting *for?*'

'We are waiting for our people to come for us. They told us to come here and wait for them. So we are waiting till they come,' the eldest girl replied.

'Yes. We are waiting till our people come for us,' said all the others in chorus.

'But,' said Frau Ebermann very patiently—'but now tell me, for I tell you that I am not in the least angry, where do you come from? Where do you come from?'

The five gave the names of two villages of which she had read in the papers,

'That is silly,' said Frau Ebermann. 'The people fired on us, and they were punished. Those places are wiped out, stamped flat.'

'Yes, yes, wiped out, stamped flat. That is why and—I have lost the ribbon off my pigtail,' said the younger girl. She looked behind her over the sofa-back.

'It is not here,' said the elder. 'It was lost before. Don't you remember?'

'Now, if you are lost, you must go and tell our police. They will take care of you and give you food,' said Frau Ebermann. 'Anna will show you the way there.'

'No,'—this was the six-year-old with the smile,—'we must wait here till our people come for us. Mustn't we, sister?'

'Of course. We wait here till our people come for us. All the world knows that,' said the eldest girl.

'Yes.' The boy in her lap had waked again. 'Little children, too—as little as Henri, and *he* doesn't wear trousers yet. As little as all that.'

'I don't understand,' said Frau Ebermann, shivering. In spite of the heat of the room and the damp breath of the steam-inhaler, the aspirin was not doing its duty.

The girl raised her blue eyes and looked at the woman for an instant.

'You see,' she said, emphasising her statements with her ring-ers, '*they* told *us* to wait *here* till *our* people came for us. So we came. We wait till our people come for us.'

'That is silly again,' said Frau Ebermann. 'It is no good for you to wait here. Do you know what this place is? You have been to school? It is Berlin, the capital of Germany.'

'Yes, yes,' they all cried; 'Berlin, capital of Germany. We know that. That is why we came.'

'So, you see, it is no good,' she said triumphantly, 'because your people can never come for you here.'

'They told us to come here and wait till our people came for us.' They delivered this as if it were a lesson in school. Then they sat still, their hands orderly folded on their laps, smiling as sweetly as ever.

'Go away! Go away!' Frau Ebermann shrieked.

'You called?' said Anna, entering.

'No. Go away! Go away!'

'Very good, old cat,' said the maid under her breath. 'Next time you *may* call,' and she returned to her friend in the kitchen.

'I ask you—ask you, *please* to go away,' Frau Ebermann pleaded. 'Go to my Anna through that door, and she will give you cakes and sweeties. It is not kind of you to come into my room and behave so badly.'

'Where else shall we go now?' the elder girl demanded, turning to her little company. They fell into discussion. One preferred the broad street with trees, another the railway station; but when she suggested an emperor's palace, they agreed with her.

'We will go then,' she said, and added half apologetically to Frau Ebermann, 'You see, they are so little they like to meet all the others.'

'What others?' said Frau Ebermann.

'The others—hundreds and hundreds and thousands and thousands of the others.'

'That is a lie. There cannot be a hundred even, much less a thousand,' cried Frau Ebermann.

'So?' said the girl politely.

'Yes. *I* tell you; and I have very good information. I know how it happened. You should have been more careful. You should not have run out to see the horses and guns passing. That is how it is done when our troops pass through. My son has written me so.'

They had clambered down from the sofa, and gathered round the bed with eager, interested eyes.

'Horses and guns going by—how fine!' someone whispered.

'Yes, yes; believe me, *that* is how the accidents to the children happen. You must know yourself that it is true. One runs out to look—'

'But I never saw any at all,' a boy cried sorrowfully. 'Only one noise I heard. That was when Aunt Emmeline's house fell down.'

'But listen to me. *I* am telling you! One runs out to look, because one is little and cannot see well. So one peeps between the man's legs, and then—you know how close those big horses and guns turn the corners—then one's foot slips and one gets run over. That's how it happens. Several times it had happened, but not many times; certainly not a hundred, perhaps not twenty. So, you see, you *must* be all. Tell me now that you are all that there are, and Anna shall give you the cakes.'

'Thousands,' a boy repeated monotonously. 'Then we all come here to wait till our people come for us.'

'But now we will go away from here. The poor lady is tired,' said the elder girl, plucking his sleeve.

'Oh, you hurt, you hurt!' he cried, and burst into tears.

'What is that for?' said Frau Ebermann. 'To cry in a room where a poor lady is sick is very inconsiderate.'

'Oh, but look, lady!' said the elder girl.

Frau Ebermann looked and saw.

'*Au revoir*, lady.' They made their little smiling bows and curtseys undisturbed by her loud cries. '*Au revoir,* lady. We will wait till our people come for us.'

When Anna at last ran in, she found her mistress on her knees, busily cleaning the floor with the lace cover from the radiator, because, she explained, it was all spotted with the blood of five children—she was perfectly certain there could not be more than five in the whole world—who had gone away for the moment, but were now waiting round the corner, and Anna was to find them and give them cakes to stop the bleeding, while her mistress swept and garnished that Our dear Lord when He came might find everything as it should be.

The Bisara of Pooree

Little Blind Fish, thou art marvellous wise,
Little Blind Fish, who put out thy eyes?
Open thy ears while I whisper my wish
Bring me a lover, thou little Blind Fish.
                                    The Charm of the Bisara.

Some natives say that it came from the other side of Kulu,
where the eleven-inch Temple Sapphire is. Others that it was
made at the Devil-Shrine of Ao-Chung in Thibet, was stolen
by a *Kafir*, from him by a Gurkha, from him again by a Lahouli,
from him by a *khitmatgar*, and by this latter sold to an Englishman, so all its virtue was lost; because, to work properly, the
Bisara of Pooree must be stolen—with bloodshed if possible,
but, at any rate, stolen.

These stories of the coming into India are all false. It was
made at Pooree ages since—the manner of its making would
fill a small book was stolen by one of the Temple dancing-girls
there, for her own purposes, and then passed on from hand to
hand, steadily northward, till it reached Hanlé: always bearing
the same name—the Bisara of Pooree. In shape it is a tiny square
box of silver, studded outside with eight small balas-rubies. Inside the box, which opens with a spring, is a little eyeless fish,
carved from some sort of dark, shiny nut and wrapped in a shred
of faded gold-cloth. That is the Bisara of Pooree, and it were
better for a man to take a king-cobra in his hand than to touch
the Bisara of Pooree.

All kinds of magic are out of date and done away with, except in India, where nothing changes in spite of the shiny, top-scum stuff that people call 'civilisation.' Any man who knows about the Bisara of Pooree will tell you what its powers are—always supposing that it has been honestly stolen. It is the only regularly working, trustworthy love-charm in the country, with one exception. (The other charm is in the hands of a trooper of the Nizam's Horse, at a place called Tuprani, due north of Hyderabad.) This can be depended upon for a fact. Someone else may explain it.

If the Bisara be not stolen, but given or bought or found, it turns against its owner in three years, and leads to ruin or death. This is another fact which you may explain when you have time. Meanwhile, you can laugh at it. At present the Bisara is safe on a hack-pony's neck, inside the blue bead-necklace that keeps off the Evil Eye. If the pony-driver ever finds it, and wears it, or gives it to his wife, I am sorry for him.

A very dirty Hill-*coolie* woman, with goitre, owned it at Theog in 1884. It came into Simla from the north before Churton's *khitmatgar* bought it, and sold it, for three times its silver value, to Churton, who collected curiosities. The servant knew no more what he had bought than the master; but a man looking over Churton's collection of curiosities Churton was an assistant commissioner by the way—saw and held his tongue. He was an Englishman, but knew how to believe. Which shows that he was different from most Englishmen. He knew that it was dangerous to have any share in the little box when working or dormant; for Love unsought is a terrible gift.

Pack—'Grubby' Pack, as we used to call him—was, in every way, a nasty little man who must have crawled into the army by mistake. He was three inches taller than his sword, but not half so strong. And the sword was a fifty-shilling, tailor-made one. Nobody liked him, and, I suppose, it was his wizenedness and worthlessness that made him fall so hopelessly in love with Miss Hollis, who was good and sweet, and five-feet-seven in her tennis-shoes. He was not content with falling in love quietly, but brought all the strength of his miserable little nature into the business. If he had not been so objectionable, one might have pitied him. He vapoured, and fretted, and fumed, and trotted up and down, and tried to make himself pleasing in Miss Hollis's big, quiet, gray eyes, and failed.

It was one of the cases that you sometimes meet, even in our country, where we marry by code, of a really blind attachment all on one side, without the faintest possibility of return. Miss Hollis looked on Pack as some sort of vermin running about the road. He had no prospects beyond captain's pay, and no wits to help that out by one penny. In a large-sized man love like his would have been touching. In a good man it would have been grand. He being what he was, it was only a nuisance.

You will believe this much. What you will not believe is what follows: Churton, and The Man who Knew what the Bisara was, were lunching at the Simla Club together. Churton was complaining of life in general. His best mare had rolled out of stable down the cliff and had broken her back; his decisions were being reversed by the upper courts more than an assistant commissioner of eight years' standing has a right to expect; he knew liver and fever, and for weeks past had felt out of sorts. Altogether, he was disgusted and disheartened.

Simla Club dining-room is built, as all the world knows, in two sections, with an arch-arrangement dividing them. Come in, turn to your own left, take the table under the window, and you cannot see anyone who has come in, turned to the right, and taken a table on the right side of the arch. Curiously enough, every word that you say can be heard, not only by the other diner, but by the servants beyond the screen through which they bring dinner. This is worth knowing; an echoing-room is a trap to be forewarned against.

Half in fun, and half hoping to be believed, The Man who Knew told Churton the story of the Bisara of Pooree at rather greater length than I have told it to you in this place; winding up with a suggestion that Churton might as well throw the little box down the hill and see whether all his troubles would go with it. In ordinary ears, English ears, the tale was only an interesting bit of folklore. Churton laughed, said that he felt better for his *tiffin*, and went out. Pack had been *tiffining* by himself to the right of the arch, and had heard everything. He was nearly mad with his absurd infatuation for Miss Hollis, that all Simla had been laughing about.

It is a curious thing that, when a man hates or loves beyond reason, he is ready to go beyond reason to gratify his feelings; which he would not do for money or power merely. Depend upon it, Solomon would never have built altars to Ashtaroth and all those ladies with queer names, if there had not been trouble of some kind in his *zenana*, and nowhere else. But this is beside the story. The facts of the case are these: Pack called on Churton next day when Churton was out, left his card, and stole the Bisara of Pooree from its place under the clock on the mantelpiece! Stole it like the thief he was by nature. Three days later all Simla was electrified by the news that Miss Hollis had accepted Pack—the shrivelled rat, Pack! Do you desire clearer evidence than this? The Bisara of Pooree had been stolen, and it worked as it had always done when won by foul means.

There are three or four times in a man's life when he is justified in meddling with other people's affairs to play Providence.

The Man who Knew felt that he was justified; but believing and acting on a belief are quite different things. The insolent satisfaction of Pack as he ambled by the side of Miss Hollis, and Churton's striking release from liver, as soon as the Bisara of Pooree had gone, decided The Man. He explained to Churton, and Churton laughed, because he was not brought up to believe that men on the Government House List steal at least little things. But the miraculous acceptance by Miss Hollis of that tailor, Pack, decided him to take steps on suspicion. He vowed that he only wanted to find out where his ruby-studded silver box had vanished to. You cannot accuse a man on the Government House List of stealing; and if you rifle his room, you are a thief yourself. Churton, prompted by The Man who Knew, decided on burglary. If he found nothing in Pack's room . . . but it is not nice to think of what would have happened in that case.

Pack went to a dance at Benmore—Benmore was Benmore in those days, and not an office and danced fifteen waltzes out of twenty-two with Miss Hollis. Churton and The Man took all the keys that they could lay hands on, and went to Pack's room in the hotel, certain that his servants would be away. Pack was a cheap soul. He had not purchased a decent cash-box to keep his papers in, but one of those native imitations that you buy for ten *rupees*. It opened to any sort of key, and there at the bottom, under Pack's insurance policy, lay the Bisara of Pooree!

Churton called Pack names, put the Bisara of Pooree in his pocket, and went to the dance with The Man. At least, he came in time for supper, and saw the beginning of the end in Miss Hollis's eyes. She was hysterical after supper, and was taken away by her mamma.

At the dance, with the abominable Bisara in his pocket, Churton twisted his foot on one of the steps leading down to the old Rink, and had to be sent home in a 'rickshaw, grumbling. He did not believe in the Bisara of Pooree any the more for this manifestation, but he sought out Pack and called him some ugly names; and 'thief' was the mildest of them. Pack took the names with the nervous smile of a little man who wants both soul and body to resent an insult, and went his way. There was no public scandal.

A week later Pack got his definite dismissal from Miss Hollis. There had been a mistake in the placing of her affections, she said. So he went away to Madras, where he can do no great harm even if he lives to be a colonel.

Churton insisted upon The Man who Knew taking the Bisara of Pooree as a gift. The Man took it, went down to the Cart Road at once, found a cart-pony with a blue bead-necklace, fastened the Bisara of Pooree inside the necklace with a piece of shoe-string and thanked Heaven that he was rid of a danger. Remember, in case you ever find it, that you must not destroy the Bisara of Pooree. I have not time to explain why just now, but the power lies in the little wooden fish. Mister Gubernatis or Max Müller could tell you more about it than I.

You will say that all this story is made up. Very well. If ever you come across a little, silver, ruby-studded box, seven-eighths of an inch long by three-quarters wide, with a dark brown wooden fish, wrapped in gold cloth, inside it, keep it. Keep it for three years, and then you will discover for yourself whether my story is true or false.

Better still, steal it as Pack did, and you will be sorry that you had not killed yourself in the beginning.

Bertban and Bimi

The orang-outang in the big iron cage lashed to the sheep-pen began the discussion. The night was stiflingly hot, and as I and Hans Breitmann, the big-beamed German, passed him, dragging our bedding to the fore-peak of the steamer, he roused himself and chattered obscenely. He had been caught somewhere in the Malayan Archipelago, and was going to England to be exhibited at a shilling a head. For four days he had struggled, yelled, and wrenched at the heavy bars of his prison without ceasing, and had nearly slain a lascar, incautious enough to come within reach of the great hairy paw.

'It would be well for you, mine friend, if you was a liddle seasick,' said Hans Breitmann, pausing by the cage. 'You haf too much ego in your Cosmos.'

The orang-outang's arm slid out negligently from between the bars. No one would have believed that it would make a sudden snakelike rush at the German's breast. The thin silk of the sleeping-suit tore out; Hans stepped back unconcernedly to pluck a banana from a bunch hanging close to one of the boats.

'Too much ego,' said he, peeling the fruit and offering it to the caged devil, who was rending the silk to tatters.

Then we laid out our bedding in the bows among the sleeping lascars, to catch any breeze that the pace of the ship might give us. The sea was like smoky oil, except where it turned to fire under our forefoot and whirled back into the dark in smears of dull flame. There was a thunderstorm some miles away; we could see the glimmer of the lightning. The ship's cow, distressed by the heat and the smell of the ape-beast in the cage, lowed unhappily from time to time in exactly the same key as that in which the look-out man answered the hourly call from the bridge. The trampling tune of the engines was very distinct, and the jarring of the ash-lift, as it was tipped into the sea, hurt the procession of hushed noise. Hans lay down by my side and lighted a goodnight cigar.

This was naturally the beginning of conversation. He owned a voice as soothing as the wash of the sea, and stores of experiences as vast as the sea itself; for his business in life was to wander up and down the world, collecting orchids and wild beasts and ethnological specimens for German and American dealers. I watched the glowing end of his cigar wax and wane in the gloom, as the sentences rose and fell, till I was nearly asleep. The orang-outang, troubled by some dream of the forests of his freedom, began to yell like a soul in purgatory, and to pluck madly at the bars of the cage.

'If he was out now dere would not be much of us left hereabout,' said Hans lazily. 'He screams goot. See, now, how I shall tame him when he stops himself.'

There was a pause in the outcry, and from Hans' mouth came an imitation of a snake's hiss, so perfect that I almost sprang to my feet. The sustained murderous sound ran along the deck, and the wrenching at the bars ceased. The orang-outang was quaking in an ecstasy of pure terror.

'Dot stopped him,' said Hans. 'I learned dot trick in Mogoung Tanjong when I was collecting liddle monkeys for some peoples in Berlin. Efery one in der world is afraid of der monkeys—except der snake. So I blay snake against monkey, and he keep quite still. Dere was too much Ego in his Cosmos. Dot is der soul-custom of monkeys. Are you asleep, or will you listen, and I will tell a dale dot you shall not pelief?'

'There's no tale in the wide world that I can't believe,' I said.

'If you haf learned pelief you haf learned somedings. Now I shall try your pelief. Goot! When I was collecting dose liddle monkeys—it was in '79 or '80, *und* I was in der islands of der Archipelago—over dere in der dark'—he pointed southward to New Guinea generally '*Mein Gott!* I would sooner collect life red devils than liddle monkeys. When dey do not bite off your thumbs dey are always dying from nostalgia—homesick—for dey haf der imperfect soul, which is midway arrested in defelopment *und* too much ego. I was dere for nearly a year, *und* dere I found a man dot was called Bertran. He was a Frenchman, *und* he was *goot* man—naturalist to his bone. Dey said he was an escaped convict, but he was naturalist, *und* dot was enough for me. He would call all der life beasts from *der* forest, *und* dey would come. I said he was St. Francis of Assizi in a new dransmigration produced, *und* he laughed *und* said he haf never preach to der fishes. He sold dem for tripang—*béche-de-mer.*

'*Und* dot man, who was king of beasts-tamer men, he had in der house shust such anoder as dot devil-animal in der cage—a great orang-outang dot thought he was a man. He haf found him when he was a child—der orang-outang—*und* he was child *und* brother *und* *opera comique* all round to Betran. He had his room in dot house—not a cage, but a room—*mit* a bed *und* sheets, *und* he would go to bed *und* get up in der morning *und* smoke his cigar *und* eat his dinner *mit* Bertrau, *und* walk *mit* him hand in hand, which was most horrible.

'*Herr Gott!* I haf seen dot beast throw himself back in his chair *und* laugh when Bertran haf made fun of me. He was *not* a beast; he was a man, *und* he talked to Bertran, *und* Bertran comprehend, for I have seen dem. *Und* he was always politeful to me except when I talk too long to Bertran *und* say nodings at all to him. Den he would pull me away—dis great, dark devil, *mit* his enormous paws—shust as if I was a child. He was not a beast; he was a man. Dis I saw pefore I know him three months, *und* Bertran he haf saw the same; and Bimi, der orang-outang, haf understood us both, *mit* his cigar between his big dog-teeth *und* der blue gum.

'I was dere a year, dere *und* at dere oder islands—somedimes for monkeys *und* somedimes for butterflies *und* orchits. One time Bertran says to me dot he will be married, because he haf found a girl dot was goot, *und* he enquire if this marrying idee was right. I would not say, pecause it was not me dot was going to be married. Den he go off courting der girl—she was a half-caste French girl—very pretty. Haf you got a new light for my cigar? *Ouf!* Very pretty. Only I say, "Haf you thought of Bimi? If he pull me away when I talk to you, what will he do to your wife? He will pull her in pieces. If I was you, Bertran, I would gif my wife for wedding-present der stuff figure of Bimi." By dot time I had learned some dings about der monkey peoples. "Shoot him?" suys Bertran. "He is your beast," I said; "if he was mine he would be shot now!"

'Den I felt at der back of my neck, der fingers of Birni. *Mein Gott!* I tell you dot he talked through dose fingers. It was der deaf-and-dumb alphabet all gomplete. He slide his hairy arm round my neck, *und* he tilt up my chin *und* look into my face, shust to see if I understood his talk so well as he understood mine.

'"See now dere!" says Bertran, "*und* you would shoot him while he is cuddlin' you? Dot is der Tenton ingrate!"

'But I knew dot I had made Bimi a life's-enemy, pecause his fingers haf talk murder through the back of my neck. Next dime I see Bimi dere was a pistol in my belt, *und* he touch it once, *und* I open der breech to show him it was loaded. He haf seen der liddle monkeys killed in der woods: he understood.

'So Bertran he was married, and he forgot clean about Bimi dot was skippin' alone on der beach *mit* der half of a human soul in his belly. I was see him skip, *und* he took a big bough *und* thrash der sand till he haf made a great hole like a grave. So I says to Bertran, "For any sakos. kill Bimi. He is mad *mit* der jealousy."

'Bertran haf said "He is not mad at all. He haf obey *und* lofe my wife, *und* if she speak he will get her slippers," *und* he looked at his wife agross der room. She was a very pretty girl.

'Den I said to him, "Dost dou pretend to know monkeys *und* dis beast dot is lashing himself mad upon der sands, pecause you do not talk to him? Shoot him when he comes to der house, for he haf der light in his eye dot means killing—*und* killing." Bimi come to der house, but dere was no light in his eye. It was all put away, cunning—so cunning *und* he fetch der girl her slippers, *und* Bertran turn to me *und* say, "Dost dou know him in nine months more dan I haf known him in twelve years? Shall a child stab his fader? I haf fed him, *und* he was my child. Do not speak this nonsense to my wife or to me anymore."

'Dot next day Bertran came to my house to help me make some wood cases for der specimens, *und* he tell me dot he haf left his wife a liddle while *mit* Bimi in der garden. Den I finish my cases quick, *und* I say, "Let us go to your houses *und* get a trink." He laugh and say, "Come along, dry mans."

'His wife was not in der garden, *und* Bimi did not come when Bertran called. *Und* his wife did not come when he called, *und* he knocked at her bedroom door *und* dot was shut tight— locked. Den he look at me, *und* his face was white. I broke down der door *mit* my shoulder, *und* der thatch of der roof was torn into a great hole, *und* der sun came in upon der floor. Haf you ever seen paper in der waste-basket, or cards at whist on der table scattered? Dere was no wife dot could be seen. I tell you dere was nodings in dot room dot might be a woman. Dere was stuff on der floor *und* dot was all. I looked at dese things *und* I was very sick; but Bertran looked a liddle longer at what was upon the floor *und* der walls, *und* der hole in der thatch. Den he pegan to laugh, soft *und* low, *und* I knew *und* thank Gott dot he was mad. He nefer cried, he nefer prayed. He stood all still in der doorway *und* laugh to himself. Den he said, "She haf locked herself in dis room, and he haf torn up der thatch. *Fi done!* Dot is so. We will mend der thatch *und* wait for Bimi. He will surely come."

'I tell you we waited ten days in dot house, after der room was made into a room again, *und* once or twice we saw Bimi comin' a liddle way from der woods. He was afraid pecause he haf done wrong. Bertran called him when he was come to look on the tenth day, *und* Bimi come skipping along der beach *und* making noises, *mit* a long piece of black hair in his hands. Den Bertran laugh and say, "*Fi done!*" shust as if it was a glass broken upon der table; *und* Bimi come nearer, *und* Bertran was honey-sweet in his voice *und* laughed to himself. For three days he made love to Bimi, pecause Bimi would not let himself be touched. Den Bimi come to dinner at der same table *mit* us, *und* the hair on his hands was all black *und* thick *mit* mit what had dried on der hands. Bertran gave him *sangaree* till Bimi was drunk and stupid, *und* den—'

Hans paused to puff at his cigar.

'And then?' said I.

'Und den Bertran he kill him *mit* his hands, *und* I go for a walk upon der beach. It was Bertran's own piziness. When I come back der ape he was dead, *und* Bertran he was dying abofe him; but still he laughed liddle *und* low *und* he was quite content. Now you know der formula of der strength of der orang-outang—it is more as seven to one in relation to man. But Bertran, he haf killed Bimi *mit* sooch dings as *Gott* gif him. Dot was der miracle.'

The infernal clamour in the cage recommenced. 'Aha! Dot friend of ours haf still too much ego in his Cosmos. Be quiet, dou!'

Hans hissed long and venomously. We could hear the great beast quaking in his cage.

'But why in the world didn't you help Bertran instead of letting him be killed ?' I asked.

'My friend,' said Hans, composedly stretching himself to slumber,' it was not nice even to mineself dot I should live after I haf seen dot room *mit* der hole in der thatch. *Und* Bertran, he was her husband. Gootnight, *und*—sleep well.'

The Eye of Allah

The cantor of St. Illod's being far too enthusiastic a musician to concern himself with its library, the sub–cantor, who idolised every detail of the work, was tidying up, after two hours' writing and dictation in the scriptorium. The copying-monks handed him in their sheets—it was a plain Four Gospels ordered by an abbot at Evesham—and filed out to vespers. John Otho, better known as John of Burgos, took no heed. He was burnishing a tiny boss of gold in his miniature of the annunciation for his Gospel of St. Luke, which it was hoped that Cardinal Falcodi, the Papal Legate, might later be pleased to accept.

'Break off, John,' said the sub–cantor in an undertone.

'Eh? Gone, have they? I never heard. Hold a minute, Clement.'

The sub–cantor waited patiently. He had known John more than a dozen years, coming and going at St. Illod's, to which monastery John, when abroad, always said he belonged. The claim was gladly allowed, for, more even than other Fitz Othos, he seemed to carry all the arts under his hand, and most of their practical receipts under his hood.

The sub–cantor looked over his shoulder at the pinned-down sheet where the first words of the *Magnificat* were built up in gold washed with red-lac for a background to the Virgin's hardly yet fired halo. She was shown, hands joined in wonder, at a lattice of infinitely intricate arabesque, round the edges of which sprays of orange-bloom seemed to load the blue hot air that carried back over the minute parched landscape in the middle distance.

'You've made her all Jewess,' said the sub–cantor, studying the olive-flushed cheek and the eyes charged with foreknowledge.

'What else was Our Lady?' John slipped out the pins. 'Listen, Clement. If I do not come back, this goes into my Great Luke, whoever finishes it.' He slid the drawing between its guard-papers.

'Then you're for Burgos again—as I heard?'

'In two days. The new Cathedral yonder—but they're slower than the Wrath of God, those masons—is good for the soul.'

'Thy soul?' The sub–cantor seemed doubtful.

'Even mine, by your permission. And down south—on the edge of the conquered countries–Granada way—there's some Moorish diaper-work that's wholesome. It allays vain thought and draws it toward the picture—as you felt, just now, in my annunciation.'

'She—it was very beautiful. No wonder you go. But you'll not forget your absolution, John?'

'Surely.' This was a precaution John no more omitted on the eve of his travels than he did the recutting of the tonsure which he had provided himself with in his youth, somewhere near Ghent. The mark gave him privilege of clergy at a pinch, and a certain consideration on the road always.

'You'll not forget, either, what we need in the scriptorium. There's no more true ultramarine in this world now. They mix it with that German blue. And as for vermilion—'

'I'll do my best always.'

'And Brother Thomas' (this was the *infirmarian* in charge of the monastery hospital) 'he needs—'

'He'll do his own asking. I'll go over his side now, and get me re-tonsured.'

John went down the stairs to the lane that divides the hospital and cook-house from the back-cloisters. While he was being barbered, Brother Thomas (St. Illod's meek but deadly persistent *infirmarian*) gave him a list of drugs that he was to bring back from Spain by hook, crook, or lawful purchase. Here they were

237

surprised by the lame, dark Abbot Stephen, in his fur-lined night-boots. Not that Stephen de Sautre was any spy; but as a young man he had shared an unlucky Crusade, which had ended, after a battle at Mansura, in two years' captivity among the Saracens at Cairo where men learn to walk softly. A fair huntsman and hawker, a reasonable disciplinarian, but a man of science above all, and a Doctor of Medicine under one Ranulphus, Canon of St. Paul's, his heart was more m the monastery's hospital work than its religious. He checked their list interestedly, adding items of his own. After the *infirmarian* had withdrawn, he gave John generous absolution, to cover lapses by the way; for he did not hold with chance—bought Indulgences.

'And what seek you this journey?' he demanded, sitting on the bench beside the mortar and scales in the little warm cell for stored drugs.

'Devils, mostly,' said John, grinning.

'In Spain? Are not Abana and Phar-par—?'

John, to whom men were but matter for drawings, and well-born to boot (since he was a de Sanford on his mother's side), looked the Abbot full in the face and—'Did you find it so?' said he.

'No. They were in Cairo too. But what's your special need of 'em?'

'For my Great Luke. He's the masterhand of all Four when it comes to devils.'

'No wonder. He was a physician. You're not.'

'Heaven forbid! But I'm weary of our Church-pattern devils. They're only apes and goats and poultry conjoined. 'Good enough for plain red-and-black Hells and Judgment Days—but not for me.'

'What makes you so choice in them?'

'Because it stands to reason and art that there are all musters of devils in Hell's dealings. Those Seven, for example, that were haled out of the Magdalene. They'd be she-devils—no kin at all to the beaked and horned and bearded devils-general.'

The abbot laughed.

'And see again! The devil that came out of the dumb man. What use is snout or bill to him? He'd be faceless as a leper. Above all—God send I live to do it!—the devils that entered the Gadarene swine. They'd be—they'd be—I know not yet what they'd be, but they'd be surpassing devils. I'd have 'em diverse as the saints themselves. But now, they're all one pattern, for wall, window, or picture-work.'

'Go on, John. You're deeper in this mystery than I'

'Heaven forbid! But I say there's respect due to devils, damned tho' they be.'

'Dangerous doctrine.'

'My meaning is that if the shape of anything be worth man's thought to picture to man, it's worth his best thought.'

'That's safer. But I'm glad I've given you absolution.'

'There's less risk for a craftsman who deals with the outside shapes of things—for Mother Church's glory.'

'Maybe so, but, John'—the abbot's hand almost touched John's sleeve—'tell me, now, is—is she Moorish or—or Hebrew?'

'She's mine,' John returned.

'Is that enough?'

'I have found it so.'

'Well—ah well! It's out of my jurisdiction, but—how do they look at it down yonder?'

'Oh, they drive nothing to a head in Spain—neither Church nor king, bless them! There's too many Moors and Jews to kill them all, and if they chased 'em away there'd be no trade nor farming. Trust me, in the conquered countries, from Seville to Granada, we live lovingly enough together—Spaniard, Moor, and Jew. Ye see, we ask no questions.'

'Yes—yes,' Stephen sighed. 'And always there's the hope she may be converted.'

'Oh yes, there's always hope.'

The abbot went on into the hospital. It was an easy age before Rome tightened the screw as to clerical connections. If the lady were not too forward, or the son too much his father's beneficiary in ecclesiastical preferments and levies, a good deal was overlooked. But, as the abbot had reason to recall, unions between Christian and *infidel* led to sorrow. None the less, when John with mule, mails, and man, clattered off down the lane for Southampton and the sea, Stephen envied him.

★★★★★★

He was back, twenty months later, in good hard case, and loaded down with fairings. A lump of richest lazuli, a bar of orange-hearted vermilion, and a small packet of dried beetles which make most glorious scarlet, for the sub-cantor. Besides that, a few cubes of milky marble, with yet a pink flush in them, which could be slaked and ground down to incomparable background-stuff. There were quite half the drugs that the abbot and Thomas had demanded, and there was a long deep-red cornelian necklace for the abbot's lady–Anne of Norton. She received it graciously, and asked where John had come by it.

'Near Granada,' he said.

'You left all well there?' Anne asked. (Maybe the abbot had told her something of John's confession.)

'I left all in the hands of God.'

'Ah me! How long since?'

'Four months less eleven days.'

'Were you—with her?'

'In my arms. Childbed.'

'And?'

'The boy too. There is nothing now.'

Anne of Norton caught her breath.

'I think you'll be glad of that,' she said after a while.

'Give me time, and maybe I'll compass it. But not now.'

'You have your handiwork and your art, and—John—remember there's no jealousy in the grave.'

'Ye-es! I have my art, and Heaven knows I'm jealous of none.'

'Thank God for that at least,' said Anne of Norton, the always ailing woman who followed the abbot with her sunk eyes. 'And be sure I shall treasure this'—she touched the beads—'as long as I shall live.'

240

'I brought—trusted—it to you for that,' he replied, and took leave. When she told the abbot how she had come by it, he said nothing, but as he and Thomas were storing the drugs that John handed over in the cell which backs on to the hospital kitchen-chimney, he observed, of a cake of dried poppy juice: 'This has power to cut off all pain from a man's body.'

'I have seen it,' said John.

'But for pain of the soul there is, outside God's Grace, but one drug; and that is a man's craft, learning, or other helpful motion of his own mind.'

'That is coming to me, too,' was the answer.

John spent the next fair May day out in the woods with the monastery swineherd and all the porkers; and returned loaded with flowers and sprays of spring, to his own carefully kept place in the north bay of the scriptorium. There, with his travelling sketch-books under his left elbow, he sunk himself past all recollections in his Great Luke.

Brother Martin, senior copyist (who spoke about once a fortnight), ventured to ask, later, how the work was going.

'All here!' John tapped his forehead with his pencil. 'It has been only waiting these months to—ah God!—be born. Are ye free of your plain-copying, Martin?'

Brother Martin nodded. It was his pride that John of Burgos turned to him, in spite of his seventy years, for really good page-work.

'Then see!' John laid out a new *vellum*—thin but flawless. 'There's no better than this sheet from here to Paris. Yes! Smell it if you choose. Wherefore—give me the compasses and I'll set it out for you—if ye make one letter lighter or darker than its next, I'll stick ye like a pig.'

'Never, John!' The old man beamed happily. 'But I will! Now, follow! Here and here, as I prick, and in script of just this height to the hair's-breadth, yell scribe the thirty-first and thirty-second verses of Eighth Luke.'

'Yes, the Gadarene Swine! "*And they besought him that he would not command them to go out into the abyss. And there was a herd of many swine*'——Brother Martin naturally knew all the Gospels by heart.

'Just so! Down to "*and he suffered them.*" Take your time to it. My Magdalene has to come off my heart first.'

Brother Martin achieved the work so perfectly that John stole some soft sweetmeats from the abbot's kitchen for his reward. The old man ate them; then repented; then confessed and insisted on penance. At which, the abbot, knowing there was but one way to reach the real sinner, set him a book called *De Virtutibus Herbarum* to fair-copy. St. Illod's had borrowed it from the gloomy Cistercians, who do not hold with pretty things, and the crabbed text kept Martin busy just when John wanted him for some rather specially spaced letterings.

'See now,' said the sub–cantor improvingly. 'You should not do such things, John. Here's Brother Martin on penance for your sake—'

'No—for my Great Luke. But I've paid the abbot's cook. I've drawn him till his own scullions cannot keep straight-faced. He'll not tell again.'

'Unkindly done! And you're out of favour with the abbot too. He's made no sign to you since you came back—never asked you to high table.'

'I've been busy. Having eyes in his head, Stephen knew it. Clement, there's no librarian from Durham to Torre fit to clean up after you.'

The sub–cantor stood on guard; he knew where John's compliments generally ended.

'But outside the scriptorium—'

'Where I never go.' The sub–cantor had been excused even digging in the garden, lest it should mar his wonderful book-binding hands.

'In all things outside the scriptorium you are the master-fool of *Christendie*. Take it from me, Clement. I've met many.'

'I take everything from you,' Clement smiled benignly. 'You use me worse than a singing-boy.

They could hear one of that suffering breed in the cloister

below, squalling as the cantor pulled his hair.

'God love you! So I do! But have you ever thought how I lie and steal daily on my travels—yes, and for aught you know, murder—to fetch you colours and earths?'

'True,' said just and conscience-stricken Clement. 'I have often thought that were I in the world—which God forbid!—I might be a strong thief in some matters.'

Even Brother Martin, bent above his loathed *De Virtutibus*, laughed.

★★★★★★

But about mid-summer, Thomas the *infirmarian* conveyed to John the abbot's invitation to supper in his house that night, with the request that he would bring with him anything that he had done for his Great Luke.

'What's toward?' said John, who had been wholly shut up in his work.

'Only one of his "wisdom" dinners. You've sat at a few since you were a man.'

'True: and mostly good. How would Stephen have us—?'

'Gown and hood over all. There will be a doctor from Salerno—one Roger, an Italian. Wise and famous with the knife on the body. He's been in the infirmary some ten days, helping me—even me!'

"Never heard the name. But our Stephen's *physicus* before *sacerdos*, always.'

'And his lady has a sickness of some time. Roger came hither in chief because of her.'

'Did he? Now I think of it, I have not seen the Lady Anne for a while.'

'Ye've seen nothing for a long while. She has been housed near a month—they have to carry her abroad now.'

'So bad as that, then?'

'Roger of Salerno will not yet say what he thinks. But—'

'God pity Stephen! . . . Who else at table, besides thee?'

'An Oxford friar. Roger is his name also. A learned and famous philosopher. And he holds his liquor too, valiantly.'

'Three doctors—counting Stephen. I've always found that means two atheists.'

Thomas looked uneasily down his nose. 'That's a wicked proverb,' he stammered. 'You should not use it.'

'Hoh! Never come you the monk over me, Thomas! You've been *infirmarian* at St. Illod's eleven years—and a lay-brother still. Why have you never taken orders, all this while?'

'I—I am not worthy.'

'Ten times worthier than that new fat swine—Henry Who's-his-name—that takes the Infirmary Masses. He bullocks in with the Viaticum, under your nose, when a sick man's only faint from being bled. So the man dies—of pure fear. Ye know it! I've watched your face at such times. Take orders, Didymus. You'll have a little more medicine and a little less Mass with your sick then; and they'll live longer.'

'I am unworthy—unworthy,' Thomas repeated pitifully.

'Not you—but—to your own master you stand or fall. And now that my work releases me for awhile, I'll drink with any philosopher out of any school. And, Thomas,' he coaxed, 'a hot bath for me in the infirmary before vespers.'

★★★★★★

When the abbot's perfectly cooked and served meal had ended, and the deep-fringed naperies were removed, and the prior had sent in the keys with word that all was fast in the monastery, and the keys had been duly returned with the word, 'Make it so till Prime,' the abbot and his guests went out to cool themselves in an upper cloister that took them, by way of the leads, to the South Choir side of the triforium. The summer sun was still strong, for it was barely six o'clock, but the abbey church, of course, lay in her wonted darkness. Lights were being lit for choir-practice thirty feet below.

'Our cantor gives them no rest,' the abbot whispered. 'Stand by this pillar and we'll hear what he's driving them at now.'

'Remember, all!' the cantor's hard voice came up. 'This is the soul of Bernard himself, attacking our evil world. Take it quicker than yesterday, and throw all your words clean-bitten from you.

In the loft there! Begin!'

The organ broke out for an instant, alone and raging. Then the voices crashed together into that first fierce line of the '*De Contemptu Mundi.*'

'*Hora novissima—tempora pessima*'—a dead pause till the assenting sound broke, like a sob, out of the darkness, and one boy's voice, clearer than silver trumpets, returned the long-drawn *vigilemus.*

'*Ecce minaciter, imminet Arbiter*' (organ and voices were leashed together in terror and warning, breaking away liquidly to the '*ille supremus*'). Then the tone-colours shifted for the prelude to '*Imminet, imminet, ut mala terminet—*'

'Stop! Again!' cried the cantor; and gave his reasons a little more roundly than was natural at choir-practice.

'Ah! Pity o' man's vanity! He's guessed we are here. Come away!' said the abbot. Anne of Norton, in her carried chair, had been listening too, further along the dark triforium, with Roger of Salerno. John heard her sob. On the way back, he asked Thomas how her health stood. Before Thomas could reply the sharp-featured Italian doctor pushed between them. 'Following on our talk together, I judged it best to tell her,' said he to Thomas.

'What?' John asked simply enough.

'What she knew already.' Roger of Salerno launched into a Greek quotation to the effect that every woman knows all about everything.

'I have no Greek,' said John stiffly. Roger of Salerno had been giving them a good deal of it, at dinner.

'Then I'll come to you in Latin. Ovid hath it neatly. "*Utque malum late solet immedicabile cancer—*" but doubtless you know the rest, worthy Sir.'

'Alas! My school-Latin's but what I've gathered by the way from fools professing to heal sick women. "*Hocus-pocus—*" but doubtless you know the rest, worthy Sir.'

Roger of Salerno was quite quiet till they regained the dining-room, where the fire had been comforted and the dates, raisins, ginger, figs, and cinnamon-scented sweetmeats set out, with the choicer wines, on the after-table. The abbot seated himself, drew off his ring, dropped it, that all might hear the tinkle, into an empty silver cup, stretched his feet towards the hearth, and looked at the great gilt and carved rose in the barrel-roof. The silence that keeps from *compline* to *matins* had closed on their world. The bull-necked friar watched a ray of sunlight split itself into colours on the rim of a crystal salt-cellar; Roger of Salerno had re-opened some discussion with Brother Thomas on a type of spotted fever that was baffling them both in England and abroad; John took note of the keen profile, and—it might serve as a note for the Great Luke—his hand moved to his bosom. The abbot saw, and nodded permission. John whipped out silver-point and sketch-book.

'Nay—modesty is good enough—but deliver your own opinion,' the Italian was urging the infirmarian. Out of courtesy to the foreigner nearly all the talk was in table-Latin; more formal and more copious than monk's patter. Thomas began with his meek stammer.

'I confess myself at a loss for the cause of the fever unless—as Varro saith in his *De Re Rustica*—certain small animals which the eye cannot follow enter the body by the nose and mouth, and set up grave diseases. On the other hand, this is not in Scripture.'

Roger of Salerno hunched head and shoulders like an angry cat. 'Always that!' he said, and John snatched down the twist of the thin lips.

'Never at rest, John.' The abbot smiled at the artist. 'You should break off every two hours for prayers, as we do. St. Benedict was no fool. Two hours is all that a man can carry the edge of his eye or hand.'

'For copyists—yes. Brother Martin is not sure after one hour. But when a man's work takes him, he must go on till it lets him go.'

'Yes, that is the demon of Socrates,' the friar from Oxford rumbled above his cup.

'The doctrine leans toward presumption,' said the abbot. 'Remember, "Shall mortal man be more just than his Maker?"'

'There is no danger of justice'; the friar spoke bitterly. 'But at least man might be suffered to go forward in his art or his thought. Yet if Mother Church sees or hears him move anyward, what says she? "No!" Always "No."'

'But if the little animals of Varro be invisible'—this was Roger of Salerno to Thomas—'how are we any nearer to a cure?'

'By experiment'—the friar wheeled round on them suddenly. 'By reason and experiment. The one is useless without the other. But Mother Church—'

'Ay!' Roger de Salerno dashed at the fresh bait like a pike. 'Listen, Sirs. Her bishops—our princes—strew our roads in Italy with carcasses that they make for their pleasure or wrath. Beautiful corpses! Yet if I—if we doctors—so much as raise the skin of one of them to look at God's fabric beneath, what says Mother Church? "Sacrilege! Stick to your pigs and dogs, or you burn!"'

'And not Mother Church only!' the friar chimed in. 'Every way we are barred—barred by the words of some man, dead a thousand years, which are held final. Who is any son of Adam that his one say-so should close a door towards truth? I would not except even Peter Peregrinus, my own great teacher.'

'Nor I Paul of Aegina,' Roger of Salerno cried. 'Listen, Sirs! Here is a case to the very point. *Apuleius affirmeth, if a man eat fasting of the juice of the cut-leaved buttercup-sceleratus* we call it, which means "rascally"'—this with a condescending nod towards John—'*his soul will leave his body laughing*. Now this is the lie more dangerous than truth, since truth of a sort is in it.'

'He's away!' whispered the abbot despairingly.

'For the juice of that herb, I know by experiment, burns, blisters, and wries the mouth. I know also the rictus, or pseudo-laughter, on the face of such as have perished by the strong poisons of herbs allied to this *ranunculus*. Certainly that spasm resembles laughter. It seems then, in my judgment, that Apuleius, having seen the body of one thus poisoned, went off at score and wrote that the man died laughing.'

'Neither staying to observe, nor to confirm observation by

experiment,' added the friar, frowning.

Stephen the abbot cocked an eyebrow toward John.

'How think you?' said he.

'I'm no doctor,' John returned, 'but I'd say Apuleius in all these years might have been betrayed by his copyists. They take short-cuts to save 'emselves trouble. Put case that Apuleius wrote the soul seems to leave the body laughing, after this poison. There's not three copyists in five (my judgment) would not leave out the "seems to." For who'd question Apuleius? If it seemed so to him, so it must be. Otherwise any child knows cut-leaved buttercup.'

'Have you knowledge of herbs?' Roger of Salerno asked curtly.

'Only that, when I was a boy in convent, I've made tetters round my mouth and on my neck with buttercup juice, to save going to prayer o' cold nights.'

'Ah!' said Roger. 'I profess no knowledge of tricks.' He turned aside, stiffly.

'No matter! Now for your own tricks, John,' the tactful abbot broke in. 'You shall show the doctors your Magdalene and your Gadarene Swine and the devils.'

'Devils? Devils? I have produced devils by means of drugs; and have abolished them by the same means. Whether devils be external to mankind or immanent, I have not yet pronounced.' Roger of Salerno was still angry.

'Ye dare not,' snapped the friar from Oxford. 'Mother Church makes Her own devils.'

'Not wholly! Our John has come back from Spain with brand-new ones.' Abbot Stephen took the vellum handed to him, and laid it tenderly on the table. They gathered to look. The Magdalene was drawn in palest, almost transparent, *grisaille*, against a raging, swaying background of woman-faced devils, each broke to and by her special sin, and each, one could see, frenziedly straining against the Power that compelled her.

'I've never seen the like of this grey shadowwork,' said the abbot. 'How came you by it?'

'*Non nobis!* It came to me,' said John, not knowing he was a generation or so ahead of his time in the use of that medium.

'Why is she so pale?' the friar demanded.

'Evil has all come out of her—she'd take any colour now.'

'Ay, like light through glass. I see.'

Roger of Salerno was looking in silence—his nose nearer and nearer the page. 'It is so,' he pronounced finally. 'Thus it is in epilepsy—mouth, eyes, and forehead—even to the droop of her wrist there. Every sign of it! She will need restoratives, that woman, and, afterwards, sleep natural. No poppy juice, or she will vomit on her waking. And thereafter—but I am not in my schools.' He drew himself up. 'Sir,' said he, 'you should be of Our calling. For, by the Snakes of Aesculapius, you see!'

The two struck hands as equals.

'And how think you of the Seven Devils?' the Abbot went on.

These melted into convoluted flower- or flame-like bodies, ranging in colour from phosphorescent green to the black purple of outworn iniquity, whose hearts could be traced beating through their substance. But, for sign of hope and the sane workings of life, to be regained, the deep border was of conventionalised spring flowers and birds, all crowned by a kingfisher in haste, atilt through a clump of yellow iris.

Roger of Salerno identified the herbs and spoke largely of their virtues.

'And now, the Gadarene Swine,' said Stephen. John laid the picture on the table.

Here were devils dishoused, in dread of being abolished to the Void, huddling and hurtling together to force lodgement by every opening into the brute bodies offered. Some of the swine fought the invasion, foaming and jerking; some were surrendering to it, sleepily, as to a luxurious back-scratching; others, wholly possessed, whirled off in bucking droves for the lake beneath. In one corner the freed man stretched out his limbs all restored to his control, and Our Lord, seated, looked at him as questioning what he would make of his deliverance.

'Devils indeed!' was the friar's comment. 'But wholly a new

249

sort.'

Some devils were mere lumps, with lobes and protuberances—a hint of a fiend's face peering through jelly-like walls. And there was a family of impatient, globular devillings who had burst open the belly of their smirking parent, and were revolving desperately toward their prey. Others patterned themselves into rods, chains and ladders, single or conjoined, round the throat and jaws of a shrieking sow, from whose ear emerged the lashing, glassy tail of a devil that had made good his refuge. And there were granulated and conglomerate devils, mixed up with the foam and slaver where the attack was fiercest. Thence the eye carried on to the insanely active backs of the downward-racing swine, the swineherd's aghast face, and his dog's terror.

Said Roger of Salerno, 'I pronounce that these were begotten of drugs. They stand outside the rational mind.'

'Not these,' said Thomas the *infirmarian*, who as a servant of the monastery should have asked his abbot's leave to speak. 'Not these—look!—in the bordure.'

The border to the picture was a diaper of irregular but balanced compartments or cellules, where sat, swam, or weltered, devils in blank, so to say—things as yet uninspired by Evil—indifferent, but lawlessly outside imagination. Their shapes resembled, again, ladders, chains, scourges, diamonds, aborted buds, or gravid phosphorescent globes—some well-nigh starlike.

Roger of Salerno compared them to the obsessions of a churchman's mind.

'Malignant?' the friar from Oxford questioned.

'"*Count everything unknown for horrible,*"' Roger quoted with scorn.

'Not I. But they are marvellous—marvellous. I think—'

The friar drew back. Thomas edged in to see better, and half opened his mouth.

'Speak,' said Stephen, who had been watching him. 'We are all in a sort doctors here.'

'I would say then'—Thomas rushed at it as one putting out his life's belief at the stake—'that these lower shapes in the bordure may not be so much hellish and malignant as models and patterns upon which John has tricked out and embellished his proper devils among the swine above there!'

'And that would signify?' said Roger of Salerno sharply.

'In my poor judgment, that he may have seen such shapes—without help of drugs.'

'Now who—who,' said John of Burgos, after a round and unregarded oath, 'has made thee so wise of a sudden, my doubter?'

'I wise? God forbid! Only John, remember—one winter six years ago—the snow-flakes melting on your sleeve at the cook-house-door. You showed me them through a little crystal, that made small things larger.'

'Yes. The Moors call such a glass the Eye of *Allah*,' John confirmed.

'You showed me them melting—six-sided. You called them, then, your patterns.'

'True. Snow-flakes melt six-sided. I have used them for diaper-work often.'

'Melting snow-flakes as seen through a glass? By art optical?' the friar asked.

'Art optical? I have never heard!' Roger of Salerno cried.

'John,' said the Abbot of St. Illod's commandingly, 'was it—is it so?'

'In some sort,' John replied, 'Thomas has the right of it. Those shapes in the bordure were my workshop-patterns for the devils above. In my craft, Salerno, we dare not drug. It kills hand and eye. My shapes are to be seen honestly, in nature.'

The abbot drew a bowl of rose-water towards him. 'When I was prisoner with—with the Saracens after Mansura,' he began, turning up the fold of his long sleeve, 'there were certain magicians—physicians—who could show—' he dipped his third finger delicately in the water—'all the firmament of Hell, as it were, in' he shook off one drop from his polished nail on to the polished table—'even such a *supernaculum* as this.'

'But it must be foul water—not clean,' said John.

251

'Show us then—all—all,' said Stephen. 'I would make sure—once more.' The abbot's voice was official.

John drew from his bosom a stamped leather box, some six or eight inches long, wherein, bedded on faded velvet, lay what looked like silver-bound compasses of old box-wood, with a screw at the head which opened or closed the legs to minute fractions. The legs terminated, not in points, but spoon-shapedly, one spatula pierced with a metal-lined hole less than a quarter of an inch across, the other with a half-inch hole. Into this latter John, after carefully wiping with a silk rag, slipped a metal cylinder that carried glass or crystal, it seemed, at each end.

'Ah! Art optic!' said the friar. 'But what is that beneath it?'

It was a small swivelling sheet of polished silver no bigger than a florin, which caught the light and concentrated it on the lesser hole. John adjusted it without the friar's proffered help.

'And now to find a drop of water,' said he, picking up a small brush.

'Come to my upper cloister. The sun is on the leads still,' said the abbot, rising.

They followed him there. Half-way along, a drip from a gutter had made a greenish puddle in a worn stone. Very carefully, John dropped a drop of it into the smaller hole of the compass leg, and, steadying the apparatus on a coping, worked the screw m the compass joint, screwed the cylinder, and swung the swivel of the mirror till he was satisfied.

'Good!' He peered through the thing. 'My Shapes are all here. Now look, Father! If they do not meet your eye at first, turn this nicked edge here, left—or right-handed.'

'I have not forgotten,' said the abbot, taking his place. 'Yes! They are here—as they were in my time—my time past. There is no end to them, I was told . . . There is no end!'

'The light will go. Oh, let me look! Suffer me to see, also!' the friar pleaded, almost shouldering Stephen from the eye-piece. The abbot gave way. His eyes were on time past. But the friar, instead of looking, turned the apparatus in his capable hands.

'Nay, nay,' John interrupted, for the man was already fiddling at the screws. 'Let the doctor see.'

Roger of Salerno looked, minute after minute. John saw his blue-veined cheek-bones turn white. He stepped back at last, as though stricken.

'It is a new world—a new world, and—Oh, God Unjust!—I am old!'

'And now Thomas,' Stephen ordered.

John manipulated the tube for the *infirmarian*, whose hands shook, and he too looked long. 'It is Life,' he said presently in a breaking voice. 'No Hell! Life created and rejoicing—the work of the Creator. They live, even as I have dreamed. Then it was no sin for me to dream. No sin—O God—no sin!'

He flung himself on his knees and began hysterically the *Benedicite omnia* opera.

'And now I will see how it is actuated,' said the friar from Oxford, thrusting forward again.

'Bring it within. The place is all eyes and ears,' said Stephen.

They walked quietly back along the leads, three English counties laid out in evening sunshine around them; church upon church, monastery upon monastery, cell after cell, and the bulk of a vast cathedral moored on the edge of the banked shoals of sunset.

When they were at the after-table once more they sat down, all except the friar, who went to the window and huddled bat-like over the thing. 'I see! I see!' he was repeating to himself.

'He'll not hurt it,' said John. But the abbot, staring in front of him, like Roger of Salerno, did not hear. The *infirmarian's* head was on the table between his shaking arms.

John reached for a cup of wine.

'It was shown to me,' the abbot was speaking to himself, 'in Cairo, that man stands ever between two infinities—of greatness and littleness. Therefore, there is no end—either to life—or—'

'And I stand on the edge of the grave,' snarled Roger of Salerno. 'Who pities me?'

'Hush!' said Thomas the *infirmarian*. 'The little creatures shall be sanctified—sanctified to the service of His sick.'

'What need?' John of Burgos wiped his lips. 'It shows no more than the shapes of things. It gives good pictures. I had it at Granada. It was brought from the East, they told me.'

Roger of Salerno laughed with an old man's malice. 'What of Mother Church? Most Holy Mother Church? If it comes to Her ears that we have spied into Her Hell without Her leave, where do we stand?'

'At the stake,' said the Abbot of St. Illod's, and, raising his voice a trifle 'You hear that? Roger Bacon, heard you that?'

The friar turned from the window, clutching the compasses tighter.

'No, no!' he appealed. 'Not with Falcodi—not with our English-hearted Foulkes made Pope. He's wise—he's learned. He reads what I have put forth. Foulkes would never suffer it.'

'"Holy Pope is one thing, Holy Church another,"' Roger quoted.

'But I—I can bear witness it is no art magic,' the friar went on. 'Nothing is it, except art optical—wisdom after trial and experiment, mark you. I can prove it, and—my name weighs with men who dare think.'

'Find them!' croaked Roger of Salerno. 'Five or six in all the world. That makes less than fifty pounds by weight of ashes at the stake. I have watched such men—reduced.'

'I will not give this up!' The friar's voice cracked in passion and despair. 'It would be to sin against the Light.'

'No, no! Let us—let us sanctify the little animals of Varro,' said Thomas.

Stephen leaned forward, fished his ring out of the cup, and slipped it on his finger. 'My sons,' said he, 'we have seen what we have seen.'

'That it is no magic but simple art,' the friar persisted.

'"Avails nothing. In the eyes of Mother Church we have seen more than is permitted to man.'

'But it was life—created and rejoicing,' said Thomas.

'To look into Hell as we shall be judged—as we shall be proved—to have looked, is for priests only.'

'Or green-sick virgins on the road to sainthood who, for cause any midwife could give you—'

The abbot's half-lifted hand checked Roger of Salerno's outpouring.

'Nor may even priests see more in Hell than Church knows to be there. John, there is respect due to Church as well as to devils.'

'My trade's the outside of things,' said John quietly. 'I have my patterns.'

'But you may need to look again for more,' the friar said.

'In my craft, a thing done is done with. We go on to new shapes after that.'

'And if we trespass beyond bounds, even in thought, we lie open to the judgment of the Church,' the abbot continued.

'But thou knowest—knowest!' Roger of Salerno had returned to the attack. 'Here's all the world in darkness concerning the causes of things—from the fever across the lane to thy Lady's—throe own Lady's—eating malady. Think!'

'I have thought upon it, Salerno! I have thought indeed.'

Thomas the *infirmarian* lifted his head again; and this time he did not stammer at all. 'As in the water, so in the blood must they rage and war with each other! I have dreamed these ten years—I thought it was a sin—but my dreams and Varro's are true! Think on it again! Here's the Light under our very hand!'

'Quench it! You'd no more stand to roasting than any other. I'll give you the case as Church—as I myself—would frame it. Our John here returns from the Moors, and shows us a hell of devils contending in the compass of one drop of water. Magic past clearance! You can hear the faggots crackle.'

'But thou knowest! Thou hast seen it all before! For man's poor sake! For old friendship's sake—Stephen!' The friar was trying to stuff the compasses into his bosom as he appealed.

'What Stephen de Sautre knows, you his friends know also. I would have you, now, obey the Abbot of St. Illod's. Give to me!' He held out his ringed hand.

'May I—may John here—not even make a drawing of one—

one screw?' said the broken friar, in spite of himself.

'Nowise!' Stephen took it over. 'Your dagger, John. Sheathed will serve.'

He unscrewed the metal cylinder, laid it on the table, and with the dagger's hilt smashed some crystal to sparkling dust which he swept into a scooped hand and cast behind the hearth.

'It would seem,' said he, 'the choice lies between two sins. To deny the world a Light which is under our hand, or to enlighten the world before her time. What you have seen, I saw long since among the physicians at Cairo. And I know what doctrine they drew from it. Hast thou dreamed, Thomas? I also—with fuller knowledge. But this birth, my sons, is untimely. It will be but the mother of more death, more torture, more division, and greater darkness in this dark age. Therefore I, who know both my world and the Church, take this choice on my conscience. Go! It is finished.'

He thrust the wooden part of the compasses deep among the beech logs till all was burned.

The Mark of the Beast

Your Gods and my Gods—do you or I know which are the
stronger?   Native Proverb.

East of Suez, some hold, the direct control of Providence
ceases; Man being there handed over to the power of the Gods
and Devils of Asia, and the Church of England Providence only
exercising an occasional and modified supervision in the case of
Englishmen.

This theory accounts for some of the more unnecessary horrors of life in India: it may be stretched to explain my story.

My friend Strickland of the police, who knows as much of
natives of India as is good for any man, can bear witness to the
facts of the case. Dumoise, our doctor, also saw what Strickland
and I saw. The inference which he drew from the evidence was
entirely incorrect. He is dead now; he died in a rather curious
manner, which has been elsewhere described.

When Fleete came to India he owned a little money and
some land in the Himalayas, near a place called Dharmsala. Both
properties had been left him by an uncle, and he came out to
finance them. He was a big, heavy, genial, and inoffensive man.
His knowledge of natives was, of course, limited, and he complained of the difficulties of the language.

He rode in from his place in the hills to spend New Year in
the station, and he stayed with Strickland. On New Year's Eve
there was a big dinner at the club, and the night was excus-
ably wet. When men foregather from the uttermost ends of the
empire, they have a right to be riotous. The Frontier had sent

down a contingent o' Catch-'em-Alive-O's who had not seen twenty white faces for a year, and were used to ride fifteen miles to dinner at the next fort at the risk of a Khyberee bullet where their drinks should lie. They profited by their new security, for they tried to play pool with a curled-up hedgehog found in the garden, and one of them carried the marker round the room in his teeth.

Half a dozen planters had come in from the south and were talking 'horse' to the biggest liar in Asia, who was trying to cap all their stories at once. Everybody was there, and there was a general closing up of ranks and taking stock of our losses in dead or disabled that had fallen during the past year. It was a very wet night, and I remember that we sang 'Auld Lang Syne' with our feet in the Polo Championship Cup, and our heads among the stars, and swore that we were all dear friends. Then some of us went away and annexed Burma, and some tried to open up the Soudan and were opened up by Fuzzies in that cruel scrub out-side Suakim, and some found stars and medals, and some were married, which was bad, and some did other things which were worse, and the others of us stayed in our chains and strove to make money on insufficient experiences.

Fleete began the night with sherry and bitters, drank cham-pagne steadily up to dessert, then raw, rasping Capri with all the strength of whisky, took Benedictine with his coffee, four or five whiskies and sodas to improve his pool strokes, beer and bones at half-past two, winding up with old brandy. Consequently, when he came out, at half-past three in the morning, into fourteen degrees of frost, he was very angry with his horse for coughing, and tried to leapfrog into the saddle. The horse broke away and went to his stables; so Strickland and I formed a Guard of Dis-honour to take Fleete home.

Our road lay through the bazaar, close to a little temple of Hanuman, the Monkey-god, who is a leading divinity worthy of respect. All gods have good points, just as have all priests. Person-ally, I attach much importance to Hanuman, and am kind to his people—the great gray apes of the hills. One never knows when one may want a friend.

There was a light in the temple, and as we passed, we could hear voices of men chanting hymns. In a native temple, the priests rise at all hours of the night to do honour to their god. Before we could stop him, Fleete dashed up the steps, patted two priests on the back, and was gravely grinding the ashes of his cigar-butt into the forehead of the red, stone image of Hanuman. Strickland tried to drag him out, but he sat down and said solemnly:

'Shee that? 'Mark of the B—beasht! *I* made it. Ishn't it fine?'

In half a minute the temple was alive and noisy, and Strickland, who knew what came of polluting gods, said that things might occur. He, by virtue of his official position, long residence in the country, and weakness for going among the natives, was known to the priests and he felt unhappy. Fleete sat on the ground and refused to move. He said that 'good old Hanuman' made a very soft pillow.

Then, without any warning, a Silver Man came out of a recess behind the image of the god. He was perfectly naked in that bitter, bitter cold, and his body shone like frosted silver, for he was what the Bible calls 'a leper as white as snow.' Also he had no face, because he was a leper of some years' standing, and his disease was heavy upon him. We two stooped to haul Fleete up, and the temple was filling and filling with folk who seemed to spring from the earth, when the Silver Man ran in under our arms, making a noise exactly like the mewing of an otter, caught Fleete round the body and dropped his head on Fleete's breast before we could wrench him away. Then he retired to a corner and sat mewing while the crowd blocked all the doors.

The priests were very angry until the Silver Man touched Fleete. That nuzzling seemed to sober them.

At the end of a few minutes' silence one of the priests came to Strickland and said, in perfect English, 'Take your friend away. He has done with Hanuman, but Hanuman has not done with him.' The crowd gave room and we carried Fleete into the road.

Strickland was very angry. He said that we might all three have been knifed, and that Fleete should thank his stars that he had escaped without injury.

Fleete thanked no one. He said that he wanted to go to bed. He was gorgeously drunk.

We moved on, Strickland silent and wrathful, until Fleete was taken with violent shivering fits and sweating. He said that the smells of the bazaar were overpowering, and he wondered why slaughter-houses were permitted so near English residences. 'Can't you smell the blood?' said Fleete.

We put him to bed at last, just as the dawn was breaking, and Strickland invited me to have another whisky and soda. While we were drinking he talked of the trouble in the temple, and admitted that it baffled him completely. Strickland hates being mystified by natives, because his business in life is to overmatch them with their own weapons. He has not yet succeeded in doing this, but in fifteen or twenty years he will have made some small progress.

'They should have mauled us,' he said, 'instead of mewing at us. I wonder what they meant. I don't like it one little bit.'

I said that the managing committee of the temple would in all probability bring a criminal action against us for insulting their religion. There was a section of the Indian Penal Code which exactly met Fleete's offence. Strickland said he only hoped and prayed that they would do this. Before I left I looked into Fleete's room, and saw him lying on his right side, scratching his left breast. Then I went to bed cold, depressed, and unhappy, at seven o'clock in the morning.

At one o'clock I rode over to Strickland's house to inquire after Fleete's head. I imagined that it would be a sore one. Fleete was breakfasting and seemed unwell. His temper was gone, for he was abusing the cook for not supplying him with an underdone chop. A man who can eat raw meat after a wet night is a curiosity. I told Fleete this and he laughed.

'You breed queer mosquitoes in these parts,' he said. 'I've been bitten to pieces, but only in one place.'

' Let's have a look at the bite,' said Strickland, 'it may have gone down since this morning.'

While the chops were being cooked, Fleete opened his shirt and showed us, just over his left breast, a mark, the perfect double of the black rosettes—the five or six irregular blotches arranged in a circle—on a leopard's hide. Strickland looked and said, 'It was only pink this morning It's grown black now.'

Fleete ran to a glass.

'By Jove!' he said, 'this is nasty. What is it?'

We could not answer. Here the chops came in, all red and juicy, and Fleete bolted three in a most offensive manner. He ate on his right grinders only, and threw his head over his right shoulder as he snapped the meat. When he had finished, it struck him that he had been behaving strangely, for he said apologetically, ' I don't think I ever felt so hungry in my life. I've bolted like an ostrich.'

After breakfast Strickland said to me, 'Don't go. Stay here, and stay for the night.'

Seeing that my house was not three miles from Strickland's, this request was absurd. But Strickland insisted, and was going to say something when Fleete interrupted by declaring in a shamefaced way that he felt hungry again. Strickland sent a man to my house to fetch over my bedding and a horse, and we three went down to Strickland's stables to pass the hours until it was time to go out for a ride. The man who has a weakness for horses never wearies of inspecting them; and when two men are killing time in this way they gather knowledge and lies the one from the other.

There were five horses in the stables, and I shall never forget the scene us we tried to look them over. They seemed to have gone mad. They reared and screamed and nearly tore up their pickets; they sweated and shivered and lathered and were distraught with fear. Strickland's horses used to know him as well as his dogs; which made the matter more curious. We left the stable for fear of the brutes throwing themselves in their panic. Then Strickland turned back and called me. The horses were still frightened, but they let us 'gentle' and make much of them, and put their heads in our bosoms.

'They aren't afraid of *us*,' said Strickland. 'D'you know, I'd give three months' pay if Outrage here could talk.'

But Outrage was dumb, and could only cuddle up to his master and blow out his nostrils, as is the custom of horses when they wish to explain things but can't. Fleete came up when we were in the stalls, and as soon as the horses saw him, their fright broke out afresh. It was all that we could do to escape from the place unkicked. Strickland said, 'They don't seem to love you, Fleete.'

'Nonsense,' said Fleete; 'my mare will follow me like a dog.' He went to her; she was in a loose-box; but as he slipped the bars she plunged, knocked him down, and broke away into the garden. I laughed, but Strickland was not amused. He took his moustache in both fists and pulled at it till it nearly came out. Fleete, instead of going off to chase his property, yawned, saying that he felt sleepy. He went to the house to lie down, which was a foolish way of spending New Year's Day.

Strickland sat with me in the stables and asked if I had noticed anything peculiar in Fleete's manner. I said that he ate his food like a beast; but that this might have been the result of living alone in the hills out of the reach of society as refined and elevating as ours for instance. Strickland was not amused. I do not think that he listened to me, for his next, sentence referred to the mark on Fleete's breast, and I said that it might have been caused by blister-flies, or that it was possibly a birthmark newly born and now visible for the first time. We both agreed that it was unpleasant to look at, and Strickland found occasion to say that I was a fool.

'I can't tell you what I think now,' said he, 'because you would call me a madman; but you must stay with me for the next few days, if you can. I want you to watch Fleete, but don't tell me what you think till I have made up my mind.'

'But I am dining out tonight,' I said.

'So am I,' said Strickland, 'and so is Fleete. At least if he doesn't change his mind.'

We walked about the garden smoking, but saying nothing because we were friends, and talking spoils good tobacco—till our pipes were out. Then we went to wake up Fleete. He was wide awake and fidgeting about his room.

'I say, I want some more chops,' he said. 'Can I get them?''

We laughed and said, 'Go and change. The ponies will be round in a minute.'

'All right,' said Fleete. 'I'll go when I get the chops—underdone ones, mind.'

He seemed to be quite in earnest. It was four o'clock, and we had had breakfast at one; still, for a long time, he demanded those underdone chops. Then he changed into riding clothes and went out into the verandah. His pony—the mare had not been caught—would not let him come near. All three horses were unmanageable—mad with fear—and finally Fleete said that he would stay at home and get something to eat. Strickland and I rode out wondering. As we passed the temple of Hanuman, the Silver Man came out and mewed at us.

'He is not one of the regular priests of the temple,' said Strickland. 'I think I should peculiarly like to lay my hands on him.'

There was no spring in our gallop on the racecourse that evening. The horses were stale, and moved as though they had been ridden out.

'The fright after breakfast has been too much for them,' said Strickland.

That was the only remark he made through the remainder of the ride. Once or twice I think he swore to himself; but that did not count.

We came back in the dark at seven o'clock, and saw that there were no lights in the bungalow. 'Careless ruffians my servants are!' said Strickland.

My horse reared at something on the carriage drive, and Fleete stood up under its nose.

'What are you doing, grovelling about the garden?' said Strickland.

But both horses bolted and nearly threw us. We dismounted by the stables and returned to Fleete, who was on his hands and knees under the orange-bushes.

'What the devil's wrong with you?' said Strickland.

'Nothing, nothing in the world,' said Fleete, speaking very quickly and thickly. 'I've been gardening—botanising you know. The smell of the earth is delightful. I think I'm going for a walk—a long walk—all night.'

Then I saw that there was something excessively out of order somewhere, and I said to Strickland, 'I am not dining out.'

'Bless you!' said Strickland. 'Here, Fleete, get up. You'll catch fever there. Come in to dinner and let's have the lamps lit. We'll all dine at home.'

Fleete stood up unwillingly, and said, ' No lamps no lamps. It's much nicer here. Let's dine outside and have some more chops—lots of 'em and underdone—bloody ones with gristle.'

Now a December evening in Northern India is bitterly cold, and Fleete's suggestion was that of a maniac.

'Come in,' said Strickland sternly. 'Come in at once.'

Fleete came, and when the lamps were brought, we saw that he was literally plastered with dirt from head to foot. He must have been rolling in the garden. He shrank from the light and went to his room. His eyes were horrible to look at. There was a green light behind them, not in them, if you understand, and the man's lower lip hung down.

Strickland said, 'There is going to be trouble—big trouble— tonight. Don't you change your riding-things.'

We waited and waited for Fleete's reappearance, and ordered dinner in the meantime. We could hear him moving about his own room, but there was no light there. Presently from the room came the long-drawn howl of a wolf.

People write and talk lightly of blood running cold and hair standing up and things of that kind. Both sensations are too horrible to be trifled with. My heart stopped as though a knife had been driven through it, and Strickland turned as white as the tablecloth.

The howl was repeated, and was answered by another howl far across the fields.

That set the gilded roof on the horror. Strickland dashed into Fleete's room. I followed, and we saw Fleete getting out of the window, he made beast-noises in the back of his throat. He could not answer us when we shouted at him. He spat.

I don't quite remember what followed, but I think that Strickland must have stunned him with the long boot-jack or else I should never have been able to sit on his chest. Fleete could not speak, he could only snarl, and his snarls were those of a wolf, not of a man. The human spirit must have been giving way all day and have died out with the twilight. We were dealing with a beast that had once been Fleete.

The affair was beyond any human and rational experience. I tried to say 'Hydrophobia,' but the word wouldn't come, because I knew that I was lying.

We bound this beast with leather thongs of the *punkah*-rope, and tied its thumbs and big toes together, and gagged it with a shoe-horn, which makes a very efficient gag if you know how to arrange it. Then we carried it into the dining-room, and sent a man to Dumoise, the doctor, telling him to come over at once. After we had despatched the messenger and were drawing breath, Strickland said, 'It's no good. This isn't any doctor's work.' I, also, knew that he spoke the truth.

The beast's head was free, and it threw it about from side to side. Anyone entering the room would have believed that we were curing a wolf's pelt. That was the most loathsome accessory of all.

Strickland sat with his chin in the heel of his fist, watching the beast as it wriggled on the ground, but saying nothing. The shirt had been torn open in the scuffle and showed the black rosette mark on the left breast. It stood out like a blister.

In the silence of the watching we heard something without mewing like a she-otter. We both rose to our feet, and, I answer for myself, not Strickland, felt sick—actually and physically sick. We told each other, as did the men in *Pinafore*, that it was the cat.

Dumoise arrived, and I never saw a little man so unprofessionally shocked. He said that it was a heart-rending case of hydrophobia, and that nothing could be done. At least any palliative measures would only prolong the agony. The beast was foaming at the mouth. Fleete, as we told Dumoise, had been bitten by dogs once or twice. Any man who keeps half a dozen terriers must expect a nip now and again. Dumoise could offer no help. He could only certify that Fleete was dying of hydrophobia. The beast was then howling, for it had managed to spit out the shoe-horn. Dumoise said that he would be ready to certify to the cause of death, and that the end was certain. He was a good little man, and he offered to remain with us; but Strickland refused the kindness. He did not wish to poison Dumoise's New Year. He would only ask him not to give the real cause of Fleete's death to the public.

So Dumoise left, deeply agitated; and as soon as the noise of the cart-wheels had died away, Strickland told me, in a whisper, his suspicions. They were so wildly improbable that he dared not say them out aloud; and I, who entertained all Strickland's beliefs, was so ashamed of owning to them that I pretended to disbelieve.

'Even if the Silver Man had bewitched Fleete for polluting the image of Hanuman, the punishment could not have fallen so quickly.'

As I was whispering this the cry outside the house rose again, and the beast fell into a fresh paroxysm of struggling till we were afraid that the thongs that held it would give way.

'Watch!' said Strickland. 'If this happens six times I shall take the law into my own hands. I order you to help me.'

He went into his room and came out in a few minutes with the barrels of an old shot-gun, a piece of fishing-line, some thick cord, and his heavy wooden bedstead. I reported that the convulsions had followed the cry by two seconds in each case, and the beast seemed perceptibly weaker.

Strickland muttered, 'But he can't take away the life! He can't take away the life!'

I said, though I knew that I was arguing against myself, 'It may be a cat. It must be a cat. If the Silver Man is responsible, why does he dare to come here?'

Strickland arranged the wood on the hearth, put the gun-barrels into the glow of the fire, spread the twine on the table and broke a walking stick in two. There was one yard of fishing line, gut, lapped with wire, such as is used for *mahseer*-fishing, and he tied the two ends together in a loop.

Then he said, ' How can we catch him? He must be taken alive and unhurt.'

I said that we must trust in Providence, and go out softly with polo-sticks into the shrubbery at the front of the house. The man or animal that made the cry was evidently moving round the house as regularly as a night-watchman. We could wait in the bushes till he came by and knock him over.

Strickland accepted this suggestion, and we slipped out from a bathroom window into the front verandah and then across the carriage drive into the bushes.

In the moonlight we could see the leper coming round the corner of the house. He was perfectly naked, and from time to time he mewed and stopped to dance with his shadow. It was an unattractive sight, and thinking of poor Fleete, brought to such degradation by so foul a creature, I put away all my doubts and resolved to help Strickland from the heated gun-barrels to the loop of twine—from the loins to the head and back again—with all tortures that might be needful.

The leper halted in the front porch for a moment and we jumped out on him with the sticks. He was wonderfully strong, and we were afraid that he might escape or be fatally injured before we caught him. We had an idea that lepers were frail creatures, but this proved to be incorrect. Strickland knocked his legs from under him and I put my foot on his neck. He mewed hideously, and even through my riding-boots I could feel that his flesh was not the flesh of a clean man.

He struck at us with his hand and feet-stumps. We looped the lash of a dog-whip round him, under the arm- pits, and dragged him backwards into the hall and so into the dining-room where the beast lay. There we tied him with trunk-straps. He made no attempt to escape, but mewed.

When we confronted him with the beast the scene was beyond description. The beast doubled backwards into a bow as though he had been poisoned with strychnine, and moaned in the most pitiable fashion. Several other things happened also, but they cannot be put down here.

'I think I was right,' said Strickland. 'Now we will ask him to cure this case.'

But the leper only mewed. Strickland wrapped a towel round his hand and took the gun-barrels out of the fire. I put the half of the broken walking stick through the loop of fishing-line and buckled the leper comfortably to Strickland's bedstead. I understood then how men and women and little children can endure to see a witch burnt alive; for the beast was moaning on the floor, and though the Silver Man had no face, you could see horrible feelings passing through the slab that took its place, exactly as waves of heat play across red-hot iron—gun-barrels for instance.

Strickland shaded his eyes with his hands for a moment and we got to work. This part is not to be printed.

★★★★★★

The dawn was beginning to break when the leper spoke. His mewings had not been satisfactory up to that point. The beast had fainted from exhaustion and the house was very still. We unstrapped the leper and told him to take away the evil spirit. He crawled to the beast and laid his hand upon the left breast. That was all. Then he fell face down and whined, drawing in his breath as he did so.

We watched the face of the beast, and saw the soul of Fleete coming back into the eyes. Then a sweat broke out on the forehead and the eyes—they were human eyes—closed. We waited for an hour but Fleete still slept. We carried him to his room and bade the leper go, giving him the bedstead, and the sheet on the bedstead to cover his nakedness, the gloves and the towels with which we had touched him, and the whip that had been hooked round his body. He put the sheet about him and went out into the early morning without speaking or mewing.

Strickland wiped his face and sat down. A night-gong, far away in the city, made seven o'clock.

'Exactly four-and -twenty hours!' said Strickland. 'And I've done enough to ensure my dismissal from the service, besides permanent quarters in a lunatic asylum. Do you believe that we are awake?'

The red-hot gun-barrel had fallen on the floor and was singeing the carpet. The smell was entirely real.

That morning at eleven we two together went to wake up Fleete. We looked and saw that the black leopard-rosette on his chest had disappeared. He was very drowsy and tired, but as soon as he saw us, he said, 'Oh! Confound you fellows. Happy New Year to you. Never mix your liquors. I'm nearly dead.'

'Thanks for your kindness, but you're over time,' said Strickland. 'Today is the morning of the second. You've slept the clock round with a vengeance.'

The door opened, and little Dumoise put his head in. He had come on foot, and fancied that we were laying out Fleete.

'I've brought a nurse,' said Dumoise. 'I suppose that she can come in for . . . what is necessary.'

'By all means,' said Fleete cheerily, sitting up in bed. 'Bring on your nurses.'

Dumoise was dumb. Strickland led him out and explained that there must have been a mistake in the diagnosis. Dumoise remained dumb and left the house hastily. He considered that his professional reputation had been injured, and was inclined to make a personal matter of the recovery. Strickland went out too. When he came back, he said that he had been to call on the Temple of Hanuman to offer redress for the pollution of the god, and had been solemnly assured that no white man had ever touched the idol and that he was an incarnation of all the virtues labouring under a delusion. ' What do you think ?' said

Strickland.

I said, '*There are more things . . .*'

But Strickland hates that quotation. He says that I have worn it threadbare.

One other curious thing happened which frightened me as much as anything in all the night's work. When Fleete was dressed he came into the dining-room and sniffed. He had a quaint trick of moving his nose when he sniffed. 'Horrid doggy smell, here,' said he. 'You should really keep those terriers of yours in better order. Try sulphur, Strick.'

But Strickland did not answer. He caught hold of the back of a chair, and, without warning, went into an amazing fit of hysterics. It is terrible to see a strong man overtaken with hysteria. Then it struck me that we had fought for Fleete's soul with the Silver Man in that room, and had disgraced ourselves as Englishmen forever, and I laughed and gasped and gurgled just as shamefully as Strickland, while Fleete thought that we had both gone mad. We never told him what we had done.

Some years later, when Strickland had married and was a church-going member of society for his wife's sake, we reviewed the incident dispassionately, and Strickland suggested that I should put it before the public.

I cannot myself see that this step is likely to clear up the mystery; because, in the first place, no one will believe a rather unpleasant story, and, in the second, it is well known to every right-minded man that the gods of the heathen are stone and brass, and any attempt to deal with them otherwise is justly condemned.

The Children of the Zodiac

Though thou love her as thyself,
As a self of purer clay,
Though her parting dim the day.
Stealing grace from all alive,
Heartily know
When half Gods go
The Gods arrive.

Emerson.

Thousands of years ago, when men were greater than they are today, the Children of the Zodiac lived in the world. There were six Children of the Zodiac—the Ram, the Bull, the Lion, the Twins, and the Girl; and they were afraid of the six houses which belonged to the Scorpion, the Balance, the Crab, the Fishes, the Goat, and the Waterman. Even when they first stepped down upon the earth and knew that they were immortal Gods, they carried this fear with them; and the fear grew as they became better acquainted with mankind and heard stories of the six houses. Men treated the children as Gods and came to them with prayers and long stories of wrong, while the Children of the Zodiac listened and could not understand.

A mother would fling herself before the feet of the Twins, or the Bull, crying: 'My husband was at work in the fields and the Archer shot him and he died; and my son will also be killed by the Archer. Help me!' The Bull would lower his huge head and answer: 'What is that to me?' Or the Twins would smile and continue their play, for they could not understand why the water ran out of people's eyes. At other times a man and a woman would come to Leo or the Girl crying: 'We two are newly married and we are very happy. Take these flowers.' As they threw the flowers they would make mysterious sounds to show that they were happy, and Leo and the Girl wondered even more than the Twins why people shouted 'Ha! ha! ha!' for no cause.

This continued for thousands of years by human reckoning, till on a day, Leo met the Girl walking across the hills and saw that she had changed entirely since he had last seen her. The Girl, looking at Leo, saw that he too had changed altogether. Then they decided that it would be well never to separate again, in case even more startling changes should occur when the one was not at hand to help the other. Leo kissed the Girl and all earth felt that kiss, and the Girl sat down on a hill and the water ran out of her eyes; and this had never happened before in the memory of the Children of the Zodiac.

As they sat together a man and a woman came by, and the man said to the woman: 'What is the use of wasting flowers on those dull Gods. They will never understand, darling.'

The Girl jumped up and put her arms round the woman, crying, 'I understand. Give me the flowers and I will give you a kiss.'

Leo said beneath his breath to the man: 'What was the new name that I heard you give to your woman just now?'

The man answered, 'Darling, of course.'

'Why, of course,' said Leo; 'and if of course, what does it mean?'

'It means "very dear," and you have only to look at your wife to see why.'

'I see,' said Leo; 'you are quite right;' and when the man and the woman had gone on he called the Girl 'darling wife;' and the Girl wept again from sheer happiness. 'I think,' she said at last, wiping her eyes, 'I think that we two have neglected men and women too much. What did you do with the sacrifices they made to you, Leo?'

'I let them burn,' said Leo. 'I could not eat them. What did you do with the flowers?'

'I let them wither. I could not wear them, I had so many of my own,' said the Girl, 'and now I am sorry.'

'There is nothing to grieve for,' said Leo; 'we belong to each other.' As they were talking the years of men's life slipped by unnoticed, and presently the man and the woman came back, both white-headed, the man carrying the woman. 'We have come to the end of things,' said the man quietly. 'This that was my wife—'

'As I am Leo's wife,' said the Girl quickly, her eyes staring.

'—was my wife, has been killed by one of your houses.' The man set down his burden, and laughed.

'Which house?' said Leo angrily, for he hated all the houses equally.

'You are Gods, you should know,' said the man. 'We have lived together and loved one another, and I have left a good farm for my son: what have I to complain of except that I still live?'

As he was bending over his wife's body there came a whistling through the air, and he started and tried to run away, crying, 'It is the arrow of the Archer. Let me live a little longer—only a little longer!' The arrow struck him and he died. Leo looked at the Girl and she looked at him, and both were puzzled.

'He wished to die,' said Leo. 'He said that he wished to die, and when Death came he tried to run away. He is a coward.'

'No, he is not,' said the Girl; 'I think I feel what he felt. Leo, we must learn more about this for their sakes.'

'For *their* sakes,' said Leo, very loudly.

'Because *we* are never going to die,' said the Girl and Leo together, still more loudly.

'Now sit you still here, darling wife,' said Leo, 'while I go to the houses whom we hate, and learn how to make these men and women live as we do.'

'And love as we do,' said the Girl.

'I do not think they need to be taught that,' said Leo, and he strode away very angry, with his lion-skin swinging from his shoulder, till he came to the house where the Scorpion lives in the darkness, brandishing his tail over his back.

'Why do you trouble the children of men?' said Leo, with his heart between his teeth.

'Are you so sure that I trouble the children of men alone?' said the Scorpion. 'Speak to your brother the Bull, and see what he says.'

'I come on behalf of the children of men,' said Leo. 'I have learned to love as they do, and I wish them to live as I—as we—do.'

'Your wish was granted long ago. Speak to the Bull. He is under my special care,' said the Scorpion.

Leo dropped back to the earth again, and saw the great star Aldebaran, that is set in the forehead of the Bull, blazing very near to the earth. When he came up to it he saw that his brother the Bull, yoked to a countryman's plough, was toiling through a wet rice-field with his head bent down, and the sweat streaming from his flanks. The countryman was urging him forward with a goad.

'Gore that insolent to death,' cried Leo, 'and for the sake of our family honour come out of the mire.'

'I cannot,' said the Bull, 'the Scorpion has told me that some-day, of which I cannot be sure, he will sting me where my neck is set on my shoulders, and that I shall die bellowing.'

'What has that to do with this disgraceful exhibition?' said Leo, standing on the dyke that bounded the wet field.

'Everything. This man could not plough without my help. He thinks that I am a stray bullock.'

'But he is a mud-crusted cottar with matted hair,' insisted Leo. 'We are not meant for his use.'

'You may not be; I am. I cannot tell when the Scorpion may choose to sting me to death—perhaps before I have turned this furrow.' The Bull flung his bulk into the yoke, and the plough tore through the wet ground behind him, and the countryman goaded him till his flanks were red.

'Do you like this?' Leo called down the dripping furrows.

'No,' said the Bull over his shoulder as he lifted his hind legs from the clinging mud and cleared his nostrils.

Leo left him scornfully and passed to another country, where he found his brother the Ram in the centre of a crowd of country people who were hanging wreaths round his neck and feeding him on freshly-plucked green corn.

'This is terrible,' said Leo. 'Break up that crowd and come away, my brother. Their hands are spoiling your fleece.'

'I cannot,' said the Ram. 'The Archer told me that on some day of which I had no knowledge, he would send a dart through me, and that I should die in very great pain.'

'What has that to do with this?' said Leo, but he did not speak as confidently as before.

'Everything in the world,' said the Ram. 'These people never saw a perfect sheep before. They think that I am a stray, and they will carry me from place to place as a model to all their flocks.'

'But they are greasy shepherds, we are not intended to amuse them,' said Leo.

'You may not be; I am,' said the Ram. 'I cannot tell when the Archer may choose to send his arrow at me—perhaps before the people a mile down the road have seen me.' The Ram lowered his head that a yokel newly arrived might throw a wreath of wild garlic-leaves over it, and waited patiently while the farmers tugged his fleece.

'Do you like this?' cried Leo over the shoulders of the crowd.

'No,' said the Ram, as the dust of the trampling feet made him sneeze, and he snuffed at the fodder piled before him.

Leo turned back intending to retrace his steps to the houses, but as he was passing down a street he saw two small children, very dusty, rolling outside a cottage door, and playing with a cat. They were the Twins.

'What are you doing here?' said Leo, indignant.

'Playing," said the Twins calmly.

'Cannot you play on the banks of the Milky Way?' said Leo.

'We did,' said they, "till the Fishes swam down and told us that some day they would come for us and not hurt us at all and carry us away. So now we are playing at being babies down here. The people like it.'

'Do you like it?' said Leo.

'No,' said the Twins, 'but there are no cats in the Milky Way,' and they pulled the cat's tail thoughtfully. A woman came out of the doorway and stood behind them, and Leo saw in her face a look that he had sometimes seen in the Girl's.

'She thinks that we are foundlings,' said the Twins, and they trotted indoors to the evening meal. Then Leo hurried as swiftly as possible to all the houses one after another; for he could not understand the new trouble that had come to his brethren.

He spoke to the Archer, and the Archer assured him that so far as that house was concerned Leo had nothing to fear. The Waterman, the Fishes, and the Goat, gave the same answer. They knew nothing of Leo, and cared less. They were the houses, and they were busied in killing men.

At last he came to that very dark house where Cancer the Crab lies so still that you might think he was asleep if you did not see the ceaseless play and winnowing motion of the feathery branches round his mouth. That movement never ceases. It is like the eating of a smothered fire into rotten timber in that it is noiseless and without haste.

Leo stood in front of the Crab, and the half darkness allowed him a glimpse of that vast blue-black back, and the motionless eyes. Now and again he thought that he heard someone sobbing, but the noise was very faint.

'Why do you trouble the children of men?' said Leo. There was no answer, and against his will Leo cried, 'Why do you trouble us? What have we done that you should trouble us?'

This time Cancer replied, 'What do I know or care? You were born into my house, and at the appointed time I shall come for you.'

'When is the appointed time?' said Leo, stepping back from the restless movement of the mouth.

'When the full moon fails to call the full tide,' said the Crab, 'I shall come for the one. When the other has taken the earth by the shoulders, I shall take that other by the throat.'

Leo lifted his hand to the apple of his throat, moistened his lips, and recovering himself, said:

'Must I be afraid for two, then?'

'For two,' said the Crab, ' and as many more as may come after.'

'My brother, the Bull, had a better fate,' said Leo, sullenly. 'He is alone.'

A hand covered his mouth before he could finish the sentence, and he found the Girl in his arms. Womanlike, she had not stayed where Leo had left her, but had hastened off at once to know the worst, and passing all the other houses, had come straight to Cancer.

'That is foolish,' said the Girl whispering, 'I have been waiting in the dark for long and long before you came. *Then* I was afraid. But now—' She put her head down on his shoulder and sighed a sigh of contentment.

'I am afraid now,' said Leo.

'That is on my account,' said the Girl. 'I know it is, because I am afraid for your sake. Let us go, husband.'

They went out of the darkness together and came back to the earth, Leo very silent, and the Girl striving to cheer him. 'My brother's fate is the better one,' Leo would repeat from time to time, and at last he said: 'Let us each go our own way and live alone till we die. We were born into the House of Cancer, and he will come for us.'

'I know; I know. But where shall I go? And where will you sleep in the evening? But let us try. I will stay here. Do you go on?'

Leo took six steps forward very slowly, and three long steps backward very quickly, and the third step set him again at the Girl's side. This time it was she who was begging him to go away and leave her, and he was forced to comfort her all through the night. That night decided them both never to leave each other for an instant, and when they had come to this decision they looked back at the darkness of the House of Cancer high above their heads, and with their arms round each other's necks laughed, 'Ha! ha! ha!' exactly as the children of men laughed. And that was the first time in their lives that they had ever laughed. Next morning they returned to their proper home and saw the flowers and the sacrifices that had been laid before their doors by the villagers of the hills. Leo stamped down the fire with his heel and the Girl flung the flower-wreaths out of sight, shuddering as she did so. When the villagers returned, as of custom, to see what had become of their offerings, they found neither roses nor burned flesh on the altars, but only a man and a woman, with frightened white faces sitting hand in hand on the altar-steps.

'Are you not Virgo?' said a woman to the Girl. 'I sent you flowers yesterday.'

'Little sister,' said the Girl, flushing to her forehead, 'do not send any more flowers, for I am only a woman like yourself.' The man and the woman went away doubtfully.

'Now, what shall we do?' said Leo.

'We must try to be cheerful, I think,' said the Girl. 'We know the very worst that can happen to us, but we do not know the best that love can bring us. We have a great deal to be glad of.'

'The certainty of death?' said Leo.

'All the children of men have that certainty also; yet they laughed long before we ever knew how to laugh. We must learn to laugh, Leo. We have laughed once, already.'

People who consider themselves Gods, as the Children of the Zodiac did, find it hard to laugh, because the immortals know nothing worth laughter or tears. Leo rose up with a very heavy heart, and he and the Girl together went to and fro among men; their new fear of death behind them. First they laughed at a naked baby attempting to thrust its fat toes into its foolish pink mouth; next they laughed at a kitten chasing her own tail; and then they laughed at a boy trying to steal a kiss from a girl, and getting his ears boxed. Lastly, they laughed because the wind blew in their faces as they ran down a hillside together, and broke panting and breathless into a knot of villagers at the bottom. The villagers laughed too at their flying clothes and wind-reddened faces; and in the evening gave them food and invited them to a dance on the grass, where everybody laughed through the mere joy of being able to dance.

That night Leo jumped up from the Girl's side crying: 'Every one of those people we met just now will die—'

'So shall we,' said the Girl sleepily. 'Lie down again, dear.' Leo could not see that her face was wet with tears.

But Leo was up and far across the fields, driven forward by the fear of death for himself and for the Girl, who was dearer to him than himself. Presently he came across the Bull drowsing in the moonlight after a hard day's work, and looking through half-shut eyes at the beautiful straight furrows that he had made.

'Ho!' said the Bull. 'So you have been told these things too. Which of the houses holds your death?'

Leo pointed upwards to the dark House of the Crab and groaned. 'And he will come for the Girl too,' he said.

'Well,' said the Bull, 'what will you do?'

Leo sat down on the dike and said that he did not know.

'You cannot pull a plough,' said the Bull, with a little touch, of contempt. 'I can, and that prevents me from thinking of the Scorpion.'

Leo was angry, and said nothing till the dawn broke, and the cultivator came to yoke the Bull to his work.

'Sing,' said the Bull, as the stiff, muddy ox-bow creaked and strained. 'My shoulder is galled. Sing one of the songs that we sang when we thought we were all Gods together.'

Leo stepped back into the canebrake, and lifted up his voice in a song of the Children of the Zodiac—the war-whoop of the young Gods who are afraid of nothing. At first he dragged the song along unwillingly, and then the song dragged him, and his voice rolled across the fields, and the Bull stepped to the tune, and the cultivator banged his flanks out of sheer light-hearted-ness, and the furrows rolled away behind the plough more and more swiftly. Then the Girl came across the fields looking for Leo, and found him singing in the cane. She joined her voice to his, and the cultivator's wife brought her spinning into the open and listened with all her children round her. When it was time for the nooning, Leo and the Girl had sung themselves both thirsty and hungry, but the cultivator and his wife gave them rye bread and milk, and many thanks; and the Bull found occasion to say: 'You have helped me to do a full half field more than I should have done. But the hardest part of the day is to come, brother.'

Leo wished to lie down and brood over the words of the Crab. The Girl went away to talk to the cultivator's wife and baby, and the afternoon ploughing began.

'Help us now,' said the Bull. 'The tides of the day are running down. My legs are very stiff. Sing, if you never sang before.'

'To a mud-spattered villager?' said Leo.

'He is under the same doom as ourselves. Are you a coward?' said the Bull. Leo flushed, and began again with a sore throat and a bad temper. Little by little he dropped away from the songs of the children and made up a song as he went along; and this was a thing he could never have done had he not met the Crab face to face. He remembered facts concerning cultivators and bullocks and rice-fields that he had not particularly noticed before the interview, and he strung them all together, growing more interested as he sang, and he told the cultivator much more about himself and his work than the cultivator knew. The Bull grunted approval as he toiled down the furrows for the last time that day, and the song ended, leaving the cultivator with a very good opinion of himself in his aching bones. The Girl came out of the hut where she had been keeping the children quiet, and talking woman-talk to the wife, and they all ate the evening meal together.

'Now yours must be a very pleasant life,' said the cultivator; 'sitting as you do on a dyke all day and singing just what comes into your head. Have you been at it long, you two—gipsies?'

'Ah!' lowed the Bull from his byre. 'That's all the thanks you will ever get from men, brother.'

'No. We have only just begun it,' said the Girl; 'but we are going to keep to it as long as we live. Are we not, Leo?'

'Yes,' said he; and they went away hand in hand.

'You can sing beautifully, Leo,' said she, as a wife will to her husband.

'What were you doing?' said he.

'I was talking to the mother and the babies,' she said. 'You would not understand the little things that make us women laugh.'

'And—and I am to go on with this—this gipsy work?' said Leo.

'Yes, dear; and I will help you.'

There is no written record of the life of Leo and of the Girl, so we cannot tell how Leo took to his new employment, which he detested. We are only sure that the Girl loved him when and wherever he sang; even when, after the song was done, she went round with the equivalent of a tambourine and collected the pence for the daily bread. There were times, too, when it was Leo's very hard task to console the Girl for the indignity of horrible praise that people gave him and her— for the silly wagging peacock feathers that they stuck in his cap, and the buttons and pieces of cloth that they sewed on his coat. Womanlike, she could advise and help to the end, but the meanness of the means revolted.

'What does it matter,' Leo would say, 'so long as the songs make them a little happier?' And they would go down the road and begin again on the old, old refrain—that whatever came or did not come the children of men must not be afraid. It was heavy teaching at first, but in process of years Leo discovered that he could make men laugh and hold them listening to him even when the rain fell. Yet there were people who would sit down and cry softly, though the crowd was yelling with delight, and there were people who maintained that Leo made them do this; and the Girl would talk to them in the pauses of the performance and do her best to comfort them. People would die, too, while Leo was talking and singing and laughing; for the Archer and the Scorpion and the Crab and the other houses were as busy as ever. Sometimes the crowd broke, and were frightened, and Leo strove to keep them steady by telling them that this was cowardly; and sometimes they mocked at the Houses that were killing them, and Leo explained that this was even more cowardly than running away.

In their wanderings they came across the Bull, or the Ram, or the Twins, but all were too busy to do more than nod to each other across the crowd, and go on with their work. As the years rolled on even that recognition ceased, for the Children of the Zodiac had forgotten that they had ever been Gods working for the sake of men. The star Aldebaran was crusted with caked dirt on the Bull's forehead, the Ram's fleece was dusty and torn, and the Twins were only babies fighting over the cat on the doorstep. It was then that Leo said, 'Let us stop singing and making jokes.'

And it was then that the Girl said, 'No—' but she did not know why she said 'No' so energetically. Leo maintained that it was perversity, till she herself, at the end of a dusty day, made the same suggestion to him, and he said, 'Most certainly not!' and they quarrelled miserably between the hedgerows, forgetting the meaning of the stars above them. Other singers and other talkers sprang up in the course of the years, and Leo, forgetting that there could never be too many of these, hated them for dividing the applause of the children of men, which he thought should be all his own. The Girl would grow angry too, and then the songs would be broken, and the jests fall flat for weeks to come, and the children of men would shout: 'Go home, you two gipsies. Go home and learn something worth singing.' After one of these sorrowful, shameful days, the Girl, walking by Leo's side through the fields, saw the full moon coming up over the trees, and she clutched Leo's arm, crying: 'The time has come now. Oh, Leo, forgive me!'

'What is it?' said Leo. He was thinking of the other singers.

'My husband!' she answered, and she laid his hand upon her breast, and the breast that he knew so well was hard as stone. Leo groaned, remembering what the Crab had said.

'Surely we were Gods once,' he cried.

'Surely we are Gods still,' said the Girl. 'Do you not remember when you and I went to the House of the Crab and—were not very much afraid? And since then . . . we have forgotten what we were singing for—we sang for the pence, and, oh, we fought for them!—We, who are the Children of the Zodiac!'

'It was my fault,' said Leo.

'How can there be any fault of yours that is not mine too?' said the Girl. 'My time has come, but you will live longer, and—' The look in her eyes said all she could not say.

'Yes, I will remember that we are Gods,' said Leo. It is very hard, even for a child of the Zodiac who has forgotten his Godhead, to see his wife dying slowly, and to know that he cannot help her. The Girl told Leo in those last months of all that she had said and done among the wives and the babies at the back of the roadside performances, and Leo was astonished that he knew so little of her who had been so much to him. When she was dying she told him never to fight for pence or quarrel with the other singers; and, above all, to go on with his singing immediately after she was dead.

Then she died, and after he had buried her he went down the road to a village that he knew, and the people hoped that he would begin quarrelling with a new singer that had sprung up while he had been away. But Leo called him ' my brother.' The new singer was newly married—and Leo knew it—and when he had finished singing Leo straightened himself, and sang the *Song of the Girl*, which he had made coming down the road. Every man who was married, or hoped to be married, whatever his rank or colour, understood that song—even the bride leaning on the new husband's arm understood it too—and presently when the song ended, and Leo's heart was bursting in him, the men sobbed. 'That was a sad tale,' they said at last, 'now make us laugh.'

Because Leo had known all the sorrow that a man could know, including the full knowledge of his own fall who had once been a God—he, changing his song quickly, made the people laugh till they could laugh no more. They went away feeling ready for any trouble in reason, and they gave Leo more peacock feathers and pence than he could count. Knowing that pence led to quarrels and that peacock feathers were hateful to the Girl, he put them aside and went away to look for his brothers, to remind them that they too were Gods.

He found the Bull goring the undergrowth in a ditch, for the Scorpion had stung him, and he was dying, not slowly, as the Girl had died, but quickly.

'I know all,' the Bull groaned, as Leo came up. 'I had forgotten too, but I remember now. Go and look at the fields I ploughed. The furrows are straight. I forgot that I was a God, but I drew the plough perfectly straight, for all that. And you, brother?'

'I am not at the end of the ploughing,' said Leo. 'Does Death hurt?'

'No; but dying does,' said the Bull, and he died. The cultivator who then owned him was much annoyed, for there was a field still unploughed.

It was after this that Leo made the *Song of the Bull* who had been a God and forgotten the fact, and he sang it in such a manner that half the young men in the world conceived that they too might be Gods without knowing it. A half of that half grew impossibly conceited, and died early. A half of the remainder strove to be Gods and failed, but the other half accomplished four times more work than they would have done under any other delusion.

Later, years later, always wandering up and down, and making the children of men laugh, he found the Twins sitting on the bank of a stream waiting for the Fishes to come and carry them away. They were not in the least afraid, and they told Leo that the woman of the house had a real baby of her own, and that when that baby grew old enough to be mischievous he would find a well-educated cat waiting to have its tail pulled. Then the Fishes came for them, but all that the people saw was two children drowning in a brook; and though their foster-mother was very sorry, she hugged her own real baby to her breast, and was grateful that it was only the foundlings.

Then Leo made the *Song of the Twins* who had forgotten that they were Gods, and had played in the dust to amuse a foster-mother. That song was sung far and wide among the women. It caused them to laugh and cry and hug their babies closer to their hearts all in one breath; and some of the women who re-membered the Girl said: 'Surely that is the voice of Virgo. Only she could know so much about ourselves.'

After those three songs were made, Leo sang them over and over again, till he was in danger of looking upon them as so many mere words, and the people who listened grew tired, and there came back to Leo the old temptation to stop singing once and for all. But he remembered the Girl's dying words and per-sisted.

One of his listeners interrupted him as he was singing. 'Leo,' said he, 'I have heard you telling us not to be afraid for the past forty years. Can you not sing something new now?'

'No,' said Leo; 'it is the only song that I am allowed to sing. You must not be afraid of the houses, even when they kill you.' The man turned to go, wearily, but there came a whistling through the air, and the arrow of the Archer was seen skimming low above the earth, pointing to the man's heart. He drew him-self up, and stood still waiting till the arrow struck home.

'I die,' he said, quietly. 'It is well for me, Leo, that you sang for forty years.'

'Are you afraid?' said Leo, bending over him.

'I am a man, not a God,' said the man. 'I should have run away but for your songs. My work is done, and I die without making a show of my fear.'

'I am very well paid,' said Leo to himself. 'Now that I see what my songs are doing, I will sing better ones.'

He went down the road, collected his little knot of listeners, and began the *Song of the Girl*. In the middle of his singing he felt the cold touch of the Crab's claw on the apple of his throat. He lifted his hand, choked, and stopped for an instant.

'Sing on, Leo,' said the crowd. 'The old song runs as well as ever it did.'

Leo went on steadily till the end, with the cold fear at his heart. When his song was ended, he felt the grip on his throat tighten. He was old, he had lost the Girl, he knew that he was losing more than half his power to sing, he could scarcely walk to the diminishing crowds that waited for him, and could not see their faces when they stood about him. None the less he cried angrily to the Crab:

'Why have you come for me *now?*'

'You were born under my care. How can I help coming for you?' said the Crab, wearily. Every human being whom the Crab killed had asked that same question.

'But I was just beginning to know what my songs were doing,' said Leo.

'Perhaps that is why,' said the Crab, and the grip tightened.

'You said you would not come till I had taken the world by the shoulders,' gasped Leo, falling back.

'I always keep my word. You have done that three times, with three songs. What more do you desire?'

'Let me live to see the world know it,' pleaded Leo. 'Let me be sure that my songs—'

'Make men brave?' said the Crab. 'Even then there would be one man who was afraid. The Girl was braver than you are. Come.'

Leo was standing close to the restless, insatiable mouth.

'I forgot,' said he, simply. 'The Girl was braver. But I am a God too, and I am not afraid.'

'What is that to me?' said the Crab.

Then Leo's speech was taken from him, and he lay still and dumb, watching Death till he died. Leo was the last of the Children of the Zodiac. After his death there sprang up a breed of little mean men, whimpering and flinching and howling because the houses killed them and theirs, who wished to live forever without any pain. They did not increase their lives, but they increased their own torments miserably, and there were no Children of the Zodiac to guide them, and the greater part of

Leo's songs were lost.

Only he had carved on the Girl's tombstone the last verse of the *Song of the Girl*, which stands at the head of this story.

One of the children of men, coming thousands of years later, rubbed away the lichen, read the lines, and applied them to a trouble other than the one Leo meant. Being a man, men believed that he had made the verses himself; but they belong to Leo, the Child of the Zodiac, and teach, as he taught, that what comes or does not come, we must not be afraid.

On the Gate: A Tale of '16

If the Order Above be but the reflection of the Order Below (as that Ancient affirms, who had some knowledge of the Order), it is not outside the Order of Things that there should have been confusion also in the Department of Death. The world's steadily falling death-rate, the rising proportion of scientifically prolonged fatal illnesses, which allowed months of warning to all concerned, had weakened initiative throughout the Necrological Departments. When the War came, these were as unprepared as civilised mankind; and, like mankind, they improvised and recriminated in the face of Heaven.

As Death himself observed to St. Peter, who had just come off The Gate for a rest: 'One does the best one can with the means at one's disposal, but—'

'I know,' said the good saint sympathetically. 'Even with what help I can muster, I'm on The Gate twenty-two hours out of the twenty-four.'

'Do you find your volunteer staff any real use?' Death went on. 'Isn't it easier to do the work oneself than—'

'One must guard against that point of view,' St. Peter returned, 'but I know what you mean. Office officialises the best of us— What is it now?' He turned to a prim-lipped seraph who had followed him with an expulsion-form for signature. St. Peter glanced it over. 'Private R. M. Buckland,' he read, 'on the charge of saying that there is no God. 'That all?'

'He says he is prepared to prove it, sir, and—according to the rules—'

'If you will make yourself acquainted with the rules, you'll find they lay down that "the fool says in his heart, there is no God." That decides it; probably shell-shock. Have you tested his reflexes?'

'No, sir. He kept on saying that there—'

'Pass him in at once! Tell off someone to argue with him and give him the best of the argument till St. Luke's free. Anything else?'

'A hospital-nurse's record, sir. She has been nursing for two years.'

'A long while.' St. Peter spoke severely. 'She may very well have grown careless.'

'It's her civilian record, sir. I judged best to refer it to you.' The seraph handed him a vivid scarlet docket.

'The next time,' said St. Peter, folding it down and writing on one corner, 'that you get one of these—er—tinted forms, mark it Q.M.A. and pass bearer at once. Don't worry over trifles.' The seraph flashed off and returned to the clamorous Gate.

'Which department is Q.M.A.?' said Death. St. Peter chuckled .

'It's not a department. It's a Ruling. "*Quia multum amavit.*" A most useful ruling. I've stretched it to . . . Now, I wonder what that child actually did die of.'

'I'll ask,' said Death, and moved to a public telephone nearby. 'Give me War Check and Audit: English side: non-combatant,' he began. 'Latest returns . . . Surely you've got them posted up to date by now! . . . Yes! Hospital Nurse in France . . . No! Not "nature and aliases." I said—what-was-nature-of-illness? . . . Thanks.' He turned to St. Peter. 'Quite normal,' he said. 'Heart-failure after neglected pleurisy following overwork.'

'Good!' St. Peter rubbed his hands. 'That brings her under the higher allowance G.L.H. scale—"*Greater love hath no man*—" But my people ought to have known that from the first.'

'Who is that clerk of yours?' asked Death. 'He seems rather a stickler for the proprieties.'

'The usual type nowadays,' St. Peter returned. 'A young power in charge of some half-baked Universe. Never having dealt with life yet, he's somewhat nebulous.'

Death sighed. 'It's the same with my old departmental heads. Nothing on earth will make my fossils on the Normal Civil Side realise that we are dying in a new age. Come and look at them. They might interest you.'

'Thanks, I will, but—Excuse me a minute! Here's my zealous young assistant on the wing once more.'

The seraph had returned to report the arrival of overwhelmingly heavy convoys at The Gate, and to ask what the saint advised.

'I'm just off on an inter-departmental inspection which will take me some time,' said St. Peter. 'You must learn to act on your own initiative. So I shall leave you to yourself for the next hour or two, merely suggesting (I don't wish in any way to sway your judgment) that you invite St. Paul, St. Ignatius (Loyola, I mean) and—er—St. Christopher to assist as supervising assessors on the Board of Admission. Ignatius is one of the subtlest intellects we have, and an officer and a gentleman to boot. I assure you'—the saint turned towards Death—'he revels in dialectics. If he's allowed to prove his case, he's quite capable of letting off the offender. St. Christopher, of course, will pass anything that looks wet and muddy.'

'They are nearly all that now, sir,' said the seraph.

'So much the better; and—as I was going to say—St. Paul is an embarrass—a distinctly strong colleague. Still—we all have our weaknesses. Perhaps a well-timed reference to his seamanship in the Mediterranean—by the way, look up the name of his ship, will you? Alexandria register, I think-might be useful in some of those sudden maritime cases that crop up. I needn't tell you to be firm, of course. That's your besetting—er—I mean—reprimand 'em severely and publicly, but—' the saint's voice broke—'oh, my child, you don't know what it is to need forgiveness. Be gentle with'em—be very gentle with 'em!'

Swiftly as a falling shaft of light the seraph kissed the sandalled feet and was away.

'Aha!' said St. Peter. 'He can't go far wrong with that Board of Admission as I've—er—arranged it.'

They walked towards the great central office of Normal Civil Death, which, buried to the knees in a flood of temporary structures, resembled a closed cribbage-board among spilt dominoes.

They entered an area of avenues and cross-avenues, flanked by long, low buildings, each packed with seraphs working wing to folded wing.

'Our temporary buildings,' Death explained. 'Always being added to. This is the War-side. You'll find nothing changed on the Normal Civil Side. They are more human than mankind.'

'It doesn't lie in my mouth to blame them,' said St. Peter.

'No, I've yet to meet the soul you wouldn't find excuse for,' said Death tenderly; 'but then I don't—er—arrange my Boards of Admission.'

'If one doesn't help one's staff, one's staff will never help itself,' St. Peter laughed, as the shadow of the main porch of the Normal Civil Death Offices darkened above them.

'This facade rather recalls the Vatican, doesn't it?' said the saint.

'They're quite as conservative. 'Notice how they still keep the old Holbein uniforms?'Morning, Sergeant Fell. How goes it?' said Death as he swung the dusty doors and nodded at a commissionaire, clad in the grim livery of Death, even as Hans Holbein has designed it.

'Sadly. Very sadly indeed, sir,' the commissionaire replied. 'So many pore ladies and gentlemen, sir, 'oo might well 'ave lived another few years, goin' off, as you might say, in every direction with no time for the proper obsequities.'

'Too bad,' said Death sympathetically. 'Well, we're none of us as young as we were, sergeant.'

They climbed a carved staircase, behung with the whole millinery of undertaking at large. Death halted on a dark Aberdeen granite landing and beckoned a messenger.

'We're rather busy today, sir,' the messenger whispered, 'but I think His Majesty will see you.'

'Who is the head of this department if it isn't you?' St. Peter whispered in turn.

'You may well ask,' his companion replied. 'I'm only—' he checked himself and went on. 'The fact is, our Normal Civil Death side is controlled by a being who considers himself all that I am and more. He's Death as men have made him—in their own image.' He pointed to a brazen plate, by the side of a black-curtained door, which read: 'Normal Civil Death, K.G., K.T., K.P., P.C., etc.' 'He's as human as mankind.'

'I guessed as much from those letters. What do they mean?'

'Titles conferred on him from time to time. King of Ghosts; King of Terrors; King of Phantoms; Pallid Conqueror, and so forth. There's no denying he's earned every one of them. A first-class mind, but just a leetle bit of a sn—'

'His Majesty is at liberty,' said the messenger.

Civil Death did not belie his name. No monarch on earth could have welcomed them more graciously; or, in St. Peter's case, with more of that particularity of remembrance which is the gift of good kings. But when Death asked him how his office was working, he became at once the Departmental Head with a grievance.

'Thanks to this abominable war,' he began testily, 'my N.C.D. has to spend all its time fighting for mere existence. Your new War-side seems to think that nothing matters except the war. I've been asked to give up two-thirds of my archives basement (E. 7-E. 64) to the Polish Civilian Casualty Check and Audit. Preposterous! Where am I to move my archives? And they've just been cross-indexed, too!'

'As I understood it,' said Death, 'our War-side merely applied for desk-room in your basement. They were prepared to leave your archives *in situ*.'

'Impossible! We may need to refer to them at any moment. There's a case now which is interesting Us all—a Mrs. Ollerby. Worcestershire by extraction—dying of an internal hereditary complaint. At any moment, We may wish to refer to her dossier, and how can we if our basement is given up to people over whom we exercise no departmental control? This war has been made excuse for slackness in every direction.'

'Indeed!' said Death. 'You surprise me. I thought nothing made any difference to the N.C.D.'

'A few years ago I should have concurred,' Civil Death replied. 'But since this—this recent outbreak of unregulated mortality there has been a distinct lack of respect toward certain aspects of our administration. The attitude is bound to reflect itself in the office. The official is, in a large measure, what the public makes him. Of course, it is only temporary reaction, but the merest outsider would notice what I mean. Perhaps you would like to see for yourself?' Civil Death bowed towards St. Peter, who feared that he might be taking up his time.

'Not in the least. If I am not the servant of the public, what am I?' Civil Death said, and preceded them to the landing. 'Now, this'—he ushered them into an immense but badly lighted office—'is our International Mortuary Department—the I.M.D. as we call it. It works with the check and audit. I should be sorry to say offhand how many billion sterling it represents, invested in the funeral ceremonies of all the races of mankind.' He stopped behind a very bald-headed clerk at a desk. 'And yet We take cognizance of the minutest detail, do not we?' he went on. 'What have we here, for example?'

'Funeral expenses of the late Mr. John Shenks Tanner.' The clerk stepped aside from the redruled book. 'Cut down by the executors on account of the war from £173:19:1 to £47:18:4. A sad falling off, if I may say so, Your Majesty.'

'And what was the attitude of the survivors?' Civil Death asked.

'Very casual. It was a motor-hearse funeral.'

'A pernicious example, spreading, I fear, even in the lowest classes,' his superior muttered. 'Haste, lack of respect for the dread summons, carelessness in the subsequent disposition of the corpse and—'

'But as regards people's real feelings?' St. Peter demanded of the clerk.

'That isn't within the terms of our reference, Sir,' was the answer. 'But we do know that, as often as not, they don't even buy black-edged announcement-cards nowadays.'

'Good Heavens!' said Civil Death swellingly. 'No cards! I must look into this myself. Forgive me, St. Peter, but we servants of humanity, as you know, are not our own masters. No cards, indeed!' He waved them off with an official hand, and immersed himself in the ledger.

'Oh, come along,' Death whispered to St. Peter. 'This is a blessed relief!'

They two walked on till they reached the far end of the vast dim office. The clerks at the desks here scarcely pretended to work. A messenger entered and slapped down a small autophonic reel.

'Here you are!' he cried. 'Mister Wilbraham Lattimer's last dying speech and record. He made a shockin' end of it.'

'Good for Lattimer!' a young voice called from a desk. 'Chuck it over!'

'Yes,' the messenger went on. 'Lattimer said to his brother: "Bert, I haven't time to worry about a little thing like dying these days, and what's more important, you haven't either. You go back to your Somme doin's, and I'll put it through with Aunt Maria. It'll amuse her and it won't hinder you." That's nice stuff for your boss!' The messenger whistled and departed. A clerk groaned as he snatched up the reel.

'How the deuce am I to knock this into official shape?' he began. 'Pass us the edifying Gantry Tubnell. I'll have to crib from him again, I suppose.'

'Be careful!' a companion whispered, and shuffled a typewritten form along the desk. 'I've used Tubby twice this morning already.'

The late Mr. Gantry Tubnell must have demised on approved departmental lines, for his record was much thumbed. Death and St. Peter watched the editing with interest.

'I can't bring in Aunt Maria any way,' the clerk broke out at last. 'Listen here, every one! She has heart-disease. She dies just as she's lifted the dropsical Lattimer to change his sheets. She says: "Sorry, Willy! I'd make a dam' pore 'ospital nurse!"'; Then she sits down and croaks. Now I call that good! I've a great mind to take it round to the War-side as an indirect casualty and get a breath of fresh air.'

'Then you'll be hauled over the coals,' a neighbour suggested.

'I'm used to that, too,' the clerk sniggered.

'Are you?' said Death, stepping forward suddenly from behind a high map-stand. 'Who are you?' The clerk cowered in his skeleton jacket.

'I'm not on the regular establishment, Sir,' he stammered. 'I'm a—volunteer. I—I wanted to see how people behaved when they were in trouble.'

'Did you? Well, take the late Mr. Wilbraham Lattimer's and Miss Maria Lattimer's papers to the War-side General Reference Office. When they have been passed upon, tell the attendance clerk that you are to serve as probationer in—let's see—in the Domestic Induced Casualty Side—7 G.S.'

The clerk collected himself a little and spoke through dry lips.

'But—but I'm—I slipped in from the lower establishment, Sir,' he breathed.

There was no need to explain. He shook from head to foot as with the palsy; and under all Heaven none tremble save those who come from that class which 'also believe and tremble.'

'Do you tell Me this officially, or as one created being to another?' Death asked after a pause.

'Oh, non-officially, Sir. Strictly non-officially, so long as you know all about it.'

His awe-stricken fellow-workers could not restrain a smile at Death having to be told about anything. Even Death bit his lips.

'I don't think you will find the War-side will raise any objection,' said he. 'By the way, they don't wear that uniform over there.'

Almost before Death ceased speaking, it was ripped off and flung on the floor, and that which had been a sober clerk of Normal Civil Death stood up an unmistakable, curly-haired, bat-winged, faun-eared imp of the pit. But where his wings joined his shoulders there was a patch of delicate dove-coloured feathering that gave promise to spread all up the pinion. St. Peter saw it and smiled, for it was a known sign of grace.

'Thank Goodness!' the ex-clerk gasped as he snatched up the Lattimer records and sheered sideways through the skylight.

'Amen!' said Death and St. Peter together, and walked through the door.

'Weren't you hinting something to me a little while ago about my lax methods?' St. Peter demanded, innocently.

'Well, if one doesn't help one's staff, one's staff will never help itself,' Death retorted. 'Now, I shall have to pitch in a stiff demi-official asking how that young fiend came to be taken on in the N.C.D. without examination. And I must do it before the N.C.D. complain that I've been interfering with their de- partmental transfers. Aren't they human? If you want to go back to The Gate I think our shortest way will be through here and across the War–Sheds.'

They came out of a side-door into Heaven's full light. A pha- lanx of Shining Ones swung across a great square singing

'To Him Who made the Heavens abide, yet cease not from their motion.

To Him Who drives the cleansing tide twice a day round ocean—
Let His Name be magnified in all poor folks' devotion!'
Death halted their leader, and asked a question.

'We're Volunteer Aid Serving Powers,' the seraph explained, 'reporting for duty in the Domestic Induced Casualty Depart- ment—told off to help relatives, where we can.'

The shift trooped on—such an array of Powers, Honours, Glories, Toils, Patiences, Services, Faiths and Loves as no man may conceive even by favour of dreams. Death and St. Peter fol- lowed them into a D.I.C.D. shed on the English side where, for the moment, work had slackened. Suddenly a name flashed on the telephone-indicator. 'Mrs. Arthur Bedott, 317, Portsmouth Avenue, Brondesbury. Husband badly wounded. One child.' Her special weakness was appended.

A seraph on the raised dais that overlooked the volunteer aids waiting at the entrance, nodded and crooked a finger. One of the new shift—a temporary acting glory—hurled himself from his place and vanished earthward.

'You may take it,' Death whispered to St. Peter, 'there will be a sustaining epic built up round Private Bedott's wound for his wife and Baby Bedott to cling to. And here—'they heard wings that flapped wearily—'here, I suspect, comes one of our failures.'

A seraph entered and dropped, panting, on a form. His plumage was ragged, his sword splintered to the hilt; and his face still worked with the passions of the world he had left, as his soiled vesture reeked of alcohol.

'Defeat,' he reported hoarsely, when he had given in a woman's name. 'Utter defeat! Look!' He held up the stump of his sword. 'I broke this on her gin-bottle.'

'So? We try again,' said the impassive chief seraph. Again he beckoned, and there stepped forward that very imp whom Death had transferred from the N.C.D.

'Go you!' said the seraph. 'We must deal with a fool according to her folly. Have you pride enough?'

There was no need to ask. The messenger's face glowed and his nostrils quivered with it. Scarcely pausing to salute, he poised and dived, and the papers on the desks spun beneath the draught of his furious vans.

St. Peter nodded high approval. 'I see!' he said. 'He'll work on her pride to steady her. By all means—"*if by all means*," as my good Paul used to say. Only it ought to read "*by any manner of possible means*." Excellent!'

'It's difficult, though,' a soft-eyed Patience whispered. 'I fail again and again. I'm only fit for an old-maid's tea-party.'

Once more the record flashed—a multiple-urgent appeal on

behalf of a few thousand men, worn-out body and soul. The Patience was detailed.

'Oh, me!' she sighed, with a comic little shrug of despair, and took the void softly as a summer breeze at dawning.

'But how does this come under the head of Domestic Casualties? Those men were in the trenches. I heard the mud squelch,' said St. Peter.

'Something wrong with the installation—as usual. Waves are always jamming here,' the seraph replied.

'So it seems,' said St. Peter as a wireless cut in with the muffled note of someone singing (sorely out of tune), to an accompaniment of desultory poppings:

'Unless you can love as the angels love With the breadth of Heaven be—'

'Twixt!' It broke off. The record showed a name. The waiting seraphs stiffened to attention with a click of tense quills.

'As you were!' said the chief seraph. 'He's met her.'

'Who is she?' said St. Peter.

'His mother. You never get over your weakness for romance,' Death answered, and a covert smile spread through the office.

'Thank Heaven, I don't. But I really ought to be going—'

'Wait one minute. Here's trouble coming through, I think,' Death interposed.

A recorder had sparked furiously in a broken run of S.O.S.'s that allowed no time for inquiry.

'Name! Name!' an impatient young Faith panted at last. 'It can't be blotted out.' No name came up. Only the reiterated appeal.

'False alarm!' said a hard-featured Toil, well used to mankind. 'Some fool has found out that he owns a soul. 'Wants work. I'd cure him! . . . '

'Hush!' said a Love in Armour, stamping his mailed foot. The office listened.

"Bad case?' Death demanded at last.

'Rank bad, Sir. They are holding back the name,' said the chief seraph. The S.O.S. signals grew more desperate, and then ceased with an emphatic thump. The Love in Armour winced.

'Firing-party,' he whispered to St. Peter. "Can't mistake that noise!'

'What is it?' St. Peter cried nervously.

'Deserter; spy; murderer,' was the chief seraph's weighed answer. 'It's out of my department now. No—hold the line! The name's up at last.'

It showed for an instant, broken and faint as sparks on charred wadding, but in that instant a dozen pens had it written. St. Peter with never a word gathered his robes about him and bundled through the door, headlong for The Gate.

'No hurry,' said Death at his elbow. 'With the present rush your man won't come up for ever so long.'

"Never can be sure these days. Anyhow, the Lower Establishment will be after him like sharks. He's the very type they'd want for propaganda. Deserter-traitor-murderer. Out of my way, please, babies!'

A group of children round a red-headed man who was telling them stories, scattered laughing. The man turned to St. Peter.

'Deserter, traitor, murderer,' he repeated. 'Can I be of service?'

'You can!' St. Peter gasped. 'Double on ahead to The Gate and tell them to hold up all expulsions till I come. Then,' he shouted as the man sped off at a long hound-like trot, 'go and picket the outskirts of the convoys. Don't let anyone break away on any account. Quick!'

But Death was right. They need not have hurried. The crowd at The Gate was far beyond the capacities of the Examining Board even though, as St. Peter's Deputy informed him, it had been enlarged twice in his absence.

'We're doing our best,' the seraph explained, 'but delay is inevitable, Sir. The Lower Establishment are taking advantage of it, as usual, at the tail of the convoys. I've doubled all pickets there, and I'm sending more. Here's the extra list, Sir—Arc J., Bradlaugh C., Bunyan J., Calvin J. Iscariot J. reported to me just now, as under your orders, and took 'em with him. Also Shakespeare W.

and—'

'Never mind the rest,' said St. Peter. I—I'm going there myself. Meantime, carry on with the passes—don't fiddle over 'em—and give me a blank or two.' He caught up a thick block of free passes, nodded to a group in khaki at a passport table, initialled their commanding officer's personal pass as for 'Officer and Party,' and left the numbers to be filled in by a quite competent-looking quarter-master-sergeant. Then, Death beside him, he breasted his way out of The Gate against the incoming multitude of all races, tongues, and creeds that stretched far across the plain.

An old lady, firmly clutching a mottle-nosed, middle-aged major by the belt, pushed across a procession of keen-faced *poilus*, and blocked his path, her captive held in that terrible mother-grip no Power has yet been able to unlock.

'I found him! I've got him! Pass him!' she ordered.

St. Peter's jaw fell. Death politely looked elsewhere.

'There are a few formalities,' the saint began.

'With Jerry in this state? Nonsense! How like a man! My boy never gave me a moment's anxiety in—'

'Don't, dear—don't!' The major looked almost as uncomfortable as St. Peter.

'Well, nothing compared with what he would give me if he weren't passed.'

'Didn't I hear you singing just now?' Death asked, seeing that his companion needed a breathing-space.

'Of course you did,' the mother intervened. 'He sings beautifully. And that's another reason! You're bass, aren't you now, darling?'

St. Peter glanced at the agonised major and hastily initialled him a pass. Without a word of thanks the mother hauled him away.

'Now, under what conceivable ruling do you justify that?' said Death.

'I.W.—the Importunate Widow. It's scandalous!' St. Peter groaned. Then his face darkened as he looked across the great plain beyond The Gate. 'I don't like this,' he said. 'The Lower Establishment is out in full force tonight. I hope our pickets are strong enough—'

The crowd here had thinned to a disorderly queue flanked on both sides by a multitude of busy, discreet emissaries from the Lower Establishment who continually edged in to do business with them, only to be edged off again by a line of watchful pickets. Thanks to the khaki everywhere, the scene was not unlike that which one might have seen on earth any evening of the old days outside the refreshment-room by the arch at Victoria Station, when the army trains started. St. Peter's appearance was greeted by the usual outburst of cock-crowing from the lower establishment.

'Dirty work at the cross-roads,' said Death dryly.

'I deserve it!' St. Peter grunted, 'but think what it must mean for Judas.'

He shouldered into the thick of the confusion where the pickets coaxed, threatened, implored, and in extreme cases bodily shoved the wearied men and women past the voluble and insinuating spirits who strove to draw them aside.

A Shropshire Yeoman had just accepted, together with a forged pass, the assurance of a genial runner of the Lower Establishment that Heaven lay round the corner, and was being stealthily steered thither, when a large hand jerked him back, another took the runner in the chest, and someone thundered: 'Get out, you crimp!' The situation was then vividly explained to the soldier in the language of the barrack-room.

'Don't blame me, guv'nor,' the man expostulated. 'I 'aven't seen a woman, let alone angels, for umpteen months. I'm from Joppa. Where d'you from?'

'Northampton,' was the answer. 'Rein back and keep by me.'

'What? You ain't ever Charley B. that my dad used to tell about? I thought you always said—'

'I shall say a deal more soon. Your sergeant's talking to that woman in red. Fetch him in quick!'

Meantime, a sunken-eyed Scots officer, utterly lost to the riot around, was being button-holed by a person of reverend aspect who explained to him that, by the logic of his own ancestral creed, not only was the Highlander irrevocably damned, but that his damnation had been predetermined before earth was made.

'It's unanswerable—just unanswerable,' said the young man sorrowfully. 'I'll be with ye.' He was moving off, when a smallish figure interposed, not without dignity.

'*Monsieur*,' it said, 'would it be of any comfort to you to know that I am—I was—John Calvin?' At this the reverend one cursed and swore like the lost Soul he was, while the Highlander turned to discuss with Calvin, pacing towards The Gate, some alterations in the fabric of a work of fiction called the *Institutio*.

Others were not so easily held. A certain woman, with loosened hair, bare arms, flashing eyes and dancing feet, shepherded her knot of waverers, hoarse and exhausted. When the taunt broke out against her from the opposing line: 'Tell 'em what you were! Tell 'em if you dare!' she answered unflinchingly, as did Judas, who, worming through the crowd like an Armenian carpet-vendor, peddled his shame aloud that it might give strength to others.

'Yes,' he would cry, 'I am everything they say, but if I'm here it must be a moral cert for you gents. This way, please. Many mansions, gentlemen! Go-ood billets! Don't you notice these low people, Sar. Plees keep hope, gentlemen!'

When there were cases that cried to him from the ground—poor souls who could not stick it but had found their way out with a rifle and a boot-lace, he would tell them of his own end, till he made them contemptuous enough to rise up and curse him. Here St. Luke's imperturbable bedside manner backed and strengthened the other's almost too oriental flux of words.

In this fashion and step by step, all the day's convoy were piloted past that danger-point where the Lower Establishment are, for reasons not given us, allowed to ply their trade. The pickets dropped to the rear, relaxed, and compared notes.

'What always impresses me most,' said Death to St. Peter, 'is the sheeplike simplicity of the intellectual mind.' He had been watching one of the pickets apparently overwhelmed by the arguments of an advanced atheist who—so hot in his argument that he was deaf to the offers of the Lower Establishment to make him a god—had stalked, talking hard—while the picket always gave ground before him—straight past the Broad Road.

'He was plaiting of long-tagged epigrams,' the sober-faced picket smiled. 'Give that sort only an ear and they'll follow ye gobbling like turkeys.'

'And John held his peace through it all,' a full fresh voice broke in. '"It may be so," says John. "Doubtless, in your belief, it is so," says John. "Your words move me mightily," says John, and gorges his own beliefs like a pike going backwards. And that young fool, so busy spinning words-words-words—that he trips past Hell Mouth without seeing it! . . . Who's yonder, Joan?'

'One of your English. 'Always late. Look!' A young girl with short-cropped hair pointed with her sword across the plain towards a single faltering figure which made at first as though to overtake the convoy, but then turned left towards the lower establishment, who were enthusiastically cheering him as a leader of enterprise.

'That's my traitor,' said St. Peter. 'He has no business to report to the Lower Establishment before reporting to convoy.'

The figure's pace slackened as he neared the applauding line. He looked over his shoulder once or twice, and then fairly turned tail and fled again towards the still convoy.

'Nobody ever gave me credit for anything I did,' he began, sobbing and gesticulating. 'They were all against me from the first. I only wanted a little encouragement. It was a regular conspiracy, but I showed 'em what I could do! I showed 'em! And— and—' he halted again. 'Oh, God! What are you going to do with me?'

No one offered any suggestion. He ranged sideways like a doubtful dog, while across the plain the Lower Establishment murmured seductively. All eyes turned to St. Peter.

'At this moment,' the saint said half to himself, 'I can't recall any precise ruling under which—'

'My own case?' the ever-ready Judas suggested.

'No-o! That's making too much of it. And yet—'

'Oh, hurry up and get it over,' the man wailed, and told them all that he had done, ending with the cry that none had ever recognised his merits; neither his own narrow-minded people, his inefficient employers, nor the snobbish jumped-up officers of his battalion.

'You see,' said St. Peter at the end. 'It's sheer vanity. It isn't even as if we had a woman to fall back upon.'

'Yet there was a woman or I'm mistaken,' said the picket with the pleasing voice who had praised John.

'Eh—what? When?' St. Peter turned swiftly on the speaker. 'Who was the woman?'

'The wise woman of Tekoah,' came the smooth answer. 'I remember, because that verse was the private heart of my plays—some of 'em.'

But the Saint was not listening. 'You have it!' he cried. 'Samuel Two, Double Fourteen. To think that I should have forgotten! *"For we must needs die and are as water spilled on the ground which cannot be gathered up again. Neither doth God respect any person, yet—"* Here, you! Listen to this!'

The man stepped forward and stood to attention. Someone took his cap as Judas and the picket John closed up beside him.

'*"Yet doth He devise means* (d'you understand that?) *devise means that His banished be not expelled from Him!"* This covers your case. I don't know what the means will be. That's for you to find out. They'll tell you yonder.' He nodded towards the now silent Lower Establishment as he scribbled on a pass. 'Take this paper over to them and report for duty there. You'll have a thin time of it; but they won't keep you a day longer than I've put down. Escort!'

'Does—does that mean there's any hope?' the man stammered.

'Yes—I'll show you the way,' Judas whispered. 'I've lived there—a very long time.'

'I'll bear you company a piece,' said John, on his left flank.

'There'll be Despair to deal with. Heart up, Mr. Littlesoul!'

The three wheeled off, and the convoy watched them grow smaller and smaller across the plain.

St. Peter smiled benignantly and rubbed his hands.

'And now we're rested,' said he, 'I think we might make a push for billets this evening, gentlemen, eh?'

The pickets fell in, guardians no longer but friends and companions all down the line. There was a little burst of cheering and the whole convoy strode away towards the not so distant Gate.

The saint and Death stayed behind to rest awhile. It was a heavenly evening. They could hear the whistle of the low-flighting cherubim, clear and sharp, under the diviner note of some released seraph's wings, where, his errand accomplished, he plunged three or four stars deep into the cool Baths of Hercules; the steady dynamo-like hum of the nearer planets on their axes; and, as the hush deepened, the surprised little sigh of some new-born sun a universe of universes away. But their minds were with the convoy that their eyes followed.

Said St. Peter proudly at last: 'If those people of mine had seen that fellow stripped of all hope in front of 'em, I doubt if they could have marched another yard tonight. Watch 'em stepping out now, though! Aren't they human?'

'To whom do you say it?' Death answered, with something of a tired smile. 'I'm more than human. I've got to die some time or other. But all other created Beings—afterwards ... '

'I know,' said St. Peter softly. 'And that is why I love you, O Azrael!'

For now they were alone Death had, of course, returned to his true majestic shape—that only One of all created beings who is doomed to perish utterly, and knows it.

'Well, that's that—for me!' Death concluded as he rose. 'And yet—' he glanced towards the empty plain where the Lower Establishment had withdrawn with their prisoner. '"*Yet doth He devise means.*"'

The Judgment of Dungara

They tell the tale even now among the groves of the Berbulda
Hill, and for corroboration point to the roofless and windowless
Mission-house. The great God Dungara, the God of Things as
They Are, Most Terrible, One-eyed, Bearing the Red Elephant
Tusk, did it all; and he who refuses to believe in Dungara will
assuredly be smitten by the Madness of Yat—the madness that
fell upon the sons and the daughters of the Buria Kol when
they turned aside from Dungara and put on clothes. So says
Athon Dazé, who is high priest of the shrine and warden of the
Red Elephant Tusk. But if you ask the assistant collector and
agent in charge of the Buria Kol, he will laugh—not because he
bears any malice against missions, but because he himself saw the
vengeance of Dungara executed upon the spiritual children of
the Reverend Justus Krenk, pastor of the Tubingen Mission, and
upon Lotta, his virtuous wife.

Yet if ever a man merited good treatment of the Gods it was
the Reverend Justus, one time of Heidelberg, who, on the faith
of a call, went into the wilderness and took the blonde, blue-
eyed Lotta with him. 'We will these Heathen now by idolatrous
practices so darkened better make,' said Justus in the early days
of his career. 'Yes,' he added with conviction, 'they shall be good
and shall with their hands to work learn. For all good Christians
must work.' And upon a stipend more modest even than that of
an English lay-reader, Justus Krenk kept house beyond Kamala
and the gorge of Malair, beyond the Berbulda River close to the
foot of the blue hill of Panth on whose summit stands the Tem-

ple of Dungara—in the heart of the country of the Buria Kol—the naked, good-tempered, timid, shameless, lazy Buria Kol.

Do you know what life at a mission outpost means? Try to imagine a loneliness exceeding that of the smallest station to which government has ever sent you—isolation that weighs upon the waking eyelids and drives you by force headlong into the labours of the day. There is no post, there is no one of your own colour to speak to, there are no roads: there is, indeed, food to keep you alive, but it is not pleasant to eat; and whatever of good or beauty or interest there is in your life, must come from yourself and the grace that may be planted in you.

In the morning, with a patter of soft feet, the converts, the doubtful, and the open scoffers, troop up to the veranda. You must be infinitely kind and patient, and, above all, clear-sighted, for you deal with the simplicity of childhood, the experience of man, and the subtlety of the savage. Your congregation have a hundred material wants to be considered; and it is for you, as you believe in your personal responsibility to your Maker, to pick out of the clamouring crowd any grain of spirituality that may lie therein. If to the cure of souls you add that of bodies, your task will be all the more difficult, for the sick and the maimed will profess any and every creed for the sake of healing, and will laugh at you because you are simple enough to believe them.

As the day wears and the impetus of the morning dies away, there will come upon you an overwhelming sense of the uselessness of your toil. This must be striven against, and the only spur in your side will be the belief that you are playing against the Devil for the living soul. It is a great, a joyous belief; but he who can hold it unwavering for four and twenty consecutive hours, must be blessed with an abundantly strong physique and equable nerve.

Ask the gray heads of the Bannockburn Medical Crusade what manner of life their preachers lead; speak to the Racine Gospel Agency, those lean Americans whose boast is that they go where no Englishman dare follow; get a pastor of the Tubingen Mission to talk of his experiences—if you can. You will be referred to the printed reports, but these contain no mention of the men who have lost youth and health, all that a man may lose except faith, in the wilds; of English maidens who have gone forth and died in the fever-stricken jungle of the Panth Hills, knowing from the first that death was almost a certainty. Few pastors will tell you of these things any more than they will speak of that young David of St. Bees, who, set apart for the Lord's work, broke down in utter desolation, and returned half distraught to the head mission, crying: 'There is no God, but I have walked with the Devil!'

The reports are silent here, because heroism, failure, doubt, despair, and self-abnegation on the part of a mere cultured white man are things of no weight as compared to the saving of one half-human soul from a fantastic faith in wood-spirits, goblins of the rock, and river-fiends.

And Gallio, the assistant collector of the countryside, 'cared for none of these things.' He had been long in the district, and the Buria Kol loved him and brought him offerings of speared fish, orchids from the dim moist heart of the forests, and as much game as he could eat. In return, he gave them quinine, and with Athon Dazé, the high priest, controlled their simple policies.

'When you have been some years in the country,' said Gallio at the Krenks' table, 'you grow to find one creed as good as another. I'll give you all the assistance in my power, of course, but don't hurt my Buria Kol. They are a good people and they trust me.'

'I will them the word of the Lord teach,' said Justus, his round face beaming with enthusiasm, 'and I will assuredly to their prejudices no wrong hastily without thinking make. But, O my friend, this in the mind impartiality-of-creed-judgment-be-looking is very bad.'

'Heigh-ho!' said Gallio, 'I have their bodies and the district to see to, but you can try what you can do for their souls. Only don't behave as your predecessor did, or I'm afraid that I can't guarantee your life.'

'And that?' said Lotta sturdily, handing him a cup of tea.

'He went up to the Temple of Dungara—to be sure he was new to the country—and began hammering old Dungara over the head with an umbrella; so the Buria Kol turned out and hammered *him* rather savagely. I was in the district, and he sent a runner to me with a note saying: "Persecuted for the Lord's sake. Send wing of regiment." The nearest troops were about two hundred miles off, but I guessed what he had been doing. I rode to Panth and talked to old Athon Dazé like a father, telling him that a man of his wisdom ought to have known that the *sahib* had sunstroke and was mad. You never saw a people more sorry in your life.

'Athon Dazé apologised, sent wood and milk and fowls and all sorts of things; and I gave five *rupees* to the shrine and told Macnamara that he had been injudicious. He said that I had bowed down in the House of Rimmon; but if he had only just gone over the brow of the hill and insulted Palin Deo, the idol of the Suria Kol, he would have been impaled on a charred bamboo long before I could have done anything, and then I should have had to have hanged some of the poor brutes. Be gentle with them, Padri—but I don't think you'll do much.'

'Not I,' said Justus, 'but my master. We will with the little children begin. Many of them will be sick—that is so. After the children the mothers; and then the men. But I would greatly that you were in internal sympathies with us prefer.'

Gallio departed to risk his life in mending the rotten bamboo bridges of his people, in killing a too persistent tiger here or there, in sleeping out in the reeking jungle, or in tracking the Suria Kol raiders who had taken a few heads from their brethren of the Buria clan. He was a knock-kneed, shambling young man, naturally devoid of creed or reverence, with a longing for absolute power which his undesirable district gratified.

'No one wants my post,' he used to say grimly, 'and my collector only pokes his nose in when he's quite certain that there is no fever. I'm monarch of all I survey, and Athon Dazé is my viceroy.'

Because Gallio prided himself on his supreme disregard of human life—though he never extended the theory beyond his own—he naturally rode forty miles to the mission with a tiny brown girl-baby on his saddle-bow.

'Here is something for you, *padri*,' said he. 'The Kols leave their surplus children to die. 'Don't see why they shouldn't, but you may rear this one. I picked it up beyond the Berbulda fork. I've a notion that the mother has been following me through the woods ever since.'

'It is the first of the fold,' said Justus, and Lotta caught up the screaming morsel to her bosom and hushed it craftily; while, as a wolf hangs in the field, Matui, who had borne it and in accordance with the law of her tribe had exposed it to die, panted weary and footsore in the bamboo-brake, watching the house with hungry mother-eyes. What would the omnipotent Assistant Collector do? Would the little man in the black coat eat her daughter alive as Athon Dazé said was the custom of all men in black coats?

Matui waited among the bamboos through the long night; and, in the morning, there came forth a fair white woman, the like of whom Matui had never seen, and in her arms was Matui's daughter clad in spotless raiment. Lotta knew little of the tongue of the Buria Kol, but when mother calls to mother, speech is easy to follow. By the hands stretched timidly to the hem of her gown, by the passionate gutturals and the longing eyes, Lotta understood with whom she had to deal. So Matui took her child again—would be a servant, even a slave, to this wonderful white woman, for her own tribe would recognise her no more. And Lotta wept with her exhaustively, after the German fashion, which includes much blowing of the nose.

'First the child, then the mother, and last the man, and to the Glory of God all,' said Justus the Hopeful. And the man came, with a bow and arrows, very angry indeed, for there was no one to cook for him.

But the tale of the mission is a long one, and I have no space to show how Justus, forgetful of his injudicious predecessor, grievously smote Moto, the husband of Matui, for his brutality; how Moto was startled, but being released from the fear of instant death, took heart and became the faithful ally and first convert of Justus; how the little gathering grew, to the huge disgust of Athon Dazé; how the priest of the God of Things as They Are argued subtilely with the Priest of the God of Things as They Should Be, and was worsted; how the dues of the Temple of Dungara fell away in fowls and fish and honeycomb; how Lotta lightened the Curse of Eve among the women, and how Justus did his best to introduce the Curse of Adam; how the Buria Kol rebelled at this, saying that their God was an idle God, and how Justus partially overcame their scruples against work, and taught them that the black earth was rich in other produce than pignuts only.

All these things belong to the history of many months, and throughout those months the white-haired Athon Dazé meditated revenge for the tribal neglect of Dungara. With savage cunning he feigned friendship towards Justus, even hinting at his own conversion; but to the congregation of Dungara he said darkly: 'They of the *padri's* flock have put on clothes and worship a busy God. Therefore Dungara will afflict them grievously till they throw themselves, howling, into the waters of the Berbulda.' At night the Red Elephant Tusk boomed and groaned among the hills, and the faithful waked and said: 'The God of Things as They Are matures revenge against the backsliders. Be merciful, Dungara, to us thy children, and give us all their crops!'

Late in the cold weather, the collector and his wife came into the Buria Kol country. 'Go and look at Krenk's Mission' said Gallio. 'He is doing good work in his own way, and I think he'd be pleased if you opened the bamboo chapel that he, has managed to run up. At any rate you'll see a civilised Buria Kol.'

Great was the stir in the mission. 'Now he and the gracious lady will that we have done good work with their own eyes see, and—yes—we will him our converts in all their new clothes by their own hands constructed exhibit. It will a great day be—for the Lord always,' said Justus; and Lotta said 'Amen.'

Justus had, in his quiet way, felt jealous of the Basel Weaving Mission, his own converts being unhandy; but Athon Dazé had latterly induced some of them to hackle the glossy silky fibres of a plant that grew plenteously on the Panth Hills. It yielded a cloth white and smooth almost as the *Tappa* of the South Seas, and that day the converts were to wear for the first time clothes made therefrom. Justus was proud of his work.

'They shall in white clothes clothed to meet the collector and his well-born lady come down, singing "Now Thank We All Our God." Then he will the chapel open, and—yes—even Gallio to believe will begin. Stand so, my children, two by two, and—Lotta, why do they thus themselves bescratch? It is not seemly to wriggle, Nala, my child. The collector will be here and be pained.'

The collector, his wife, and Gallio climbed the hill to the Mission-station. The converts were drawn up in two lines, a shining band nearly forty strong. 'Hah!' said the collector, whose acquisitive bent of mind led him to believe that he had fostered the institution from the first. 'Advancing, I see, by leaps and bounds.'

Never was truer word spoken! The mission *was* advancing exactly as he had said—at first by little hops and shuffles of shamefaced uneasiness, but soon by the leaps of fly-stung horses and the bounds of maddened kangaroos. From the hill of Panth the Red Elephant Tusk delivered a dry and anguished blare. The ranks of the converts wavered, broke and scattered with yells and shrieks of pain, while Justus and Lotta stood horror-stricken.

'It is the Judgment of Dungara!' shouted a voice. 'I burn! I burn! To the river or we die!'

The mob wheeled and headed for the rocks that over-hung the Berbulda, writhing, stamping, twisting and shedding its garments as it ran, pursued by the thunder of the trumpet of Dungara. Justus and Lotta fled to the collector almost in tears.

'I cannot understand! Yesterday,' panted Justus, 'they had the Ten Commandments.—What is this? Praise the Lord all good spirits by land and by sea. Nala! Oh, shame!'

With a bound and a scream there alighted on the rocks above their heads, Nala, once the pride of the mission, a maiden of fourteen summers, good, docile, and virtuous—now naked as the dawn and spitting like a wild-cat.

'Was it for this!' she raved, hurling her petticoat at Justus; 'was it for this I left my people and Dungara—for the fires of your Bad Place? Blind ape, little earthworm, dried fish that you are, you said that I should never burn! O Dungara, I burn now! I burn now! Have mercy, God of Things as They Are!'

She turned and flung herself into the Berbulda, and the trumpet of Dungara bellowed jubilantly. The last of the converts of the Tubingen Mission had put a quarter of a mile of rapid river between herself and her teachers.

'Yesterday,' gulped Justus, 'she taught in the school A,B,C,D.— Oh! It is the work of Satan!'

But Gallio was curiously regarding the maiden's petticoat where it had fallen at his feet. He felt its texture, drew back his shirt-sleeve beyond the deep tan of his wrist and pressed a fold of the cloth against the flesh. A blotch of angry red rose on the white skin.

'Ah!' said Gallio calmly, 'I thought so.'

'What is it?' said Justus.

'I should call it the Shirt of Nessus, but—Where did you get the fibre of this cloth from?'

'Athon Dazé,' said Justus. 'He showed the boys how it should manufactured be.'

'The old fox! Do you know that he has given you the Nilgiri Nettle—scorpion—*Girardenia heterophylla*—to work up? No wonder they squirmed! Why, it stings even when they make bridge-ropes of it, unless it's soaked for six weeks. The cunning brute! It would take about half an hour to burn through their thick hides, and then—!'

Gallio burst into laughter, but Lotta was weeping in the arms of the Collector's wife, and Justus had covered his face with his hands.

'*Girardenia heterophylla!*' repeated Gallio. 'Krenk, why *didn't* you tell me? I could have saved you this. Woven fire! Anybody but a naked Kol would have known it, and, if I'm a judge of their ways, you'll never get them back.'

He looked across the river to where the converts were still wallowing and wailing in the shallows, and the laughter died out of his eyes, for he saw that the Tubingen Mission to the Buria Kol was dead.

Never again, though they hung mournfully round the deserted school for three months, could Lotta or Justus coax back even the most promising of their flock. No! The end of conversion was the fire of the Bad Place—fire that ran through the limbs and gnawed into the bones. Who dare a second time tempt the anger of Dungara? Let the little man and his wife go elsewhere. The Buria Kol would have none of them. An unofficial message to Athon Dazé that if a hair of their heads were touched, Athon Dazé and the priests of Dungara would be hanged by Gallio at the temple shrine, protected Justus and Lotta from the stumpy poisoned arrows of the Buria Kol, but neither fish nor fowl, honeycomb, salt nor young pig were brought to their doors any more. And, alas! man cannot live by grace alone if meat be wanting.

'Let us go, mine wife,' said Justus; 'there is no good here, and the Lord has willed that some other man shall the work take—in good time—in His own good time. We will go away, and I will—yes—some botany bestudy.'

If anyone is anxious to convert the Buria Kol afresh, there lies at least the core of a mission-house under the hill of Panth. But the chapel and school have long since fallen back into jungle.

At the Pit's Mouth

Men say it was a stolen tide—
The Lord that sent it he knows all,
But in mine ear will aye abide
The message that the bells let fall,
And awesome bells they were to me,
That in the dark rang, "Enderby."

— Jean Ingelow.

Once upon a time there was a man and his wife and a Tertium Quid.

All three were unwise, but the wife was the unwisest. The man should have looked after his wife, who should have avoided the Tertium Quid, who, again, should have married a wife of his own, after clean and open flirtations, to which nobody can possibly object, round Jakko or Observatory Hill. When you see a young man with his pony in a white lather, and his hat on the back of his head flying down-hill at fifteen miles an hour to meet a girl who will be properly surprised to meet him, you naturally approve of that young man, and wish him staff appointments, and take an interest in his welfare, and, as the proper time comes, give them sugar-tongs or side-saddles, according to your means and generosity.

The Tertium Quid flew downhill on horseback, but it was to meet the man's wife; and when he flew up-hill it was for the same end. The man was in the Plains, earning money for his Wife to spend on dresses and four-hundred-*rupee* bracelets, and inexpensive luxuries of that kind. He worked very hard, and sent her a letter or a post-card daily. She also wrote to him daily, and said that she was longing for him to come up to Simla. The Tertium Quid used to lean over her shoulder and laugh as she wrote the notes. Then the two would ride to the post office together.

Now, Simla is a strange place and its customs are peculiar; nor is any man who has not spent at least ten seasons there qualified to pass judgment on circumstantial evidence. which is the most untrustworthy in the courts. For these reasons, and for others which need not appear, I decline to state positively whether there was anything irretrievably wrong in the relations between the man's wife and the Tertium Quid. If there was, and hereon you must form your own opinion, it was the man's wife's fault. She was kittenish in her manners, wearing generally an air of soft and fluffy innocence. But she was deadly learned and evil-instructed; and, now and again, when the mask dropped, men saw this, shuddered and almost drew back. Men are occasionally particular, and the least particular men are always the most exacting.

Simla is eccentric in its fashion of tearing friendships. Certain attachments which have set and crystallized through half a dozen seasons acquire almost the sanctity of the marriage bond, and are revered as such. Again, certain attachments equally old, and, to all appearance, equally venerable, never seem to win any recognized official status; while a chance-sprung acquaintance now two months born, steps into the place which by right belongs to the senior. There is no law reducible to print which regulates these affairs.

Some people have a gift which secures them infinite toleration, and others have not. The man's wife had not. If she looked over the garden wall, for instance, women taxed her with stealing their husbands. She complained pathetically that she was not allowed to choose her own friends. When she put up her big white muff to her lips, and gazed over it and under her eyebrows at you as she said this thing, you felt that she had been infamously misjudged, and that all the other women's instincts were all wrong; which was absurd. She was not allowed to own the Tertium Quid in peace; and was so strangely constructed that she would not have enjoyed peace had she been so permitted. She preferred some semblance of intrigue to cloak even her most commonplace actions.

After two months of riding, first round Jakko, then Elysium, then Summer Hill, then Observatory Hill, then under Jutogh, and lastly up and down the Cart Road as far as the Tara Devi gap in the dusk, she said to the Tertium Quid, "Frank, people say we are too much together, and people are so horrid."

The Tertium Quid pulled his moustache, and replied that horrid people were unworthy of the consideration of nice people.

"But they have done more than talk—they have written—written to my hubby—I'm sure of it," said the man's wife, and she pulled a letter from her husband out of her saddle-pocket and gave it to the Tertium Quid.

It was an honest letter, written by an honest man, then stewing in the Plains on two hundred *rupees* a month (for he allowed his wife eight hundred and fifty), and in a silk banian and cotton trousers. It is said that, perhaps, she had no thought of the unwisdom of allowing her name to be so generally coupled with the Tertium Quid's; that she was too much of a child to understand the dangers of that sort of thing; that he, her husband, was the last man in the world to interfere jealously with her little amusements and interests, but that it would be better were she to drop the Tertium Quid quietly and for her husband's sake. The letter was sweetened with many pretty little pet names, and it amused the Tertium Quid considerably. He and She laughed over it, so that you, fifty yards away, could see their shoulders shaking while the horses slouched along side by side.

Their conversation was not worth reporting. The upshot of it was that, next day, no one saw the man's wife and the Tertium Quid together. They had both gone down to the cemetery, which, as a rule, is only visited officially by the inhabitants of Simla.

A Simla funeral with the clergyman riding, the mourners riding, and the coffin creaking as it swings between the bearers, is one of the most depressing things on this earth, particularly when the procession passes under the wet, dank dip beneath the Rockcliffe Hotel, where the sun is shut out and all the hill streams are wailing and weeping together as they go down the valleys

Occasionally folk tend the graves, but we in India shift and are transferred so often that, at the end of the second year, the dead have no friends—only acquaintances who are far too busy amusing themselves up the hill to attend to old partners. The idea of using a cemetery as a rendezvous is distinctly a feminine one. A man would have said simply "Let people talk. We'll go down the Mall." A woman is made differently, especially if she be such a woman as the man's wife. She and the Tertium Quid enjoyed each other's society among the graves of men and women whom they had known and danced with aforetime.

They used to take a big horse-blanket and sit on the grass a little to the left of the lower end, where there is a dip in the ground and where the occupied graves stop short and the ready-made ones are not ready. Each well-regulated India Cemetery keeps half a dozen graves permanently open for contingencies and incidental wear and tear. In the Hills these are more usually baby's size, because children who come up weakened and sick from the Plains often succumb to the effects of the rains in the hills or get pneumonia from their *ayahs* taking them through damp pine-woods after the sun has set. In cantonments, of course, the man's size is more in request; these arrangements varying with the climate and population.

One day when the man's wife and the Tertium Quid had just arrived in the cemetery, they saw some *coolies* breaking ground. They had marked out a full-size grave, and the Tertium Quid asked them whether any *sahib* was sick. They said that they did not know; but it was an order that they should dig a *sahib's* grave.

"Work away," said the Tertium Quid, "and let's see how it's

done."

The *coolies* worked away, and the man's wife and the Tertium Quid watched and talked for a couple of hours while the grave was being deepened Then a coolie, taking the earth in blankets as it was thrown up, jumped over the grave.

"That's queer," said the Tertium Quid. "Where's my ulster?"

"What's queer?" said the man's wife.

"I have got a chill down my back just as if a goose had walked over my grave."

"Why do you look at the thing, then?" said the man's wife. "Let us go."

The Tertium Quid stood at the head of the grave, and stared without answering for a space. Then he said, dropping a pebble down, "It is nasty and cold; horribly cold. I don't think I shall come to the cemetery any more. I don't think grave-digging is cheerful."

The two talked and agreed that the cemetery was depressing. They also arranged for a ride next day out from the cemetery through the Mashobra Tunnel up to Fagoo and back, because all the world was going to a garden-party at Viceregal Lodge, and all the people of Mashobra would go too.

Coming up the cemetery road, the Tertium Quid's horse tried to bolt up hill, being tired with standing so long, and managed to strain a back sinew.

"I shall have to take the mare tomorrow," said the Tertium Quid, "and she will stand nothing heavier than a snaffle."

They made their arrangements to meet in the cemetery, after allowing all the Mashobra people time to pass into Simla. That night it rained heavily, and next day, when the Tertium Quid came to the trysting-place, he saw that the new grave had a foot of water in it, the ground being a tough and sour clay.

"'Jove! That looks beastly," said the Tertium Quid. "Fancy being boarded up and dropped into that well!"

They then started off to Fagoo, the mare playing with the snaffle and picking her way as though she were shod with satin, and the sun shining divinely. The road below Mashobra to Fagoo

319

is officially styled the Himalayan-Thibet Road; but in spite of its name it is not much more than six feet wide in most places, and the drop into the valley below must be anything between one and two thousand feet.

"Now we're going to Thibet," said the man's wife merrily, as the horses drew near to Fagoo. She was riding on the cliff-side.

"Into Thibet," said the Tertium Quid, "ever so far from people who say horrid things, and hubbies who write stupid letters. With you—to the end of the world!"

A *coolie* carrying a log of wood came round a corner, and the mare went wide to avoid him—forefeet in and haunches out, as a sensible mare should go.

"To the world's end," said the man's wife, and looked unspeakable things over her near shoulder at the Tertium Quid.

He was smiling, but, while she looked, the smile froze stiff as it were on his face, and changed to a nervous grin—the sort of grin men wear when they are not quite easy in their saddles. The mare seemed to be sinking by the stem, and her nostrils cracked while she was trying to realize what was happening. The rain of the night before had rotted the drop-side of the Himalayan-Thibet Road, and it was giving way under her. "What are you doing?" said the man's wife. The Tertium Quid gave no answer. He grinned nervously and set his spurs into the mare, who rapped with her forefeet on the road, and the struggle began. The man's wife screamed, "Oh, Frank, get off!"

But the Tertium Quid was glued to the saddle—his face blue and white—and he looked into the man's wife's eyes. Then the man's wife clutched at the mare's head and caught her by the nose instead of the bridle. The brute threw up her head and went down with a scream, the Tertium Quid upon her, and the nervous grin still set on his face.

The man's wife heard the tinkle-tinkle of little stones and loose earth falling off the roadway, and the sliding roar of the man and horse going down. Then everything was quiet, and she called on Frank to leave his mare and walk up. But Frank did not answer. He was underneath the mare, nine hundred feet below, spoiling a patch of Indian corn.

As the revellers came back from Viceregal Lodge in the mists of the evening, they met a temporarily insane woman, on a temporarily mad horse, swinging round the corners, with her eyes and her mouth open, and her head like the head of the Medusa. She was stopped by a man at the risk of his life, and taken out of the saddle, a limp heap, and put on the bank to explain herself. This wasted twenty minutes, and then she was sent home in a lady's 'rickshaw, still with her mouth open and her hands picking at her riding-gloves.

She was in bed through the following three days, which were rainy; so she missed attending the funeral of the Tertium Quid, who was lowered into eighteen inches of water, instead of the twelve to which he had first objected.

Through the Fire

The policeman rode through the Himalayan forest, under the moss-draped oaks, and his orderly trotted after him.

'It's an ugly business, Bhere Singh,' said the policeman. 'Where are they?'

'It is a very ugly business,' said Bhere Singh; 'and as for *them*, they are, doubtless, now frying in a hotter fire than was ever made of spruce-branches.'

'Let us hope not,' said the policeman, 'for, allowing for the difference between race and race, it's the story of Francesca da Rimini, Bhere Singh.'

Bhere Singh knew nothing about Francesca da Rimini, so he held his peace until they came to the charcoal-burners' clearing where the dying flames said '*whit, whit, whit*' as they fluttered and whispered over the white ashes. It must have been a great fire when at full height. Men had seen it at Donga Pa across the valley winking and blazing through the night, and said that the charcoal-burners of Kodru were getting drunk. But it was only Suket Singh, *sepoy* of the 102nd Punjab Native Infantry, and Athira, a woman, burning—burning—burning.

This was how things befell; and the policeman's diary will bear me out.

Athira was the wife of Madu, who was a charcoal-burner, one-eyed and of a malignant disposition. A week after their marriage, he beat Athira with a heavy stick. A month later, Suket Singh, *sepoy*, came that way to the cool hills on leave from his regiment, and electrified the villagers of Kodru with tales

322

of service and glory under the government, and the honour in which he, Suket Singh, was held by the Colonel Sahib Bahadur. And Desdemona listened to Othello as Desdemonas have done all the world over, and, as she listened, she loved.

'I've a wife of my own,' said Suket Singh, 'though that is no matter when you come to think of it. I am also due to return to my regiment after a time, and I cannot be a deserter—I who intend to be *havildar.*' There is no Himalayan version of 'I could not love thee, dear, as much, Loved I not Honour more;' but Suket Singh came near to making one.

'Never mind,' said Athira, 'stay with me, and, if Madu tries to beat me, you beat him.'

'Very good,' said Suket Singh; and he beat Madu severely, to the delight of all the charcoal-burners of Kodru.

'That is enough,' said Suket Singh, as he rolled Madu down the hillside. 'Now we shall have peace.' But Madu crawled up the grass slope again, and hovered round his hut with angry eyes.

'He'll kill me dead,' said Athira to Suket Singh. 'You must take me away.'

'There'll be a trouble in the Lines. My wife will pull out my beard; but never mind,' said Suket Singh, 'I will take you.'

There was loud trouble in the Lines, and Suket Singh's beard was pulled, and Suket Singh's wife went to live with her mother and took away the children. 'That's all right,' said Athira; and Suket Singh said, 'Yes, that's all right.'

So there was only Madu left in the hut that looks across the valley to Donga Pa; and, since the beginning of time, no one has had any sympathy for husbands so unfortunate as Madu.

He went to Juseen Dazé, the wizard-man who keeps the Talking Monkey's Head.

'Get me back my wife,' said Madu.

'I can't,' said Juseen Dazé, 'until you have made the Sutlej in the valley run up the Donga Pa.'

'No riddles,' said Madu, and he shook his hatchet above Juseen Dazé's white head.

'Give all your money to the headmen of the village,' said

Juseen Dazé, 'and they will hold a communal council, and the council will send a message that your wife must come back.'

So Madu gave up all his worldly wealth, amounting to twenty-seven *rupees*, eight *annas*, three *pice*, and a silver chain, to the Council of Kodru. And it fell as Juseen Dazé foretold.

They sent Athira's brother down into Suket Singh's regiment to call Athira home. Suket Singh kicked him once round the Lines, and then handed him over to the *havildar*, who beat him with a belt.

'Come back,' yelled Athira's brother.

'Where to?' said Athira.

'To Madu,' said he.

'Never,' said she.

'Then Juseen Dazé will send a curse, and you will wither away like a barked tree in the springtime,' said Athira's brother. Athira slept over these things.

Next morning she had rheumatism. 'I am beginning to wither away like a barked tree in the springtime,' she said. 'That is the curse of Juseen Dazé.'

And she really began to wither away because her heart was dried up with fear, and those who believe in curses die from curses. Suket Singh, too, was afraid because he loved Athira better than his very life. Two months passed, and Athira's brother stood outside the regimental Lines again and yelped, 'Aha! You are withering away. Come back.'

'I will come back,' said Athira.

'Say rather that *we* will come back,' said Suket Singh.

'*Ai*; but when?' said Athira's brother.

'Upon a day very early in the morning,' said Suket Singh; and he tramped off to apply to the Colonel Sahib Bahadur for one week's leave.

'I am withering away like a barked tree in the spring,' moaned Athira.

'You will be better soon,' said Suket Singh; and he told her what was in his heart, and the two laughed together softly, for they loved each other. But Athira grew better from that hour.

They went away together, travelling third-class by train as the regulations provided, and then in a cart to the low hills, and on foot to the high ones. Athira sniffed the scent of the pines of her own hills, the wet Himalayan hills. 'It is good to be alive,' said Athira.

'Hah!' said Suket Singh. 'Where is the Kodru road and where is the Forest Ranger's house?'...

'It cost forty *rupees* twelve years ago,' said the Forest Ranger, handing the gun.

'Here are twenty,' said Suket Singh, 'and you must give me the best bullets.'

'It is *very* good to be alive,' said Athira wistfully, sniffing the scent of the pine-mould; and they waited till the night had fallen upon Kodru and the Donga Pa. Madu had stacked the dry wood for the next day's charcoal-burning on the spur above his house. 'It is courteous in Madu to save us this trouble,' said Suket Singh as he stumbled on the pile, which was twelve foot square and four high. 'We must wait till the moon rises.'

When the moon rose, Athira knelt upon the pile. 'If it were only a government Snider,' said Suket Singh ruefully, squinting down the wire-bound barrel of the Forest Ranger's gun.

'Be quick,' said Athira; and Suket Singh was quick; but Athira was quick no longer. Then he lit the pile at the four corners and climbed on to it, reloading the gun.

The little flames began to peer up between the big logs atop of the brushwood. 'The government should teach us to pull the triggers with our toes,' said Suket Singh grimly to the moon. That was the last public observation of Sepoy Suket Singh.

★★★★★★

Upon a day, early in the morning, Madu came to the pyre and shrieked very grievously, and ran away to catch the policeman who was on tour in the district.

'The base-born has ruined four *rupees'* worth of charcoal wood,' Madu gasped. 'He has also killed my wife, and he has left a letter which I cannot read, tied to a pine bough.'

In the stiff, formal hand taught in the regimental school, Sepoy Suket Singh had written—

> Let us be burned together, if anything remain over, for
> we have made the necessary prayers. We have also cursed
> Madu, and Malak the brother of Athira—both evil men.
> Send my service to the Colonel Sahib Bahadur.

The policeman looked long and curiously at the marriage
bed of red and white ashes on which lay, dull black, the barrel
of the ranger's gun. He drove his spurred heel absently into a
half-charred log, and the chattering sparks flew upwards. 'Most
extraordinary people,' said the policeman.

'*Whe-w, whew, ouiou,*' said the little flames.

The policeman entered the dry bones of the case, for the
Punjab Government does not approve of romancing, in his diary.

'But who will pay me those four *rupees*?' said Madu.

The Sending of Dana Da

When the Devil rides on your chest remember the chamar.—
Native Proverb.

Once upon a time, some people in India made a new Heaven and a new Earth out of broken tea-cups, a missing brooch or two, and a hair-brush. These were hidden under bushes, or stuffed into holes in the hillside, and an entire Civil Service of subordinate Gods used to find or mend them again; and every one said: '*There are more things in Heaven and Earth than are dreamt of in our philosophy.*' Several other things happened also, but the religion never seemed to get much beyond its first manifestations; though it added an air-line postal service, and orchestral effects in order to keep abreast of the tunes, and choke off competition.

This religion was too elastic for ordinary use. It stretched itself and embraced pieces of everything that the medicine-men of all ages have manufactured. It approved of and stole from Freemasonry; looted the Latter-day Rosicrucians of half their pet words; took any fragments of Egyptian philosophy that it found in the *Encyclopaedia Britannica*; annexed as many of the Vedas as had been translated into French or English, and talked of all the rest; built in the German versions of what is left of the Zend Avesta; encouraged White, Gray and Black Magic, including spiritualism, palmistry, fortune-telling by cards, hot chestnuts, double-kernelled nuts and tallow droppings; would have adopted Voodoo and Oboe had it known anything about them, and showed itself, in every way, one of the most accommodating arrangements that had ever been invented since the birth of the sea.

When it was in thorough working order, with all the machinery, down to the subscriptions, complete, Dana Da came from nowhere, with nothing in his hands, and wrote a chapter in its history which has hitherto been unpublished. He said that his first name was Dana, and his second was Da. Now, setting aside Dana of the New York *Sun*, Dana is a Bhil name, and Da fits no native of India unless you except the Bengali De as the original spelling. Da is Lap or Finnish; and Dana Da was neither Finn, Chin, Bhil, Bengali, Lap, Nair, Gond, Romaney, Magh, Bokhariot, Kurd, Armenian, Levantine, Jew, Persian, Punjabi, Madrasi, Parsee, nor anything else known to ethnologists. He was simply Dana Da, and declined to give further information. For the sake of brevity and as roughly indicating his origin, he was called 'The Native.' He might have been the original Old Man of the Mountains, who is said to be the only authorised head of the Tea-cup Creed. Some people said that he was; but Dana Da used to smile and deny any connection with the cult; explaining that he was an 'Independent Experimenter.'

As I have said, he came from nowhere, with his hands behind his back, and studied the Creed for three weeks; sitting at the feet of those best competent to explain its mysteries. Then he laughed aloud and went away, but the laugh might have been either of devotion or derision.

When he returned he was without money, but his pride was unabated. He declared that he knew more about the Things in Heaven and Earth than those who taught him, and for this contumacy was abandoned altogether.

His next appearance in public life was at a big cantonment in Upper India, and he was then telling fortunes with the help of three leaden dice, a very dirty old cloth, and a little tin box of opium pills. He told better fortunes when he was allowed half a bottle of whiskey; but the things which he invented on the opium were quite worth the money. He was in reduced circumstances. Among other people's he told the fortune of an Englishman who had once been interested in the Simla Creed, but who, later on, had married and forgotten all his old knowledge in the study of babies and things. The Englishman allowed Dana Da to tell a fortune for charity's sake, and gave him five *rupees*, a dinner, and some old clothes. When he had eaten, Dana Da professed gratitude, and asked if there were anything he could do for his host—in the esoteric line.

'Is there anyone that you love?' said Dana Da. The Englishman loved his wife, but had no desire to drag her name into the conversation. He therefore shook his head.

'Is there anyone that you hate?' said Dana Da. The Englishman said that there were several men whom he hated deeply.

'Very good,' said Dana Da, upon whom the whiskey and the opium were beginning to tell. 'Only give me their names, and I will despatch a Sending to them and kill them.'

Now a Sending is a horrible arrangement, first invented, they say, in Iceland. It is a Thing sent by a wizard, and may take any form, but, most generally, wanders about the land in the shape of a little purple cloud till it finds the Sendee, and him it kills by changing into the form of a horse, or a cat, or a man without a face. It is not strictly a native patent, though *chamars* of the skin and hide castes can, if irritated, despatch a Sending which sits on the breast of their enemy by night and nearly kills him. Very few natives care to irritate *chamars* for this reason.

'Let me despatch a Sending,' said Dana Da; 'I am nearly dead now with want, and drink, and opium, but I should like to kill a man before I die. I can send a Sending anywhere you choose, and in any form except in the shape of a man.'

The Englishman had no friends that he wished to kill, but partly to soothe Dana Da, whose eyes were rolling, and partly to see what would be done, he asked whether a modified Sending could not be arranged for—such a Sending as should make a man's life a burden to him, and yet do him no harm. If this were possible, he notified his willingness to give Dana Da ten *rupees* for the job.

'I am not what I was once,' said Dana Da, 'and I must take the money because I am poor. To what Englishman shall I send it?'

'Send a Sending to Lone Sahib,' said the Englishman, naming a man who had been most bitter in rebuking him for his apostasy from the Tea-cup Creed. Dana Da laughed and nodded.

'I could have chosen no better man myself,' said he. 'I will see that he finds the Sending about his path and about his bed.'

He lay down on the hearth-rug, turned up the whites of his eyes, shivered all over and began to snort. This was Magic, or Opium, or the Sending, or all three. When he opened his eyes he vowed that the Sending had started upon the war-path, and was at that moment flying up to the town where Lone Sahib lives.

'Give me my ten *rupees*,' said Dana Da wearily, 'and write a letter to Lone Sahib, telling him, and all who believe with him, that you and a friend are using a power greater than theirs. They will see that you are speaking the truth.'

He departed unsteadily, with the promise of some more rupees if anything came of the Sending.

The Englishman sent a letter to Lone Sahib, couched in what he remembered of the terminology of the Creed. He wrote: 'I also, in the days of what you held to be my backsliding, have obtained Enlightenment, and with Enlightenment has come Power.' Then he grew so deeply mysterious that the recipient of the letter could make neither head nor tail of it, and was proportionately impressed; for he fancied that his friend had become a 'fifth-rounder.' When a man is a 'fifth-rounder' he can do more than Slade and Houdin combined.

Lone Sahib read the letter in five different fashions, and was beginning a sixth interpretation when his bearer dashed in with the news that there was a cat on the bed. Now if there was one thing that Lone Sahib hated more than another, it was a cat. He scolded the bearer for not turning it out of the house. The bearer said that he was afraid. All the doors of the bedroom had been shut throughout the morning, and no *real* cat could possibly have entered the room. He would prefer not to meddle with the creature.

Lone Sahib entered the room gingerly, and there, on the pillow of his bed, sprawled and whimpered a wee white kitten; not a jumpsome, frisky little beast, but a slug-like crawler with its eyes barely opened and its paws lacking strength or direction—a kitten that ought to have been in a basket with its mamma. Lone Sahib caught it by the scruff of its neck, handed it over to the sweeper to be drowned, and fined the bearer four *annas*.

That evening, as he was reading in his room, he fancied that he saw something moving about on the hearth-rug, outside the circle of light from his reading-lamp. When the thing began to myowl, he realised that it was a kitten—a wee white kitten, nearly blind and very miserable. He was seriously angry, and spoke bitterly to his bearer, who said that there was no kitten in the room when he brought in the lamp, and *real* kittens of tender age generally had mother-cats in attendance.

'If the Presence will go out into the veranda and listen,' said the bearer, 'he will hear no cats. How, therefore, can the kitten on the bed and the kitten on the hearth-rug be real kittens?'

Lone Sahib went out to listen, and the bearer followed him, but there was no sound of anyone mewing for her children. He returned to his room, having hurled the kitten down the hillside, and wrote out the incidents of the day for the benefit of his co-religionists. Those people were so absolutely free from superstition that they ascribed anything a little out of the common to agencies. As it was their business to know all about the agencies, they were on terms of almost indecent familiarity with manifestations of every kind.

Their letters dropped from the ceiling—unstamped—and spirits used to squatter up and down their staircases all night; but they had never come into contact with kittens. Lone Sahib wrote out the facts, noting the hour and the minute, as every psychical observer is bound to do, and appending the English-man's letter because it was the most mysterious document and might have had a bearing upon anything in this world or the next. An outsider would have translated all the tangle thus: 'Look out! You laughed at me once, and now I am going to make you sit up.'

Lone Sahib's co-religionists found that meaning in it; but their translation was refined and full of four-syllable words. They held a sederunt, and were filled with tremulous joy, for, in spite of their familiarity with all the other worlds and cycles, they had a very human awe of things sent from Ghost-land. They met in Lone Sahib's room in shrouded and sepulchral gloom, and their conclave was broken up by a clinking among the photo-frames on the mantelpiece. A wee white kitten, nearly blind, was looping and writhing itself between the clock and the candlesticks. That stopped all investigations or doubtings. Here was the manifestation in the flesh. It was, so far as could be seen, devoid of purpose, but it was a manifestation of undoubted authenticity.

They drafted a Round Robin to the Englishman, the backslider of old days, adjuring him in the interests of the Creed to explain whether there was any connection between the embodiment of some Egyptian God or other (I have forgotten the name) and his communication. They called the kitten Ra, or Toth, or Tum, or something; and when Lone Sahib confessed that the first one had, at his most misguided instance, been drowned by the sweeper, they said consolingly that in his next life he would be a 'bounder,' and not even a 'bounder' of the lowest grade. These words may not be quite correct, but they accurately express the sense of the house.

When the Englishman received the Round Robin—it came by post—he was startled and bewildered. He sent into the bazar for Dana Da, who read the letter and laughed. 'That is my Sending,' said he. 'I told you I would work well. Now give me another ten *rupees.*'

'But what in the world is this gibberish about Egyptian Gods?' asked the Englishman.

'Cats,' said Dana Da with a hiccough, for he had discovered the Englishman's whiskey bottle. 'Cats, and cats, and cats! Never was such a Sending. A hundred of cats. Now give me ten more *rupees* and write as I dictate.'

Dana Da's letter was a curiosity. It bore the Englishman's signature, and hinted at cats—at a Sending of Cats. The mere words on paper were creepy and uncanny to behold.

'What have you done, though?' said the Englishman; 'I am as much in the dark as ever. Do you mean to say that you can actually send this absurd Sending you talk about?'

'Judge for yourself,' said Dana Da. 'What does that letter mean? In a little time they will all be at my feet and yours, and I—O Glory!—will be drugged or drunk all daylong.'

Dana Da knew his people.

When a man who hates cats wakes up in the morning and finds a little squirming kitten on his breast, or puts his hand into his ulster-pocket and finds a little half-dead kitten where his gloves should be, or opens his trunk and finds a vile kitten among his dress-shirts, or goes for a long ride with his mackintosh strapped on his saddle-bow and shakes a little squawling kitten from its folds when he opens it, or goes out to dinner and finds a little blind kitten under his chair, or stays at home and finds a writhing kitten under the quilt, or wriggling among his boots, or hanging, head downwards, in his tobacco-jar, or being mangled by his terrier in the veranda,—when such a man finds one kitten, neither more nor less, once a day in a place where no kitten rightly could or should be, he is naturally upset.

When he dare not murder his daily trove because he believes it to be a manifestation, an emissary, an embodiment, and half a dozen other things all out of the regular course of nature, he is more than upset. He is actually distressed. Some of Lone Sahib's co-religionists thought that he was a highly favoured individual; but many said that if he had treated the first kitten with proper respect—as suited a Toth-Ra-Tum-Sennacherib Embodiment— all this trouble would have been averted. They compared him to the Ancient Mariner, but none the less they were proud of him and proud of the Englishman who had sent the manifestation. They did not call it a Sending because Icelandic magic was not in their programme.

After sixteen kittens, that is to say after one fortnight, for there were three kittens on the first day to impress the fact of the Sending, the whole camp was uplifted by a letter—it came fly-

ing through a window-from the Old Man of the Mountains—
the head of all the Creed—explaining the manifestation in the
most beautiful language and soaking up all the credit of it for
himself. The Englishman, said the letter, was not there at all.
He was a backslider without power or asceticism, who couldn't
even raise a table by force of volition, much less project an army
of kittens through space. The entire arrangement, said the letter, was strictly orthodox, worked and sanctioned by the highest
authorities within the pale of the Creed.

There was great joy at this, for some of the weaker brethren
seeing that an outsider who had been working on independent
lines could create kittens, whereas their own rulers had never
gone beyond crockery—and broken at best—were showing a
desire to break line on their own trail. In fact, there was the
promise of a schism. A second Round Robin was drafted to the
Englishman, beginning: 'O Scoffer,' and ending with a selec-
tion of curses from the Rites of Mizraim and Memphis and the
Commination of Jugana, who was a 'fifth-rounder,' upon whose
name an upstart 'third-rounder' once traded. A papal excommu-
nication is a *billet-doux* compared to the commination of Jugana.
The Englishman had been proved, under the hand and seal of
the Old Man of the Mountains, to have appropriated Virtue and
pretended to have Power which, in reality, belonged only to the
Supreme Head. Naturally the Round Robin did not spare him.

He handed the letter to Dana Da to translate into decent
English. The effect on Dana Da was curious. At first he was furiously angry, and then he laughed for five minutes.

'I had thought,' he said, 'that they would have come to me. In
another week I would have shown that I sent the Sending, and
they would have discrowned the Old Man of the Mountains
who has sent this Sending of mine. Do you do nothing. The
time has come for me to act. Write as I dictate, and I will put
them to shame. But give me ten more *rupees*.'

At Dana Da's dictation the Englishman wrote nothing less
than a formal challenge to the Old Man of the Mountains. It
wound up: 'And if this manifestation be from your hand, then let

it go forward; but if it be from my hand, I will that the Sending shall cease in two days' time. In that day there shall be twelve kittens and thenceforward none at all. The people shall judge between us.' This was signed by Dana Da, who added pentacles and pentagrams, and a *crux ansata*, and half a dozen *swastikas*, and a Triple Tau to his name, just to show that he was all he laid claim to be.

The challenge was read out to the gentlemen and ladies, and they remembered then that Dana Da had laughed at them some years ago. It was officially announced that the Old Man of the Mountains would treat the matter with contempt; Dana Da being an independent investigator without a single 'round' at the back of him. But this did not soothe his people. They wanted to see a fight. They were very human for all their spirituality. Lone Sahib, who was really being worn out with kittens, submitted meekly to his fate. He felt that he was being 'kittened to prove the power of Dana Da,' as the poet says.

When the stated day dawned, the shower of kittens began. Some were white and some were tabby, and all were about the same loathsome age. Three were on his hearth-rug, three in his bath-room, and the other six turned up at intervals among the visitors who came to see the prophecy break down. Never was a more satisfactory Sending. On the next day there were no kittens, and the next day and all the other days were kittenless and quiet. The people murmured and looked to the Old Man of the Mountains for an explanation.

A letter, written on a palm-leaf, dropped from the ceiling, but everyone except Lone Sahib felt that letters were not what the occasion demanded. There should have been cats, there should have been cats,—full-grown ones. The letter proved conclusively that there had been a hitch in the psychic current which, colliding with a dual identity, had interfered with the percipient activity all along the main line. The kittens were still going on, but owing to some failure in the developing fluid, they were not materialised. The air was thick with letters for a few days afterwards. Unseen hands played Gluck and Beethoven on finger-bowls and clock-shades; but all men felt that psychic life was a mockery without materialised kittens. Even Lone Sahib shouted with the majority on this head. Dana Da's letters were very insulting, and if he had then offered to lead a new departure, there is no knowing what might not have happened.

But Dana Da was dying of whiskey and opium in the Englishman's *godown*, and had small heart for honours.

'They have been put to shame,' said he. 'Never was such a Sending. It has killed me.'

'Nonsense,' said the Englishman, 'you are going to die, Dana Da, and that sort of stuff must be left behind. I'll admit that you have made some queer things come about. Tell me honestly, now, how was it done?'

'Give me ten more *rupees*,' said Dana Da faintly, 'and if I die before I spend them, bury them with me.' The silver was counted out while Dana Da was fighting with Death. His hand closed upon the money and he smiled a grim smile.

'Bend low,' he whispered. The Englishman bent.

'*Bunnia*—Mission-school—expelled—*box-wallah* (peddler)—Ceylon pearl-merchant—all mine English education—outcasted, and made up name Dana Da—England with American thought-reading man and—and—you gave me ten *rupees* several times—I gave the *sahib's* bearer two—eight a month for cats—little, little cats. I wrote, and he put them about—very clever man. Very few kittens now in the *bazar*. Ask Lone Sahib's sweeper's wife.'

So saying, Dana Da gasped and passed away into a land where, if all be true, there are no materialisations and the making of new creeds is discouraged.

But consider the gorgeous simplicity of it all!

The Mother Hive

If the stock had not been old and overcrowded, the wax-moth would never have entered; but where bees are too thick on the comb there must be sickness or parasites. The heat of the hive had risen with the June honey-flow, and though the fanners worked, until their wings ached, to keep people cool, everybody suffered.

A young bee crawled up the greasy trampled alighting-board. "Excuse me," she began, "but it's my first honey-flight. Could you kindly tell me if this is my—"

"—own hive?" the guard snapped. "Yes! Buzz in, and be foul-brooded to you! Next!"

"Shame!" cried half a dozen old workers with worn wings and nerves, and there was a scuffle and a hum.

The little grey wax-moth, pressed close in a crack in the alighting-board, had waited this chance all day. She scuttled in like a ghost, and, knowing the senior bees would turn her out at once, dodged into a brood-frame, where youngsters who had not yet seen the winds blow or the flowers nod discussed life. Here she was safe, for young bees will tolerate any sort of stranger. Behind her came the bee who had been slanged by the guard.

"What is the world like, Melissa?" said a companion.

"Cruel! I brought in a full load of first-class stuff, and the guard told me to go and be foul-brooded!" She sat down in the cool draught across the combs.

"If you'd only heard," said the wax-moth silkily, "the insolence of the guard's tone when she cursed our sister. It aroused the entire community." She laid an egg. She had stolen in for that purpose.

"There *was* a bit of a fuss on the gate," Melissa chuckled. "You were there, Miss —— ?" She did not know how to address the slim stranger.

"Don't call me 'Miss.' I'm a sister to all in affliction—just a working-sister. My heart bled for you beneath your burden." The wax-moth caressed Melissa with her soft feelers and laid another egg.

"You mustn't lay here," cried Melissa. "You aren't a queen."

"My dear child, I give you my most solemn word of honour those aren't eggs. Those are my principles, and I am ready to die for them." She raised her voice a little above the rustle and tramp round her. "If you'd like to kill me, pray do."

"Don't be unkind, Melissa," said a young bee, impressed by the chaste folds of the wax-moth's wing, which hid her ceaseless egg-dropping.

"*I* haven't done anything," Melissa answered. "She's doing it all."

"Ah, don't let your conscience reproach you later, but when you've killed me, write me, at least, as one that loved her fellow-workers."

Laying at every sob, the wax-moth backed into a crowd of young bees, and left Melissa bewildered and annoyed. So she lifted up her little voice in the darkness and cried, "Stores!" till a gang of cell-fillers hailed her, and she left her load with them.

"I'm afraid I foul-brooded you just now," said a voice over her shoulder. "I'd been on the gate for three hours, and one would foul-brood the queen herself after that. No offence meant."

"None taken," Melissa answered cheerily. "I shall be on guard myself, some day. What's next to do?"

"There's a rumour of death's head moths about. Send a gang of youngsters to the gate, and tell them to narrow it in with a couple of stout scrap-wax pillars. It'll make the hive hot, but we can't have death's headers in the middle of our honey-flow."

"My only wings! I should think not!" Melissa had all a sound bee's hereditary hatred against the big, squeaking, feathery thief of the hives. "Tumble out!" she called across the youngsters' quarters. "All you who aren't feeding babies, show a leg. Scrap-wax pillars for the ga-ate!" She chanted the order at length.

"That's nonsense," a downy, day-old bee answered. "In the first place, I never heard of a death's header coming into a hive. People don't do such things. In the second, building pillars to keep 'em out is purely a Cypriote trick, unworthy of British bees. In the third, if you trust a death's head, he will trust you. Pillar-building shows lack of confidence. Our dear sister in grey says so."

"Yes. Pillars are un-English and provocative, and a waste of wax that is needed for higher and more practical ends," said the wax-moth from an empty store-cell.

"The safety of the hive is the highest thing I've ever heard of. You mustn't teach us to refuse work," Melissa began.

"You misunderstand me, as usual, love. Work's the essence of life; but to expend precious unreturning vitality and real labour against imaginary danger, *that* is heartbreakingly absurd! If I can only teach a—a little toleration—a little ordinary kindness here toward that absurd old bogey you call the death's header, I shan't have lived in vain."

"She *hasn't* lived in vain, the darling!" cried twenty bees together. "You should see her saintly life, Melissa! She just de-votes herself to spreading her principles, and—and—she looks lovely!"

An old, baldish bee came up the comb.

"Pillar-workers for the gate! Get out and chew scraps. Buzz off!" she said. The wax-moth slipped aside.

The young bees trooped down the frame, whispering.

"What's the matter with 'em?" said the oldster. "Why do they call each other 'ducky' and 'darling'? 'Must be the weather." She sniffed suspiciously. "Horrid stuffy smell here. Like stale quilts. Not wax-moth, I hope, Melissa ?"

"Not to my knowledge," said Melissa, who, of course, only

knew the wax-moth as a lady with principles, and had never thought to report her presence. She had always imagined Wax-moths to be like blood-red dragon-flies.

"You had better fan out this corner for a little," said the old bee and passed on. Melissa dropped her head at once, took firm hold with her fore-feet, and fanned obediently at the regulation stroke—three hundred beats to the second. Fanning tries a bee's temper, because she must always keep in the same place where she never seems to be doing any good, and, all the while, she is wearing out her only wings. When a bee cannot fly, a bee must not live; and a bee knows it. The wax-moth crept forth, and caressed Melissa again.

"I see," she murmured, "that at heart you are one of us."

"I work with the hive," Melissa answered briefly.

"It's the same thing. We and the Hive are one."

"Then why are your feelers different from ours?" Don't cuddle so."

"Don't be provincial, *carissima*. You can't have all the world alike—yet."

"But why do you lay eggs?" Melissa insisted. "You lay 'em like a queen—only you drop them in patches all over the place. I've watched you."

"Ah, Brighteyes, so you've pierced my little subterfuge? Yes, they are eggs. By and by they'll spread our principles. Aren't you glad ?"

"You gave me your most solemn word of honour that they were not eggs."

"That was my little subterfuge, dearest—for the sake of the cause. Now I must reach the young." The wax-moth tripped towards the fourth brood-frame where the young bees were busy feeding the babies.

It takes some time for a sound bee to realize a malignant and continuous lie. "She's very sweet and feathery," was all that Melissa thought, "but her talk sounds like ivy honey tastes. I'd better get to my field-work again."

She found the gate in a sulky uproar. The youngsters told off to the pillars had refused to chew scrap-wax because it made their jaws ache, and were clamouring for virgin stuff.

"Anything to finish the job!" said the badgered guards. "Hang up, some of you, and make wax for these slack-jawed sisters."

Before a bee can make wax she must fill herself with honey. Then she climbs to safe foothold and hangs, while other gorged bees hang on to her in a cluster. There they wait in silence till the wax comes. The scales are either taken out of the maker's pockets by the workers, or tinkle down on the workers while they wait. The workers chew them (they are useless unchewed) into the all-supporting, all-embracing wax of the hive.

But now, no sooner was the wax-cluster in position than the workers below broke out again.

"Come down!" they cried. "Come down and work! Come on, you Levantine parasites! Don't think to enjoy yourselves up there while we're sweating down here!"

The cluster shivered, as from hooked fore-foot to hooked hind-foot it telegraphed uneasiness. At last a worker sprang up, grabbed the lowest wax-maker, and swung, kicking above her companions.

"I can make wax too!" she bawled. "Give me a full gorge and I'll make tons of it."

"Make it, then," said the bee she had grappled. The spoken word snapped the current through the cluster. It shook and glistened like a cat's fur in the dark. "Unhook!" it murmured. "No wax for anyone today."

"You lazy thieves! Hang up at once and produce our wax," said the bees below.

"Impossible! The sweat's gone. To make your wax we must have stillness, warmth, and food. Unhook! Unhook!"

They broke up as they murmured, and disappeared among the other bees, from whom, of course, they were undistinguishable.

"Seems as if we'd have to chew scrap-wax for these pillars, after all," said a worker.

"Not by a whole comb," cried the young bee who had broken the cluster. "Listen here! I've studied the question more than twenty minutes. It's as simple as falling off a daisy. You've heard of Cheshire, Root and Langstroth?"

They had not, but they shouted "Good old Langstroth!" just the same.

"Those three know all that there is to be known about making hives. One or t'other of 'em must have made ours, and if they've made it, they're bound to look after it. Ours is a 'guaranteed patent hive.' You can see it on the label behind."

"Good old guarantee! Hurrah for the label behind!" roared the bees.

"Well, such being the case, I say that when we find they've betrayed us, we can exact from them a terrible vengeance."

"Good old vengeance! Good old Root! 'Nuff said! Chuck it!" The crowd cheered and broke away as Melissa dived through.

" D'you know where Langstroth, Root and Cheshire live if you happen to want 'em?" she asked of the proud and panting orator.

"Gum me if I know they ever lived at all! But aren't they beautiful names to buzz about? Did you see how it worked up the sisterhood?"

"Yes; but it didn't defend the Gate," she replied.

"Ah, perhaps that's true, but think how delicate *my* position is, sister. I've a magnificent appetite, and I don't like working. It's bad for the mind. My instinct tells me that I can act as a restraining influence on others. They would have been worse, but for me."

But Melissa had already risen clear, and was heading for a breadth of virgin white clover, which to an overtired bee is as soothing as plain knitting to a woman.

"I think I'll take this load to the nurseries," she said, when she had finished. "It was always quiet there in my day," and she topped off with two little pats of pollen for the babies.

She was met on the fourth brood-comb by a rush of excited sisters all buzzing together.

"One at a time! Let me put down my load. Now, what is it,

Sacharissa?" she said.

" Grey Sister—that fluffy one, I mean—she came and said we ought to be out in the sunshine gathering honey, because life was short. She said any old bee could attend to our babies, and some day old bees would. That isn't true, Melissa, is it? No old bees can take us away from our babies, can they?"

"Of course not. You feed the babies while your heads are soft. When your heads harden, you go on to field-work. Any one knows that."

"We told her so! We *told* her so; but she only waved her feelers, and said we could all lay eggs like queens if we chose. And I'm afraid lots of the weaker sisters believe her, and are trying to do it. So unsettling!"

Sacharissa sped to a sealed worker-cell whose lid pulsated, as the bee within began to cut its way out.

"Come along, precious!" she murmured, and thinned the frail top from the other side. A pale, damp, creased thing hoisted itself feebly on to the comb. Sacharissa's note changed at once. "No time to waste! Go up the frame and preen yourself!" she said. "Report for nursing-duty in my ward tomorrow evening at six. Stop a minute. What's the matter with your third right leg ?"

The young bee held it out in silence—unmistakably a drone leg incapable of packing pollen.

"Thank you. You needn't report till the day after tomorrow." Sacharissa turned to her companion. "That's the fifth oddity hatched in my ward since noon. I don't like it."

"There's always a certain number of 'em," said Melissa. "You can't stop a few working sisters from laying, now and then, when they overfeed themselves. They only raise dwarf drones."

"But we're hatching out drones with workers' stomachs; workers with drones' stomachs; and albinoes and mixed-leggers who can't pack pollen—like that poor little beast yonder. I don't mind dwarf drones any more than you do (they all die in July), but this steady hatch of oddities frightens me, Melissa!"

"How narrow of you! They are all so delightfully clever and unusual and interesting," piped the wax-moth from a crack above them. "Come here, you dear, downy duck, and tell us all about your feelings."

"I wish she'd go!" Sacharissa lowered her voice. "She meets these—er—oddities as they dry out, and cuddles 'em in corners."

"I suppose the truth is that we're over-stocked and too well fed to swarm," said Melissa.

"That is the truth," said the queen's voice behind them. They had not heard the heavy royal footfall which sets empty cells vibrating. Sacharissa offered her food at once. She ate and dragged her weary body forward. " Can you suggest a remedy?" she said.

"New principles!" cried the wax-moth from her crevice. "We'll apply them quietly—later."

"Suppose we sent out a swarm?" Melissa suggested. "It's a little late, but it might ease us off."

"It would save us, but—I know the hive! You shall see for yourself." The old queen cried the swarming cry, which to a bee of good blood should be what the trumpet was to Job's war-horse. In spite of her immense age (three years), it rang between the canon-like frames as a pibroch rings in a mountain pass; the fanners changed their note, and repeated it up in every gallery; and the broad-winged drones, burly and eager, ended it on one nerve-thrilling outbreak of bugles: *La Reine le veult! Swarm! Swar-rm! Swar-r-rm!*"

But the roar which should follow the call was wanting. They heard a broken grumble like the murmur of a falling tide.

"Swarm? What for? Catch me leaving a good bar-frame hive, with fixed foundations, for a rotten old oak out in the open where it may rain any minute! *We're* all right! It's a 'patent guaranteed hive.' Why do they want to turn us out? Swarming be gummed! Swarming was invented to cheat a worker out of her proper comforts. Come on off to bed!"

The noise died out as the bees settled in empty cells for the night.

"You hear?" said the queen. "I know the hive!"

"Quite between ourselves, *I* taught them that," cried the wax-moth. "Wait till my principles develop, and you'll see the light from a new quarter."

"You speak truth for once," the queen said suddenly, for she recognized the wax-moth. "That light will break into the top of the hive. A hot smoke will follow it, and your children will not be able to hide in any crevice."

"Is it possible?" Melissa whispered. "I—we have sometimes heard a legend like it."

"It is no legend," the old queen answered. "I had it from my mother, and she had it from hers. After the wax-moth has grown strong, a shadow will fall across the gate; a voice will speak from behind a veil; there will be light, and hot smoke, and earthquakes, and those who live will see everything that they have done, all together in one place, burned up in one great fire." The old queen was trying to tell what she had been told of the bee master's dealings with an infected hive in the apiary, two or three seasons ago; and, of course, from her point of view the affair was as important as the Day of Judgment.

"And then?" asked horrified Sacharissa.

"Then, I have heard that a little light will burn in a great darkness, and perhaps the world will begin again. Myself, I think not."

"Tut! Tut!" the wax-moth cried. "You good, fat people always prophesy ruin if things don't go exactly your way. But I grant you there will be changes."

There were. When her eggs hatched, the wax was riddled with little tunnels, coated with the dirty clothes of the caterpillars. Flannelly lines ran through the honey-stores, the pollen-larders, the foundations, and, worst of all, through the babies in their cradles, till the sweeper guards spent half their time tossing out useless little corpses. The lines ended in a maze of sticky webbing on the face of the comb. The caterpillars could not stop spinning as they walked, and as they walked everywhere, they smarmed and garmed everything. Even where it did not hamper the bees' feet, the stale, sour smell of the stuff put them

345

off their work; though some of the bees who had taken to egg-laying said it encouraged them to be mothers and maintain a vital interest in life.

When the caterpillars became moths, they made friends with the ever-increasing oddities—albinoes, mixed-leggers, single-eyed composites, faceless drones, half-queens and laying sisters; and the ever-dwindling band of the old stock worked themselves bald and fray-winged to feed their queer charges. Most of the oddities would not, and many, on account of their malformations, could not, go through a day's field-work; but the wax-moths, who were always busy on the brood-comb, found pleasant home occupations for them. One albino, for instance, divided the number of pounds of honey in stock by the number of bees in the hive, and proved that if every bee only gathered honey for seven and three quarter minutes a day, she would have the rest of the time to herself, and could accompany the drones on their mating flights. The drones were not at all pleased.

Another, an eyeless drone with no feelers, said that all brood-cells should be perfect circles, so as not to interfere with the grub or the workers. He proved that the old six-sided cell was solely due to the workers building against each other on opposite sides of the wall, and that if there were no interference, there would be no angles. Some bees tried the new plan for a while, and found it cost eight times more wax than the old six-sided specification; and, as they never allowed a cluster to hang up and make wax in peace, real wax was scarce.

However, they eked out their task with varnish stolen from new coffins at funerals, and it made them rather sick. Then they took to cadging round sugar-factories and breweries, because it was easiest to get their material from those places, and the mixture of glucose and beer naturally fermented in store and blew the store-cells out of shape, besides smelling abominably. Some of the sound bees warned them that ill-gotten gains never prosper, but the oddities at once surrounded them and balled them to death. That was a punishment they were almost as fond of as they were of eating, and they expected the sound bees to feed them. Curiously enough the age-old instinct of loyalty and devotion towards the hive made the sound bees do this, though their reason told them they ought to slip away and unite with some other healthy stock in the apiary.

"What about seven and three-quarter minutes' work now?" said Melissa one day as she came in. "I've been at it for five hours, and I've only half a load."

"Oh, the hive subsists on the hival honey which the hive produces," said a blind oddity squatting in a store-cell.

"But honey is gathered from flowers outside—two miles away sometimes," cried Melissa.

"Pardon me," said the blind thing, sucking hard. "But this is the hive, is it not ?"

"It was. Worse luck, it is."

"And the hival honey is here, is it not?" It opened a fresh store-cell to prove it.

"Ye-es, but it won't be long at this rate," said Melissa.

"The rates have nothing to do with it. This hive produces the hival honey. You people never seem to grasp the economic simplicity that underlies all life."

" Oh, me!" said poor Melissa, "haven't you ever been beyond the gate?"

"Certainly not. A fool's eyes are in the ends of the earth. Mine are in my head." It gorged till it bloated.

Melissa took refuge in her poorly paid field-work and told Sacharissa the story.

"Hut!" said that wise bee, fretting with an old maid of a this-tle. "Tell us something new. The hive's full of such as him—it, I mean."

"What's the end to be? All the honey going out and none coming in. Things can't last this way!" said Melissa.

"Who cares?" said Sacharissa. "I know now how drones feel the day before they're killed. A short life and a merry one for me."

"If it only were merry! But think of those awful, solemn, lop-sided oddities waiting for us at home—crawling and clambering

347

and preaching—and dirtying things in the dark."

"I don't mind that so much as their silly songs, after we've fed 'em, all about '*work among the merry, merry blossoms*,'" said Sacharissa from the deeps of a stale canterbury bell.

"I do. How's our queen?" said Melissa.

"Cheerfully hopeless, as usual. But she lays an egg now and then."

"Does she so?" Melissa backed out of the next bell with a jerk. "Suppose now, we sound workers tried to raise a princess in some clean corner?"

"You'd be put to it to find one. The hive's all wax-moth and muckings. But—well?"

"A princess might help us in the time of the voice behind the veil that the queen talks of. And anything is better than working for oddities that chirrup about work that they can't do, and waste what we bring home."

"Who cares?" said Sacharissa. "I'm with you, for the fun of it. The oddities would ball us to death, if they knew. Come home, and we'll begin."

★★★★★★

There is no room to tell how the experienced Melissa found a far-off frame so messed and mishandled by abandoned cell-building experiments that, for very shame, the bees never went there. How in that ruin she blocked out a royal cell of sound wax, but disguised by rubbish till it looked like a *kopje* among deserted *kopjes*. How she prevailed upon the hopeless queen to make one last effort and lay a worthy egg. How the queen obeyed and died. How her spent carcass was flung out on the rubbish heap, and how a multitude of laying sisters went about dropping drone-eggs where they listed, and said there was no more need of queens. How, covered by this confusion, Sacharissa educated certain young bees to educate certain new-born bees in the almost lost art of making royal jelly. How the nectar for it was won out of hours in the teeth of chill winds.

How the hidden egg hatched true—no drone, but blood royal. How it was capped, and how desperately they worked to feed and double-feed the now swarming oddities, lest any break in the food-supplies should set them to instituting inquiries, which, with songs about work, was their favourite amusement. How in an auspicious hour, on a moonless night, the princess came forth—a princess indeed, and how Melissa smuggled her into a dark empty honey-magazine, to bide her time; and how the drones, knowing she was there, went about singing the deep disreputable love-songs of the old days—to the scandal of the laying sisters, who do not think well of drones. These things are written in the *Book of Queens*, which is laid up in the hollow of the Great Ash Ygdrasil.

After a few days the weather changed again and became glorious. Even the oddities would now join the crowd that hung out on the alighting-board, and would sing of work among the merry, merry blossoms till an untrained ear might have received it for the hum of a working hive. Yet, in truth, their store-honey had been eaten long ago. They lived from day to day on the efforts of the few sound bees, while the wax-moth fretted and consumed again their already ruined wax. But the sound bees never mentioned these matters. They knew, if they did, the oddities would hold a meeting and ball them to death.

"Now you see what we have done," said the wax-moths. "We have created new material, a new convention, a new type, as we said we would."

"And new possibilities for us," said the laying sisters gratefully. "You have given us a new life's work, vital and paramount."

"More than that," chanted the oddities in the sunshine; "you have created a new heaven and a new earth. Heaven, cloudless and accessible" (it was a perfect August evening) "and earth teeming with the merry, merry blossoms, waiting only our honest toil to turn them all to good. The—er—aster, and the crocus, and the—er—ladies' smock in her season, the chrysanthemum after her kind, and the Guelder Rose bringing forth abundantly withal."

"Oh, Holy Hymettus!" said Melissa, awestruck. "I knew they didn't know how honey was made, but they've forgotten the order of the flowers! What will become of them?"

A shadow fell across the alighting-board as the bee master and his son came by. The oddities crawled in and a voice behind a veil said: "I've neglected the old hive too long. Give me the smoker."

Melissa heard and darted through the gate. "Come, oh come!" she cried. "It is the destruction the old queen foretold. Princess, come!"

"Really, you are too archaic for words," said an oddity in an alley-way. "A cloud, I admit, may have crossed the sun; but why hysterics? Above all, why princesses so late in the day? Are you aware it's the hival tea-time? Let's sing grace."

Melissa clawed past him with all six legs. Sacharissa had run to what was left of the fertile brood-comb. "Down and out!" she called across the brown breadth of it. "Nurses, guards, fanners, sweepers—out! Never mind the babies. They're better dead. Out, before the light and the hot smoke!"

The princess's first clear fearless call (Melissa had found her) rose and drummed through all the frames. "*La Reine le veult! Swarm! Swar-rm! Swar-r-rm!*"

The hive shook beneath the shattering thunder of a stuck-down quilt being torn back.

"Don't be alarmed, dears," said the wax-moths. "That's our work. Look up, and you'll see the dawn of the new day."

Light broke in the top of the hive as the queen had prophesied—naked light on the boiling, bewildered bees.

Sacharissa rounded up her rearguard, which dropped head-long off the frame, and joined the princess's detachment thrusting toward the gate. Now panic was in full blast, and each sound bee found herself embraced by at least three oddities. The first instinct of a frightened bee is to break into the stores and gorge herself with honey; but there were no stores left, so the oddities fought the sound bees.

"You must feed us, or we shall die!" they cried, holding and clutching and slipping, while the silent scared earwigs and little spiders twisted between their legs. "Think of the hive, traitors!

The holy hive!"

"You should have thought before!" cried the sound bees. "Stay and see the dawn of your new day."

They reached the gate at last over the soft bodies of many to whom they had ministered.

"On! Out! Up!" roared Melissa in the princess's ear. "For the hive's sake! To the old oak!"

The princess left the alighting-board, circled once, flung herself at the lowest branch of the old oak, and her little loyal swarm—you could have covered it with a pint mug—followed, hooked, and hung.

"Hold close!" Melissa gasped. "The old legends have come true! Look!"

The hive was half hidden by smoke, and figures moved through the smoke. They heard a frame crack stickily, saw it heaved high and twirled round between enormous hands—a blotched, bulged, and perished horror of grey wax, corrupt brood, and small drone-cells, all covered with crawling oddities, strange to the sun.

"Why, this isn't a hive! This is a museum of curiosities," said the voice behind the veil. It was only the bee master talking to his son.

" Can you blame 'em, father ?" said a second voice. "It's rotten with wax-moth. See here!"

Another frame came up. A finger poked through it, and it broke away in rustling flakes of ashy rottenness.

"Number Four Frame! That was your mother's pet comb once," whispered Melissa to the princess. "Many's the good egg I've watched her lay there."

"Aren't you confusing *post hoc* with *propter hoc*?" said the bee master. "wax-moth only succeed when weak bees let them in." A third frame crackled and rose into the light. "All this is full of laying workers' brood. That never happens till the stock's weakened. Phew!"

He beat it on his knee like a tambourine, and it also crumbled to pieces.

The little swarm shivered as they watched the dwarf drone-grubs squirm feebly on the grass. Many sound bees had nursed on that frame, well knowing their work was useless; but the actual sight of even useless work destroyed disheartens a good worker.

"No, they have some recuperative power left," said the second voice. "Here's a queen cell!"

" But it's tucked away among—— What on earth has come to the little wretches? They seem to have lost the instinct of cell-building." The father held up the frame where the bees had experimented in circular cell-work. It looked like the pitted head of a decaying toadstool.

"Not altogether," the son corrected. "There's one line, at least, of perfectly good cells."

"My work," said Sacharissa to herself. "I'm glad man does me justice before—"

That frame, too, was smashed out and thrown atop of the others and the foul earwiggy quilts.

As frame after frame followed it, the swarm beheld the upheaval, exposure, and destruction of all that had been well or ill done in every cranny of their hive for generations past. There was black comb so old that they had forgotten where it hung; orange, buff, and ochre-varnished store-comb, built as bees were used to build before the days of artificial foundations; and there was a little, white, frail new work. There were sheets on sheets of level, even brood-comb that had held in its time unnumbered thousands of unnamed workers; patches of obsolete drone-comb, broad and high-shouldered, showing to what marks the male grub was expected to grow; and two-inch deep honey-magazines, empty, but still magnificent, the whole gummed and glued into twisted scrap-work, awry on the wires; half-cells, beginnings abandoned, or grandiose, weak-walled, composite cells pieced out with rubbish and capped with dirt.

Good or bad, every inch of it was so riddled by the tunnels of the wax-moth that it broke in clouds of dust as it was flung on the heap.

"Oh, see!" cried Sacharissa. "The great burning that our queen foretold. Who can bear to look?"

A flame crawled up the pile of rubbish, and they smelt singeing wax.

The figures stooped, lifted the hive and shook it upside down over the pyre. A cascade of oddities, chips of broken comb, scale, fluff, and grubs slid out, crackled, sizzled, popped a little, and then the flames roared up and consumed all that fuel.

"We must disinfect," said a voice. "Get me a sulphur-candle, please."

The shell of the hive was returned to its place, a light was set in its sticky emptiness, tier by tier the figures built it up, closed the entrance, and went away. The swarm watched the light leaking through the cracks all the long night. At dawn one wax-moth came by, fluttering impudently.

"There has been a miscalculation about the new day, my dears," she began; "one can't expect people to be perfect all at once. That was our mistake."

"No, the mistake was entirely ours," said the princess.

"Pardon me," said the wax-moth. "When you think of the enormous upheaval—call it good or bad—which our influence brought about, you will admit that we, and we alone—"

"You?" said the princess. "Our stock was not strong. So *you* came—as any other disease might have come. Hang close, all my people."

When the sun rose, veiled figures came down, and saw their swarm at the bough's end waiting patiently within sight of the old hive—a handful, but prepared to go on.

The Wish House

The new church visitor had just left after a twenty minutes' call. During that time, Mrs. Ashcroft had used such English as an elderly, experienced, and pensioned cook should, who had seen life in London. She was the readier, therefore, to slip back into easy, ancient Sussex (Ts softening to 'd's as one warmed) when the 'bus brought Mrs. Fettley from thirty miles away for a visit, that pleasant March Saturday. The two had been friends since childhood; but, of late, destiny had separated their meetings by long intervals.

Much was to be said, and many ends, loose since last time, to be ravelled up on both sides, before Mrs. Fettley, with her bag of quilt-patches, took the couch beneath the window commanding the garden, and the football-ground in the valley below.

'Most folk got out at Bush Tye for the match there,' she explained, 'so there weren't no one for me to cushion agin, the last five mile. An' she do just-about bounce ye.'

'You've took no hurt,' said her hostess. 'You don't brittle by agein', Liz.'

Mrs. Fettley chuckled and made to match a couple of patches to her liking. 'No, or I'd ha' broke twenty year back. You can't ever mind when I was so's to be called round, can ye?'

Mrs. Ashcroft shook her head slowly—she never hurried—and went on stitching a sack-cloth lining into a list-bound rush tool-basket. Mrs. Fettley laid out more patches in the Spring light through the geraniums on the window-sill, and they were silent awhile.

'What like's this new Visitor o' yourn?' Mrs. Fettley inquired, with a nod towards the door. Being very short-sighted, she had, on her entrance, almost bumped into the lady.

Mrs. Ashcroft suspended the big packing-needle judicially on high, ere she stabbed home. 'Settin' aside she don't bring much news with her yet, I dunno as I've anythin' special agin her.'

'Ourn, at Keyneslade,' said Mrs. Fettley, 'she's full o' words an' pity, but she don't stay for answers. Ye can get on with your thoughts while she clacks.'

'This 'un don't clack. She's aimin' to be one o' those high church nuns, like.'

'Ourn's married, but, by what they say, she've made no great gains of it . . . ' Mrs. Fettley threw up her sharp chin. 'Lord! How they dam' cherubim do shake the very bones o' the place!'

The tile-sided cottage trembled at the passage of two specially chartered forty-seat charabancs on their way to the Bush Tye match; a regular Saturday' shopping' 'bus, for the county's capital, fumed behind them; while, from one of the crowded inns, a fourth car backed out to join the procession, and held up the stream of through pleasure-traffic.

'You're as free-tongued as ever, Liz,' Mrs. Ashcroft observed.

'Only when I'm with you. Otherwhiles, I'm granny—three times over. I lay that basket's for one o' your gran'chiller—ain't it?'

''Tis for Arthur—my Jane's eldest.'

'But he ain't workin' nowheres, is he?'

'No. 'Tis a picnic-basket.'

'You're let off light. My Willie, he's allus at me for money for them aireated wash-poles folk puts up in their gardens to draw the music from Lunnon, like. An' I give it 'im pore fool me!'

'An' he forgets to give you the promise-kiss after, don't he?' Mrs. Ashcroft's heavy smile seemed to strike inwards.

'He do. 'No odds 'twixt boys now an' forty year back. 'Take all an' give naught—an' we to put up with it! Pore fool we! Three shillin' at a time Willie'll ask me for!'

'They don't make nothin' o' money these days,' Mrs. Ashcroft said.

'An' on'y last week,' the other went on, 'me daughter, she ordered a quarter pound suet at the butchers's; an' she sent it back to 'im to be chopped. She said she couldn't bother with choppin' it.'

'I lay he charged her, then.'

'I lay he did. She told me there was a whisk-drive that afternoon at the Institute, an' she couldn't bother to do the choppin'.'

'Tck!'

Mrs. Ashcroft put the last firm touches to the basket-lining. She had scarcely finished when her sixteen-year-old grandson, a maiden of the moment in attendance, hurried up the garden-path shouting to know if the thing were ready, snatched it, and made off without acknowledgment. Mrs. Fettley peered at him closely.

'They're goin' picnickin' somewheres,' Mrs. Ashcroft explained.

'Ah,' said the other, with narrowed eyes. 'I lay he won't show much mercy to any he comes across, either. Now 'oo the dooce do he remind me of, all of a sudden?'

'They must look arter theirselves—'same as we did.' Mrs. Ashcroft began to set out the tea.

'No denyin' you could, Gracie,' said Mrs. Fettley.

'What's in your head now?'

'Dunno . . . But it come over me, sudden-like—about dat woman from Rye—I've slipped the name—Barnsley, wadn't it?'

'Batten—Polly Batten, you're thinkin' of.'

'That's it—Polly Batten. That day she had it in for you with a hay-fork—'time we was all hayin' at Smalldene—for stealin' her man.'

'But you heered me tell her she had my leave to keep him?'

Mrs. Ashcroft's voice and smile were smoother than ever.

'I did—an' we was all looking that she'd prod the fork spang through your breasts when you said it.'

'No-oo. She'd never go beyond bounds—Polly. She shruck too much for reel doin's.'

'Allus seems to me,' Mrs. Fettley said after a pause, 'that a man 'twixt two fightin' women is the foolishest thing on earth. 'Like a dog bein' called two ways.'

'Mebbe. But what set ye off on those times, Liz?'

'That boy's fashion o' carryin' his head an' arms. I haven't rightly looked at him since he's growed. Your Jane never showed it, but—him! Why, 'tis Jim Batten and his tricks come to life again! . . . Eh?'

'Mebbe. There's some that would ha' made it out so—bein' barren-like, themselves.'

'Oho! Ah well! Dearie, dearie me, now! . . . An' Jim Batten's been dead this—'

'Seven and twenty year,' Mrs. Ashcroft answered briefly. 'Won't ye draw up, Liz?'

Mrs. Fettley drew up to buttered toast, currant bread, stewed tea, bitter as leather, some home-preserved pears, and a cold boiled pig's tail to help down the muffins. She paid all the proper compliments.

'Yes. I dunno as I've ever owed me belly much,' said Mrs. Ashcroft thoughtfully. 'We only go through this world once.'

'But don't it lay heavy on ye, sometimes?' her guest suggested.

'Nurse says I'm a sight liker to die o' me indigestion than me leg.' For Mrs. Ashcroft had a long-standing ulcer on her shin, which needed regular care from the village nurse, who boasted (or others did, for her) that she had dressed it one hundred and three times already during her term of office.

'An' you that was so able, too! It's all come on ye before your full time, like. I've watched ye goin'.' Mrs. Fettley spoke with real affection.

'Somethin's bound to find ye sometime. I've me 'eart left me still,' Mrs. Ashcroft returned.

'You was always big-hearted enough for three. That's somethin' to look back on at the day's end.'

'I reckon you've your back-lookin's, too,' was Mrs. Ashcroft's answer.

'You know it. But I don't think much regardin' such matters excep' when I'm along with you, Gra'. 'Takes two sticks to make a fire.'

Mrs. Fettley stared, with jaw half-dropped, at the grocer's bright calendar on the wall. The cottage shook again to the roar of the motortraffic, and the crowded football-ground below the garden roared almost as loudly; for the village was well set to its Saturday leisure.

★★★★★★

Mrs. Fettley had spoken very precisely for some time without interruption, before she wiped her eyes. 'And,' she concluded, 'they read 'is death-notice to me, out o' the paper last month. O' course it wadn't any o' my becomin' concerns—let be I 'adn't set eyes on him for so long. O' course I couldn't say nor show nothin'. Nor I've no rightful call to go to Eastbourne to see 'is grave, either. I've been schemin' to slip over there by the 'bus some day; but they'd ask questions at 'ome past endurance. So I 'aven't even that to stay me.'

'But you've 'ad your satisfactions?'

'Godd! Yess! Those four years 'e was workin' on the rail near us. An' the other drivers they gave him a brave funeral, too.'

'Then you've naught to cast-up about. 'Nother cup o' tea?'

★★★★★★

The light and air had changed a little with the sun's descent, and the two elderly ladies closed the kitchen-door against chill. A couple of jays squealed and skirmished through the undraped apple-trees in the garden. This time, the word was with Mrs. Ashcroft, her elbows on the tea-table, and her sick leg propped on a stool . . .

'Well I never! But what did your 'usband say to that?' Mrs. Fettley asked, when the deep-toned recital halted.

''E said I might go where I pleased for all of 'im. But seein' 'e was bedrid, I said I'd 'tend 'im out. 'E knowed I wouldn't take no advantage of 'im in that state. 'E lasted eight or nine week.

358

Then he was took with a seizure-like; an' laid stone-still for days. Then 'e propped 'imself up abed an' says: "You pray no man'll ever deal with you like you've dealed with some." "An' you?" I says, for you know, Liz, what a rover 'e was. "It cuts both ways," says 'e, "but I'm death-wise, an' I can see what's comin' to you." He died a-Sunday an' was buried a-Thursday . . . An' yet I'd set a heap by him—one time or—did I ever?'

'You never told me that before,' Mrs. Fettley ventured.

'I'm payin' ye for what ye told me just now. Him bein' dead, I wrote up, sayin' I was free for good, to that Mrs. Marshall in Lunnon—which gave me my first place as kitchen-maid—Lord, how long ago! She was well pleased, for they two was both gettin' on, an' I knowed their ways. You remember, Liz, I used to go to 'em in service between whiles, for years—when we wanted money, or—or my 'usband was away—on occasion.'

''E did get that six months at Chichester, didn't 'e?' Mrs. Fettley whispered. 'We never rightly won to the bottom of it.'

''E'd ha' got more, but the man didn't die.'

"None o' your doin's, was it, Gra'?'

'No! 'Twas the woman's husband this time. An' so, my man bein' dead, I went back to them Marshall's, as cook, to get me legs under a gentleman's table again, and be called with a handle to me name. That was the year you shifted to Portsmouth.'

'Cosham,' Mrs. Fettley corrected. 'There was a middlin' lot o' new buildin' bein' done there. My man went first, an' got the room, an' I follered.'

'Well, then, I was a year-abouts in Lunnon, all at a breath, like, four meals a day an' livin' easy. Then, 'long towards autumn, they two went travellin', like, to France; keepin' me on, for they couldn't do without me. I put the house to rights for the caretaker, an' then I slipped down 'ere to me sister Bessie—me wages in me pockets, an' all 'ands glad to be 'old of me.'

'That would be when I was at Cosham,' said Mrs. Fettley.

'You know, Liz, there wasn't no cheap-dog pride to folk, those days, no more than there was cinemas nor whisk-drives. Man or woman 'ud lay hold o' any job that promised a shillin' to the backside of it, didn't they? I was all peaked up after Lunnon, an' I thought the fresh airs 'ud serve me. So I took on at Smalldene, obligin' with a hand at the early potato-liftin, stubbin' hens, an' such-like. They'd ha' mocked me sore in my kitchen in Lunnon, to see me in men's boots, an me petticoats all shorted.'

'Did it bring ye any good?' Mrs. Fettley asked.

''Twadn't for that I went. You know, 's'well's me, that na'un happens to ye till it 'as 'appened. Your mind don't warn ye before'and of the road ye've took, till you're at the far eend of it. We've only a backwent view of our proceedin's.'

''Oo was it?'

''Arry Mockler.' Mrs. Ashcroft's face puckered to the pain of her sick leg.

Mrs. Fettley gasped. ''Arry? Bert Mockler's son! An' I never guessed!'

Mrs. Ashcroft nodded. 'An' I told myself—an' I beleft it—that I wanted field-work.'

'What did ye get out of it?'

'The usuals. Everythin' at first—worse than naught after. I had signs an' warnings a-plenty, but I took no heed of 'em. For we was burnin' rubbish one day, just when we'd come to know how 'twas with—with both of us. 'Twas early in the year for burnin', an' I said so. "No!" says he. "The sooner dat old stuff's off an' done with," 'e says, "the better." 'Is face was harder'n rocks when he spoke. Then it come over me that I'd found me master, which I 'adn't ever before. I'd allus owned 'em, like.'

'Yes! Yes! They're yourn or you're theirn,' the other sighed. 'I like the right way best.'

'I didn't. But 'Arry did . . . 'Long then, it come time for me to go back to Lunnon. I couldn't. I clean couldn't! So, I took an' tipped a dollop o' scaldin' water out o' the copper one Monday mornin' over me left 'and and arm. Dat stayed me where I was for another fortnight.'

'Was it worth it?' said Mrs. Fettley, looking at the silvery scar on the wrinkled fore-arm.

Mrs. Ashcroft nodded. 'An' after that, we two made it up

'twixt us so's 'e could come to Lunnon for a job in a liv'rystable not far from me. 'E got it. I 'tended to that. There wadn't no talk nowhere. His own mother never suspicioned how 'twas. He just slipped up to Lunnon, an' there we abode that winter, not 'alf a mile 'tother from each.'

'Ye paid 'is fare an' all, though'; Mrs. Fettley spoke convincedly.

Again Mrs. Ashcroft nodded. 'Dere wadn't much I didn't do for him. 'E was me master, an'—O God, help us!—we'd laugh over it walkin' together after dark in them paved streets, an' me corns fair wrenchin' in me boots! I'd never been like that before. Ner he! Ner he!'

Mrs. Fettley clucked sympathetically.

'An' when did ye come to the eend?' she asked.

'When 'e paid it all back again, every penny. Then I knowed, but I wouldn't suffer meself to know. "You've been mortal kind to me," he says. "Kind!" I said. "'Twixt us?" But 'e kep' all on tellin' me 'ow kind I'd been an' 'e'd never forget it all his days. I held it from off o' me for three evenin's, because I would not believe. Then 'e talked about not bein' satisfied with 'is job in the stables, an' the men there puttin' tricks on 'im, an' all they lies which a man tells when 'e's leavin' ye. I heard 'im out, neither 'elpin' nor 'inderin'. At the last, I took off a fiddle brooch which he'd give me an' I says: "Dat'll do. I ain't askin' na'un'." An' I turned me round an' walked off to me own sufferin's. 'E didn't make 'em worse. 'E didn't come nor write after that. 'E slipped off 'ere back 'ome to 'is mother again.'

'An' 'ow often did ye look for 'en to come back?' Mrs. Fettley demanded mercilessly.

'More'n once—more'n once! Goin' over the streets we'd used, I thought de very pave-stones 'ud shruck out under me feet.'

'Yes,' said Mrs. Fettley. 'I dunno but dat don't 'urt as much as aught else. An' dat was all ye got?'

'No. 'Twadn't. That's the curious part, if you'll believe it, Liz.'

'I do. I lay you're further off lyin' now than in all your life, Gra'.'

'I am . . . An' I suffered, like I'd not wish my most arrantest enemies to. God's Own Name! I went through the hoop that spring! One part of it was 'eddicks which I'd never known all me days before. Think o' me with an 'eddick! But I come to be grateful for 'em. They kep' me from thinkin' . . . '

''Tis like a tooth,' Mrs. Fettley commented. 'It must rage an' rugg till it tortures itself quiet on ye; an' then—then there's na'un left.'

'I got enough lef' to last me all my days on earth. It come about through our charwoman's fiddle girl—Sophy Ellis was 'er name—all eyes an' elbers an' hunger. I used to give 'er vittles. Otherwhiles, I took no special notice of 'er, an' a sight less, o' course, when me trouble about 'Arry was on me. But—you know how fiddle maids first feel it sometimes—she come to be crazy-fond o' me, pawin' an' cuddlin' all whiles; an' I 'adn't the 'eart to beat 'er off . . . One afternoon, early in spring 'twas, 'er mother 'ad sent 'er round to scutchel up what vittles she could off of us. I was settin' by the fire, me apern over me head, halfmad with the 'eddick, when she slips in. I reckon I was middlin' short with 'er. "Lor'!" she says. "Is that all? I'll take it off you in two-twos!" I told her not to lay a finger on me, for I thought she'd want to stroke my forehead; an'—I ain't that make. "I won't tech ye," she says, an' slips out again.

'She 'adn't been gone ten minutes 'fore me old 'eddick took off quick as bein' kicked. So I went about my work. Prasin'ly, Sophy comes back, an' creeps into my chair quiet as a mouse. 'Er eyes was deep in 'er 'ead an''er face all drawed. I asked 'er what 'ad 'appened. "Nothin'," she says. "On'y I've got it now." "Got what?" I says. "Your 'eddick," she says, all hoarse an' sticky-tipped. "I've took it on me." "Nonsense," I says, "it went of it-self when you was out. Lay still an' I'll make ye a cup o' tea." "'Twon't do no good," she says, "till your time's up. 'Ow long do your 'eddicks last?" "Don't talk silly," I says, "or I'll send for the doctor." It looked to me like she might be hatchin' de measles.

"Oh, Mrs. Ashcroft," she says, stretchin' out 'er fiddle thin arms. "I do love ye." There wasn't any holdin' agin that. I took 'er into me lap an' made much of 'er. "Is it truly gone?" she says. "Yes," I says, "an' if 'twas you took it away, I'm truly grateful." "'Twas me," she says, layin' 'er cheek to mine. "No one but me knows how." An' then she said she'd changed me 'eddick for me at a Wish 'Ouse.'

'Whatt?' Mrs. Fettley spoke sharply.

'A Wish House. No! I'adn't 'eard o' such things, either. I couldn't get it straight at first, but, puttin' all together, I made out that a Wish 'Ouse 'ad to be a house which 'ad stood unlet an' empty long enough for someone, like, to come an' in'abit there. She said a fiddle girl that she'd played with in the livery-stables where 'Arry worked 'ad told 'er so. She said the girl 'ad belonged in a caravan that laid up, o' winters, in Lunnon. Gipsy, I judge.'

'Ooh! There's no sayin' what Gippos know, but I've never 'eard of a Wish 'Ouse, an' I know—some things,' said Mrs. Fettley.

'Sophy said there was a Wish 'Ouse in Wadloes Road just a few streets off, on the way to our green-grocer's. All you 'ad to do, she said, was to ring the bell an' wish your wish through the slit o' the letter-box. I asked 'er if the fairies give it 'er? "Don't ye know," she says, "there's no fairies in a Wish 'Ouse? There's on'y a Token."'

'Goo' Lord A'mighty! Where did she come by that word?' cried Mrs. Fettley; for a Token is a wraith of the dead or, worse still, of the living.

'The caravan-girl 'ad told 'er, she said. Well, Liz, it troubled me to 'ear 'er, an' lyin' in me arms she must ha' felt it. "That's very kind o' you," I says, holdin' 'er tight, "to wish me 'eddick away. But why didn't ye ask somethin' nice for yourself?" "You can't do that," she says. "All you'll get at a Wish 'Ouse is leave to take someone else's trouble. I've took Ma's 'eddicks, when she's been kind to me; but this is the first time I've been able to do aught for you. Oh, Mrs. Ashcroft, I do just about love you." An'

363

she goes on all like that. Liz, I tell you my 'air e'en a'most stood on end to 'ear 'er. I asked 'er what like a Token was. "I dunno," she says, "but after you've ringed the bell, you'll 'ear it run up from the basement, to the front door. Then say your wish," she says, "an' go away."

'"The Token don't open de door to ye, then?" I says. "Oh no," she says. "You on'y 'ear gigglin', like, be'ind the front door. Then you say you'll take the trouble off of 'oo ever 'tis you've chose for your love; an' yell get it," she says. I didn't ask no more—she was too 'ot an' fevered. I made much of 'er till it come time to light de gas, an' a fiddle after that, 'er 'eddick—mine, I suppose—took off, an' she got down an' played with the cat.'

'Well, I never!' said Mrs. Fettley. 'Did—did ye foller it up, anyways?'

'She askt me to, but I wouldn't 'ave no such dealin's with a child.'

'What did ye do, then?'

"Sat in me own room 'stid o' the kitchen when me 'eddicks come on. But it lay at de back o' me mind.'

''Twould. Did she tell ye more, ever?'

'No. Besides what the Gippo girl 'ad told 'er, she knew naught, 'cept that the charm worked. An', next after that—in May 'twas—I suffered the summer out in Lunnon. 'Twas hot an' windy for weeks, an' the streets stinkin' o' dried 'orsedung blowin' from side to side an' lyin' level with the kerb. We don't get that nowadays. I 'ad my 'ol'day just before hoppin', an' come down 'ere to stay with Bessie again. She noticed I'd lost flesh, an' was all poochy under the eyes.'

'Did ye see 'Arry?'

Mrs. Ashcroft nodded. 'The fourth—no, the fifth day. Wednesday 'twas. I knowed 'e was workin' at Smalldene again. I asked 'is mother in the street, bold as brass. She 'adn't room to say much, for Bessie—you know 'er tongue—was talkin' full-clack. But that Wednesday, I was walkin' with one o' Bessie's chillern hangin' on me skirts, at de back o' Chanter's Tot. Prasin'ly, I felt 'e was be'ind me on the footpath, an' I knowed by 'is tread 'e'd changed 'is nature. I slowed, an' I heard 'im slow. Then I fussed a piece with the child, to force him past me, like. So 'e 'ad to come past. 'E just says "Good-evenin'," and goes on, tryin' to pull 'isself together.'

'Drunk, was he?' Mrs. Fettley asked.

'Never! S'runk an' wizen; 'is clothes 'angin' on 'im like bags, an' the back of 'is neck whiter'n chalk. 'Twas all I could do not to oppen my arms an' cry after him. But I swallered me spittle till I was back 'ome again an' the chillern abed. Then I says to Bessie, after supper, "What in de world's come to 'Arry Mockler?" Bessie told me 'e'd been a-hospital for two months, 'long o' cuttin' 'is foot wid a spade, muckin' out the old pond at Smalldene. There was poison in de dirt, an' it rooshed up 'is leg, like, an' come out all over him. 'E 'adn't been back to 'is job—carterin' at Smalldene—more'n a fortnight. She told me the doctor said he'd go off, likely, with the November frostes; an' 'is mother 'ad told 'er that 'e didn't rightly eat nor sleep, an' sweated 'imself into pools, no odds 'ow chill 'e lay. An' spit terrible o' mornin's. "Dearie me," I says. "But, mebbe, hoppin' 'll set 'im right again," an' I licked me thread-point an' I fetched me needle's eye up to it an' I threads me needle under de lamp, steady as rocks. An' dat night (me bed was in de wash-house) I cried an' I cried. An' you know, Liz—for you've been with me in my throes—it takes summat to make me cry.'

'Yes; but chile-bearin' is on'y just pain,' said Mrs. Fettley.

'I come round by cock-crow, an' dabbed cold tea on me eyes to take away the signs. Long towards nex' evenin'—I was settin' out to lay some flowers on me 'usband's grave, for the look o' the thing—I met 'Arry over against where the War Memorial is now. 'E was comin' back from 'is 'orses, so 'e couldn't not see me. I looked 'im all over, an' "'Arry," I says twix' me teeth, "come back an' rest-up in Lunnon." "I won't take it," he says, "for I can give ye naught." "I don't ask it," I says. "By God's Own Name, I don't ask na'un! On'y come up an' see a Lunnon doctor." 'E lifts 'is two 'eavy eyes at me: "'Tis past that, Gra'," 'e says. "I've but a few months left." "'Arry!" I says. "My man!" I says. I couldn't say no more. 'Twas all up in me throat. "Thank ye kindly, Gra'," 'e says (but 'e never says "my woman"), an' 'e went on upstreet an' 'is mother—Oh, damn 'er!—she was watchin' for 'im, an' she shut de door be'ind 'im.'

Mrs. Fettley stretched an arm across the table, and made to finger Mrs. Ashcroft's sleeve at the wrist, but the other moved it out of reach.

'So I went on to the churchyard with my flowers, an' I remembered my 'usband's warnin' that night he spoke. 'E was death-wise, an' it 'ad 'appened as 'e said. But as I was settin' down de jam-pot on the grave-mound, it come over me there was one thing I could do for 'Arry. Doctor or no doctor, I thought I'd make a trial of it. So I did. Nex' mornin', a bill came down from our Lunnon green-grocer. Mrs. Marshall, she'd lef' me petty cash for suchlike—o' course—but I tole Bess 'twas for me to come an' open the 'ouse. So I went up, afternoon train.'

'An'—but I know you 'adn't—'adn't you no fear?'

'What for? There was nothin' front o' me but my own shame an' God's croolty. I couldn't ever get 'Arry—'ow could I? I knowed it must go on burnin' till it burned me out.'

'Aie!' said Mrs. Fettley, reaching for the wrist again, and this time Mrs. Ashcroft permitted it.

'Yit 'twas a comfort to know I could try this for 'im. So I went an' I paid the green-grocer's bill, an' put 'is receipt in me hand-bag, an' then I stepped round to Mrs. Ellis—our char—an' got the 'ouse-keys an' opened the 'ouse. First, I made me bed to come back to (God's Own Name! Me bed to lie upon!). Nex' I made me a cup o' tea an' sat down in the kitchen thinkin', till 'long towards dusk. Terrible close, 'twas. Then I dressed me an' went out with the receipt in me 'and-bag, feignin' to study it for an address, like.

'Fourteen, Wadloes Road, was the place—a liddle basement-kitchen 'ouse, in a row of twenty-thirty such, an' tiddy strips o' walled garden in front—the paint off the front doors, an' na'un done to na'un since ever so long. There wasn't 'ardly no one in the streets 'cept the cats. 'Twas 'ot, too! I turned into the gate bold as brass; up de steps I went an' I ringed the front-door bell. She pealed loud, like it do in an empty house. When she'd all ceased, I 'eard a cheer, like, pushed back on de floor o' the kitchen. Then I 'eard feet on de kitchen-stairs, like it might ha' been a heavy woman in slippers. They come up to de stairhead, acrost the hall—I 'eard the bare boards creak under 'em—an' at de front door dey stopped. I stooped me to the letter-box slit, an' I says: "Let me take everythin' bad that's in store for my man, 'Arry Mockler, for love's sake." Then, whatever it was 'tother side de door let its breath out, like, as if it 'ad been holdin' it for to 'ear better.'

'Nothin' was said to ye?' Mrs. Fettley demanded.

'Na'un. She just breathed out—a sort of A-ah, like. Then the steps went back an' downstairs to the kitchen—all draggy—an' I heard the cheer drawed up again.'

'An' you abode on de doorstep, throughout all, Gra'?'

Mrs. Ashcroft nodded.

'Then I went away, an' a man passin' says to me: "Didn't you know that house was empty?" "No," I says. "I must ha' been give the wrong number." An' I went back to our 'ouse, an' I went to bed; for I was fair flogged out. 'Twas too 'ot to sleep more'n snatches, so I walked me about, lyin' down betweens, till crack o' dawn. Then I went to the kitchen to make me a cup o' tea, an' I hitted meself just above the ankle on an old roastin' jack o' mine that Mrs. Ellis had moved out from the corner, her last cleanin'. An' so—nex' after that—I waited till the Marshalls come back o' their holiday.'

'Alone there? I'd ha' thought you'd 'ad enough of empty houses,' said Mrs. Fettley, horrified.

'Oh, Mrs. Ellis an' Sophy was runnin' in an' out soon's I was back, an' 'twixt us we cleaned de house again top-to-bottom. There's allus a hand's turn more to do in every house. An' that's 'ow 'twas with me that autumn an' winter, in Lunnon.'

'Then na'un hap—overtook ye for your doin's?'

Mrs. Ashcroft smiled. 'No. Not then. 'Long in November I sent Bessie ten shillin's.'

'You was allus free-'anded,' Mrs. Fettley interrupted.

'An' I got what I paid for, with the rest o' the news. She said the hoppin' 'ad set 'im up wonderful. 'E'd 'ad six weeks of it, and now 'e was back again carterin' at Smalldene. No odds to me 'ow it 'ad 'appened—'slong's it 'ad. But I dunno as my ten shillin's eased me much. 'Arry bein' dead, like, 'e'd ha' been mine, till Judgment. 'Arry bein' alive,'e'd like as not pick up with some woman middlin' quick. I raged over that. Come spring, I 'ad somethin' else to rage for. I'd growed a nasty little weepin' boil, like, on me shin, just above the boot-top, that wouldn't heal no shape. It made me sick to look at it, for I'm clean-fleshed by nature. Chop me all over with a spade, an' I'd heal like turf. Then Mrs. Marshall she set 'er own doctor at me. 'E said I ought to ha' come to him at first go-off, 'stead o' drawn' all manner o' dyed stockm's over it for months. 'E said I'd stood up too much to me work, for it was settin' very close atop of a big swelled vein, like, behither the small o' me ankle. "Slow come, slow go," 'e says. "Lay your leg up on high an' rest it," he says, "an' 'twill ease off. Don't let it close up too soon. You've got a very fine leg, Mrs. Ashcroft," 'e says. An' he put wet dressin's on it.'

''E done right.' Mrs. Fettley spoke firmly. 'Wet dressin's to wet wounds. They draw de humours, same's a lamp-wick draws de oil.'

'That's true. An' Mrs. Marshall was allus at me to make me set down more, an' dat nigh healed it up. An' then after a while they packed me off down to Bessie's to finish the cure; for I ain't the sort to sit down when I ought to stand up. You was back in the village then, Liz.'

'I was. I was, but—never did I guess!'

'I didn't desire ye to.' Mrs. Ashcroft smiled. 'I saw 'Arry once or twice in de street, wonnerful fleshed up an'restored back. Then, one day I didn't see 'im, an' 'is mother told me one of 'is 'orses 'ad lashed out an' caught 'im on the 'ip. So 'e was abed an' middlin' painful. An' Bessie, she says to his mother, 'twas a pity 'Arry 'adn't a woman of 'is own to take the nursin' off 'er. And the old lady was mad! She told us that 'Arry 'ad never looked after any woman in 'is born days, an' as long as she was atop the mowlds, she'd contrive for 'im till 'er two 'ands dropped off. So I knowed she'd do watch-dog for me, 'thout askin' for bones.'

Mrs. Fettley rocked with small laughter.

'That day,' Mrs. Ashcroft went on, 'I'd stood on me feet nigh all the time, watchin' the doctor go in an' out; for they thought it might be 'is ribs, too. That made my boil break again, issuin' an' weepin'. But it turned out 'twadn't ribs at all, an"Arry 'ad a good night. When I heard that, nex' mornin', I says to meself, "I won't lay two an' two together yit. I'll keep me leg down a week, an' see what comes of it." It didn't hurt me that day, to speak of—'seemed more to draw the strength out o' me like— an' 'Arry 'ad another good night. That made me persevere; but I didn't dare lay two an' two together till the weekend, an' then, 'Arry come forth e'en a'most 'imself again—na'un hurt outside ner in of him. I nigh fell on me knees in de washhouse when Bessie was up-street. "I've got ye now, my man," I says. "You'll take your good from me 'thout knowin' it till my life's end. O God, send me long to live for 'Arry's sake!" I says. An' I dunno that didn't still me ragin's.'

'For good?' Mrs. Fettley asked.

'They come back, plenty times, but, let be how 'twould, I knowed I was doin' for 'im. I knowed it. I took an' worked me pains on an' off, like regulatin' my own range, till I learned to 'ave 'em at my commandments. An' that was funny, too. There was times, Liz, when my trouble 'ud all s'rink an' dry up, like. First, I used to try an' fetch it on again; bein' fearful to leave 'Arry alone too long for anythin' to lay 'old of. Prasin'ly I come to see that was a sign he'd do all right awhile, an' so I saved myself'

"'Ow long for?' Mrs. Fettley asked, with deepest interest.

'I've gone de better part of a year onct or twice with na'un more to show than the liddle weepin' core of it, like. All s'rinked up an' dried off. Then he'd inflame up—for a warnin'—an' I'd suffer it. When I couldn't no more—an' I 'ad to keep on goin' with my Lunnon work—I'd lay me leg high on a cheer till it eased. Not too quick. I knowed by the feel of it, those times, dat

369

'Arry was in need. Then I'd send another five shillin's to Bess, or somethin' for the chillern, to find out if, mebbe, 'e'd took any hurt through my neglects. 'Twas so! Year in, year out, I worked it dat way, Liz, an' 'e got 'is good from me 'thout knowin'—for years and years.'

'But what did you get out of it, Gra'?' Mrs. Fettley almost wailed. 'Did ye see 'im reg'lar?'

'Times—when I was 'ere on me 'ol'days. An' more, now that I'm 'ere for good. But 'e's never looked at me, ner any other woman 'cept 'is mother. 'Ow I used to watch an' listen! So did she.'

'Years an' years!' Mrs. Fettley repeated. 'An' where's 'e workin' at now?'

'Oh, 'e's give up carterin' quite a while. He's workin' for one o' them big tractorisin' firms—ploughin' sometimes, an' sometimes off with lorries—fur as Wales, I've 'eard. He comes 'ome to 'is mother 'tween whiles; but I don't set eyes on him now, fer weeks on end. No odds! 'Is job keeps 'im from continuin' in one stay anywheres.'

'But just for de sake o' sayin' somethin'—s'pose 'Arry did get married?' said Mrs. Fettley.

Mrs. Ashcroft drew her breath sharply between her still even and natural teeth. 'Dat ain't been required of me,' she answered. 'I reckon my pains 'ull be counted agin that. Don't you, Liz?'

'It ought to be, dearie. It ought to be.'

'It do 'urt sometimes. You shall see it when nurse comes. She thinks I don't know it's turned.'

Mrs. Fettley understood. Human nature seldom walks up to the word 'cancer.'

'Be ye certain sure, Gra'?' she asked.

'I was sure of it when old Mr. Marshall 'ad me up to 'is study an' spoke a long piece about my faithful service. I've obliged 'em on an' off for a goodish time, but not enough for a pension. But they give me a weekly 'lowance for life. I knew what that sinnified—as long as three years ago.'

'Dat don't prove it, Gra'.'

'To give fifteen bob a week to a woman 'oo'd live twenty year in the course o' nature? It do!'

'You're mistook! You're mistook!' Mrs. Fettley insisted.

'Liz, there's no mistakin' when the edges are all heaped up, like—same as a collar. You'll see it. An' I laid out Dora Wickwood, too. She 'ad it under the arm-pit, like.'

Mrs. Fettley considered awhile, and bowed her head in finality.

''Ow long d'you reckon 'twill allow ye, countin' from now, dearie?'

'Slow come, slow go. But if I don't set eyes on ye 'fore next hoppin', this'll be goodbye, Liz.'

'Dunno as I'll be able to manage by then—not 'thout I have a liddle dog to lead me. For de chillern, dey won't be troubled, an'—O Gra'! I'm blindin' up—I'm blindin' up!'

'Oh, dat was why you didn't more'n finger with your quiltpatches all this while! I was wonderin'... But the pain do count, don't ye think, Liz? The pain do count to keep 'Arry where I want 'im. Say it can't be wasted, like.'

'I'm sure of it—sure of it, dearie. You'll 'ave your reward.'

'I don't want no more'n this—if de pain is taken into de reckonin'.'

''Twill be—'twill be, Gra'.'

There was a knock on the door.

'That's nurse. She's before 'er time,' said Mrs. Ashcroft. 'Open to 'er.'

The young lady entered briskly, all the bottles in her bag clicking. 'Evenin', Mrs. Ashcroft,' she began. 'I've come raound a little earlier than usual because of the Institute dance to-na-ite. You won't ma-ind, will you?'

'Oh, no. Me dancin' days are over.' Mrs. Ashcroft was the self-contained domestic at once.

'My old friend, Mrs. Fettley 'ere, has been settin' talkin' with me a while.'

'I hope she 'asn't been fatiguing you?' said the nurse a little frostily.

'Quite the contrary. It 'as been a pleasure. Only—only—just at the end I felt a bit—a bit flogged out like.'

'Yes, yes.' The Nurse was on her knees already, with the washes to hand. 'When old ladies get together they talk a deal too much, I've noticed.'

'Mebbe we do,' said Mrs. Fettley, rising. 'So now I'll make myself scarce.'

'Look at it first, though,' said Mrs. Ashcroft feebly. 'I'd like ye to look at it.'

Mrs. Fettley looked, and shivered. Then she leaned over, and kissed Mrs. Ashcroft once on the waxy yellow forehead, and again on the faded grey eyes.

'It do count, don't it—de pain?' The lips that still kept trace of their original moulding hardly more than breathed the words.

Mrs. Fettley kissed them and moved towards the door.

What is a God beside Woman? Dust and derision!

The Solid Muldoon

Did ye see John Malone, wid his shinin', brand-new hat?
Did ye see how he walked like a grand aristocrat?
There was flags an' banners wavin' high, an' dhress and shtyle
were shown,
But the best av all the company was Misther John Malone.

John Malone.

There had been a royal dog-fight in the ravine at the back of the rifle-butts, between Learoyd's Jock and Ortheris's Blue Rot—both mongrel Rampur hounds, chiefly ribs and teeth. It lasted for twenty happy, howling minutes, and then Blue Rot collapsed and Ortheris paid Learoyd three *rupees*, and we were all very thirsty. A dog-fight is a most heating entertainment, quite apart from the shouting, because Rampurs fight over a couple of acres of ground. Later, when the sound of belt-badges clicking against the necks of beer-bottles had died away, conversation drifted from dog to man-fights of all kinds. Humans resemble red-deer in some respects. Any talk of fighting seems to wake up a sort of imp in their breasts, and they bell one to the other, exactly like challenging bucks. This is noticeable even in men who consider themselves superior to privates of the line: it shows the refining influence of civilisation and the march of progress.

Tale provoked tale, and each tale more beer. Even dreamy Learoyd's eyes began to brighten, and he unburdened himself of a long history in which a trip to Malham Cove, a girl at Pateley Brigg, a ganger, himself and a pair of clogs were mixed in drawling tangle.

'An' so Ah coot's yead oppen from t' chin to t' hair, an' he was abed for t' matter o' a month,' concluded Learoyd pensively.

Mulvaney came out of a reverie—he was lying down—and flourished his heels in the air. 'You're a man, Learoyd,' said he critically, 'but you've only fought wid men, an' that's an ivry-day expayrience; but I've stud up to a ghost, an' that was *not* an ivry-day expayrience.'

'No?' said Ortheris, throwing a cork at him. 'You git up an' address the 'ouse—you an' yer expayriences. Is it a bigger one nor usual?'

''Twas the livin' trut'!' answered Mulvaney, stretching out a huge arm and catching Ortheris by the collar. 'Now where are ye, me son? Will ye take the wurrud av the Lorrd out av my mouth another time?' He shook him to emphasise the question.

'No, somethin' else, though,' said Ortheris, making a dash at Mulvaney's pipe, capturing it and holding it at arm's length; 'I'll chuck it acrost the ditch if you don't let me go!'

'You maraudin' hathen! 'Tis the only cutty I iver loved. Handle her tinder, or I'll chuck *you* acrost the nullah. If that poipe was bruk—Ah! Give her back to me, Sorr!'

Ortheris had passed the treasure to my hand. It was an absolutely perfect clay, as shiny as the black ball at Pool. I took it reverently, but I was firm.

'Will you tell us about the ghost-fight if I do?' I said.

'Is ut the shtory that's troublin' you? Av course I will. I mint to all along. I was only gettin' at ut my own way, as Popp Doggle said whin they found him thrying to ram a cartridge down the muzzle. Orth'ris, fall away!'

He released the little Londoner, took back his pipe, filled it, and his eyes twinkled. He has the most eloquent eyes of any one that I know.

'Did I iver tell you,' he began, 'that I was wanst the divil av a man?'

'You did,' said Learoyd with a childish gravity that made Ortheris yell with laughter, for Mulvaney was always impressing upon us his great merits in the old days.

'Did I iver tell you,' Mulvaney continued calmly, 'that I was wanst more av a divil than I am now?'

'Mer—ria! You don't mean it?' said Ortheris.

'Whin I was corp'ril—I was rejuced aftherwards—but, as I say, *whin* I was corp'ril, I was a divil of a man.'

He was silent for nearly a minute, while his mind rummaged among old memories and his eye glowed. He bit upon the pipe-stem and charged into his tale.

'Eyah! They was great times. I'm ould now; me hide's wore off in patches; sinthrygo has disconceited me, an' I'm a married man tu. But I've had my day—I've had my day, an' nothin' can take away the taste av that! Oh my time past, whin I put me fut through ivry livin' wan av the Tin Commandmints between Revelly and Lights Out, blew the froth off a pewter, wiped me moustache wid the back av me hand, an' slept on ut all as quiet as a little child! But ut's over—ut's over, an' 'twill niver come back to me; not though I prayed for a week av Sundays. Was there *any* wan in the ould rig'mint to touch Corp'ril Terence Mulvaney whin that same was turned out for sedukshin? I niver met him. Ivry woman that was not a witch was worth the run-nin' afther in those days, an' ivry man was my dearest frind or—I had stripped to him an' we knew which was the betther av the tu.

'Whin I was corp'ril I wud not ha' changed wid the colo-nel—no, nor yet the commandher-in-chief. I wud be a sargint. There was nothin' I wud not be! Mother av Hivin, look at me! Fwhat am I *now?*

'We was quartered in a big cantonmint—'tis no manner av use namin' names, for ut might give the barricks disrepitation—an' I was the Imperor av the Earth to my own mind, an' wan or tu women thought the same. Small blame to thim. Afther we had lain there a year, Bragin, the colour sargint av E Comp'ny, wint an' took a wife that was lady's maid to some big lady in the station. She's dead now is Annie Bragin—died in child-bed at Kirpa Tal, or ut may ha' been Almorah—seven—nine years gone, an' Bragin he married agin. But she was a pretty woman whin Bragin inthrojuced her to cantonmint society. She had eyes like the brown av a buttherfly's wing whin the sun catches ut, an' a waist no thicker than my arm, an' a little sof' button av a mouth I would ha' gone through all Asia bristlin' wid bay'nits to get the kiss av. An' her hair was as long as the tail av the colonel's charger—forgive me mentionin' that blunderin' baste in the same mouthful with Annie Bragin—but 'twas all shpun gold, an' time was when a lock av ut was more than di'monds to me. There was niver pretty woman yet, an' I've had thruck wid a few, cud open the door to Annie Bragin.

"'Twas in the Cath'lic Chapel I saw her first, me oi rolling round as usual to see fwhat was to be seen.

"You're too good for Bragin, my love," thinks I to mesilf, "but that's a mistake I can put straight, or my name is not Terence Mulvaney."

'Now take my wurrd for ut, you Orth'ris there an' Learoyd, an' kape out av the married quarters—as I did not. No good iver comes av ut, an' there's always the chance av your bein' found wid your face in the dirt, a long picket in the back av your head, an' your hands playing the fifes on the tread av another man's doorstep. 'Twas so we found O'Hara, he that Rafferty killed six years gone, when he wint to his death wid his hair oiled, whistlin' *Larry O'Rourke* betune his teeth. Kape out av the married quarters, I say, as I did not. 'Tis onwholesim, 'tis dangerous, an' 'tis ivrything else that's bad, but—O my sowl, 'tis swate while ut lasts!

'I was always hangin' about there whin I was off duty an' Bragin wasn't, but niver a sweet word beyon' ordinar' did I get from Annie Bragin. "'Tis the pervarsity av the sect," sez I to mesilf, an' gave my cap another cock on my head an' straightened my back—'twas the back av a dhrum major in those days—an' wint off as tho' I did not care, wid all the women in the married quarters laughin', I was pershuaded—most bhoys *are* I'm thinkin'—that no woman born av woman cud stand against me av I hild up my little finger. I had reason fer thinkin' that way—

till I met Annie Bragin.

'Time an' agin whin I was blandandherin' in the dusk a man wud go past me as quiet as a cat. "That's quare," thinks I, "for I am, or I should be, the only man in these parts. Now what divilment can Annie be up to?" Thin I called myself a blayguard for thinkin' such things; but I thought thim all the same. An' that, mark you, is the way av a man.

'Wan evenin' I said:—"Mrs. Bragin, manin' no disrespect to you, who is that corp'ril man"—I had seen the stripes though I cud niver get sight av his face—"*who* is that corp'ril man that comes in always whin I'm goin' away?"

'"Mother av God!" sez she, turnin' as white as my belt, "have *you* seen him too?"

'"Seen him!" sez I; "av coorse I have. Did ye want me not to see him, for"—we were standin' talkin' in the dhark, outside the veranda av Bragin's quarters—"you'd betther tell me to shut me eyes. Onless I'm mistaken, he's come now."

'An', sure enough, the corp'ril was walkin' to us, hangin' his head down as though he was ashamed av himsilf.

'"Goodnight, Mrs. Bragin," sez I, very cool; "'tis not for me to interfere wid your *a-moors;* but you might manage things wid more dacincy. I'm off to canteen," I sez.

'I turned on my heel an' wint away, swearin' I wud give that man a dhressin' that wud shtop him messin' about the married quarters for a month an' a week. I had not tuk ten paces before Annie Bragin was hangin' on to my arm, an' I cud feel that she was shakin' all over.

'"Stay wid me, Mister Mulvaney," sez she; "you're flesh an' blood, at the least—are ye not?"

'"I'm *all* that," sez I, an' my anger wint away in a flash. "Will I want to be asked twice, Annie?"

'Wid that I slipped my arm round her waist, for, begad, I fancied she had surrindered at discretion, an' the honours av war were mine.

'"Fwhat nonsinse is this?" sez she, dhrawin' hersilf up on the tips av her dear little toes. "Wid the mother's milk not dhry on your impident mouth? Let go!" she sez.

"'Did ye not say just now that I was flesh an' blood?" sez I. "I have not changed since," I sez; an' I kep' my arm where ut was.

"'Your arms to yoursilf!" sez she, an' her eyes sparkild.

"'Sure, 'tis only human nature," sez I, an' I kep' my arm where ut was.

"'Nature or no nature," sez she, "you take your arm away or I'll tell Bragin, an' he'll alter the nature av your head. Fwhat d'you take me for?" she sez.

"'A woman," sez I; "the prettiest in barricks."

"'A *wife*," sez she; "the straightest in cantonmints!"

'Wid that I dropped my arm, fell back tu paces, an' saluted, for I saw that she mint fwhat she said.'

'Then you know something that some men would give a good deal to be certain of. How could you tell?' I demanded in the interests of science.

"'Watch the hand," said Mulvaney; "av she shuts her hand tight, thumb down over the knuckle, take up your hat an' go. You'll only make a fool av yoursilf av you shtay. But av the hand lies opin on the lap, or av you see her thryin' to shut ut, an' she can't,—go on! She's not past reasonin' wid."

'Well, as I was sayin', I fell back, saluted, an' was goin' away.

"'Shtay wid me," she sez. "Look! He's comin' again."

'She pointed to the veranda, an' by the hoight av impart'nince, the corp'ril man was comin' out av Bragin's quarters.

"'He's done that these five evenin's past," sez Annie Bragin. "Oh, fwhat will I do!"

"He'll not do ut again," sez I, for I was fightin' mad.

'Kape away from a man that has been a thrifle crossed in love till the fever's died down. He rages like a brute beast.

'I wint up to the man in the veranda, manin', as sure as I sit, to knock the life out av him. He slipped into the open. "Fwhat are you doin' philanderin' about here, ye scum av the gutter?" sez I polite, to give him his warnin', for I wanted him ready.

'He niver lifted his head, but sez, all mournful an' melancolius, as if he thought I wud be sorry for him: "I can't find her," sez he.

'"My troth," sez I, "you've lived too long—you an' your seekin's an' findin's in a dacint married woman's quarters! Hould up your head, ye frozen thief av Genesis," sez I, "an' you'll find all you want an' more!"

'But he niver hild up, an' I let go from the shoulther to where the hair is short over the eyebrows.

'"That'll do your business," sez I, but it nearly did mine instid. I put my bodyweight behind the blow, but I hit nothing at all, an' near put my shoulther out. The corp'ril man was not there, an' Annie Bragin, who had been watchin' from the veranda, throws up her heels, an' carries on like a cock whin his neck's wrung by the dhrummer-bhoy. I wint back to her, for a livin' woman, an' a woman like Annie Bragin, is more than a p'rade-groun' full av ghosts. I'd niver seen a woman faint before, an' I stud like a shtuck calf, askin' her whether she was dead, an' prayin' her for the love av me, an' the love av her husband, an' the love av the Virgin, to opin her blessed eyes again, an' callin' mesilf all the names undher the canopy av Hivin for plaguin' her wid my miserable *a-moors* whin I ought to ha' stud betune her an' this Corp'ril man that had lost the number av his mess.

'I misremimber fwhat nonsinse I said, but I was not so far gone that I cud not hear a fut on the dirt outside. 'Twas Bragin comin' in, an' by the same token Annie was comin' to. I jumped to the far end av the veranda an' looked as if butter wudn't melt in my mouth. But Mrs. Quinn, the quarter-master's wife that was, had tould Bragin about my hangin' round Annie.

'"I'm not pleased wid you, Mulvaney," sez Bragin, unbucklin' his sword, for he had been on duty.

'"That's bad hearin'," I sez, an' I knew that the pickets were dhriven in. "What for, sargint?" sez I.

'"Come outside," sez he, "an' I'll show you why."

'"I'm willin'," I sez; "but my stripes are none so ould that I can afford to loses him. Tell me now, *who* do I go out wid?" sez I.

'He was a quick man an' a just, an' saw fwhat I wud be afther.

379

"Wid Mrs. Bragin's husband," sez he. He might ha' known by me askin' that favour that I had done him no wrong.

'We wint to the back av the arsenal an' I stripped to him, an' for ten minutes 'twas all I cud do to prevent him killin' himself against my fistes. He was mad as a dumb dog—just frothing wid rage; but he had no chanst wid me in reach, or learnin', or anything else.

"'Will ye hear reason?" sez I, whin his first wind was run out.

"'Not whoile I can see," sez he. Wid that I gave him both, one after the other, smash through the low gyard that he'd been taught whin he was a boy, an' the eyebrow shut down on the cheek-bone like the wing av a sick crow.

"'Will ye hear reason now, ye brave man?" sez I.

"'Not whoile I can speak," sez he, staggerin' up blind as a stump. I was loath to do ut, but I wint round an' swung into the jaw side-on an' shifted ut a half pace to the lef'.

"'Will ye hear reason now?" sez I; "I can't keep my timper much longer, an' 'tis like I will hurt you."

"'Not whoile I can stand," he mumbles out av one corner av his mouth. So I closed an' threw him—blind, dumb, an' sick, an' jammed the jaw straight.

"'You're an ould fool, *Mister* Bragin," sez I.

"'You're a young thief," sez he, "an' you've bruk my heart, you an' Annie betune you!"

'Thin he began cryin' like a child as he lay. I was sorry as I had niver been before. 'Tis an awful thing to see a strong man cry.

"'I'll swear on the Cross!" sez I.

"'I care for none av your oaths," sez he.

"'Come back to your quarters," sez I, "an' if you don't believe the livin', begad, you shall listen to the dead," I sez.

'I hoisted him an' tuk him back to his quarters. "Mrs. Bragin," sez I, "here's a man that you can cure quicker than me."

"'You've shamed me before my wife," he whimpers.

"'Have I so?" sez I. "By the look on Mrs. Bragin's face I think

I'm for a dhressin'–down worse than I gave you."

'An' I was! Annie Bragin was woild wid indignation. There was not a name that a dacint woman cud use that was not given my way. I've had my colonel walk roun' me like a cooper roun' a cask for fifteen minutes in ord'ly room, bekaze I wint into the corner shop an' unstrapped lewnatic; but all I iver tuk from his rasp av a tongue was ginger-pop to fwhat Annie tould me. An' that, mark you, is the way av a woman.

'Whin ut was done for want av breath, an' Annie was bendin' over her husband, I sez: "'Tis all thrue, an' I'm a blayguard an' you're an honest woman; but will you tell him of wan service that I did you?"

'As I finished speakin' the corp'ril man came up to the veranda, an' Annie Bragin shquealed. The moon was up, an' we cud see his face.

'"I can't find her," sez the corp'ril man, an' wint out like the puff av a candle.

'"Saints stand betune us an' evil!" sez Bragin, crossin' himself; "that's Flahy av the Tyrone."

'"Who was he?" I sez, "for he has given me a dale av fightin' this day."

'Bragin tould us that Flahy was a corp'ril who lost his wife av cholera in those quarters three years gone, an' wint mad, an' *walked* afther they buried him, huntin' for her.

'"Well," sez I to Bragin, "he's been hookin' out av Purgathory to kape company wid Mrs. Bragin ivry evenin' for the last fortnight. You may tell Mrs. Quinn, wid my love, for I know that she's been talkin' to you, an' you've been listenin', that she ought to ondherstand the differ 'twixt a man an' a ghost. She's had three husbands," sez I, "an' *you*'ve got a wife too good for you. Instid av which you lave her to be boddered by ghosts an'—an' all manner av evil spirruts. I'll niver go talkin' in the way av politeness to a man's wife again. Goodnight to you both," sez I; an' wid that I wint away, havin' fought wid woman, man and Divil all in the heart av an hour. By the same token I gave Father Victor wan *rupee* to say a Mass for Flahy's soul, me havin' discommoded him by shticking my fist into his systim.'

'Your ideas of politeness seem rather large, Mulvaney,' I said.

'That's as you look at ut,' said Mulvaney calmly; 'Annie Bragin niver cared for me. For all that, I did not want to leave anything behin' me that Bragin could take hould av to be angry wid her about—whin an honust wurrd cud ha' cleared all up. There's nothing like opin-speakin'. Orth'ris, ye scutt, let me put me oi to that bottle, for my throat's as dhry as whin I thought I wud get a kiss from Annie Bragin. An' that's fourteen years gone! Eyah! Cork's own city an' the blue sky above ut—an' the times that was—the times that was!'

The Recrudescence of Imray
(A.k.a. *The Return of Imray*)

The doors were wide, the story saith,
Out of the night came the patient wraith,
He might not speak, and he could not stir
A hair of the Baron's minniver—
Speechless and strengthless, a shadow thin,
He roved the castle to seek his kin.
And oh, 'twas a piteous thing to see
The dumb ghost follow his enemy!

The Baron

Imray achieved the impossible. Without warning, for no conceivable motive, in his youth, at the threshold of his career he chose to disappear from the world—which is to say, the little Indian station where he lived.

Upon a day he was alive, well, happy, and in great evidence among the billiard-tables at his club. Upon a morning, he was not, and no manner of search could make sure where he might be. He had stepped out of his place; he had not appeared at his office at the proper time, and his dogcart was not upon the public roads. For these reasons, and because he was hampering, in a microscopical degree, the administration of the Indian Empire, that empire paused for one microscopical moment to make inquiry into the fate of Imray. Ponds were dragged, wells were plumbed, telegrams were despatched down the lines of railways and to the nearest seaport town—twelve hundred miles away; but Imray was not at the end of the drag-ropes nor the telegraph wires. He was gone, and his place knew him no more. Then the work of the great Indian Empire swept forward, because it could not be delayed, and Imray from being a man became a mystery—such a thing as men talk over at their tables in the club for a month, and then forget utterly. His guns, horses, and carts were sold to the highest bidder. His superior officer wrote an altogether absurd letter to his mother, saying that Imray had unaccountably disappeared, and his bungalow stood empty.

After three or four months of the scorching hot weather had gone by, my friend Strickland, of the police, saw fit to rent the bungalow from the native landlord. This was before he was engaged to Miss Youghal—an affair which has been described in another place—and while he was pursuing his investigations into native life. His own life was sufficiently peculiar, and men complained of his manners and customs. There was always food in his house, but there were no regular times for meals. He ate, standing up and walking about, whatever he might find at the sideboard, and this is not good for human beings. His domestic equipment was limited to six rifles, three shot-guns, five saddles, and a collection of stiff-jointed *mahseer*-rods, bigger and stronger than the largest salmon-rods.

These occupied one-half of his bungalow, and the other half was given up to Strickland and his dog Tietjens—an enormous Rampur slut who devoured daily the rations of two men. She spoke to Strickland in a language of her own; and whenever, walking abroad, she saw things calculated to destroy the peace of Her Majesty the Queen Empress, she returned to her master and laid information. Strickland would take steps at once, and the end of his labours was trouble and fine and imprisonment for other people. The natives believed that Tietjens was a familiar spirit, and treated her with the great reverence that is born of hate and fear.

One room in the bungalow was set apart for her special use. She owned a bedstead, a blanket, and a drinking-trough, and if any one came into Strickland's room at night her custom was to knock down the invader and give tongue till someone came with a light. Strickland owed his life to her, when he was on the Frontier, in search of a local murderer, who came in the gray dawn to send Strickland much farther than the Andaman Islands. Tietjens caught the man as he was crawling into Strickland's tent with a dagger between his teeth; and after his record of iniquity was established in the eyes of the law he was hanged. From that date Tietjens wore a collar of rough silver, and employed a monogram on her night-blanket; and the blanket was of double woven Kashmir cloth, for she was a delicate dog.

Under no circumstances would she be separated from Strickland; and once, when he was ill with fever, made great trouble for the doctors, because she did not know how to help her master and would not allow another creature to attempt aid. Macarnaght, of the Indian Medical Service, beat her over her head with a gun-butt before she could understand that she must give room for those who could give quinine.

A short time after Strickland had taken Imray's bungalow, my business took me through that station, and naturally, the club quarters being full, I quartered myself upon Strickland. It was a desirable bungalow, eight-roomed and heavily thatched against any chance of leakage from rain. Under the pitch of the roof ran a ceiling-cloth which looked just as neat as a white-washed ceiling. The landlord had repainted it when Strickland took the bungalow. Unless you knew how Indian bungalows were built you would never have suspected that above the cloth lay the dark three-cornered cavern of the roof, where the beams and the underside of the thatch harboured all manner of rats, bats, ants, and foul things.

Tietjens met me in the verandah with a bay like the boom of the bell of St. Paul's, putting her paws on my shoulder to show she was glad to see me. Strickland had contrived to claw together a sort of meal which he called lunch, and immediately after it was finished went out about his business. I was left alone with Tietjens and my own affairs. The heat of the summer had broken up and turned to the warm damp of the rains. There was no motion in the heated air, but the rain fell like ramrods on the earth, and flung up a blue mist when it splashed back. The bamboos, and the custard-apples, the poinsettias, and the mango-trees in the garden stood still while the warm water lashed through them, and the frogs began to sing among the aloe hedges. A little before the light failed, and when the rain was at its worst, I sat in the back verandah and heard the water roar from the eaves, and scratched myself because I was covered with the thing, called prickly-heat. Tietjens came out with me and put her head in my lap and was very sorrowful; so I gave her biscuits when tea was ready, and I took tea in the back verandah on account of the little coolness found there. The rooms of the house were dark behind me. I could smell Strickland's saddlery and the oil on his guns, and I had no desire to sit among these things.

My own servant came to me in the twilight, the muslin of his clothes clinging tightly to his drenched body, and told me that a gentleman had called and wished to see someone. Very much against my will, but only because of the darkness of the rooms, I went into the naked drawing-room, telling my man to bring the lights. There might or might not have been a caller waiting—it seemed to me that I saw a figure by one of the windows but when the lights came there was nothing save the spikes of the rain without, and the smell of the drinking earth in my nostrils. I explained to my servant that he was no wiser than he ought to be, and went back to the verandah to talk to Tietjens. She had gone out into the wet, and I could hardly coax her back to me; even with biscuits with sugar tops. Strickland came home, dripping wet, just before dinner, and the first thing he said was,

'Has anyone called?'

I explained, with apologies, that my servant had summoned me into the drawing-room on a false alarm; or that some loafer had tried to call on Strickland, and thinking better of it had fled after giving his name. Strickland ordered dinner, without comment, and since it was a real dinner with a white tablecloth attached, we sat down.

At nine o'clock Strickland wanted to go to bed, and I was tired too. Tietjens, who had been lying underneath the table, rose up, and swung into the least exposed verandah as soon as her master moved to his own room, which was next to the stately chamber set apart for Tietjens. If a mere wife had wished to sleep out of doors in that pelting rain it would not have mattered; but Tietjens was a dog, and therefore the better animal. I looked at Strickland, expecting to see him flay her with a whip. He smiled queerly, as a man would smile after telling some unpleasant domestic tragedy. 'She has done this ever since I moved in here,' said he. 'Let her go.'

The dog was Strickland's dog, so I said nothing, but I felt all that Strickland felt in being thus made light of. Tietjens encamped outside my bedroom window, and storm after storm came up, thundered on the thatch, and died away. The lightning spattered the sky as a thrown egg spatters a barn-door, but the light was pale blue, not yellow; and, looking through my split bamboo blinds, I could see the great dog standing, not sleeping, in the verandah, the hackles alift on her back and her feet anchored as tensely as the drawn wire-rope of a suspension bridge. In the very short pauses of the thunder I tried to sleep, but it seemed that someone wanted me very urgently. He, whoever he was, was trying to call me by name, but his voice was no more than a husky whisper. The thunder ceased, and Tietjens went into the garden and howled at the low moon. Somebody tried to open my door, walked about and about through the house and stood breathing heavily in the verandahs, and just when I was falling asleep I fancied that I heard a wild hammering and clamouring above my head or on the door.

I ran into Strickland's room and asked him whether he was ill, and had been calling for me. He was lying on his bed half dressed, a pipe in his mouth. 'I thought you'd come,' he said. 'Have I been walking round the house recently?'

I explained that he had been tramping in the dining-room and the smoking-room and two or three other places; and he laughed and told me to go back to bed. I went back to bed and slept till the morning, but through all my mixed dreams I was sure I was doing some one an injustice in not attending to his wants. What those wants were I could not tell; but a fluttering, whispering, bolt-fumbling, lurking, loitering Someone was reproaching me for my slackness, and, half awake, I heard the howling of Tietjens in the garden and the threshing of the rain.

I lived in that house for two days. Strickland went to his office daily, leaving me alone for eight or ten hours with Tietjens for my only companion. As long as the full light lasted I was comfortable, and so was Tietjens; but in the twilight she and I moved into the back verandah and cuddled each other for company. We were alone in the house, but none the less it was much too fully occupied by a tenant with whom I did not wish to interfere. I never saw him, but I could see the curtains between the rooms quivering where he had just passed through; I could hear the chairs creaking as the bamboos sprung under a weight that had just quitted them; and I could feel when I went to get a book from the dining-room that somebody was waiting in the shadows of the front verandah till I should have gone away. Tietjens made the twilight more interesting by glaring into the darkened rooms with every hair erect, and following the motions of something that I could not see. She never entered the rooms, but her eyes moved interestedly: that was quite sufficient. Only when my servant came to trim the lamps and make all light and habitable she would come in with me and spend her time sitting on her haunches, watching an invisible extra man as he moved about behind my shoulder. Dogs are cheerful companions.

I explained to Strickland, gently as might be, that I would go over to the club and find for myself quarters there. I admired his hospitality, was pleased with his guns and rods, but I did not much care for his house and its atmosphere. He heard me out to the end, and then smiled very wearily, but without contempt, for he is a man who understands things. 'Stay on,' he said, 'and see what this thing means. All you have talked about I have known since I took the bungalow. Stay on and wait. Tietjens has left me. Are you going too?'

I had seen, him through one little affair, connected with a

heathen idol, that had brought me to the doors of a lunatic asylum, and I had no desire to help him through further experiences. He was a man to whom unpleasantnesses arrived as do dinners to ordinary people.

Therefore I explained more clearly than ever that I liked him immensely, and would be happy to see him in the daytime; but that I did not care to sleep under his roof. This was after dinner, when Tietjens had gone out to lie in the verandah.

''Pon my soul, I don't wonder,' said Strickland, with his eyes on the ceiling-cloth. 'Look at that!'

The tails of two brown snakes were hanging between the cloth and the cornice of the wall. They threw long shadows in the lamplight.

'If you are afraid of snakes of course—' said Strickland.

I hate and fear snakes, because if you look into the eyes of any snake you will see that it knows all and more of the mystery of man's fall, and that it feels all the contempt that the Devil felt when Adam was evicted from Eden. Besides which its bite is generally fatal, and it twists up trouser legs.

'You ought to get your thatch overhauled,' I said. 'Give me a *mahseer*-rod, and we'll poke 'em down.'

' They'll hide among the roof-beams,' said Strickland. 'I can't stand snakes overhead. I'm going up into the roof. If I shake 'em down, stand by with a cleaning-rod and break their backs.'

I was not anxious to assist Strickland in his work, but I took the cleaning-rod and waited in the dining-room, while Strickland brought a gardener's ladder from the verandah, and set it against the side of the room. The snake-tails drew themselves up and disappeared. We could hear the dry rushing scuttle of long bodies running over the baggy ceiling-cloth. Strickland took a lump with him, while I tried to make clear to him the danger of hunting roof-snakes between a ceiling-cloth and a thatch, apart from the deterioration of property caused by ripping out ceiling-cloths.

'Nonsense!' said Strickland. 'They're sure to hide near the walls by the cloth. The bricks are too cold for 'em, and the heat of the room is just what they like.' He put his hand to the corner of the stuff and ripped it from the cornice. It gave with a great sound of tearing, and Strickland put his head through the opening into the dark of the angle of the roof-beams. I set my teeth and lifted the rod, for I had not the least knowledge of what might descend.

'H'm!' said Strickland, and his voice rolled and rumbled in the roof. 'There's room for another set of rooms up here, and, by Jove, someone is occupying 'em!'

'Snakes?' I said from below.

'No. It's a buffalo. Hand me up the two last joints of a *mahseer*-rod, and I'll prod it. It's lying on the main roof-beam.'

I handed up the rod.

'What a nest for owls and serpents! No wonder the snakes live here,' said Strickland, climbing farther into the roof. I could see his elbow thrusting with the rod. 'Come out of that, whoever you are! Heads below there! It's falling.'

I saw the ceiling cloth nearly in the centre of the room bag with a shape that was pressing it downwards and downwards towards the lighted lamp on the table. I snatched the lamp out of danger and stood back. Then the cloth ripped out from the walls, tore, split, swayed, and shot down upon the table something that I dared not look at, till Strickland had slid down the ladder and was standing by my side.

He did not say much, being a man of few words; but he picked up the loose end of the tablecloth and threw it over the remnants on the table.

'It strikes me,' said he, putting down the lamp, 'our friend Imray has come back. Oh! you would, would you?'

There was a movement under the cloth, and a little snake wriggled out, to be back-broken by the butt of the *mahseer*-rod. I was sufficiently sick to make no remarks worth recording.

Strickland meditated, and helped himself to drinks. The arrangement under the cloth made no more signs of life.

'Is it Imray?' I said.

Strickland turned back the cloth for a moment, and looked.

'It is Imray,' he said; 'and his throat is cut from ear to ear.'

Then we spoke, both together and to ourselves: 'That's why he whispered about the house.'

Tietjens, in the garden, began to bay furiously. A little later her great nose heaved open the dining-room door.

She snuffed and was still. The tattered ceiling-cloth hung down almost to the level of the table, and there was hardly room to move away from the discovery.

Tietjens came in and sat down; her teeth bared under her lip and her forepaws planted. She looked at Strickland.

'It's a bad business, old lady,' said he. 'Men don't climb up into the roofs of their bungalows to die, and they don't fasten up the ceiling cloth behind 'em. Let's think it out.'

'Let's think it out somewhere else,' I said.

'Excellent idea! Turn the lamps out. We'll get into my room.'

I did not turn the lamps out. I went into Strickland's room first, and allowed him to make the darkness. Then he followed me, and we lit tobacco and thought. Strickland thought. I smoked furiously, because I was afraid.

'Imray is back,' said Strickland. 'The question is—who killed Imray? Don't talk, I've a notion of my own. When I took this bungalow I took over most of Imray's servants. Imray was guileless and inoffensive, wasn't he?'

I agreed; though the heap under the cloth had looked neither one thing nor the other.

'If I call in all the servants they will stand fast in a crowd and lie like Aryans. What do you suggest?'

'Call 'em in one by one,' I said.

'They'll run away and give the news to all their fellows,' said Strickland. 'We must segregate 'em. Do you suppose your servant knows anything about it?'

'He may, for aught I know; but I don't think it's likely. He has only been here two or three days,' I answered. 'What's your notion?'

'I can't quite tell. How the dickens did the man get the wrong side of the ceiling-cloth?'

There was a heavy coughing outside Strickland's bedroom door. This showed that Bahadur Khan, his body-servant, had waked from sleep and wished to put Strickland to bed.

'Come in,' said Strickland. 'It's a very warm night, isn't it?'

Bahadur Khan, a great, green-turbaned, six-foot Mahomedan, said that it was a very warm night; but that there was more rain pending, which, by His Honour's favour, would bring relief to the country.

'It will be so, if God pleases,' said Strickland, tugging off his boots. 'It is in my mind, Bahadur Khan, that I have worked thee remorselessly for many days—ever since that time when thou first earnest into my service. What time was that?'

'Has the Heaven-born forgotten? It was when Imray Sahib went secretly to Europe without warning given; and I—even I-came into the honoured service of the protector of the poor.'

'And Imray Sahib went to Europe?'

'It is so said among those who were his servants.'

'And thou wilt take service with him when he returns?'

'Assuredly, *sahib*. He was a good master, and cherished his dependants.'

'That is true. I am very tired, but I go buck-shooting tomorrow. Give me the little sharp rifle that I use for black-buck; it is in the case yonder.'

The man stooped over the case; handed barrels, stock, and fore-end to Strickland, who fitted all together, yawning dolefully. Then he reached down to the gun-case, took a solid-drawn cartridge, and slipped it into the breech of the .360 Express.

'And Imray Sahib has gone to Europe secretly! That is very strange, Bahadur Khan, is it not?'

'What do I know of the ways of the white man, Heaven-born?'

'Very little, truly. But thou shalt know more *anon*. It has reached me that Imray Sahib has returned from his so long journeyings, and that even now he lies in the next room, waiting his servant.'

'*Sahib!*'

The lamplight slid along the barrels of the rifle as they levelled themselves at Bahadur Khan's broad breast.

'Go and look!' said Strickland. 'Take a lamp. Thy master is
tired, and he waits thee. Go!'

The man picked up a lamp, and went into the dining-room,
Strickland following, and almost pushing him with the muzzle
of the rifle. He looked for a moment at the black depths behind
the ceiling-cloth; at the writhing snake under foot; and last, a
gray glaze settling on his face, at the thing under the tablecloth.

'Hast thou seen?' said Strickland after a pause.

'I have seen. I am clay in the white man's hands. What does
the Presence do?'

'Hang thee within the month. What else?'

'For killing him? Nay, *sahib*, consider. Walking among us, his
servants, he cast his eyes upon my child, who was four years old.
Him he bewitched, and in ten days he died of the fever—my
child!'

'What said Imray Sahib?'

'He said he was a handsome child, and patted him on the
head; wherefore my child died. Wherefore I killed Imray Sahib
in the twilight, when he had come back from office, and was
sleeping. Wherefore I dragged him up into the roof-beams and
made all fast behind him. The Heaven-born knows all things. I
am the servant of the Heaven-born.'

Strickland looked at me above the rifle, and said, in the vernacular, 'Thou art witness to this saying? He has killed.'

Bahadur Khan stood ashen gray in the light of the one lamp.
The need for justification came upon him very swiftly. 'I am
trapped,' he said, 'but the offence was that man's. He cast an evil
eye upon my child, and I killed and hid him. Only such as are
served by devils,' he glared at Tietjens, couched stolidly before
him, 'only such could know what I did.'

'It was clever. But thou shouldst have lashed him to the beam
with a rope. Now, thou thyself wilt hang by a rope. Orderly!'

A drowsy policeman answered Strickland's call. He was followed by another, and Tietjens sat wondrous still.

'Take him to the police-station,' said Strickland. 'There is a case toward.'

'Do I hang, then?' said Bahadur Khan, making no attempt to escape, and keeping his eyes on the ground.

'If the sun shines or the water runs—yes!' said Strickland.

Bahadur Khan stepped back one long pace, quivered, and stood still. The two policemen waited further orders.

'Go!' said Strickland.

'Nay; but I go very swiftly,' said Bahadur Khan. 'Look! I am even now a dead man.'

He lifted his foot, and to the little toe there clung the head of the half-killed snake, firm fixed in the agony of death.

'I come of land-holding stock,' said Bahadur Khan, rocking where he stood. 'It were a disgrace to me to go to the public scaffold: therefore I take this way. Be it remembered that the *sahib's* shirts are correctly enumerated, and that there is an extra piece of soap in his washbasin. My child was bewitched, and I slew the wizard. Why should you seek to slay me with the rope? My honour is saved, and—and—I die.'

At the end of an hour he died, as they die who are bitten by the little brown *karait*, and the policemen bore him and the thing under the tablecloth to their appointed places. All were needed to make clear the disappearance of Imray.

'This,' said Strickland, very calmly, as he climbed into bed, 'is called the nineteenth century. Did you hear what that man said?'

'I heard,' I answered. 'Imray made a mistake.'

'Simply and solely through not knowing the nature of the Oriental, and the coincidence of a little seasonal fever. Bahadur Khan had been with him for four years.'

I shuddered. My own servant had been with me for exactly that length of time. When I went over to my own room I found my man waiting, impassive as the copper head on a penny, to pull off my boots.

'What has befallen Bahadur Khan?' said I.

'He was bitten by a snake and died. The rest the *sahib* knows,' was the answer.

'And how much of this matter hast thou known?'

'As much as might be gathered from One coming in in the twilight to seek satisfaction. Gently, *sahib*. Let me pull off those boots.'

I had just settled to the sleep of exhaustion when I heard Strickland shouting from his side of the house—

'Tietjens has come back to her place!'

And so she had. The great deerhound was couched stately on her own bedstead on her own blanket, while, in the next room, the idle, empty, ceiling-cloth waggled as it trailed on the table.

The Miracle of Saint Jubanus

The visitor had been drawn twenty kilometres beyond the end of the communal road under construction, by a rumour of a small window of thirteenth-century glass, said to represent a haloed saint in a helmet—none other, indeed, than Saint Julian of Auvergne—and to be found in the village church of Saint Jubans, down the valley.

But there was a wedding in the church, followed by the usual collection for charity. After the bridal procession had passed into the sunshine, two small acolytes began fighting over an odd *sou*. In a stride the tall old priest was upon them, knocked their heads together, unshelled them from their red, white-laced robes of office, and they rolled—a pair of black-gabardined gamins locked in war—out over the threshold on to the steep hillside.

He stood at the church door and looked down into the village beneath, half buried among the candles of the horse-chestnuts. It climbed up, house by house, from a busy river, to sharp, turfed slopes that lapped against live rock, whence, dominating the red valley, rose enormous ruins of an old *château* with bastions, curtains, and keeps, and a flying bridge that spanned the dry moat. Valerian and lilac in flower sprang wherever there was foothold.

'All acolytes are little devils,' said the priest benignly, and descended to the wedding-breakfast, which one could see in plan, set out by the stream in a courtyard of cut limes. His bearing was less that of a *curé* than a soldier, for his *soutane* swung like a marching-overcoat, and he lacked that bend of the neck, 'the priest's stoop,' with which his Church stamps her sons when they are caught young.

The wedding-feast had ended, and the heat of the day was abated before he climbed up again, beneath an enormous umbrella, to find the visitor among the ruins beside the little church.

'I make a rule not to smoke unless it is offered. A thousand thanks! . . . This ought to be Smyrna . . . ' He exhaled the smoke through his finely-cut nostrils. 'Yes, it is Smyrna . . . Good! And *Monsieur* appreciates our "Marylands" also? Hmm. I remember the time when our government tobaccos were a national infamy . . . How long here am I? Close upon forty years . . . No. Never much elsewhere. It suffices me . . . '

'A good people. Composed of a few old clans—Meilhac—Leclos—Falloux—Poivrain—Ballart. *Monsieur* may have observed their names upon our monument.' He pointed downward to the little cast-iron *poilu*, which seemed to be standard pattern for war memorials in that region. 'Neither rich nor poor. When the charabanc-road through the valley is made they will be richer . . . Postcards for the tourists, an hotel, and an antiquity shop, for sure, here beside the church. A syndicate of initiative has, indeed, approached me to write on the attractions of the district, as well as on the life of Saint Jubanus . . . But surely he existed!

'He was a Gaul commanding a Gaulish legion at the time when Christianity was spreading in the Roman Army. We were—he was engaged against the Bo—the Alemanni—and was on the eve of attack when some of his officers chose that moment to throw down their swords and embrace the Cross. Knowing that he had been baptized, they assumed his sympathy; but he charged them to wait till the battle was finished. He said, in effect "*Render unto Caesar the things that are Caesar's, and to God the things that are God's.*" Some obeyed. Some did not. But even with defeatist and demoralised forces he won the day. They would then have given him a triumph, but he put aside the laurel wreath, and from his own chariot publicly renounced his profession and the old deities. So—I expect it was necessary for discipline to be kept—he was beheaded on the field he had won. That is the legend . . .

'His miracles? But one only on record. He called a dying man back to life by whispering in his ear, and the man sat up and laughed. (I wish I knew that joke.) That is why we have a proverb in our valley: "It would take Saint Jubans himself to make you smile." I imagine him as an old soldier, strict in his duty, but also something of a farceur. Every year I deliver on his day a discourse in his honour. And you will perceive that when the War came his life applied with singular force to the situation . . .

'They called up the priests? Assuredly! I went . . . It is droll to re-enter the old life in a double capacity. You see, one can sometimes—er—replace a casualty if—if—one has been—had experience. In that event, one naturally speaks secularly on secular subjects. A moment later one gives them absolution as they advance. But they were good—good boys. And so wastefully used! . . . That is why I am of all matchmakers in our village the least scrupulous. Ask the old women! . . . Yes, *monsieur* . . . and I returned without a scar . . .

'The good God spared me also the darkness of soul which covered, and which covers still, so many—the doubt—the defiance—the living damnation. I had thought—may He pardon me!—that it was hard to reach the hearts of my people here. I saw them, after the war, split open! Some entered hells of whose existence they had not dreamed—of whose terrors they lacked words to tell. So they—men distraught—needed more care in the years that followed the war than even at Chemin des Dames . . . Yes, I was there, also, when it seemed that hope had quitted France. I know now how a man can lay hands upon himself out of pure fear!

'And there were those, untouched, whom the war had immobilised from the soul outwards. In special, there was Martin Ballart, the only one of his family who returned—the son of a good woman who died at his birth. Him, frankly, I loved from the beginning, and, I think, he loved me. Yes, even when

I took him for one of my acolytes—you saw the type at the wedding?—and I had very often to correct him. He was not clever nor handsome, but he had the eyes of a joyous faithful dog, and the laugh of Pan himself. And he came back at the last blasted, withered, dumb—a ghost that gnawed itself. There had been his girl, too . . . When they met again he did not know her. She said: "No matter. I will wait." But he remained as he was. He lived, at first, with his aunt down there.

'Oh, he worked—it was no time for idleness—but the work did not restore. And he would hide himself for an hour or two and come back visibly replunged in his torments. I watched him, of course. It was a little photograph—one of those accursed Kodak pictures, of a young man in a trench, dancing languorously with a skeleton. It was the nail of his obsession . . . I left it with him. Had I taken it, there might have been a crisis. Short of that, I tried every expedient, even to exorcism . . . But why not? You call them mick-robs. We call them devils . . . One thing only gave me hope. He took pleasure in my company. He looked at me with the eyes of a dog in pain, and followed me always. It came about in effect that he lived up here. He would sit still while I played piquet with our schoolmaster, Falloux . . .

'Ah, that was a type upon whom our war had done bad work! No, he had not served. He had some internal trouble, which I told him always was a mere constipation of Atheism. Oh yes—he was enormously a freethinker! A man with a thick black beard, and an intellect (he carried it in front of him like his stomach) never happy unless it was dirtily rude to the *Bon Dieu* and His Saints. Little unclean stories and epigrams, you understand. He called Saint Jubanus a militarist and an impostor—this defeatist of a Zeppelinistic belly! But he could play piquet, and he was safer at my house than infecting our estaminet with his witticisms. I told him always that he would be saved on account of "invincible ignorance." Then he would thunder:

'"But if your God has any logic, I shall be damned!"'

'"Be content," I would reply. "The *Bon Dieu* will never hear your name. You will be certified, together with the cartel, by some totally inferior specialist of a demon as incapable of receiving even rudimentary instruction."

'Then he would clutch at his beard and throw down the cards, which poor Martin picked up for us. But apart from his rudeness to God and the Hierarchy, he was of exemplary life. *Pardi*, he had to be! She charged herself with that. Not believing in God, he had naturally married a devil before whom he trembled. She took him to Mass. That was why he was always most extravagant at my house on Monday evenings. His atheism, *Monsieur*, was, after all, but the *panache* without which a good little Frenchman cannot exist. A fond, there are few atheists in France. But, I concede, there are several arrivistes. Knowing this (and her), I hardly troubled to pray for him.

'It was for poor Martin that I prayed always but not with full passion until his aunt told me she would take him to Lourdes . . Every man, besides being all the other base characters in Scripture, is a *Naaman* at heart. You have seen Lourdes, *Monsieur*? A-ah! . . .

'So I exposed this new trouble and my own mean little soul to the *Bon Dieu*. It was He—I remember the very night—Who put it into my heart to pray seriously to Saint Jubanus. I had prayed to him, oh, many times before; but it occurred to me at that hour that my past demands had not, in view of his secular career, been sufficiently precised or underlined. The idea kept me awake. I got up. I went to the church, which is, as you see, not three steps. There—it is—it was—an old duty of my life in the world—I kept my—I walked up and down in the dark. At last I found myself, constating my case, not formally to a saint, but officially as to my commanding officer. I said—substantially:

'"*Mon General*, the time has come for action. You gave your single life to uphold the honour of your military obligation. There are some two million Gauls who have given up theirs for much the same object, as well as twenty-three out of your very own village here. Surely some of these must by now have appeared before you! I address you simply, then, as an old moustache who is trying to beat off an attack of the Devil on the soul of Martin Ballart, Corporal, 743rd of the Line, two citations. (One must be precise always with the hierarchy.) I am at the end of my resources. God has ordered that I should report to you. I ask no obvious miracles, because, between ourselves, I do not in the least desire this pleasant retreat of ours to develop into a Lourdes. I beg only your help as my officer in the case of a good boy who, by fortune of war, is descending alive into Hell." I concluded, textually: "*Mon* General, many reputations rest upon a single action. That also is the fortune of war. But I submit, with respect, after your sixteen-hundred years in retreat, it is not too much that an old and very tired combatant of your own race should signal for a small reinforcement from his *commandant* . . . "

'I think—I know, indeed, from what happened afterwards—he was moved by this last thrust. It was as though all God's goodnight had chuckled above me. I went to my bed again and slept in confidence . . .

'Did I look for a sign? Did Gouraud give any when he took our revenge for Chemin des Dames—when he let the enemy fall into the trap by their own momentum? No! I continued my work, and always I prayed for Martin. Then there came down the valley—as he does yearly—the itinerant mender of umbrellas, for whom my housekeeper stores up her repairs. She had acquired a piece of material to re-cover my umbrella, which, as you can see, is somewhat formidable in point of size, and of a certain antiquity. Indeed, I do not know whether there still exists another effective machine of its type, constructed, see you, from the authentic bone of the whale. Look! Vast as it is, it was still more vast when that artist arrived. My Mathilde's piece of material was found to be inadequate in extent. But the man said that, with a small cutting down of the tips of the ribs, he could accommodate the area to the fabric. The result you behold. A fraction smaller, but essentially the same. And equally strong. *Mon Dieu*, that was needed! . . . Yes, sometimes I dare to think that that crapulous vagrant might have been Saint Jubanus himself! . . .

'This was in the interval—while the good saint prepared his second line just like our Gouraud. During that time I listened to poor Martin's aunt making her arrangements to take him to Lourdes, of which officially I had to approve. For, what miracle had we to offer? Further, I endured the attacks of' that Falloux. Something that I may have said in respect to The Almighty diverted his dirtinesses from that quarter, and he fell back on Saint Jubanus. My own vanity—the syndicate of initiative having approached me, as I have told you, to write his life for prospective tourists—drew that on my head. I fear that, once or twice, I may have lost my dignity with him as a priest. He asserts that I swore like a Foot *chausseur*, which had been his service. (Poor little rats of the Line!) . . .

'And our Saint's Day that year, was wet, so I knew all the world would attend. I had been summoned out of the village before the discourse—a couple of kilometres down the road. On my return, because it dripped water by rivers, I set my repaired umbrella to dry . . . But we will go over to the church. It is not three steps, and I will show you the place. Also, it will be cooler in there . . . It is true we are in horrible neglect, but, as you say, that window is a jewel. It represents beyond doubt Saint Jubanus . . .

'My umbrella? I deposited that behind this pillar here, outside the sacristy. And by the side of the pillar, as you see, is as much as we have of a vestiary—this press, with its shelves. Remark that I laid my umbrella, always open, in this spot, on its side. Thus! For myself, when I preach, though I am not an orator, I prefer the naked *soutane*—it hampers action less; but—out of respect for our Saint—I put on the *cotta*. At the same time I tell my two acolytes—who are of precisely the type you saw after the wedding; it is fixed by the Devil—to prepare me the vestments for the service of the Benediction which would succeed my discourse. It was to them to extract these vestments with some decency from that press there. In this there was a little delay. I stepped aside to look, for—an acolyte is capable of anything—it seemed to me that they had chosen that hour to amuse themselves with my umbrella. I demanded why they did not leave it alone. One replied that he could not; and the other opened that terrible giggle of the nervous small boy. Heaven pardon me, but I am of limited patience! I signified that I had means of enforcing my orders. There is a reverberation in this place effective for the voice at dramatic moments.

'But it was my umbrella which at that moment began to take the stage. It receded from me with those two young attached to different points of its circumference. At the same time it gyrated painfully in that shadow there. I followed, stupefied, and demanded some explanation of the outrage. It replied in two voices of an equal regret that it was attached and could not free itself. I hastened to aid. They said afterwards they misconstrued my motives. All I know is that my umbrella, open always, but tortured by unequal compressions, descended indescribably those three steps here into the body of the church, where the congregation awaited my discourse. On one side of its large circle, which you see, was an acolyte, facing inwards, clawing at the laces on his bosom and his elbow.

'On another was his companion, inextricably caught high up under the armpit, which he could not reach with the other hand, because he was facing outwards, pinned there by his vestments. The central effect, *Monsieur*, was that of an undevout *pagoda* conducting a *pas de trois* in a sacred edifice, to the accompaniment of increasing whimpers. This was before they collapsed, those young. Whether by accident or design, the child facing inwards snatched at the back of the head of the other. We shave our boys' heads in France, fortunately; but he had nails, that one, and the other protested . . .

'I? I followed, men said, step by step, slowly, with my mouth open. Some instinct doubtless warned me not to approach lest I should be—er—caught up by that chariot. Also, which often happens to me inopportunely, the incident struck me as humorous. I desired to see the end . . . But this was but the beginning. My people gasped. My umbrella pursued its career, undecidedly but continuously. Then one of the little juggernauts—if that be the word—began to weep. The other followed . . . And then? Then, *Monsieur*, that Falloux—that practical and logical atheist, who believes reason is the source of all leapt into the breach, crying: "But they are attached! Stand still, and I will detach you." But that they would not do. My perambulating mosque of an umbrella resumed command. Its handle, see, tripped and slid over the stone floor like the pointed foot of a danseuse. This, with the natural elasticity of the ribs, furnished all the motifs of the ballet.

'As Falloux stooped to the rim of its circumference—being short-sighted in all respects—one side elevated itself, and the point of a rib caught him in the beard beneath the chin. It appeared then that he could not disengage. He made several gestures. Then he cried: "But it is I who am also attached! Stand still, you misbegotten little brats, till I detach myself!" And he laboured with his hands in the thickets of his beard like a suicide who has no time to lose. But he remained—he rested there—conforming with yelps of agony to the agonies of the rival circus, into whose orbit had now projected itself, at their own level, the head of their abominated preceptor, distorted and menacing . . . And then? . . .

'There are occasions, *Monsieur*, when one must lead or oneself mount the tumbril. I exploded a fraction of a second before my people, saving, doubtless, some a ruptured blood-vessel. We did not—see you—laugh greatly. We were beyond that point when we began. Soon—very soon—we could no more. We could but ache aloud, which I assure you is most painful—while my insolent umbrella promenaded its three adherents through pagan undulations and genuflexions. It was Salome's basin, you understand, dancing by itself with every appearance of enjoyment, and offering to all quarters the head of the Apostle and of two of the Innocents. But not the Holy Ones!

'Then she rose in her place, and said: "Imbecile! But stand still. I will bring the scissors."

'And she went out. It was cruel of the Saint to force us to recommence. We could do nothing except continue to ache and

hiccough and implore Falloux to stand still. He would not—
he could not—on account of those young, who, weeping with
shame, continued to endeavour to extricate themselves indi-
vidually. Falloux followed their movements in every particular.
You see, he was attached to his troupe by hairs, which it hurts to
pull—oh, exquisitely! But he did his best. I have never conceived
such motions, even in dreams. You will comprehend, *Monsieur*,
that there are certain physical phenomena inseparable from the
contortions of a globose man labouring through unaccustomed
exercises. These also were vouchsafed to us! . . .

'It is said that I was on my knees beating my forehead against
the back of a *prie-Dieu*, when we heard, above all, the laugh of
Faunus himself—the dear, natural voice of my Martin, rich with
innocent delight, crying: "But, do it again! If you love me, Uncle
Falloux, do it all again!"

'We turned as one, and Martin's girl, who sits always where
she can see him, took him in her arms. The miracle had happened! . . . Yes, from that moment Falloux lost the centre of his
stage. Then she returned—like Atropos. She cut him free; she
threw down the shears; she led him out . . . I? I picked them up
and I conducted my autopsy on my acolytes with more of cir-
cumspection. Beards renew themselves, but not our poor little
church vestments when they are torn . . .

'The explanation? Modern and scientific, *Monsieur*. Saint
Jubanus—the repairer of umbrellas—had, as I have told you,
shortened the ribs of my umbrella. Look! He had then capped
the point of each rib with a large, stamped, tin tip, which you
perceive locks down. It bears some likeness to the old snap-hook
on the pole of an artillery waggon, and is perfectly calculated to
catch in any fabric—or hair. But, to make sure, that inspired
scoundrel had, in pushing on his labour-saving capsules—which
are marked S.G.D.G. (that ought to be "A.M.D.G.")—bent back
the terminal *laminae*—fibres—what do you call them?—of the
whale's bone. You can see them protruding hungrily from the
neck of each rib-cap, and also from the slits at the side of it . . .
Have you forgotten those heads of grass with which one used to

entangle and wind up the silky hairs in the nape of a girl's neck? Just that, *Monsieur*; but in a sufficiently gross beard, inextricable, and causing supreme torture at every twitch ...

'Yes. We were all stilled after Martin had laughed, except Martin and his girl. They wept together—the tears from the soul. I said to them:

'"Go out, my children. All the world is for you today Paradise. Enter there!"

'I had reason. They would never have listened to my beautiful discourse. Ah! It was necessary to reconstruct that while we regained our gravity, because at that moment (it is true, *Monsieur*, that the Devil's favourite lair is beneath the altar), at that moment came my temptation! Falloux had been delivered into my hands by Saint Jubanus. He who had mocked and thrust out his chin against God and the Saints had, logically, by that very chin been caught and shaken in the face of the souk, as I myself—as I have seen a man handled at Sidi bel Abbas! Never should he survive it! With my single tongue I would unstick him from his office, his civilisation, and his self-respect. But I recalled that he was a Gaul who had been shamed in public, and was, therefore, now insane. One did—one should—not mock afresh a man who has thus suffered. For so I have seen many good soldiers lost to France. Also, he was a soul in my charge ...

'Yet, you will concede, the volte-face demanded skill. At that moment Saint Jubanus came to my aid. It was as though he himself had signalled: "To the next objective—charge! Martin is saved! Save now by any means the man whom I have used as his saviour. If necessary, old comrade, lie! Lie for the honour of the legion!" ('*Pristi!* What a commander he must have been in his prime!) I took at once for my text our saying: "It would need Saint Jubans himself to make you laugh."

'I made plain to them first, of course, that his merits were wide enough to cover the sin of laughing in church. I demonstrated what that laughter had effected for our poor Martin, whose agonies they knew all. I told them—and it is true—that the *Bon Dieu* demands nothing better from honest people than honest laughter, and that he who awakens it is a benefactor. Then I extolled the instrument by which the miracle had been wrought. That is to say, I extolled Falloux, who had lent himself so willingly and with such self-sacrifice to this happy accident. (After all, he had sworn creditably enough—for a foot *chasseur*!) I said that we two had often discussed Martin together. (My orders were to lie, and I interpreted them liberally.) I made clear how a smaller-minded man than he would have broken loose (which he could not have done except by her scissors) before the experiment had terminated; but that he, Falloux, was of a moral stature sufficient to advance under a mitraille of derision to the complete awakening of Martin's soul.

'I said that though a freethinker, Falloux—this same animal Falloux—realised the value of moral therapeuthy. (They were enormously delighted at this. They thought it was a new vice from Paris.) For Falloux himself, who—she told me later—was biting his nails in the hen-house convulsed with shame, I extemporised a special citation. No. Our village does not read Rabelais, but he did. So I compared—Heaven forgive me!—that unhappy costive soul with all its belly to Gargantua. Oh, only by implication, *Monsieur*! I stated that the *grandeur* of his moral gesture of self-effacement was Gargantuan in its abandon. That phrase impressed them also. They realised now that it was not a comedy at which they had assisted, but a miracle . . .

'And thus I laboured with my people. *Mon Dieu*, but I sweated like an ox! At last they swung in the furrow, and I claimed their homage for him. And I succeeded! I led them down the hill to offer it en masse! He came out upon us like a wild beast. But when I had explained our objective, he—this enormity Falloux—was convinced that he had scientifically lent himself to a Gargantuan jest of abandoned self-abnegation because he was an expert in moral therapeutics! . . . That, setting aside my discourse, which was manifestly inspired, was the second miracle, *Monsieur*—the abasement of Falloux on—my faith!—his tenderest point. And his redemption! For it is she who is more the unbeliever of the two these days. She is a woman. She knows that I can be, on occasion, a liar almost as formidable . . .

'But this has been an orgy of the most excellent cigarettes, and, for me, a debauch of conversation. It demands at least that I offer a cup of coffee which may not be too detestable. Let us go . . . But my little house is here—under the hand, see you—not three steps . . . But think of the pleasure you give me, *Monsieur!* . . . What? What? What is it that thou singest to me there? . . . A thousand pardons for the phrase! But Saint Julian of Auvergne has no affinity whatever with Saint Jubanus. They are uniquely different. I implore you to abandon that heresy! Auvergne! Auvergne! "Famous for its colleges and kettles," as I once read somewhere in the world. Impossible a million times! Saint Julian was a Roman officer—doubtless of unimpeachable sanctity—but a Latin; whereas our general was a Gaul—as Gallic as—'

He beckoned to a young man of the large-boned, well-fleshed, post-war type, who was ascending the hill from the fields behind a yoke of gold and silver oxen with sheepskin wigs. He moved up slowly, smiling.

'As Gallic as he,' the priest went on. 'Look at him! He was that one who was pinned to my umbrella by his back on that day and—tell *Monsieur* what they call you in the village now.'

The youth's smile widened to a heavenly grin. '*Parapluie, Monsieur*,' said he, and climbed on.

The priest stopped at his own door. 'Mathilde,' he cried, 'the larger bottle—er—from Martinique; thy gingerbread; and my African coffee for two. *Pardi, Monsieur*, forty years ago there would have been two pistols also, had I known or cared anything about the Saints in those days! . . . Saint Julian of Auvergne, indeed! But I will explain.'

A Deal in Cotton

Long and long ago, when Devadatta was King of Benares, I wrote some tales concerning Strickland of the Punjab police (who married Miss Youghal), and Adam, his son. Strickland has finished his Indian service, and lives now at a place in England called Weston-super-Mare, where his wife plays the organ in one of the churches. Semi-occasionally he comes up to London, and occasionally his wife makes him visit his friends. Otherwise he plays golf and follows the harriers for his figure's sake.

If you remember that Infant who told a tale to Eustace Cleever the novelist, you will remember that he became a baronet with a vast estate. He has, owing to cookery, a little lost his figure, but he never loses his friends. I have found a wing of his house turned into a hospital for sick men, and there I once spent a week in the company of two dismal nurses and a specialist in "Sprue." Another time the place was full of schoolboys—sons of Anglo-Indians—whom the Infant had collected for the holidays, and they nearly broke his keeper's heart.

But my last visit was better. The Infant called me up by wire, and I fell into the arms of a friend of mine, Colonel A. L. Corkran, so that the years departed from us, and we praised *Allah*, who had not yet terminated the *delights*, nor separated the *companions*.

Said Corkran, when he had explained how it felt to command a native infantry regiment on the border: "The Strides are coming for tonight—with their boy."

"I remember him. The little fellow I wrote a story about," I said. " Is he in the service?"

"No. Strick got him into the Centro-Euro-Africo Protectorate. He's assistant-commissioner at Dupé—wherever that is. Somaliland, ain't it, Stalky?" asked the Infant.

Stalky puffed out his nostrils scornfully. "You're only three thousand miles out. Look at the atlas."

"Anyhow, he's as rotten full of fever as the rest of you," said the Infant, at length on the big divan. "And he's bringing a native servant with him. Stalky be an athlete, and tell Ipps to put him in the stable room."

"Why? Is he a Yao—like the fellow Wade brought here—when your housekeeper had fits?" Stalky often visits the Infant, and has seen some odd things.

"No. He's one of old Strickland's Punjabi policemen—and quite European—I believe."

"Hooray! Haven't talked Punjabi for three months—and a Punjabi from Central Africa ought to be amusin'."

We heard the chuff of the motor in the porch, and the first to enter was Agnes Strickland, whom the Infant makes no secret of adoring.

He is devoted, in a fat man's placid way, to at least eight designing women; but she nursed him once through a bad bout of Peshawur fever, and when she is in the house, it is more than all hers.

"You didn't send rugs enough," she began. "Adam might have taken a chill."

"It's quite warm in the *tonneau*. Why did you let him ride in front?"

"Because he wanted to," she replied, with the mother's smile, and we were introduced to the shadow of a young man leaning heavily on the shoulder of a bearded Punjabi Mohammedan.

"That is all that came home of him," said his father to me. "There was nothing in it of the child with whom I had journeyed to Dalhousie centuries since."

"And what is this uniform?" Stalky asked of Imam Din, the servant, who came to attention on the marble floor.

"The uniform of the Protectorate troops, *sahib*. Though I am the little *sahib's* body-servant, it is not seemly for us white men to be attended by folk dressed altogether as servants."

"And—and you white men wait at table on horseback? " Stalky pointed to the man's spurs.

"These I added for the sake of honour when I came to England," said Imam Din.

Adam smiled the ghost of a little smile that I began to remember, and we put him on the big couch for refreshments. Stalky asked him how much leave he had, and he said " Six months."

"But he'll take another six on medical certificate," said Agnes anxiously. Adam knit his brows.

"You don't want to—eh? *I* know. 'Wonder what my second in command is doing." Stalky tugged his moustache, and fell to thinking of his Sikhs.

"Ah!" said the Infant. "I've only a few thousand pheasants to look after. Come along and dress for dinner. We're just ourselves. What flower is your honour's ladyship commanding for the table?"

" Just ourselves?" she said, looking at the crotons in the great hall. "Then let's have marigolds—the little cemetery ones."

So it was ordered.

Now, marigolds to us mean hot weather, discomfort, parting, and death. That smell in our nostrils, and Adam's servant in waiting, we naturally fell back more and more on the old slang, recalling at each glass those who had gone before. We did not sit at the big table, but in the bay window overlooking the park, where they were carting the last of the hay. When twilight fell we would not have candles, but waited for the moon, and continued our talk in the dusk that makes one remember.

Young Adam was not interested in our past except where it had touched his future. I think his mother held his hand beneath the table. Imam Din—shoeless, out of respect to the floors— brought him his medicine, poured it drop by drop, and asked for orders.

411

"Wait to take him to his cot when he grows weary," said his mother, and Imam Din retired into the shadow by the ancestral portraits.

"Now what d'you expect to get *out* of your country?" the Infant asked, when—our India laid aside—we talked Adam's Africa. It roused him at once.

"Rubber—nuts—gums—and so on," he said. "But our real future is cotton. I grew fifty acres of it last year in my district."

"My district!" said his father. "Hear him, Mummy!"

"I did though! I wish I could show you the sample. Some Manchester chaps said it was as good as any Sea Island cotton on the market."

"But what made you a cotton-planter, my son?" she asked.

"My chief said every man ought to have a *shouk* (a hobby) of sorts, and he took the trouble to ride a day out of his way to show me a belt of black soil that was just the thing for cotton."

"Ah! What was your chief like?" Stalky asked, in his silkiest tones.

"The best man alive—absolutely. He lets you blow your own nose yourself. The people call him"—Adam jerked out some heathen phrase—"that means the Man with the Stone Eyes, you know."

"I'm glad of that. Because I've heard—from other quarters"— Stalky's sentence burned like a slow match, but the explosion was not long delayed. "Other quarters!" Adam threw out a thin hand. "Every dog has his fleas. If you listen to *them*, of course!" The shake of his head was as I remembered it among his father's policemen twenty years before, and his mother's eyes shining through the dusk called on me to adore it. I kicked Stalky on the shin. One must not mock a young man's first love or loyalty.

A lump of raw cotton appeared on the table.

"I thought there might be a need. Therefore I packed it between our shirts," said the voice of Imam Din.

"Does he know as much English as that?" cried the Infant, who had forgotten his East.

We all admired the cotton for Adam's sake, and, indeed, it was very long and glossy.

"It's—it's only an' experiment," he said. "We're such awful paupers we can't even pay for a mailcart in my district. We use a biscuit-box on two bicycle wheels. I only got the money for that"—he patted the stuff—"by a pure fluke."

"How much did it cost?" asked Strickland.

"With seed and machinery—about two hundred pounds. I had the labour done by cannibals."

"That sounds promising." Stalky reached for a fresh cigarette.

"No, thank you," said Agnes. "I've been at Weston-super-Mare a little too long for cannibals. I'll go to the music-room and try over next Sunday's hymns."

She lifted the boy's hand lightly to her lips, and tripped across the acres of glimmering floor to the music-room that had been the Infant's ancestors' banqueting hall. Her grey and silver dress disappeared under the musicians' gallery; two electrics broke out, and she stood backed against the lines of gilded pipes.

"There's an abominable self-playing attachment here!" she called.

"Me!" the Infant answered, his napkin on his shoulder. "That's how I play *Parsifal*."

" I prefer the direct expression. Take it away, Ipps."

We heard old Ipps skating obediently all over the floor.

"Now for the direct expression," said Stalky, and moved on the Burgundy recommended by the faculty to enrich fever-thinned blood.

"It's nothing much. Only the belt of cotton-soil my chief showed me ran right into the Sheshaheli country. We haven't been able to prove cannibalism against that tribe in the courts; but when a Sheshaheli offers you four pounds of woman's breast, tattoo marks and all, skewered up in a plantain leaf before breakfast, you—"

"Naturally burn the villages before lunch," said Stalky.

Adam shook his head. "No troops," he sighed. "I told my chief about it, and he said we must wait till they chopped a

413

white man. He advised me if ever I felt like it not to commit a—a barren *felo de se*, but to let the Sheshaheli do it. Then he could report, and then we could mop 'em up! "

"Most immoral! That's how we got—" Stalky quoted the name of a province won by just such a sacrifice.

"Yes, but the beasts dominated one end of my cotton-belt like anything. They chivied me out of it when I went to take soil for analysis—me and Imam Din."

"*Sahib!* Is there a need?" The voice came out of the darkness, and the eyes shone over Adam's shoulder ere it ceased.

"None. The name was taken in talk." Adam abolished him with a turn of the finger. "I couldn't make a *casus belli* of it just then, because my chief had taken all the troops to hammer a gang of slave kings up north. Did you ever hear of our war against Ibn Makarrah? He precious nearly lost us the Protectorate at one time, though he's an ally of ours now."

"Wasn't he rather a pernicious brute, even as they go?" said Stalky. "Wade told me about him last year."

"Well, his nickname all through the country was 'The Merciful,' and he didn't get that for nothing. None of our people ever breathed his proper name. They said 'He' or 'That One,' and they didn't say it aloud, either. He fought us for eight months."

"I remember. There was a paragraph about it in one of the papers," I said.

"We broke him, though. No—the slavers don't come our way, because our men have the reputation of dying too much, the first month after they're captured. That knocks down profits, you see."

"What about your charming friends, the Sheshahelis?" said the Infant.

"There's no market for Sheshaheli. People would as soon buy crocodiles. I believe, before we annexed the country, Ibn Makarrah dropped down on 'em once—to train his young men—and simply hewed 'em in pieces. The bulk of my people are agriculturists—just the right stamp for cotton-growers. . . . What's mother playing?—*Once in royal?*"

414

The organ that had been crooning as happily as a woman over her babe restored, steadied to a tune.

"Magnificent! Oh, magnificent!" said the Infant loyally. I had never heard him sing but once, and then, though it was early in the tolerant morning, his mess had rolled him into a lotus pond.

"How did you get your cannibals to work for you? " asked Strickland.

"They got converted to civilization after my chief smashed Ibn Makarrah—just at the time I wanted 'em. You see my chief had promised me in writing that if I could scrape up a surplus he would not bag it for his roads this time, but I might have it for my cotton game. I only needed two hundred pounds. Our revenues didn't run to it."

"What is your revenue?" Stalky asked in the vernacular. .

"With hut-tax, traders', game and mining licenses, not more than fourteen thousand *rupees*; every penny of it ear-marked months ahead." Adam sighed.

"Also there is a fine for dogs straying in the *sahib's* camp. Last year it exceeded three *rupees*," Imam Din said quietly.

"Well, I thought that was fair. They howled so. We were rather strict on fines. I worked up my native clerk—Bulaki Ram—to a ferocious pitch of enthusiasm. He used to calculate the profits of our cotton-scheme to three points of decimals, after office. I tell you I envied your magistrates here hauling money out of motorists every week! I had managed to make our ordinary revenue and expenditure just about meet, and I was crazy to get the odd two hundred pounds for my cotton. That sort of thing grows on a chap when he's alone—and talks aloud!"

"Hul-lo! Have you been there already?" the father said, and Adam nodded.

"Yes. Used to spout what I could remember of *Marmion* to a tree, sir. Well *then* my luck turned. One evening an English-speaking nigger came in towing a corpse by the feet. (You get used to little things like that.) He said he'd found it, and please would I identify, because if it was one of Ibn Makarrah's men there might be a reward. It was an old Mohammedan, with a strong dash of Arab—a small-boned, bald-headed chap, and I was just wondering how it had kept so well in our climate when it sneezed. You ought to have seen the nigger! He fetched a howl and bolted like—like the dog in *Tom Sawyer*, when he sat on the what's-its-name beetle. He yelped as he ran, and the corpse went on sneezing. I could see it had been *sarkied*. (That's a sort of gum-poison, pater, which attacks the nerve centres. Our chief medical officer is writing a monograph about it.) So Imam Din and I emptied out the corpse one time, with my shaving soap and trade gunpowder, and hot water.

"I'd seen a case of *sarkie* before; so when the skin peeled off his feet, and he stopped sneezing, I knew he'd live. He *was* bad, though; lay like a log for a week while Imam Din and I massaged the paralysis out of him. Then he told us he was a Hajji—had been three times to Mecca—come in from French Africa, and that he'd met the nigger by the wayside— just like a case of *thuggee*, in India—and the nigger had poisoned him. That seemed reasonable enough by what I knew of Coast niggers."

"You believed him?" said his father keenly.

"There was no reason I shouldn't. The nigger never came back, and the old man stayed with me for two months," Adam returned. "You know what the best type of a Mohammedan gentleman can be, pater? He was that."

"None finer, none finer," was the answer.

"Except a Sikh," Stalky grunted.

"He'd been to Bombay; he knew French Africa inside out; he could quote poetry and the *Koran* all day long. He played chess—you don't know what that meant to me—like a master. We used to talk about the regeneration of Turkey and the Sheik-ul- Islam between moves. Oh, everything under the sun we talked about! He was awfully open-minded. He believed in slavery, of course, but he quite saw that it would have to die out. That's why he agreed with me about developing the resources of the district—by cotton-growing, you know."

"You talked of that too?" said Strickland.

"Rather. We discussed it for hours. You don't know what it meant to me. A wonderful man. Imam Din, was not our Hajji marvellous?"

"Most marvellous! It was all through the Hajji that we found the money for our cotton-play." Imam Din had moved, I fancy, behind Strickland's chair.

"Yes. It must have been dead against his convictions too. He brought me news when I was down with fever at Dupé that one of Ibn Makarrah's men was parading through my district with a bunch of slaves—in the Fork!"

"What's the matter with the Fork, that you can't abide it?" said Stalky. Adam's voice had risen at the last word.

"Local etiquette, sir," he replied, too earnest to notice Stalky's atrocious pun. "If a slaver runs slaves through British territory he ought to pretend that they're his servants. Hawkin' 'em about in the Fork—the forked stick that you put round their necks, you know—is insolence—same as not backing your topsails in the old days. Besides, it unsettles the district."

"I thought you said slavers didn't come your way," I put in.

"They don't. But my chief was smoking 'em out of the North all that season, and they were bolting into French territory any road they could find. My orders were to take no notice so long as they circulated, but open slave-dealing in the—Fork, was too much. I couldn't go myself, so I told a couple of our Makalali police and Imam Din to make talk with the gentleman one time. It was rather risky, and it might have been expensive, but it turned up trumps. They were back in a few days with the slaver (he didn't show fight) and a whole crowd of witnesses, and we tried him in my bedroom, and fined him properly. Just to show you how demoralized the brute must have been (Arabs often go dotty after a defeat), he'd snapped up four or five utterly useless Sheshaheli, and was offering 'em to all and sundry along the road. Why, he offered 'em to you, didn't he, Imam Din?"

"I was witness that he offered man-eaters for sale," said Imam Din.

"Luckily for my cotton-scheme, that landed him both ways.

You see, he had slaved *and* exposed slaves for sale in British territory. That meant the double fine if I could get it out of him."

"What was his defence?" said Strickland, late of the Punjab police.

"As far as I remember—but I had a temperature of 104 degrees at the time—he'd mistaken the meridians of longitude. Thought he was in French territory. Said he'd never do it again, if we'd let him off with a fine. I could have shaken hands with the brute for that. He paid up cash like a motorist and went off one time."

"Did you see him?"

"Ye-es. Didn't I, Imam Din?"

"Assuredly the *sahib* both saw and spoke to the slaver. And the *sahib* also made a speech to the man-eaters when he freed them, and they swore to supply him with labour for all his cotton-play. The *sahib* leaned on his own servant's shoulder the while."

"I remember something of that. I remember Bulaki Ram giving me the papers to sign, and I distinctly remember him locking up the money in the safe—two hundred and ten beautiful English sovereigns. You don't know what that meant to me! I believe it cured my fever; and as soon as I could, I staggered off with the Hajji to interview the Sheshaheli about labour. *Then* I found out why they had been so keen to work! It wasn't gratitude. Their big village had been hit by lightning and burned out a week or two before, and they lay flat in rows around me asking me for a job. I gave it 'em."

"And so you were very happy?" His mother had stolen up behind us. "You liked your cotton, dear?" She tidied the lump away.

"By Jove, I was happy!" Adam yawned. "Now if anyone," he looked at the Infant, "cares to put a little money into the scheme, it'll be the making of my district. I can't give you figures, sir, but I assure—"

"You'll take your arsenic, and Imam Din'll take you up to bed, and I'll come and tuck you in."

Agnes leaned forward, her rounded elbows on his shoulders,

hands joined across his dark hair, and—"Isn't he a darling?" she said to us, with just the same heart-rending lift to the left eyebrow and the same break of her voice as sent Strickland mad among the horses in the year '84. We were quiet when they were gone. We waited till Imam Din returned to us from above and coughed at the door, as only dark-hearted Asia can.

"Now," said Strickland, "tell us what truly befell, son of my servant."

"All befell as our *sahib* has said. Only—only there was an arrangement—a little arrangement on account of his cotton-play."

"Tell! Sit! I *beg* your pardon, Infant," said Strickland.

But the Infant had already made the sign, and we heard Imam Din hunker down on the floor. One gets little out of the East at attention.

"When the fever came on our *sahib* in our roofed house at Dupé," he began, "the Hajji listened intently to his talk. He expected the names of women; though I had already told him that our virtue was beyond belief or compare, and that our sole desire was this cotton-play. Being at last convinced, the Hajji breathed on our *sahib's* forehead, to sink into his brain news concerning a slave-dealer in his district who had made a mock of the law. *sahib*," Imam Din turned to Strickland, "our *sahib* answered to those false words as a horse of blood answers to the spur. He sat up. He issued orders for the apprehension of the slave-dealer. Then he fell back. Then we left him."

"Alone—servant of my son, and son of my servant?" said his father.

"There was an old woman which belonged to the Hajji. She had come in with the Hajji's money-belt. The Hajji told her that if our *sahib* died, she would die with him. And truly our *sahib* had given me orders to depart."

"Being mad with fever—eh?"

"What could we do, *sahib?* This cotton-play was his heart's desire. He talked of it in his fever. Therefore it was his heart's desire that the Hajji went to fetch. Doubtless the Hajji could have given him money enough out of hand for ten cotton-plays; but in this respect also our *sahib's* virtue was beyond belief or compare. Great Ones do not exchange moneys. Therefore the Hajji said—and I helped with my counsel—that we must make arrangements to get the money in all respects conformable with the English Law. It was great trouble to us, but—the law is the law. And the Hajji showed the old woman the knife by which she would die if our *sahib* died. So I accompanied the Hajji."

"Knowing who he was?" said Strickland.

"No! Fearing the man. A virtue went out from him overbearing the virtue of lesser persons. The Hajji told Bulaki Ram the clerk to occupy the seat of government at Dupé till our return. Bulaki Ram feared the Hajji, because the Hajji had often gloatingly appraised his skill in figures at five thousand *rupees* upon any slave-block. The Hajji then said to me: 'Come, and we will make the man-eaters play the cotton-game for my delight's delight.' The Hajji loved our *sahib* with the love of a father for his son, of a saved for his saviour, of a Great One for a Great One. But I said: 'We cannot go to that Sheshaheli place without a hundred rifles. We have here five.' The Hajji said: 'I have untied a knot in my head-handkerchief which will be more to us than a thousand.' I saw that he had so loosed it that it lay flagwise on his shoulder. Then I knew that he was a Great One with virtue in him.

"We came to the highlands of the Sheshaheli on the dawn of the second day—about the time of the stirring of the cold wind. The Hajji walked delicately across the open place where their filth is, and scratched upon the gate which was shut. When it opened I saw the man-eaters lying on their cots under the eaves of the huts. They rolled off: they rose up, one behind the other the length of the street, and the fear on their faces was as leaves whitening to a breeze. The Hajji stood in the gate guarding his skirts from defilement. The Hajji said: 'I am here once again. Give me six and yoke up.' They zealously then pushed to us with poles six, and yoked them with a heavy tree.

"The Hajji then said: 'Fetch fire from the morning hearth,

and come to windward,' The wind is strong on those headlands at sunrise, so when each had emptied his crock of fire in front of that which was before him, the broadside of the town roared into flame, and all went. The Hajji then said: 'At the end of a time there will come here the white man ye once chased for sport. He will demand labour to plant such and such stuff. Ye are that labour, and your spawn after you.' They said, lifting their heads a very little from the edge of the ashes: 'We are that labour, and our spawn after us.' The Hajji said: 'What is also my name?' They said: 'Thy name is also The Merciful.' The Hajji said: 'Praise then my mercy'; and while they did this, the Hajji walked away, I following."

The Infant made some noise in his throat, and reached for more Burgundy.

"About noon one of our six fell dead. Fright—only fright, *sahib!* None had—none could—touch him. Since they were in pairs, and the other of the Fork was mad and sang foolishly, we waited for some heathen to do what was needful. There came at last Angari men with goats. The Hajji said: 'What do ye see?' They said: 'Oh, our Lord, we neither see nor hear.' The Hajji said: 'But I command ye to see and to hear and to say.' They said: 'Oh, our. Lord, it is to our commanded eyes as though slaves stood in a Fork.' The Hajji said: 'So testify before the officer who waits you in the town of Dupé.' They said: 'What shall come to us after?' The Hajji said: 'The just reward for the informer. But if ye do not testify, then a punishment which shall cause birds to fall from the trees in terror and monkeys to scream for pity.' Hearing this, the Angari men hastened to Dupé. The Hajji then said to me: 'Are those things sufficient to establish our case, or must I drive in a village full?'

"I said that three witnesses amply established any case, but as yet, I said, the Hajji had not offered his slaves for sale. It is true, as our *sahib* said just now, there is one fine for catching slaves, and yet another for making to sell them. And it was the double fine that we needed, *sahib*, for our *sahib's* cotton-play. We had fore-arranged all this with Bulaki Ram, who knows the English law, and I thought the Hajji remembered, but he grew angry, and cried out: 'O God, Refuge of the Afflicted, must I, who am what I am, peddle this dog's meat by the roadside to gain his delight for my heart's delight?" None the less, he admitted it was the English law, and so he offered me the six—five—in a small voice, with an averted head. The Sheshaheli do not smell of sour milk as heathen should. They smell like leopards, *sahib*. This is because they eat men."

"Maybe," said Strickland. "But where were thy wits? One witness is not sufficient to establish the fact of a sale."

"What could we do, *sahib?* There was the Hajji's reputation to consider. We could not have called in a heathen witness for such a thing. And, moreover, the *sahib* forgets that the defend-ant himself was making this case. He would not contest his own evidence. Otherwise, I know the law of evidence well enough.

"So then we went to Dupé, and while Bulaki Ram waited among the Angari men, I ran to see our *sahib* in bed. His eyes were very bright, and his mouth was full of upside-down orders, but the old woman had not loosened her hair for death. The Hajji said: 'Be quick with my trial. I am not Job!' The Hajji was a learned man. We made the trial swiftly to a sound of sooth-ing voices round the bed. Yet—*yet*, because no man can be sure whether a *sahib* of that blood sees, or does not see, we made it strictly in the manner of the forms of the English law. Only the witnesses and the slaves and the prisoner we kept without for his nose's sake."

"Then he did not see the prisoner?" said Strickland.

"I stood by to shackle up an Angari in case he should de-mand it, but by God's favour he was too far fevered to ask for one. It is quite true he signed the papers. It is quite true he saw the money put away in the safe—two hundred and ten English pounds—and it is quite true that the gold wrought on him as a strong cure. But as to his seeing the prisoner, and having speech with the man-eaters—the Hajji breathed all that on his forehead to sink into his sick brain. A little, as ye have heard, has remained. . . . Ah, but when the fever broke, and our *sahib* called for the fine-book, and the thin little picture-books from Europe with the pictures of ploughs and hoes, and cotton-mills—ah, then he laughed as he used to laugh, *sahib*. It was his heart's desire, this cotton-play. The Hajji loved him, as who does not? It was a little, little arrangement, *sahib*, of which—*is* it necessary to tell all the world?"

"And when didst thou know who the Hajji was?" said Strickland.

"Not for a certainty till he and our *sahib* had returned from their visit to the Sheshaheli country. It is quite true as our *sahib* says, the man-eaters lay flat around his feet, and asked for spades to cultivate cotton. That very night, when I was cooking the dinner, the Hajji said to me: 'I go to my own place, though God knows whether the Man with the Stone Eyes have left me an ox, a slave, or a woman.' I said: 'Thou art then That One?' The Hajji said: 'I am ten thousand *rupees* reward into thy hand. Shall we make another law-case and get more cotton machines for the boy?' I said: 'What dog am I to do this? May God prolong thy life a thousand years!' The Hajji said: 'Who has seen tomorrow? God has given me as it were a son in my old age, and I praise Him. See that the breed is not lost!'

"He walked then from the cooking-place to our *sahib's* office-table under the tree, where our *sahib* held in his hand a blue envelope of service newly come in by runner from the North. At this, fearing evil news for the Hajji, I would have restrained him, but he said: 'We be both Great Ones. Neither of us will fail.' Our *sahib* looked up to invite the Hajji to approach before he opened the letter, but the Hajji stood off till our *sahib* had well opened and well read the letter. Then the Hajji said: 'Is it permitted to say farewell ?' Our *sahib* stabbed the letter on the file with a deep and joyful breath and cried a welcome. The Hajji said: 'I go to my own place,' and he loosed from his neck a chained heart of ambergris set in soft gold and held it forth. Our *sahib* snatched it swiftly in the closed fist, down turned, and said : 'If thy name be written hereon, it is needless, for a name is already engraved on my heart.' The Hajji said: 'And on mine also is a name engraved; but there is no name on the amulet.' The Hajji stooped to our *sahib's* feet, but our *sahib* raised and embraced him, and the Hajji covered his mouth with his shoulder-cloth, because it worked, and so he went away."

"And what order was in the service letter?" Stalky murmured.

"Only an order for our *sahib* to write a report on some new cattle sickness. But all orders come in the same make of envelope. We could not tell what order it might have been."

"When he opened the letter—my son—made he no sign? A cough? An oath?" Strickland asked.

"None, *sahib*. I watched his hands. They did not shake. Afterward he wiped his face, but he was sweating before from the heat."

"Did he know? Did he know who the Hajji was?" said the Infant in English.

"I am a poor man. Who can say what a *sahib* of that get knows or does not know? But the Hajji is right. The breed should not be lost. It is not very hot for little children in Dupé, and as regards nurses, my sister's cousin at Jull—"

"H'm! That is the boy's own concern. I wonder if his chief ever knew?" said Strickland.

"Assuredly," said Imam Din. " On the night before our *sahib* went down to the sea, the Great Sahib—the Man with the Stone Eyes—dined with him in his camp, I being in charge of the table. They talked a long while and the Great Sahib said: 'What didst thou think of *That* One?' (*We* do not say Ibn Makarrah yonder.) Our *sahib* said: 'Which one?' The Great Sahib said: 'That One which taught thy maneaters to grow cotton for thee. He was in thy district three months to my certain knowledge, and I looked by every runner that thou wouldst send me in his head.' Our *sahib* said: 'If his head had been needed, another man should have been appointed to govern my district, for he was my friend.'

"The Great Sahib laughed and said: 'If I had needed a lesser man in thy place be sure I would have sent him, as, if I had needed the head of That One, be sure I would have sent men to bring it to me. But tell me now, by what means didst thou twist him to thy use and our profit in this cotton-play?' Our *sahib* said: 'By God, I did not use that man in any fashion whatever. He was my friend.' The Great Sahib said: '*Toh Vau!* (Bosh!) Tell!' Our *sahib* shook his head as he does—as he did when a child—and they looked at each other like sword-play men in the ring at a fair. The Great Sahib dropped his eyes first and he said: 'So be it. I should perhaps have answered thus in my youth. No matter. I have made treaty with That One as an ally of the State. Some day he shall tell me the tale.' Then I brought in fresh coffee, and they ceased. But I do not think That One will tell the Great Sahib more than our *sahib* told him."

"Wherefore?" I asked.

"Because they are both great ones, and I have observed in my life that great ones employ words very little between each other in their dealings; still less when they speak to a third concerning those dealings. Also they profit by silence. . . . Now I think that the mother has come down from the room, and I will go rub his feet till he sleeps."

His ears had caught Agnes's step at the stair-head, and presently she passed us on her way to the music-room humming the *Magnificat*.

At the End of the Passage

The sky is lead and our faces are red,
And the gates of Hell are opened and riven,
And the winds of Hell are loosened and driven,
And the dust flies up in the face of Heaven,
And the clouds come down in a fiery sheet,
Heavy to raise and hard to be borne.
And the soul of man is turned from his meat,
Turned from the trifles for which he has striven
Sick in his body, and heavy hearted,
And his soul flies up like the dust in the sheet
Breaks from his flesh and is gone and departed,
As the blasts they blow on the cholera-horn.

Himalayan.

Four men, each entitled to 'life, liberty, and the pursuit of happiness,' sat at a table playing whist. The thermometer marked—for them—one hundred and one degrees of heat. The room was darkened till it was only just possible to distinguish the pips of the cards and the very white faces of the players. A tattered, rotten *punkah* of whitewashed calico was puddling the hot air and whining dolefully at each stroke. Outside lay gloom of a November day in London. There was neither sky, sun, nor horizon,—nothing but a brown purple haze of heat. It was as though the earth were dying of apoplexy.

From time to time clouds of tawny dust rose from the ground without wind or warning, flung themselves tablecloth-wise among the tops of the parched trees, and came down again. Then a whirling dust-devil would scutter across the plain for a couple of miles, break, and fall outward, though there was nothing to check its flight save a long low line of piled railway-sleepers white with the dust, a cluster of huts made of mud, condemned rails, and canvas, and the one squat four-roomed bungalow that belonged to the assistant engineer in charge of a section of the Gaudhari State line then under construction.

The four, stripped to the thinnest of sleeping-suits, played whist crossly, with wranglings as to leads and returns. It was not the best kind of whist, but they had taken some trouble to arrive at it. Mottram of the Indian Survey had ridden thirty and railed one hundred miles from his lonely post in the desert since the night before; Lowndes of the Civil Service, on special duty in the political department, had come as far to escape for an instant the miserable intrigues of an impoverished native State whose king alternately fawned and blustered for more money from the pitiful revenues contributed by hard-wrung peasants and despairing camel-breeders; Spurstow, the doctor of the line, had left a cholera-stricken camp of coolies to look after itself for forty-eight hours while he associated with white men once more. Hummil, the assistant engineer, was the host. He stood fast and received his friends thus every Sunday if they could come in. When one of them failed to appear, he would send a telegram to his last address, in order that he might know whether the defaulter were dead or alive. There are very many places in the East where it is not good or kind to let your acquaintances drop out of sight even for one short week.

The players were not conscious of any special regard for each other. They squabbled whenever they met; but they ardently desired to meet, as men without water desire to drink. They were lonely folk who understood the dread meaning of loneliness. They were all under thirty years of age,—which is too soon for any man to possess that knowledge.

'Pilsener?' said Spurstow, after the second rubber, mopping his forehead.

'Beer's out, I'm sorry to say, and there's hardly enough soda-water for tonight,' said Hummil.

'What filthy bad management!' Spurstow snarled.

'Can't help it. I've written and wired; but the trains don't come through regularly yet. Last week the ice ran out,—as Lowndes knows.'

'Glad I didn't come. I could ha' sent you some if I had known, though. Phew! it's too hot to go on playing bumblepuppy.' This with a savage scowl at Lowndes, who only laughed. He was a hardened offender.

Mottram rose from the table and looked out of a chink in the shutters.

'What a sweet day!' said he.

The company yawned all together and betook themselves to an aimless investigation of all Hummil's possessions,—guns, tattered novels, saddlery, spurs, and the like. They had fingered them a score of times before, but there was really nothing else to do.

'Got anything fresh?' said Lowndes.

'Last week's *Gazette of India*, and a cutting from a home paper. My father sent it out. It's rather amusing.'

'One of those vestrymen that call 'emselves M.P.'s again, is it?' said Spurstow, who read his newspapers when he could get them.

'Yes. Listen to this. It's to your address, Lowndes. The man was making a speech to his constituents, and he piled it on. Here's a sample:

"And I assert unhesitatingly that the Civil Service in India is the preserve—the pet preserve—of the aristocracy of England. What does the democracy—what do the masses—get from that country, which we have step by step fraudulently annexed? I answer, nothing whatever. It is farmed with a single eye to their own interests by the scions of the aristocracy. They take good care to maintain their lavish scale of incomes, to avoid or stifle any inquiries into the nature and conduct of their administration, while they themselves force the unhappy peasant to pay with the sweat of his brow for all the luxuries in which they are lapped."

Hummil waved the cutting above his head. ''Ear! 'ear!' said his audience.

Then Lowndes, meditatively: 'I'd give I'd give three months' pay to have that gentleman spend one month with me and see how the free and independent native prince works things. Old Timbersides'—this was his flippant title for an honoured and decorated feudatory prince—'has been wearing my life out this week past for money. By Jove, his latest performance was to send me one of his women as a bribe!'

'Good for you! Did you accept it?' said Mottram.

'No. I rather wish I had, now. She was a pretty little person, and she yarned away to me about the horrible destitution among the king's women-folk. The darlings haven't had any new clothes for nearly a month, and the old man wants to buy a new drag from Calcutta,—solid silver railings and silver lamps, and trifles of that kind. I've tried to make him understand that he has played the deuce with the revenues for the last twenty years and must go slow. He can't see it.'

'But he has the ancestral treasure-vaults to draw on. There must be three millions at least in jewels and coin under his palace,' said Hummil.

'Catch a native king disturbing the family treasure! The priests forbid it except as the last resort. Old Timbersides has added something like a quarter of a million to the deposit in his reign.'

'Where the mischief does it all come from? ' said Mottram.

'The country. The state of the people is enough to make you sick. I've known the tax-men wait by a milch-camel till the foal was born and then hurry off the mother for arrears. And what can I do? I can't get the court clerks to give me any accounts; I can't raise anything more than a fat smile from the commander-in-chief when I find out the troops are three months in arrears; and old Timbersides begins to weep when I speak to him. He has taken to the King's Peg heavily,—liqueur brandy for whisky, and Heidsieck for soda-water.'

'That's what the Rao of Jubela took to. Even a native can't last long at that,' said Spurstow. 'He'll go out.'

'And a good thing, too. Then I suppose we'll have a council of regency, and a tutor for the young prince, and hand him back his kingdom with ten years' accumulations.'

'Whereupon that young prince, having been taught all the vices of the English, will play ducks and drakes with the money and undo ten years' work in eighteen months. I've seen that business before,' said Spurstow. 'I should tackle the king with a light hand, if I were you, Lowndes. They'll hate you quite enough under any circumstances.'

' That's all very well. The man who looks on can talk about the light hand; but you can't clean a pigsty with a pen dipped in rose-water. I know my risks; but nothing has happened yet. My servant's an old Pathan, and he cooks for me. They are hardly likely to bribe him, and I don't accept food from my true friends, as they call themselves. Oh, but it's weary work! I'd sooner be with you, Spurstow. There's shooting near your camp.'

'Would you? I don't think it. About fifteen deaths a day don't incite a man to shoot anything but himself. And the worst of it is that the poor devils look at you as though you ought to save them. Lord knows, I've tried everything. My last attempt was empirical, but it pulled an old man through. He was brought to me apparently past hope, and I gave him gin and Worcester sauce with cayenne. It cured him; but I don't recommend it.'

' How do the cases run generally?' said Hummil.

'Very simply indeed. Chlorodyne, opium pill, chlorodyne, collapse, nitre, bricks to the feet, and then the burning-*ghat*. The last seems to be the only thing that stops the trouble. It's black cholera, you know. Poor devils! But, I will say, little Bunsee Lal, my apothecary, works like a demon. I've recommended him for promotion if he comes through it all alive.'

'And what are your chances, old man?' said Mottram.

'Don't know; don't care much; but I've sent the letter in. What are you doing with yourself generally?'

'Sitting under a table in the tent and spitting on the sextant to keep it cool,' said the man of the survey. 'Washing my eyes to avoid ophthalmia, which I shall certainly get, and trying to make a sub-surveyor understand that an error of five degrees in an angle isn't quite so small as it looks. I'm altogether alone, y' know, and shall be till the end of the hot weather.'

'Hummil's the lucky man,' said Lowndes, flinging himself into a long chair. 'He has an actual roof—torn as to the ceiling-cloth, but still a roof—over his head. He sees one train daily. He can get beer and soda-water and ice 'em when God is good. He has books, pictures,'—they were torn from the *Graphic*,—'and the society of the excellent sub-contractor Jevins, besides the pleasure of receiving us weekly.'

Hummil smiled grimly. 'Yes, I'm the lucky man, I suppose. Jevins is luckier.'

'How? Not—'

'Yes. Went out. Last Monday.'

'By his own hand?' said Spurstow quickly, hinting the suspicion that was in everybody's mind. There was no cholera near Hummil's section. Even fever gives a man at least a week's grace, and sudden death generally implied self-slaughter.

'I judge no man this weather,' said Hummil. 'He had a touch of the sun, I fancy; for last week, after you fellows had left, he came into the verandah and told me that he was going home to see his wife, in Market Street, Liverpool, that evening.

'I got the apothecary in to look at him, and we tried to make him lie down. After an hour or two he rubbed his eyes and said he believed he had had a fit,—hoped he hadn't said anything rude. Jevins had a great idea of bettering himself socially. He was very like Chucks in his language.'

'Well?'

'Then he went to his own bungalow and began cleaning a rifle. He told the servant that he was going to shoot buck in the morning. Naturally he fumbled with the trigger, and shot himself through the head—accidentally. The apothecary sent in a report to my chief, and Jevins is buried somewhere out there. I'd have wired to you, Spurstow, if you could have done anything.'

'You're a queer chap,' said Mottram. 'If you'd killed the man yourself you couldn't have been more quiet about the business.'

'Good Lord! what does it matter?' said Hummil calmly. 'I've got to do a lot of his overseeing work in addition to my own. I'm the only person that suffers. Jevins is out of it,—by pure accident, of course, but out of it. The apothecary was going to write a long screed on suicide. Trust a *babu* to drivel when he gets the chance.'

'Why didn't you let it go in as suicide?' said Lowndes.

'No direct proof. A man hasn't many privileges in this country, but he might at least be allowed to mishandle his own rifle. Besides, some day I may need a man to smother up an accident to myself. Live and let live. Die and let die.'

'You take a pill,' said Spurstow, who had been watching Hummil's white face narrowly. 'Take a pill, and don't be an ass. That sort of talk is skittles. Anyhow, suicide is shirking your work. If I were Job ten times over, I should be so interested in what was going to happen next that I'd stay on and watch.'

'Ah! I've lost that curiosity,' said Hummil.

'Liver out of order?' said Lowndes feelingly.

'No. Can't sleep. That's worse.'

' By Jove, it is!' said Mottram. 'I'm that way every now and then, and the fit has to wear itself out. What do you take for it?'

'Nothing. What's the use? I haven't had ten minutes' sleep since Friday morning.'

'Poor chap! Spurstow, you ought to attend to this,' said Mottram. 'Now you mention it, your eyes are rather gummy and swollen.'

Spurstow, still watching Hummil, laughed lightly. 'I'll patch him up, later on. Is it too hot, do you think, to go for a ride?'

'Where to?' said Lowndes wearily. 'We shall have to go away at eight, and there'll be riding enough for us then. I hate a horse, when I have to use him as a necessity. Oh, heavens! what is there to do?'

'Begin whist again, at *chick* points ('a *chick*' is supposed to be eight shillings) and a gold *mohur* on the rub,' said Spurstow promptly.

'Poker. A month's pay all round for the pool,—no limit,—and fifty-*rupee* raises. Somebody would be broken before we got up,' said Lowndes.

'Can't say that it would give me any pleasure to break any man in this company,' said Mottram. 'There isn't enough excitement in it, and it's foolish.' He crossed over to the worn and battered little camp-piano,—wreckage of a married household that had once held the bungalow,—and opened the case.

'It's used up long ago,' said Hummil. 'The servants have picked it to pieces.'

The piano was indeed hopelessly out of order, but Mottram managed to bring the rebellious notes into a sort of agreement, and there rose from the ragged keyboard something that might once have been the ghost of a popular music-hall song. The men in the long chairs turned with evident interest as Mottram banged the more lustily.

'That's good!' said Lowndes. 'By Jove! the last time I heard that song was in '79, or thereabouts, just before I came out.'

'Ah !' said Spurstow with pride, 'I was home in '80.' And he mentioned a song of the streets popular at that date.

Mottram executed it roughly. Lowndes criticised and volunteered emendations. Mottram dashed into another ditty, not of the music-hall character, and made us if to rise.

'Sit down,' said Hummil. 'I didn't know that you had any music in your composition. Go on playing until you can't think of anything more. I'll have that piano tuned up before you come again. Play something festive.'

Very simple indeed were the tunes to which Mottram's art and the limitations of the piano could give effect, but the men listened with pleasure, and in the pauses talked all together of what they had seen or heard when they were last at home. A dense dust-storm sprung up outside, and swept roaring over the house, enveloping it in the choking darkness of midnight, but Mottram continued unheeding, and the crazy tinkle reached the ears of the listeners above the napping of the tattered ceiling-cloth.

In the silence after the storm he glided from the more direct-ly personal songs of Scotland, half humming them as he played, into the Evening Hymn.

'Sunday,' said he, nodding his head.

'Go on. Don't apologise for it,' said Spurstow.

Hummil laughed long and riotously. 'Play it, by all means. You're full of surprises today. I didn't know you had such a gift of finished sarcasm. How does that thing go?'

Mottram took up the tune.

'Too slow by half. You miss the note of gratitude,' said Hum-mil. 'It ought to go to the "*Grasshopper's Polka*,"—this way.' And he chanted, *prestissimo*,—

Glory to thee, my God, this night,
For all the blessings of the light.

'That shows we really feel our blessings. How does it go on?—

If in the night I sleepless lie,
My soul with sacred thoughts supply;
May no ill dreams disturb my rest,—

'Quicker, Mottram!—

Or powers of darkness me molest!

'Bah! what an old hypocrite you are!'

'Don't be an ass,' said Lowndes. 'You are at full liberty to make fun of anything else you like, but leave that hymn alone. It's associated in my mind with the most sacred recollections—'

'Summer evenings in the country,—stained-glass window, light going out, and you and she jamming your heads together over one hymn-book,' said Mottram.

' Yes, and a fat old cockchafer hitting you in the eye when you walked home. Smell of hay, and a moon as big as a bandbox sitting on the top of a haycock; bats,—roses,—milk and midges,' said Lowndes.

' Also mothers. I can just recollect my mother singing me to

434

sleep with that when I was a little chap,' said Spurstow.

The darkness had fallen on the room. They could hear Hummil squirming in his chair.

'Consequently,' said he testily, 'you sing it when you are seven fathom deep in Hell! It's an insult to the intelligence of the Deity to pretend we're anything but tortured rebels.'

'Take *two* pills,' said Spurstow; 'that's tortured liver.'

'The usually placid Hummil is in a vile bad temper. I'm sorry for his *coolies* tomorrow,' said Lowndes, as the servants brought in the lights and prepared the table for dinner.

As they were settling into their places about the miserable goat-chops, and the smoked tapioca pudding, Spurstow took occasion to whisper to Mottram, 'Well done, David!'

'Look after Saul, then,' was the reply.

'What are you two whispering about? 'said Hummil suspiciously.

'Only saying that you are a damned poor host. This fowl can't be cut,' returned Spurstow with a sweet smile. 'Call this a dinner?'

'I can't help it. You don't expect a banquet, do you?'

Throughout that meal Hummil contrived laboriously to insult directly and pointedly all his guests in succession, and at each insult Spurstow kicked the aggrieved persons under the table; but he dared not exchange a glance of intelligence with either of them. Hummil's face was white and pinched, while his eyes were unnaturally large. No man dreamed for a moment of resenting his savage personalities, but as soon as the meal was over they made haste to get away.

'Don't go. You're just getting amusing, you fellows. I hope I haven't said anything that annoyed you. You're such touchy devils.' Then, changing the note into one of almost abject entreaty, Hummil added, ' I say, you surely aren't going?'

'In the language of the blessed Jorrocks, where I dines I sleeps,' said Spurstow. 'I want to have a look at your *coolies* tomorrow, if you don't mind. You can give me a place to lie down in, I suppose?'

The others pleaded the urgency of their several duties next day, and, saddling up, departed together, Hummil begging them to come next Sunday. As they jogged off, Lowndes unbosomed himself to Mottram—

'. . . And I never felt so like kicking a man at his own table in my life. He said I cheated at whist, and reminded me I was in debt! Told you you were as good as a liar to your face! You aren't half indignant enough over it.'

'Not I,' said Mottram. 'Poor devil! Did you ever know old Hummy behave like that before or within a hundred miles of it?'

'That's no excuse. Spurstow was hacking my shin all the time, so I kept a hand on myself. Else I should have—'

'No, you wouldn't. You'd have done as Hummy did about Jevins; judge no man this weather. By Jove! the buckle of my bridle is hot in my hand! Trot out a bit, and 'ware rat-holes.'

Ten minutes' trotting jerked out of Lowndes one very sage remark when he pulled up, sweating from every pore—

"Good thing Spurstow's with him tonight.'

'Ye-es. Good man, Spurstow. Our roads turn here. See you again next Sunday, if the sun doesn't bowl me over.'

'S'pose so, unless old Timbersides' finance minister manages to dress some of my food. Goodnight, and—God bless you!'

'What's wrong now?'

'Oh, nothing.' Lowndes gathered up his whip, and, as he nicked Mottram's mare on the flank, added, 'You're not a bad little chap,—that's all.' And the mare bolted half a mile across the sand, on the word.

In the assistant engineer's bungalow Spurstow and Hummil smoked the pipe of silence together, each narrowly watching the other. The capacity of a bachelor's establishment is as elastic as its arrangements are simple. A servant cleared away the dining-room table, brought in a couple of rude native bedsteads made of tape strung on a light wood frame, flung a square of cool Calcutta matting over each, set them side by side, pinned two towels to the *punkah* so that their fringes should just sweep clear of the sleepers' nose and mouth, and announced that the couches were ready.

The men flung themselves down, ordering the *punkah-coolies* by all the powers of Hell to pull. Every door and window was shut, for the outside air was that of an oven. The atmosphere within was only 104°, as the thermometer bore witness, and heavy with the foul smell of badly-trimmed kerosene lamps; and this stench, combined with that of native tobacco, baked brick, and dried earth, sends the heart of many a strong man down to his boots, for it is the smell of the Great Indian Empire when she turns herself for six months into a house of torment. Spurstow packed his pillows craftily so that he reclined rather than lay, his head at a safe elevation above his feet. It is not good to sleep on a low pillow in the hot weather if you happen to be of thick-necked build, for you may pass with lively snores and gugglings from natural sleep into the deep slumber of heat-apoplexy.

'Pack your pillows,' said the doctor sharply, as he saw Hummil preparing to lie down at full length.

The night-light was trimmed; the shadow of the *punkah* wavered across the room, and the '*flick*' of the *punkah*-towel and the soft whine of the rope through the wall-hole followed it. Then the *punkah* flagged, almost ceased. The sweat poured from Spurstow's brow. Should he go out and harangue the *coolie*? It started forward again with a savage jerk, and a pin came out of the towels. When this was replaced, a *tom-tom* in the *coolie*-lines began to beat with the steady throb of a swollen artery inside some brain-fevered skull. Spurstow turned on his side and swore gently. There was no movement on Hummil's part. The man had composed himself as rigidly as a corpse, his hands clinched at his sides. The respiration was too hurried for any suspicion of sleep. Spurstow looked at the set face. The jaws were clinched, and there was a pucker round the quivering eyelids.

'He's holding himself as tightly as ever he can,' thought Spurstow. 'What in the world is the matter with him?—Hummil!'

'Yes,' in a thick constrained voice.

'Can't you get to sleep?'

'No.'

'Head hot? 'Throat feeling bulgy? or how?'

'Neither, thanks. I don't sleep much, you know.'

"Feel pretty bad?'

'Pretty bad, thanks. There is a *tom-tom* outside, isn't there? I thought it was my head at first. . . . Oh Spurstow, for pity's sake give me something that will put me asleep,—sound asleep,—if it's only for six hours!' He sprang up, trembling from head to foot. 'I haven't been able to sleep naturally for days, and I can't stand it!—I can't stand it!'

'Poor old chap!'

'That's no use. Give me something to make me sleep. I tell you I'm nearly mad. I don't know what I say half my time. For three weeks I've had to think and spell out every word that has come through my lips before I dared say it. Isn't that enough to drive a man mad? I can't see things correctly now, and I've lost my sense of touch. My skin aches—my skin aches! Make me sleep. Oh, Spurstow, for the love of God make me sleep sound. It isn't enough merely to let me dream. Let me sleep!'

'All right, old man, all right. Go slow; you aren't half as bad as you think.'

The flood-gates of reserve once broken, Hummil was clinging to him like a frightened child. ' You're pinching my arm to pieces.'

'I'll break your neck if you don't do something for me. No, I didn't mean that. Don't be angry, old fellow.' He wiped the sweat off himself as he fought to regain composure. ' I'm a bit restless and off my oats, and perhaps you could recommend some sort of sleeping mixture,—bromide of potassium.'

'Bromide of skittles! Why didn't you tell me this before? Let go of my arm, and I'll see if there's anything in my cigarette-case to suit your complaint.' Spurstow hunted among his day-clothes, turned up the lump, opened a little silver cigarette-case, and advanced on the expectant Hummil with the daintiest of fairy squirts.

'The last appeal of civilisation,' said he, 'and a thing I hate to use. Hold out your arm. Well, your sleeplessness hasn't ruined your muscle; and what a thick hide it is! Might as well inject a buffalo subcutaneously. Now in a few minutes the morphia will begin working. Lie down and wait.'

A smile of unalloyed and idiotic delight began to creep over Hummil's face. 'I think,' he whispered,—'I think I'm going off now. Gad! it's positively heavenly! Spurstow, you must give me that case to keep; you—' The voice ceased as the head fell back.

'Not for a good deal,' said Spurstow to the unconscious form. 'And now, my friend, sleeplessness of your kind being very apt to relax the moral fibre in little matters of life and death, I'll just take the liberty of spiking your guns.'

He paddled into Hummil's saddle-room in his bare feet and uncased a twelve-bore rifle, an express, and a revolver. Of the first he unscrewed the nipples and hid them in the bottom of a saddlery-case; of the second he abstracted the lever, kicking it behind a big wardrobe. The third he merely opened, and knocked the doll-head bolt of the grip up with the heel of a riding-boot.

'That's settled,' he said, as he shook the sweat off his hands. 'These little precautions will at least give you time to turn. You have too much sympathy with gun-room accidents.'

And as he rose from his knees, the thick muffled voice of Hummil cried in the doorway, 'You fool!'

Such tones they use who speak in the lucid intervals of delirium to their friends a little before they die.

Spurstow started, dropping the pistol. Hummil stood in the doorway, rocking with helpless laughter.

'That was awf'ly good of you, I'm sure,' he said, very slowly, feeling for his words. 'I don't intend to go out by my own hand at present. I say, Spurstow, that stuff won't work. What shall I do? What shall I do?' And panic terror stood in his eyes.

'Lie down and give it a chance. Lie down at once.'

'I daren't. It will only take me halfway again, and I shan't be able to get away this time. Do you know it was all I could do to come out just now? Generally I am as quick as lightning; but you had clogged my feet. I was nearly caught.'

'Oh yes, I understand. Go and lie down.'

'No, it isn't delirium; but it was an awfully mean trick to play on me. Do you know I might have died?'

As a sponge rubs a slate clean, so some power unknown to Spurstow had wiped out of Hummil's face all that stamped it for the face of a man, and he stood at the doorway in the expression of his lost innocence. He had slept back into terrified childhood.

'Is he going to die on the spot?' thought Spurstow. Then, aloud, 'All right, my son. Come back to bed, and tell me all about it. You couldn't sleep; but what was all the rest of the nonsense?'

'A place,—a place down there,' said Hummil, with simple sincerity. The drug was acting on him by waves, and he was flung from the fear of a strong man to the fright of a child as his nerves gathered sense or were dulled.

'Good God! I've been afraid of it for months past, Spurstow. It has made every night hell to me; and yet I'm not conscious of having done anything wrong.'

'Be still, and I'll give you another dose. We'll stop your nightmares, you unutterable idiot!'

'Yes, but you must give me so much that I can't get away. You must make me quite sleepy,—not just a little sleepy. It's so hard to run then.'

'I know it; I know it. I've felt it myself. The symptoms are exactly as you describe.'

'Oh, don't laugh at me, confound you! Before this awful sleeplessness came to me I've tried to rest on my elbow and put a spur in the bed to sting me when I fell back. Look!'

'By Jove! the man has been rowelled like a horse! Ridden by the nightmare with a vengeance! And we all thought him sensible enough. Heaven send us understanding! You like to talk, don't you?'

'Yes, sometimes. Not when I'm frightened. *Then* I want to

run. Don't you?'

'Always. Before I give you your second dose try to tell me exactly what your trouble is.'

Hummil spoke in broken whispers for nearly ten minutes, whilst Spurstow looked into the pupils of his eyes and passed his hand before them once or twice.

At the end of the narrative the silver cigarette-case was produced, and the last words that Hummil said as he fell back for the second time were, 'Put me quite to sleep; for if I'm caught I die,—I die!'

'Yes, yes; we all do that sooner or later,—thank Heaven who has set a term to our miseries,' said Spurstow, settling the cushions under the head. 'It occurs to me that unless I drink something I shall go out before my time. I've stopped sweating,— and I wear a seventeen-inch collar.' He brewed himself scalding hot tea, which is an excellent remedy against heat-apoplexy if you take three or four cups of it in time. Then he watched the sleeper.

'A blind face that cries and can't wipe its eyes, a blind face that chases him down corridors! H'm! Decidedly, Hummil ought to go on leave as soon as possible; and, sane or otherwise, he undoubtedly did rowel himself most cruelly. Well, Heaven send us understanding!'

At mid-day Hummil rose, with an evil taste in his mouth, but an unclouded eye and a joyful heart.

'I was pretty bad last night, wasn't I?' said he.

'I have seen healthier men. You must have had a touch of the sun. Look here: if I write you a swingeing medical certificate, will you apply for leave on the spot?'

'No.'

'Why not? You want it.'

'Yes, but I can hold on till the weather's a little cooler.'

'Why should you, if you can get relieved on the spot?'

'Burkett is the only man who could be sent; and he's a born fool.'

'Oh, never mind about the line. You aren't so important as all that. Wire for leave, if necessary.'

Hummil looked very uncomfortable.

'I can hold on till the rains,' he said evasively.

'You can't. Wire to headquarters for Burkett.'

'I won't. If you want to know why, particularly, Burkett is married, and his wife's just had a kid, and she's up at Simla, in the cool, and Burkett has a very nice billet that takes him into Simla from Saturday to Monday. That little woman isn't at all well. If Burkett was transferred she'd try to follow him. If she left the baby behind she'd fret herself to death. If she came,— and Burkett's one of those selfish little beasts who are always talking about a wife's place being with her husband,—she'd die. It's murder to bring a woman here just now. Burkett hasn't the physique of a rat. If he came here he'd go out; and I know she hasn't any money, and I'm pretty sure she'd go out too. I'm salted in a sort of way, and I'm not married. Wait till the rains, and then Burkett can get them down here. It'll do him heaps of good.'

'Do you mean to say that you intend to face—what you have faced, till the rains break?'

'Oh, it won't be so bad, now you've shown me a way out of it. I can always wire to you. Besides, now I've once got into the way of sleeping, it'll be all right. Anyhow, I shan't put in for leave. That's the long and the short of it.'

'My great Scott! I thought all that sort of thing was dead and done with.'

'Bosh! You'd do the same yourself. I feel a new man, thanks to that cigarette-case. You're going over to camp now, aren't you?'

'Yes; but I'll try to look you up every other day, if I can.'

'I'm not bad enough for that. I don't want you to bother. Give the *coolies* gin and ketchup.'

'Then you feel all right?'

'Fit to fight for my life, but not to stand out in the sun talking to you. Go along, old man, and bless you!'

Hummil turned on his heel to face the echoing desolation of his bungalow, and the first thing he saw standing in the verandah was the figure of himself. He had met a similar apparition once before, when he was suffering from overwork and the strain of the hot weather.

'This is bad,—already,' he said, rubbing his eyes. 'If the thing slides away from me all in one piece, like a ghost, I shall know it is only my eyes and stomach that are out of order. If it walks— my head is going.'

He approached the figure, which naturally kept at an unvarying distance from him, as is the use of all spectres that are born of overwork. It slid through the house and dissolved into swimming specks within the eyeball as soon as it reached the burning light of the garden. Hummil went about his business till even. When he came in to dinner he found himself sitting at the table. The vision rose and walked out hastily. Except that it cast no shadow it was in all respects real.

No living man knows what that week held for Hummil. An increase of the epidemic kept Spurstow in camp among the *coolies*, and all he could do was to telegraph to Mottram, bidding him go to the bungalow and sleep there. But Mottram was forty miles away from the nearest telegraph, and knew nothing of anything save the needs of the survey till he met, early on Sunday morning, Lowndes and Spurstow heading towards Hummil's for the weekly gathering.

'Hope the poor chap's in a better temper,' said the former, swinging himself off his horse at the door. 'I suppose he isn't up yet.'

'I'll just have a look at him,' said the doctor. 'If he's asleep there's no need to wake him.'

And an instant later, by the tone of Spurstow's voice calling upon them to enter, the men knew what had happened. There was no need to wake him.

The *punkah* was still being pulled over the bed, but Hummil had departed this life at least three hours.

The body lay on its back, hands clinched by the side, as Spurstow had seen it lying seven nights previously. In the staring eyes was written terror beyond the expression of any pen.

Mottram, who had entered behind Lowndes, bent over the

dead and touched the forehead lightly with his lips. 'Oh, you lucky, lucky devil!' he whispered.

But Lowndes had seen the eyes, and withdrew shuddering to the other side of the room.

'Poor chap! poor old chap! And the last time I met him I was angry. Spurstow, we should have watched him. Has he—?'

Deftly Spurstow continued his investigations, ending by a search round the room.

'No, he hasn't,' he snapped. 'There's no trace of anything. Call the servants.'

They came, eight or ten of them, whispering and peering over each other's shoulders.

'When did your *sahib* go to bed?' said Spurstow.

'At eleven or ten, we think,' said Hummil's personal servant.

'He was well then? But how should you know?'

'He was not ill, as far as our comprehension extended. But he had slept very little for three nights. This I know, because I saw him walking much, and specially in the heart of the night.'

As Spurstow was arranging the sheet, a big straight-necked hunting-spur tumbled on the ground. The doctor groaned. The personal servant peeped at the body.

'What do you think, Chuma?' said Spurstow, catching the look on the dark face.

'Heaven-born, in my poor opinion, this that was my master has descended into the Dark Places, and there has been caught because he was not able to escape with sufficient speed. We have the spur for evidence that he fought with fear. Thus have I seen men of my race do with thorns when a spell was laid upon them to overtake them in their sleeping hours and they dared not sleep.'

'Chuma, you're a mud-head. Go out and prepare seals to be set on the *sahib's* property.'

'God has made the Heaven-born. God has made me. Who are we, to inquire into the dispensations of God? I will bid the other servants hold aloof while you are reckoning the tale of the *sahib's* property. They are all thieves, and would steal.'

'As far as I can make out, he died from—oh, anything; stoppage of the heart's action, heat-apoplexy, or some other visitation,' said Spurstow to his companions. 'We must make an inventory of his effects, and so on.'

'He was scared to death,' insisted Lowndes. 'Look at those eyes! For pity's sake don't let him be buried with them open!'

'Whatever it was, he's clear of all the trouble now,' said Mottram softly.

Spurstow was peering into the open eyes.

' Come here,' said he. 'Can you see anything there?'

'I can't face it!' whimpered Lowndes. 'Cover up the face! Is there any fear on earth that can turn a man into that likeness? It's ghastly. Oh, Spurstow, cover it up!'

'No fear—on earth,' said Spurstow. Mottram leaned over his shoulder and looked intently.

'I see nothing except some gray blurs in the pupil. There can be nothing there, you know.'

'Even so. Well, let's think. It'll take half a day to knock up any sort of coffin; and he must have died at midnight. Lowndes, old man, go out and tell the *coolies* to break ground next to Jevins's grave. Mottram, go round the house with Chuma and see that the seals are put on things. Send a couple of men to me here, and I'll arrange.'

The strong-armed servants when they returned to their own kind told a strange story of the doctor *sahib* vainly trying to call their master back to life by magic arts, to wit,—the holding of a little green box that clicked to each of the dead man's eyes, and of a bewildered muttering on the part of the doctor *sahib*, who took the little green box away with him.

The resonant hammering of a coffin-lid is no pleasant thing to hear, but those who have experience maintain that much more terrible is the soft swish of the bed-linen, the reeving and unreeving of the bed-tapes, when he who has fallen by the roadside is apparelled for burial, sinking gradually as the tapes are tied over, till the swaddled shape touches the floor and there is no protest against the indignity of hasty disposal.

At the last moment Lowndes was seized with scruples of conscience. 'Ought you to read the service,—from beginning to end?' said he to Spurstow.

'I intend to. You're my senior as a civilian. You can take it if you like.'

'I didn't mean that for a moment. I only thought if we could get a chaplain from somewhere,—I'm willing to ride anywhere,—and give poor Hummil a better chance. That's all.'

'Bosh!' said Spurstow, as he framed his lips to the tremendous words that stand at the head of the burial service.

★★★★★★

After breakfast they smoked a pipe in silence to the memory of the dead. Then Spurstow said absently—

''Tisn't in medical science.'

'What?'

'Things in a dead man's eye.'

'For goodness' sake leave that horror alone!' said Lowndes. 'I've seen a native die of pure fright when a tiger chivied him. I know what killed Hummil.'

'The deuce you do! I'm going to try to see.' And the doctor retreated into the bathroom with a Kodak camera. After a few minutes there was the sound of something being hammered to pieces, and he emerged, very white indeed.

'Have you got a picture?' said Mottram. 'What does the thing look like?'

'It was impossible, of course. You needn't look, Mottram. I've torn up the films. There was nothing there. It was impossible.'

'That,' said Lowndes, very distinctly, watching the shaking hand striving to relight the pipe, 'is a damned lie.'

Mottram laughed uneasily. 'Spurstow's right.' he said. 'We're all in such a state now that we'd believe anything. For pity's sake let's try to be rational.'

There was no further speech for a long time. The hot wind whistled without, and the dry trees sobbed. Presently the daily train, winking brass, burnished steel, and spouting steam, pulled up panting in the intense glare. 'We'd better go on on that,' said

Spurstow. 'Go back to work. I've written my certificate. We can't do any more good here, and work'll keep our wits together. Come on.'

No one moved. It is not pleasant to face railway journeys at mid-day in June. Spurstow gathered up his hat and whip, and, turning in the doorway, said—

There may be Heaven,—there must be Hell.
Meantime, there is our life here. We-ell?

Neither Mottram nor Lowndes had any answer to the question.

By Word of Mouth

Not though you die tonight,
O Sweet, and wail,
A spectre at my door,
Shall mortal Fear make
Love immortal fail—
I shall but love you more,
Who, from Death's house returning, give me still
One moment's comfort in my matchless ill.

Shadow Houses.

This tale may be explained by those who know how souls are made, and where the bounds of the Possible are put down. I have lived long enough in this India to know that it is best to know nothing, and can only write the story as it happened.

Dumoise was our civil surgeon at Meridki, and we called him 'Dormouse,' because he was a round little, sleepy little man. He was a good doctor and never quarrelled with anyone, not even with our deputy commissioner who had the manners of a bargee and the tact of a horse. He married a girl as round and as sleepy-looking as himself. She was a Miss Hillardyce, daughter of 'Squash' Hillardyce of the Berars, who married his chief's daughter by mistake. But this is another story.

A honeymoon in India is seldom more than a week long; but there is nothing to hinder a couple from extending it over two or three years. India is a delightful country for married folk who are wrapped up in one another. They can live absolutely alone and without interruption—just as the Dormice did. Those two little people retired from the world after their marriage, and were very happy. They were forced, of course, to give occasional dinners, but they made no friends thereby, and the station went its own way and forgot them; only saying, occasionally, that Dormouse was the best of good fellows though dull. A civil surgeon who never quarrels is a rarity, appreciated as such.

Few people can afford to play Robinson Crusoe anywhere— least of all in India, where we are few in the land and very much dependent on each other's kind offices. Dumoise was wrong in shutting himself from the world for a year, and he discovered his mistake when an epidemic of typhoid broke out in the station in the heart of the cold weather, and his wife went down. He was a shy little man, and five days were wasted before he realised that Mrs. Dumoise was burning with something worse than simple fever, and three days more passed before he ventured to call on Mrs. Shute, the engineer's wife, and timidly speak about his trouble.

Nearly every household in India knows that doctors are very helpless in typhoid. The battle must be fought out between Death and the Nurses minute by minute and degree by degree. Mrs. Shute almost boxed Dumoise's ears for what she called his 'criminal delay,' and went off at once to look after the poor girl. We had seven cases of typhoid in the Station that winter and, as the average of death is about one in every five cases, we felt certain that we should have to lose somebody. But all did their best. The women sat up nursing the women, and the men turned to and tended the bachelors who were down, and we wrestled with those typhoid cases for fifty-six days, and brought them through the Valley of the Shadow in triumph. But, just when we thought all was over, and were going to give a dance to celebrate the victory, little Mrs. Dumoise got a relapse and died in a week, and the station went to the funeral. Dumoise broke down utterly at the brink of the grave, and had to be taken away.

After the death Dumoise crept into his own house and refused to be comforted. He did his duties perfectly, but we all felt that he should go on leave, and the other men of his own service told him so. Dumoise was very thankful for the suggestion—he was thankful for anything in those days—and went to Chini on a walking-tour. Chini is some twenty marches from Simla, in the heart of the Hills, and the scenery is good if you are in trouble. You pass through big, still deodar forests, and under big, still cliffs, and over big, still grass-downs swelling like a woman's breasts; and the wind across the grass, and the rain among the deodars say—'Hush—hush—hush.' So little Dumoise was packed off to Chini, to wear down his grief with a full-plate camera and a rifle. He took also a useless bearer, because the man had been his wife's favourite servant. He was idle and a thief, but Dumoise trusted everything to him.

On his way back from Chini, Dumoise turned aside to Bagi, through the Forest Reserve which is on the spur of Mount Huttoo. Some men who have travelled more than a little say that the march from Kotegarh to Bagi is one of the finest in creation. It runs through dark wet forest, and ends suddenly in bleak, nipped hillside and black rocks. Bagi *dâk*-bungalow is open to all the winds and is bitterly cold. Few people go to Bagi. Perhaps that was the reason why Dumoise went there. He halted at seven in the evening, and his bearer went down the hillside to the village to engage *coolies* for the next day's march. The sun had set and the night-winds were beginning to croon among the rocks. Dumoise leaned on the railing of the verandah, waiting for his bearer to return. The man came back almost immediately after he had disappeared, and at such a rate that Dumoise fancied he must have crossed a bear. He was running as hard as he could up the face of the hill

But there was no bear to account for his terror. He raced to the verandah and fell down, the blood spurting from his nose and his face iron-gray. Then he gurgled—'I have seen the *Memsahib*! I have seen the *Memsahib*!'

'Where?' said Dumoise.

'Down there, walking on the road to the village. She was in a blue dress, and she lifted the veil of her bonnet and said—"Ram Dass, give my *salaams* to the *Sahib*, and tell him that I shall meet him next month at Nuddea." Then I ran away, because I was afraid.'

What Dumoise said or did I do not know. Ram Dass declares that he said nothing, but walked up and down the verandah all the cold night, waiting for the *Memsahib* to come up the hill, and stretching out his arms into the dark like a madman. But no *Memsahib* came, and, next day, he went on to Simla cross-questioning the bearer every hour.

Ram Dass could only say that he had met Mrs. Dumoise, and that she had lifted up her veil and given him the message which he had faithfully repeated to Dumoise. To this statement Ram Dass adhered. He did not know where Nuddea was, had no friends at Nuddea, and would most certainly never go to Nuddea, even though his pay were doubled.

Nuddea is in Bengal, and has nothing whatever to do with a doctor serving in the Punjab. It must be more than twelve hundred miles south of Meridki.

Dumoise went through Simla without halting, and returned to Meridki, there to take over charge from the man who had been officiating for him during his tour. There were some dispensary accounts to be explained, and some recent orders of the surgeon-general to be noted, and, altogether, the taking-over was a full day's work. In the evening Dumoise told his *locum tenens*, who was an old friend of his bachelor days, what had happened at Bagi; and the man said that Ram Dass might as well have chosen Tuticorin while he was about it.

At that moment a telegraph-*peon* came in with a telegram from Simla, ordering Dumoise not to take over charge at Meridki, but to go at once to Nuddea on special duty. There was a nasty outbreak of cholera at Nuddea, and the Bengal Government being short-handed, as usual, had borrowed a surgeon from the Punjab.

Dumoise threw the telegram across the table and said—'Well?'

The other doctor said nothing. It was all that he could say.

Then he remembered that Dumoise had passed through

Simla on his way from Bagi; and thus might, possibly, have heard first news of the impending transfer.

He tried to put the question and the implied suspicion into words, but Dumoise stopped him with—'If I had desired *that*, I should never have come back from Chini. I was shooting there. I wish to live, for I have things to do . . . but I shall not be sorry.'

The other man bowed his head, and helped, in the twilight, to pack up Dumoise's just opened trunks. Ram Dass entered with the lamps.

'Where is the *Sahib* going?' he asked.

'To Nuddea,' said Dumoise softly.

Ram Dass clawed Dumoise's knees and boots and begged him not to go. Ram Dass wept and howled till he was turned out of the room. Then he wrapped up all his belongings and came back to ask for a character. He was not going to Nuddea to see his *Sahib* die and, perhaps, to die himself.

So Dumoise gave the man his wages and went down to Nuddea alone, the other doctor bidding him goodbye as one under sentence of death.

Eleven days later he had joined his *Memsahib*; and the Bengal Government had to borrow a fresh doctor to cope with that epidemic at Nuddea. The first importation lay dead in Chooadanga *dâk*- bungalow.

Haunted Subalterns

So long as the 'Inextinguishables' confined themselves to running picnics, gymkhanas, flirtations and innocences of that kind, no one said anything. But when they ran ghosts, people put up their eyebrows. 'Man can't feel comfy with a regiment that entertains ghosts on its establishment. It is against general orders. The 'Inextinguishables' said that the ghosts were private and not regimental property. They referred you to Tesser for particulars; and Tesser told you to go to—the hottest cantonment of all. He said that it was bad enough to have men making hay of his bedding and breaking his banjo-strings when he was out, without being chaffed afterwards; and he would thank you to keep your remarks on ghosts to yourself. This was before the 'Inextinguishables' had sworn by their several lady-loves that they were innocent of any intrusion into Tesser's quarters. Then Horrocks mentioned casually at mess, that a couple of white figures had been bounding about his room the night before, and he didn't approve of it. The 'Inextinguishables' denied, energetically, that they had had any hand in the manifestations, and advised Horrocks to consult Tesser.

I don't suppose that a subaltern believes in anything except his chances of a company; but Horrocks and Tesser were exceptions. They came to believe in their ghosts. They had reason.

Horrocks used to find himself, at about three o'clock in the morning, staring wide-awake, watching two white Things hopping about his room and jumping up to the ceiling. Horrocks was of a placid turn of mind. After a week or so spent in watching his servants, and lying in wait for strangers, and trying to keep awake all night, he came to the conclusion that he was haunted, and that, consequently, he need not bother. He wasn't going to encourage these ghosts by being frightened of them. Therefore, when he woke—as usual—with a start and saw these Things jumping like kangaroos, he only murmured:—' Go on! Don't mind me!' and went to sleep again.

Tesser said:—'It's all very well for you to make fun of your show. You can see your ghosts. Now I can't see mine, and I don't half like it.'

Tesser used to come into his room of nights, and find the whole of his bedding neatly stripped, as if it had been done with one sweep of the hand, from the top right-hand corner of the charpoy to the bottom left-hand corner. Also his lamp used to lie weltering on the floor, and generally his pet screw-head, inlaid, nickel-plated banjo was lying on the charpoy, with all its strings broken. Tesser took away the strings, on the occasion of the third manifestation, and the next night a man complimented him on his playing the best music ever got out of a banjo, for half an hour.

'Which half hour?' said Tesser.

'Between nine and ten,' said the man. Tesser had gone out to dinner at 7.30, and had returned at midnight.

He talked to his bearer and threatened him with unspeakable things. The bearer was gray with fear:—'I'm a poor man,' said he. 'If the *Sahib* is haunted by a devil, what can I do?'

'Who says I'm haunted by a devil?' howled Tesser, for he was angry.

'I have seen *it*,' said the bearer, 'at night, walking round and round your bed; and that is why everything is *ulta-pulta* in your room. I am a poor man, but I never go into your room alone. The *bhisti* comes with me.'

Tesser was thoroughly savage at this, and he spoke to Horrocks, and the two laid traps to catch that devil, and threatened their servants with dog-whips if any more '*shaitan-ke*-hanky-panky' took place. But the servants were soaked with fear, and it was no use adding to their tortures. When Tesser went out at night, four of his men, as a rule, slept in the verandah of his quarters, until the banjo without the strings struck up, and then they fled.

One day, Tesser had to put in a month at a fort with a detachment of 'Inextinguishables.' The fort might have been Govindghar, Jumrood, or Phillour; but it wasn't. He left cantonments rejoicing, for his devil was preying on his mind; and with him went another subaltern, a junior. But the devil came too. After Tesser had been in the fort about ten days he went out to dinner. When he came back he found his subaltern doing sentry on a banquette across the fort ditch, as far removed as might be from the officers' quarters.

'What's wrong?' said Tesser.

The subaltern said, 'Listen!' and the two, standing under the stars, heard from the officers' quarters, high up in the wall of the fort, the '*strumty tumty tumty*' of the banjo; which seemed to have an *oratorio* on hand.

'That performance,' said the subaltern, 'has been going on for three mortal hours. I never wished to desert before, but I do now. I say, Tesser, old man, you are the best of good fellows, I'm sure, but . . . I say . . . look here, now, you are quite unfit to live with. 'Tisn't in my commission, you know, that I'm to serve under a . . . a . . . man with devils.'

'Isn't it?' said Tesser. 'If you make an ass of yourself I'll put you under arrest . . . and in my room!'

'You can put me where you please, but I'm not going to assist at these infernal concerts. 'Tisn't right. 'Tisn't natural. Look here, I don't want to hurt your feelings, but—try to think now— haven't you done something—committed some—murder that has slipped your memory—or forged something . . .?'

'Well! For an all-round, double-shotted, half-baked fool you are the . . . '

'I dare say I am,' said the subaltern. 'But you don't expect me to keep my wits with that row going on, do you?'

The banjo was rattling away as if it had twenty strings. Tesser sent up a stone, and a shower of broken window-pane fell into the fort ditch; but the banjo kept on. Tesser hauled the other subaltern up to the quarters, and found his room in frightful confusion—lamp upset, bedding all over the floor, chairs over-turned, and table tilted sideways. He took stock of the wreck and said despairing:—'Oh, this is lovely!'

The subaltern was peeping in at the door.

'I'm glad you think so,' he said. "Tisn't lovely enough for me. I *locked up* your room directly after you had gone out. See here, I think you had better apply for Horrocks to come out in my place. He's troubled with your complaint, and this business will make me a jabbering idiot if it goes on.'

Tesser went to bed amid the wreckage, very angry, and next morning he rode into cantonments and asked Horrocks to ar-range to relieve 'that fool with me now.'

'You've got 'em again, have you' said Horrocks. 'So've I. *Three* white figures this time. We'll worry through the entertainment together.'

So Horrocks and Tesser settled down in the fort together, and the 'Inextinguishables' said pleasant things about 'seven other devils.' Tesser didn't see where the joke came in. His room was thrown upside-down three nights out of seven. Horrocks was not troubled in any way, so his ghosts must have been purely local ones. Tesser, on the other hand, was personally haunted; for his devil had moved with him from cantonments to the fort. Those two boys spent three parts of their time trying to find out *who* was responsible for the riot in Tesser's rooms. At the end of a fortnight they tried to find out *what* was responsible; and seven days later they gave it up as a bad job. Whatever It was, It refused to be caught; even when Tesser went out of the fort ostenta-tiously, and Horrocks lay under Tesser's *charpoy* with a revolver. The servants were afraid—more afraid than ever—and all the evidence showed that they had been playing no tricks. As Tesser said to Horrocks:—'A haunted subaltern is a joke, but s'pose this keeps on. Just think what a haunted colonel would be! And look here—s'pose I marry! D'you s'pose a girl would live a week

456

with me *and* this devil?'

'I don't know,' said Horrocks. 'I haven't married often; but I knew a woman once who lived with her husband when he had D. T. He's dead now, and I dare say *she* would marry you if you asked her. She isn't exactly a girl though, but she has a large experience of the *other* devils—the blue variety. She's a government pensioner now, and you might write, y' know. Personally, if I hadn't suffered from ghosts of my own, I should rather avoid you.'

'That's just the point,' said Tesser. 'This devil thing will end in getting me *budnamed*, and you know I've lived on lemon-squashes and gone to bed at ten for weeks past.'

''Tisn't that sort of devil,' said Horrocks. 'It's either a first-class fraud for which someone ought to be killed, or else you've offended one of these Indian devils. It stands to reason that such a beastly country should be full of fiends of all sorts.'

'But why should the creature fix on *me*,' said Tesser, 'and why won't he show himself and have it out like a—like a devil?'

They were talking outside the mess after dark, and, even as they spoke, they heard the banjo begin to play in Tesser's room, about twenty yards off.

Horrocks ran to his own quarters for a shot-gun and a revolver, and Tesser and he crept up quietly, the banjo still playing, to Tesser's door.

'Now we've got It!' said Horrocks, as he threw the door open and let fly with the twelve-bore; Tesser squibbing off all six barrels into the dark, as hard as he could pull trigger.

The furniture was ruined, and the whole fort was awake; but that was all. No one had been killed, and the banjo was lying on the dishevelled bedclothes as usual.

Then Tesser sat down in the verandah, and used language that would have qualified him for the companionship of unlimited devils. Horrocks said things too; but Tesser said the worst.

When the month in the fort came to an end, both Horrocks and Tesser were glad. They held a final council of war, but came to no conclusion.

"Seems to me, your best plan would be to make your devil stretch himself. Go down to Bombay with the time-expired men,' said Horrocks. 'If he really is a devil, he'll come in the train with you.'

"'Tisn't good enough,' said Tesser. 'Bombay's no fit place to live in at this time of the year. But I'll put in for depot duty at the hills.' And he did.

Now here the tale rests. The devil stayed below, and Tesser went up and was free. If I had invented this story, I should have put in a satisfactory ending—explained the manifestations as somebody's practical joke. My business being to keep to facts, I can only say what I have said. The devil may have been a hoax. If so, it was one of the best ever arranged. If it was not a hoax—but you must settle that for yourselves.

In the House of Suddhoo

A stone's throw out on either hand
From that well-ordered road we tread,
And all the world is wild and strange:
Churel and ghoul and Djinn and sprite
Shall bear us company tonight,
For we have reached the Oldest Land
Wherein the Powers of Darkness range.
                    From the Dusk to the Dawn.

The house of Suddhoo, near the Taksali Gate, is two-storied, with four carved windows of old brown wood, and a flat roof. You may recognise it by five red hand prints arranged like the Five of Diamonds on the whitewash between the upper windows. Bhagwan Dass the grocer and a man who says he gets his living by seal-cutting live in the lower storey with a troop of wives, servants, friends, and retainers. The two upper rooms used to be occupied by Janoo and Azizun, and a little black-and-tan terrier that was stolen from an Englishman's house and given to Janoo by a soldier. Today, only Janoo lives in the upper rooms. Suddhoo sleeps on the roof generally, except when he sleeps in the street. He used to go to Peshawar in the cold weather to visit his son who sells curiosities near the Edwardes' Gate, and then he slept under a real mud roof.

Suddhoo is a great friend of mine, because his cousin had a son who secured, thanks to my recommendation, the post of head-messenger to a big firm in the station. Suddhoo says that God will make me a lieutenant-governor one of these days. I daresay his prophecy will come true. He is very, very old, with white hair and no teeth worth showing, and he has outlived his wits—outlived nearly everything except his fondness for his son at Peshawar. Janoo and Azizun are Kashmiris, Ladies of the City, and theirs was an ancient and more or less honourable profession; but Azizun has since married a medical student from the North West and has settled down to a most respectable life somewhere near Bareilly. Bhagwan Dass is an extortionate and an adulterator. He is very rich. The man who is supposed to get his living by seal-cutting pretends to be very poor. This lets you know as much as is necessary of the four principal tenants in the house of Suddhoo. Then there is me of course; but I am only the chorus that comes in at the end to explain things. So I do not count.

Suddhoo was not clever. The man who pretended to cut seals was the cleverest of them all—Bhagwan Dass only knew how to lie—except Janoo. She was also beautiful, but that was her own affair,

Suddhoo's son at Peshawar was attacked by pleurisy, and old Suddhoo was troubled. The seal-cutter man heard of Suddhoo's anxiety and made capital out of it. He was abreast of the times. He got a friend in Peshawar to telegraph daily accounts of the son's health. And here the story begins.

Suddhoo's cousin's son told me, one evening, that Suddhoo wanted to see me; that he was too old and feeble to come personally, and that I should be conferring an everlasting honour on the House of Suddhoo if I went to him. I went; but I think, seeing how well off Suddhoo was then, that he might have sent something better than an *ekka*, which jolted fearfully, to haul out a future lieutenant-governor to the city on a muggy April evening. The *ekka* did not run quickly. It was full dark when we pulled up opposite the door of Ranjit Singh's tomb near the main gate of the fort. Here was Suddhoo, and he said that by reason of my condescension, it was absolutely certain that I should become a lieutenant-governor while my hair was yet black. Then we talked about the weather and the state of my health, and the wheat crops, for fifteen minutes, in the Huzuri

Bagh, under the stars.

Suddhoo came to the point at last. He said that Janoo had told him that there was an order of the *Sirkar* against magic, because it was feared that magic might one day kill the Empress of India, I didn't know anything about the state of the law; but I fancied that something interesting was going to happen, I said that so far from magic being discouraged by the government it was highly commended. The greatest officials of the State practised it themselves. (If the financial statement isn't magic, I don't know what is.) Then, to encourage him further, I said that, if there was any *jadoo* afoot, I had not the least objection to giving it my countenance and sanction, and to seeing that it was clean *jadoo*—white magic, as distinguished from the unclean *jadoo* which kills folk.

It took a long time before Suddhoo admitted that this was just what he had asked me to come for. Then he told me, in jerks and quavers, that the man who said he cut seals was a sorcerer of the cleanest kind; that every day he gave Suddhoo news of the sick son in Peshawar more quickly than the lightning could fly, and that this news was always corroborated by the letters. Further, that he had told Suddhoo how a great danger was threatening his son, which could be removed by clean *jadoo*; and, of course, heavy payment. I began to see exactly how the land lay, and told Suddhoo that I also understood a little *jadoo* in the Western line, and would go to his house to see that everything was done decently and in order. We set off together; and on the way Suddhoo told me that he had paid the seal-cutter between one hundred and two hundred *rupees* already; and the *jadoo* of that night would cost two hundred more. Which was cheap, he said, considering the greatness of his son's danger; but I do not think he meant it.

The lights were all cloaked in the front of the house when we arrived. I could hear awful noises from behind the seal-cutter's shop-front, as if someone were groaning his soul out. Suddhoo shook all over, and while we groped our way upstairs told me that the *jadoo* had begun. Janoo and Azizun met us at the stairhead, and told us that the *jadoo*-work was coming off in their rooms, because there was more space there. Janoo is a lady of a free-thinking turn of mind. She whispered that the *jadoo* was an invention to get money out of Suddhoo, and that the seal-cutter would go to a hot place when he died. Suddhoo was nearly crying with fear and old age. He kept walking up and down the room in the half-light, repeating his son's name over and over again, and asking Azizun if the seal-cutter ought not to make a reduction in the case of his own landlord. Janoo pulled me over to the shadow in the recess of the carved bow-windows. The boards were up, and the rooms were only lit by one tiny oil-lamp. There was no chance of my being seen if I stayed still.

Presently, the groans below ceased, and we heard steps on the staircase. That was the seal-cutter. He stopped outside the door as the terrier barked and Azizun fumbled at the chain, and he told Suddhoo to blow out the lamp. This left the place in jet darkness, except for the red glow from the two *huqas* that belonged to Janoo and Azizun. The seal-cutter came in, and I heard Suddhoo throw himself down on the floor and groan. Azizun caught her breath, and Janoo backed on to one of the beds with a shudder. There was a clink of something metallic, and then shot up a pale blue-green flame near the ground. The light was just enough to show Azizun, pressed against one corner of the room with the terrier between her knees; Janoo, with her hands clasped, leaning forward as she sat on the bed; Suddhoo, face down, quivering, and the seal-cutter.

I hope I may never see another man like that seal-cutter. He was stripped to the waist, with a wreath of white jasmine as thick as my wrist round his forehead, a salmon coloured loin-cloth round his middle, and a steel bangle on each ankle. This was not awe-inspiring. It was the face of the man that turned me cold. It was blue-gray in the first place. In the second, the eyes were rolled back till you could only see the whites of them; and, in the third, the face was the face of a demon—a ghoul—anything you please except of the sleek, oily old ruffian who sat in the daytime over his turning-lathe downstairs. He was lying on his stomach with his arms turned and crossed behind him, as if he had been thrown down pinioned. His head and neck were the only parts of him off the floor.

They were nearly at right angles to the body, like the head of a cobra at spring. It was ghastly. In the centre of the room, on the bare earth floor, stood a big, deep, brass basin, with a pale blue-green light floating in the centre like a night-light. Round that basin the man on the floor wriggled himself three times. How he did it I do not know. I could see the muscles ripple along his spine and fall smooth again; but I could not see any other motion. The head seemed the only thing alive about him, except that slow curl and uncurl of the labouring back-muscles. Janoo from the bed was breathing seventy to the minute; Azizun held her hands before her eyes; and old Suddhoo, fingering at the dirt that had got into his white beard, was crying to himself. The horror of it was that the creeping, crawly thing made no sound—only crawled! And, remember, this lasted for ten minutes, while the terrier whined, and Azizun shuddered, and Janoo gasped, and Suddhoo cried.

I felt the hair lift at the back of my head, and my heart thump like a thermantidote paddle. Luckily, the seal-cutter betrayed himself by his most impressive trick and made me calm again. After he had finished that unspeakable triple crawl, he stretched his head away from the floor as high as he could, and sent out a jet of fire from his nostrils. Now I knew how fire-spouting is done I can do it myself so I felt at ease. The business was a fraud. If he had only kept to that crawl without trying to raise the effect, goodness knows what I might not have thought. Both the girls shrieked at the jet of fire and the head dropped, chin-down on the floor, with a thud; the whole body lying then like a corpse with its arms trussed.

There was a pause of five full minutes after this, and the blue-green flame died down. Janoo stooped to settle one of her anklets, while Azizun turned her face to the wall and took the terrier in her arms. Suddhoo put out an arm mechanically to Janoo's *huqa*, and she slid it across the floor with her foot. Directly above the body and on the wall were a couple of flaming portraits, in stamped-paper frames, of the Queen and the Prince of Wales. They looked down on the performance, and to my thinking, seemed to heighten the grotesqueness of it all.

Just when the silence was getting unendurable, the body turned over and rolled away from the basin to the side of the room, where it lay stomach-up. There was a faint 'plop' from the basin—exactly like the noise a fish makes when it takes a fly—and the green light in the centre revived.

I looked at the basin, and saw, bobbing in the water, the dried, shrivelled, black head of a native baby open eyes, open mouth, and shaved scalp. It was worse, being so very sudden, than the crawling exhibition. We had no time to say anything before it began to speak.

Read Poe's account of the voice that came from the mesmerised dying man, and you will realise less than one-half of the horror of that head's voice.

There was an interval of a second or two between each word, and a sort of 'ring, ring, ring,' in the note of the voice, like the timbre of a bell. It pealed slowly, as if talking to itself, for several minutes before I got rid of my cold sweat. Then the blessed solution struck me, I looked at the body lying near the doorway, and saw, just where the hollow of the throat joins on the shoulders, a muscle that had nothing to do with any man's regular breathing twitching away steadily. The whole thing was a careful reproduction of the Egyptian *teraphin* that one reads about sometimes; and the voice was as clever and as appalling a piece of ventriloquism as one could wish to hear.

All this time the head was 'lip-lip-lapping' against the side of the basin, and speaking. It told Suddhoo, on his face again whining, of his son's illness and of the state of the illness up to the evening of that very night. I always shall respect the seal' cutter for keeping so faithfully to the time of the Peshawar telegrams. It went on to say that skilled doctors were night and day watching over the man's life; and that he would eventually recover if the fee to the potent sorcerer, whose servant was the head in the basin, were doubled.

Here the mistake from the artistic point of view came in. To ask for twice your stipulated fee in a voice that Lazarus might have used when he rose from the dead, is absurd. Janoo, who is really a woman of masculine intellect, saw this as quickly as I did. I heard her say '*Asli nahinl Fareib!*' scornfully under her breath; and just as she said so the light in the basin died out, the head stopped talking, and we heard the room door creak on its hinges. Then Janoo struck a match, lit the lamp, and we saw that head, basin, and seal-cutter were gone. Suddhoo was wringing his hands, and explaining to anyone who cared to listen, that, if his chances of eternal salvation depended on it, he could not raise another two hundred *rupees*. Azizun was nearly in hysterics in the corner; while Janoo sat down composedly on one of the beds to discuss the probabilities of the whole thing being a *bunao*, or 'make-up.'

I explained as much as I knew of the seal-cutter's way of *jadoo*; but her argument was much more simple—'The magic that is always demanding gifts is no true magic,' said she. 'My mother told me that the only potent love-spells are those which are told you for love. This seal-cutter man is a liar and a devil. I dare not tell, do anything, or get anything done, because I am in debt to Bhagwan Dass the *bunnia* for two gold rings and a heavy anklet. I must get my food from his shop. The seal-cutter is the friend of Bhagwan Dass, and he would poison my food. A fool's *jadoo* has been going on for ten days, and has cost Suddhoo many *rupees* each night. The seal-cutter used black hens and lemons and *mantras* before. He never showed us anything like this till tonight. Azizun is a fool, and will be a *purdahnashin* soon. Suddhoo has lost his strength and his wits. See now! I had hoped to get from Suddhoo many *rupees* while he lived, and many more after his death; and behold, he is spending everything on that offspring of a devil and a she-ass, the seal-cutter!'

Here I said, 'But what induced Suddhoo to drag me into the business? Of course I can speak to the seal-cutter, and he shall refund. The whole thing is child's talk—shame—and senseless.'

'Suddhoo *is* an old child,' said Janoo. 'He has lived on the roofs these seventy years and is as senseless as a milch-goat. He brought you here to assure himself that he was not breaking any law of the *Sirkar*, whose salt he ate many years ago. He worships the dust off the feet of the seal-cutter, and that cow-devourer has forbidden him to go and see his son. What does Suddhoo know of your laws or the lightning-post? I have to watch his money going day by day to that lying beast below.'

Janoo stamped her foot on the floor and nearly cried with vexation; while Suddhoo was whimpering under a blanket in the corner, and Azizun was trying to guide the pipe-stem to his foolish old mouth.

★★★★★★

Now, the case stands thus. Unthinkingly, I have laid myself open to the charge of aiding and abetting the seal-cutter in obtaining money under false pretences, which is forbidden by Section 420 of the Indian Penal Code. I am helpless in the matter for these reasons. I cannot inform the police. What witnesses would support my statements? Janoo refuses flatly, and Azizun is a veiled woman somewhere near Bareilly lost in this big India of ours. I dare not again take the law into my own hands, and speak to the seal-cutter; for certain am I that, not only would Suddhoo disbelieve me, but this step would end in the poisoning of Janoo, who is bound hand and foot by her debt to the *bunnia*. Suddhoo is an old dotard; and whenever we meet mumbles my idiotic joke that the *Sirkar* rather patronises the Black Art than otherwise. His son is well now; but Suddhoo is completely under the influence of the seal-cutter, by whose advice he regulates the affairs of his life. Janoo watches daily the money that she hoped to wheedle out of Suddhoo taken by the seal-cutter, and becomes daily more furious and sullen.

She will never tell, because she dare not; but, unless something happens to prevent her, I am afraid that the seal-cutter will die of cholera—the white arsenic kind—about the middle of May. And thus I shall be privy to a murder in the House of Suddhoo.

My Own True Ghost Story

As I came through the Desert thus it was—
As I came through the Desert.
                    The City of Dreadful Night,

Somewhere in the other world, where there are books and
pictures and plays and shop-windows to look at, and thousands
of men who spend their lives in building up all four, lives a gentleman who writes real stories about the real insides of people;
and his name is Mr, Walter Besant. But he will insist upon treating his ghosts—he has published half a workshopful of them—
with levity. He makes his ghost-seers talk familiarly, and, in some
cases, flirt outrageously, with the phantoms. You may treat anything, from a viceroy to a vernacular paper, with levity; but you
must behave reverently towards a ghost, and particularly an Indian one.

There are, in this land, ghosts who take the form of fat, cold,
pobby corpses, and hide in trees near the roadside till a traveller
passes. Then they drop upon his neck and remain. There are also
terrible ghosts of women who have died in child-bed. These
wander along the pathways at dusk, or hide in the crops near a
village, and call seductively. But to answer their call is death in
this world and the next. Their feet are turned backwards that all
sober men may recognize them. There are ghosts of little children who have been thrown into wells. These haunt well-curbs

and the fringes of jungles, and wail under the stars, or catch women by the wrist and beg to be taken up and carried. These and the corpse-ghosts, however, are only vernacular articles and do not attack *sahibs*. No native ghost has yet been authentically reported to have frightened an Englishman; but many English ghosts have scared the life out of both white and black.

Nearly every other station owns a ghost. There are said to be two at Simla, not counting the woman who blows the bellows at Syree *dâk*-bungalow on the Old Road; Mussoorie has a house haunted of a very lively thing; a White Lady is supposed to do night-watchman round a house in Lahore; Dalhousie says that one of her houses "repeats" on autumn evenings all the incidents of a horrible horse-and-precipice accident; Murree has a merry ghost, and, now that she has been swept by cholera, will have room for a sorrowful one; there are officers quarters, in Mian Mir whose doors open without reason, and whose furniture is guaranteed to creak, not with the heat of June but with the weight of invisibles who come to lounge in the chairs; Peshawar possesses houses that none will willingly rent; and there is something—not fever—wrong with a big bungalow in Allahabad. The older provinces simply bristle with haunted houses, and march phantom armies along their main thorough-fares.

Some of the *dâk*-bungalows on the Grand Trunk Road have handy little cemeteries in their compound—witnesses to the "changes and chances of this mortal life" in the days when men drove from Calcutta to the Northwest. These bungalows are objectionable places to put up in. They are generally very old, always dirty, while the khansamah is as ancient as the bungalow. He either chatters senilely, or falls into the long trances of age. In both moods he is useless. If you get angry with him, he refers to some *sahib* dead and buried these thirty years, and says that when he was in that *sahib's* service not a *khansamah* in the province could touch him. Then he jabbers and mows and trembles and fidgets among the dishes and you repent of your irritation.

In these *dâk*-bungalows, ghosts are most likely to be found, and when found, they should be made a note of. Not long ago it was my business to live in *dâk*-bungalows. I never inhabited the same house for three nights running, and grew to be learned in the breed. I lived in government-built ones with red brick walls and rail ceilings, an inventory of the furniture posted in every room, and an excited snake at the threshold to give welcome. I lived in "converted" ones—old houses officiating as *dâk*-bunga-lows—where nothing was in its proper place and there wasn't even a fowl for dinner.

I lived in second-hand palaces where the wind blew through open-work marble tracery just as uncomfortably as through a broken pane. I lived in *dâk*-bungalows where the last entry in the visitors' book was fifteen months old, and where they slashed off the curry-kid's head with a sword. It was my good luck to meet all sorts of men, from sober travelling missionaries and deserters flying from British regiments, to drunken loafers who threw whisky bottles at all who passed; and my still greater good fortune just to escape a maternity case. Seeing that a fair proportion of the tragedy of our lives out here acted itself in *dâk*-bungalows, I wondered that I had met no ghosts. A ghost that would volntarily hang about a *dâk*-bungalow would be mad of course; but so many men have died mad in *dâk*-bungalows that there must be a fair percentage of lunatic ghosts.

In due time I found my ghost, or ghosts rather, for there were two of them. Up till that hour I had sympathized with Mr. Be-sant's method of handling them, as shown in *The Strange Case of Mr. Lucraft and other Stories*. I am now in the opposition.

We will call the bungalow Katmal *dâk*-bungalow. But *that* was the smallest part of the horror. A man with a sensitive hide has no right to sleep in *dâk*-bungalows. He should marry. Kat-mal *dâk*-bungalow was old and rotten and unrepaired. The floor was of worn brick, the walls were filthy, and the windows were nearly black with grime. It stood on a by-path largely used by native sub-deputy assistants of all kinds, from finance to forests; but real *sahibs* were rare, The *khansamah*, who was nearly bent double with old age, said so.

When I arrived, there was a fitful, undecided rain on the face

469

of the land, accompanied by a restless wind, and every gust made a noise like the rattling of dry bones in the stiff toddy-palms outside. The *khansamah* completely lost his head on my arrival. He had served a *sahib* once. Did I know that *sahib?* He gave me the name of a well-known man who has been buried for more than a quarter of a century, and showed me an ancient *daguerreotype* of that man in his prehistoric youth. I had seen a steel engraving of him at the head of a double volume of *Memoirs* a month before, and I felt ancient beyond telling.

The day shut in and the *khansamah* went to get me food. He did not go through the pretence of calling it *"khana"*—man's victuals. He said *"ratub"* and that means, among other things, "grub"—dog's rations. There was no insult in his choice of the term. He had forgotten the other word, I suppose.

While he was cutting up the dead bodies of animals, I settled myself down, after exploring the *dâk*-bungalow. There were three rooms, beside my own, which was a corner kennel, each giving into the other through dingy white doors fastened with long iron bars. The bungalow was a very solid one, but the partition-walls of the rooms were almost jerry-built in their flimsiness. Every step or bang of a trunk echoed from my room down the other three, and every footfall came back tremulously from the far walls. For this reason I shut the door. There were no lamps—only candles in long glass shades. An oil wick was set in the bath-room.

For bleak, unadulterated misery that *dâk*-bungalow was the worst of the many that I had ever set foot in. There was no fireplace, and the windows would not open; so a brazier of charcoal would have been useless. The rain and the wind splashed and gurgled and moaned round the house, and the toddy-palms rattled and roared. Half a dozen jackals went through the compound singing, and a hyena stood afar off and mocked them. A hyena would convince a *sadducee* of the resurrection of the dead—the worst sort of dead. Then came the *ratub*—a curious meal, half native and half English in composition with the old *khansamah* babbling behind my chair about dead and gone English people, and the wind-blown candles playing shadow-bo-peep with the bed and the mosquito-curtains.

It was just the sort of dinner and evening to make a man think of every single one of his past sins, and of all the others that he in-tended to commit if he lived.

Sleep, for several hundred reasons, was not easy. The lamp in the bathroom threw the most absurd shadows into the room, and the wind was beginning to talk nonsense.

Just when the reasons were drowsy with bloodsucking I heard the regular—"Let-us-take-and-heave-him-over" grunt of *dool-ie*-bearers in the compound. First one *doolie* came in, then a second, and then a third. I heard the *doolies* dumped on the ground, and the shutter in front of my door shook. "That's someone trying to come in," I said. But no one spoke, and I persuaded myself that it was the gusty wind. The shutter of the room next to mine was attacked, flung back, and the inner door opened. "That's some sub-deputy assistant," I said, "and he has brought his friends with him. Now they'll talk and spit and smoke for an hour."

But there were no voices and no footsteps. No one was putting his luggage into the next room. The door shut, and I thanked Providence that I was to be left in peace. But I was curious to know where the *doolies* had gone. I got out of bed and looked into the darkness. There was never a sign of a *doolie*. Just as I was getting into bed again, I heard, in the next room, the sound that no man in his senses can possibly mistake—the whir of a billiard ball down the length of the slates when the striker is stringing for break. No other sound is like it. A minute afterwards there was another whir, and I got into bed. I was not frightened—indeed I was not. I was very curious to know what had become of the *doolies*. I jumped into bed for that reason.

Next minute I heard the double click of a cannon and my hair sat up. It is a mistake to say that hair stands up. The skin of the head tightens and you can feel a faint, prickly bristling all over the scalp. That is the hair sitting up.

There was a whir and a click, and both sounds could only

471

have been made by one thing—a billiard ball. I argued the matter out at great length with myself; and the more I argued the less probable it seemed that one bed, one table, and two chairs—all the furniture of the room next to mine—could so exactly duplicate the sounds of a game of billiards. After another cannon, a three-cushion one to judge by the whir, I argued no more. I had found my ghost and would have given worlds to have escaped from that *dâk*-bungalow. I listened, and with each listen the game grew clearer. There was whir on whir and click on click. Sometimes there was a double click and a whir and another click. Beyond any sort of doubt, people were playing billiards in the next room. And the next room was not big enough to hold a billiard table!

Between the pauses of the wind I heard the game go forward—stroke after stroke. I tried to believe that I could not hear voices; but that attempt was a failure.

Do you know what fear is? Not ordinary fear of insult, injury or death, but abject, quivering dread of something that you cannot see—fear that dries the inside of the mouth and half of the throat—fear that makes you sweat on the palms of the hands, and gulp in order to keep the uvula at work? This is a fine fear—a great cowardice, and must be felt to be appreciated. The very improbability of billiards in a *dâk*-bungalow proved the reality of the thing. No man—drunk or sober—could imagine a game at billiards, or invent the spitting crack of a "screw-cannon."

A severe course of *dâk*-bungalows has this disadvantage—it breeds infinite credulity. If a man said to a confirmed *dâk*-bungalow-haunter:—"There is a corpse in the next room, and there's a mad girl in the next but one, and the woman and man on that camel have just eloped from a place sixty miles away," the hearer would not disbelieve because he would know that nothing is too wild, grotesque, or horrible to happen in a *dâk*-bungalow.

This credulity, unfortunately, extends to ghosts. A rational person fresh from his own house would have turned on his side and slept. I did not. So surely as I was given up as a bad carcass by the scores of things in the bed because the bulk of my blood was in my heart, so surely did I hear every stroke of a long game at billiards played in the echoing room behind the iron-barred door. My dominant fear was that the players might want a marker. It was an absurd fear; because creatures who could play in the dark would be above such superfluities. I only know that that was my terror; and it was real.

After a long long while, the game stopped, and the door banged. I slept because I was dead tired. Otherwise I should have preferred to have kept awake. Not for everything in Asia would I have dropped the door-bar and peered into the dark of the next room.

When the morning came, I considered that I had done well and wisely and inquired for the means of departure.

"By the way, *khansamah*" I said, " what were those three *doolies* doing in my compound in the night?"

"There were no *doolies*," said the *khansamah*.

I went into the next room and the daylight streamed through the open door. I was immensely brave. I would, at that hour, have played Black Pool with the owner of the big Black Pool down below.

"Has this place always been a *dâk*-bungalow?" I asked.

"No," said the *khansamah*. "Ten or twenty years ago, I have forgotten how long, it was a billiard-room."

"A how much?"

"A billiard-room for the *sahibs* who built the railway. I was *khansamah* then in the big house where all the railway-*sahibs* lived, and I used to come across with brandy-*shrab*. These three rooms were all one, and they held a big table on which the *sahibs* played every evening. But the *sahibs* are all dead now, and the railway runs, you say, nearly to Kabul."

"Do you remember anything about the *sahibs*?"

"It is long ago, but I remember that one *sahib*, a fat man and always angry, was playing here one night, and he said to me:— 'Mangal Khan, brandy *pani do*,' and I filled the glass, and he bent over the table to strike, and his head fell lower and lower till it hit the table, and his spectacles came off, and when we—the *sahibs*—and I myself ran to lift him he was dead. I helped to carry him out. Aha, he was a strong *sahib!* But he is dead and I, old Mangal Khan, am still living, by your favour."

That was more than enough! I had my ghost—a first-hand, authenticated article. I would write to the Society for Psychical Research—I would paralyse the empire with the news! But I would, first of all, put eighty miles of assessed crop-land between myself and that *dâk*-bungalow before nightfall. The society might send their regular agent to investigate later on.

I went into my own room and prepared to pack after noting down the facts of the case. As I smoked I heard the game begin again,—with a miss in balk this time, for the whir was a short one.

The door was open and I could see into the room. *Click—click!* That was a cannon. I entered the room without fear, for there was sunlight within and a fresh breeze without. The unseen game was going on at a tremendous rate. And well it might, when a restless little rat was running to and fro inside the dingy ceiling-cloth, and a piece of loose window-sash was making fifty breaks off the window-bolt as it shook in the breeze!

Impossible to mistake the sound of billiard balls! Impossible to mistake the whir of a ball over the slate! But I was to be excused. Even when I shut my enlightened eyes the sound was marvellously like that of a fast game.

Entered angrily the faithful partner of my sorrows, Kadir Baksh.

"This bungalow is very bad and low-caste! No wonder the Presence was disturbed and is speckled. Three sets of *doolie*-bearers came to the bungalow late last night when I was sleeping outside, and said that it was their custom to rest in the rooms set apart for the English people! What honour has the *khansamah?* They tried to enter, but I told them to go. No wonder, if these *Oorias* have been here, that the Presence is sorely spotted. It is shame, and the work of a dirty man."

Kadir Baksh did not say that he had taken from each gang

two *annas* for rent in advance, and then, beyond my earshot, had beaten them with the big green umbrella whose use I could never before divine. But Kadir Baksh has no notions of morality.

There was an interview with the *khansamah*, but as he promptly lost his head, wrath gave place to pity, and pity led to a long conversation, in the course of which he put the fat engineer-*sahib's* tragic death in three separate stations—two of them fifty miles away. The third shift was to Calcutta, and there the *sahib* died while driving a dog-cart.

If I had encouraged him the *khansamah* would have wandered all through Bengal with his corpse.

I did not go away as soon as I intended. I stayed for the night, while the wind and the rat and the sash and the window-bolt played a ding-dong " hundred and fifty up." Then the wind ran out and the billiards stopped, and I felt that I had ruined my one genuine, hall-market ghost story.

Had I only stopped at the proper time, I could have made *anything* out of it.

That was the bitterest thought of all!

The Bull that Thought

Westward from a town by the Mouths of the Rhone, runs a road so mathematically straight, so barometrically level, that it ranks among the world's measured miles and motorists use it for records.

I had attacked the distance several times, but always with a Mistral blowing, or the unchancy cattle of those parts on the move. But once, running from the East, into a high-piled, almost Egyptian, sunset, there came a night which it would have been sin to have wasted. It was warm with the breath of summer in advance; moonlit till the shadow of every rounded pebble and pointed cypress wind-break lay solid on that vast flat-floored waste; and my Mr. Leggatt, who had slipped out to make sure, reported that the roadsurface was unblemished.

'Now,' he suggested, 'we might see what she'll do under strict road-conditions. She's been pullin' like the Blue de Luxe all day. Unless I'm all off, it's her night out.'

We arranged the trial for after dinner—thirty kilometres as near as might be; and twenty-two of them without even a level crossing.

There sat beside me at *table d'hote* an elderly, bearded Frenchman wearing the rosette of by no means the lowest grade of the Legion of Honour, who had arrived in a talkative Citroen. I gathered that he had spent much of his life in the French Colonial Service in Annam and Tonquin. When the war came, his years barring him from the front line, he had supervised Chinese wood-cutters who, with axe and dynamite, deforested the centre of France for trench-props. He said my chauffeur had told him that I contemplated an experiment. He was interested in cars—had admired mine—would, in short, be greatly indebted to me if I permitted him to assist as an observer. One could not well refuse; and, knowing my Mr. Leggatt, it occurred to me there might also be a bet in the background.

While he went to get his coat, I asked the proprietor his name.

'Voiron—Monsieur Andre Voiron,' was the reply.

'And his business?'

'*Mon Dieu!* He is Voiron! He is all those things, there!' The proprietor waved his hands at brilliant advertisements on the dining-room walls, which declared that Voiron Freres dealt in wines, agricultural implements, chemical manures, provisions and produce throughout that part of the globe.

He said little for the first five minutes of our trip, and nothing at all for the next ten—it being, as Leggatt had guessed, Esmeralda's night out. But, when her indicator climbed to a certain figure and held there for three blinding kilometres, he expressed himself satisfied, and proposed to me that we should celebrate the event at the hotel. 'I keep yonder,' said he, 'a wine on which I should value your opinion.'

On our return, he disappeared for a few minutes, and I heard him rumbling in a cellar. The proprietor presently invited me to the dining-room, where, beneath one frugal light, a table had been set with local dishes of renown. There was, too, a bottle beyond most known sizes, marked black on red, with a date. Monsieur Voiron opened it, and we drank to the health of my car. The velvety, perfumed liquor, between fawn and topaz, neither too sweet nor too dry, creamed in its generous glass. But I knew no wine composed of the whispers of angels' wings, the breath of Eden and the foam and pulse of Youth renewed. So I asked what it might be.

'It is champagne,' he said gravely.

'Then what have I been drinking all my life?'

'If you were lucky, before the war, and paid thirty shillings a bottle, it is possible you may have drunk one of our better-class tisanes.'

'And where does one get this?'

'Here, I am happy to say. Elsewhere, perhaps, it is not so easy. We growers exchange these real wines among ourselves.'

I bowed my head in admiration, surrender, and joy. There stood the most ample bottle, and it was not yet eleven o'clock. Doors locked and shutters banged throughout the establishment. Some last servant yawned on his way to bed. Monsieur Voiron opened a window and the moonlight flooded in from a small pebbled court outside. One could almost hear the town of Chambres breathing in its first sleep. Presently, there was a thick noise in the air, the passing of feet and hooves, lowings, and a stifled bark or two. Dust rose over the courtyard wall, followed by the strong smell of cattle.

'They are moving some beasts,' said Monsieur Voiron, cocking an ear. 'Mine, I think. Yes, I hear Christophe. Our beasts do not like automobiles—so we move at night. You do not know our country—the Crau, here, or the Camargue? I was—I am now, again—of it. All France is good; but this is the best.' He spoke, as only a Frenchman can, of his own loved part of his own lovely land.

'For myself, if I were not so involved in all these affairs'— he pointed to the advertisements—'I would live on our farm with my cattle, and worship them like a Hindu. You know our cattle of the Camargue, *Monsieur?* No? It is not an acquaintance to rush upon lightly. There are no beasts like them. They have a mentality superior to that of others. They graze and they ruminate, by choice, facing our mistral, which is more than some automobiles will do. Also they have in them the potentiality of thought—and when cattle think—I have seen what arrives.'

'Are they so clever as all that?' I asked idly.

'*Monsieur*, when your sportif chauffeur camouflaged your limousine so that she resembled one of your army lorries, I would not believe her capacities. I bet him—ah—two to one— she would not touch ninety kilometres. It was proved that she could. I can give you no proof, but will you believe me if I tell you what a beast who thinks can achieve?'

'After the war,' said I spaciously, 'everything is credible.'

'That is true! Everything inconceivable has happened; but still we learn nothing and we believe nothing. When I was a child in my father's house—before I became a Colonial Administrator—my interest and my affection were among our cattle. We of the old rock live here—have you seen?— in big farms like castles. Indeed, some of them may have been Saracenic. The barns group round them—great white-walled barns, and yards solid as our houses. One gate shuts all. It is a world apart; an administration of all that concerns beasts. It was there I learned something about cattle. You see, they are our playthings in the Camargue and the Crau. The boy measures his strength against the calf that butts him in play among the manure-heaps. He moves in and out among the cows, who are—not so amiable. He rides with the herdsmen in the open to shift the herds.

'Sooner or later, he meets as bulls the little calves that knocked him over. So it was with me—till it became necessary that I should go to our colonies.' He laughed. 'Very necessary. That is a good time in youth, *Monsieur*, when one does these things which shock our parents. Why is it always papa who is so shocked and has never heard of such things—and mamma who supplies the excuses? ...And when my brother—my elder who stayed and created the business—begged me to return and help him, I resigned my colonial career gladly enough. I returned to our own lands, and my well-loved, wicked white and yellow cattle of the Camargue and the Crau. My Faith, I could talk of them all night, for this stuff unlocks the heart, without making repentance in the morning ...Yes! It was after the war that this happened.

'There was a calf, among Heaven knows how many of ours—a bull-calf—an infant indistinguishable from his companions. He was sick, and he had been taken up with his mother into the big farmyard at home with us. Naturally the children of our herdsmen practised on him from the first. It is in their blood. The Spaniards make a cult of bull-fighting. Our little devils down here bait bulls as automatically as the English child kicks or throws balls. This calf would chase them with his eyes open, like a cow when she hunts a man. They would take refuge behind our tractors and wine-carts in the centre of the yard: he would chase them in and out as a dog hunts rats. More than that, he would study their psychology, his eyes in their eyes. Yes, he watched their faces to divine which way they would run. He himself, also, would pretend sometimes to charge directly at a boy. Then he would wheel right or left— one could never tell— and knock over some child pressed against a wall who thought himself safe.

'After this, he would stand over him, knowing that his companions must come to his aid; and when they were all together, waving their jackets across his eyes and pulling his tail, he would scatter them—how he would scatter them! He could kick, too, sideways like a cow. He knew his ranges as well as our gunners, and he was as quick on his feet as our Carpentier. I observed him often. Christophe—the man who passed just now—our chief herdsman, who had taught me to ride with our beasts when I was ten—Christophe told me that he was descended from a yellow cow of those days that had chased us once into the marshes. "He kicks just like her," said Christophe. "He can side-kick as he jumps. Have you seen, too, that he is not deceived by the jacket when a boy waves it? He uses it to find the boy. They think they are feeling him. He is feeling them always. He thinks, that one." I had come to the same conclusion. Yes—the creature was a thinker along the lines necessary to his sport; and he was a humorist also, like so many natural murderers. One knows the type among beasts as well as among men. It possesses a curious truculent mirth—almost indecent but infallibly significant—'

Monsieur Voiron replenished our glasses with the great wine that went better at each descent.

'They kept him for some time in the yards to practise upon. Naturally he became a little brutal; so Christophe turned him out to learn manners among his equals in the grazing lands, where the Camargue joins the Crau. How old was he then? About eight or nine months, I think. We met again a few months later—he and I. I was riding one of our little half-wild horses, along a road of the Crau, when I found myself almost unseated. It was he! He had hidden himself behind a wind-break till we passed, and had then charged my horse from behind. Yes, he had deceived even my little horse! But I recognised him. I gave him the whip across the nose, and I said: "Apis, for this thou goest to Arles! It was unworthy of thee, between us two." But that creature had no shame. He went away laughing, like an Apache. If he had dismounted me, I do not think it is I who would have laughed—yearling as he was.'

'Why did you want to send him to Arles?' I asked.

'For the bull-ring. When your charming tourists leave us, we institute our little amusements there. Not a real bull-fight, you understand, but young bulls with padded horns, and our boys from hereabouts and in the city go to play with them. Naturally, before we send them we try them in our yards at home. So we brought up Apis from his pastures. He knew at once that he was among the friends of his youth—he almost shook hands with them—and he submitted like an angel to padding his horns. He investigated the carts and tractors in the yards, to choose his lines of defence and attack. And then—he attacked with an *élan*, and he defended with a tenacity and forethought that delighted us.

'In truth, we were so pleased that I fear we trespassed upon his patience. We desired him to repeat himself, which no true artist will tolerate. But he gave us fair warning. He went out to the centre of the yard, where there was some dry earth; he kneeled down and—you have seen a calf whose horns fret him thrusting and rooting into a bank? He did just that, very deliberately, till he had rubbed the pads off his horns. Then he rose, dancing on those wonderful feet that twinkled, and he said: "Now, my friends, the buttons are off the foils. Who begins?" We understood. We finished at once. He was turned out again on the pastures till it should be time to amuse them at our little metropolis.

481

'But, some time before he went to Arles—yes, I think I have it correctly—Christophe, who had been out on the Crau, informed me that Apis had assassinated a young bull who had given signs of developing into a rival. That happens, of course, and our herdsmen should prevent it. But Apis had killed in his own style—at dusk, from the ambush of a wind-break—by an oblique charge from behind which knocked the other over. He had then disembowelled him. All very possible, but—the murder accomplished— Apis went to the bank of a wind-break, knelt, and carefully, as he had in our yard, cleaned his horns in the earth. Christophe, who had never seen such a thing, at once borrowed (do you know, it is most efficacious when taken that way?) some Holy Water from our little chapel in those pastures, sprinkled Apis (whom it did not affect), and rode in to tell me.

'It was obvious that a thinker of that bull's type would also be meticulous in his toilette; so, when he was sent to Arles, I warned our consignees to exercise caution with him. Happily, the change of scene, the music, the general attention, and the meeting again with old friends—all our bad boys attended—agreeably distracted him. He became for the time a pure farceur again; but his wheelings, his rushes, his rat-huntings were more superb than ever. There was in them now, you understand, a breadth of technique that comes of reasoned art, and, above all, the passion that arrives after experience. Oh, he had learned, out there on the Crau! At the end of his little turn, he was, according to local rules, to be handled in all respects except for the sword, which was a stick, as a professional bull who must die. He was manoeuvred into, or he posed himself in, the proper attitude; made his rush; received the point on his shoulder and then—turned about and cantered toward the door by which he had entered the arena.

'He said to the world: "My friends, the representation is ended. I thank you for your applause. I go to repose myself." But our Arlesians, who are—not so clever as some, demanded an encore, and Apis was headed back again. We others from his country, we knew what would happen. He went to the centre of the ring, kneeled, and, slowly, with full parade, plunged his horns alternately in the dirt till the pads came off. Christophe shouts: "Leave him alone, you straight-nosed imbeciles! Leave him before you must." But they required emotion; for Rome has always debauched her loved Provincia with bread and circuses. It was given. Have you, *Monsieur*, ever seen a servant, with pan and broom, sweeping round the base-board of a room? In a half-minute Apis has them all swept out and over the barrier. Then he demands once more that the door shall be opened to him. It is opened and he retires as though—which, truly, is the case—loaded with laurels.'

Monsieur Voiron refilled the glasses, and allowed himself a cigarette, which he puffed for some time.

'And afterwards?' I said.

'I am arranging it in my mind. It is difficult to do it justice. Afterwards—yes, afterwards—Apis returned to his pastures and his mistresses and I to my business. I am no longer a scandalous old "*sportif*" in shirt-sleeves howling encouragement to the yellow son of a cow. I revert to Voiron Freres-wines, chemical manures, *et cetera*. And next year, through some chicane which I have not the leisure to unravel, and also, thanks to our patriarchal system of paying our older men out of the increase of the herds, old Christophe possesses himself of Apis. Oh, yes, he proves it through descent from a certain cow that my father had given his father before the Republic. Beware, *Monsieur*, of the memory of the illiterate man! An ancestor of Christophe had been a soldier under our Soult against your Beresford, near Bayonne. He fell into the hands of Spanish guerrillas. Christophe and his wife used to tell me the details on certain Saints' Days when I was a child. Now, as compared with our recent war, Soult's campaign and retreat across the Bidassoa—'

'But did you allow Christophe just to annex the bull?' I demanded.

'You do not know Christophe. He had sold him to the Spaniards before he informed me. The Spaniards pay in coin—*douros* of very pure silver. Our peasants mistrust our paper. You know the saying: "A thousand *francs* paper; eight hundred metal, and the cow is yours." Yes, Christophe sold Apis, who was then two and a half years old, and to Christophe's knowledge thrice at least an assassin.'

'How was that?' I said.

'Oh, his own kind only; and always, Christophe told me, by the same oblique rush from behind, the same sideways overthrow, and the same swift disembowelment, followed by this levitical cleaning of the horns. In human life he would have kept a manicurist—this Minotaur. And so, Apis disappears from our country. That does not trouble me. I know in due time I shall be advised. Why? Because, in this land, *Monsieur*, not a hoof moves between Berre and the Saintes Maries without the knowledge of specialists such as Christophe. The beasts are the substance and the drama of their lives to them. So when Christophe tells me, a little before Easter Sunday, that Apis makes his debut in the bull-ring of a small Catalan town on the road to Barcelona, it is only to pack my car and trundle there across the frontier with him. The place lacked importance and manufactures, but it had produced a matador of some reputation, who was condescending to show his art in his native town. They were even running one special train to the place. Now our French railway system is only execrable, but the Spanish—'

'You went down by road, didn't you?' said I.

'Naturally. It was not too good. Villamarti was the *matador's* name. He proposed to kill two bulls for the honour of his birthplace. Apis, Christophe told me, would be his second. It was an interesting trip, and that little city by the sea was ravishing. Their bull-ring dates from the middle of the seventeenth century. It is full of feeling. The ceremonial too—when the horsemen enter and ask the mayor in his box to throw down the keys of the bull-ring—that was exquisitely conceived. You know, if the keys are caught in the horseman's hat, it is considered a good omen. They were perfectly caught. Our seats were in the front row beside the gates where the bulls enter, so we saw everything.

'Villamarti's first bull was not too badly killed. The second *matador*, whose name escapes me, killed his without distinction—a foil to Villamarti. And the third, Chisto, a laborious, middle-aged professional who had never risen beyond a certain dull competence, was equally of the background. Oh, they are as jealous as the girls of the *Comedie Francaise*, these *matadors!* Villamarti's *troupe* stood ready for his second bull. The gates opened, and we saw Apis, beautifully balanced on his feet, peer *coquettishly* round the corner, as though he were at home.

'A *picador*—a mounted man with the long lance-goad—stood near the barrier on his right. He had not even troubled to turn his horse, for the capeadors—the men with the cloaks—were advancing to play Apis—to feel his psychology and intentions, according to the rules that are made for bulls who do not think . . . I did not realise the murder before it was accomplished! The wheel, the rush, the oblique charge from behind, the fall of horse and man were simultaneous. Apis leaped the horse, with whom he had no quarrel, and alighted, all four feet together (it was enough), between the man's shoulders, changed his beautiful feet on the carcass, and was away, pretending to fall nearly on his nose. Do you follow me?

'In that instant, by that stumble, he produced the impression that his adorable assassination was a mere bestial blunder. Then, *Monsieur*, I began to comprehend that it was an artist we had to deal with. He did not stand over the body to draw the rest of the troupe. He chose to reserve that trick. He let the attendants bear out the dead, and went on to amuse himself among the *capeadors*. Now to Apis, trained among our children in the yards, the cloak was simply a guide to the boy behind it. He pursued, you understand, the person, not the propaganda—the proprietor, not the journal. If a third of our electors of France were as wise, my friend! . . . But it was done leisurely, with humour and a touch of truculence. He romped after one man's cloak as a clumsy dog might do, but I observed that he kept the man on his terrible left side. Christophe whispered to me: "Wait for his mother's kick. When he has made the fellow confident it will arrive."

'It arrived in the middle of a gambol. My God! He lashed

out in the air as he frisked. The man dropped like a sack, lifted one hand a little towards his head, and—that was all. So you see, a body was again at his disposition; a second time the cloaks ran up to draw him off, but, a second time, Apis refused his grand scene. A second time he acted that his murder was accident and he convinced his audience! It was as though he had knocked over a bridge-gate in the marshes by mistake. Unbelievable? I saw it.'

The memory sent Monsieur Voiron again to the champagne, and I accompanied him.

'But Apis was not the sole artist present. They say Villamarti comes of a family of actors. I saw him regard Apis with a new eye. He, too, began to understand. He took his cloak and moved out to play him before they should bring on another *picador*. He had his reputation. Perhaps Apis knew it. Perhaps Villamarti reminded him of some boy with whom he had practised at home. At any rate Apis permitted it—up to a certain point; but he did not allow Villamarti the stage. He cramped him throughout. He dived and plunged clumsily and slowly, but always with menace and always closing in. We could see that the man was conforming to the bull—not the bull to the man; for Apis was playing him towards the centre of the ring, and, in a little while—I watched his face—Villamarti knew it. But I could not fathom the creature's motive. "Wait," said old Christophe. "He wants that *picador* on the white horse yonder.

'When he reaches his proper distance he will get him. Villamarti is his cover. He used me once that way." And so it was, my friend! With the clang of one of our own Seventy-fives, Apis dismissed Villamarti with his chest—breasted him over—and had arrived at his objective near the barrier. The same oblique charge; the head carried low for the sweep of the horns; the immense sideways fall of the horse, broken-legged and half-paralysed; the senseless man on the ground, and—behold Apis between them, backed against the barrier—his right covered by the horse; his left by the body of the man at his feet.

'The simplicity of it! Lacking the carts and tractors of his early parade-grounds he, being a genius, had extemporised with the materials at hand, and dug himself in. The *troupe* closed up again, their left wing broken by the kicking horse, their right immobilised by the man's body which Apis bestrode with significance. Villamarti almost threw himself between the horns, but—it was more an appeal than an attack. Apis refused him. He held his base. A *picador* was sent at him—necessarily from the front, which alone was open. Apis charged—he who, till then, you realise, had not used the horn! The horse went over backwards, the man half beneath him. Apis halted, hooked him under the heart, and threw him to the barrier. We heard his head crack, but he was dead before he hit the wood.

'There was no demonstration from the audience. They, also, had begun to realise this Foch among bulls! The arena occupied itself again with the dead. Two of the *troupe* irresolutely tried to play him—God knows in what hope!— but he moved out to the centre of the ring. "Look!" said Christophe. "Now he goes to clean himself. That always frightened me." He knelt down; he began to clean his horns. The earth was hard. He worried at it in an ecstasy of absorption. As he laid his head along and rattled his ears, it was as though he were interrogating the devils themselves upon their secrets, and always saying impatiently: "Yes, I know that—and that—and that! Tell me more—more!' In the silence that covered us, a woman cried: "He digs a grave! Oh, Saints, he digs a grave!" Some others echoed this—not loudly— as a wave echoes in a grotto of the sea.'

'And when his horns were cleaned, he rose up and studied poor Villamarti's *troupe*, eyes in eyes, one by one, with the gravity of an equal in intellect and the remote and merciless resolution of a master in his art. This was more terrifying than his *toilette*.'

'And they—Villamarti's men?' I asked.

'Like the audience, were dominated. They had ceased to posture, or stamp, or address insults to him. They conformed to him. The two other *matadors* stared. Only Chisto, the oldest, broke silence with some call or other, and Apis turned his head towards him. Otherwise he was isolated, immobile—sombre—

meditating on those at his mercy. Ah!

For some reason the trumpet sounded for the *banderillas*—those gay hooked darts that are planted in the shoulders of bulls who do not think, after their neck-muscles are tired by lifting horses. When such bulls feel the pain, they check for an instant, and, in that instant, the men step gracefully aside. Villamarti's *banderillero* answered the trumpet mechanically—like one condemned. He stood out, poised the darts and stammered the usual patter of invitation . . . And after? I do not assert that Apis shrugged his shoulders, but he reduced the episode to its lowest elements, as could only a bull of Gaul. With his truculence was mingled always—owing to the shortness of his tail—a certain Rabelaisian abandon, especially when viewed from the rear. Christophe had often commented upon it.

'Now, Apis brought that quality into play. He circulated round that boy, forcing him to break up his beautiful poses. He studied him from various angles, like an incompetent photographer. He presented to him every portion of his anatomy except his shoulders. At intervals he feigned to run in upon him. My God, he was cruel! But his motive was obvious. He was playing for a laugh from the spectators which should synchronise with the fracture of the human morale. It was achieved. The boy turned and ran towards the barrier. Apis was on him before the laugh ceased; passed him; headed him—what do I say?—herded him off to the left, his horns beside and a little in front of his chest: he did not intend him to escape into a refuge. Some of the *troupe* would have closed in, but Villamarti cried: "If he wants him he will take him. Stand!" They stood. Whether the boy slipped or Apis nosed him over I could not see. But he dropped, sobbing. Apis halted like a car with four brakes, struck a pose, smelt him very completely and turned away. It was dismissal more ignominious than degradation at the head of one's battalion. The representation was finished. Remained only for Apis to clear his stage of the subordinate characters.

'Ah! His gesture then! He gave a dramatic start—this Cyrano of the Camargue—as though he was aware of them for the first time. He moved. All their beautiful breeches twinkled for an instant along the top of the barrier. He held the stage alone! But Christophe and I, we trembled! For, observe, he had now involved himself in a stupendous drama of which he only could supply the third act. And, except for an audience on the razor-edge of emotion, he had exhausted his material. Moliere himself—we have forgotten, my friend, to drink to the health of that great soul—might have been at a loss. And tragedy is but a step behind failure. We could see the four or five civil guards, who are sent always to keep order, fingering the breeches of their rifles. They were but waiting a word from the mayor to fire on him, as they do sometimes at a bull who leaps the barrier among the spectators. They would, of course, have killed or wounded several people—but that would not have saved Apis.'

Monsieur Voiron drowned the thought at once, and wiped his beard.

'At that moment Fate—the genius of France, if you will— sent to assist in the incomparable finale, none other than Chisto, the eldest, and I should have said (but never again will I judge!) the least inspired of all; mediocrity itself, but at heart—and it is the heart that conquers always, my friend—at heart an artist. He descended stiffly into the arena, alone and assured. Apis regarded him, his eyes in his eyes. The man took stance, with his cloak, and called to the bull as to an equal: "Now, *Senor*, we will show these honourable *caballeros* something together." He advanced thus against this thinker who at a plunge—a kick—a thrust— could, we all knew, have extinguished him.

'My dear friend, I wish I could convey to you something of the unaffected *bonhomie*, the humour, the delicacy, the consideration bordering on respect even, with which Apis, the supreme artist, responded to this invitation. It was the master, wearied after a strenuous hour in the atelier, unbuttoned and at ease with some not inexpert but limited disciple. The telepathy was instantaneous between them. And for good reason! Christophe said to me: "All's well. That Chisto began among the bulls. I was sure of it when I heard him call just now. He has been a herdsman. He'll pull it off." There was a little feeling and adjustment, at first, for mutual distances and allowances.

Oh, yes! And here occurred a gross impertinence of Villamarti. He had, after an interval, followed Chisto—to retrieve his reputation. My Faith! I can conceive the elder Dumas slamming his door on an intruder precisely as Apis did. He raced Villamarti into the nearest refuge at once. He stamped his feet outside it, and he snorted: "Go! I am engaged with an artist." Villamarti went—his reputation left behind forever.

'Apis returned to Chisto saying: "Forgive the interruption. I am not always master of my time, but you were about to observe, my dear confrere . . .?" Then the play began. Out of compliment to Chisto, Apis chose as his objective (every bull varies in this respect) the inner edge of the cloak—that nearest to the man's body. This allows but a few millimetres clearance in charging. But Apis trusted himself as Chisto trusted him, and, this time, he conformed to the man, with inimitable judgment and temper. He allowed himself to be played into the shadow or the sun, as the delighted audience demanded. He raged enormously; he feigned defeat; he despaired in statuesque abandon, and thence flashed into fresh paroxysms of wrath—but always with the detachment of the true artist who knows he is but the vessel of an emotion whence others, not he, must drink. And never once did he forget that honest Chisto's cloak was to him the gauge by which to spare even a hair on the skin. He inspired Chisto too. My God! His youth returned to that meritorious beef-sticker— the desire, the grace, and the beauty of his early dreams.

'One could almost see that girl of the past for whom he was rising, rising to these present heights of skill and daring. It was his hour too—a miraculous hour of dawn returned to gild the sunset. All he knew was at Apis' disposition. Apis acknowledged it with all that he had learned at home, at Arles and in his lonely murders on our grazing-grounds. He flowed round Chisto like a river of death—round his knees, leaping at his shoulders, kicking just clear of one side or the other of his head; behind his back, hissing as he shaved by; and once or twice—inimitable!— he reared wholly up before him while Chisto slipped back from beneath the avalanche of that instructed body. Those two, my dear friend, held five thousand people dumb with no sound but of their breathings— regular as pumps. It was unbearable. Beast and man realised together that we needed a change of note—a detente. They relaxed to pure buffoonery. Chisto fell back and talked to him outrageously. Apis pretended he had never heard such language. The audience howled with delight.

'Chisto slapped him; he took liberties with his short tail, to the end of which he clung while Apis pirouetted; he played about him in all postures; he had become the herdsman again— gross, careless, brutal, but comprehending. Yet Apis was always the more consummate clown. All that time (Christophe and I saw it) Apis drew off towards the gates of the *toril* where so many bulls enter but—have you ever heard of one that returned? We knew that Apis knew that as he had saved Chisto, so Chisto would save him. Life is sweet to us all; to the artist who lives many lives in one, sweetest. Chisto did not fail him. At the last, when none could laugh any longer, the man threw his cape across the bull's back, his arm round his neck. He flung up a hand at the gate, as Villamarti, young and commanding but not a herdsman, might have raised it, and he cried: "Gentlemen, open to me and my honourable little donkey." They opened—I have misjudged Spaniards in my time!—those gates opened to the man and the bull together, and closed behind them. And then?

From the mayor to the *Guardia Civil* they went mad for five minutes, till the trumpets blew and the fifth bull rushed out—an unthinking black Andalusian. I suppose someone killed him. My friend, my very dear friend, to whom I have opened my heart, I confess that I did not watch. Christophe and I, we were weeping together like children of the same mother. Shall we drink to her?'

The City of Dreadful Night

The dense wet heat that hung over the face of land, like a blanket, prevented all hope of sleep in the first instance. The *cicalas* helped the heat; and the yelling jackals the *cicalas*. It was impossible to sit still in the dark, empty, echoing house and watch the *punkah* beat the dead air. So, at ten o'clock of the night, I set my walking-stick on end in the middle of the garden, and waited to see how it would fall. It pointed directly down the moonlit road that leads to the City of Dreadful Night. The sound of its fall disturbed a hare. She limped from her form and ran across to a disused Mahomedan burial-ground, where the jawless skulls and rough-butted shank-bones, heartlessly exposed by the July rains, glimmered like mother o' pearl on the rain-channelled soil. The heated air and the heavy earth had driven the very dead upward for coolness' sake. The hare limped on; snuffed curiously at a fragment of a smoke-stained lamp-shard, and died out, in the shadow of a clump of tamarisk trees.

The mat-weaver's hut under the lee of the Hindu temple was full of sleeping men who lay like sheeted corpses. Overhead blazed the unwinking eye of the moon. Darkness gives at least a false impression of coolness. It was hard not to believe that the flood of light from above was warm. Not so hot as the sun, but still sickly warm, and heating the heavy air beyond what was our due. Straight as a bar of polished steel ran the road to the City of Dreadful Night; and on either side of the road lay corpses disposed on beds in fantastic attitudes—one hundred and seventy bodies of men. Some shrouded all in white with bound-up mouths; some naked and black as ebony in the strong light; and one—that lay face upwards with dropped jaw, far away from the others silvery white and ashen gray.

'A leper asleep; and the remainder wearied *coolies*, servants, small shopkeepers, and drivers from the hackstand hard by. The scene—a main approach to Lahore city, and the night a warm one in August.' This was all that there was to be seen; but by no means all that one could see. The witchery of the moonlight was everywhere; and the world was horribly changed. The long line of the naked dead, flanked by the rigid silver statue, was not pleasant to look upon. It was made up of men alone. Were the womenkind, then, forced to sleep in the shelter of the stifling mud-huts as best they might? The fretful wail of a child from a low mud-roof answered the question.

Where the children are the mothers must be also to look after them. They need care on these sweltering nights. A black little bullet-head peeped over the coping, and a thin—a painfully thin—brown leg was slid over on to the gutter pipe. There was a sharp clink of glass bracelets; a woman's arm showed for an instant above the parapet, twined itself round the lean little neck, and the child was dragged back, protesting, to the shelter of the bedstead. His thin, high-pitched shriek died out in the thick air almost as soon as it was raised; for even the children of the soil found it too hot to weep.

More corpses; more stretches of moonlit, white road, a string of sleeping camels at rest by the wayside; a vision of scudding jackals; *ekka*-ponies asleep—the harness still on their backs, and the brass- studded country carts, winking in the moonlight— and again more corpses. Wherever a grain cart atilt, a tree trunk, a sawn log, a couple of bamboos and a few handfuls of thatch cast a shadow, the ground is covered with them. They lie—some face downwards, arms folded, in the dust; some with clasped hands flung up above their heads; some curled up dog-wise; some thrown like limp gunny-bags over the side of the grain carts; and some bowed with their brows on their knees in the full glare of the moon.

It would be a comfort if they were only given to snoring; but they are not, and the likeness to corpses is unbroken in all respects save one. The lean dogs snuff at them and turn away. Here and there a tiny child lies on his father's bedstead, and a protecting arm is thrown round it in every instance. But, for the most part, the children sleep with their mothers on the house-tops. Yellow-skinned white-toothed pariahs are not to be trusted within reach of brown bodies.

A stifling hot blast from the mouth of the Delhi Gate nearly ends my resolution of entering the City of Dreadful Night at this hour. It is a compound of all evil savours, animal and veg-etable, that a walled city can brew in a day and a night. The tem-perature within the motionless groves of plantain and orange-trees outside the city walls seems chilly by comparison. Heaven help all sick persons and young children within the city tonight! The high house-walls are still radiating heat savagely, and from obscure side gullies fetid breezes eddy that ought to poison a buffalo. But the buffaloes do not heed. A drove of them are pa-rading the vacant main street; stopping now and then to lay their ponderous muzzles against the closed shutters of a grain-dealer's shops and to blow thereon like grampuses.

Then silence follows—the silence that is full of the night noises of a great city. A stringed instrument of some kind is just, and only just, audible. High overhead someone throws open a window, and the rattle of the wood-work echoes down the empty street. On one of the roofs, a *hookah* is in full blast; and the men are talking softly as the pipe gutters. A little farther on, the noise of conversation is more distinct. A slit of light shows itself between the sliding shutters of a shop. Inside, a stubble-bearded, weary-eyed trader is balancing his account-books among the bales of cotton prints that surround him. Three sheeted figures bear him company, and throw in a remark from time to time. First he makes an entry, then a remark; then passes the back of his hand across his streaming forehead. The heat in the built-in street is fearful. Inside the shops it must be almost unendurable. But the work goes on steadily; entry, guttural growl, and uplifted hand-stroke succeeding each other with the precision of clock-work.

A policeman—turbanless and fast asleep—lies across the road on the way to the Mosque of Wazir Khan. A bar of moonlight falls across the forehead and eyes of the sleeper, but he never stirs. It is close upon midnight, and the heat seems to be increasing. The open square in front of the Mosque is crowded with corpses; and a man must pick his way carefully for fear of treading on them. The moonlight stripes the Mosque's high front of coloured enamel work in broad diagonal bands; and each separate dreaming pigeon in the niches and corners of the masonry throws a squab little shadow. Sheeted ghosts rise up wearily from their pallets, and flit into the dark depths of the building. Is it possible to climb to the top of the great Minars, and thence to look down on the city?

At all events the attempt is worth making, and the chances are that the door of the staircase will be unlocked. Unlocked it is; but a deeply sleeping janitor lies across the threshold, face turned to the moon. A rat dashes out of his turban at the sound of approaching footsteps. The man grunts, opens his eyes for a minute, turns round, and goes to sleep again. All the heat of a decade of fierce Indian summers is stored in the pitch-black, polished walls of the corkscrew staircase. Half-way up, there is something alive, warm, and feathery; and it snores. Driven from step to step as it catches the sound of my advance, it flutters to the top and reveals itself as a yellow-eyed, angry kite. Dozens of kites are asleep on this and the other Minars, and on the domes below. There is the shadow of a cool, or at least a less sultry breeze at this height; and, refreshed thereby, turn to look on the City of Dreadful Night.

Doré might have drawn it! Zola could describe it—this spectacle of sleeping thousands in the moonlight and in the shadow of the moon. The roof-tops are crammed with men, women, and children; and the air is full of undistinguishable noises. They are restless in the City of Dreadful Night; and small wonder. The marvel is that they can even breathe. If you gaze intently at the multitude, you can see that they are almost as uneasy as a daylight crowd; but the tumult is subdued. Everywhere, in the strong light, you can watch the sleepers turning to and fro; shifting their beds and again resettling them. In the pit-like courtyards of the houses there is the same movement.

The pitiless moon shows it all. Shows, too, the plains outside the city, and here and there a hand's-breadth of the Ravee without the walls. Shows lastly, a splash of glittering silver on a house-top almost directly below the mosque Minar. Some poor soul has risen to throw a jar of water over his fevered body; the tinkle of the falling water strikes faintly on the ear. Two or three other men, in far-off corners of the City of Dreadful Night, follow his example, and the water flashes like heliographic signals.

A small cloud passes over the face of the moon, and the city and its inhabitants—clear drawn in black and white before— fade into masses of black and deeper black. Still the unrestful noise continues, the sigh of a great city overwhelmed with the heat, and of a people seeking in vain for rest. It is only the lower-class women who sleep on the house-tops. What must the torment be in the latticed *zenanas*, where a few lamps are still twinkling? There are footfalls in the court below. It is the *muezzin*—faithful minister; but he ought to have been here an hour ago to tell the Faithful that prayer is better than sleep—the sleep that will not come to the city.

The *muezzin* fumbles for a moment with the door of one of the Minars, disappears awhile, and a bull-like roar—a magnificent bass thunder— tells that he has reached the top of the Minar. They must hear the cry to the banks of the shrunken Ravee itself! Even across the courtyard it is almost overpowering. The cloud drifts by and shows him outlined in black against the sky, hands laid upon his ears, and broad chest heaving with the play of his lungs—'*Allah ho Akbar*'; then a pause while another *Muezzin* somewhere in the direction of the Golden Temple takes up the call—'*Allah ho Akbar.*' Again and again; four times in all; and from the bedsteads a dozen men have risen up already.—'I bear witness that there is no God but God.'

What a splendid cry it is, the proclamation of the creed that brings men out of their beds by scores at midnight! Once again he thunders through the same phrase, shaking with the vehemence of his own voice; and then, far and near, the night air rings with 'Mahomed is the Prophet of God.' It is as though he were flinging his defiance to the far-off horizon, where the summer lightning plays and leaps like a bared sword. Every *Muezzin* in the city is in full cry, and some men on the roof-tops are beginning to kneel. A long pause precedes the last cry, '*La ilaha Illallah*,' and the silence closes up on it, as the ram on the head of a cotton-bale.

The *Muezzin* stumbles down the dark stairway grumbling in his beard. He passes the arch of the entrance and disappears. Then the stifling silence settles down over the City of Dreadful Night. The kites on the Minar sleep again, snoring more loudly, the hot breeze comes up in puffs and lazy eddies, and the moon slides down towards the horizon. Seated with both elbows on the parapet of the tower, one can watch and wonder over that heat-tortured hive till the dawn. 'How do they live down there? What do they think of? When will they awake?' More tinkling of sluiced water-pots; faint jarring of wooden bedsteads moved into or out of the shadows; uncouth music of stringed instruments softened by distance into a plaintive wail, and one low grumble of far-off thunder.

In the courtyard of the mosque the janitor, who lay across the threshold of the Minar when I came up, starts wildly in his sleep, throws his hands above his head, mutters something, and falls back again. Lulled by the snoring of the kites—they snore like over-gorged humans—I drop off into an uneasy doze, conscious that three o'clock has struck, and that there is a slight—a very slight—coolness in the atmosphere. The city is absolutely quiet now, but for some vagrant dog's love-song. Nothing save dead heavy sleep.

Several weeks of darkness pass after this. For the moon has gone out. The very dogs are still, and I watch for the first light of the dawn before making my way homeward. Again the noise of shuffling feet. The morning call is about to begin, and my night watch is over. '*Allah ho Akbar! Allah ho Akbar!*' The east grows gray, and presently saffron; the dawn wind comes up as though the *muezzin* had summoned it; and, as one man, the City of Dreadful Night rises from its bed and turns its face towards the dawning day. With return of life comes return of sound. First a low whisper, then a deep bass hum; for it must be remembered that the entire city is on the house-tops. My eyelids weighed down with the arrears of long deferred sleep, I escape from the Minar through the courtyard and out into the square beyond, where the sleepers have risen, stowed away the bedsteads, and are discussing the morning hookah. The minute's freshness of the air has gone, and it is as hot as at first.

'Will the *sahib*, out of his kindness, make room?' What is it? Something borne on men's shoulders comes by in the half-light, and I stand back. A woman's corpse going down to the burning-*ghât*, and a bystander says, 'She died at midnight from the heat.' So the city was of Death as well as Night after all.

The Enemies to Each Other

With Apologies to the Shade of Mirza Mirkhond

It is narrated (and God knows best the true state of the case) by Abu Ali Jafir Bin Yakub-ul-Isfahani that when, in His determinate Will, The Benefactor had decided to create the Greatest Substitute (Adam), He despatched, as is known, the faithful and the excellent Archangel Jibrail to gather from Earth clays, loams, and sands endowed with various colours and attributes, necessary for the substance of our pure Forefather's body. Receiving the Command and reaching the place, Jibrail put forth his hand to take them, but Earth shook and lamented and supplicated him. Then said Jibrail: 'Lie still and rejoice, for out of thee He will create that than which (there) is no handsomer thing — to wit a Successor and a Wearer of the Diadem over thee through the ages.' Earth said: 'I adjure thee to abstain from thy purpose, lest evil and condemnation of that person who is created out of me should later overtake him, and the Abiding (sorrow) be loosed upon my head. I have no power to resist the Will of the Most High, but I take refuge with Allah from thee.' So Jibrail was moved by the lamentations and helplessness of Earth, and returned to the Vestibule of the Glory with an empty hand.

After this, by the Permission, the Just and Terrible Archangel Michael next descended, and he, likewise, hearing and seeing the abjection of Earth, returned with an empty hand. Then was sent the Archangel Azrael, and when Earth had once again implored God, and once again cried out, he closed his hand upon her bosom and tore out the clays and sands necessary.

Upon his return to the Vestibule it was asked if Earth had again taken refuge with *Allah* or not? Azrael said: 'Yes.'

It was answered 'If it took refuge with Me why didst thou not spare?'

Azrael answered: 'Obedience (to Thee) was more obligatory than Pity (for it).'

It was answered: 'Depart! I have made thee the Angel of Death to separate the souls from the bodies of men.'

Azrael wept, saying: 'Thus shall all men hate me.'

It was answered: 'Thou hast said that Obedience is more obligatory than Pity. Mix thou the clays and the sands and lay them to dry between Tayif and Mecca till the time appointed.'

So, then, Azrael departed and did according to the command. But in his haste he perceived not that he had torn out from Earth clays and minerals that had lain in her at war with each other since the first; nor did he withdraw them and set them aside. And in his grief that he should have been decreed the Separator of Companions, his tears mingled with them in the mixing, so that the substance of Adam's body was made unconformable and ill-assorted, pierced with burning drops, and at issue with itself before there was (cause of) strife.

This, then, lay out to dry for forty years between Tayif and Mecca and, through all that time, the Beneficence of the Almighty leavened it and rained upon it the mercy and the blessing, and the properties necessary to the adornment of the successorship. In that period, too, it is narrated that the angels passed to and fro above it, and among them Eblis the Accursed, who smote the predestined creation while it was drying, and it rang hollow. Eblis then looked more closely and observing that of which it was composed to be diverse and ill-assorted and impregnated with bitter tears, he said: 'Doubt not I shall soon attain authority over this; and his ruin shall be easy.' (This, too, lay in the foreknowledge of The Endless.)

When time was that the chain of cause and effect should be surrendered to man's will, and the vessels of desire and intention entrusted to his intelligence, and the tent of his body illuminated by the lamp of vitality, the soul was despatched, by command of the Almighty, with the Archangel Jibrail, towards that body. But the soul being thin and subtle refused, at first, to enter the thick and diverse clays, saying: 'I have fear of that (which is) to be.'

This it cried twice, till it received the word: 'Enter unwillingly, and unwillingly depart.' Then only it entered.

And when that agony was accomplished, the word came: 'My compassion exceedeth My wrath.' It is narrated that these were the first words of which our pure Forefather had cognisance.

Afterwards, by the operation of the determinate will, there arose in Adam a desire for a companion, and an intimate and a friend in the Garden of the Tree. It is narrated that he first took counsel of Earth (which had furnished) his body. Earth said: 'Forbear. Is it not enough that one should have dominion over me?'

Adam answered: 'There is but one who is One in earth or Heaven. All paired things point to the Unity, and my soul, which came not from thee, desires unutterably.'

Earth said: 'Be content in innocence, and let thy body, which I gave unwillingly, return thus to (me) thy mother.'

Adam said: 'I am motherless. What should I know?'

At that time came Eblis the Accursed who had long prepared an evil stratagem and a hateful device against our pure Forefather, being desirous of his damnation, and anxious to multiply causes and occasions thereto. He addressed first his detestable words to the peacock among the birds of the Garden, saying: 'I have great amity towards thee because of thy beauty; but, through no fault of mine, I am forbidden the Garden. Hide me, then, among thy tail-feathers that I may enter it, and worship both thee and our Lord Adam, who is master of thee.'

The peacock said: 'Not by any contrivance of mine shaft thou enter, lest a judgment fall on my beauty and my excellence. But there is in the Garden a Serpent of loathsome aspect who shall make thy path easy.' He then despatched the serpent to the gate and after conversation and by contrivance and a malign artifice, Eblis hid himself under the tongue of the serpent, and was thus conveyed past the barrier. He then worshipped Adam and ceased not to counsel him to demand a companion and an intimate that the delights might be increased, and the succession assured to the regency of earth. For he foresaw that, among multitudes, many should come to him. Adam therefore made daily supplication for that blessing.

It was answered him: 'How knowest thou if the gratification of thy desire be a blessing or a curse?'

Adam said: 'By no means; but I will abide the chance.'

Then the somnolence fell upon him, as is narrated; and upon waking he beheld our Lady Eve (upon whom be the Mercy and the Forgiveness).

Adam said: 'O my lady and light of my universe, who art thou?'

Eve said: 'O my lord and summit of my contentment, who art thou?'

Adam said: 'Of a surety I am thine.'

Eve said: 'Of a surety I am throe.'

Thus they ceased to inquire further into the matter, but were united, and became one flesh and one soul, and their felicity was beyond comparison or belief or imagination or apprehension.

Thereafter, it is narrated that Eblis the Stoned consorted with them secretly in the Garden, and the peacock with him; and they jested and made mirth for our Lord Adam and his Lady Eve and propounded riddles and devised occasions for the stringing of the ornaments and the threading of subtleties. And upon a time when their felicity was at its height, and their happiness excessive, and their contentment expanded to the uttermost, Eblis said: 'O my master and my mistress, declare to us, if it pleases, some comparison or similitude that lies beyond the limits of possibility.'

Adam said: 'This is easy. That the sun should cease in Heaven or that the rivers should dry in the Garden is beyond the limits of possibility.'

And they laughed and agreed, and the peacock said: 'O our lady, tell us now something of a jest as unconceivable and as beyond belief as this saying of thy Lord.'

Our Lady Eve then said: 'That my lord should look upon me otherwise than is his custom is beyond this saying.' And when they had laughed abundantly, she said: 'O our servitors, tell us now something that is further from possibility or belief than my saying.'

Then the peacock said: 'O our Lady Eve, except that thou shouldst look upon thy lord otherwise than is thy custom, there is nothing further than thy saying from possibility or belief or imagination.'

Then said Eblis: 'Except that the one of you should be made an enemy to the other, there is nothing, O my lady, further than thy saying from possibility, or belief, or imagination, or apprehension.' And they laughed immoderately all four together in the Garden.

But when the peacock had gone and Eblis had seemed to depart, our Lady Eve said to Adam 'My lord and disposer of my soul, by what means did Eblis know our fear?'

Adam said: 'O my Lady, what fear?'

Eve said: 'The fear which was in our hearts from the first, that the one of us might be made an enemy to the other.'

Then our pure forefather bowed his head on her bosom and said: 'O Companion of my heart, this has been my fear also from the first, but how didst thou know?'

Eve said: 'Because I am thy flesh and thy soul. What shall we do?'

Thus, then, they came at moonrise to the tree that had been forbidden to them, and Eblis lay asleep under it. But he waked merrily and said 'O my master and my mistress, this is the Tree of Eternity. By eating her fruit, felicity is established for ever among mankind; nor after eating it shall there be any change whatever in the disposition of the hearts of the eaters.'

Eve then put out her hand to the fruit, but Adam said: 'It is forbidden. Let us go.'

Eve said: 'O my lord and my sustainer, upon my head be it, and upon the heads of my daughters after me. I will first taste of this tree, and if misfortune fall on me, do thou intercede for me; or else eat likewise, so that eternal bliss may come to us together.'

Thus she ate, and he after her; and at once the ornaments of paradise disappeared from round them, and they were delivered to shame and nudity and abjection. Then, as is narrated, Adam accused Eve in the presence; but our Lady Eve (upon whom be the pity and the recompense) accepted (the blame of) all that had been done.

When the serpent and the peacock had each received their portion for their evil contrivances (for the punishment of Eblis was reserved) the Divine Decree of Expulsion was laid upon Adam and Eve in these words: 'Get ye down, the one of you an enemy to the other.'

Adam said: 'But I have heard that thy compassion exceeds thy wrath.'

It was answered: 'I have spoken. The decree shall stand in the place of all curses.' So they went down, and the barriers of the Garden of the tree were made fast behind them.

It is further recorded by the stringers of the pearls of words and the narrators of old, that when our pure forefather the Lord Adam and his adorable consort Eve (upon whom be the glory and the sacrifice) were thus expelled, there was lamentation among the beasts in the Garden whom Adam had cherished and whom our Lady Eve had comforted. Of those unaffected there remained only the mole, whose custom it was to burrow in earth and to avoid the light of the sun. His nature was malignant and his body inconspicuous, but, by the Power of the Omnipotent, whose name be exalted, he was then adorned with eyes far-seeing both in the light and the darkness.

When the mole heard the Divine Command of Expulsion, it entered his impure mind that he would extract profit and advancement from a secret observation and a hidden espial. So he followed our forefather and his august consort, under the earth, and watched those two in their affliction and their abjection and their misery, and the Garden was without his presence for that time.

When his watch was complete and his observation certain, he turned him swiftly underneath the earth and came back saying to the guardians of the gate: 'Make room! I have a sure and a terrible report.' So his passage was permitted, and he lay till evening in the Garden. Then he said: 'Can the accursed by any means escape the decree?'

It was answered: 'By no means can they escape or avoid.'

Then the mole said 'But I have seen that they have escaped.'

It was answered:

'Declare thy observation.'

The mole said: 'The enemies to each other have altogether departed from Thy worship and Thy adoration. Nor are they in any sort enemies to each other, for they enjoy together the most perfect felicity, and moreover they have made them a new God.'

It was answered: 'Declare the shape of the God.'

The mole said: 'Their God is of small stature, pinkish in colour, unclothed, fat and smiling. They lay it upon the grass and, filling its hands with flowers, worship it and desire no greater comfort.'

It was answered: 'Declare the name of the God.'

The mole said: 'Its name is Quabil (Cain), and I testify upon a sure observation that it is their God and their uniter and their comforter.'

It was answered: 'Why hast thou come to us?'

The mole said: 'Through my zeal and my diligence; for honour and in hope of reward.'

It was answered: 'Is this, then, the best that thou canst do with the eyes which We gave thee?'

The mole said: 'To the extreme of my ability!'

It was answered: 'There is no need. Thou hast not added to their burden, but to thine own. Be darkened henceforward, upon earth and under earth. It is not good to spy upon any creature of God to whom alleviation is permitted.'

So, then, the mole's eyes were darkened and contracted, and

his lot was made miserable upon and under the earth to this day.

But to those two, Adam and Eve, the alleviation was permitted, till Habil and Quabil and their sisters Labuda and Aqlemia had attained the age of maturity. Then there came to the greatest substitute and his consort, from out of Kabul the Stony, that peacock, by whose contrivance Eblis the Accursed had first obtained admission into the Garden of the tree. And they made him welcome in all their ways and into all their imaginings; and he sustained them with false words and flagitious counsels, so that they considered and remembered their forfeited delights in the Garden both arrogantly and impenitently.

Then came the word to the Archangel Jibrail the Faithful, saying: 'Follow those two with diligence, and interpose the shield of thy benevolence where it shall be necessary; for though We have surrendered them for awhile (to Eblis) they shall not achieve an irremediable destruction.'

Jibrail therefore followed our first substitute and the Lady Eve—upon whom is the grace and a forgetfulness—and kept watch upon them in all the lands appointed for their passage through the world. Nor did he hear any lamentations in their mouths for their sins. It is recorded that for an hundred years they were continuously upheld by the Peacock under the detestable power of Eblis the Stoned, who by means of magic multiplied the similitudes of meat and drink and rich raiment about them for their pleasure, and came daily to worship them as Gods. (This also lay in the predestined will of the inscrutable.) Further, in that age, their eyes were darkened and their minds were made turbid, and the faculty of laughter was removed from them. The Excellent Archangel Jibrail, when he perceived by observation that they had ceased to laugh, returned and bowed himself among the servitors and cried: 'The last evil has fallen upon Thy creatures whom I guard! They have ceased to laugh and are made even with the ox and the camel.'

It was answered: 'This also was foreseen. Keep watch.'

After yet another hundred years Eblis, whose doom is assured, came to worship Adam as was his custom and said: 'O my Lord and my Advancer and my Preceptor in Good and Evil, whom hast thou ever beheld in all thy world, wiser and more excellent than thyself?'

Adam said: 'I have never seen such an one.'

Eblis asked: 'Hast thou ever conceived of such an one?'

Adam answered: 'Except in dreams I have never conceived of such an one.'

Eblis then answered: 'Disregard dreams. They proceed from superfluity of meat. Stretch out thy hand upon the world which thou hast made and take possession.'

So Adam took possession of the mountains which he had levelled and of the rivers which he had diverted and of the upper and lower fires which he had made to speak and to work for him, and he named them as possessions for himself and his children for ever. After this, Eblis asked: 'O, my Upholder and Crown of my Belief, who has given thee these profitable things?'

Adam said: 'By my hand and my head, I alone have given myself these things.'

Eblis said: 'Praise we the giver!'

So, then, Adam praised himself in a loud voice, and built an altar and a mirror behind the altar; and he ceased not to adore himself in the mirror, and to extol himself daily before the altar, by the name and under the attributes of the Almighty.

The historians assert that on such occasions it was the custom of the peacock to expand his tail and stand beside our first substitute and to minister to him with flatteries and adorations.

After yet another hundred years, the Omnipotent, Whose Name be exalted, put a bitter remorse into the bosom of the peacock, and that bird closed his tail and wept upon the mountains of Serendib. Then said the Excellent and Faithful Archangel Jibrail: 'How has the vengeance overtaken thee, O thou least desirable of fowl?'

The peacock said: 'Though I myself would by no means consent to convey Eblis into the Garden of the Tree, yet as is known to thee and to the All-Seeing, I referred him to the serpent for a subtle device, by whose malice and beneath whose tongue did Eblis secretly enter that Garden. Wherefore did *Allah* change my attuned voice to a harsh cry and my beauteous legs to unseemly legs, and hurled me into the district of Kabul the Stony. Now I fear that He will also deprive me of my tail, which is the ornament of my days and the delight of my eye. For that cause and in that fear I am penitent, O Servant of God.'

Jibrail then said: 'Penitence lies not in confession, but in restitution and visible amendment.'

The peacock said: 'Enlighten me in that path and prove my sincerity.'

Jibrail said: 'I am troubled on account of Adam who, through the impure magic of Eblis, has departed from humility, and worships himself daily at an altar and before a mirror, in such and such a manner.'

The peacock said: 'O Courier of the Thrones, hast thou taken counsel of the Lady Eve?'

Jibrail asked: 'For what reason?'

The peacock said: 'For the reason that when the Decree of Expulsion was issued against those two, it was said: "Get ye down, the one of you an enemy unto the other," and this is a sure word.'

Jibrail answered: 'What will that profit?'

The peacock said: 'Let us exchange our shapes for a time and I will show thee that profit.'

Jibrail then exacted an oath from the peacock that he would return him his shape at the expiration of a certain time without dishonour or fraud, and the exchange was effected, and Jibrail retired himself into the shape of the peacock, and the peacock lifted himself into the illustrious similitude of Jibrail and came to our Lady Eve and said: 'Who is God?'

The Lady Eve answered him: 'His name is Adam.'

The peacock said: 'How is he God?'

The Lady Eve answered: 'For that he knows both good and evil.'

The peacock asked: 'By what means attained he to that

knowledge?'

The Lady Eve answered: 'Of a truth it was I who brought it to him between my hands from off a tree in the Garden.'

The peacock said: 'The greater then thy modesty and thy meekness, O my Lady Eve,' and he removed himself from her presence, and came again to Jibrail a little before the time of the evening prayer. He said to that excellent and trusty one: 'Continue, I pray, to serve in my shape at the time of the worship at the altar.'

So Jibrail consented and preened himself and spread his tail and pecked between his claws, after the manner of created peacocks, before the altar until the entrance of our pure forefather and his august consort.

Then he perceived by observation that when Adam kneeled at the mirror to adore himself the Lady Eve abode unwillingly, and in time she asked: 'Have I then no part in this worship?'

Adam answered: 'A great and a redoubtable part hast thou, O my Lady, which is to praise and worship me constantly.'

The Lady Eve said: 'But I weary of this worship. Except thou build me an altar and make a mirror to me also I will in no wise be present at this worship, nor in thy bed.' And she withdrew her presence.

Adam then said to Jibrail whom he esteemed to be the peacock: 'What shall we do? If I build not an altar, the woman who walks by my side will be a reproach to me by day and a penance by night, and peace will depart from the earth.'

Jibrail answered, in the voice of the peacock: 'For the sake of peace on earth build her also an altar.' So they built an altar with a mirror in all respects conformable to the Altar which Adam had made, and Adam made proclamation from the ends of the earth to the ends of the earth that there were now two Gods upon earth—the one man, and the other woman.

Then came the peacock in the likeness of Jibrail to the Lady Eve and said: 'O Lady of Light, why is thy altar upon the left hand and the altar of my Lord upon the right?'

The Lady Eve said: 'It is a remediable error,' and she remedied it with her own hands, and our pure forefather fell into a great anger.

Then entered Jibrail in the likeness of the peacock and said to Adam: 'O my lord and very interpreter, what has vexed thee?'

Adam said: 'What shall we do? The woman who sleeps in my bosom has changed the honourable places of the altars, and if I suffer not the change she will weary me by night and day, and there will be no refreshment upon earth.'

Jibrail said, speaking in the voice of the peacock: 'For the sake of refreshment suffer the change.' So they worshipped at the changed altars, the altar to the woman upon the right, and to the man upon the left.

Then came the peacock, in the similitude of Jibrail the Trusty One, to our Lady Eve and said: 'O Incomparable and All–Creating, art thou by chance the mother of Quabil and Habil (Cain and Abel)?'

The Lady Eve answered: 'By no chance but by the immutable ordinance of nature am I their mother.'

The peacock said, in the voice of Jibrail: 'Will they become such as Adam?'

The Lady Eve answered: 'Of a surety, and many more also.'

The peacock, as Jibrail, said: 'O Lady of Abundance, enlighten me now which is the greater, the mother or the child?'

The Lady Eve answered: 'Of a surety, the mother.'

The disguised peacock then said: 'O my Lady, seeing that from thee alone proceed all the generations of man who calls himself God, what need of any altar to man?'

The Lady Eve answered: 'It is an error. Doubt not it shall be rectified,' and at the time of the worship she smote down the left-hand altar.

Adam said: 'Why is this, O my lady and my co-equal?'

The Lady Eve answered: 'Because it has been revealed that in me is all excellence and increase, splendour, terror, and power. Bow down and worship.'

Adam answered: 'O my lady, but thou art Eve my mate and no sort of goddess whatever. This have I known from the beginning. Only for peace' sake I suffered thee to build an altar to thyself.'

The Lady Eve answered: 'O my Lord, but thou art Adam my mate, and by many universes removed from any sort of God-head, and this have I known from the first. Nor for the sake of any peace whatever will I cease to proclaim it.' She then pro-claimed it aloud, and they reproached each other and disputed and betrayed their thoughts and their inmost knowledges until the peacock lifted himself in haste from their presence and came to Jibrail and said: 'Let us return each to his own shape; for en-lightenment is at hand.'

So restitution was made without fraud or dishonour and they returned to the temple each in his proper shape with his at-tributes, and listened to the end of that conversation between the first substitute and his august consort who ceased not to reprehend each other upon all matters within their observation and their experience and their imagination.

When the steeds of recrimination had ceased to career across the plains of memory, and when the drum of evidence was no longer beaten by the drumstick of malevolence, and the bird of argument had taken refuge in the rocks of silence, the Excellent and Trustworthy Archangel Jibrail bowed himself before our pure forefather and said: 'O my lord and fount of all power and wisdom, is it permitted to worship the visible God?'

Then by the operation of the mercy of *Allah*, the string was loosed in the throat of our first substitute and the oppression was lifted from his lungs and he laughed without cessation and said: 'By *Allah*, I am no God but the mate of this most detestable woman whom I love, and who is necessary to me beyond all the necessities.' But he ceased not to entertain Jibrail with tales of the follies and the unreasonableness of our Lady Eve till the night time.

The peacock also bowed before the Lady Eve and said: 'Is it permitted to adore the source and the excellence?' and the string was loosened in the Lady Eve's throat and she laughed aloud and merrily and said: 'By *Allah* I am no goddess in any sort, but the mate of this mere Man whom, in spite of all, I love beyond and above my soul.' But she detained the peacock with tales of the stupidity and the childishness of our pure forefather till the sun rose.

Then Adam entered, and the two looked upon each other laughing. Then said Adam: 'O my lady and crown of my torments, is it peace between us?'

And our Lady Eve answered: 'O my lord and sole cause of my unreason, it is peace till the next time and the next occasion.'

And Adam said: 'I accept, and I abide the chance.'

Our Lady Eve said: 'O man, wouldst thou have it otherwise upon any composition?'

Adam said: 'O woman, upon no composition would I have it otherwise—not even for the return to the Garden of the tree; and this I swear on thy head and the heads of all who shall proceed from thee.'

And Eve said: 'I also.' So they removed both altars and laughed and built a new one between.

Then Jibrail and the peacock departed and prostrated themselves before the throne and told what had been said.

It was answered: 'How left ye them?'

They said: 'Before one altar.'

It was answered: 'What was written upon the altar?'

They said: 'The Decree of Expulsion as it was spoken—"Get ye down, the one of you an enemy unto the other."'

And it was answered: 'Enough! It shall stand in the place of both our curse and our blessing.'

They

One view called me to another; one hill top to its fellow, half across the county, and since I could answer at no more trouble than the snapping forward of a lever, I let the country flow under my wheels. The orchid-studded flats of the East gave way to the thyme, ilex, and grey grass of the downs; these again to the rich cornland and fig-trees of the lower coast, where you carry the beat of the tide on your left hand for fifteen level miles; and when at last I turned inland through a huddle of rounded hills and woods I had run myself clean out of my known marks. Beyond that precise hamlet which stands godmother to the capital of the United States, I found hidden villages where bees, the only things awake, boomed in eighty-foot lindens that overhung grey Norman churches; miraculous brooks diving under stone bridges built for heavier traffic than would ever vex them again; tithe-barns larger than their churches, and an old smithy that cried out aloud how it had once been a hall of the Knights of the Temple. Gipsies I found on a common where the gorse, bracken, and heath fought it out together up a mile of Roman road; and a little farther on I disturbed a red fox rolling dog-fashion in the naked sunlight.

As the wooded hills closed about me I stood up in the car to take the bearings of that great down whose ringed head is a landmark for fifty miles across the low countries. I judged that the lie of the country would bring me across some westward running road that went to his feet, but I did not allow for the confusing veils of the woods. A quick turn plunged me first into a green cutting brimful of liquid sunshine, next into a gloomy tunnel where last year's dead leaves whispered and scuffled about my tyres. The strong hazel stuff meeting overhead had not been cut for a couple of generations at least, nor had any axe helped the moss-cankered oak and beech to spring above them. Here the road changed frankly into a carpeted ride on whose brown velvet spent primrose-clumps showed like jade, and a few sickly, white-stalked bluebells nodded together. As the slope favoured I shut off the power and slid over the whirled leaves, expecting every moment to meet a keeper; but I only heard a jay, far off, arguing against the silence under the twilight of the trees.

Still the track descended. I was on the point of reversing and working my way back on the second speed ere I ended in some swamp, when I saw sunshine through the tangle ahead and lifted the brake.

It was down again at once. As the light beat across my face my fore-wheels took the turf of a great still lawn from which sprang horsemen ten feet high with levelled lances, monstrous peacocks, and sleek round-headed maids of honour—blue, black, and glistening—all of clipped yew. Across the lawn—the marshalled woods besieged it on three sides—stood an ancient house of lichened and weather-worn stone, with mullioned windows and roofs of rose-red tile. It was flanked by semi-circular walls, also rose-red, that closed the lawn on the fourth side, and at their feet a box hedge grew man-high. There were doves on the roof about the slim brick chimneys, and I caught a glimpse of an octagonal dove-house behind the screening wall.

Here, then, I stayed; a horseman's green spear laid at my breast; held by the exceeding beauty of that jewel in that setting.

"If I am not packed off for a trespasser, or if this knight does not ride a wallop at me," thought I, "Shakespeare and Queen Elizabeth at least must come out of that half-open garden door and ask me to tea."

A child appeared at an upper window, and I thought the little thing waved a friendly hand. But it was to call a companion, for presently another bright head showed. Then I heard a laugh among the yew-peacocks, and turning to make sure (till then I had been watching the house only) I saw the silver of a fountain behind a hedge thrown up against the sun. The doves on the roof cooed to the cooing water; but between the two notes I caught the utterly happy chuckle of a child absorbed in some light mischief.

The garden door—heavy oak sunk deep in the thickness of the wall—opened further: a woman in a big garden hat set her foot slowly on the time-hollowed stone step and as slowly walked across the turf. I was forming some apology when she lifted up her head and I saw that she was blind.

"I heard you," she said. "Isn't that a motor car?"

"I'm afraid I've made a mistake in my road. I should have turned off up above—I never dreamed"—I began.

"But I'm very glad. Fancy a motorcar coming into the garden I It will be such a treat " She turned and made as though looking about her. "You—you haven't seen any one have you—perhaps?"

"No one to speak to, but the children seemed interested at a distance."

"Which?"

"I saw a couple up at the window just now, and I think I heard a little chap in the grounds."

"Oh, lucky you!" she cried, and her face brightened. "I hear them, of course, but that's all. You've seen them and heard them?"

"Yes," I answered. "And if I know anything of children one of them's having a beautiful time by the fountain yonder. Escaped, I should imagine."

"You're fond of children?"

I gave her one or two reasons why I did not altogether hate them.

"Of course, of course," she said. "Then you understand. Then you won't think it foolish if I ask you to take your car through the gardens, once or twice—quite slowly. I'm sure they'd like to see it. They see so little, poor things. One tries to make their

515

life pleasant, but " she threw out her hands towards the woods. "We're so out of the world here."

"That will be splendid," I said. "But I can't cut up your grass."

She faced to the right. "Wait a minute," she said. "We're at the South gate, aren't we? Behind those peacocks there's a flagged path. We call it the Peacock's Walk. You can't see it from here, they tell me, but if you squeeze along by the edge of the wood you can turn at the first peacock and get on to the flags.

It was sacrilege to wake that dreaming house-front with the clatter of machinery, but I swung the car to clear the turf, brushed along the edge of the wood and turned in on the broad stone path where the fountain-basin lay like one star-sapphire.

"May I come too?" she cried. "No, please don't help me. They'll like it better if they see me."

She felt her way lightly to the front of the car, and with one foot on the step she called: "Children, oh, children! Look and see what's going to happen!"

The voice would have drawn lost souls from the Pit, for the yearning that underlay its sweetness, and I was not surprised to hear an answering shout behind the yews. It must have been the child by the fountain, but he fled at our approach, leaving a little toy boat in the water. I saw the glint of his blue blouse among the still horsemen.

Very disposedly we paraded the length of the walk and at her request backed again. This time the child had got the better of his panic, but stood far off and doubting.

"The little fellow's watching us," I said. "I wonder if he'd like a ride."

"They're very shy still. Very shy. But, oh, lucky you to be able to see them! Let's listen."

I stopped the machine at once, and the humid stillness, heavy with the scent of box, cloaked us deep. Shears I could hear where some gardener was clipping; a mumble of bees and broken voices that might have been the doves.

"Oh, unkind!" she said wearily.

"Perhaps they're only shy of the motor. The little maid at the window looks tremendously interested."

"Yes?" She raised her head. "It was wrong of me to say that. They are really fond of me. It's the only thing that makes life worth living—when they're fond of you, isn't it? I daren't think what the place would be without them. By the way, is it beautiful?"

I think it is the most beautiful place I have ever seen."

"So they all tell me. I can feel it, of course, but that isn't quite the same thing."

"Then have you never ?" I began, but stopped abashed.

"Not since I can remember. It happened when I was only a few months old, they tell me. And yet I must remember something, else how could I dream about colours. I see light in my dreams, and colours, but I never *see* them. I only hear them just as I do when I'm awake."

"It's difficult to see faces in dreams. Some people can, but most of us haven't the gift," I went on, looking up at the window where the child stood all but hidden.

"I've heard that too," she said. "And they tell me that one never sees a dead person's face in a dream. Is that true?"

"I believe it is—now I come to think of it"

"But how is it with yourself—yourself?" The blind eyes turned towards me.

"I have never seen the faces of my dead in any dream," I answered.

"Then it must be as bad as being blind."

The sun had dipped behind the woods and the long shades were possessing the insolent horsemen one by one. I saw the light die from off the top of a glossy-leaved lance and all the brave hard green turn to soft black. The house, accepting another day at end, as it had accepted an hundred thousand gone, seemed to settle deeper into its rest among the shadows.

"Have you ever wanted to?" she said after the silence.

"Very much sometimes," I replied. The child had left the window as the shadows closed upon it.

"Ah! So've I, but I don't suppose it's allowed. . . .Where d'you live?"

"Quite the other side of the county—sixty miles and more, and I must be going back. I've come without my big lamp."

"But it's not dark yet. I can feel it."

"I'm afraid it will be by the time I get home. Could you lend me someone to set me on my road at first? I've utterly lost myself."

"I'll send Madden with you to the cross-roads. We are so out of the world, I don't wonder you were lost! I'll guide you round to the front of the house; but you will go slowly, won't you, till you're out of the grounds? It isn't foolish, do you think?"

" I promise you I'll go like this," I said, and let the car start herself down the flagged path.

We skirted the left wing of the house, whose elaborately cast lead guttering alone was worth a day's journey; passed under a great rose-grown gate in the red wall, and so round to the high front of the house which in beauty and stateliness as much excelled the back as that all others I had seen.

"Is it so very beautiful?" she said wistfully when she heard my raptures. "And you like the lead-figures too? There's the old azalea garden behind. They say that this place must have been made for children. Will you help me out, please? I should like to come with you as far as the cross-roads, but I mustn't leave them. Is that you, Madden? I want you to show this gentleman the way to the cross-roads. He has lost his way but—he has seen them."

A butler appeared noiselessly at the miracle of old oak that must be called the front door, and slipped aside to put on his hat. She stood looking at me with open blue eyes in which no sight lay, and I saw for the first time that she was beautiful.

" Remember," she said quietly, "if you are fond of them you will come again," and disappeared within the house.

The butler in the car said nothing till we were nearly at the lodge gates, where catching a glimpse of a blue blouse in a shrubbery I swerved amply lest the devil that leads little boys to play should drag me into child-murder.

"Excuse me," he asked of a sudden, "but why did you do that. Sir?"

"The child yonder."

"Our young gentleman in blue?"

"Of course."

"He runs about a good deal. Did you see him by the fountain, Sir?"

"Oh, yes, several times. Do we turn here?"

"Yes, Sir. And did you 'appen to see them upstairs too?"

"At the upper window? Yes."

"Was that before the mistress come out to speak to you. Sir?"

"A little before that. Why d'you want to know?"

He paused a little. "Only to make sure that—that they had seen the car, Sir, because with children running about, though I'm sure you're driving particularly careful, there might be an accident. That was all. Sir. Here are the cross-roads. You can't miss your way from now on. Thank you, Sir, but that isn't our custom, not with—"

"I beg your pardon," I said, and thrust away the British silver.

"Oh, it's quite right with the rest of 'em as a rule. Goodbye, Sir."

He retired into the armour-plated conning tower of his caste and walked away. Evidently a butler solicitous for the honour of his house, and interested, probably through a maid, in the nursery.

Once beyond the signposts at the cross-roads I looked back, but the crumpled hills interlaced so jealously that I could not see where the house had lain. When I asked its name at a cottage along the road, the fat woman who sold sweetmeats there gave me to understand that people with motor cars had small right to live—much less to "go about talking like carriage folk." They were not a pleasant-mannered community.

When I retraced my route on the map that evening I was little wiser. Hawkin's Old Farm appeared to be the survey title of the place, and the old *County Gazetteer*, generally so ample, did not allude to it. The big house of those parts was Hodnington Hall, Georgian with early Victorian embellishments, as an atrocious steel engraving attested. I carried my difficulty to a neighbour—a deep-rooted tree of that soil—and he gave me a name of a family which conveyed no meaning.

A month or so later—I went again, or it may have been that my car took the road of her own volition. She over-ran the fruitless downs, threaded every turn of the maze of lanes below the hills, drew through the high-walled woods, impenetrable in their full leaf, came out at the cross roads where the butler had left me, and a little further on developed an internal trouble which forced me to turn her in on a grass way-waste that cut into a summer-silent hazel wood. So far as I could make sure by the sun and a six-inch Ordnance map, this should be the road flank of that wood which I had first explored from the heights above.

I made a mighty serious business of my repairs and a glittering shop of my repair kit, spanners, pump, and the like, which I spread out orderly upon a rug. It was a trap to catch all childhood, for on such a day, I argued, the children would not be far off. When I paused in my work I listened, but the wood was so full of the noises of summer (though the birds had mated) that I could not at first distinguish these from the tread of small cautious feet stealing across the dead leaves. I rang my bell in an alluring manner, but the feet fled, and I repented, for to a child a sudden noise is very real terror. I must have been at work half an hour when I heard in the wood the voice of the blind woman crying: "Children, oh children, where are you?" and the stillness made slow to close on the perfection of that cry. She came towards me, half feeling her way between the tree boles, and though a child it seemed clung to her skirt, it swerved into the leafage like a rabbit as she drew nearer.

"Is that you?" she said, "from the other side of the county?"

"Yes, it's me from the other side of the county."

"Then why didn't you come through the upper woods? They

were there just now."

"They were here a few minutes ago. I expect they knew my car had broken down, and came to see the fun."

"Nothing serious, I hope? How do cars break down?"

"In fifty different ways. Only mine has chosen the fifty first."

She laughed merrily at the tiny joke, cooed with delicious laughter, and pushed her hat back.

"Let me hear," she said.

"Wait a moment," I cried, "and I'll get you a cushion."

She set her foot on the rug all covered with spare parts, and stooped above it eagerly. "What delightful things!" The hands through which she saw glanced in the chequered sunlight. "A box here—another box! Why you've arranged them like playing shop!"

"I confess now that I put it out to attract them. I don't need half those things really."

"How nice of you! I heard your bell in the upper wood. You say they were here before that?"

"I'm sure of it. Why are they so shy? That little fellow in blue who was with you just now ought to have got over his fright. He's been watching me like a Red Indian."

"It must have been your bell," she said. "I heard one of them go past me in trouble when I was coming down. They're shy—so shy even with me." She turned her face over her shoulder and cried again: "Children! Oh, children! Look and see!"

"They must have gone off together on their own affairs," I suggested, for there was a murmur behind us of lowered voices broken by the sudden squeaking giggles of childhood. I returned to my tinkerings and she leaned forward, her chin on her hand, listening inter-stedly.

"How many are they?" I said at last. The work was finished, but I saw no reason to go.

Her forehead puckered a little in thought. "I don't quite know," she said simply. "Sometimes more—sometimes less. They come and stay with me because I love them, you see."

"That must be very jolly," I said, replacing a drawer, and as I spoke I heard the inanity of my answer.

"You—you aren't laughing at me," she cried. " I—I haven't any of my own. I never married. People laugh at me sometimes about them because—because—"

"Because they're savages," I returned. "It's nothing to fret for. That sort laugh at everything that isn't in their own fat lives."

"I don't know. How should I? I only don't like being laughed at about *them*. It hurts; and when one can't see. . . . I don't want to seem silly," her chin quivered like a child's as she spoke, " but we blindies have only one skin, I think. Everything outside hits straight at our souls. It's different with you. You've such good defences in your eyes—looking out—before anyone can really pain you in your soul. People forget that with us."

I was silent reviewing that inexhaustible matter-the more than inherited (since it is also carefully taught) brutality of the Christian peoples, .beside which the mere heathendom of the West Coast nigger is clean and restrained. It led me a long distance into myself.

"Don't do that!" she said of a sudden, putting her hands before her eyes.

"What?"

She made a gesture with her hand.

"That! It's— it's all purple and black. Don't! That colour hurts."

"But, how in the world do you know about colours?" I exclaimed, for here was a revelation indeed.

"Colours as colours?" she asked.

"No. *Those* colours which you saw just now."

"You know as well as I do," she laughed, "else you wouldn't have asked that question. They aren't in the world at all. They're in *you*—when you went so angry."

"D'you mean a dull purplish patch, like port-wine mixed with ink?" I said.

"I've never seen ink or port-wine, but the colours aren't mixed. They are separate—all separate."

"Do you mean black streaks and jags across the purple?"

522

She nodded. "Yes—if they are like this," and zigzagged her finger again, "but it's more red than purple—that bad colour."

"And what are the colours at the top of the—whatever you see?"

Slowly she leaned forward and traced on the rug the figure of the egg itself.

"I see them so," she said, pointing with a grass stem, "white, green, yellow, red, purple, and when people are angry or bad, black across the red—as you were just now."

"Who told you anything about it—in the beginning?" I demanded.

"About the colours? No one. I used to ask what colours were when I was little—in table-covers and curtains and carpets, you see—because some colours hurt me and some made me happy. People told me; and when I got older that was how I saw people." Again she traced the outline of the egg which it is given to very few of us to see.

"All by yourself?" I repeated.

"All by myself. There wasn't anyone else. I only found out afterwards that other people did not see the colours."

She leaned against the tree-bole plaiting and unplaiting chance-plucked grass stems. The children in the wood had drawn nearer. I could see them with the tail of my eye frolicking like squirrels.

"Now I am sure you will never laugh at me," she went on after a long silence. "Nor at *them*."

" Goodness! No!" I cried, jolted out of my train of thought. "A man who laughs at a child—unless the child is laughing too—is a heathen."

"I didn't mean that of course. You'd never laugh *at* children, but I thought—I used to think—that perhaps you might laugh about *them*. So now I beg your pardon. . . . What are you going to laugh at?"

I had made no sound, but she knew.

"At the notion of your begging my pardon. If you had done your duty as a pillar of the state and a landed proprietress you ought to have summoned me for trespass when I barged through your woods the other day. It was disgraceful of me—inexcusable."

She looked at me, her head against the tree trunk—long and steadfastly—this woman who could see the naked soul.

"How curious," she half whispered. "How very curious."

"Why, what have I done?"

"You don't understand . . . and yet you understood about the colours. Don't you understand?"

She spoke with a passion that nothing had justified, and I faced her bewilderedly as she rose. The children had gathered themselves in a roundel behind a bramble bush. One sleek head bent over something smaller, and the set of the little shoulders told me that fingers were on lips. They, too, had some child's tremendous secret. I alone was hopelessly astray there in the broad sunlight.

"No," I said, and shook my head as though the dead eyes could note. "Whatever it is, I don't understand yet. Perhaps I shall later—if you'll let me come again."

"You will come again," she answered. "You will surely come again and walk in the wood."

"Perhaps the children will know me well enough by that time to let me play with them—as a favour. You know what children are like."

"It isn't a matter of favour but of right," she replied, and while I wondered what she meant, a dishevelled woman plunged round the bend of the road, loose-haired, purple, almost lowing with agony as she ran. It was my rude, fat friend of the sweetmeat shop. The blind woman heard and stepped forward. "What is it, Mrs. Madehurst?" she asked.

The woman flung her apron over her head and literally grovelled in the dust, crying that her grandchild was sick to death, that the local doctor was away fishing, that Jenny, the mother was at her wits end, and so forth, with repetitions and bellowings.

Where's the next nearest doctor?" I asked between paroxysms.

"Madden will tell you. Go round to the house and take him with you. I'll attend to this. Be quick!" She half-supported the fat woman into the shade. In two minutes I was blowing all the horns of Jericho under the front of the House Beautiful, and Madden, in the pantry, rose to the crisis like a butler and a man.

A quarter of an hour at illegal speeds caught us a doctor five miles away. Within the half-hour we had decanted him, much interested in motors, at the door of the sweetmeat shop, and drew up the road to await the verdict.

"Useful things cars," said Madden, all man and no butler. "If I'd had one when mine took sick she wouldn't have died."

"How was it?" I asked.

"Croup. Mrs. Madden was away. No one knew what to do. I drove eight miles in a tax cart for the doctor. She was choked when we came back. The car'd ha' saved her. She'd have been close on ten now."

"I'm sorry," I said. "I thought you were rather fond of children from what you told me going to the cross-roads the other day."

" Have you seen 'em again. Sir—this mornin'?"

"Yes, but they're well broke to cars. I couldn't get any of them within twenty yards of it."

He looked at me carefully as a scout considers a stranger— not as a menial should lift his eyes to his divinely appointed superior.

"I wonder why," he said just above the breath that he drew.

We waited on. A light wind from the sea wandered up and down the long lines of the woods, and the wayside grasses, whitened already with summer dust, rose and bowed in sallow waves.

A woman, wiping the suds off her arms, came out of the cottage next the sweetmeat shop.

"I've be'n listenin' in de backyard," she said cheerily. He says Arthur's unaccountable bad. Did ye hear him shruck just now? Unaccountable bad. I reckon t'will come Jenny's turn to walk in

525

de wood nex' week along, Mr. Madden."

"Excuse me, Sir, but your lap-robe is slipping," said Madden deferentially. The woman started, dropped a curtsey, and hurried away.

"What does she mean by 'walking in the wood'?" I asked.

"It must be some saying they use hereabouts. I'm from Norfolk myself," said Madden. "They're an independent lot in this county. She took you for a chauffeur. Sir."

I saw the doctor come out of the cottage followed by a draggle-tailed wench who clung to his arm as though he could make treaty for her with death. "Dat sort," she wailed—"dey're just as much to us dat has 'em as if dey was lawful born. Just as much— just as much I an' Grod he'd be just as pleased if you saved 'un doctor. Don't take it from me. Miss Florence will tell ye de very same. Don't leave 'im, doctor!"

" I know. I know," said the man, " but he'll be quiet for a while now. We'll get the nurse and the medicine as fast as we can." He signalled me to come forward with the car, and I strove not to be privy to what followed; but I saw the girl's face, blotched and frozen grief, and I felt the hand without a ring clutching at my knees when we moved away.

The doctor was a man of some humour, for I remember he claimed my car under the Oath of Æsculapius, and used it and me without mercy. First we convoyed Mrs. Madehurst and the blind woman to wait by the sick bed till the nurse should come. Next we invaded a neat county town for prescriptions (the doctor said the trouble was cerebro-spinal meningitis), and when the County Institute, banked and flanked with scared maricet cattle, reported itself out of nurses for the moment we literally flung ourselves loose upon the county. We conferred with the owners of great houses—magnates at the ends of overarching avenues whose big-boned womenfolk strode away from their tea-tables to listen to the imperious doctor.

At last a white-haired lady sitting under a cedar of Lebanon and surrounded by a court of magnificent Borzois—all hostile to motors—gave the doctor, who received them as from a princess, written orders which we bore many miles at top speed, through a park, to a French nunnery, where we took over in exchange a pallid-faced and trembling sister. She knelt at the bottom of the tonneau telling her beads without pause till, by short cuts of the doctor's invention, we had her to the sweetmeat shop once more. It was a long afternoon crowded with mad episodes that rose and dissolved like the dust of our wheels; cross-sections of remote and incomprehensible lives through which we raced at right angles; and I went home in the dusk, wearied out, to dream of the clashing horns of cattle; round-eyed nuns walking in a garden of graves; pleasant tea-parties beneath shaded trees; the carbolic-scented, grey-painted corridors of the County Institute; the steps of shy children in the wood, and the hands that clung to my knees as the motor began to move.

★★★★★★

I had intended to return in a day or two, but it pleased Fate to hold me from that side of the county, on many pretexts, till the elder and the wild rose had fruited. There came at last a brilliant day, swept clear from the south-west, that brought the hills within hand's reach—a day of unstable airs and high filmy clouds. Through no merit of my own I was free, and set the car for the third time on that known road. As I reached the crest of the downs I felt the soft air change, saw it glaze under the sun; and, looking down at the sea, in that instant beheld the blue of the Channel turn through polished silver and dulled steel to dingy pewter. A laden collier hugging the coast steered outward for deeper water and, across copper-coloured haze, I saw sails rise one by one on the anchored fishing-fleet.

In a deep dene behind me an eddy of sudden wind drummed through sheltered oaks, and spun aloft the first day sample of autumn leaves. When I reached the beach road the sea-fog fumed over the brickfields, and the tide was telling all the groins of the gale beyond Ushant. In less than an hour summer England vanished in chill grey. We were again the shut island of the North, all the ships of the world bellowing at our perilous gates; and between their outcries ran the piping of bewildered gulls. My cap dripped moisture, the folds of the rug held it in pools or sluiced it away in runnels, and the salt-rime stuck to my lips.

Inland the smell of autumn loaded the thickened fog among the trees, and the drip became a continuous shower. Yet the late flowers—mallow of the wayside, scabious of the field, and dahlia of the garden—showed gay in the mist, and beyond the sea's breath there was little sign of decay in the leaf. Yet in the villages the house doors were all open, and bare-legged, bare-headed children sat at ease on the damp doorsteps to shout " pip-pip" at the stranger.

I made bold to call at the sweetmeat shop, where Mrs. Madehurst met me with a fat woman's hospitable tears. Jenny's child, she said, had died two days after the nun had come. It was, she felt, best out of the way, even though insurance offices, for reasons which she did not pretend to follow, would not willingly insure such stray lives. "Not but what Jenny didn't tend to Arthur as though he'd come all proper at de end of de first year—like Jenny herself." Thanks to Miss Florence, the child had been buried with a pomp which, in Mrs. Madehurst's opinion, more than covered the small irregularity of its birth. She described the coffin, within and without, the glass hearse, and the evergreen lining of the grave.

But how's the mother?" I asked. Jenny? Oh, she'll get over it. I've felt dat way with one or two o' my own. She'll get over. She's walkin' in de wood now."

"In this weather?"

Mrs. Madehurst looked at me with narrowed eyes across the counter.

"I dunno but it opens de 'eart like. Yes, it opens de 'eart. Dat's where losin' and bearin' comes so alike in de long run, we do say."

Now the wisdom of the old wives is greater than that of all the Fathers, and this last oracle sent me thinking so extendedly as I went up the road, that I nearly ran over a woman and a child at the wooded comer by the lodge gates of the House Beautiful.

"Awful weather!" I cried, as I slowed dead for the turn.

"Not so bad," she answered placidly out of the fog. "Mine's used to 'un. You'll find yours indoors, I reckon."

Indoors, Madden received me with professional courtesy, and kind inquiries for the health of the motor, which he would put under cover.

I waited in a still, nut-brown hall, pleasant with late flowers and warmed with a delicious wood fire—a place of good influence and great peace. (Men and women may sometimes, after great effort, achieve a creditable lie; but the house, which is their temple, cannot say anything save the truth of those who have lived in it.) A child's cart and a doll lay on the black-and-white floor, where a rug had been kicked back. I felt that the children had only just hurried away—to hide themselves, most like—in the many turns of the great adzed staircase that climbed statelily out of the hall, or to crouch at gaze behind the lions and roses of the carven gallery above. Then I heard her voice above me, singing as the blind sing—from the soul:—

In the pleasant orchard-closes.

And all my early summer came back at the call.

In the pleasant orchard-closes,
God bless all our gains say we—
But may God bless all our losses,
Better suits with our degree.

She dropped the marring fifth line, and repeated—

Better suits with our degree!

I saw her lean over the gallery, her linked hands white as pearl against the oak.

"Is that you—from the other side of the county?" she called.

"Yes, me—from the other side of the county," I answered laughing.

"What a long time before you had to come here again." She ran down the stairs, one hand lightly touching the broad rail. "It's two months and four days. Summer's gone!"

"I meant to come before, but Fate prevented."

"I knew it. Please do something to that fire. They won't let me play with it, but I can feel it's behaving badly. Hit it!"

I looked on either side of the deep fireplace, and found but a half-charred hedge-stake with which I punched a black log into flame.

" It never goes out, day or night," she said, as though explaining. "In case anyone comes in with cold toes, you see."

"It's even lovelier inside than it was out," I murmured. The red light poured itself along the age-polished dusky panels till the Tudor roses and lions of the gallery took colour and motion. An old eagle-topped convex mirror gathered the picture into its mysterious heart, distorting afresh the distorted shadows, and curving the gallery lines into the curves of a ship. The day was shutting down in half a gale as the fog turned to stringy scud. Through the uncurtained mullions of the broad window I could see valiant horsemen of the lawn rear and recover against the wind that taunted them with legions of dead leaves.

"Yes, it must be beautiful," she said. "Would you like to go over it? There's still light enough upstairs."

I followed her up the unflinching, wagon-wide staircase to the gallery whence opened the thin fluted Elizabethan doors.

"Feel how they put the latch low down for the sake of the children." She swung a light door inward.

"By the way, where are they?" I asked. "I haven't even heard them today."

She did not answer at once. Then, " I can only hear them," she replied softly. "This is one of their rooms—everything ready, you see."

She pointed into a heavily-timbered room. There were little low gate tables and children's chairs. A doll's house, its hooked front half open, faced a great dimpled rocking-horse, from whose padded saddle it was but a child's scramble to the broad window-seat overlooking the lawn. A toy gun lay in a corner beside a gilt wooden cannon.

"Surely they've only just gone," I whispered. In the failing light a door creaked cautiously. I heard the rustle of a frock and the patter of feet—quick feet through a room beyond.

"I heard that," she cried triumphantly. "Did you? Children, O children, where are you?"

The voice filled the walls that held it lovingly to the last perfect note, but there came no answering shout such as I had heard in the garden. We hurried on from room to oak-floored room; up a step here, down three steps there; among a maze of passages; always mocked by our quarry. One might as well have tried to work an unstopped warren with a single ferret. There were bolt-holes innumerable—recesses in walls, embrasures of deep slitten windows now darkened, whence they could start up behind us; and abandoned fireplaces, six feet deep in the masonry, as well as the tangle of communicating doors.

Above all, they had the twilight for their helper in our game. I had caught one or two joyous chuckles of evasion, and once or twice had seen the silhouette of a child's frock against some darkening window at the end of a passage; but we returned empty-handed to the gallery, just as a middle-aged woman was setting a lamp in its niche.

"No, I haven't seen her either this evening, Miss Florence," I heard her say, "but that Turpin he says he wants to see you about his shed."

"Oh, Mr. Turpin must want to see me very badly. Tell him to come to the hall, Mrs. Madden."

I looked down into the hall whose only light was the dulled fire, and deep in the shadow I saw them at last. They must have slipped down while we were in the passages, and now thought themselves perfectly hidden behind an old gilt leather screen. By child's law, my fruitless chase was as good as an introduction, but since I had taken so much trouble I resolved to force them to come forward later by the simple trick, which children detest, of pretending not to notice them. They lay close, in a little huddle, no more than shadows except when a quick flame betrayed an outline.

"And now we'll have some tea," she said. " I believe I ought to have offered it you at first, but one doesn't arrive at manners somehow when one lives alone and is considered—h'm—peculiar." Then with very pretty scorn, "would you like a lamp to see to eat by?"

"The firelight's much pleasanter, I think." We descended into that delicious gloom and Madden brought tea.

I took my chair in the direction of the screen ready to surprise or be surprised as the game should go, and at her permission, since a hearth is always sacred, bent forward to play with the fire.

"Where do you get these beautiful short faggots from?" I asked idly. "Why, they are tallies!"

"Of course," she said. "As I can't read or write I'm driven back on the early English tally for my accounts. Give me one and I'll tell you what it meant."

I passed her an unburned hazel-tally, about a foot long, and she ran her thumb down the nicks.

"This is the milk-record for the home farm for the month of April last year, in gallons," said she. "I don't know what I should have done without tallies. An old forester of mine taught me the system. It's out of date now for everyone else; but my tenants respect it. One of them's coming now to see me. Oh, it doesn't matter. He has no business here out of office hours. He's a greedy, ignorant man—very greedy or—he wouldn't come here after dark."

"Have you much land then?"

" Only a couple of hundred acres in hand, thank goodness. The other six hundred are nearly all let to folk who knew my folk before me, but this Turpin is quite a new man—and a highway robber."

"But are you sure I sha'n't be ?"

" Certainly not. You have the right. He hasn't any children."

"Ah, the children!" I said, and slid my low chair back till it nearly touched the screen that hid them. "I wonder whether they'll come out for me."

There was a murmur of voices—Madden's and a deeper

note—at the low, dark side door, and a ginger-headed, canvas-gaitered giant of the unmistakable tenant farmer type stumbled or was pushed in.

"Come to the fire, Mr. Turpin," she said.

"If—if you please. Miss, I'll—I'll be quite as well by the door." He clung to the latch as he spoke like a frightened child. Of a sudden I realised that he was in the grip of some. almost overpowering fear.

"Well?"

"About that new shed for the young stock—that was all. These first autumn storms settin' in . . . but I'll come again, Miss." His teeth did not chatter much more than the door latch.

"I think not," she answered levelly. "The new shed—m'm. What did my agent write you on the 15th?"

"I—fancied p'raps that if I came to see you—ma—man to man like. Miss. But—"

His eyes rolled into every corner of the room wide with horror. He half opened the door through which he had entered, but I noticed it shut again—from without and firmly.

"He wrote what I told him," she went on. "You are overstocked already. Dunnett's Farm never carried more than fifty bullocks—even in Mr. Wright's time. And he used cake. You've sixty-seven and you don't cake. You've broken the lease in that respect. You're dragging the heart out of the farm."

"I'm—I'm getting some minerals—superphosphates—next week. I've as good as ordered a truck-load already. I'll go down to the station tomorrow about 'em. Then I can come and see you man to man like, Miss, in the daylight. . . . That gentleman's not going away, is he?" He almost shrieked.

I had only slid the chair a little further back, reaching behind me to tap on the leather of the screen, but he jumped like a rat.

"No. Please attend to me, Mr. Turpin." She turned in her chair and faced him with his back to the door. It was an old and sordid little piece of scheming that she forced from him—his plea for the new cowshed at his landlady's expense, that he might with the covered manure pay his next year's rent out of the valuation after, as she made clear, he had bled the enriched pastures to the bone. I could not but admire the intensity of his greed, when I saw him out-facing for its sake whatever terror it was that ran wet on his forehead.

I ceased to tap the leather—was, indeed, calculating the cost of the shed—when I felt my relaxed hand taken and turned softly between the soft hands of a child. So at last I had triumphed. In a moment I would turn and acquaint myself with those quick-footed wanderers. . . .

The little brushing kiss fell in the centre of my palm—as a gift on which the fingers were, once, expected to close: as the all faithful half-reproachful signal of a waiting child not used to neglect even when grown-ups were busiest—a fragment of the mute code devised very long ago.

Then I knew. And it was as though I had known from the first day when I looked across the lawn at the high window.

I heard the door shut. The woman turned to me in silence, and I felt that she knew.

What time passed after this I cannot say. I was roused by the fall of a log, and mechanically rose to put it back. Then I returned to my place in the chair very close to the screen.

"Now you understand," she whispered, across the packed shadows.

"Yes, I understand—now. Thank you."

"I—I only hear them." She bowed her head in her hands. "I have no right, you know—no other right. I have neither borne nor lost—neither borne nor lost!"

"Be very glad then," said I, for my soul was torn open within me.

"Forgive me!"

She was still, and I went back to my sorrow and my joy.

"It was because I loved them so," she said at last, brokenly. "*That* was why it was, even from the first—even before I knew that they—they were all I should ever have. And I loved them so!"

She stretched out her arms to the shadows and the shadows

within the shadow.

"They came because I loved them—because I needed them. I—I must have made them come. Was that wrong, think you?"

"No— no."

"I—I grant you that the toys and—and all that sort of thing were nonsense, but—but I used to so hate empty rooms myself when I was little." She pointed to the gallery. "And the passages all empty. . . . And how could I ever bear the garden door shut? Suppose—"

"Don't! For pity's sake, don't!" I cried. The twilight had brought a cold rain with gusty squalls that plucked at the leaded windows.

"And the same thing with keeping the fire in all night. I don't think it so foolish— do you?"

I looked at the broad brick hearth, saw, through tears I believe, that there was no unpassable iron on or near it, and bowed my head.

"I did all that and lots of other things—just to make believe. Then they came. I heard them, but I didn't know that they were not mine by right till Mrs. Madden told me—"

"The butler's wife? What?"

"One of them—I heard—she saw. And knew. Hers! *Not* for me. I didn't know at first. Perhaps I was jealous. Afterwards, I began to understand that it was only because I loved them, not because . . . Oh, you *must* bear or lose," she said piteously. "There is no other way—and yet they love me. They mustl Don't they?"

There was no sound in the room except the lapping voices of the fire, but we two listened intently, and she at least took comfort from what she heard. She recovered herself and half rose. I sat still in my chair by the screen.

"Don't think me a wretch to whine about myself like this, but—but I'm all in the dark, you know, and you can see."

In truth I could see, and my vision confirmed me in my resolve, though that was like the very parting of spirit and flesh. Yet a little longer I would stay since it was the last time.

"You think it is wrong, then?" she cried sharply, though I had

535

said nothing.

"Not for you. A thousand times no. For you it is right. . . . I am grateful to you beyond words. For me it would be wrong. For me only. . . . "

"Why?" she said, but passed her hand before her face as she had done at our second meeting in the wood. "Oh, I see," she went on simply as a child. "For you it would be wrong." Then with a little indrawn laugh, "and, d'you remember, I called you lucky—once—at first. You who must never come here again!"

She left me to sit a little longer by the screen, and I heard the sound of her feet die out along the gallery above.

LEONAUR

ALSO FROM LEONAUR
AVAILABLE IN SOFTCOVER OR HARDCOVER WITH DUST JACKET

THE COMPLETE FOUR JUST MEN: VOLUME 2 *by Edgar Wallace—The Law of the Four Just Men & The Three Just Men*—disillusioned with a world where the wicked and the abusers of power perpetually go unpunished, the Just Men set about to rectify matters according to their own standards, and retribution is dispensed on swift and deadly wings.

THE COMPLETE RAFFLES: 1 *by E. W. Hornung—The Amateur Cracksman & The Black Mask*—By turns urbane gentleman about town and accomplished cricketer, life is just too ordinary for Raffles and that sets him on a series of adventures that have long been treasured as a real antidote to the 'white knights' who are the usual heroes of the crime fiction of this period.

THE COMPLETE RAFFLES: 2 *by E. W. Hornung—A Thief in the Night & Mr Justice Raffles*—By turns urbane gentleman about town and accomplished cricketer, life is just too ordinary for Raffles and that sets him on a series of adventures that have long been treasured as a real antidote to the 'white knights' who are the usual heroes of the crime fiction of this period.

THE COLLECTED SUPERNATURAL AND WEIRD FICTION OF WILKIE COLLINS: VOLUME 1 *by Wilkie Collins*—Contains one novel 'The Haunted Hotel', one novella 'Mad Monkton', three novelettes 'Mr Percy and the Prophet', 'The Biter Bit' and 'The Dead Alive' and eight short stories to chill the blood.

THE COLLECTED SUPERNATURAL AND WEIRD FICTION OF WILKIE COLLINS: VOLUME 2 *by Wilkie Collins*—Contains one novel 'The Two Destinies', three novellas 'The Frozen deep', 'Sister Rose' and 'The Yellow Mask' and two short stories to chill the blood.

THE COLLECTED SUPERNATURAL AND WEIRD FICTION OF WILKIE COLLINS: VOLUME 3 *by Wilkie Collins*—Contains one novel 'Dead Secret,' two novelettes 'Mrs Zant and the Ghost' and 'The Nun's Story of Gabriel's Marriage' and five short stories to chill the blood.

FUNNY BONES *selected by Dorothy Scarborough*—An Anthology of Humorous Ghost Stories.

MONTEZUMA'S CASTLE AND OTHER WEIRD TALES *by Charles B. Cory*—Cory has written a superb collection of eighteen ghostly and weird stories to chill and thrill the avid enthusiast of supernatural fiction.

SUPERNATURAL BUCHAN *by John Buchan*—Stories of Ancient Spirits, Uncanny Places & Strange Creatures.

www.ingramcontent.com/pod-product-compliance
Lightning Source LLC
Chambersburg PA
CBHW030922020726
47498CB00001B/76